GHOST OF THE
TRUTHSEEKER
STRUNGBOUND

GHOST OF THE TRUTHSEEKER

BOOK 3

A CULTIVATION LITRPG

STRUNGBOUND

Timeless
Wind

First published by Timeless Wind Publishing LLC 2024

Copyright © 2024 by Strungbound.

This novel is entirely a work of fiction. The names, characters and incidents portrayed in it are the work of the author's imagination. Any resemblance to actual persons, living or dead, events or localities is entirely coincidental.

Strungbound asserts the moral right to be identified as the author of this work.

First edition

Editing by Silas Sontag and QueenStiletto.

Cover art by Macarious. Typography designed by Sarah Anderson.

RECAP OF BOOK 2

After dealing with Anthony Ricci's attempted invasion, Alistair is forced right back into action with the fourth Quest, [Territorial Dominance], that rewards the denizens of Earth based on the size of their territories. But first, he is saddled with a debt he has taken on as the inheritor of Anthony's freehold.

Alistair then investigates the surrounding groups, including Port Locasta, ruled by a bookish cultivator named Caren Locasta. Alistair joins with Caren and other elites of the town to eradicate a horde of mutated snakes, led by their king, Sessen Esshei.

After a somewhat difficult fight, he defeats the King of the Serpents. It turns out that the beast is an experiment, created by beings called Devil Kings. Devil Kings are those who have their blood replaced by demon blood. They experience a manyfold increase in power, but are afflicted with madness and permanent deaths, not entering the cycle of Samsara.

With a new Skill called [Blood Hand], Alistair extracts a memory from Sessen Esshei of one of the thirteen Devil Kings, named Saturn. The thirteen Devil Kings were chosen from some of the most powerful evildoers on the planet, including George Moulin, an ice-based cultivator Alistair has previously clashed with.

Alistair returns home and builds up his freehold, recruiting more and more talented cultivators to help run the day-to-day affairs as he focuses on hunting down Saturn and the Devil Kings at large. Soon after, they get a hint of Devil King activity on the outskirts of their territory. Alistair investigates with Alexandra and Oliver.

They find a mysterious mansion in the depths of a dense forest. Accepting a Dungeon prompt, they must find and defeat Saturn, the master of the manor. While exploring the mysterious interior of the mansion, they encounter two extremely powerful opponents. One is Pharaoh, otherwise known as Wandering Hobo, #1 on the leaderboards, and the other is Whimsy, a Devil King herself, but freed from George's control. Alistair engages Pharaoh in a protracted battle that ends in a draw as Pharaoh reveals he was just testing our hero, though Alistair was on the back foot.

Together, they discover that Saturn, the Ninth Devil King, is already dead, killed by Pharaoh's former partner, Jakk, who betrays them and takes Saturn's mantle. Pharaoh and Alistair agree to be partners, and they go their separate ways. Alistair trains hard and continues to grow stronger, reaching over 1,000 subregions before the end of [Territorial Dominance], though this is not even close to the top 10.

For the next Quest, [The Game of Life], he participates in a trial against anonymous opponents, where he has to use his wits rather than his strength. They play for subregions, and Alistair comes out on top in his group. In the next round of the Quest, he is reunited with his allies for "Capture the Beacon," where they construct a base and hide a beacon inside it. To win, they can steal their opponent's beacon and bring it back to their base, or eliminate all the members of the opposing teams.

After ten iterations of teams clashing with one another, a change occurs in the Quest. The Pathfinder AI interferes with the Quest to expedite it, to the chagrin of the sects, houses, and corporations invested in their sponsees. The expedition is so that the sixth Quest, [Armageddon], can happen sooner. The sponsors are especially angry because the new sixth Quest has a high mortality rate and is replacing the relatively safe previously planned Quest. As for the current Quest, all the iterations are condensed into one single battle royale between all remaining teams.

With the help of three non-Northeast Order Freehold cultivators, Alistair's team comes out on top, after a long and difficult battle. The Devil Kings are clearly stronger than everyone else, but with teamwork and thinking outside the box, they defeat them.. This includes Dragonus, the Third Devil King, former #1 on the leaderboard and possessor of a storied black dragon bloodline, and Admiral, the Fourth Devil King and Alexandra's father. In a final confrontation between Lucius Wood, the father of Bartholomew and Alfred Wood, two of Alistair's former allies in Felons vs. Fellows, Alistair comes out on top with the help of Caren Locasta, who had been hiding a vampiric Class.

His victory in [The Game of Life] vaults Alistair to both #1 on the leaderboards and the owner of the most subregions in the world. This doesn't spare his territory from the devastating impacts of Earth Asunder, the first wave of [Armageddon], that sends unbelievably destructive natural disasters all over the world. In the midst of this danger, Dragonus and Admiral strike.

Alistair fights them 1v2 at first, before Alexandra and Oliver swoop in to help. Alistair takes on Dragonus, defeating him with the help of his new blood dragon ghost's bloodline, Dev'rox, and a breakthrough in the Dao. Alexandra and Oliver have difficulty with their opponent, but Alistair is in no condition to help after his testing battle with the Third Devil King. All hope seems lost, and it appears they are about to be killed by Admiral when Dev'rox feeds Alexandra the vial of blood Alistair kept from Sessen Esshei. She becomes a quasi-Devil King and defeats her father, saving the day.

Alistair recovers from his injuries and wakes up several days later. After commiserating with Alexandra, he goes forth and prepares for his next fight, knowing that there will always be another as long as he seeks to reach the Peak and change the multiverse.

1 THE WASTELAND

ALISTAIR TESTED out his rusty muscles as he ran through the city. He still felt stiff from his five-day-long coma, but his **[Carmela's Happy Pies]** and his substantial amount of Endurance worked wonders. Even after only a few minutes of moving around, he was close to 100%.

Alistair went over his status screen like he was supposed to before he'd passed out after fighting the Devil Kings. The first thing on the docket was a hefty 225 Upgrade Points to allocate.

A ninth Badge slot would cost 400 Points, while 225 would go a long way for any individual branch of his Talent Trees. But Alistair instead invested them in a Badge—"Deliverance of Justice."

That put the Skill at 290/500 Upgrade Points to leveling up. As far as he could tell, the Badge refused to earn points naturally at a reasonable pace. Like a Skill, "Deliverance of Justice" upgraded itself over the course of ordinary usage, but it was far more stringent than a Skill. However, with the requirement for upgrading to the next Tier jumping from 100 to 500, Alistair assumed that the benefits would be astronomical in kind.

Urgent messages flooded his inbox from a variety of sources. While without a specialized Class one had to enter the Soulnet to receive or send mail, it was possible to spend a hefty amount of drachma to prioritize a message, meaning that it would appear as a notification.

Alistair checked them over, getting a read on the situation. The earthquakes and lava golems affecting the thousand-subregion zone around the capital were mostly dealt with. By slaying the enormous boss golem at the center of the rift, he had reduced the power of the natural disaster and the subsequent aftershocks. His top operatives had dealt with the remaining zones in the intervening days. There were still small echoes that popped up every so often, but nothing major.

That left an apprehensive atmosphere over everyone. It was obvious that this was not the end—but no one knew when the next disaster was coming. They were not alone. No area on the planet had been hit with a second storm yet.

But that was just the capital. The outer regions of the Northeast Order Freehold were a massacre. Alistair's heart dropped as he read that a rough estimate said that almost ten percent of his freehold's population had died in the first assault. It was an unconscionable amount of death and suffering.

The web of seemingly unimportant decisions he had made all led up to this point, where he had been unable to place Land Store protections for his border territories in time. His map of territories was ablaze, thousands of subregions seized by the enemy. Hordes of demon-blooded men and beasts assaulted his lands.

"Don't be so hard on yourself," Dev'rox offered. "Just put a fist through George's face and everything will be fine."

"Like that'll be easy," Alistair grumbled. He had pushed himself to his limits fighting Dragonus, who was merely the Third Devil King. Oracle had to be stronger than Dragonus, and therefore the leader of the Devil Kings was unfathomably powerful.

At least he had Dev'rox to help. The imp was proving to be more than just an auxiliary combatant. In the last fight, he had summoned giant magical arrays that could displace vast quantities of Mana. But perhaps the more interesting development was his ability to swap places with a chosen target.

With the snap of his fingers, the imp could trade places with almost anything. Objects of spiritual density, mostly meaning powerful foes with lots of Dao energy, were more difficult, requiring permission or a huge amount of Mana. In addition, the further the distance, the more Mana was required.

Alistair cooked up all kinds of ways he could take advantage of the ability, while also setting goals for himself to grow capable of defeating George

Moulin. He still had to gather enough insight to create his finishing Skill. A proto-Domain was also something he had been considering. If George had a proto-Domain himself, it would be difficult for Alistair to win without one.

But as he came upon the collapsed buildings and makeshift rescue centers, all his other thoughts ceased entirely. Despite the long break, [Ghost Whispers] still tingled with remnant spectral energy, filling him with extra power. It was a testament to the scale of the atrocity.

Over half the buildings in the area he ran through were at least partially destroyed, and half of those almost fully destroyed. From the obsidian that stained the pavement and parts of the buildings, it was obvious the rift hadn't been closed before the lava golems had run rampant.

However, despite all the damages, people remained vibrant. That was how it was these days. Anyone who survived had lost family, friends, and colleagues. Constant death had become an unavoidable fact of life.

Alistair ignored the streams of air and space Mana that served as their public transportation. They seemed to be fully functional, but he was faster, jumping onto the roofs of the buildings and running at near full speed.

People stood and stared at their fearless leader speeding over the skyline. Alistair's blood pumped and adrenaline rushed through his body as he became one with the wind. With the airwalking aspect of [Dash], he could make one leap through the air before touching down.

It was the first step toward true flight. Based on what he knew of the higher realms, even cultivators without wings or fire abilities could fly through their own power at a certain point. Perhaps Visionary, he wasn't sure.

He landed on top of a new structure, right where the old headquarters used to be. All signs of a destructive earthquake were gone, including the rubble of the previous building. In its place was a dome that appeared to be made from frosted glass, with one tall spire in the center.

That tower was the antenna of Celeste Mendoza, the head of communications. Alistair could feel her electromagnetic waves oscillate through him, spreading out into the world as she picked up snippets of information from all across the lands.

Alistair chuckled as he saw that the tower served a dual-purpose. There was a chimney at the top, with a small hole. Felix had a sense of humor, knowing his boss was wont to go on aerial escapades. Alistair leaped a distance over half a football field onto the dome. The frosted material was ambrosic glass, an addition to the Land Store that appeared during his nap, which was even stronger than valyrik.

Hoisting himself down the hole, he felt dozens of layers of warding pass by. No alarm or blockage came up, as it was attuned to his personal aura signature.

Alistair already felt the attention of everyone inside the building turn to him, as he didn't cloak his aura. He was used to it by now. All the watching, hopeful, grateful eyes.

The chute led right to an oval office. It was spare, only containing the bare necessities. His most important officers were already in the room, having made their way after sensing his presence.

Oliver was the first to speak up. "Look who finally got out of bed? Who would have thought I would be the first one up and going out of all of us."

"Bah, you were the least injured," Alistair joked back. "Not all of us can have a personal attendant made out of bones."

There were fewer people than Alistair was expecting; it was only Oliver, Caren, Celeste, and a few of the less physically capable officers.

"Where is everyone?" he asked.

"In the field," Celeste replied, flipping her long, black hair braided into a ponytail. She was obviously still at work even as she talked to him, weird gadgets sticking out of electronic ports all over her body. "We've stabilized this region in your absence, but there are still ongoing disasters elsewhere."

She used her eye beam projectors to show Alistair the situation. Floods, hurricanes, landslides, and wildfires assaulted civilization. He glimpsed some of his allies, like John and Blaise, or Lily and Robert, dealing with the disasters.

"For our three highest population centers, which would be here, Ricciton, and Carmen's old capital, we have the situation under control. In terms of population, the rifts are under control for 80% of all subregions, but 20% are almost completely untouched. There are still millions of people in those subregions, unfortunately."

"Where is it the worst?" Alistair immediately asked.

"The Wasteland," she said.

Alistair raised an eyebrow. "Wasteland?"

"I thought you would know that already. You really need to keep up with your geography," Celeste said, though after realizing how her words could be interpreted, she hastily added, "sir... Uh, sorry, the Wasteland is an area across what used to be the western United States, around the Rocky Mountains. It's over a hundred thousand square miles large, created by the destructive rampage of Vritra."

"That snake? Shouldn't be a problem," Alistair said, remembering the Reptile Emperor. At his pace, he should have leapfrogged the beast entirely.

"Well, he shouldn't be an issue, regardless. Since the start of [Armageddon], he hasn't been spotted at all in the Wasteland. His former subjects are going crazy trying to find their master."

"That figures. They teamed up during the last Quest. I wouldn't be surprised if George made them Devil Princes... which would be problematic to say the least." Alistair stroked his chin. "What happened during the Devil Kings' attack?"

"We weren't their only targets," Celeste said. "They hit everywhere. In fact, we probably got off easy compared to Lucius and the United Polities. We still don't know where Lucius's whereabouts are. He's probably dead, and we know for certain Carmen and Richard are dead."

"No way!" Alistair exclaimed. While he had his share of difficulties with the Spanish mage, he never even imagined that she would have died. Come to think of it, it was the first death of a top 10 ranker that he knew of for certain, besides Anthony. "Are you positive they're dead?"

"The Devil Kings posted a video on the Soulnet with their bodies. I can show you, if you want. Oracle publicly took responsibility."

"How crude," Alistair muttered. "So Oracle is the one in charge now?"

"Correct. She seems to have taken over Dragonus's duties as the primary Devil King active in the world. And from what we've seen, she's far stronger than Dragonus. Her abilities include Karmic cultivation and its resulting control over Fate, prognostication, and bodily puppeteering."

"Bodily puppeteering?" Alistair knew those other two powers, but the third was new to him.

"Based on your sister's research and your needle, we now understand that all Devil Kings have a level of control over anybody they give their blood to. But her control goes far beyond that."

Celeste changed her eye hologram to a fuzzy video of Oracle. She had long black hair and tan skin, her eyes green pools of fire. That made them similar to Alexandra's, but Alistair felt like the true Devil King had a more sickly, evil hue, slightly lighter and less welcoming.

In the footage, Oracle looked like a mad puppeteer, forcing a group of people to dance via slim green strings attached to her fingers.

"I see. I'll keep an eye out for that. Anything else?"

No one else had anything to say, so they adjourned the meeting there. Oliver stayed after to catch up with Alistair.

"How's everything going?" Alistair asked. It felt like he hadn't talked to the Necromancer in forever. Oliver was an important asset of the freehold, and he had been busy with constant missions.

"Good," Oliver said, reclining in his chair as one of his zombies fed him potato chips. "Goddamn, it always feels like you're two steps ahead of me. Just feeling your aura now is sickening."

"What can I say—I've been lucky."

"Luck's something to do with it, that's for sure," Oliver jabbed. "But we're not even in the same category, so who cares. I'm a support, and you can bet I'm the best support in the world." He gave a thumbs up. "You like my new trick I used in the fight with the sword in the portal? Got the idea from— Never mind, you probably wouldn't know it."

"Guess I'm not cool enough for that." Alistair shrugged. "But I did think that was a really neat idea. You've been practicing it?"

"For sure," Oliver said. "I have tons of weapons in storage now. I was the one who brought the idea to the build manual, but the build manual adapted fast, and it helped me unlock a plague-related Talent Tree. So now I can throw my corpses on people and infect them with virulent plagues."

"Remind me to never piss you off."

"You're headed out to the Wasteland now? Mind if I join?" Oliver did his best to sound innocent despite his aura of pure death.

"Yeah, I was just about to. You don't have anywhere to be?"

"Nah, remember I just got out of the hospital, too. I'm itching to fight again. I have to replenish my zombie stores after Admiral re-killed most of them. Is Alexandra going to come too?"

A lonely image of Alexandra sitting on the meadow entered his mind. She was still dealing with the effects of her transformation.

"Let's give her some time." Alistair brushed off some dust from his shirt. "Wait," he said, looking down at his outfit. It wasn't his **Mammothskin Raiment,** but a white hospital gown. "Where's my robe?"

———

It turned out that Felix, the weapons master and crafter, had seen Alistair's torn raiment and wanted to improve it. And so he had.

Alistair gingerly accepted the folded outfit from the Kenyan man. His work was only getting better, the clear mark of a crafting Dao imparted within his clothing.

"I gave them a little extra." Felix smiled.

"I can see that," Alistair replied. The fluffy and somewhat cumbersome robes now looked sleek and sexy. Black with laminated dark gray trims, it still retained its characteristic puffy cuffs and collar that felt nice and cozy against his skin. But more than the appearance, its nature had changed. When he scanned the item, it had skipped all the way from Uncommon to Legendary rarity.

"For general protection, it's better than anything that's not been specially crafted or dropped by a Quest. The heat and cold insulation should be more than doubled, and it will heal itself as long as you're wearing it. You'd have to completely demolish it in order to break it."

"Thank you," Alistair said, unfolding the item. There was a badge sewn onto the area above the heart. An insignia of a tri-colored fist of gold, coral, and baby blue that made him grin uncontrollably. It was his freehold's emblem, a visual representation of his path. The badge's three colors were that of his three Dao Nodes. "That's a nice touch."

"You did my boots too?" Alistair asked, seeing his **Fall of Fleet** on the crafter's worktable.

"Oh yes, I almost forgot," Felix said, grabbing the pair of boots. "There's not much you can do for an item like that, but I added a jumping effect which complements the falling. You should be able to jump twice as high now. Good luck on your journey, sir. I should be getting back to work now. Have a stack of spears as tall as this building to take care of."

"Of course, I wouldn't want to hold you up."

Alistair took in a last look of admiration at Felix's workshop. It was a hot, humid chamber full of bronze machines and steam that rose up for stories and stories. There was a conveyor belt that slithered around the room, containing everything from fully finished products to mere proto-types. It made Alistair bashful to see such genius. He only had one skill—fighting.

Though perhaps Karma can count for another skill, Alistair bargained. When he wasn't in combat, his positive Karma sat unused within him. All that accrued merit going to waste, since his natural regeneration would have gained it back, anyway. He decided to burn a little over his regeneration rate, just to see what it would do. Maybe he would get lucky.

Alistair hummed over some ideas for other talents he could develop as he walked out of the workshop. Talents as in actual talents, not from the Talent Tree. Singing or playing an instrument would be nice. There had to be cultivator musicians thousands of times better than a mortal could ever be.

He headed straight for the nearest **Teleportation Circle,** when Dev'rox whispered in his ear, "Watch out."

Alistair snapped to attention, his **[Fighter's Instinct]** taking over. The Skill was his highest at Tier 4, and even close to upgrading once more. But he was too late to intercept the attack.

By attack, he meant a girl stabbing him. The rusty knife shattered upon hitting his robe, the young girl falling over. Alistair grabbed her hand before she hit the ground, hoisting her up. She immediately began to cry.

Dev'rox snickered and commented on his failure to detect her. "Looks like that confirms my theory of how a danger sense would react to a weakling."

Alistair focused his attention on the girl, giving off a light amount of his aura. Not enough to be harmful, but enough to impress his power upon her.

"What is this?" he asked.

"You killed my mom!"

Tears ran down the girl's face. A quick **[Eyes of Truth]** revealed her name to be Julia. Looking at her closely, she wasn't as young as he initially thought, maybe about ten or eleven.

"Julia, you can't go around stabbing people. Do you know who I am?"

"Of course I know you," she said in between sobs. "You killed my mom!"

"Sweetie, what are you talking about?" Alistair asked.

"You left us behind. My mommy got stuck under rocks in that cave. We were trying to get her out. Daddy was calling for you to help, but you ran away. But then Daddy let her die too."

Alistair started to piece together what the girl was talking about. It had to be from when he fought Johnny Choi, the fire wielder that had attacked when he was evacuating the tunnels. The shelter partially collapsed, killing some and trapping others under the debris. Alistair didn't have enough time to go back and save everyone, as he already had to deal with everyone else who was fleeing.

From what he parsed, Julia's mom got trapped under the rocks, and her family tried to get her out. Most likely, after seeing the futility of their task and the imminent danger of the situation, her father had picked her up and fled.

"Where is your daddy?" Alistair asked her.

"He's dead too," she said, more solemnly than he thought possible for a girl of ten. "From the earthquake."

Alistair was at a loss for words for a moment. Thoughts raced through his mind. Should he try to defend his actions, which he didn't regret? Should he apologize, empathizing with Julia?

"Who are you living with?" Alistair ended up on.

Julia pouted and tried to run away, but he kept his grip on her hand. Eventually, she relented and answered. "Ms. Richards with the other kids who don't have parents anymore."

"And what would Ms. Richards say about you stealing a knife and trying to stab someone?"

"I don't know," she said with some attitude.

Alistair raised an eyebrow, waiting for a proper response.

"I guess she'd say that you shouldn't do that. But she's not my mom."

"She's the closest thing you have to a mom now," Alistair retorted. From the way she flinched a little, he could tell that statement got to her. *That might have been a little too soon.* "Everyone's lost someone by now. My mom is gone. We have to cling to what we have left. I'm sorry about what happened to your family, but I didn't kill them. They did." He pointed at the sky. "And I won't rest until they're gone. Does that make you feel better?"

"No," she said.

"I didn't think it would. You can blame me if you want, but I think we both know that's not what you really feel. You're not stupid. You knew that you wouldn't hurt me at all, I'd wager. What do you really want?"

Alistair peered into the vicissitudes of Fate as he drew upon his Karma to look at the girl. It was his first time utilizing Lesser Samatha, which allowed him to see inner truths. What he saw was a person with vast potential. A temperament not so dissimilar to his own, in fact.

"I don't know," she admitted. In Alistair's vision, he could see that she wished to say she wanted her parents back. But even at her young age, Julia knew that was impossible, a juvenile dream befit of a toddler. *Or a dream like me.*

She said she didn't know, but as Alistair looked into her soul, he felt a change.

"No more messing around," Alistair said. As he was talking, he barely picked up a quiet sound of chattering children in the distance. "If you stab people, you go to jail. You know that, right? Even if they can't be hurt by it. Go back to Ms. Richards and behave yourself."

Alistair let go of her hand and sent her off. He wasn't sure if he had done the right thing. Then again, he wasn't expecting an assassination attempt from a ten-year-old girl.

"I say you should have smacked her," Dev'rox said. "Just send her flying in the air. Regicide is punishable by souldeath where I'm from."

"Forgive me if I don't model my society based on Hell," Alistair shot back. "Offense intended."

"Touché."

Alistair decided to take the public streams instead of running on the rooftops, not wanting to receive unwanted attention. The tunnels of space and air Mana were quite efficient and brought him back to the headquarters in no time.

Alistair snuck through the building with the Dao of the Ghost. While the ambrosic glass was naturally resistant to both Mana and the Dao and they had extra enchantments, he was using his Dao to remain invisible and intangible. He still passed through the checkpoints like normal.

He unveiled himself right in front of the **Teleportation Circle** room. There were five of them in a row, with enough space in between them for a group of people to get on or off at once.

Oliver was waiting for him, and he had his eyes locked straight on where Alistair was even before he uncloaked.

"Ghost is similar enough to death. I could feel you," Oliver explained. "Let's go."

Alistair looked at the directory near the entrance, finding the one that would bring him closest to the Wasteland. Many of the options were grayed out in the aftermath of Earth Asunder.

He pressed his destination, stepped onto the platform with Oliver and closed his eyes. The blue light of the circle washed over him. The city was nice, but it felt cramped. In the wilderness, he was truly free.

2 MANA STORMS

OF COURSE, the **Teleportation Circle** didn't bring Alistair and Oliver directly to the Wasteland. They first had to take an intermediate stop at a town that had once been in Pharaoh's domain.

His territorial domain, not his proto-Domain. Alistair was jealous of the ease that the mysterious Egyptologist had with his Dao. Alistair himself was nowhere near the creation of his own Dao field, let alone a proto-Domain.

From what he had gleaned from Dev'rox, a Dao field was the first step to creating a proto-Domain. Unfortunately, his Daos were more conceptual in nature compared to Pharaoh, Alexandra, or Admiral. Any attempt he made to impose his Dao into his surroundings ended in failure. Not an absolute failure—he could do it, somewhat, but it served no purpose in combat. He could fill the air with the Dao of the Fist, but it didn't suddenly create an army of flying fists to smite his opponents. That was completely out of his purview.

Alistair started to wonder about that golden gourd that Dragonus had used in their fight. It contained an incense that felt like a stolen piece of the Heavens, fueling his Dao-wrought fires to absurd levels of heat and size.

Maybe if I had that… Alistair thought woefully.

"Hey, I have something for you," Oliver said as they walked off the **Teleportation Circle**. *Speak of the Devil*, Alistair thought. It was the gourd he was talking about, complete with an embossed Chinese dragon. "You need this thing?"

"Don't mind if I do," Alistair said, taking the jug. He was hesitant to uncork it out in the open, not knowing if the incense would go free. That was if there *was* still incense, which he wasn't entirely sure. Luckily, the item would fit inside his inventory. An inspection revealed it was called **Heavenly Nectar Incense,** and it was a Legendary rarity item. It was fortunate happenstance that he had just vacated his **Laser Gun II's** spot in his inventory.

They arrived in Logista, a medium-sized settlement going from the directory. Alistair was going to look at his freehold profile for more information, but a sudden prickle of danger popped up in his danger sense, accompanied by blazing sirens.

They were suddenly in a pitch black room, which Alistair could tell was supernaturally dark. His aura sense was blocked by an unknown presence in the air.

Alistair tried moving his arm, but it was stuck. Confused, he looked down, feeling his arm without his vision. There was some kind of chain or enormous band locking his limbs in place. While he hadn't moved with even close to all of his might, his Strength should have been high enough to shatter almost any restraint a medium-sized town could muster.

While he wasn't worried for his own life, Oliver's worst stat was Constitution. Alistair revved into action, seeing through the preternatural darkness with **[Eyes of Truth]**. Right away, he followed up with his new Skill—**[Draconic Roar]**.

Alistair focused force affinity Mana into the Skill, though most of its power came from his *nue*. Like how Mana seemed to exit from the soulcore and Dao energy from his Dao Nodes, *nue* felt like it came from his mind.

He imagined it as a misty cloud of intangible creative essence that was bathed in the Logos—his willpower made manifest. The common epithet, killing intent, was therefore somewhat misplaced, though not entirely so. When sharpened by a warrior's nature, it took on a different, more belligerent flavor.

The **[Draconic Roar]** dispersed the darkness and destroyed its source. Alistair cast down a **[Lightning of Justice]**, which was very close to reaching Tier 2. The golden bolt of lightning soared down from the ceiling of what appeared to be a medieval-style tower, striking the ground in front of Alistair and illuminating it.

They were in the lion's den. A few dozen feet above them, there was a platform with ten men and women holding bows, all knocked out.

With their interlocutors unconscious, Alistair broke the chains around him and Oliver with a **[Frozen Claw]** and his teeth, biting the embrittled cuffs.

"Thanks for the assist," Oliver said. "I was not expecting that. But neither were they. What do you think happened?"

"I honestly have no idea. But we should clear our names before this becomes more trouble than it's worth."

Alistair felt a group of people approaching from behind. He turned around, pressing open the thick door with a single finger.

"Everyone! Stop it! It's me, Alistair. Why are you attacking us?"

The group of five just outside the door looked like they were on death's door. Replete in tattered plate armor, they had a weary look in their eyes. There were two women and three men, one of the women having a clearly stronger aura than the others. Alistair primarily addressed her with his question.

She was unusually tall, around his height, with a healthy amount of lean muscle covered by dilapidated bronze plates. Alistair estimated her to be on par with one of his squad leaders, so around level 40.

After feeling his aura close up, she nearly fell over. She bowed deeply, apologizing profusely. "I'm so sorry for this mix-up. I had no idea it was you. I'm Lexie, the woman in charge of Logista."

Oliver's face scrunched up in a scowl. "Why the hell would you think that was a good idea in the first place?"

Lexie grimaced. "Sir, it appears that, well, uh, your aura might have ticked off our sensors. This is a dangerous area, and we haven't fully dealt with the Earth Asunder wave yet. If we were to be attacked from the inside, it would be fatal. I made the executive decision to purchase an aura sensor that would react to Devil Kings and monsters. But I guess it thought you were an enemy?"

"That's what I get for being a Necromancer, I guess," Oliver grumbled.

Alistair pointed at the unconscious people above. "Sorry about the mess. I held back on my roar, so I wouldn't kill them."

"Thanks," Lexie said, looking unnerved by how easily he took them out. "What are you doing here?"

"We're here to help, actually. Why don't you show me around? I think we can get off to a better start than this."

———

Alistair was astonished by the state of his frontier territories. When he was on-world, he had mostly stuck to the East Coast, and specifically the former northeast of the United States. When he had gone out to other areas, it was before the start of [Armageddon], before they had bolstered their defenses and started empire-building.

If there wasn't that much of a difference between the core and outlying territories a few months ago, now it was like night and day.

Logista had a population of over fifty thousand, yet their tallest building was three stories. Many of them were half-falling over, cracks and destroyed walls everywhere. Alistair didn't see any valyrik or ambrosic glass or any other high-end material. In fact, most of them looked like they were constructed with wood from the region itself.

The people were just as downtrodden as their town. Alistair saw a lot of jutting bones and tired eyes among the people. There were whole swaths of blocks that were completely obliterated. He even thought he saw a couple of dead bodies. No one seemed to care, not even Lexie and her group.

It was a sober reminder of the dynamics of power. While New Boston and its nearby territories had suffered greatly over the course of the initiation, they always had Alistair. They had never experienced a total breakdown of society. And before him, there'd been Sofia. He still felt a pang of guilt thinking about his former boss. While at first, he had thought her cold and unfeeling, in the end he knew that she deeply cared about her people. If only he had been a little stronger, he could have saved her.

"Your town is a piece of shit," Oliver said nonchalantly. Alistair gave him a pointed look.

"We do what we can," said a man who followed Lexie the closest. "After Wandering Hobo left us, it's been difficult."

Alistair had to mentally adjust "Wandering Hobo" back to "Pharaoh" in his brain, since he had spent much more time thinking of the inexplicable former #1 as "Pharaoh." He still didn't understand why that man had chosen that ridiculous name as his moniker, and also how the Corlyon Company allowed such a childish act.

Oliver whistled. "So he let you guys out to dry completely? Sounds like an ass."

"This boy is quite unlike that sheltered otaku that you first met," Dev'rox wryly commented. As to where the imp had learned the word "otaku," Alistair didn't even want to know.

To his surprise, Lexie tried defending Pharaoh. "He protected us from the worst. Handing us over to you is better than nothing."

Oliver didn't respond to that.

They jogged for several minutes, eventually making their way through the small city and up to a hill in the east. From that vantage point, they could see out in the distance to the horizon.

Alistair now understood why they called it the Wasteland. In its lack of vitality, it reminded him of the dead zone near the serpent cave and Selephita's flaming dominion, but there were a few key differences.

For one, as far as he could tell, the zone was literally black and white. But the objects inside it were not colored black and white, it was the light itself that was changing. Somehow, with maybe his understanding of deeper insight or even his sense of smell, he understood that the underlying material hadn't changed colors. It was an ether in the air, poisoning color itself.

Besides the color, it was plain *disgusting*. Putrid fumes of dissolving animal corpses wafted in the air, reaching all the way to the hill. Pools of a sickly dark liquid stained the terrain in amorphous formations all over the land.

Though it was named the Wasteland, it was actually less lifeless than the other two special zones he had seen before. There was still shrubbery, and with his impressive mastery of life force, he detected some small mammals, perhaps kangaroo rats or desert shrews.

It was a rocky desert, with large cracks. The Wasteland part was still in the distance, though not so far that Logista could feel comfortable. The cracked over and flat look of the ground reminded him of popular images of Death Valley, only with the addition of random puddles.

Death Valley was a good description. Even with the physical rearrangement of the world, Alistair assumed that he had to be looking at a part of the Mojave Desert. The small signs of life were there, but they felt off.

Like they were sapped of their life force. Alistair didn't know precisely how to explain it. It was just off.

"Take it in," Lexie said. "We forbid anyone from going into it. It's far too dangerous, even with Vritra gone. This patch of land has been growing ever since the start of the initiation, I suppose, though no one was keeping track of it back then. Once Vritra took over, it ballooned in size."

"And the other reptiles. I heard they're going crazy?" Alistair asked.

"That's correct. Some of the damages you saw in Logista were from raging salamanders. But the primary concern is Earth Asunder. You might be able to understand the problem. Since we can't go inside because of the remaining beasts, we can't close the disaster rifts. And if we can't close the disaster rifts, they keep getting bigger and bigger. And the elemental beasts that come from within the rifts keep getting stronger."

The man added, "Honestly, we're kinda hoping that the elemental beasts and the reptile beasts will finish each other off, but that's a tall ask."

"I see," Alistair said. "But what is the disaster? I don't really see anything from here."

"You're already seeing it," Lexie said.

Alistair rubbed his eyes and looked closer. *Wait a second,* he thought. When he first saw it, he thought the black and white appearance was the result of the reptiles. But what if that was Earth Asunder?

"Whatever it is, there's not a name for it on Earth." Lexie shook her head. "The records we've found call it a Mana Storm. It sucks out Mana and there are periodic surges that make the strongest hurricanes look like nothing. Not to mention, there are pure Mana elemental beasts."

"Sounds interesting, right, Alistair?" Oliver grinned.

"I suppose," Alistair said. "How fast is it growing?"

"That's the thing. It stopped two days ago. We've been in the process of evacuating." Lexie pointed to the division between the black-and-white section and the normal terrain. "People are people. Ever since the growth stopped, the urgency to leave plummeted."

"We'll take care of it," Alistair said. "In the meantime, get everyone out of here. Tell them it's on my direct orders."

"Will do," Lexie said, motioning to her people. "We'll let you do your thing now."

They descended the hill, leaving Alistair and Oliver alone.

"Don't forget me," Dev'rox said. Alistair groaned internally. There had to be something down the line for ghost cultivation that would let him shield his thoughts. Practicing his *nue* seemed to help to some degree, though Dev'rox was coy about whether it was an effective pathway.

Oliver peered over the hill's edge, a steep, multi-story drop. "I don't suppose you want to go down like a normal person."

Alistair was already in free fall by the time the last words reached his ears. "You know me too well."

————

It didn't take them long to reach the Wasteland. Alistair began to regret jumping off, as Oliver wouldn't stop bugging him. Surely he had enough Constitution to weather the fall easily, Alistair reckoned. Alistair himself had *mostly* gotten over his fear of heights out of sheer necessity.

Now that he didn't have to keep Dev'rox a secret from Oliver, at least the imp could make himself busy distracting Oliver. Apparently, Dev'rox had taken to reading manga. When Alistair asked how that was possible, he only responded by saying that he was accessing the memories of Japanese ghosts that Alistair had felt.

Alistair was the one to take the first step inside. The line between the normal desert and the Wasteland was clearly demarcated, beige soil contrasting with complete grayscale. Alistair tossed a rock over the border. The moment it crossed, it turned a dull gray.

Why don't—

"Don't even think about it," Dev'rox said.

"Fine."

Alistair took a deep breath. Why was he filled with so much trepidation, anyway? He could feel little animals scurrying about. Clearly, whatever was going on wasn't inherently deadly.

He lifted his foot and gingerly stepped inside the Wasteland. If he was expecting anything crazy to happen, his imagination would be disappointed. There was no difference except the sudden lack of color.

After seeing Alistair go in successfully, Oliver joined as well. The two of them carefully trekked forward, paying close attention to their surroundings.

"Not so bad, was it?" Dev'rox said.

"Shut up. You didn't even want to go."

"I'm not the one with a tough, draconic body. Your life force is like that of an Adept already. My dainty ectoplasmic form would have been swept away by the tiniest surge of a Mana Storm."

"You know what a Mana Storm is?"

"Of course. They're quite common in the Asura Hell."

"And can you tell me what they are?" Alistair asked.

"I can, because you could easily find out yourself. Which is an indictment of your poor education in and of itself. A Mana Storm is a natural phenomenon that occurs just about everywhere that has a high enough concentration of Mana. It doesn't take much at all, though I guess this planet would still be too weak. Perhaps they'll start happening naturally once Earth reaches the Basic quality? Not sure. Of course, they scale in strength depending on how advanced the planet is. As I'm sure you recall, Dao archetypes are the reason why there are many similar species all across the multiverse. But it doesn't only apply to physical or cultural concepts. The patterns of nature—such as storms—exist everywhere."

"So, what's a Mana Storm look like?" Alistair asked, but even as he said those words, his aura sense stirred as he felt a presence in the distance.

"I think you're about to find out."

3 HEART OF THE STORM

AT FIRST, Alistair didn't understand why everything was in grayscale. He felt something was off from afar, and the life force of the living beings inside the Wasteland felt strange, but he couldn't quite come up with a full explanation.

But now that he was inside, he was beginning to understand. It was Mana. The ambient Mana that suffused the entirety of the air was thinner, around a third to half density, but that wasn't it. The difference was that it lacked animus. It was without the spark of vigor that gave Mana its energetic essence.

That took a visual form in the absence of color. His internal Mana leaked out in wisps of color, the only pigmentation except for the growing presence in the distance.

Alistair felt like it was Mana's answer to a Heavenly tribulation. But this was no wrath of the Heavens, but of nature itself. A great mass of Mana of every flavor gathered on the horizon, washing the black-and-white landscape in temporary swathes of the rainbow. It reminded him of the facsimile Dao Heart, but this force of the cosmos was no pretty condensation of colorful mist.

It looked like a combination of different types of weather phenomena. The torrential downpour of a hurricane, manifested in glowing liquid affinity Mana. Cycling, hypersonic winds of a tornado, in emerald wind affinity Mana. Firestorms, lightning, and hard-to-describe masses of death and time—Mana congealed together into an amorphous storm of unbelievable proportions.

Red lightning obliterated the ground in columns of plasma taller than the highest skyscrapers. It was a wild twin to the lightning of Heavenly tribulation, smiting the ground with the fury of the natural world. Wrathful scarlet flames emerged from the destroyed earth, searing everything in a blaze similar to that of the firebird Selephita. Strange tiny ravens made of death aura spread with the flames, like carriers of the plague.

The Mana Storm spread over ten miles, but it was moving towards them at a rapid pace. While the storm wasn't actually conscious, Alistair swore he felt anger from the mass of affinities. It was directed at him and Oliver, a fury that wanted to reclaim their greedy bodies that had stolen so much of the precious aura of the cosmos.

As cultivators, they were stealing Heaven's providence: the immortality of the body, enlightenment of the mind, and purification of the soul. It was nature's wont to reclaim that stolen Mana. Even though the technology of the Sublimed Machine through the Final Frontier Empire had placated natural law, they could not fully stop it.

"What are we going to do?" Oliver shouted over the blasting winds, which had picked up once the storm became visible. "It's coming straight for us! You can feel that right?"

Alistair nodded. If they merely tried to run it would chase them. He didn't have to ascribe a malevolent consciousness for that—Mana was attracted to Mana. At its current speed, he could outrun without a hitch, but Oliver was too slow. He had a solution for that, but he worried it was dangerously foolish.

"Why don't we tame the storm?" Alistair posed. "We probably can get some goodies from this thing. The bigger they are, the more goodies they give?"

"That sounds crazy, but I'm down. As long as you promise to get me out if it gets too dangerous."

"Promise."

Alistair took a deep breath and looked at the Mana Storm head-on. He took in every minute detail, admiring its majesty. This was what he expected of planets in the Imperial Heartlands—something beyond what his mortal mind could imagine.

The flames and death Mana ravens expanded faster than the storm itself, laying waste to the land. As they reached further and further away from the heart of the Mana Storm, they slowly lost their color.

When they got close, Oliver held up a hand—scaring Alistair, if only for a moment.

Alistair hadn't had any opportunity to see Oliver in action since before the fifth Quest, [The Game of Life]. While they briefly joined forces against Dragonus and Admiral, that quickly devolved into two separate fights, and he had only seen the end of Oliver and Alexandra's struggle against the naval Devil King.

For a single moment, a wave of fear washed over his body as Oliver's Dao energy exploded out of his body. For an ephemeral moment, he doubted his own understanding of Black and White Impermanence, of himself as a psychopomp and representation of death. For a fleeting moment, he saw the finality of the death: the end.

Oliver's Dao energy was the unsullied death that all living beings refused to countenance. The accidental death energy of the Mana Storm obeyed him absolutely, fading away to nothingness.

Alistair helped out with the flames, casting a [Frozen Claw] that froze the blaze into scarlet ice crystals. But the columns of lightning still encroached, seemingly getting faster as the storm grew nearer.

The winds were raging now. With his 266 Constitution, Alistair's body was incredibly dense, making him harder to move. The gales were still strong enough to push him back, and Oliver, who was much lighter, had to dig his hands into the ground to stay put.

That made it impossible to communicate through normal methods. Luckily, since Oliver knew about Dev'rox, they used the imp as an intermediary for communication. Alistair had Dev'rox tell Oliver his plan, who nodded in response.

Alistair was no storm chaser, especially not of a Mana Storm. But he had his instincts. [Fighter's Instinct] was on the verge of advancing to Tier 5, and he had the assistance of Dev'rox's formidable experience. He had a strong feeling that the storm would attempt to strike down power.

Alistair closed his eyes for a moment, gathering his aura. Then he let it out. Maybe there was a small part of him that wanted to one-up Oliver. Only a small part, of course.

At this point, his soulcore was entirely saturated with properly attuned

Mana. His Skills no longer had any use for the ad hoc conversion sieves within his meridians that turned pure Mana into the proper affinity. Now, his soulcore had his four affinities in their full substance—force, lightning, ice, and blood.

Vibrant color temporarily coated the dull landscape. The storm stirred in the distance in response to a rival energy. Faster than seemed possible, the lightning changed angles, arcing toward Alistair like an angry swarm of bees.

Oliver was right there to defend him. As planned, he opened one of his empty **[Otherworld Gates]**, a square of darkness in the sky. Oliver had moved far beyond his tiny portals that could only house human-sized objects. The **[Otherworld Gate]** he produced blotted out almost the entire sky from Alistair's sight.

Lightning rained down into the portal, disappearing into a pocket dimension. Oliver grimaced as it happened. Dev'rox relayed to Alistair that he could only absorb so much energy before it would burst.

Alistair didn't need that long. With Oliver's Skill redirecting a decent portion of the Mana Storm's wrath, Alistair could proceed with his crazy idea—trying to capture the storm. Lightning in a bottle, so to speak.

Alistair uncorked the **Heavenly Nectar Incense,** raising it above his head. As the new owner of the item, the smoky incense inside heeded his command, staying inside its container. While the material held a formidable presence, it had no real power in the world without the addition of an outside force.

Still, as a piece of an unblemished celestial realm, its presence was out of place in the Wasteland. The Mana Storm recognized that, refocusing its attention on Alistair and his gourd. Alistair braced himself as a thick bolt of lightning came down from the sky.

He used every piece of defense he had to defy the will of the skies. Mana, Dao energy, and *nue* flooded his body, reinforcing his very existence. Alistair still cried out in unimaginable agony. The lightning suffused his cells with wild, untamed, natural Mana.

However, the amount that struck him wasn't even half of the total lightning's output. Almost all the energy poured into the gourd, combining with the incense. To finish it off, Alistair poured his own Dao energy into the mix.

The Dao that aligned most with lightning was obviously Justice, so Alistair unleashed his Justice Node into the gourd. The Dao energy left him far faster than he anticipated, as the gourd *pulled* on it like it had a mind of its own. Through gritted teeth, Alistair acquiesced to the item's greedy desires, not holding anything back.

The Mana Storm responded in turn. Many smaller bolts came down from the sky, joining together with the main, continuous stream of lightning that refused to stop. The **Heavenly Nectar Incense** couldn't handle the additional load, passing it along to Alistair.

He stood on the verge of losing consciousness. Something had to give. He could feel the Justice and lightning combine into that same form of quasi-physical substance he remembered Dragonus using. At last, Alistair lowered his arm and bottled the gourd, haggardly **[Dashing]** away.

The Mana Storm was relentless in its fury, sending a different type of attack against Alistair in lieu of the red lightning. A column of time and space affinity Mana shot down from the heart of the clouds, possessing congealed energy even denser than the lightning.

Alistair turned and readied himself to stop it, but Oliver already had it covered.

With one portal, he unleashed the **Sun's End Vanquishment Sword.** He had it attached to a launcher within the **[Otherworld Gate]**, and fired it at the column in a blur of motion. Yet that wasn't all that came with the sword. Alistair glimpsed something attached to the hilt of the sword—or someone.

It was Anthony's skeleton, though it looked more like a living creature, with semi-transparent rings of flesh-like ectoplasm surrounding the bones. Oliver had clearly beefed up one of his strongest summons since last time.

In another portal, he unveiled a titanic snake—the body of Sessen Esshei. Alistair almost wanted to complain that it was unfair Oliver was getting more powerful off of Alistair's fallen enemies.

The serpentine corpse opened its mouth and unleashed a black hole. The gravitational pull warped the air, and it shot toward the spacetime column.

Oliver clearly had supreme confidence in his zombie if he was willing to risk the skeleton against the Mana Storm's wrath. As Anthony's skeleton swung his majestic katana in a huge arc, the black hole exploded upon contact with the stream of Mana, sucking in a large portion into its eternal void. In an instant, it took up half the energy and collapsed in on itself, leaving no trace behind.

The slash of the **Sun's End Vanquishment Sword** took care of the rest. Void and destruction Mana combined in a bipartisan beam that swept away the incoming attack. Channeling the power of chaos, it turned the sky to daisies and butterflies, which floated down harmlessly.

Alistair gave Oliver an approving nod. *Certainly more elegant than what I would have done,* he thought.

"That's for sure," Dev'rox said. "You would have punched it like a caveman."

With its two major attacks thwarted, Alistair could feel as plain as day that the Mana Storm had expended a fair amount of its power. Even its rumbles and monumental gusts felt more muted. Which offered an opportunity.

Alistair activated [Eyes of Truth], peering into the heart of the storm. While observing it with his aura sense was essentially a higher-fidelity version of his normal vision, Karmic sight was a different story. Even his aura sense couldn't penetrate the incredibly dense inner core of the storm, but his Karmic sight could.

Using his perception of threads of Fate, he found something strange at the center. A rift in reality, with a sentient being at the center. An elemental beast, of pure Mana affinity.

The storm started running away immediately, leaving him with little time to think. Alistair didn't warn Oliver of what he was about to do, crouching to the ground and springing into the air with the coiled release of his immensely powerful hamstrings. He flew over a hundred feet into the air, bolstered by the newly improved **Fall of Fleet.**

Dev'rox had already felt his intentions, moving into position smoothly. Alistair activated [Dash], using Dev'rox's head as a stepping stone. The rest of the way lacked solid ground, so he was still subject to gravity like any other flying object, but his current momentum would last long enough for him to reach the eye of the storm.

Alistair pressed together his hands, using himself as the grounding for his electrical Skill.

Skill Upgraded: [Lightning of Justice] (Tier 2 Legendary Skill): *Strike the Earthly ground and bring down the illuminating Lightning of Justice from afar.* Mana Cost: 60. Upgradeable (0/200).

Alistair frowned for a moment at the Skill text. Wasn't there a change to the wording, adding "illuminating" to the description? That had never happened before.

In any case, the golden lightning obliterated the sanctum of the clouds. Rainbow-colored Mana burst away like blood spatter from a bullet wound. His target was in sight—the Mana was thick enough to swim in at that point, and Alistair did, frenziedly thrusting himself forward.

The being at the center of the storm was humanoid but with no features at all. It was a mass of pure affinity Mana, presenting as a mixture of glowing blue and white Mana, in a form that could not quite be described as a solid, liquid, or gas, but a strange mixture of all three.

With no face, Alistair thought it could pass as a horror movie villain. It seemed surprised to see an intruder in its sacred abode. The beast floated in a mass of condensed rainbow Mana above a thin, thirty-foot rift.

Alistair recognized it as the same type of construction as he had found in the earthquake lava rifts back in New Boston. Once you destroyed the final boss, the rift disappeared.

For all the power that the storm possessed, the beast was easy pickings. Perhaps it was weakened from expending so much energy. Alistair cut it in half with a simple **[Blood Hand],** savoring the life force afterward.

The moment he killed the beast, the rift disappeared, as well as the resulting Mana Storm. In less than ten seconds, the immense cloud of Mana all across the spectrum dissipated into the atmosphere. No longer drawn to a single point by the rift and beast, Mana settled back into the land where it belonged, returning some color to the region.

Alistair casually fell from the sky. With his improved **Fall of Fleet,** it was like jumping an inch onto a cushioned pillow.

The ground didn't feel the same way, with his boots distributing his immense weight into the earth, creating a small crater. Alistair dusted the dirt off his robes, breathing deeply. The wound in the world was gone. Mana had returned.

Already the color was returning to the soil, sky and tiny lifeforms. Off in the distance, it was still black-and-white, but at least in their vicinity, they saw the beauty of color.

Oliver caught up to him. "You dropped this."

He handed him the golden gourd that now contained a justice-fueled Dao material.

"I was worried it would explode in my hands," Oliver told him. "I have a feeling it will be useful, if you can manage to keep it safe."

Alistair understood the meaning of his words when he tried to put it in his inventory. It just wouldn't work. Unfortunately, that made a lot of sense. The inventory was an interior physical location dug into their soulcore. According to the records, such an ability should have only been capable for an Adept and up, but the Sublimed Machine Faction played loose with the rules of cultivation with their technological abilities.

His nascent soul couldn't handle the ridiculous amount of concentrated quintessence. Which presented a problem. He would have to keep the gourd on his person at all times, at least if he wanted it to be useful in a pinch. If George Moulin popped out of nowhere, having it in a safe back home would be useless.

Alistair was lucky that his **Mammothskin Raiment** had ample pockets, and that Felix had kept those pockets intact and even expanded them. He placed the gourd inside his robe and turned to Oliver.

"Looks like we're going to have to go storm chasing."

4 THE HOLY RAVINE

ALISTAIR CONSTANTLY FELT for his lightning-filled gourd. He knew it was in his pocket and that it hadn't fallen out, but he still obsessively checked. It still felt so unstable. He understood that the chance of it actually coming out was minuscule, but he was a worrier by nature. Like the card that Farsa Strongbite gave him or the Cabal marble, it wouldn't fit in his inventory, though unlike those items, it didn't appear to be soulbound. That meant that he could actually lose it, whereas those other things would always return to him.

Over the course of the next few hours, they trekked the Wasteland looking for storms. However, they came up empty. They only caught glimpses of Mana Storms on the horizon, yet when they tried getting closer, the storms also moved further away, almost as if they were avoiding them.

Considering that Alistair had uncovered that there was an elemental beast inside the storms that appeared to control them, it was a less crazy hypothesis than at first glance.

"What are those pure Mana beasts called, anyway?" Oliver asked.

"Uh, I don't know," Alistair said. "I forgot to inspect it."

"Devonic Purebreeds," Dev'rox offered up. "Ironic, since they're impure mutts, at least compared to the greater ones. The 'pure' purebreeds are some of the most haughty beings in the multiverse."

Oliver was used to the imp at this point, not hesitating at all at his sudden manifestation. "What do you know about the Devonic type?"

"They seek to purify all other types of Mana. Absorb, refine, destroy. You send one youth onto a planet without sufficient defenses, and in a few years' time, it will be a mass of pure affinity Mana."

"Well, we can't let that happen," Alistair said. "But also, that doesn't seem to match this Wasteland in a one-to-one correspondence. This area hasn't been turned to pure Mana—it's lacking the vitality of Mana altogether."

"I'm not sure about that one," Dev'rox admitted. "Maybe they're siphoning off the pure affinity Mana they're making somewhere else."

Besides the lack of Mana Storms, they also didn't see any of the reptiles that were said to be going haywire at the disappearance of their king, Vritra. There were signs that they had once been there, with abandoned tunnels, cylindrical slithering indents, and pools of acid. But no living creatures. It was a complete ghost town.

Considering the Wasteland was the size of Montana, their options were limited. Oliver wanted to use Alistair's speed to go all in chasing a storm down, whereas Alistair wanted to try going to the center. In the end, he convinced Oliver by reminding him he would have to stay on Alistair's back the entire time.

Alistair's logic was that the center always was the place to go. When in doubt, head straight for the center.

Even after accounting for Oliver's slower speed, it still only took them a bit over two hours to make it there. That was the advantage of cultivation improving their bodies. As far as he understood, their planet would grow in time as well. Based on some reports on distances, it probably had already grown slightly. For now, their superior physiques would expedite travel immensely, though after seeing the solar system-sized worlds in his bloodline vision, Alistair knew convenient travel wasn't a given.

Alistair checked back at his subregion map multiple times to keep them on course. He didn't want any shenanigans like when they were going through the forest to Saturn's château.

Speaking of Saturn, the count in his [Vanquishing the Devil Kings] Quest updated from 0/12 to 2/12. Like how the Devil Kings had a Quest that took a snapshot of the top 10 humans at a certain point in time, the humans would have to kill the Devil Kings from a certain point in time, likely those from the beginning of the Quest.

If George raised any more Devil Princes to Devil Kings like he had done with Jakk, they wouldn't count. Alistair wasn't especially worried about that. At his strength, defeating future replacement Devil Kings would be like taking candy from a baby.

Still, the current ten Devil Kings left sounded daunting, but Alistair thought it was easier than it seemed. He had defeated Dragonus fair and square, so he could certainly take on almost all the others in a one-on-one fight. He really just had to be careful about George or Oracle.

While he let his mind wander, they arrived close to the position Alistair calculated to be the center of the Wasteland.

It was nothing like they expected. Firstly, Alistair was hoping to see a concentration of Mana Storms, but it was black-and-white like everywhere else. But what they did see in the distance were two enormous mountains.

"I'm not going crazy, am I?" Oliver asked. "Those are mountains, right?"

Alistair squinted, finding it difficult to get a good look with the lack of color. "I think so."

One of the mountains looked black, while the other was pure white. Alistair got the sense that there was something in the middle between them, hidden by their bulk. Most likely a valley.

As they grew closer to the peaks, their size became more clear. While he was not a perfect judge of height, the mountains looked to be verging on the size of the largest on Earth, close to twenty thousand feet tall. After everything Alistair had seen, not overly impressive.

However, even if it wasn't that impressive, in order to get to whatever they were guarding, they still had to climb them.

The white peak was the closer one. It essentially looked like a normal mountain, except it was pure white. There were slight variations in color based on the shading of the snow and rocks. Being entirely barren of life, you could see cleanly from the bottom to the top. Snow piled up even at the bottom, showing just how cold it was.

They started climbing right away. Both Alistair and Oliver had never gone mountain climbing before, but with their Attributes it wasn't that difficult. The only problem was that its sheer size made the ascent tedious. Alistair remembered reading that it would take climbers several weeks to ascend Mount Everest.

Luckily, they wouldn't have to wait weeks. They were going way faster than any normal human could. The troubles were the freezing temperatures and unsteady nature of the mountain. Multiple times, Alistair's foothold crumbled underneath him. Only thanks to his lightning quick reflexes and extraordinary strength did he avoid falling.

Oliver might not have been able to avoid such a disaster, so he stayed behind Alistair, who acted as the lead climber. By shadowing his every action, Oliver dodged many unsteady holds.

The sun bore down on them stronger the higher they climbed, but never raised the temperature. Even though he remained focused on the ascent, Alistair couldn't help but admire the untouched grandeur of the pearly peak. In the before, he might have dismissed mountaineering as a reckless hobby. He had never felt more unified with nature than now, when he put one hand above the other in non-stop motion.

Ten hours in and it was growing cold. Not for him, who had the unfettered protection of **Mammothskin Raiment.** Alistair thought he could have scaled it in thirty minutes, but he had to wait up for Oliver.

The difference in their abilities was very discrete—at Alistair's level of Agility and Strength he could almost run up the cliff face like a mountain goat, while Oliver had much more difficulty, having to approach it more like a normal person. That slowed down their climb by over a factor of ten.

Alistair wasn't willing to risk having another person on his back if they fell off. But there was something else odd about their climbing. It was far more difficult than it should have been. Even Alistair was huffing and puffing for air at the halfway mark. That shouldn't have been possible with his ability to convert basic physiological processes to Mana consumption, but somehow it was happening.

"Can we take… a break?" Oliver stammered out, hanging on for dear life to the sheer cliff face. His fingertips were covered in frost, a result of the plummeting temperatures.

"That sounds like a good idea." Alistair turned his back to the mountain, holding himself against a small ledge as he overlooked the Wasteland. Secretly, he had been hoping for a break himself, but he wasn't going to ask for a rest first.

At their elevation, snow was piling up everywhere, making it that much more difficult to climb, on top of the mysterious fatigue. Alistair couldn't imagine what goodies would lie on the other side of the mountainous wall. Surely, if it was this hard to scale, there had to be something good, right?

"Don't look down," Dev'rox said mischievously.

"Go to hell," Alistair replied, though he took the dare and had a gander. He regretted it instantly. For some reason, despite having fallen off flying komodo dragons and giant fireworms, standing on a cliff edge still gave him goosebumps. *Why is this scarier than being in the Mana Storm? It's higher up, but terminal velocity means our fall would only be maybe 50% faster at the end.*

"Don't rub it in, you bastard," Dev'rox said. "That's what I'm trying to do."

"What do you think is on the other side?" Oliver asked.

"No clue," Alistair replied. "It better be good, though."

"I'm thinking it's an entire civilization of Mana Storms. All living together like a happy family."

"Perfect, then we can slaughter all of them at once," Alistair said. "No more happy family."

"And I thought I was the one who was morbid," Oliver said. "Okay, let's get back to climbing."

On the way up, Alistair had to hand Oliver his coat, since it was getting too cold for him. Alistair would brave the freezing temperatures shirtless, since he had stopped wearing undershirts out of laziness.

"The ladies must love that," Dev'rox cooed, though Alistair ignored him. After another three hours, they had almost made it to the summit. This was in spite of choosing the shortest part of the white mountain to climb.

At last, the end was in sight. Alistair sped up, digging his fingertips into the voluminous amounts of snow as he dragged himself to the top. The fatigue had fully permeated his body. It wasn't anything compared to some of the pains he had experienced in battle, but it still wasn't pleasant.

Oliver sounded like a dying billy goat. Dev'rox helped him out, lazily floating to the small clearing at the summit. He looked down on the Necromancer, who was wheezing in exhaustion fifteen feet below.

"What will you do for me if I swap places with you?" Dev'rox asked.

"This... isn't... funny," Oliver said. "C'mon, just do it."

"Dev'rox," Alistair warned, giving him a pointed look.

"Fine. You're no fun." Dev'rox snapped his fingers and swapped places with Oliver, who promptly collapsed into a pile of snow.

Alistair nudged Oliver, who was still face-planted in the snow. "You're going to want to see this."

Alistair couldn't believe his eyes. As he stood on the mountaintop, taking in the view below, he almost wanted to hit himself in the head. It didn't make any sense.

There was an enormous, luscious valley cradled between the two mountains. Verdant, colorful, and full of life, it was in stark contrast to the rest of the colorless Wasteland.

The valley was split in two by a beautiful, winding river, which flowed through the centerpiece of the valley—a sprawling and lively village. Terrace farms covered the inner slopes of the mountain, while smoke billowed from chimneys into the open air. It was an idyllic scene of some fairy tale countryside that felt completely out of place.

"What the hell?" Oliver said, having gathered himself to his knees. "What is this?"

What is this, indeed, Alistair thought. He could barely make out some human figures toiling on the farms, but he also would've sworn he could see reptilian silhouettes as well.

Not able to make out much more from their position, they started climbing down. The other side of the cliff was much less snowy and was full of grass just a few hundred feet down from the peak.

So far, it didn't seem like anyone had noticed them. Alistair and Oliver were a stealthy duo, well-practiced at suppressing their auras. Alistair felt like his cloak was especially effective today, with essentially zero Mana emanating out of his skin. Too close to zero, in fact.

Alistair looked inward to Dev'rox for advice. But he didn't need the imp's opinion to realize what had happened. It wasn't only his outward aura that had disappeared—it was everything. When he tried to access his Dao Nodes or his soulcore, it was like they had been sealed away. He had never felt anything like that before. Even when he had been inside a proto-Domain, the suppression wasn't anywhere near what it was now.

Oliver looked toward him with fearful recognition. The two of them scrambled back up the mountain, intent on escaping whatever death trap lay ahead of them in the false bucolic paradise below.

Alistair felt like a mortal again. His limbs were heavy, his body ached in strange ways that he hadn't experienced for months. His diaphragm hurt, his lungs wailed, and his heart struggled to pump oxygen to his greedy body.

While it was a steep mountain, it was almost as if he was weaker than he was before the initiation. Perhaps the internal Mana that enriched his muscles and skeleton took over so much of his bodily functions that his true natural ability had decayed. Or maybe he was just being dramatic.

It was embarrassing to see Oliver easily keeping up with him as they hiked up the cliff face. They both were exhausted by the time they reached the top. Alistair wasn't sure where the exact border was, but considering that Dev'rox had been able to use his Skill quite close to the summit, it had to be around where they crossed over.

They could regroup later on and figure out what was happening here. It wasn't even their main priority—dealing with the Mana Storms was. And even—

Alistair fell back onto his bottom, yelping in pain as blood streamed down his nose. Based on the sickening crack concomitant with the pain, he had broken his nose. Blood dripped down onto the pure white snow.

His mind lost focus for a moment from the pain and shock, but Alistair wasn't some sheltered college kid anymore. He recollected himself and realized what had happened. He had haphazardly jogged nose-first into an invisible wall.

Oliver, seeing Alistair's injury, walked up to the pathway they had crossed over not ten minutes before. He tentatively reached out a palm, only for it to be stopped midair. Oliver didn't have much Strength to begin with, so without his cultivation boost, he was a scrawny teenager, but he tried pushing against the invisible barrier, anyway. To no avail.

"I can't believe this," Oliver muttered. "There's no way."

Alistair joined him in investigating the mysterious barrier, pinching his nose at the same time.

"Dev'rox, do you know what's going on?"

"I'm guessing the three of us stumbled into a Devonic Elision Field. Like the name suggests, it's a technology built from the Beast Cores and purified ancestral material of mature Devonic Purebreeds. Using their innate purification methods, the field creates both a barrier that traps and absorbs quintessence—Mana, Dao energy, *nue*—all of it. They even have them in the Asura Hell—that's how widespread they are. Even you have seen something related in those power dampening handcuffs. I'm quite sure they also use Devonic Purebreed matter."

"Great," Alistair huffed out, giving up on physically pounding in the wall after his hands started hurting. At least his nosebleed had let up. "Any suggestions?"

"Well, to put it simply, you're incredibly screwed unless those people down there are helpful. You have the body of a mortal now, meaning you'll die in however long your biology can withstand a lack of water."

"That's just about what I thought," Alistair said. "Oliver, I think we're going to have to make contact."

5 SILVER COMET SECT

"DON'T BE IMPERTINENT, PLEASE." Alistair smiled, though with a small degree of underlying sharpness. "We really have to be as congenial as we can, if that will save our lives."

"You sound so old," Oliver complained. "That was possibly the lamest way to phrase that."

"Like you're a normal kid at all," Alistair shot back. "Aren't you turning nineteen in a few months, anyway? I'm only three years older than you."

"3.5, you're rounding down."

"Whatever, you understand my point. This is serious. In all honesty, this might be the stickiest situation we've ever been in."

"'Stickiest situation'? Really?"

Alistair gave him a serious glance. "I mean it."

"Yeah, yeah, I understand. I won't do anything weird, I promise. This is life and death we're talking about."

"Don't make me regret bringing you along. Let's get going."

———

Alistair also tried accessing his items and his status screen. All his items that were trapped in his inventory were inaccessible, while the items that were on his person didn't seem to work. **Devilsbane Gauntlets** remained inert crimson bracelets, unable to turn into gloves.

His status screen was also completely inoperable. It returned an error message, saying "Access Unavailable At This Time," and flickered uselessly.

Dev'rox didn't know what to make of it, though he hadn't encountered a Devonic Elision Field in an area that had the Pathfinder AI. Was it a quirk of the interaction of Mana? A specific Pathfinder limitation for this region? They had no way of knowing.

Alistair silently prayed for the safety of the Northeast Order. There was nothing he could do—it was completely out of his hands. He could only trust in Alexandra, John, and others to protect everyone. *And to protect themselves.* The looming threat of George Moulin was like an executioner's blade.

They trekked down the outward facing hill with no trouble. There appeared to be hundreds of acres of farmland leading to a bustling village in the center, so there weren't many people in the outlying areas.

In some villages, he noted reptiles as beasts of burden. While he couldn't use his Skills to say for certain, based on their behavior they were most likely below the threshold of sophonce—for beasts of paltry pedigree, level 30.

Now that Alistair thought about it, Selephita implied that the most decorated species achieved sophonce early as well. It was funny then that in the middle, the vast majority of the beast species throughout the multiverse gained intelligence much later at Half-Step Immortal, which Alistair thought might have been either Profound, Visionary, or some transitional special beast Realm. That created an intriguing bell curve, with both the lowest and highest beast species reaching intelligence early.

The first people they encountered were a family attending their wheat fields. Alistair and Oliver approached them as harmlessly as possible, waving to them as soon as they reached the edge of their fields.

The man that saw them first was young, though he looked hardened like a farm boy, with a deep tan. He was wearing a practical set of silk robes. Alistair thought it looked somewhat funny for what was ostensibly a peasant to be wearing such a fine fabric, but things weren't always a one-to-one correlation to Earth norms.

"Who're ya?" he said, with a thick accent that Alistair couldn't place.

Alistair bowed his head deeply, forcing Oliver to do the same. "We are two humble travelers from a faraway land. We seek refuge from the turbulent forces outside these lands, and any gratitude shown shall be repaid tenfold."

"Ah, yar Earthlins, aren't ya? Always a miracle to hear ya speaking New Moi, ain't that right? We gots a few Earthlins here. Tha name's Grag, what's about you two?" Grag bowed to both of them.

"Alistair Tan, and this is my friend Oliver Cambry." They returned the gesture.

"Well, nice to meet ya. This har is me family's farm. Yar welcome to stay here for a while, but I'd reckon yar gonna wanna go to tha town center." Grag pointed a finger down the beaten path they were on to a location deeper and lower inside the valley. Because of their elevation, they could make out a cluster of buildings from above.

"Thank you, Grag," Alistair said. "If I may ask, where do you people come from?"

"Us? Well, we've just about been here in tha Holy Ravine since time began, I reckon, though I gots some Moi blood in mah from my mama's side. If ya mean how'ds we get from over yonder to yar neck of the valley, I haven't tha faintest idea. A little over a year ago, we woke up to tha Holy Ravine having new neighbors. We didn't notice much at first cuz we ain't have tha tendency to leave this har valley oft'n. From what we've heard from ya Earthlins, we're kinda in a similar situation. Our planet ain't have any of that Mana nonsense either, or any such things as a Pathfinder AI."

A little over a year... Alistair thought to himself. *Time dilation?* The initiation had started four months ago, so the timeline didn't make any sense as presented. Since Alistair had seen the Pathfinder using time dilation before, it didn't seem outlandish, as they already had the Devonic Elision Field surrounding their valley.

"Well, thank you very much, Grag. Is there anything else we should know?"

Grag stroked his chin. "Be wary of tha Church of the Holy Ones. Most of us ain't got a problem with outsiders, but they aren't too keen on ya. But even they wouldn't dare attack ya without ya attackin' 'em first. The Holy Ravine hasn't seen bloodshed in a hundred generations."

Alistair and Oliver exchanged a look at Grag's last statement. Even if they weren't affected by the war against the Devil Kings, he didn't imagine the Final Frontier Empire to be a very peaceful place.

Before they could leave, Grag invited his entire family to meet the mysterious Earthlings. There was Grag's pa, his ma, and then his five brothers and four sisters. Alistair didn't want to be rude, since Grag was so nice, but they kept asking question after question. It was obvious they didn't get many visitors.

But then it exploded from there. Nearby villagers came over to see what the fuss was about. Then they told their neighbors, and they told their neighbors. Alistair and Oliver kept walking toward the town center, but behind them gathered a crowd of over a hundred people.

Alistair confirmed his suspicions about the place by asking about the reptiles people were using on the farms. Vritra had, for a brief period, lived with the villagers in the Holy Ravine along with some of his brood, but left several months ago. Apparently, some of the villagers had negotiated with the Reptile Emperor to use some of the cow-sized lizards as farm animals.

Just hearing that Vritra had managed to leave perked Alistair up. He would have to ask more knowledgeable people about how that had happened.

Talking to Grag gave him information on important aspects of their culture. They were a hardened people, despite what Grag had said about warfare. What he said was literally true—the Holy Ravine proper had not seen warfare within its borders for a hundred generations. But that was only because of their unrivaled martial strength and the nigh impregnable mountain passes. They were under constant siege from enemy forces.

In addition, whatever planet they had come from halfway across the universe had no modern technology. In fact, militarily, they seemed to not have *any* technology. From what Alistair gathered on the way into the town, they fought all their battles unarmed in hand-to-hand combat.

Alistair supposed he couldn't dig at them too hard. After all, the difference between the Final Frontier Empire and Earth was dozens of times larger than the difference between Earth and the Holy Ravine.

As he walked, a stray thought occurred to Alistair—what about his debt? If it was impossible to access the system at all, he was screwed in terms of making payments. Not only that, but he already had a late payment. But he dismissed those worries. Right now, he was more concerned about surviving and getting back to everyone.

Their posse continued downward. They continuously lost and gained followers the entire time. It was a ten-mile walk from the peak of the valley down to the fertile trough. People had their own lives to live, and they couldn't stay the whole way.

Without their normal speed, it took several hours to reach the more populated area. Alistair didn't recall ever walking so far in his life, at least at their current pace. It was especially difficult since all the people of the valley were much more fit than them. Their stamina felt endless. For people without Mana, it was odd, to say the least.

The domiciles began increasing in density a few miles out of the true town square. Farmland shrunk and became concentrated on smaller yield crops like berries or ginseng. Smoke rose from chimneys into what felt like the purest air Alistair had ever felt in his life.

The natural beauty of the valley was unparalleled. Interestingly, while there were the enormous guardian mountains of black and white that defended the Holy Ravine from outsiders, the center of the valley was quite hilly.

Acres upon acres of the most fertile farmland Alistair had ever seen led into a deciduous forest biome. It was thicker on the outskirts of the hills, while deeper in, he could make out tall pagodas and sprawling estates. Paved roads crossed the landscape, intersecting with the hills and forest. Yet even in the deepest part of the valley, there were still trees.

At the very center of it all was a huge building that looked like a hybrid of a Buddhist temple and a church. While it might have been the tallest structure in the town, because of how the valley worked, it was at the exact deepest point. Ten stories tall at the center, there was a cerulean twelve-pointed star at its peak.

With all the commotion Alistair and Oliver had tossed up, an envoy came to meet with them at the start of the hilly zone.

By the time they grew close to the town, the crowd had mostly dispersed. Alistair had the sense that there was some tension between the rural and the less rural villagers. He said less rural because the combined population of the entire valley couldn't have possibly been over fifty to sixty thousand. For a city kid like himself, that was rural, especially when considering the landscape.

The envoy sent out to greet them was headed by a short old man in a tattered set of beige robes. He wore a black headband around his forehead and walked with a wooden cane. While he looked like nothing special,

Alistair perceived a solidity to his movement that was unusual for a man of his age, or a man of any age, for that matter.

A group of robust young men followed him, all with shaved heads and similar robes that displayed muscular chests. Some of them wore red headbands, while others wore purple.

"Earthlings, welcome to the Holy Ravine! I am Ko Pao, Head Apostle of the Silver Comet Sect. You are the first Earthlings we have had come to our lands in many months. What tidings do you bring from beyond our mountains?"

Alistair immediately noticed that Ko Pao lacked the heavy accent of Grag. Alistair was so grateful that the Pathfinder AI's translation service was still working, or they would have really been screwed.

"I assume that my fellow Earthlings must have told you about the initiation and everything that came along with that. As of right now, we're in the sixth and final Quest—the Quest that determines the fate of this planet. And since I don't think that the Pathfinder AI is going to send you back, you're a part of this planet too. Let me explain everything."

Alistair took a glance at the dozen men that Ko Pao brought with him. The youngest had to be in his teens, while the oldest was in his thirties or forties. However, they acted in unison, all holding their heads and gaze slightly down with their hands clasped behind their backs respectfully. It was uncanny. While he didn't have any of his powers, he could tell that they weren't pushovers.

Alistair took Ko Pao aside, explaining the delicate nature of the situation. He wanted only the Head Apostle to hear his next words, but the old man insisted on bringing one other of the bald men to listen.

He gave an abridged version of his post-initiation story, explaining all the Quests and filling in the details that the Earthling stragglers weren't privy to. Ko Pao nodded and hummed along, not once interrupting him.

At the end, Alistair explained the Devil Kings and the sponsors and Final Frontier Empire, along with a rough idea of how the Pathfinder AI worked. During the course of his explanation, he touched on Selephita, which made him wonder about whether there were other pockets of alien civilization like Selephita's domain and the Holy Ravine. He hadn't considered that possibility before, but it made sense—the Pathfinder AI was trying to create novel and divergent situations to test Earth, and if it could also test some other places that needed integration as well, why not?

Alistair got the sense that Oliver was less than thrilled at how much information he was divulging to Ko Pao. And yes, it was a bit risky to reveal how important he was. But Alistair felt like he could trust them, at least to a certain extent. While he lacked his **[Eyes of Truth]**, something deep inside him said that they were trustworthy. Also, it wasn't like anything he was saying was top secret information.

"You spin an interesting tale, outsider," said Ko Pao's presumed disciple. He was one of the largest of the bunch, standing half a head taller than Alistair with even more impressive muscles. He was beardless with a cutting jawline and a distinctive diagonal scar coming down from his forehead over his nose, and wore a red headband. Now that Alistair thought about it, it looked similar to a Muay Thai Mongkhon. "How do we know what you say is true?"

"That is enough, Pike," Ko Pao said. "Have you forgotten your hospitality? These two poor souls have been through enough. Questioning their integrity is a step too far. I apologize for my student's rudeness. Please, come back with us to our temple and join us for supper. We can discuss what lies in store for you in the Holy Ravine."

"Can I have a moment to talk with my friend?" Alistair asked.

Ko Pao nodded his head.

Alistair pulled Oliver aside. He could tell that Oliver wasn't as enthusiastic as he was. "What's your read on things?" he asked.

"That I've resigned myself to die. I don't trust these guys further than I could throw them. But what can we do? We can't leave and we can't use our powers. If we tried to get away from them, I'm sure it'd piss them off, and if they wanted to, they could easily throw us in jail or worse."

Dev'rox couldn't manifest himself without Mana, but Alistair could relay his mental messages to Oliver as an intermediary. "Do you think the system would let promising candidates like you die so easily? Is what Dev'rox just said."

"You think the Herald of the Pathfinder is gonna show up and pluck us out of here if we get in trouble?" Oliver asked incredulously.

"Dev'rox says that he didn't say that, but that it's an AI vastly more powerful than the human mind and its plans are inscrutable and impossible to see. That doesn't guarantee our safety by any means—the law of the jungle is king and we might be tested here, but it's unlikely for random events outside our control to be fatal without recourse. Is what Dev'rox says."

"You don't have to convince me anymore, imp, I understand," Oliver said. "I can't do anything about it, so why resist?"

"We'd be delighted to accept," Alistair said to Ko Pao. "What kind of sect is the Silver Comet, anyway?"

Ko Pao gave a warm, but slightly impish smile. "I'm glad you asked."

––––––––

The Silver Comet Sect wasn't located in the town proper, but on a hill on the outskirts. One of the hills so deeply covered in forest, Alistair couldn't even make out the temple. It was a simple compound of stone bricks partially built into the hill itself. You could tell right away the temple was hundreds, if not thousands of years old. The ancient character was evident in everything, from the worn out metal door handles to the color of the rocks.

But while the temple was ancient, the dwellers inside were full of life. Chatter and laughter could be heard from every wing and corner. The members of the Silver Comet Sect appeared to be all male, ranging from adolescents to old men, all wearing a colored headband. Based on the general distribution of the colors, it seemed like there was a hierarchy, with black at the top and white on the bottom.

Wherever Ko Pao walked, the sect members bowed. He obviously commanded respect, despite his lack of physical strength compared to the rest of them, most of whom looked ridiculously proportioned, like comic book heroes.

He led them down a sparsely decorated main hall. The ceiling was so low that it grazed the hair of the tall man who'd challenged him before, giving it a claustrophobic feeling. However, instead of bringing them to guest quarters or their dining hall for supper, Alistair and Oliver found themselves in a blistering hot room.

It was gigantic, large enough to fit a house, and sparsely decorated. The walls were the same stone as everything else, but the floor was matted with a light, spongy material.

The first thing he noticed once he was inside was that the heat was overbearing. Alistair couldn't tell where it was coming from, but it was as hot as a Russian sauna.

There were dozens of men inside the room, all fiercely sparring with one another. They were blurs of movement, masters of martial arts.

"What's this?" Oliver asked, clearly not dealing with the heat any better than Alistair was.

"Oh, forgive me," Ko Pao said. "I forget that outsiders aren't familiar with our customs. The Holy Ravine's most sacred art and law is that of the fist. All guests must be challenged first, and then treated with the utmost respect."

6 ENTRY DUEL

As soon as Ko Pao entered and stepped onto the matted portion of the floor, all the men stopped fighting.

Even those in the middle of a punch arrested their movement midair, dropping their arms to their sides with complete sincerity and respect.

"Excuse me?" Oliver asked. "Challenged?"

"Yes. I will find an appropriate fighter for you. Naturally, you are not required to win your bout, but you must show proper respect for your opponent."

Oliver gulped and looked at Alistair, who shrugged. *When in Rome, do as the Romans.* Oliver returned an exasperated look.

"Who wishes to go first?" Ko Pao asked.

"May as well get this over with," Oliver said. "I'll go."

Ko Pao took out his cane and started prodding Oliver, who winced in pain as the old man jabbed his stomach.

"Hmm," the master said, stroking his long, triangular beard. "Jaron, come forward."

Alistair heard Jaron's light footsteps before he saw him. A boy no older than eight, reaching just above Oliver's waist. Alistair almost chuckled. Even Oliver, who knew that he was no hand-to-hand fighter, would have his pride wounded by that.

"This is my opponent?" Oliver asked, clearly a little miffed, as Alistair expected.

Dev'rox laughed inside Alistair's head, though it felt restrained. His consciousness seemed to be dampened by the suppression field, so even the act of internal thought transfer took effort. "I can't wait to see this."

"Do not underestimate him," Ko Pao replied. "He has been training since birth."

"So what, I have to fight him? What's allowed?"

"Anything is allowed except for weapons. That said, I wouldn't recommend trying to gouge out his eyes. He might really kill you then, though I would then have to kill him for breaking guest right."

"Okay," Oliver gulped. He jumped up and down a few times. Alistair thought that the Necromancer would have resisted this extremely peculiar scenario more, so he appreciated that Oliver was on his best behavior. Plus, it wasn't like this kid could actually hurt Oliver, right?

The crowd of sect members dispersed, creating a circular ring. The little boy did his best to look menacing with his shaved head and stern expression, but it only ended up looking cute.

Meanwhile, Alistair was doing his best to hype Oliver up, but it wasn't working well.

"You got this man," Alistair said, patting him on the back.

"Shut up," Oliver whispered back. "I'm fighting a goddamn little kid."

"That's why it will look really bad when you get your ass beat."

"Nah, I totally got this, dude," Oliver said. "I've watched your fights before. Lemme show you my moves."

Oliver did a series of shadow-boxing moves. It didn't look half-bad—if you were a beginner, that was. While he was fluid in his jabs and straights, he didn't shift his weight properly. Not that it should have mattered, fighting a little boy.

Alistair was happy to see that the suppression field didn't take away everything. His knowledge of martial arts was baked into his muscle memory. While he wouldn't be as fluid with certain connections to the Dao severed, he could still throw hands.

Ko Pao took center stage, lifting his cane into the air. "Our first guest, citizen of Earth, Oliver Cambry! And our white rank apostle, Jaron Silvus. May the blessed Mother of War grant a fair and beneficial match. The winner shall be the one to get the first knockdown. All techniques are permitted."

"Apologies if I injure you, honored guest," the boy said without a hint of sarcasm. In fact, Alistair would have sworn the look on his face was that of a heavyweight boxer sparring against a middleweight in training camp—he was afraid of hurting his opponent.

"There's no need for that," Oliver replied, putting up his dukes. His uneasy glance back at Alistair suggested he was both afraid of losing, but also curious how on Earth a four-and-a-half foot tall child could defeat him.

Back before the initiation, Alistair would say there was literally a zero percent chance Jaron could beat Oliver in a fist-fight. The young man had a solid physique and, as he said, he had picked up some moves from Alistair over time. And right now they were in a region without Mana, and with either trace amounts or no amount of the Dao.

But a hunch told Alistair to not count out this Jaron.

Ko Pao raised his hands and brought them down in a chopping motion. "Begin!"

Oliver circled around Jaron, slowly approaching the boy. Alistair could tell that he still felt uncomfortable with the idea of fighting a kid, so Jaron was going to have to make the first move. But like a sage-like master, the boy simply walked forward with his hands at his sides.

Then he struck. Jaron threw a perfectly executed right straight, aiming up at Oliver's solar plexus. But the Necromancer caught the punch easily, as was expected. Oliver unleashed an open palm strike that was more of a slap, intending to finish the match in one blow and also not injure the boy too much.

In a split second, Oliver's face was on the ground.

Since he was without his improved eyesight and visual dynamic acuity, Alistair had almost missed what happened. Jaron had moved with supernatural agility, performing a leg sweep at the exact fulcrum point of Oliver's weight, which had shifted due to his slap. Oliver became the slightest amount unbalanced, shifting slightly too far forward. Then, he'd punched him in the nose with blinding speed. Oliver face-planted from both the reap and the punch.

"Victory to Jaron Silvus!" Ko Pao declared, issuing a hearty laugh, though the fellow pupils in the crowd remained stone-faced.

Alistair could hardly believe what he saw. For that kid to see all of that in such a short amount of time and execute those techniques with the speed he did—it didn't seem possible. Was Jaron just a prodigy of prodigies? Alistair could have sworn that Jaron touched upon the Dao, despite it feeling so far away for himself.

Oliver pulled himself up to his knees, drops of blood dripping out of his nose. Alistair worried that he would be a little hot-headed and mad that a child beat him up, but he seemed in good spirits.

"Good job," Oliver said, bowing to his opponent, perhaps thinking it was the proper custom from reading a ton of murim manhwa.

Luckily, Oliver was correct with his assumption, and Jaron bowed back. "Well met. Thank you for your fists."

Ko Pao offered a hand to Oliver and pulled him up with a mysterious amount of strength coming from his tiny body. The Necromancer returned to Alistair's side, giving him a sheepish look. "Hope you do better, or I'll be reminding you of that grin you have on your face."

Both participants made a handshake in the traditional style of the Holy Ravine, clasping each other by what was supposed to be the elbow. Because of the massive size difference, Jaron could not fully reach the elbow of his former opponent, though he tried valiantly.

Alistair could feel the tension in the room rise. It was obvious even from the way that he walked that Oliver was no martial artist. But that wasn't the case for himself. Every seeker wanted to test their mettle.

It had to be said that Alistair had never fought someone with only hand-to-hand combat. He was always using his powers in some way or another. The closest was against Red, the mysterious Cabal recruit he'd encountered during his time in Felons vs. Fellows. That, of course, had ended in an embarrassing loss, Alistair unable to lay even one finger on the red-haired man.

I could use that style though, he absently thought to himself, remembering Red's suave all-white outfit. A bone-chilling feeling snapped him out of his reverie, Alistair immediately looking toward the source. It was his opponent.

Alistair couldn't deny he was pleased that the man who stood in front of him was a man, and not a child. He was muscular, like all the other members of the sect. His hair was longer than most of his compatriots, though no more than half an inch, his hairline covered by an orange Mongkhon-style headband.

Because of his plain white robes and harmonious facial features, Alistair thought that he would do a good job standing in for Red. Because if he imagined someone as Red, he wouldn't feel bad for beating them up.

Ko Pao introduced the man, who gazed at him with pure focus. He stood a few inches taller than Alistair, his stance completely sturdy, like the world was attached to him rather than him standing on the world.

"This is Apol-Xin, recently promoted to orange rank apostle. He shall be a good match for you, Alistair Tan of Earth. For this higher level duel, the fight will be to surrender or incapacitation. Do not fret, I will prevent any serious injuries. Once more, I beseech the Mother of War for a fair and beneficial match. Begin!"

The other apostles widened the circle this time, stepping back in unison, with Oliver slightly delayed. They formed a ring twice the size of a UFC octagon, giving more than ample room for movement.

Alistair stared at his opponent, taking a deep breath and focusing. While he couldn't enter the Kai'tazake Mutra, he still remembered the deep feeling of calm, the flow of heightened concentration. While his Skills had been severed, he had been living the movements of {Assassin Fist} and {Psychopomp's Discipline} for months. While he couldn't execute the moves as perfectly as before without the closeness of the Dao, he still had the principles in mind.

Fluid, then still. Soft, then hard. The Kiss of Death. Alistair repeated the mantra of the World Titan Zenaitsu Morogoni, and raised his hands in preparation for the bout. Apol-Xin, however, kept his hands at his sides, like he was some kind of unbothered master.

Well, I'll show him that he's underestimating me, Alistair thought. *Let's start with a jab.*

He unleashed his fastest attack, a left jab straight at his opponent's nose. He could see the path of his arm, the exact way it would connect with his opponent's face. And it looked like it did. Yet he touched only air.

Alistair didn't make the same mistake of overextending and losing his balance like Oliver did. His balance was stable, and his movements were solid. Missing that blow didn't throw him out of sync, and he felt Apol-Xin out with a series of jabs.

None of them landed. Alistair paid attention to Apol-Xin's feet, which barely moved as he dodged each jab with the most subtle of movements. He gritted his teeth, remembering how Red had done the same. This time would be different.

All of his limbs became whips of water as he embodied the mantra of {Psychopomp's Discipline}. There was no doubt that Apol-Xin was superior in experience, so Alistair had to implement an unorthodox strategy.

He threw an arcing haymaker that was full of inefficiencies, in an apparent attempt to knock his opponent out in one blow. Apol-Xin easily backstepped and avoided it, but Alistair was expecting that. He lunged forward with all the speed his body would give him, going for a flying knee straight toward Apol-Xin's chest.

The orange rank apostle caught the knee with both hands. This was Alistair's second ruse. He grabbed onto the left sleeve of his opponent's robe with his own left hand and the collar with his right hand, performing what a judoka would call a harai goshi, a sweeping hip toss. Apol-Xin landed on the ground with a heavy thud.

Alistair followed his opponent to the ground and brought his fist up to ground and pound, but when he looked down, a seed of doubt grew in his mind.

Why does he look so nonplussed? Alistair would have expected some emotion on his face—he had just been thrown hard onto the matted floor. But Apol-Xin's face was completely blank, like a statue carved out of granite.

That moment of hesitation was all the apostle needed. The heat of the training room on top of the exertion had caused a large amount of sweat to collect in Alistair's hair. Unlike the members of the Silver Comet Sect, he lacked a headband and had a large mass of fashionable hair.

Finding the exact focus point of weight, Apol-Xin hip-bridged with a surprising amount of force. Alistair's vision suffered, and he didn't see it coming, though there was no guarantee he would have anticipated it under any conditions. Alistair tried to adjust his weight and stay mounted, but the sweat in his eyes distracted him enough that he misjudged the distance.

He fell off on Apol-Xin's right hip, who immediately followed up with a capoeira-style kick, spinning upward off of his palm and slamming his heel into Alistair's face.

Shooting pain spiked through the nerves of his face, and his brain ricocheted in his skull. The metallic taste of blood felt like the bitter throes of defeat. Alistair gathered all of his willpower and charged Apol-Xin, delivering an uppercut straight into Apol-Xin's stomach.

Thud. Alistair's fist met abs of unthinkable toughness. *What's with this body?*

Those were Alistair's last thoughts before he went lights out.

Apol-Xin tried a blindingly fast elbow strike, aiming right for where he kicked Alistair to deal the most damage. Alistair somehow partially parried the blow despite his condition, even managing to land a hook to his opponent's liver, but it was too weak to do anything.

An elbow struck outside his perception. That Alistair managed to block it even a little bit was a testament to Alistair's battle-tested instincts and innate talent, the movements of {Psychopomp's Discipline} baked into his DNA.

The Silver Comet Sect apprentice unleashed a burst of air in preparation for an arcing punch. Alistair fell unconscious with a smile on his face.

7 DAILY TRAINING

"WHY'D you get beat so hard, man?" Oliver asked.

"I concur with the skeleton boy," Dev'rox said. "That was an embarrassing showing."

Alistair opened his eyes. His head throbbed, and his limbs felt like they were being weighed down by anchors. He was still on the floor of the training hall, still sweating like a pig.

"How long have I been out for?" Alistair asked.

"Just a few minutes. They dragged you over here to recover."

Alistair lifted his head off the ground and observed his surroundings. The apostles of the Silver Comet Sect were sparring with each other. He and Oliver were in the corner, along with Ko Pao.

"I should have had two solid hits on him," Alistair said. "But he's made of stone or something. I don't understand."

Ko Pao chuckled. "That is the famous Steel Body that our sect prides itself for. You, boy, you have potential. I can shape you into a masterpiece if you stay with us for three months."

"Three months?" Alistair questioned. "We can't stay here for three months. We have to get out of here as soon as possible. I have millions of people relying on me."

Ko Pao's venerable smile didn't reach his eyes. "I am afraid that it might be more difficult to return than you imagine. I have yet to explain the crux of the situation, and for that I apologize. It was not my intention to withhold or mislead, but the circumstances were not proper until now.

"The Holy Ravine is under the control of one organization—the Church of the Holy Ones. You have most likely seen their building already—the temple in the middle of town with a twelve-pointed star. The Church of the Holy Ones was once a sect like us. By the letter of the law, they are still a sect, but in practice they serve as the entire government.

"There are seven martial sects that have existed for a thousand years in these lands. The Silver Comet Sect, the Raging Bull Sect, the Viper's Fangs Sect, Kodaidaemin, the Sworn Sisters, the Slaves of Shadow, and the Church of the Holy Ones. For the majority of our history, the Holy Ravine has been in flux between these sects, with different ones coming to the forefront at different periods. That is, until thirty years ago.

"The governance of the Holy Ravine is determined by the winner of the triennial Dragon's Equinox Festival. Each sect sends three fighters under the age of forty, and the sect of the winner is declared the governing body of the Holy Ravine for the next three years. In our entire thousand-year recorded history, there has never been a four-time repeat victor. Sects have won four times in a row, but never with the same fighter, and never five in a row. Twenty-four years ago, a man from the Church of the Holy Ones appeared. His name was Silvanio Apostolos, and he became the youngest ever governor at the age of seventeen. Then, to the eternal shame of the other six factions, he went on to win seven more times in a row."

Alistair did some mental math. "So then he's forty-one now? Meaning that he's aged out, unless they changed the rules."

"Correct. As he is now older than forty, he is ineligible to compete in next year's Dragon's Equinox Festival. Even Silvanio has not gone so far as to change the sacred ruleset, but his control over the Holy Ravine is strong. Ten years ago, after the fifth victory, they rebuilt the town center with the enormous temple you see today. Even though we might not like his rule, we all respect his strength, though all the other sects wonder if his young heir shall be up for the task in next year's tournament. Or even if he shall relinquish power upon a loss. Alas, these concerns have no bearing on you. All that applies to you and your friend is that Silvanio has a deep distrust of outsiders. By making the decision to harbor you, we have made ourselves enemies of the Holy Ones more than we already were. If Silvanio can control this field you speak of that is limiting your powers, he would never tell you willingly, and he will not let you leave."

Alistair shook his head. "I'm sorry if we're a burden. I had no idea."

"Nonsense. I was the one who said to take you in," Ko Pao said. "I did it on a hunch. The other outsiders told us of the great changes to the world, but nothing compared to what you said. Your exploits sound legendary."

"Don't butter him up too much," Oliver said. "He's already got people worshiping him like a god back on Earth. Well, the other parts of Earth."

"Hah. As if," Alistair said. "If the tournament is going to take another year, what's this about three months? How are we going to get out of here?"

Ko Pao held up a finger. "One thing before that, if we agree to train you, you must do something for us in the future. We aren't so altruistic as to do this for free."

"Something?" Alistair asked.

"One favor. I can't tell you exactly what for, since I do not know yet."

Alistair stroked his chin. "I can't promise you anything. There are certain things I won't do. But within reason, you have yourself a deal."

"That is sufficient," Ko Pao replied. "It's not as if we are moving heaven and earth for you in the first place. Both of your training will be in our routines."

"Both?" Oliver asked.

Ko Pao glared at him. "Refusing our hospitality would be unwise, young one. You have much to learn from our teachings. While you may not have the hardware or talent of your friend, all canvases can be painted upon. Now, to your previous question, it is simple. All contests in the Holy Ravine can be determined with the fist. If you want to leave, you'll have to defeat one of Silvanio's five champions and ask for a favor. He will respect that tradition."

"Five champions?" Alistair looked incredulous. "If the Church of the Holy Ones is the most powerful sect, wouldn't that mean that one of his champions would be equivalent to your strongest apostle? Or at the very least, one of your strongest? I lost to a guy that's in the middle of your rankings. How am I supposed to defeat one of his champions?"

Ko Pao tapped his cane on the ground. "As a newcomer without renown in our martial world, you will certainly fight the weakest of his champions. Indeed, this champion is not the top five of Silvanio's sect, but has reached his position for his potential. That does not mean he is weak, but he is not at the level of the other champions, or someone like Pike."

"Pike, the tall guy with the scar and red headband? But isn't red a rank below black?" Alistair gestured around to the several individuals with black headbands. There were five, excluding Ko Pao.

"I have yet to promote Pike not out of his lack of strength. He is the strongest of the younger generation of this sect. Now, enough talking. Your training begins."

———

"Master, I don't understand." Pike stood leaning against the wall of the training room with his arms crossed. "Why are we placing our bets on this random outsider? We don't even know if the tall tales he spins about his position in the outside world are true. He could be a liar."

They observed the first hour of training for their two guests. The tempering of the body came before any technique drilling. Alistair was with the yellow and orange headbands doing intense calisthenics, while Oliver trained with the white headbands practicing both cardiovascular endurance and the strength of their knuckles by punching wooden dummies over and over.

"What he said corresponds to what the others have said. And have you not felt the Mother's Presence on him?"

Pike snorted. "Whatever you wish, Master."

But Pike knew that Ko Pao was correct. It didn't mean that everything this Alistair spoke was true, but the Mother's Presence was undeniable. The overall amount of Mother's Presence had exploded since the displacement of the Holy Ravine onto the planet called Earth, but this man in particular had an obscene amount, rivaling the Master himself. His techniques were pitiable and his physique laughable, but that meant something. It wasn't just a case of all outsiders being blessed—the other Earthlings were even more deficient than the average yellow headband. Except Vritra.

Pike disliked that arrogant snake, and was glad that he had vanished. But his power was undeniable. He had defeated Silvanio's strongest champion with unthinkable speed and strength. If Alistair's words were true, he was even stronger than Vritra since he had defeated the Reptile Emperor in combat.

"You will be his personal instructor," Ko Pao said.

"What? But surely you would be a superior choice, Master. I am but a candle to your sun as an instructor."

"You underestimate yourself." Ko Pao smiled. "I think not only of this moment, but of all future moments. By training this man, you yourself shall reach further heights. In next year's Dragon's Equinox Festival, you will defeat Elerie Apostolos."

"Truly?" Pike's eyebrows shot up. Ko Pao was not a man to flatter or exaggerate.

"Are you doubting your master's words now? Go join the others. I must meditate for an hour."

With that, Ko Pao dismissed Pike, returning to his private meditation chambers deep in the recesses of the temple.

Meanwhile, Pike stayed inside the training hall and performed the ancient breathing ritual of the Seventh Sworn Brother, exorcising all the little demons within his dantian. How much had Master Ko Pao done for him, a wretched delinquent? The elderly apostle had taken in Pike as a troubled young man, who fought in the streets every day and night. He owed everything to that old-timer. He would train the outsider. But he wouldn't go easy on him. If Alistair died from not being able to handle Pike's routine, that wasn't his fault, was it?

———

The first two weeks, Alistair didn't train in martial arts at all, nor did he see Oliver except for the free time at the end of the day and the ten minutes when all the apostles gathered for a morning and evening hymn under Master Ko Pao.

All his time was spent "tempering the body." And by tempering the body, Apostle Pike meant torturing him in new and exquisite ways that would have the worst war criminal blushing.

Alistair had thought he had known pain before. He had thought he had known what hard work was, what struggle was. Those foolish pretensions had long left his system.

What he lived before was called a sheltered existence. In the Holy Ravine, there was no power-up coming, no special Quest. No guidance, and no way out.

He bunked with the yellow headbands, which was the second-lowest rank. They had six in total, white, yellow, orange, purple, red, and black. He only performed half of the yellow headband daily activities, the other half coming from personal tutoring under Apostle Pike.

Pike turned out to be the strongest apostle of the Silver Comet Sect under the age of forty. In fact, he was only twenty-five, just three years older than Alistair, though Alistair thought he looked thirty-five with his rough features.

Wake-up time was two hours before dawn with the other yellow head-bands. Every day, they went on an hour run at a breakneck pace that Alistair felt was verging on Olympic-level fast. And that was just the beginning. After the run was an hour of "toughness instruction." What they didn't explain was that it was the most absurd form of self-flagellation Alistair had ever seen.

The members of the Silver Comet Sect punched and kicked and slammed and elbowed each other over every part of their body in the name of improving durability and endurance. They played a game where each person got one hit on the other, and the first one to touch the ground with any part of their body except their feet lost.

After that ridiculous training with only their unarmed body, they would move on to hammer time, which was as crazy as the name sounded. There was a position that rotated among trainees called the Smith, who would go up to each of them and smash them with a hammer. Oh, but lest Alistair forget, the head was off limits. As if that made things okay.

The first time Alistair took a hammer to the stomach, he collapsed to his knees and threw up his dinner.

After toughness instruction they had breakfast, along with a special secret herbal medicine developed from the plants only found deep in their forest. His instructors claimed that it sped up healing and recovery, which terrified him, since what would the training be like without the tincture?

Then was an hour of strength training, consisting of both calisthenics and weight training with discs of stone. That was Alistair's favorite part of the day. While it was extremely difficult as they took each exercise to beyond failure with dropsets, supersets, and partial reps, it wasn't literally crazy like the other training types.

After strength training were three hours of drilling techniques and light sparring, but Alistair wasn't allowed to participate in that. Instead, he had personal tutoring with Pike Zenbatty.

The first day, Ko Pao had let them rest after "light" training, which was actually the most grueling physical exercise Alistair had ever done. Therefore, the next day was their first "real" day.

Three and a half hours after waking up, Alistair reported to one of the private training rooms. Dying.

Alistair drank from his canteen with wanton thirst. He could barely feel his limbs at that point, anyway. The kind of training he was doing was beyond reasonable, and on pre-initiation Earth would have led to rhabdomyolysis, an extremely dangerous medical condition where damaged muscle tissue released its proteins and electrolytes into the bloodstream.

That he was relatively healthy further confirmed his suspicions that there was something funky going on with these Holy Raviners. While not even close to the physical capability of an actual cultivator, they were clearly stronger, faster, more durable, and more cardiovascularly fit than any human from before.

By his best reckoning, it was related to the Dao. He could feel it within all the apostles, very faintly. A small inkling that powered up their bodies when they expressed their hardened willpower, and improved their techniques beyond the humanly possible. But no matter how hard he tried, he couldn't reach the Dao of the Fist within himself. He could feel it, ever so faintly, but it was locked behind an impenetrable wall of darkness.

Pike Zenbatty stood with his arms crossed in the middle of the training room. It was a small enclave deep within the Silver Comet temple, plainly adorned with engravings of comets in the stone walls, along with the names and faces of past sect leaders. With his near seven-foot frame, Pike's shaved head almost reached the ceiling.

Alistair almost fell to his knees upon entering the sweltering room, even hotter than the main training room. *When will this end?*

His whole body was screaming for mercy. His skin was bruised and battered. His muscles were exhausted. Every breath was agony, and the sweltering heat that the Silver Comet Sect mandated in every single training room didn't help.

At least they were allowed an ample amount of water. Alistair took a swig from his canteen, relishing in the ice-cold fresh water.

He had forgotten everything. Overdue debt payments? His parents and friends? The future of Earth? When the body is put under extreme stress, the mind goes blank. Alistair was no longer capable of stringing together chains of coherent thought, only small snippets of conscious volition.

Collapsing to his knees on the floor of the small training room was the first time he had been off his feet in an inordinate amount of time. Finally, his body had a chance to rest.

"I would love to see you give in, outsider," Pike sneered. "Master Ko Pao puts too much trust in you. The Silver Comet Sect's reputation will suffer if you fail your challenge."

"This... is impossible," Alistair managed to say. "You're going to kill me."

"Nonsense. All that reveals is that your will is weak. When I was a junior apostle, I suffered ten times worse. Where the mind wills, the body follows. This is the basic principle of martial arts, and also of the Mother's Presence."

Alistair stayed silent for a few seconds, drinking out of his canteen and trying to stop panting from exertion.

"Mother's Presence?" Alistair finally asked.

"The Mother of War is our patron goddess. You can feel her presence in every art of war—when you raise your fist; when you breathe the bellicose air; when you dedicate your body, mind, and soul to the pursuit of victory."

"The Dao?" Alistair tried to center his imbalanced breathing and concentrate. Without the easy mechanism of his Dao Nodes within his soulcore, the Dao felt so very faint. But there was a trace, unable to be fully constrained by the suppression field.

"Perhaps. I know not of the outsiders' techniques."

"What are we going to do?"

Pike took a deep breath, then straightened his posture. "You're going to hit me."

"Uh, what?"

"You will strike me for the next three hours without respite. If you can survive that, I will consider you worthy."

Alistair wanted to say that that's not what Master Ko Pao said, but he refrained. The old man wasn't here to save him. Plus, he wasn't about to give Pike the satisfaction.

"Isn't that a technique?" Alistair asked.

"No. I will not be teaching you any specific moves or styles. You are free to hit any part of my body, including my face, with anything you want."

"And what about down there—"

"No."

"Okay, that clears things up." Alistair stretched his fingers, opening and closing them in a fist several times. His breathing was under control and the pain of fatigue had faded into a dull ache. Maybe Pike was right about this mind over matter stuff. The Mother's Presence. The Dao.

"Maybe—" Alistair decided to be cheeky, throwing a powerful straight right directly at Pike's face. Was it against the rules? Alistair thought not, and he wanted to see how the red headband apostle would react. Attacking while talking was practically his signature move at this point.

"Disappointing."

Alistair immediately started cradling his fist, which hurt like hell after connecting. *What the hell are these people made of?* Alistair wondered. Even striking their faces felt like punching steel. Pike tanked his punch without even moving an inch, absorbing the entire kinetic chain of the blow with impassable conviction.

"Again," Pike commanded.

Alistair calmed down. If a sucker punch wasn't effective, he needed to try something more orthodox. Jumping up and down to get blood pumping to his legs, Alistair soared into the air, performing a perfectly executed tornado kick straight into Pike's face.

This time, the pain from hitting the absolute unit that was Pike's skull bones was lessened since the area of contact was spread over his shinbone. Yet the apostle's face was still implacable. This time, Alistair noted that the apostle's feet shifted upon impact, even if it was less than an inch.

"Better. Now—"

Alistair interrupted Pike's next words, delivering a left hook to the side, an elbow to the cheek, and then a full power uppercut straight into his tutor's stomach in quick succession. A loud thud met each blow, with Pike not even flinching in the slightest. Alistair put his hands on his knees after his combo, panting for the humid air.

"Again." Pike loomed over him with his giant frame like an angry deva. Alistair was in for a long first day.

8 FUNDAMENTALS

AFTER THE THREE-HOUR training with Pike came lunch, a welcome respite in Alistair's day. Lunch was a full hour, and he ate with the other yellow headbands, who were welcoming enough of the outsider. Alistair spent the entire time recuperating as much as was physically possible, and luckily, they were allowed to drink more of the herbal tea mixture that sped up healing.

After lunch was another break, this time, meditation. Before that, they gave him a nice shave, making him bald-headed like all the other apostles. They spent two hours in solitude, contemplating the deeper mysteries.

Alistair was expected to join them, yet he wasn't taught anything about their specific meditative techniques. Somehow, despite being promised that he would learn the secret of the Silver Comet Sect's Steel Body and the martial arts belonging to their style, the details of their meditation were forbidden to him.

Alistair spent the time trying to feel "the Mother's Presence" as the Holy Raviners called it, to no avail. At least it served as a good rest. It was the easiest thing in the world to sit in peaceful, dark loneliness, away from the sweltering heat of the training room. The non-heated areas of the Silver Comet Sect were quite cool.

The next three hours were physical training in the inverse of the start of the day, so weight training, then toughness training, then another run.

Saving the run for last made it twice as difficult. The yellow headbands were instructed to go easy on him during toughness training, but not everyone got the memo. He was just happy he hadn't died from internal bleeding, a major concern of his going into the training. Whether it was the tea or his willpower shaping up his flesh, he didn't care as long as he survived.

Dinner came after the run, and then the other yellow headbands had technique and sparring. Alistair instead went back to one-on-one sessions with Pike, but instead of punching the man, he had to knock down a set number of weighted dolls within a certain time frame, or receive a beating from the apostle.

After two hours of that, there was finally an hour and a half of free time before sleeping and starting the whole thing over again.

On the first day, Alistair was too tired to do anything but lie down and nurse his wounds. He did so with company, at least. The Silver Comet Sect forced Alistair and Oliver to bunk separately, but they spent their free time in his room, which he shared with three other yellow headbands.

"What's wrong with you?" Oliver said, who was lounging on one of the hard stone beds. He looked in much better condition than Alistair, who didn't even want to rest on the heated bed, lest he be unnecessarily reminded of his sweltering training. Instead, he closed his eyes and laid down on the ground.

The only reason Oliver was so chipper was because he had been worked much less hard than Alistair. Unlike some systems where the higher ranks did less work, in the Silver Comet Sect, the workload commensurately increased for the headbands, except perhaps for the black rank. Alistair hadn't seen Master Ko Pao participating in any of the hard training.

Alistair didn't respond, closing his eyes in silence and pretending like his body didn't exist.

Oliver continued to talk to his quiet friend. "Are we really going to get out of here?"

Alistair was in no mood to talk, feeling overwhelmed with fatigue. He wanted to blow up and tell Oliver what a stupid question that was—how was Alistair supposed to know any better than him? They were in the same situation. But he couldn't. Not when Oliver sounded like a scared little kid. It was Alistair's duty to stay strong.

"Of course," Alistair said. "I can't lose in a fist fight for the third time, especially if their weakest champion is a nepotism hire."

"Third time? When did you lose the first time?"

Alistair realized that he had never told anyone else about what happened. Only Dev'rox was there to witness his beating. He reluctantly retold the story to Oliver.

"And here I was thinking you were the strongest at our level," Oliver said at the end. "Looks like I have higher heights to aim for now."

"Red was still like thirty levels higher than me at the time? My level now is probably still under where he was back then."

"But it sounds like he didn't even use a fraction of his full power?"

"Shut up."

"It's a very sore topic for him," Dev'rox added.

"Shut up."

"But I didn't say anything?" Oliver gave him a confused look.

"Oh, I forgot. Dev'rox can't speak to you because of the Devonic Elision Field. Looks like I'm the only one that has to hear his annoying voice."

"Ah. Say hello to Dev'rox for me."

"I can hear you, boy," Dev'rox replied.

Oliver stood up from his stone cot, a luxury that Alistair couldn't perform. "I wonder what changes the Pathfinder AI is going to make once we return. Surely all this training can't be for nothing?"

"You might become a pugilist yourself," Alistair said absently.

"How horrific," Oliver replied. "Our team has enough brutes already. Where's the sophistication?"

"Hey," Alistair interjected. "I'm sorry, but can I get some rest?"

"Oh yeah, my bad. I'll shut up now."

Alistair felt a little bad that he was dampening Oliver's youthful spirits, but he needed his rest. Tomorrow was going to be even worse.

———

One week into his training, Alistair was running on empty. He had long passed his physical limits, only his willpower pushing his body to continue.

It was the seventh of his morning sessions with Pike when he began to understand the deeper mysteries his teacher had been trying to impart.

All the light had vanished from Alistair's eyes. All his lofty ideals and goals had been subsumed and left to the wayside. The willpower that drove him wasn't his desire for justice or to avenge the weak, but his base hatred of losing.

He could hardly remember his own name or what he was here to do. All that lay ahead was pain and more pain. A single thought passed through his mind—*don't lose.*

"Again."

Alistair punched Pike's hardened frame with all his might, moving the man back less than an inch.

"Again."

Alistair kicked Pike in the vulnerable spot of a man, ignoring his teacher's previous prohibition. He didn't do it on purpose, but he acted purely on instinct since his conscious faculties no longer controlled his movements. From his body's perspective, he was in a fight for his life and nothing was off limits.

Alistair's sucker kick moved Pike even less than his punch. Not even a grimace flashed over Pike's chiseled face. He shook his head, looking down on Alistair. "Wrong."

If Alistair had been conscious, he might have complained at the ridiculous nature of his training. Pike had not given a single explicit instruction in the entire period of training. Not one single hint or lesson. Just "again" or "better" or "worse" or "wrong" or "insufficient."

But Alistair wasn't conscious, at least not fully. So he continued. He continued for two and a half hours, striking Pike in all manner of ways. He tried throws, leg takedowns, trips, kicks, punches, elbow strikes, knees, submissions, eye pokes, knifehands. One-inch punches and fajins.

With the direct knowledge of {Psychompomp's Discipline} imbued in his muscle memory, his arsenal of moves was more vast than the most experienced MMA fighter in the world.

Pike didn't look impressed by that fact. If anything, he looked disappointed.

"Your diversity of techniques would shame even the average black headband. Yet why are they so poorly executed?"

Alistair's mind barely registered those words, following up with a question mark kick—a type of kick that appeared like a front kick, then at the last second transitioned into a roundhouse kick using only the power of the knee. Not the hardest hitting of all the vast array of kicks, its utility was in its surprise factor.

Alistair's shin smushed Pike's cheek in, who barely felt a thing. "You're not even listening, are you? Is our basic training that difficult? I knew Master Ko Pao was wrong about you. You can't even learn something so basic to save your loved ones?"

It was obviously a bait, but it worked. Alistair's anger temporarily overwhelmed his fatigue, and he attacked with a renewed flurry of blows, eschewing technicality.

His body had gotten leaner and less muscular in only a week of staying at the Silver Comet Sect, a testament to their insane training regimen. But despite the loss of muscle, his blows were far stronger than they were at the start.

After his misguided outburst, Alistair could barely breathe. His lungs screamed from the forced intake of the humid air, searing his insides. He rested his hands against his knees and panted like a dog. This was the end. This was his limit. He was going to die.

So why not try to knock that smug smile off Pike's face before he went out?

Suddenly, his vision shrank. There was only himself and Pike. They were six feet apart, but he felt infinitely close to the red headband.

Alistair tried the most basic of attacks, a right straight directed at Pike's solar plexus.

His arm was as heavy as a lead rod. His punch was slow, with little explosive force. By all rights, it should have been the weakest punch he'd thrown yet.

Alistair's eyes opened into a new universe. In his lowest moment, he found the keys to the pinnacle of martial arts. In his ragged breath. In his weak heartbeat. In his blurred vision and delirious brain. The inner workings of the flow of power.

Why had he been wasting so much energy before? The best attack was direct.

Alistair's fist collided with Pike's chest with a soft thud. No matter what secrets of power Alistair discovered, he was on death's door physically. His punch was not strong. But nonetheless, Pike took one whole step back. He did no noticeable damage, and the tall man didn't make any noise. But that one step was enough for Alistair. He collapsed instantly after seeing the aftermath of his punch.

Ko Pao felt his unconscious student's forehead with his palm. Alistair was resting quietly in the infirmary wing of their temple, attended to by their best medics. A special preparation of the herbal tea was being prepared, many times the normal concentration. It was both miraculously curative and toxic to the internal organs. The secret was that the tea cleansed the body and accelerated healing so thoroughly that it could cause complete system failure from overwork.

"One week?" Ko Pao stroked his long beard. "In the entire records of the Holy Ravine, have you heard of something like this?"

Jo Ran, a black headband of just fifty years and the last champion of the Silver Comet Sect, shook his head. "Never. There is no precedent."

"Obviously, it's different," Pike clarified. "His knowledge and arsenal of techniques exceeds mine, and perhaps even rivals yours, if I may be slightly presumptuous, Master Ko Pao. He clearly has had extensive training."

Ko Pao looked at his closest confidants. "If his statements are to be believed, he first started his journey in the fist four months ago."

Ectavian, Pike's closest rival within the sect, offered his opinion. "Further evidence to the power of this 'cultivation' the outsiders speak of. With all the information we now know, it is clear that our civilization will not remain in this state forever. Silvanio is a greedy man. Based on Vritra's departure, he knows a way to the outside world. There is no doubt he will one day venture outside to gain power beyond our imaginations. We cannot forget there is also the possibility that this Final Frontier Empire intervenes and integrates us directly."

"But this does make us more confident in the outsider's chances, does it not?" Ko Pao asked. He looked at the archivist, Davnos.

The archivist Davnos, a man of forty years who had just replaced his father in the post, shifted his spectacles. "It's still a tree colony away, Master. He may grasp the first fundamentals, but the stress we put him through here will severely delay his Steel Body training. We won't be able to push him to the state required for explosive growth for at least a month and a half."

Ko Pao assessed their situation objectively. Two sects had aligned themselves entirely to the Church of the Holy Ones. Two more were in their sphere, meaning that they pretended to stay neutral while always siding with Silvanio. One was truly neutral, and two opposed the Holy Ones—only Kodaidaemin and the Silver Comet Sect.

Kodaidaemin was the second most powerful group in the ravine, but the opposition's power slipped every year. Within another decade or two, Silvanio would have complete and uncontested control of the Holy Ravine.

In the past, Ko Pao had been worried about the poisoned fruits of such an outcome. With Silvanio's greed, he would not have been surprised if the former champion tried incursions into neighboring territory.

But now? After seeing the physical power of a being like Vritra, the answer was clear. If Silvanio was allowed to obtain the power of cultivation, the ruin he would bring on both the Holy Ravine and the outside world was untold. Based on Alistair's detailed recounting of the initiation, one's base talent and attributes contributed to both the initial level and subsequent growth of the individual in cultivation.

Ko Pao felt a pang of fear.

There was much to loathe about Silvanio Apostolos. But he was unrivaled under the heavens—the greatest talent in martial arts in the Holy Ravine for over a thousand years. He would master this Pathfinder AI in no time.

The only hope was to align with the powers of the outside world. And for all his naïveté and youthful bravado, Alistair was their only hope.

Davnos looked up. "I have no idea, if I am to be honest. This situation is unprecedented in our history."

Ko Pao suddenly tapped his cane on the floor with considerable force, causing a wave of wind to expand from the point of contact. "You have not spoken to anyone else about what Alistair told me and Brother Pike on that day?"

"Of course not, Master," Pike said, the others agreeing.

"Good. Keep that a secret and hold it to your chest. Everything hinges on Governor Silvanio's ignorance. Continue training the boy and report back to me on his progress."

Alistair went right back to training the next day. Thankfully, the Silver Comet Sect wasn't entirely mental, and they cut his workload in half, removing the toughness instruction and the first personal session with Pike.

That still left two hours of running, two hours of weight training, and two hours in his second session with Pike.

"What did I learn yesterday?" Alistair asked as he approached Pike. They switched locations for their class, taking the lesson outside. Pike stood in the middle of a shallow rapids close to a gigantic waterfall. Alistair's vision was partially obscured from the mist churned up by the falling water.

"The fundamentals of action," Pike said.

Alistair waded through the water, finding Pike's implacability astounding. He himself couldn't help but be swayed by the strong currents, while his teacher was perfectly still.

Despite his collapse from exhaustion yesterday, Alistair felt better than ever today. Actually, that was the wrong way to phrase it. His muscles still ached and he still had internal damage. No matter how strong his willpower was, his physical output was delimited.

But he was more... solid. That sounded funny since at that very moment, the river was churning him around like butter, but it wasn't fair to compare himself to Pike.

Pike continued his speech as he waited for Alistair to catch up, wading deeper into the river and closer to the waterfall's point of contact.

"To properly master the art of fighting, you must understand the 'intention' behind all of your and your opponent's movements. Nothing exists without purpose. Why do I punch or kick at a certain time? Why do I then follow up with a foot sweep or throw? You have entered the realm of fundamentals. But do not confuse this for mastery. You are far behind the peers of your generation within the Holy Ravine."

Alistair raised his hand, though evidently Pike didn't understand the gesture, based on the confusion on his face. "So what happens in a fight between two masters of fundamentals?"

"Are they exactly the same in their mastery? Such a thing is quite rare. Obviously, the one who sees farther into the depths of intention has the advantage, but their victory is not assured. There are a plenitude of other factors, such as reach, weight, technical skill, willpower, durability, stamina, speed, creativity, and others that I am not thinking of now."

"So who'd win in a fight?" Alistair asked. Pike continued backpedaling, not even looking behind. The waterfall was only a few body lengths away, the deafening noise of the crashing water forcing the two of them to shout. "You or Master Ko Pao?"

Pike chuckled. "Master Ko Pao, of course. While I surpass him in all physical categories, he is a supreme archon of the fist. In all the Holy Ravine, he is in the top three strongest fighters. Only Silvanio Apostolos and Mira Xeni surpass him. Some say Lord Xiaoli as well, but I disagree."

"A woman is at the top?" Alistair asked. Based on everything he had seen in the outside world, gender didn't matter in the least in terms of strength for cultivators. While the people of the Holy Ravine lacked Mana, they were certainly superhuman in many respects, so it wasn't necessarily shocking.

"This is unusual to you?" Pike almost had his back underneath the waterfall now. He outstretched his arm and beckoned Alistair to come forward. "Why is that the case?"

"Not unusual, per se," Alistair said. "In the arena of cultivation there isn't a difference between the genders, though since you guys don't have the same kind of outlandish powers, I had assumed it would be closer to Earth where men had an advantage in combat."

"I see. I am not well traveled, but I have heard from the archivist, Davnos, that there are certain lands where women do not fight. The Kingdom of Erazt for one. That strikes me as foolish. We cannot spare a man, woman, or child. Strike me."

Alistair lunged forward. But he stopped midway.

"What happened?" Alistair asked.

"Ah, you've seen it now," Pike replied. "You can't read the intention, can you?"

"Are you using some technique to hide it?" Alistair wondered.

"No. You unlocked your true sight under extreme duress. While a master can access it as easily as walking, you are not there yet. You will have to partially replicate the conditions."

"Didn't Master Ko Pao say that I shouldn't push myself too far? How am I supposed to do that?"

"The mind conquers all things."

Very helpful. Alistair closed his eyes and focused on his breathing. It always came down to the breathing, didn't it?

He tried to remember the sensation of seeing the principles of movement. The state of his body. At the footstep of death's door. Alistair strode toward Pike with his eyes still closed, letting his other senses take over.

The feeling of oneness returned. It reminded him somewhat of communing with his Dao Nodes, though the exact nature of that was lost to him. Ever since entering the Devonic Elision Field, it was like his specific memories and feelings that he had of anything cultivation related were sealed behind an impenetrable gate.

Slowly, piece by piece, Alistair was confident that he was learning to access the Dao manually, what the Raviners called the Mother's Presence. Compared to his full power, it was literally a microscopic droplet, which made Alistair wonder if he'd already inadvertently accessed the fundamentals while using the Dao of the Fist while he wasn't suppressed and had just forgotten about it.

Something deep inside him made him think otherwise. While his memories were partially sealed, he was sure that he had never personally seen so deeply into the machinations of combat. While he hadn't realized it before, there was a very subtle difference between his own insight and the Pathfinder AI's given insight.

With natural ease, Alistair flowed into a flurry of blows without opening his eyes. From his perspective, it was like it happened in slow motion. Every muscle moved with intention. All his strikes felt as if they landed at the same time, defying the laws of causality.

Alistair opened his eyes. He had pushed Pike back into the waterfall. But even more than that, Pike had moved. Alistair had the edge of his hand a few inches from the apostle's throat, who had blocked with his palm, catching Alistair's blow with ease.

Alistair laughed hysterically. He had gotten Pike to block!

To his credit, Pike didn't look bothered at all by his pupil's growth, despite his previous dislike of Alistair. "It's finally time to start training for real."

9 REMATCH

THE NEXT FEW DAYS, Alistair's training was focused almost entirely on technique and mastery of fundamentals. He still participated in half of the physical training, but he was allowed more breaks than the other yellow headbands. He had the feeling that they weren't thrilled about that. And he himself hated that he was getting easy treatment. But there were bodily limits. If he went too hard, he wouldn't be able to maximize his progress.

Part of the reason Alistair had to take it easy physically was that he could only tolerate a lower dose of the herbal tea, due to the massive treatment they gave him after his intensive training with Pike.

That didn't mean he didn't train hard in other ways. He took part in the technique lessons and sparring, and attacked Pike every day without fail. He was finally getting Pike to dodge and defend his blows, though the young master only needed the slightest adjustments of his feet and a single carefree hand to defend Alistair's all-out attacks. Attacks that in a real fight would have left Alistair open to innumerable counters.

Even his body was improving. After that minor blip of overtraining where he physically shrunk, he was gaining muscle mass at an inhuman pace. Pike told him that it was a combination of his body reacclimating to its previous state, as well as the secret foods and techniques of the Silver Comet Sect that had been passed down for a hundred generations.

Oliver adjusted nicely. He had no inherent talent for martial arts and was far behind even the lowest white belts, but he was learning faster than Alistair would have thought possible. The Silver Comet Sect were excellent teachers. The Necromancer would easily have beaten everyone except professional fighters in the old world, given equalized stats.

After two weeks, Alistair was thankfully back into the normal yellow headband routine, though he wasn't allowed to do the sledgehammer part of the toughness instruction, only the barehanded part.

As strength returned to his limbs, Alistair's training with Pike grew more fierce. In his thirteenth day of training, he gave the tall man his first nose bleed with a disguised spinning backfist. Of course, at any time, he could have blocked any and all of Alistair's attacks; he only let a certain number of attacks through. Even so, Alistair rejoiced.

The more he practiced with Pike, the more he realized that the entire time, the strongest youth of the Silver Comet Sect had been guiding him to make the correct moves. Alistair's discovery of the fundamentals underlying martial arts was not merely his own talent. Through tiny movements, minuscule intentional "mistakes," and subtle baits, Pike had been continuously leading Alistair to make optimal moves without him even realizing.

It honestly terrified him. That idea seemed so impossible that Alistair wanted to reject it at face value. But there was no other explanation. The kind of skill and technical execution required for such a feat was a miracle beyond Alistair's comprehension. He had seen something like that just once before, now that he remembered—Red, the Cabal recruit he had met when Nenna Spindoller escaped, had also taught Alistair through dodging.

Far from discouraging him, the feat spurned Alistair to work even harder. He couldn't let Red or Pike remain ahead of him forever.

After exactly three weeks spent at the Silver Comet Sect, Alistair was allowed a rematch with Apol-Xin, for testing into the orange headband group.

Alistair walked barefoot on the cool stone ground of the temple, his eyes closed. After he bloodied Pike's nose, in all subsequent sessions, he had to wear a blindfold. "A true martial artist is not impeded by the absence of sight," Pike had told him.

The heated sweat chamber that Alistair had his first match was not the traditional dueling room. Rather, there was a large courtyard at the center of the temple. Pentagonal in shape, it led to all five main wings of the building and could host almost two hundred, though there weren't that many apostles of the sect in total.

The seating consisted of long stone benches that filled each side of the pentagon in ascending rows, with a six-foot drop onto the dueling floor itself. The terrain for their battle was smooth gray stone, the same as what made up the rest of the temple. They had a vast area for their duel, larger than any MMA arena from the before, maybe the size of a baseball infield.

Duels traditionally took place on weekends. However, because of the urgency of Alistair's position, Ko Pao had permitted a late-night weekday event. As such, the stands were not even close to capacity. Master Ko Pao himself, along with Pike, Oliver, and several of the yellow and orange headbands, counted themselves among the observers.

Alistair finally took his blindfold off upon arriving at the antechamber to the courtyard. Apol-Xin, as the senior, came from the north end into the courtyard, while Alistair came from one of the two wings opposite to Apol-Xin's.

Pike waited for him in the antechamber.

"Are you ready?" Pike asked.

"As I'll ever be," Alistair said.

"You should win."

"Really?"

"Do you trust me?" Pike asked.

"Sort of?" Alistair replied.

"Do you trust me?"

"Yes?"

"You'll win. Just use my training." Pike patted him on the back.

"Thanks."

Alistair jumped up and down, letting the tension leave his body. He was barred from learning the special meditation techniques of the Silver Comet Sect, but he had his own Kai'tazake Mutra. It was harder to access and less supernatural while in the Holy Ravine, but its presence was still soothing.

He assessed his opponent without emotion. He had no care in the least about revenge. His victory was only the first step on the long path of achieving his goals.

Alistair had little information on Apol-Xin's personal style and arsenal of techniques—their brief battle not being nearly enough to go on. Physically, he looked to be 6'5" and 265 pounds, though with the weird Steel Body shenanigans, he might have been far heavier. While Alistair was nowhere near complete with the program, he felt heavier than his bodily appearance suggested, owing to a peculiar density of muscle.

Apol-Xin stared at him with cold eyes. Alistair felt a certain hostility behind his gaze. It was no surprise. He hadn't engendered the best relations with the average member of the sect, who were displeased with the speed of Alistair's promotion and the significant resources poured into his training. He tried his best to ease any concerns, but he couldn't be friends with everyone.

Ko Pao stood up, the rest of the apostles bowing their heads. Alistair actually managed to react in time, bowing with everyone else.

"Today brings a rematch of Apol-Xin and Alistair Tan. Alistair challenges for promotion into the orange rank. May the Mother of War grant a fair and unblemished match. Begin!"

The venerable master thrust his hand down from the sky, heralding the beginning of the battle.

Alistair let his hands down to his sides and stood very still. All of his previous battles flashed like a near-death experience. He remembered every punch, every kick, every blow. It was true that his body contained a wealth of unearned ability inherited from Zenaitsu Morogoni. A preternaturally efficient style of unarmed combat, designed for killing.

With his cultivation sealed and his Talent Tree, Dao Nodes, and Skills absent, the full motions of {Psychopomp's Discipline} were absent. Yet, Alistair felt beyond a shadow of a doubt that he was far superior now.

Would he have beaten his old self in a fight? Of course not, even if his old self had been equalized in stats to his current state. The Fist Node and true access to the Mutra and {Psychopomp's Discipline} added an insane amount of firepower, regardless of physical prowess.

But what he had now was a "foundation." He was no Shaolin monk or world champion boxer in the before. He'd taken a few kickboxing classes. Almost all of his martial arts skill had been acquired magically through Skills and Talents, and then lightly, *lightly* reinforced through practical combat.

It wasn't that he hadn't fought enough—he had fought plenty. But he didn't really get any better from those fights because he was already too good, and they weren't challenging him specifically within the domain of martial arts.

He had been through numerous fights where he barely survived—the orcs, Anthony, Dragonus and Admiral—but the crux of the difficulty came from their unique powers. They weren't pugilists.

Alistair now believed that the heart of the Dao was foundation. Without a strong foundation, you could add the highest quality building materials and still have your skyscraper collapse.

When he imagined towering Truthseekers like the Sage, he could feel the solidity in their bases. Even a Foundation realm like Lucius showed his true and total faith in the power of money. That was where his synchronicity with his Dao came from.

It was the missing element that the Silver Comet Sect and Brother Pike gave him. There were no such things as do-overs, but the Devonic Elision Field was the closest that one could get. A training experience without any cultivation, aided only by a set of disjointed techniques baked into his muscle memory. A chance to make his foundation as solid as steel.

Alistair no longer needed to trick his body into thinking it was about to die to access his opponent's intentions. It simply lay out before him as easy as reading a picture book.

Apol-Xin carefully circled around him, realizing that Alistair was not the same man as before.

Alistair stepped closer, bit by bit, trying to feel out his opponent. The orange headband then leaped forward with blinding speed, firing off a series of jabs. The tables had turned—in their last battle, Alistair was the one to make the first move, also by throwing jabs.

As a practitioner of the Steel Body for many years, Apol-Xin was faster, stronger, and more durable than his opponent. By all rights, he should have lit up Alistair's face with his attack.

Yet that did not come to pass. Alistair saw the fundamentals behind Apol-Xin's fists and parried with ease, moving almost as fast as his opponent. Yes, he was inferior physically to the orange headband—but that gap had closed immensely compared to last time.

Alistair saw a flicker of annoyance pass over Apol-Xin's face. Perfect. While he didn't have the full embrace of the Mutra, he knew that an excess of emotion in his opponent was a potential key to victory.

The two warriors exchanged a series of fast-paced strikes. To the untrained eye, they were nearly invisible.

Alistair had superior technique and Apol-Xin superior speed and power. In their understanding of fundamentals, they seemed evenly matched.

They only used their fists—a kick would leave too big of an opening, and a throw or leg grab would be too obvious.

Apol-Xin's first mistake was underestimating Alistair's power. After a fifteen-second high-level exchange of mostly jabs and straights, the larger fighter grew impatient with the standstill. Alistair could almost hear the thoughts in his head. "How is it possible for him to have improved this much? It must be an illusion."

Apol-Xin had made optimal use of his Steel Body in their previous fight, and attempted to do so again. Seeing a jab coming straight for his nose bridge, the orange apostle knew what he had to do and took the blow head-on, countering with a powerful right straight with knock-out potential.

WHACK!

His straight whooshed by open air. Blood dripped down from Apol-Xin's nose, and a sharp pain arrested his movement. Apol-Xin had trained to withstand pain, but like the plucking of a hair off someone's head, a strike to the nose bridge caused an automatic reaction.

Alistair's jab connected, slightly rocking his opponent, which sent the straight veering off in the wrong direction. It was something he could not have accomplished before his physical training. His strikes had real power behind them now, something that Apol-Xin couldn't ignore.

That was only the opening salvo—Alistair's blow did no lasting damage. However, it did imprint itself in Apol-Xin's psyche. *How did he get that strong?* Apol-Xin wondered. The orange headband wasn't privy to Alistair's growth as a member of the orange headbands. He clearly had underestimated Alistair's growth.

Alistair could almost feel those thoughts seeping off the orange headband. He saw it in the new caution of the apostle's moves as a hand wiped away blood from his mouth. That would give Alistair the advantage he needed.

It was Alistair's turn to go on the offensive, sending out a flurry of even faster punches. Those jabs surpassed his previous speed and equaled Apol-Xin's own.

Anxiety took hold of Apol-Xin's heart. Alistair's speed seemed incomprehensible. Was he holding back before? Just how high had the Earthling reached in a mere three weeks?

Caution and fear slowed down Apol-Xin's reactions, and also his better judgment.

Alistair had not been hiding his powers, or somehow broken through his limits and reached a new level of speed. He simply wasted energy, firing all of his muscles at maximum throttle in order to momentarily overwhelm his opponent.

Alistair saw deeper into the fundamentals of martial arts. Apol-Xin had the capacity to figure out his opponent's ruse, but his earlier caution led him down a mental trap. The tiniest of mistakes was all it took to lose in a close fight, Alistair knew.

Apol-Xin backpedaled, furiously working to parry Alistair's rapid onslaught.

The onslaught disappeared without a trace, Alistair's fist stopping in midair.

With Apol-Xin retreating, it was time to unleash a kick. Alistair spun around, slamming the back of his foot into the apostle's temple in a spinning wheel.

It was more than just technique; Alistair's implementation of fundamentals was sublime. It wasn't his intention to use psychological tactics from the start, but that was all part of the natural flow of combat. Use every advantage you can get. Have foresight beyond your opponent and out-predict them.

Apol-Xin did not fall from a single blow. Alistair had no way of gauging the apostle's adrenaline-boosted top speed other than an estimate based on his typical showings, but Apol-Xin exceeded his measure. The man took the blow to the head and blasted forward, aiming a straight punch right for Alistair's chest.

Alistair had no time to dodge, instead slightly swerving his body and throwing a palm strike. His attack connected with Apol-Xin's arm and sent the muscular pugilist tumbling across the stone floor of the stadium.

The rushed angle strained a tendon within Alistair's wrist. However, the force of his palm strike came at an advantageous position, making him the winner of the exchange.

Apol-Xin, the proud orange rank apostle of the lauded Silver Comet Sect, panted as he felt wooziness from the previous single spinning heel kick. He shook his head in disbelief. Alistair's kick was with the full force of his muscular frame and with perfect technique, but the Steel Body was nothing to scoff at. Apol-Xin had trained his body through toughness instruction and the final secret technique of the sect, yet in one blow, he wanted to throw up his lunch.

Alistair circled his prey, switching to a southpaw stance, so his unharmed left arm would be in prime position.

If he had thought seeing his opponent's intention was easy before, now it was like floating in a lake—completely effortless.

I just needed some real practice, didn't I?

Training with Pike was instructive, but it was only training, after all. Alistair dropped his stance and walked toward his opponent, acting like he was an arrogant villain. At this point, Alistair was confident that he had surpassed Apol-Xin's ability to see the fundamentals.

He wondered since when was it so easy to read an opponent. It was so obvious that Apol-Xin would strike when Alistair got within one hand's length of his jab range. The orange headband was confused and annoyed with his opponent's antics. A decline in function and wits led to an off-balance hook.

That blow came faster than Alistair's prediction—his fundamentals were nowhere near complete. It was still sufficient, and despite Apol-Xin's knuckles grazing and opening a wound on his cheek, he reacted in time.

He grabbed the apostle's arm and twisted downward, hip hinging and throwing his opponent onto the ground. Alistair knew it as the incomparable judo throw—the ippon seoi nage.

The force with which Apol-Xin slammed into the ground was staggering. With Alistair's powerful physique and the large man's weight, a mortal would have probably instantly died. Not a Silver Comet apostle. The Steel Body was at its best when defending against strikes in one's perception. The seoi nage was quick, but gave a small window for Apol-Xin to brace himself.

And strike back.

Apol-Xin thought quick on his feet, recognizing the matted floor would act as a spring, given the sheer force of the shoulder throw. In training, they used bouncy material to prevent serious injury, but even in a real match, the sect didn't want people dying. The Steel Body was tough, but a full power throw directly to the back of the head by someone with superhuman strength was something else.

The tall fighter rebounded off the ground from Alistair's throw, delivering a kick while upside down. His toes connected with Alistair's forehead.

But Alistair wasn't afraid. He tanked the blow with his skull, slightly slipping it so it didn't do full damage. He grabbed Apol-Xin's dangling legs with an aggressive hug, tumbling down to the floor with his opponent.

They landed in what was called north-south position, with Alistair on top and his head at Apol-Xin's legs, and Apol-Xin in the same position but on the bottom. Alistair scrambled to action first, repositioning his head and chest into a reverse scarf-hold. He pressed his right shoulder into Apol-Xin's chest and hooked his opponent's left arm with his own left arm.

Alistair exerted as much pressure as he could, guided by his muscle memory to find the optimal positions. With his bulk, it was a crushing weight, though Apol-Xin would never surrender to a mere hold.

Next came the dance. The sect member was stronger and faster than Alistair, and used that to his advantage. Alistair's foresight on the ground was worse than Apol-Xin's, owing to a lack of experience. Pike didn't train ground work nearly as much as standing.

Apol-Xin was like an otter and Alistair like an orca, the former slithering away from every submission attempt and hold while the latter chased with furious intent. And then they would switch, Apol-Xin becoming the aggressor and Alistair the defender. It was a breakneck contest of strength, flexibility, endurance, and predictions.

They grappled for three minutes, morphing between a wide array of holds and positions. Alistair worked like a dog, scrambling with youthful explosiveness. His tenacity was on display for all to see, sweat dripping from his body like it was water. Apol-Xin didn't give in either, countering every move.

Finally, there came a breaking point. Alistair adapted. While at first he held the lower hand on the ground in terms of foresight, he quickly grew. In a mere matter of minutes, he was seeing ahead of his opponent—gazing deeper and further into the intentions of his opponent's movements.

Apol-Xin's eyes widened as he saw what was happening. He couldn't believe it. A flicker of doubt crossed into his mind. Something that anyone who faced a prodigy would have to come to bear with. The inadequacy of one's own talent before those blessed by Heaven.

The idea of such a thing chilled Apol-Xin to the soul. He had been training for two decades and was from a line of prized warriors. Shaking those thoughts to the side, he prepared a rear naked choke. He had taken Alistair's back—the absolute worst position that the Magical Pugilist could be in.

Apol-Xin pressed his head against Alistair's neck and hooked his feet over Alistair's legs, securing the position. With his arms, he fought to get in position and get his opponent's neck deep into his elbow crease to obtain the choke.

It was a chokehold nearly impossible to escape from. The end was nigh. Alistair had fought valiantly, but this was as far as he would go.

Unless...

With the speed of a raging storm, Alistair reached back and tore out a clump of hair from Apol-Xin's head. He wouldn't have been able to accomplish such a feat if his opponent's hair wasn't slightly longer than the others.

For a moment, the apostle's grip weakened. Not by much—he was a trained fighter who had undergone years of pain tolerance. But like the breaking of the nose bridge, it caused an involuntary reaction. Alistair took advantage of the slip up, moving his legs away and to the side and breaking Apol-Xin's grip.

Alistair ate an uppercut to the chin. His brain rattled in its skull. If that was the price to pay for victory, so be it. He headbutted the orange headband in the nose, targeting the spot he'd already damaged.

"Aarghh!" Apol-Xin let out a cry of pain. The intriguing thing about a match between two practitioners of the Steel Body was that they mostly canceled each other out. However, in certain locations, instead of canceling out, the effect was magnified. The top of the skull was a site of constant reinforcement, while the nose remained one of the weakest spots on a Steel Body user.

Even without completing his toughness instruction, the durability of Alistair's skull bones won out—Apol-Xin tumbled over, this time with Alistair on top.

Alistair rained a series of vicious elbows down on Apol-Xin's face. The downed man did his best to raise his guard, but couldn't block all the damage.

Then an inkling of an idea came to mind. Alistair looked back at how Pike had guided him to understand the fundamentals with his own obscenely deep foresight. He wasn't even close to replicating that kind of feat, but what about something lesser? A feeling stirred within Alistair.

My Dao Node? Alistair's mind furiously tried to ascertain what had happened. *No, that's still locked away. Is it the lesser presence of the Dao that these people call 'the Mother's Presence?'* It wasn't nearly as powerful as his Fist Node, but it felt very similar. And it wasn't triggered by his supremacy over martial arts, but on a whim.

Alistair wasn't one to play with his food. He always fought with candor, never trying to purposefully belittle his opponents. However, central to his Dao was the concept of growth. The necessity of reaching the top in order to change the unjust system of the multiverse. And growth needed properly difficult moments.

He made the tiniest of errors—on purpose—letting Apol-Xin slip out of his mount and stand up. Alistair followed up with an arcing, off-balance haymaker.

Apol-Xin easily avoided it, but Alistair was expecting that. He lunged forward with all the speed his body would give him, going for a flying knee straight toward Apol-Xin's chest.

The orange rank apostle caught the knee with both hands. Alistair smiled. He grabbed onto the left sleeve of his opponent's robe with his own left hand and the collar with his right hand, and performed what a judoka would call a harai goshi—except that was what had happened in their previous fight.

No, Alistair, let things play out in the exact same way except for one. To grow. To surpass. Instead of a harai goshi, Alistair performed an ouchi gari, an inner reap, using his foot to sweep Apol-Xin's leg from the inside at the same time as he pushed and pulled the big man to the ground.

Alistair smiled at the same time as he delivered a punch with all of his power right into Apol-Xin's face. And then another. And then another. He knew how tough that bastard was. Alistair had immense respect for his opponent's warrior spirit.

Finally, after more than twenty blows, Apol-Xin stopped moving. Alistair raised a hand in jubilation. Victory was his.

10 THE CHURCH OF THE HOLY ONES

"That was sloppy," Pike said, blocking a punch from Alistair. "You could have won easier."

It was the day after Alistair's rematch against Apol-Xin, and he was already training again.

Alistair suffered a mild concussion and some bruising from his match, but nothing that would prevent him from continuing his work. That sounded weird to say. In the before, a concussion would have been a serious injury. With the advent of cultivation, he wasn't sure a concussion was even possible. Things kind of either killed you or they didn't. But in the weird, quasi-superhuman state of the Holy Ravine, the concussion was unpleasant, but treatable with sheer willpower and herbal tea.

Apol-Xin was a gracious loser, declaring Alistair to be his superior after the match, and that he would look forward to training with him. Ko Pao looked delighted, and Pike actually stood up and cheered for his student.

Then, Ko Pao dropped a bombshell—Governor Silvanio had requested to see him, and they could not refuse.

Alistair wasn't surprised—he was honestly shocked it hadn't happened sooner. Silvanio must have known about him and Oliver the moment they attracted a crowd walking into the main village. As the ruler of the Holy Ravine, it was well within his rights to see an outsider that came in, especially one that was preparing to challenge one of his champions.

On that note, Alistair wondered if Silvanio knew what he was going to ask for if he was victorious. It seemed obvious that his request would be to leave. Vritra had left after showing his overwhelming strength, taking some of the reptiles away with him. That meant that Silvanio had some way of letting people out.

If only Alistair had the innate strength of a Beast Lord. His guess was that the Devonic Elision Field considered more of Vritra's stats to be biological, therefore letting him keep more of his cultivated strength. If a dragon walked into the ravine, they wouldn't suddenly become as weak as a rat.

"And I thought your eyes were all-seeing," Alistair replied, adjusting his blindfold. Training without sight was mightily conducive to the growth of his foresight. It forced him to see without sight, looking beyond what lay in front of his eyes.

"Oh?" Pike asked.

"It's impossible to grow without a little adversity. I was trying to improve my principles. And on the plus side, I think I accessed the Dao for the first time again. I mean, the Mother's Presence."

"Ah, so that's what that was. I thought that might be the case. I must applaud your ingenuity."

Alistair prepared a beautiful tornado kick, but suddenly, his blindfold came off. He was astonished. Pike ripped it off his head with one graceful swipe, and Alistair was none the wiser. He didn't sense the initial movement at all. *I guess I still have a lot to learn.*

He had little time to think as Pike nearly took his head off with a thundering jab that made a cracking sound in the air.

"You've passed the point of attacking only," Pike announced. "Now, you must defend."

Pike executed a series of perfectly formed jabs and straights. It was like he was a paragon of martial arts, using almost *overly* perfect forms. It was stiff, and Alistair knew that he was purposefully hardening his style to teach him something. What that was would probably take several days to figure out, and he wouldn't stop paying attention.

Pike spoke while he struck. "Do you know why the Steel Body is so much better at defending against strikes inside one's perception?"

"No," Alistair made out. He had a longer explanation, but he couldn't say it with how quick Pike's attacks were.

"Every single sect in the Ravine has trained and tempered their bodies far beyond the average human. The Raging Bulls gain the Bull's Temperament, a raging state which grants superhuman strength and endurance. The Viper's Fangs practice the Snake's Spine, wherein their bodies become impossibly flexible and supple. There are benefits and downsides to the secret technique of each sect, not all of which are body tempering. By downside, I do not mean that there is any part of you that will become worse for knowing the Steel Body, but as an opportunity cost for learning it compared to the other secret techniques."

Not for the first time, Alistair thanked the translation program baked into his soulcore. It could even cover something like "opportunity cost," and wasn't affected by the suppression field. So far, it hadn't failed in translating a language, but surely it couldn't have *every* language in its files? Alistair filed that away for another time.

"If the Steel Body made it so that the user was truly invincible, guarded from all sides with a nigh-impenetrable exterior, every sect would have switched over. But it is not such a divine way, unfortunately. If only the Mother willed it so. The Steel Body is truly awe-inspiring, and in my unbiased opinion, the best in the valley, but there is a 'weakness.'

"Attacks outside of one's perception are far more damaging. Not as damaging as they were before the Steel Body, but still far more damaging. The Steel Body hardens bones, tightens muscles, connective tissue, and the willpower, but most importantly, it is a preparatory defense. By connecting to the Mother's Presence when we feel an attack, we use our willpower to nullify the offensive power. Then you can evidently see why an attack outside of one's perception would be more effective. There is no mental preparation, no gathering of willpower.

"Now, I will train your perception. Think of this as the precursor to the fundamentals. If fundamentals are how deep you can understand the flow of battle, how knowledgeable you are of your opponent, how great your understanding of the mechanics of the body—perception is the data that goes into fundamental understanding. You do not want bad data."

Alistair nodded. He did not want bad data.

And then the dance began. For as long as he lived, Alistair knew that he would never find anything as beautiful as the art of fighting. While at first he had only picked up the mantle out of necessity, now he truly enjoyed it.

Was there a conflict there between that and his commitment to justice? He thought not.

The love of fighting flowed back into his central purpose. The more he loved to fight, the more it came naturally to him. The more it came naturally to him, the more skilled he could be, and the more skilled he could be, the easier he could help others. That was why, with all the pressure on him to defeat Silvanio's champion, Alistair knew he couldn't lose.

———

Alistair's journey to the Church of the Holy Ones was with a small envoy— Master Ko Pao, Pike, Davnos, and Ko Min. While the Silver Comet Sect was an all-male sect, unlike a mixed gender sect like Kodaidaemin or the Church of the Holy Ones, women weren't forbidden on the premises like a sealed monastery. Ko Min was Ko Pao's granddaughter and often helped out around the temple.

They left the next day at the crack of dawn. Alistair could feel the tension in the air. Master Ko Pao assured him that nothing bad was going to happen, but it didn't help. It was funny to Alistair that he was more nervous for a simple meeting than facing down superpowered Devil Kings in life-or-death combat.

Obviously, it came down to his lack of power, his lack of control. Alistair wondered if this was how almost all of his citizens felt in the outside world. Powerless, subject to the whims of fate and those stronger than them. He remembered the elemental beasts that had come out of the earthquake in New Boston. He had dealt with them easily, but anyone below, say, level 35 would have a mighty hard time dealing with the lava golems and presumably the other beasts coming from the disasters. And the boss beast? You would need to be around level 45 or have some alternate method of power to contest that without a serious risk to your life.

There were three sects in the main village itself. The Church of the Holy Ones, the Viper's Fangs, and the Sworn Sisters. The second largest after the Holy Ones, Kodaidaemin, was located on a different peak of the white mountain. Their temple was a mountain retreat in the snow, and the apostles there were considered some of the toughest, though Pike claimed that the Silver Comet brothers exceeded them.

Alistair had asked if the center of the Holy Ravine had always held the Holy Ones and that their old base was smaller, or that they had constructed an entirely new building. Pike told him that they were always there, but their original building was much smaller. Their oldest records said that the original Church of the Holy Ones was a ziggurat of the local gods, abandoned over a thousand years ago when they began venerating the Moian pantheon.

Alistair found himself interested in the anthropological history of the Holy Ravine, but Pike shrugged.

"I don't concern myself with those things," he said. "That is for the scholarly man, not I."

Instead, he talked with Davnos, the archivist. And Alistair had *many* questions for the scholar.

Alistair questioned the learned man, who stood as tall as him with white and black streaks in his hair. Even the archivists of the Silver Comet Sect were buff like bodybuilders. "What do you know of the planet that you came from, before you got whisked away? And how did that all happen?"

Davnos laughed. "What do you know of your *planet*? The entire sphere? Do you take the Holy Ravine for some backwater savages with no knowledge of geography? How would you explain your knowledge of your own planet?"

Alistair flushed with embarrassment. He had phrased his question terribly. He also turned red because the answer was yes to Davnos's question about the Holy Raviners being backwater, but he wasn't just going to say that. "Forgive me, that was dumb. And uh, no, of course you're not savages. I'm just curious because a farmer I talked to sounded like he considered the Holy Ravine the entire world."

Davnos grinned, showing off a gold tooth and that he was not truly offended. "That would be the case, wouldn't it? Most of the villagers here are simple folk. To them, the Holy Ravine is the world. As for me, I've traveled far and wide in my youth, but I settled back here in my middle age. Before I can answer your question, I must confirm that the information I have obtained about this planet from the outsiders who have sheltered here is correct. You call this Earth, and there are seven continents. Water takes up 70% of the surface, and you could say there are four seasons, though many parts of the world have less. You have almost two hundred nations, and advanced technology that allows you to reach the stars and send information thousands of miles in a fraction of the second. This is all correct, yes? Although, out of date." Davnos gestured up to the sky.

"Yeah, that's how it was. I'm surprised you know all that."

"It is an archivist's job to know things," Davnos said. "I ask and I listen. I've extensively interviewed some of the refugees from Earth, asking all sorts of questions. I thought it might be useful one day, and even if not, knowledge for its own sake needs no justification. Now, as for comparison, we call our world Lisorte, though other peoples might name it differently. From what I can gather, it is much larger than Earth. We have two moons, one of which is red and nearly as large as our planet, causing devastating tides. For our lands, the Holy Ravine is one small part of the greater Martial League, one of the five largest nations on Lisorte. The Martial League, as aptly named, is a civilization where the fists determine everything. There are innumerable lands and peoples within its borders. Because of Lisorte's sheer size, our population measures within the hundreds of millions, I believe. The Holy Ravine is still but a minor, minor place in the Martial League."

"Interesting," Alistair said. "I assume your technological level was much lower than Earth."

"Quite so," Davnos said. "I am amazed by the stories your people tell of what these marvelous 'electronics' were capable of. Alas, they seem to have all failed?"

"Correct," Alistair replied. "After the initiation, all of our advanced electronics failed. Though, I've heard of cases where people's Classes allow them access to technology. My friend Alfred, he can create tiny little spy drones that function similarly to what electronic ones could do, but even better. Actually, maybe they are still electronic? This universe is part of the Final Frontier Empire, which purchased the Pathfinder AI from the Sublimed Machine Faction. I assume it means that they use more technology as part of their cultivation than other places, but I've never been outside this universe. I wouldn't have a good frame of reference."

Alistair looked at his companion and realized he was going on a tangent. "Oh, apologies, I didn't mean to go on like that. This must all be confusing."

"No, it is quite alright. You bring up some interesting points, though I do not grasp the entire situation."

"And you, why isn't the entire Holy Ravine going crazy? At least on Earth, we knew about the possibility of aliens. It sounds like Lisorte had medieval levels of technology. By medieval, I mean the level of technology Earth had a thousand years ago. Wasn't this all insanely shocking to you guys?"

Davnos laughed. "The Holy Ravine is made up of sturdy stock. For a thousand years, we have engaged in eternal war with our neighbors in the Wasted Realm. And yet, for a thousand years, the Holy Ravine has not seen civilian bloodshed within its borders. Our people are simple and hard. This situation, while not ideal, is not the worst thing that could happen. Indeed, some are hopeful that they will develop the powers they have heard about from the outsiders."

"I think that should happen," Alistair said. "But I can't guarantee anything. So, speaking on the Holy Ravine, were you the strongest in all the Martial League?"

"Despite my pride in my homeland, we cannot claim that title," Davnos said. "We are far too small. Our fighters are much stronger than the average soldier in the Martial League, but we lack enough population for the truest talents to emerge. As much as it pains me to say, the unprecedented arrival of Silvanio improved the standing of the Holy Ravine greatly. That is the major reason why his rule is not contested more. Even so, he would only be in the top twenty-five masters of the Martial League."

"What a wide world it is." Alistair found it hard to believe that anyone could be better than Pike at martial arts—he moved with such athleticism and confidence that he gave off the impression he could knock out a mountain-sized dragon with a sure punch. That is, if you didn't count Red. Alistair wasn't powerful enough at the time to truly comprehend his movements, but he gave off the aura of perfection. As much as he liked Pike, Red was something else.

Alistair shook his head. "What I would give to see him against one of those masters," he muttered.

"What was that?" Davnos asked. Alistair had forgotten that the members of the Silver Comet Sect had unusually good hearing.

"Oh, nothing. A couple of months ago, I encountered this guy who beat my ass with just one hand. Well, he didn't actually attack me at all, but he embarrassed me pretty hard. I bet he would win against Pike, honestly, even if you brought him down to the same physical condition."

"How intriguing," Davnos said, stroking his chin. "What is the name of this master, should I encounter them in the future?"

"Red," Alistair said. "I encountered him on a planet that must be billions of miles away from here, so you probably won't ever see him."

Davnos's eyes widened. "What did this fellow look like?"

"Tall, good-looking guy. Tan with red hair. Liked the color white, but that could be just his outfit of the—"

"By the Mother's great bosom, it cannot be!" The wizened man stopped mid-stride, staring directly into Alistair's eyes. "Surely you jest?"

"Nope, that's what he looked like," Alistair replied, extremely confused. "Why, do you know him?"

"His Excellency Red Harmonia," Davnos stated, as if reciting from memory. "The undisputed First Grandmaster of the Martial League, the youngest in history to become the Grand Champion of the Martial League at fourteen years old, the Unrivaled One and guarantor of the Martial League against the Drakonian Empire and the Wasted Realm. I cannot believe that you witnessed him with your own two eyes."

The reverence Davnos had for Red bordered on fanatical. Alistair wondered exactly what Red had done to earn all of those titles. But the more pressing question was, how the hell this was possible?

It can't be a coincidence, can it? The guy I meet from back then turns out to be related to these people now? Let's think about this analytically. Nenna Spindoller didn't mention that Red was from the same universe as me. That is using absence of evidence to make a positive assertion, but I think she probably would have mentioned that. So Lisorte is probably not in the same universe as the Final Frontier Empire. Plus, since their initiations happened at around the same time, their Prime Initiates would have been owning in Felons vs Fellows, right? At the time of the Felons vs. Fellows, I wasn't even a talent in the grand scheme of the empire. The Pathfinder AI wouldn't have been specifically targeting me. I'm stronger now, and it hasn't shown that kind of favoritism from what I've seen. Considering I don't know what the mission Nenna and Red were on, there is a high likelihood it had to do with a part of his planet coming here. Or parts? There could have been more than one.

Alistair scratched his head. Could parts of Earth be on Lisorte, or other far-off worlds? What if all of Harvard College or the Shaolin Monastery were currently involved in some interplanetary dispute? Alistair would feel bad for them, though he had to suppress a chuckle, since the idea was kind of funny in and of itself. He would have to investigate missing regions when he got home. A lot of things were missing in burnt portions of the world caused by Atavius Meloi, and everything was scrambled up, so it wouldn't be easy.

"Have I lost you?" Davnos asked, interrupting his thoughts.

"No, no, I was just thinking," Alistair said. "What a coincidence I have already seen your Grand Champion."

"Indeed. All the better. Perhaps you can introduce us one day."

Alistair stifled a laugh. "That would be interesting."

They made their way through the thick forest and back into the main village. It bustled with life, people on their merry way like there wasn't an apocalypse going on. To them, there was nothing wrong. Alistair couldn't help but wonder what would happen to all those people if the Devil Kings successfully managed to unify the planet. He doubted they would remain safe forever in those conditions.

The normal people of the Holy Ravine gave the Silver Comet Sect brothers a wide berth. Respectful, but also a little afraid, Alistair estimated. To the average peasant, the sects were both their protectors but also their rulers. A different caste. Still, almost everyone had a distant relative or two that was in them, so it wasn't like they were completely alien.

Davnos had told him the population of the Holy Ravine was fifty-five thousand. There were many different ethnicities despite the apparent isolation of the place, owing to multiple waves of immigration. Ko Pao's lineage in particular came from the first wave of immigration that brought the introduction of martial arts. This afforded him respect beyond his title as Head Apostle, even from Silvanio.

At last, they came upon the Church of the Holy Ones. It was as opulent as Alistair remembered, an enormous temple that reached up into the heavens, a twelve-pointed cerulean star on its steeple. The main section of the temple was a ten-story pagoda the area of the entire Silver Comet temple, with west and east wings attached to it.

There was an overhang of silvery stone that looked almost like the nave of a Gothic-style church attached to the temple. This extended forward, giving a depth to the temple that felt ancient and foreboding.

It was nothing compared to the wonders Alistair had seen on Faxor, but for the Holy Ravine, it was sheer grandiosity. It was something that the other sects had complained endlessly about. The presentation suggested that the Church of the Holy Ones was the greatest.

Are they wrong about that? They've won the championship of the Holy Ravine eight times in a row.

Unlike the Silver Comet Sect, they had two guards at the front door. A short stone stairway led up to two doors taller than two of Alistair, engraved with conquests of man over nature. Right as they arrived, the doors opened, and a man stepped out.

Right away, Alistair understood who he was. Silvanio Apostolos.

He was shorter and smaller than Alistair expected, perhaps the same size as himself before the initiation. However, in every aspect of his being, he screamed strength. He had harsh, angular features, not an ounce of fat on his face. His hair was dark and his skin pale, and he wore a fine silk cloak patterned after the starry night sky, far fancier than the clothing even the elders of the Silver Comet Sect wore.

And he was staring straight at Alistair.

11 GOVERNOR SILVANIO APOSTOLOS

"Hello, my friends," Silvanio said, his gaze moving from Alistair to Ko Pao and the others. Chills went down Alistair's spine as his nearly black eyes washed over him. Silvanio's presence felt more like a Dark Lord than an eight-time martial arts champion. "Master Ko Pao, it is good to see you again. Has it been seven months since our last encounter, when my daughter Elerie soundly defeated your prized disciple?"

Silvanio's voice was quiet and soft, with a touch of raspiness like he was whispering at full volume. However, Alistair couldn't mistake those eyes. They were that of a predator looking at its prey.

"An excellent bout, if I say so myself, Governor Silvanio," Ko Pao responded without skipping a beat. "Wouldn't a rematch be proper?"

"In good time, in good time, my elder friend. Next year's tournament seems like the perfect venue, would you not agree?"

"That would be wonderful," Ko Pao said.

"And what have you for me today? An outsider who wants a bout with one of my fighters? What is his request?" Silvanio once again stared at Alistair with that unnerving gaze of his.

"To leave, along with his friend," Ko Pao said. "That is all."

"There is a reason that none are allowed to leave the Holy Ravine until we can understand the situation better. Outsiders are dangerous. That reptilian monstrosity could have killed everyone in the Holy Ravine. This is a tall ask, outsider."

"If outsiders are so dangerous, then isn't that all the more reason to have them leave?"

"The outsiders are dangerous on the outside," Silvanio replied. "Here, they are powerless."

Left unsaid was the eventual implication to that train of logic. If the outsiders got their powers on the outside, and therefore couldn't leave, then what would happen to him and Oliver?

"We have a difference of opinion on the matter. I ask with the traditions of this place in mind, Silvanio. He may make a request of you as is within his guest right. Considering you were capable of letting the beast leave, it is not unreasonable, even if it is not to your liking. As an outsider with little training in the arts, he should face your weakest champion."

"I have no weak champions," Silvanio retorted with some bite.

"Which is why I did not say 'weak.'"

"That is true, that is true. Very well then. I do not wish to make things more impossible than they already are. He will face Brutus Caligoris in single combat for his request. In the meantime, shall I get to know this intrepid outsider? Please, come in to my humble abode."

Silvanio bowed and opened his arms wide to indicate they should come in. Behind him, the massive doors creaked open, sounding like they weighed thousands of pounds.

Alistair looked to Ko Pao, who smiled at Silvanio with a warmth that only a wizened old man could muster. "We would be delighted to."

———

The inside of the church was just as magnificent as the outside. They walked through a massive hallway decorated with huge tapestries that depicted scenes of combat. If the paintings were to be believed, from time immemorial, members of the Church of the Holy Ones had been draped in the finest silk and always fought giant men while being outnumbered by impossible odds.

Alistair found their whole temple distastefully overdone. What happened to the principles of humility for martial artists? It felt wrong that these theatrical braggarts were the strongest in the Holy Ravine.

Silvanio himself led them through the temple, showing off their various facilities. They had hot springs, cold baths, and fine eating shops *inside* the building. It was practically a five-star hotel!

There were starry-skied acolytes rushing everywhere he looked. There were far more members of the Church of the Holy Ones than members of the Silver Comet Sect, especially among the young people. The ratio of those under eighteen to those over for the Holy Ones was almost one-to-two, whereas it might have been one to four for Alistair's sect of choice. A displeasing fact for Ko Pao, no doubt, and one central reason he opposed the rule of Silvanio so doggedly.

I must remember, the Silver Comet Sect are not being entirely altruistic, Alistair thought. *I break bread with them, and they are nice to me—well, as nice as a society of battle-trained martial artists can be, but in the end, they have their own goals. I would hazard a guess that the favor they want from me is to wallop the Church of the Holy Ones once I regain my full power.*

Silvanio's eye remained on Alistair for almost the entire tour. He spoke so passionately about the glory of the Holy Ones and their advantages over the other six sects in the Holy Ravine, that it almost— *Wait,* Alistair thought. *Is he trying to recruit me?*

Alistair shook his head. How bold. Alistair needed every ounce of power that he could get, but he was no traitor. The Silver Comet Sect had taken him in and assisted him. Plus, why did he get the feeling he was better suited for their style than the Holy Ones?

That thought lasted until the moment they entered the training hall.

Scratch that, the Holy One style suits me way better.

Like their robes, the walls and ceiling of the training hall were of the night sky peppered with stars. Their hall was at least three times as large as the one back in the Silver Comet temple, if not more. A hundred disciples used dummies, weights, and sparred against each other. Despite being behind enemy lines, Alistair felt a certain sense of camaraderie.

And their style—it was enthralling. Alistair used Zenaitsu Morogoni's style, possibly named Psychopomp's Discipline, though he couldn't be sure if that was the real name or a creation of the Pathfinder AI. It was an all-out attacking style focused on killing the opponent as quickly as possible, through fluid, adaptable movements.

Fluid, then still. Soft, then hard. The Kiss of Death. That was its motto. There were many arcing movements and feints and trickery involved. Of course,

Alistair's personal tastes added a certain twist. He guessed the original style focused more heavily on striking, but somehow he had altered it over time to have more throws and grappling. Thankfully, the Dao of the Fist did not literally only apply to moves with fists or striking in general.

As a result, Alistair's default state was to not like getting hit. At all. The Steel Body violated all of his instincts. The Holy Ones, on the other hand, seemed all about dodging. They moved like the wind, always evading their opponents by a whisker. On top of that, unlike the straightforward, honest moves of the Silver Comet, they were tricky and cunning.

They moved with such grace. It was a lie to say he wasn't tempted by it. But who cared? It was good to be balanced. It wasn't a bad thing to get accustomed to other styles.

Silvanio's soft voice interrupted his thoughts. "There is my wonderful daughter. Elerie! Come here."

Alistair's breath was taken away as he saw Elerie Apostolos, the strongest champion of the Church of the Holy Ones and the daughter of Silvanio. She was beautiful. Tall and confident, she moved with preternatural grace. Every step was perfectly executed, every breath perfectly balanced. She wore a starry cloak like her father, except hers had the sleeves cut off, revealing well-muscled arms with white bands around the bicep.

She had black hair and pale skin like her father. However, instead of his pure black irises, she had red eyes, making her look positively vampiric. Alistair doubted she actually had Shaded One ancestry like Caren, though.

Elerie bowed respectfully to Ko Pao and Pike, with a shallower bow to the latter. "Welcome Master Ko Pao, Brother Pike. Who is this newcomer I see?"

Ko Pao answered. "This is Alistair Tan, my newest apostle. He comes from the outside and will challenge Brutus for permission to leave."

"A difficult bout," Elerie said. "It is almost impossible. Brutus would be a challenge for even Pike."

"Hardly," Pike shot back.

"In my bouts against him and you, I felt equal challenge, that is to say, very little."

"Children, children, this will all be settled in good time," Silvanio said. "Ko Pao, I presume Pike will be your first seed in the tournament?"

"Indeed," the old man said.

"Elerie shall be mine. May they meet in the finals."

"That would be most auspicious."

"Though," Silvanio said, appearing to look troubled for a moment. "I don't see why they can't have a rematch now? For training purposes."

"I would love that, father," Elerie said with a wide smile.

"I too, would not deny such an opportunity," said Pike.

The only one who didn't seem happy about the idea was Master Ko Pao. "This is neither the time nor the place. You know this, Silvanio—it is not within our customs."

"I have less knowledge of the customs than the esteemed Master Ko Pao, eldest of the seven sects. Very well then. However, I must entreat you to stay for a while. Alistair, I would like to be regaled with tales of the outside, if you may."

Alistair looked to Master Ko Pao who had a solemn look on his lined face. *Yeah, there's no way I'm getting out of this one. He's the ruler of the Holy Ravine, after all.*

"Of course, Governor Silvanio. I would love to."

―――

Silvanio brought them to a cozy underground grotto, lit by torches on all sides. It was hot down there, hotter than the cool autumn temperatures outside, but still at a comfortable level.

There was an entire *restaurant* carved into the cave, which had murals engraved on the walls of some kind of Titanomachy, Alistair supposed. Deified figures, including a goddess of war that Alistair assumed was the Mother, fought against a legion of burning demons. The carving was ornate and detailed, a masterwork.

The tables were carved out of the rock itself, and Silvanio seated them. Ko Pao, Pike, Davnos, Alistair, Ko Min, Elerie, and Silvanio. At one table.

Alistair thought it was the most awkward thing he had ever been a part of.

Ko Min was a quiet, mousy girl, around the same age as Oliver. She was extremely shy, though she liked to help out the apostles of the sect. She had little experience with martial arts—only what her grandfather had taught her.

Useless as an ally for mealtime conversation. What about Pike?

Pike was carving into his meat like a caveman. Not him then. What about—

Silvanio interrupted his thoughts. "Alistair, I have heard tall tales about the outside. Is it true there are creatures known as 'Devil Kings?' I have heard they are fiendish beasts without reason that can conjure fire strong enough to burn down the entire Holy Ravine in a single second."

Alistair put down his fork. "One of them maybe, but he's dead. I doubt the other one is strong enough."

Silvanio looked at him with empty eyes. Alistair coughed. "Oh, sorry, forgot you don't know anything about them. Well, they look human, except for their eyes and these weird markings that go down their heads and backs. They are human, they just have demon blood inside them that makes them stronger."

"Demon blood," Silvanio said. "It is difficult to believe unless you've seen it with your own eyes. Men and women capable of flying and destroying cities with a thought. I would hardly believe it myself if not for over a dozen witnesses to the changes. And that powerful reptile, Vritra. Even as a master unrivaled in the Holy Ravine, I thought that I would not want to try my luck against him. But you are not as powerful as him? Why is that?"

Alistair chose to answer truthfully. "As a beast, more of his power is innate to his body and cannot be negated by the suppression field in the valley. Perhaps you saw him at ten percent strength. For a human like me, it takes almost everything away. Of course, even with my full strength, I would be nothing compared to Vritra. He is one of the most powerful forces in the outside world, outstripped by less than ten people, by my estimation."

He couldn't forget that he was pulling the wool over Silvanio's eyes. If he revealed his actual position, there was no telling what the man would do. They had come up with a good persona—a decently powerful martial artist that was nowhere near the heights of his real self or the Devil Kings.

"Ten percent strength and he outmatches all of us? That is a frightening thought. And how exactly did your people acquire these powers?"

He already knows the answer, Alistair thought. *He just wants to hear what I'll say.*

Alistair had to play his cards correctly. "Dev'rox? I need some of your ancient wisdom."

"You do, finally?" the imp said. "I was waiting for when you would wake me from my slumber."

"How much should I tell him?"

"The safest answer is nothing," Dev'rox said. "Any information can be used against you by an opponent crafty enough."

"How crafty do you think Silvanio is?"

"Crafty enough. He is a hard man to read."

"Haven't you been among humans for tens of thousands of years?"

"Bah."

"Maybe. I think I have an idea. If I give him a little curiosity, I think it will help. What does he want? He is clearly interested in power—in becoming a cultivator. I'm thinking years down the line. Obviously, I want the Silver Comet Sect to win the next championship and become the ruler. I believe that Pike can do it. But what if Elerie wins? As I understand, as Global Mayor, I would be the planetary lord of Earth. I don't think these displaced people are going home. That never happened before. So the Holy Ravine is going to become a part of our world, whether we like it or not. They could become valuable allies in the far future, with how solid their foundations are compared to normal humans."

"It looks like you already made up your mind," Dev'rox said. "You've become better at thinking strategically."

"I learned from the best."

"Don't even try it. I am immune to flattery." Dev'rox beamed.

Alistair continued his conversation with Silvanio, who Alistair realized at this point was probably wondering why he'd been silent for so long.

"When Earth was initiated into the Final Frontier Empire, the Pathfinder AI opened up the Dao and gave our bodies the capability to process Mana. Your planet most likely underwent a similar process near the same time."

"Lisorte?" Silvanio asked, genuinely taken aback for the first time. "What makes you say that?"

"I saw Grandmaster Red Harmonia," Alistair said, using his proper title to show respect. "He wasn't on your planet. He was strong, probably the strongest person I've seen that was recently initiated. I think the fact that you already had some Dao energy on your world before makes you stronger starting out. And now I find out that he was already the Grand Champion of the Martial League or whatever. That puts his strength into perspective."

Silvanio went completely silent for ten seconds, making Alistair grow nervous. What if he had said the wrong thing? Was Silvanio about to go crazy and kill him for mentioning Red? Maybe they had past history and Red had humiliated him, and he would go insane at the mere mention.

"Most interesting," Silvanio finally said, relaxing in his chair. "I had wondered what was going on with Lisorte while we were transported here. Thank you for telling me this, Alistair."

"I just thought you should know."

"I am unaware of how much Master Ko Pao has informed you about Grandmaster Red," Silvanio started. "But he is no ordinary man. I had the good fortune of meeting him one time. All the greatest masters in the Martial League were called to the capital in response to wanton aggression from one of our human neighbors. They thought themselves sly as the majority of our forces dealt with a particularly large incursion from the Wasted Realm.

"Red Harmonia is a step above every human I have ever seen in the fist. The moves of a master are incomprehensible to the amateur, yet we are amateurs before his divine understanding. If he has undergone this process you speak of, then it is no wonder he is invincible."

Invincible? Alistair didn't know about that. It was a wide world out there, after all. Red couldn't be that impressive in the grand scheme of the multiverse. But he supposed that on the frontier, he might be invincible for his level, except for the strongest elites of the various universal powers.

He pushed his charisma to the maximum. "Is this process really necessary? What are you gaining by forcing me into this duel? If there's a way for Vritra to leave, then surely it's possible?"

Silvanio's black eyes gave away no information. His dead expression was the same as always. If he was offended by Alistair's impertinence, he didn't let it reach his expression.

"It cannot be done. There are larger things at work than you realize. But fear not, I shall abide by my word. If you win your battle, you are free to go."

Alistair didn't understand Silvanio's logic. It seemed completely off. Yes, there was some risk to letting him go. But wasn't there an even greater risk to pissing him off and then letting him go if he won? If he wasn't as nice as he was, he could go back and raze the Holy Ravine or even more specifically the Church of the Holy Ones for daring to defy him. It all smelled off to Alistair. Did he really have that much faith in his champion?

A lumpy presence along his thigh made itself known as he adjusted his seating. Dragonus's gourd, **Heavenly Nectar Incense.** Which now contained the concentrated power of a raging Mana Storm inside a hermetically sealed hunk of golden metal that felt inviolable.

There was no doubt in Alistair's mind that the hybrid concoction of congealed Dao energy, natural Mana, and mysterious incense was still fecund inside the gourd. Whatever the Devonic Elision Field was doing, it couldn't penetrate through the gourd's protective walls.

However, he was unsure of what would happen if he unleashed it. It was entirely possible, and more probable than not in his opinion, that the dampening would immediately affect the contents, effectively putting his hard-earned lightning to waste.

No, it was better to keep that in reserve. He had captured the lightning knowing of his future battle against George Moulin. He would withhold using its power for now. If he needed to escape as a last resort, he could try it.

The second object he had in there also made him squirm. The black marble with a thunderstorm inside of it. Given to him by Nenna Spindoller, an agent of a mysterious organization called the Cabal. It could never be lost and always returned to him no matter what. Like the gourd, it couldn't go inside of his soulcore. Would the Cabal beam down from their far-off bases and come and rescue him?

No, that was far too good to be true. In a multiverse where struggle led to power, he couldn't imagine they would or even could intervene in such a circumstance.

"I understand your position. This Brutus Caligoris, may I meet him?"

Silvanio shook his head. "It is customary for the duelists to have no contact until the moment of their bout. But besides, he is taken with other matters away from the sect."

"I can tell you all you need to know about Brutus," Elerie said, to what Alistair thought might have been the chagrin of her father. "Mad Brutus the Biter, he is called. He only joined the Holy Ones six years ago. While his technique is yet unrefined, his ferocity is second-to-none."

Silvanio gave his daughter a stern look. "Thank you, my daughter. Ko Pao, how does two months' time sound?"

"It is acceptable," Ko Pao replied. "Under the standard conditions?"

"Let us have the match cloistered," Silvanio said. "Out of respect for the delicate circumstances."

"It is acceptable."

Alistair felt like he missed something in their interaction, but he didn't concern himself too much. He had his mission before him. Defeat Brutus Caligoris, and get the hell out of the Holy Ravine. And if plan A failed, he still had his gourd as a last resort. Then there was his last, last resort, which was begging the Pathfinder AI to be let out.

A genial voice interrupted their table talk. "Esteemed masters, guests."

Alistair looked up to see a robed, kindly looking man. He was older, with crow's feet and smile lines. "Shall I introduce you to the main course for our meal?"

Ko Pao clapped joyfully. "I am famished. Governor Silvanio, what say you?"

Silvanio nodded to the waiter. "A feast fit for a king, Gorion. Nothing less for the eldest master of the Holy Ravine and his disciples."

12 RESUMED TRAINING

THE REST of the meal went by without much of note. They mostly discussed internal politics and Holy Ravine affairs. Alistair had Dev'rox absorb as much of it as possible. The infernal imp didn't even need a bribe, since he genuinely enjoyed political machinations. It gave him something to do while trapped inside Alistair's body.

Back at the sect, Alistair's training ramped up once again. They never went *easy* on him by any stretch of the word, but after nearly dying while unlocking his foresight, his body physically needed a break.

He was placed back into the regular group with the other orange headbands. That meant the runs, the toughness instruction, weight training, and sparring.

Alistair found the moves coming naturally to him after his bout with Apol-Xin. Not that he was a slow learner before, but the actual life experience of their fight increased his learning rate an appreciable amount. Alistair worked twice as hard as anyone else, so that no one thought he was coasting on his talent alone.

Every day hurt like hell, but it was doable. Pike worked him twice as hard in their personal sessions. He brought in a rotating coterie of purple headbands for him to spar with. They didn't go that hard so he could recover, but it was still tough fighting against opponents every single day.

It felt like Pike had a secret motive with his selection of opponents. He never spoke about it outright, but Alistair could feel that each was tailored to a certain weakness in him. Whatever Pike chose to focus on in their training, he would find a purple headband to match that theme.

For example, if they were training to better Alistair's foresight, the sparring partner would be someone with deep insight into the fundamentals of battle. If they were instead aiming for increased power generation, he would face a physically imposing opponent. All this served to round off Alistair's rough edges and turn him into a fighting beast.

Alistair adapted to the new schedule faster than it got harder. The Steel Body training increased all of his physical stats except speed. All in all, that meant his mind wandered more than before, when he barely had any energy to think.

His thoughts drifted to the Northeast Order Freehold. To Alexandra, his family, John, the Woods, and Pharaoh. To Donna and Tamia and all the other innocent people. Because of the time dilation, he calculated they had just finished the second week of Earth Asunder. He had missed an entire natural disaster cycle. There could be an untold amount of damage from whatever storms or quakes or floods emerged.

Based on the rate of the flow of time, he would return six days into the second wave of [Armageddon]. And he would miss out on all the Contribution Points. He really wanted the highest Contribution Score. How would the Pathfinder AI treat the sudden change in his knowledge and abilities?

Alistair smacked himself in the face. It was no use worrying about things outside his control. Whatever happened on the outside happened. He needed to focus on his training and getting stronger.

Today, Pike was taking him for special training. But he wasn't alone. Ko Pao had assigned to him a partner from a different sect, a woman named Izalia d'Fortune. She came from Kodaidaemin, an allied sect to the Silver Comet. Together, they were the last opposition to the total domination of the Church of the Holy Ones.

This was nearly two weeks after Alistair's fight against Apol-Xin. Already, he was too strong for the orange headbands. His growth was unstoppable. Apol-Xin, who had once easily defeated Alistair, was easy pickings now. They had scheduled his promotion bout to purple in two days.

Izalia was meant to bridge that gap. The other sects in the village didn't use precisely the same headband ranking system, but she was still at the top of the heap in Kodaidaemin, having a black rectangle tattooed on her forehead.

The Kodaidaemin emphasized fast and precise movements, often in combos. They weren't quite as quick as the Holy Ones, and they didn't have their whimsical sense of airiness either, but used direct, straight lines of attack. In that sense, they were somewhat similar to the Silver Comet Sect.

Alistair thought he understood why Master Ko Pao chose someone from another sect, and not internally. Since he was climbing so fast, it was embarrassing for the apostles to lose to him when he was weaker than them not a few weeks ago. By using an outsider, he didn't hurt anyone's feelings.

His progress wasn't their fault. He already knew so many techniques that once he had been given the keys to employ them, he was destined to grow leaps and bounds. Alistair looked at Izalia d'Fortune with greedy hunger. How soon would he be able to beat her?

Ouch. Alistair almost recoiled from a stream of water entering his eye.

After hours of various martial exercises, they were ending the day meditating under a waterfall. Well, maybe meditating wasn't the right word. Pike had instructed Izalia and Alistair to stand on a rock face underneath a billowing, rigorous waterfall. Tens of thousands of gallons of water fell over their heads every second. While they stood there, they had to punch continuously.

Pike had the two apostles stand facing each other to up the competitive spirit. He didn't give them any goal in particular to aim for, or any notion of when the exercise would end.

So Alistair punched away, ignoring the stray stream of water. He kept a steady but superhuman pace, punching a permanent veil in the water with his immense speed. However, even with his durability, it was incredibly painful to remain under the falling river. The pressure and weight of the water felt like a ton of rocks crushing his shoulders and head. He could barely breathe with the water trying to wade its way into every orifice.

Alistair looked over at his partner. She was tall for a woman, coming up to his eyes, with black hair and large purple eyes. Despite her height, she was very skinny, skinnier than you would expect for a martial artist, and had an unusually youthful face. She met his gaze unwaveringly, showing intense determination.

"Excellent, excellent," Pike announced after thirty minutes of their practice. At that point, Alistair's arms wanted to fall off. Punching for half an hour was normally as easy as walking for him, but the added mass of the water made it feel like he had a hundred pound weight on each arm. "Let's take a quick break."

Thank goodness, Alistair thought to himself, practically falling out of the waterfall. To his dismay, Izalia showed him up by reacting slowly to Pike's words. She stayed punching for a few moments more. *That was unnecessary.*

Pike ushered them to a cliff face overlooking the Silver Comet Sect's temple. In the distance, you could make out the smoking chimneys of the main town square, and the looming specter of the Church of the Holy Ones. In times like these, a scenic vista was something Alistair wouldn't neglect to enjoy. There was something sublime about the natural beauty of the Holy Ravine. Despite its parochial milieu, Alistair found it easy to believe how such powerful individuals would choose to remain within its borders.

"What was the purpose of that exercise?" Pike asked the two of them.

Both Alistair and Izalia shot up their hands with the vigor and enthusiasm of a teacher's pet.

Pike shook his head. "Okay, we'll take turns. Alistair, you go first."

Alistair tilted his head and stroked his chin. "Uh, because you want us to get used to acting under pressure?"

"Wrong!" Pike slammed his fist into a nearby rock, causing a massive shockwave that sent cracks running down into the ground. "That is part of the reason, but not even close to the main purpose. We can do that anywhere. Why specifically here, on the mountainside, and underneath the River Sylo? Izalia, go."

Izalia stiffened and spoke with youthful brashness. "Sir, I believe it is because the method of water is the most suffocating of all. The ancient songs of the Holy Ravine describe the exploits of the Fisher Hero Dranik who trained to face the Serpent of the Depths by standing under a waterfall."

"That's more like an extended version of Alistair's answer. The real answer is tradition." Pike performed the standard move-set of the Silver Comet Sect, what Alistair would call a kata, and the Pathfinder AI's soul translation service agreed. A series of prescribed movements in a standard order that was meant to be memorized and assist with the cohesion of one's martial arts. The kata Pike performed was simple, relying on strength and power.

Pike looked at them with a devilish grin. "What good are these moves? And when I say these moves, I mean these exact moves."

"Presumably, they are the accretion of thousands of years of users," Alistair answered. "In each generation, the best techniques are preserved for the future, with ineffective methods left to the wayside."

"You'd think that," Pike replied. "But that isn't necessarily true. The kata are great, yes, but to call them perfect would be an interesting claim. Their weight comes from tradition, not perfection."

"Tradition, but not perfection?" Alistair asked. "But why would you purposefully lessen your own techniques by passing on imperfect techniques?"

Izalia scoffed. "That's easy, newbie. Does this concept not exist on your world? Tradition is power. When a legendary hero has used a certain technique to vanquish her infamous enemies, the technique itself becomes legendary."

Alistair called up Dev'rox from his dormant state. The imp's lethargy was difficult for Alistair to contend with. He did not like thinking of what was happening to his friend. The two of them had a bond that transcended their initial pact. Without words, he knew that if he didn't get out, Dev'rox would eventually pass to nothingness.

"Is that something true of the whole multiverse?" Alistair asked Dev'rox. "Sorry to bother you, buddy."

"Buddy? That's new," Dev'rox said. If he had his material form, he certainly would have been grinning. "It's fine. I still have enough gathered spiritual presence to last for another three months, so you'll have a berth of over a month to leave. Just don't call on me too much. As for your question, while I haven't heard it in those exact terms before, it sounds correct. If I were to hazard a guess, I would say it is connected to the Akashic Records."

The Akashic Records. The mysterious location at the center of metaphysical reality. Alistair's ghost blood dragon bloodline came from the Akashic Records. It was an interesting theory. Perhaps when accessing a move that had achieved momentous accomplishments, it was stronger because of being closer to the metaphysical center of the Akashic Records.

"Ah," Alistair said, not wanting the conversation to grow awkward in silence. "Yes, I apologize, I did know that. So by changing technical imperfections in a technique, you could lose the bonus from the legendary nature?

In that case, wouldn't all the best moves be the oldest ones with the most storied histories?"

"Aha! You've stumbled onto something, my apprentice." Pike jumped onto a boulder overlooking Alistair and Izalia. "Two things—legendary accomplishments are only legendary as long as people remember them. The sands of time take all. Generally speaking, the strongest period of a legacy is two generations after it is created. Enough time to cement the story in people's minds, but within or almost within living memory, though of course there are exceptions for the truly brilliant. And then, of course, there is genius.

"Genius is like the blooming of a flower. Delicate, and fleeting. Always destined to occur. Using an ancient technique to the letter is fine. But improving upon it with your own creativity? That is sublime. That is the pinnacle we all try to reach."

"What if you aren't even modifying a known technique?" Alistair wondered. "Like, what if someone just makes something purely from their imagination, with no provenance?"

Pike flashed a high kick faster than Alistair could even dream of reacting in his current state. The large apostle's toes touched his nose, though Alistair swatted it down right away since the smell was quite gross. "Then your name would be forever remembered like Dranik or Elegion or Red Harmonia. I recommend you aim for those heights."

"Is Silvanio at that level?" Izalia asked.

"I wouldn't know," Pike said. "Now, back to my original question."

"My answer was essentially correct," Izalia complained. "Of course I knew about the tradition aspect, but I was answering from the perspective of the original user, sir."

"Very well. You get full credit for your answer. Go ahead and punch Alistair as your reward."

Izalia smirked and dashed into an elbow strike right for Alistair's stomach. Since he had forewarning, he braced for impact, diffusing the impact of the blow with the Steel Body. Still, it hurt.

"Is this really necessary, Brother Pike?" Alistair coughed. "When I get a question right, I can't hit her."

"You're more sturdy than her. Have some decency," Pike retorted with a smile. "I allow you to *try* to strike her, but you just miss every time."

Alistair sighed. That much was true. He had met Izalia d'Fortune today, and in the half-dozen times Alistair had been allowed a punch for answering a question correctly, he had hit only air.

"That's enough for this lesson," Pike said. "How about a short sparring session, and then we can go into town?"

Both Alistair and Izalia excitedly agreed. They barely got any free time, so a sojourn into the town was much needed.

Alistair rolled up his sleeves. Sparring session time it was.

———

Alistair held in his pain as the three of them ran through the forest. Putting it mildly, Izalia had beaten his ass. They hadn't gone a hundred percent since it was sparring, but he knew he was far outclassed. There was simply nothing he could do.

But for some reason, it didn't feel as bad as when he got destroyed by Apol-Xin. With his greater experience, he could plainly see the areas where the d'Fortune heir outclassed him. She was faster than him, saw deeper into the fundamentals of martial arts than him, and had superior perception than him. Her application of technique and reflexes were superior. These things could and would be improved over time.

That didn't take away the soreness from his ribs and the pain he experienced in every rapid step as they cruised through the forest.

At their rapid pace, it only took thirty minutes to sprint through the forest. Alistair requested that they pick up Oliver along the way. He knew that his friend was wilting in the Silver Comet Sect, to put it lightly. That kid had a lot of grit. *No,* Alistair thought. *I can't call him a kid anymore, can I?*

Despite not having a lick of martial arts background, Oliver had adapted as best he could. He was still in the white headband group, and near the bottom of the pack, but he never gave up. Alistair guessed that he wanted to prove to Alistair that he wasn't weak, so he had the mental fortitude to never give up.

The last week or so, Oliver had barely spoken. The intense training took its toll, and he rolled up into bed as soon as possible every night. This would be an opportunity for him to relax and have fun.

Alistair pleaded with Pike for the Necromancer's case. Technically, it wasn't allowed, but the experienced apostle pulled some strings and got permission to bring Oliver along for the ride.

The four of them made their way through the forest and joined the main trail leading into town. In a strange coincidence, Alistair saw a familiar face on the way.

"Grag?" Alistair asked. He spotted two people along the road to the town center, one of whom looked very familiar with his farmer's tan and red silk robes.

"Oh? Oh! May, it's those outsiders!" Grag exclaimed. "This har is my wife, May. Ya didn't see her last time round cuz she was at her folks' house."

"Nice to meet you, May," Alistair said, unsure of what greeting custom to use. He had found out the hard way that the clasping handshake was only for after duels or moments of great significance, and not to be used as a standard greeting.

Luckily, the woman made a simple and deep bow that he returned in kind. May was a short woman, her head reaching her husband's shoulder, with similar tanned skin.

"You know these two, Alistair?" Pike asked.

"We met them when I came here for the first time," Alistair said. "What are you two doing here?"

"A most joyous occasion! May's little sister is getting marred, and there's a gran' old fest goin' on in the Dragon's Head tavern."

"Marred?" Alistair raised an eyebrow.

"Married," Izalia supplied.

"Oh, that's wonderful," Alistair said. Oliver nodded his head vigorously.

"I'm so happy for the two of tham. Such a wonderful couple. Say what, would ya like to come along?"

"You're sure it wouldn't be an issue?" Alistair asked. "We don't know the bride or groom at all."

Grag was about to say something, but then he seemed to get a hold of his surroundings. He immediately bowed, almost to an absurd degree, testing his back's limit in flexibility.

"Mah apologies, Lord Fighter," he said, bowing many times over toward Pike. His wife copied him. "I did not see ya at first. And Lady Fighter, ma'am. Please have mercy on me and mah wife. I would not dare think o' inviting ya to the wedding."

Alistair was taken aback by how servile Grag was. It was a good reminder of the difference in status of those at the top of the Holy Ravine and those at the bottom. Grag must have recognized the red headband tied around Pike's forehead as a symbol of authority within one of the seven sects. They were the nobility of the Holy Ravine. It felt weird, since he thought of them more like warrior monks than nobles or aristocrats. Except Silvanio, he had major noblesse oblige vibes.

Pike put up an arm nonchalantly. "It's alright, I care little for political titles. You don't have to address me so formally. I'm not my great-great-great grandfather, after all. Alistair, do you want to join them? I suppose we'll have to take off our headbands to blend in."

"I think it could be fun. What do you think, Izalia?" Alistair asked.

"I'm for anything that doesn't involve more training. Let's go."

13 DRAGON'S HEAD TAVERN

ALISTAIR WAS surprised when he saw the Dragon's Head Tavern. His expectation was a rowdy, lower class, rambunctious inn, but in reality, it was remarkably high end.

Like the name suggested, there was a stone statue of a dragon's head above the entrance. A large torch burned inside its maw, making it look like the dragon was about to breathe its flames down on the incoming patrons.

While the tavern was in the town center, it was off the beaten path, at the top of one of the few hills in the valley proper. Inside, there was no loud laughter of drunkards, but the serene sounds of stringed instruments and polite discussion.

The restaurant was split into two sections; an upstairs and a downstairs, separated by a coiling marble staircase shaped to look like an eastern dragon. At the center of dozens of tables was a small stage where the musicians performed. There was one man and one woman who looked almost identical to each other. The man played an instrument that looked similar to a pipa, while the woman played something that looked like an erhu, contributing to an eastern vibe within the tavern.

Alistair's face might have given off some of his surprise, since Grag chuckled, commenting, "Don't ya look so shocked, I'll have ya know, farmers are quite important har in the Holy Ravine."

Izalia nodded. "It is true. While the Mother of War is one of our most important goddesses, the Father of Grain cannot be said to be any lesser."

"Come on, now! Mah family gots tha whole top section reserved. They say that tha Dragon's Head has tha best food in tha entire valley!"

Grag nodded to one of the servers, who wore a long silk dress that glittered like a jewel. She was beautiful, though Alistair found the large amounts of overly white makeup to be a bit strange. She escorted them up the staircase and to the rest of the wedding party.

"Grag! My cousin, who do we have har!" A burly, drunk man even larger than Alistair sauntered over from one of the many long tables on the top floor. He looked somewhat similar to Grag, with a deep tan and brown hair, blue eyes, and a sharp, aquiline nose. His eyes didn't leave Izalia, who gave him a cold glance.

Grag shook his drunken cousin with some urgency. "Hush, ya fool! Ya don't wanna show disrespect," he whispered louder than a normal person's speech. "Lord Fighter Pike, Lady Fighter Izalia, and Lord Fighter Alistair, I apologize for mah cousin's improper manners."

"No apology necessary, I can see that he's having quite the fun time," Izalia said.

"Like tha lady said! I am having a fun time!" the cousin stated. His eyes were bloodshot, and he was so inebriated he wasn't understanding Grag. But he made a mistake when he sauntered over to Izalia and put his arm around her shoulder. "What's yar name again?"

Izalia acted instantaneously, flicking the giant man with her pinkie finger. He went flying in the direction he came, crashing into his seat. "I wouldn't recommend that."

The other attendees of the wedding party looked over with concern, but upon seeing what had happened, they seemed to go back to their own business. An older woman hurried over to the scene, bowing over and over to the d'Fortune heir. Grag and his wife, May, also asked for forgiveness.

Izalia looked over at the unconscious man. Alistair wasn't sure if that was from the blow or the alcohol, maybe both. "I'm more concerned for the poor women of his village than for myself."

The older woman, perhaps the man's mother, nodded vigorously. "My deepest apologies, Lady Fighter, Kal is a big ol' fool. He handles alcohol terribly."

"Tell him what he did when he wakes up and remind him of the old laws," Izalia said. "That should scare him enough."

"How merciful," Pike commented. "We shouldn't interrupt their fun so much, Izalia."

"How would you like if one of those women put her arm around you?" she asked.

"I might enjoy it, depending on the woman. For example, if it was your sister's, I would never object."

"Leila doesn't want anything to do with you after you were mysteriously absent for your last date," Izalia retorted. "Sir."

"There was an emergency!" Pike protested. "I had to deal with an outpost at the Last River."

"You could have done it faster."

Pike shook his head. "Let's let bygones be bygones. I'd hoped that by training you she'd understand I mean well."

"So you're only training me to get to my sister? How nefarious. Sir," she added.

"Master Ko Pao personally assigned me as I am the greatest teacher in the Silver Comet Sect; I take great offense— Ah, damn it. You've beat me here."

"Hmph. I might've told her you've learned to be more humble before that boast."

Alistair butted in, seeing how the rest of the group looked quite uneasily at the exchange between the two martial artists. Pike had said to take their headbands off... but Izalia's mark as a fighter was literally etched onto her forehead and she refused to remove the silver headband holding her hair down. Anyway, it was obvious that Grag and May would tell everyone no matter what. "Ma'am, thank you for taking care of your... son?"

The woman nodded. Alistair bowed to her. "Please enjoy your party, and we will try to stay out of your affairs."

"T-thank you Lord Fighter," she stammered, grabbing May and Grag by the arms and pulling them away.

Alistair turned to his two companions. "Can't you see you were scaring the living daylights out of those two?"

"I cannot imagine what could be considered frightening about our amicable conversation," Izalia said with not a hint of shame.

"Neither do I?" Pike looked far too innocent for his actions.

Alistair shook his head. What hopeless martial artists they were, uninitiated into the careful art of sociability. Much unlike him, who was charismatic as a cult leader. *Maybe that's not the best way to describe it.*

They met with the bride and groom. Vai, May's sister, and her husbandto-be, Polomus. Like the rest of the farmers, they seemed to be slightly on edge seeing the warriors that protected the Ravine. Alistair wondered if there was bad blood between them. From what he saw of the sects, they didn't seem like the type to bully the agriculturalists.

While the martial artists were feared, many of the wedding party guests actually did come up to them. He had the feeling that seeing two high-ranking apostles of a sect was not an everyday occurrence. Pike put back on his red headband with pride after seeing the futility of hiding, while there were no bangs allowed for the Kodaidaemin.

In a strange turn of events, Oliver was the most popular of the four of them. Because of his white headband, he must have been seen as more approachable. The attrition rate for white headbands was high—many of the farmers here had sons and daughters who at one point had been white headband equivalents, or they themselves had tried joining a sect in their youth.

Oliver was swamped with questions, almost all by children who wanted to know all about his experience. He looked to Alistair for help, who shook his head, sending a clear message: "You're on your own with that."

Overall, the political system of the Silver Comet Sect felt in some ways less insane than those in Earth's history. With hard work and dedication, you could make it from the bottom to the top of the hierarchy.

Alistair guessed that the high-ranking members of the seven sects were like royalty in ancient times back on Earth. Though he imagined that they were way chiller than Earth nobles or Final Frontier Empire nobles, for that matter. That probably came from their strict discipline and training dedicated to the destruction of the ego.

After they got shopped around with a large amount of clout chasing from Grag, he offered them one of the private rooms he'd reserved. He kicked out a couple of old grandpas who were playing a game that looked like Go.

There were a bunch of private rooms at the back of the second floor, hidden behind a graceful veil hanging from the ceiling. The veil, which had an alluring siren embroidered on it, led to a hallway of rooms.

Alistair closed the paneled sliding door behind the four of them. A single red candle lit the entire room, so the lighting was dim. He peered at the curious candle, admiring the apple red flame. Alistair had never seen a candle burning red before.

The room was large enough to fit ten people, though it had no chairs. Instead, there were mats for them to sit on, surrounding a wooden table that stood only a few inches from the floor. There were partially eaten food and drinks on the table, and a four-player game of Go unfinished on a 23x23 board built into the wood.

Alistair was no expert at Go, but he had played with his grandparents and parents a number of times over the years. Seeing the game reminded him of Edward Lasker's famous quote, "If there are sentient beings on other planets, then they play Go." Though, the impact of that quote was diminished by the existence of Dao archetypes.

Go was a remarkably simple game for its complexity. In fact, one could argue it was complex because the rules were so simple. Normally it was a two-player game, one person with the black stones and one person with the white stones. They took turns placing down their stones on a grid; the victory being the person who encircled more territory at the end. There were more rules than that, but that was the essence of the game.

The board on the table was larger than he was used to, but that seemed to be because it was multiplayer oriented. There were four colors of stones on the unfinished game board—blue, red, green, and yellow.

"You wanna play?" Alistair asked his three companions.

"You know how?" Izalia raised an eyebrow.

"It looks very similar to a game on my planet called Go," Alistair said. *Though my planet is your planet now.*

"We call it War's Brother," Pike explained. "It is traditionally played by four people."

"Ah, interesting," Alistair said. "It's slightly different on Earth. It's mostly a two-person game with a slightly smaller board, 19x19."

"I've never played Go before," Oliver said. "Can you teach me?"

Pike and Izalia explained the rules to Oliver, with Alistair listening in to ascertain the changes. There were slight variations to Go as it was on Earth. Nothing major, but it did change up the game in subtle ways, and the multiplayer element and larger board were new to him. He felt flattered when they offered to play the game the way his people normally did, but he refused, stating, "When in Rome."

They stared blankly at him. Oops. Alistair forgot how the soul translation system of the Pathfinder AI often struggled at conveying idioms or extremely localized phrases.

"What's up with the political situation here?" Alistair asked, as he placed down one of his blue stones. Damn, these Holy Raviners were good at Go, or War's Brother, as they called it. He was getting thrashed, all of his attempts to gain territory failing right away. They weren't even teaming up on him either—Izalia and Pike were much more concerned with going at each other's throats than worrying about him, and he was still losing. Oliver was doing his own thing, not a threat to anyone in the slightest, though he was staring at his pieces like they would move with his mental command.

"What do you mean?" Izalia asked. She didn't even look up at him as she placed a yellow stone down and captured one of Pike's red stones, to his chagrin.

"Like the relations between the sects," Alistair said.

"You're unsealing a bucket of earthworms with that one," Pike replied. "Hmm. I suppose in order to tell the bigger picture, we have to start with the pre-Silvanio age.

"While our legends say that our people have been in the land for time immemorial, our archivists agree that our oldest written records date back a thousand years. A thousand years ago being the time when a group of Moi people fled persecution east of here. They brought both the written word and their system of martial arts. Master Ko Pao is descended from an ancient line of Moi that founded the Silver Comet Sect. All of this was five hundred years before the founding of the Martial League itself. In this entire thousand-year period, there have always been the seven sects. Silver Comet, Kodaidaemin, Raging Bull, Viper's Fangs, Sworn Sisters, Slaves of Shadow, and the Holy Ones. It is said that seven brave men and women founded these sects to eternally defend the Holy Ravine against the Wasted Realm."

Alistair butted in with a question. "I've heard you people speak about the Wasted Realm a lot, and not in a positive light. Are they your enemies?"

Izalia snorted, replying to Oliver's amateur move with a slicing maneuver that cut his territory in twain. "The Wasted Realm is the home to the immortal enemy of all mankind. Darkness forever lies over their lands, for the gods have cursed them for their immorality, so sayeth the Book of Songs, chapter 1, verse 35. They have maintained their lands west of the Akolian Mountains and east of the Poen Sea since the eldest days. Inhuman corpses that never tire and never sleep lie in the earth, waiting for flesh to consume. The Martial League is the only thing that stands between them and complete domination of mankind."

"When you say corpse, you really mean corpse?" Alistair asked. "Like a zombie?"

"Zom-bie?" Izalia sounded out the word. "I don't know what this means. But they take the dead of the places they conquer and add them to their army. Every single one of their troops we have ever encountered has been one of our dead ancestors or those of neighboring lands. The Dread King is their leader, but he never leaves the Palace of Night at the center of their kingdom. The last expedition sent by a Grandmaster of the Martial League was over a hundred years ago. A specialized strike team of some of the most renowned martial artists in the realm, including one who was almost as glorified as Red Harmonia. They tore through the land with their ruthless march, making it to the Dread City in two months. Then all communications abruptly cut off. Not one man or woman on that expedition returned. To this day, the Martial League is recovering from our losses sustained in the aftermath of that foolish journey, and the Wasted Realm has the most land it has had in a thousand years."

"Adding to what Izalia said," Pike added. "The Holy Ravine almost borders the Wasted Realm. You could make it there in a day's journey by foot if you really pushed it. Despite almost all our neighbors falling to the Wasted Realm and having to be recaptured at one point, not once have we suffered defeat."

Alistair could hear the pride for his homeland oozing out of Pike's words. Well, from what Alistair had seen, the Holy Ravine *was* pretty awesome.

"Back to your original question, though," Pike continued. "Not one of the seven sects dominated the other. Of course, there were periods of one coming to the forefront and others receding, but the balance of power was relatively stable. In the years before Silvanio, the Silver Comet Sect was the most powerful, under the champion Jo Ran, that large old man you've seen a couple of times. Silvanio changed everything. His first ally was the Sworn Sisters. The Silver Comet Sect and the Sworn Sisters have always had icy relations as the only two single sex sects. But they were quickly joined by the Raging Bull Sect and Viper's Fangs Sect. Those three, along with the Holy Ones themselves, comprise the core power of Silvanio—each of their leaders is wedded at the hip to the man. The Slaves of Shadow have remained neutral in all affairs, though practically that means they're siding with the Holy Ones. While the Silver Comet has always been their most vocal opponent, Kodaidaemin also vigorously opposes the domination of the Holy Ones."

"I take umbrage with that characterization," Izalia huffed. "Leila is the only one in our age cohort to have beaten Elerie in any match whatsoever. Something not even *you* could accomplish."

"Don't go rubbing it in."

Alistair understood at that moment that the relationship between Izalia's sister and Pike was more delicate than a silly fling. As the two strongest members of their respective sects in the younger generation, their relationship could be the biggest boon or the worst disaster.

"Your world is so hard for me to understand," Alistair said. "You barely had Mana or the Dao, yet there was a zombie horde. Any other magic stuff?"

Izalia looked up in thought. "I never would have found it odd until talking to your people, but the people of the Drakonian Empire have scaly skin and horns and stand a full head taller than humans. We think the reason we developed such advanced martial arts is to stand a chance against them. They're way stronger than normal humans. You could pass as a fourth dragonborn with those eyes of yours."

My eyes? Alistair thought. He looked at himself in one of the clean silver plates the other group had left behind. Sure enough, his pupils were taller and narrower than before. Like a dragon's. They weren't complete slits, but more like halfway in-between that of a human and a dragon. He sure hoped that he wouldn't keep taking on draconic characteristics the more he upgraded his bloodline.

A waitress knocked on the door, taking away the food of the guys who got kicked out and replacing it with freshly made dishes.

Alistair's mouth watered as he saw the new food. The sect fed them properly, but not these kinds of delicacies.

The waitress brought fried dumplings, crusted and stuck to each other, so you had to break each one off. They still sizzled with the oil used to cook them, and were filled with minced bamboo shoots, black truffle, ground beef, ginger, garlic, and more vegetables and spices that Alistair wasn't even sure existed on Earth. This was topped with a divine dipping sauce that incorporated soy, ginger, and a hint of white truffle oil, but not too much to overpower the flavor.

With that came a mouthwatering soup that looked as immaculate as it tasted. The broth was crystal clear, filled with wispy spirals of dragonfruit essence. There were julienned vegetables soaked in the limpid liquid, which only enhanced their flavor. The broth was something Alistair had never seen before, a fusion between sweet and spicy that danced between the two in a fashion impossible to Earth cuisine, like it was a living, dynamic dish designed to attack one's credulity of something tasting that good.

But that wasn't even the main course. With those two above dishes coming from the top of her cart, the two dishes below blew Alistair's palate away. It was somehow even better than the food on Faxor, better than his [Carmela's Happy Pies]. Lisorte was some planet, that was for sure. It didn't have that much of a higher Dao concentration or Mana than Earth, but still had such incredible things.

The first main dish was beef tenderloin coated in a five-spice rub, wrapped to perfection in a flaky puff pastry. The way the outside of the savory and buttered pastry crunched and the inner layers were chewy created the most sublime eating experience, combined with how the umami flavors of the meat saturated into the bread. It was lightly sauced with a red wine reduction, and there were garlic-infused mashed potatoes for a side.

Alistair couldn't say the second main dish was better than the first, but it was in no way worse. Grilled salmon fillet glazed with a shiny and colorful sauce made from fresh mango, ginger, soy, and honey. The sweetness was counterbalanced with a hefty sprinkling of sea salt, and it was garnished with sesame seeds and served on top of a fragrant jasmine rice pilaf.

The group devoured the food. Alistair couldn't name a favorite out of the four dishes. He loved them all. Yet despite wanting to scarf down the food like a starving man recently rescued from a desert island, he somehow stopped himself. The reason was because it was even better to slowly eat the food. It was so delicious his body overrode his natural desire to eat faster, and instead he ate particularly slowly, savoring each and every bite like it was his last.

"This is way better than that underground place in the Holy Ones' church," Alistair said as he licked the remains of the mashed potatoes off his spoon.

"No doubt," Pike responded, his mouth containing two dumplings at once. "I've heard Silvano has tried to poach the head chef of Dragon's Head multiple times, offering him even triple the pay he makes here. He refused every time. His father's father's father cooked here, and he'll be damned if he leaves."

"I must pay my respects to the chef," Alistair announced. "What an upright, amazing man! What a shining star for his community! We need a lot more of that in this world."

"Cheers to that!" Pike switched over to a beef pastry, soaking it in the red wine reduction. "Here's to more loyal chefs who stay with their ancestral restaurant even after greedy, conspiring men who want to take over Holy Ravine try to poach them!"

"Hear, hear!" Alistair roared in response. There was something inside him that needed this whimsical outing. His life had been fighting and training for what felt like a lifetime. The challenges of the future were deadly and not to be underestimated, but if he never had fun, would he even be a human by the time he reached the peak? He looked over at Oliver, who was laughing. He couldn't even imagine that frightened and antisocial young man acting like this. No matter how serious Alistair became, and no matter how dire the threats were, he promised to never forget to enjoy the small moments of life.

"You're drunk," Izalia dryly noted. "The red wine reduction uses a special grape whose alcohol content barely gets burned off when turned into a sauce. You too, Pike. But you have no excuse, since you already knew that."

Oliver looked at his pastry suspiciously. "You didn't tell us earlier?"

"This is betrayal," Alistair accused. His head was spinning and when he saw his reflection in his spotty clean plate, he saw that his cheeks were flushed. He hadn't been drunk in over five months, since before the initiation. He had even blocked the psychedelic mist when he went to that club in Port Locasta.

"Lighten up, Izalia," Pike said, his massive scar looking far less menacing with the genuine smile plastered over his face. "Your sister knows how to have fun better than you."

"A true martial artist remains alert at all times," Izalia recited as if reading from a creed. "His mind remains sharp, and his fists remain deadly. At any moment, his enemies could strike, and his people could fall. The world is his battlefield."

"And who would dare oppose the top disciple of the Silver Comet and the fifth disciple of Kodaidaemin?"

There was a sharp knock on their door. A feminine voice called out from behind. "Keep it down in there!"

"I'll take care of that," Pike said, sauntering over to the paneled door. It had a wooden frame with a canvas center, reminding Alistair of a traditional Japanese-style entrance, though these were more attached to the wall. Sound traveled easily through them.

Pike opened the door. "Fuck."

Standing outside their entertainment room was Elerie Apostolos, the heir of the Church of the Holy Ones.

14 THE FINAL TRIAL OF THE STEEL BODY

PIKE SHUT THE DOOR IMMEDIATELY.

The door flew open again. Elerie looked at their group with smug arrogance. "You don't close the door on me, comet boy. Has the standard within your sect fallen so low that you parade around drunk?"

Pike snickered. "There is no parading around, Elerie. Look, we are playing War's Brother! You can admit that testing one's mind under strenuous conditions is a catalyst to growth."

"Yes, of course," Elerie said, dripping with sarcasm. "That is what you were doing."

Izalia stood up and defended them. "And you're here strictly on business?"

"That's right," Elerie said. "I talked to Head Chef Koi."

"Ha," Alistair interjected. "He'll never join you."

Elerie snapped her neck to look at Alistair so fast, he thought her head might fall off. "Did I ask you, outsider? What do you know of these things?"

"More than plenty," Pike said. "He has grown accustomed to our ways with remarkable speed. No one can say he isn't a true Holy Raviner anymore. I, too, was once skeptical of this man, but he has proved me wrong."

"That remains to be seen," Elerie said. She stormed out of the room, leaving the four of them wondering what the hell that had been.

"Shall we get back to the game?" Pike asked.

Oliver nodded vigorously, stuffing his face with more beef pastries. Too bad they were almost out of food. Alistair made eye contact with Izalia, communicating something along the lines of, "These guys really don't care about what just happened?" Despite his teasing, he felt they were on a more similar page in terms of personality than he was with Pike. Turned out his gruff exterior was a front for a pretty lackadaisical guy.

Alistair didn't say anything, though, and they returned to their four-player Go game. Pike came out victorious in the end, and Alistair second, though that was only the simplistic measure of their territories. With Oliver out of contention early on, the two frontrunners in Pike and Izalia duked it out. That let Alistair creep into second by territory, but he was never in the running to win the game.

They returned to the temple an hour past midnight. He knew that in the morning, he would regret his decision. They still had to get up before the crack of dawn.

Before leaving to sleep, he asked Pike a question as they went inside the entrance hall.

"What do you plan on doing after the Holy Ravine is initiated?"

It was a simple inquiry. Alistair didn't know for certain if it would come to pass. Maybe the Holy Ravine would never be initiated. Maybe the Devil Kings would emerge victorious and annihilate their little slice of countryside.

"I don't know," Pike answered. "I want to explore those stars the outsiders have talked about. I'd also like to see you leap over a mountain too. Not sure if I quite believe it."

"Mountains might be a tall task, but you're on for that. You need to help me survive my fight if you want that to happen."

"What do you think I'm doing? You're my prized disciple. Go to sleep and don't let Master Ko Pao hear you. He'll have my head."

Alistair heeded his teacher's words and found his bed in the purple headband dormitory. His thoughts churned, but his body shut down almost instantly, falling into a dreamless sleep.

———

The next day, the Silver Comet Sect added a new element to his training—punching a giant rock.

They shuffled around his schedule to compress the previous weight training blocks into a single two-hour period dedicated to rock punching. Because of this, he no longer only trained with the purple headbands, but had dedicated periods to the black, red, and sometimes orange apostles.

There was little instruction for the rock punching period. Pike guided him to the location of a huge rock in the forest. It was twice as tall as Alistair and three times as wide.

"How did this even get here?" Alistair asked.

"Prehistoric glacial movement," Pike answered. "There are tons of them in the forest. All you have to do is keep punching this rock until you can shatter it. That's all. At the end of the two-hour period, I'll come back to check on your progress. Once you can complete this, you're ready for the next step."

Alistair nodded. It was just a rock, after all. How hard could it be?

The answer: Extremely difficult.

Two weeks later, Alistair had made almost no progress in breaking the rock. There were slight cracks running over its face, but no major internal damage.

There were two problems—its size and his delicate bones. He had chipped off a fist-sized portion of the stone, but his power barely diffused within the inner portion. In addition, his hands and feet were too weak to withstand constant, full power blows. He had to space out his attacks to give himself time to recover.

It was one of those moments where he missed his **Devilsbane Gauntlets.** Those trusty clawed gloves let him punch as hard as he wanted. They jangled helplessly off his wrists as crimson bracelets. More of a fashion statement than a deadly weapon at the moment.

Only six more weeks until my bout, Alistair thought to himself as he pummeled the rock with open palm strikes. That was the best idea he had come up with. The palm was less delicate than the knuckles, and only transferred a bit less power. He could continuously wail into the huge rock for much longer. *But I'm not ready.*

Alistair had gone through dozens and dozens of sparring matches. The conclusion—he wasn't ready to face a champion-level fighter. He was comfortably beating and surpassing purple headbands, but red headbands were still giving him the works, let alone black headbands. He still never understood why Pike wasn't a black headband, and he didn't ask. Some things were better left unsaid.

Both his experience and body were lacking. Those red and black headbands had years and years of hand-to-hand combat under their belts. Breaching that was the gap between heaven and earth. On top of that, all red and black headbands had undergone the so-called "Final Trial of the Steel Body."

While Alistair wasn't privy to exactly what that entailed, he knew it over doubled the efficiency of the Steel Body and granted a new technique.

Despite his lack of experience, the complete Steel Body was what he really wanted. Alistair knew that if he had it, he would have a fighting chance against the black headbands. After all, he had his own specialties too. No one in the sect except for possibly Master Ko Pao could match him in variety of techniques.

And creativity, or so Alistair liked to think. His sparring partners might dispute that one, since it was harder to objectively quantify.

Alistair continued to strike the rock—only five more minutes left. He reminisced about all the training that brought him to that point.

Every day, his foresight deepened, and his awareness expanded. Alistair could see five moves ahead at any given time, which was close to his [Eyes of Truth] precognitive sight. Obviously, it wasn't nearly as accurate, but he was impressed with his natural perceptions. With his new awareness of the world, he could sense the slightest vibrations in the air. From fifteen feet away and his back turned, he could detect an enemy's killing intent.

But none of this improvement helped him with the task before him. There was no such thing as predicting a rock's movement. The rock was in front of him, so his perception didn't matter.

"Having difficulty?" Pike's voice came from on top of the rock. Alistair jumped back. He had been so focused, he hadn't even realized that his mentor had climbed it from the other side.

"This is impossible," Alistair said. "You're telling me you could do this before you had the complete Steel Body?"

"I never said that," Pike countered. He spoke his next words with far more candor than usual. "Alistair, you must understand something. The Final Trial is no laughing matter. The gap between purple and red is the largest for this reason. The qualification process for a purple headband to even attempt the trial is extensive. Even with this intense screening, one in four who attempt it die. You are going far faster than we would ever normally allow. The archivist and Master Ko Pao are calculating the date for your trial that will maximize your recovery."

Alistair understood that. If he attempted the Final Trial too early, he would have a higher chance of dying. Conversely, if he waited too long, he wouldn't be recovered in time for the duel against Brutus.

"They've determined two weeks and two days to be the appropriate amount of recovery time. Since the Final Trial takes one week, you have two weeks until it begins. Even if you don't crack this rock, you'll still undergo the trial. You don't stand a chance against Brutus without it. But please, I'm begging you, give this your all. I promise, despite not being able to explain the method, this will help you out a lot. I don't want to see you die."

Alistair didn't know what to say. Pike had helped him so much over the past few months. The man who complained about outsiders the day he'd met him was gone.

Pike patted him on the back. "But I believe in you. So keep at it."

Those two weeks came and went in the blink of an eye. Despite all of his training, Alistair couldn't help but feel jittery the day of the Final Trial. The sect members were extremely tight-lipped about their pride and joy, and no one shared any information about what was going to happen, except that it was the most difficult thing they had ever done.

His imagination exceeded his reason as he conjured up all sorts of tortuous nightmares of what the Final Trial of the Steel Body could be. Surprisingly, the one who calmed him down wasn't Pike, but Oliver.

It was the morning of his appointment. Instead of his normal schedule, the various elders of the Silver Comet Sect would take him through the beginning processes of the trial. Alistair woke up early, his sleep troubled.

"What the hell!" Alistair whispered. Oliver was standing in the doorway to his room, silently pacing. Luckily, Alistair had caught himself, so he wouldn't wake up the other three apostles who bunked with him.

"Shh!" Oliver hushed, like he wasn't the one being crazy for infiltrating Alistair's room. "You'll wake them up."

Shaking his head, Alistair jumped onto the cool stone floor. He had been awake for the past hour anyway, so there wasn't a point in staying in bed. It wasn't as if he was capable of going back to sleep.

"Why are you here?" Alistair asked.

"To cheer you on, obviously," Oliver replied. "I thought I'd give you a pep talk or something."

Alistair rolled his eyes. He didn't want to wake up his roommates, so they took the discussion outside into the dormitory hallway. "Go for it, coach."

"You weren't supposed to take that seriously." Oliver threw up his hands. "I don't have anything prepared."

Alistair saw more than he let on. The little shakes in his friend's hands, the clenching of his jaw, the slightly higher pitch to his voice. "I'll survive, if that's what you're worried about. I've faced tougher things than this before. You scared, ye of little faith? When have I let you down before?"

"That's back when you had powers," Oliver countered. "Pretty over-powered ones too, I might add."

"Hey, I still have Dev'rox," Alistair said. "He could probably beat everyone here with his eyes closed."

"Of course I could," Dev'rox said, though only to Alistair.

Oliver didn't look amused. "I'm serious, Alistair. It doesn't look good. They're rushing you so fast because you don't stand a chance without the complete Steel Body, but you're not ready yet. I heard the white headbands talking about it, and they heard it from Ko Min, and she heard it from Jo Ran. They give it a 50/50 of you living or dying in the trial, and if you survive, maybe one in three of defeating Brutus. I was never that good at math, but that's a one in six chance. How are you going to do this, seriously?"

Alistair took a deep breath. Yeah, when you put it like that, it didn't sound good. Instead of responding to Oliver's concern directly, he asked a question. "When you get back, what do you want to do first? How about we visit the Hall of Math? I'm sure by then, my money will have gone to the moon, and we can purchase some higher tier information on necromancy."

"You're not fucking answering my question!" Oliver raised his voice. Teardrops formed around the corners of his eyes. "This could be it, and you're not taking it serious—"

Oliver's voice became muffled as Alistair brought the younger man in for a hug. Their height difference and Oliver's poor posture meant that the teenager's head cradled against Alistair's chest. At that point, he let it all out, sobbing uncontrollably as Alistair comforted him.

"I-I'm s-scared, Alistair," Oliver finally managed. "What's going to happen out there?"

The implication was left unspoken, but Alistair understood. Without him as a counterbalance, the Devil Kings would surely win in the end. It was only a matter of time. Even if somehow they did make it out in a few months rather than when they planned to, they might come home to a ruined planet ruled by George Moulin, all of their loved ones long dead.

Alistair patted Oliver on the back. "Believe in me like I believed in you all those months ago. Let me tell you, you're almost unrecognizable compared to the man I saved from that corrupt politician. You're brave and intelligent, and I'm sure that thousands of people owe their lives to the work you've done. I'm not sure if I ever would have thought of using the portals to store triggered weapons to fire at enemies."

Oliver wiped away his tears and chuckled, freeing himself from Alistair's embrace. "I can't claim to be the creator of that one. I got the idea from an anime."

"Gilgamesh from Fate, right?" Alistair answered. "Guess I am cool enough for that, after all."

Oliver laughed like a madman. Alistair joined in. They laughed until he physically couldn't anymore, his diaphragm too sore to continue.

"You two done with this laughing fit?"

With his awareness at maximum levels, Alistair already knew who it was. Pike Zenbatty, the prized apostle of the Silver Comet Sect, and his teacher.

Oliver bowed. "Brother Pike. Alistair, you're right. I do believe in you."

"I have to take this one to the elders now," Pike said. "Goodbye, Oliver. Your progress with the white headbands is less than I would have hoped, but you've done well to make do with what minuscule amount of talent you have."

"Yeah, yeah, no need to rub it in," Oliver said as he waved goodbye and headed back to his dormitory.

Once he was gone, Alistair gave Pike a pointed look. "You didn't have to be that harsh. He's trying hard, you know."

"Trying hard means nothing when an Undead Prince sends his legions to kill everyone you've known. Enough dallying. The elders are waiting."

In the halls of the Silver Comet temple before the morning light, Alistair walked. The crack of dawn was still an hour away. The only light came from piles of the glowing blue moss attached to stone walls.

The aged stones beneath him were cool to the touch. Pike brought him deeper into the temple than he had ever gone before.

"The ancient parts of the temple are mysterious, even to us," Pike whispered. "They seem to have existed even before the Silver Comet. It seems that we repurposed an older building and renovated it over time. Now, we enter the original temple."

They crawled through a cramped tunnel built into the lower part of one of the walls close to Master Ko Pao's office. There was a marked shift in the color of the stones as Pike and Alistair crossed into the old section. The grays of the stone turned into a bronze-colored metal that shined with unnatural brightness despite the meager amount of light.

It made little sense. Even if the older structure was much smaller, who would use this much metal for a building? Looking at the construction, Alistair was astounded by how complex it looked. The walls were composed of millions of pieces of interlocking parts, almost like a jigsaw puzzle, but the intersections were only orthogonal.

"Wondrous, isn't it?" Pike asked. "To this day, we do not know how this section was constructed, who did it, or what purpose it served. These types of ancient ruins exist all over the Holy Ravine, and even across the Martial League in general. Madmen claimed that it was evidence of the existence of a magical civilization in the past that could rend cities to ash with a thought. Maybe those madmen weren't as mad as we thought."

The tunnel led to a cavernous hall that almost looked like the inside of a church. There was a stained-glass image of a flaming sword high on the ceiling, and five balconies that housed rows of seats. They overlooked a dais at the center where a chunk of silver metal sat, illuminated by light filtering from the stained-glass above. It was small, only a little larger than a softball.

The room was mostly dark, but that metal shone bright from a single beam of light. Alistair felt drawn to the metal the moment he laid eyes on it. Now that he thought about it, the silvery-black piece reminded him of when he went on school trips to museums. What was that again?

It was a piece of an asteroid, Alistair realized. *This must be the 'silver comet' the sect is named after.*

In the shadowed terraces above the dais, there were cloaked figures. The elders of the Silver Comet Sect. This was it. There was no turning back. Not that he would have in any circumstance. Would he have to fight someone? Fast for a week while standing on coals?

"Approach," announced one of the figures above. Based on the voice, it sounded like Master Ko Pao, but he was speaking funny, so Alistair wasn't entirely sure. "Brother Pike, thank you for your services. You are dismissed."

Pike bowed. He gave Alistair a slap on the back. "You will do this as I did before you. No doubt within my mind."

When Pike put it like that, Alistair couldn't let his mentor down, could he?

A different figure spoke. "Today, you face the Final Trial of the Steel Body. You pass the point of no return. Do you wish to continue?"

"Yes." Alistair spoke loud and with conviction. There was no doubt within his heart.

"Very well," another said. "Approach the dais."

At the same time that Alistair walked up to the mysterious pedestal containing the lit chunk, one of the cloaked figures walked down from the stairs leading to the upper section. He could tell by the shape under her clothes that she was a woman.

Ko Min? Alistair wondered. She was the only woman that lived in the Silver Comet temple, as far as he could tell. Master Ko Pao's daughter—Ko Min's mother—died in childbirth, and her father died in a skirmish with the Wasted Realm.

She gingerly carried a huge ceremonial knife almost as large as her forearm with both her palms. It was silver, similar to the silver of the metal on the pedestal, except more polished. There were intricate carvings along the blade's edge in mesmerizing spiral patterns.

Ko Min and Alistair arrived at the center at the same time. From this spot, he could see the source of the light when he looked up. At first glance, you might think that the flaming stained-glass sword on the ceiling was etched that way, but when Alistair examined it closer, he realized that it was an effect of something above it.

The flames' light was filtering through the glass and focused onto the pedestal, where it illuminated the silvery metal. His heart pounded as he looked at the centerpiece. There was no way it was an ordinary rock.

Something ancient pulsed through its core, something that he had no words to describe.

Ko Min drew closer to him, closer than Alistair was comfortable with. She whispered into his ear, "You must etch this symbol into your chest."

"What symbol?" he asked, leaning back awkwardly.

She moved quick as a rabbit to the rock. From within her robes, she drew out a glass bottle of a teal liquid and poured it over the metal chunk. Within seconds of the liquid coating the rock, a glowing symbol of the same teal appeared on the surface.

The writing was unlike anything Alistair had ever seen. It was not English writing, or Chinese characters, or even Old Moi. It was something that he knew in his soul to be older, more profound. The symbol flickered with new meaning every second.

"Impossible..." Dev'rox stirred within him for the first time in a while. "The Language of the Pure Dao. The First Script of the Heavens and the Earth."

Alistair started sweating the moment he heard Dev'rox's words. "How is that even possible? Should this world not be crumbling in the might of the 'First Script'? That sounds like something of unimaginable power."

"The Language of the Pure Dao is the true tongue of the divine progeny and demons. Its power comes as much from its speaker as its inherent nature. Though, this is not an original carving. It has clearly been copied hundreds of times, losing some of its meaning in each iteration. An unadulterated character of the First Script would be far too much for this universe, let alone this planet, to handle."

"Can you understand what it says?" Alistair asked.

"Spirit's Fists Overcoming Struggle," Dev'rox said.

Upon hearing the translation, everything made sense. The symbol had already resonated with him before, but now it became obvious. So obvious. He was coming home. There was no reason to fear anything going forward.

Alistair took the knife from Ko Min's hands and stripped his robes. The symbol pulsed with unblemished meaning. Even if it was a copy of a copy of a copy, something like this had been used by the first beings in the multiverse, if Dev'rox knew what he was talking about.

What a strange planet, Alistair thought. *One day I'll have to visit it myself.* By the time he could get there, it would most likely be years and years later, since it sounded like Lisorte was in an adjacent universe.

Alistair placed the tip of the knife against his chest while he started at the beauty of the First Script. Slowly, he pierced his skin. Warm blood dripped down his stomach as he replicated the symbol as best he could.

Ko Min nodded once she saw that he had finished. She approached the pedestal containing the silver comet chunk with all the reverence in the world. With the rub of her fingers, she collected the liquid she'd poured on the rock. Alistair saw that the surface of the metal slightly deformed with her touch, and she collected some liquidized metal on her fingers.

Alistair stood in rapt attention, unsure of what would happen next. The cut into his chest began to hurt, the pain taken away by his adrenaline earlier. His heart pounded.

Ko Min whispered into the hand she'd grazed the metal chunk with. Too low to hear, she stepped in front of Alistair and then outstretched her arm underneath the blue light.

All the cloaked figures began chanting, quiet as a whisper. The acoustics of the chamber carried their sound farther than it should have gone, but Alistair did not understand the words. This was probably Old Moi and not the verbal form of the First Script, if such a thing existed, as Dev'rox did not speak up.

After a minute of the woman holding up her arm, with no warning, she swiftly dug her fingers into Alistair's wound.

It took all his mental strength to stop himself from screaming in pain, compounded by the sudden nature of the move. Alistair gritted his teeth and closed his eyes.

Ko Min continued to brush her fingers with his cut. Alistair realized she was putting the metal stuff in his body. Was this the secret of the Steel Body? Strange elements infused within the system?

After a painful minute, she ceased transferring the substance into his bloodstream. Alistair didn't feel any different, besides the added pain. Nothing like the sturdiness that he knew the Steel Body to grant its users, though surely the trial was only beginning.

Master Ko Pao spoke once more. "Long ago, before humans were granted the gift of reason by the gods, a star fell from the skies. What stands before you is a small piece of that fallen star. Since the beginning of the Silver Comet Sect, we have used the power from this metal to strengthen our bodies. The archivists say that a thousand years ago, it was as large as a person. This small chunk is all that remains."

The shadowed figure of his master moved right up to the edge of the balcony. He held up his hands, almost as in prayer.

"You must cherish this gift, Alistair. If all else remains the same, the generation to come will be the last of the Steel Body. Prepare yourself. You must remain standing."

All the apostles in the room began a deep hum. Alistair had never heard anything quite like it. Almost religious in feeling, the low baritone vibrations shook everything in sight. Not a substantial amount, but enough to make everything look slightly blurry.

Alistair got that tickling feeling in his chest that accompanied low frequency vibrations, like a monk version of ASMR. The symbol on the metal comet glowed more vibrantly and pulsed.

The ceiling collapsed.

Though he heard no sound of glass breaking, a column of blue fire came down upon him. It was as if the flaming sword above had fallen like an executioner's blade, slicing off his head.

The entire dais became engulfed in a pillar of fire extending from the ceiling sixty feet in the air to the floor. All Alistair knew was pain.

It wasn't the most excruciating pain he had ever felt. He could still think and move. The problem was that it was unceasing. Pain usually came in ebbs and flows, even serious injuries. This gave absolutely no respite, no waves. Each and every second was torture.

Alistair was completely trapped. There were no more sounds and no more sights, only flames.

If he was being honest, he almost failed in the first five seconds. His knees wobbled, and he came close to falling. But with a gargantuan effort, he forced himself still.

These were no ordinary flames. While the pain was intense, it wasn't like his skin was melting off. They were hot, but not unbearably so, more like the heat of a potentially illegal sauna.

But Alistair was more worried about something else—Master Ko Pao hadn't given him a time limit. Just how long was he supposed to stay in the fire?

15 TRIPARTITE PURIFICATION

ALISTAIR DIDN'T KNOW how long it took before the visions came. Time was in flux inside the fire. The pain erased his perception of its flow. Ten minutes or five days could have passed.

He had to focus on two things—both staying conscious and preventing himself from running out like a coward. The unfortunate problem was that those two things were diametrically opposed.

Forcing himself to stay conscious despite the pain and stress to his body required a concentrated force of will. It was impossible to meditate under the circumstances, even for him, so he focused more on being alive rather than some equanimous mental state.

That led to the issue of realizing his own weakness. Not that he was a weak person, but everyone had their limits. There was only so much pain that a human could withstand before breaking. By making himself more conscious of his own life, that increased his desire to flee and preserve that very life.

Alistair rocked back and forth between these two extremes for an unknown amount of time. Dev'rox, housed deep within his soulcore, shared the pain through their mental link.

Thank you. The imp remained silent, but a feeling of gruff acknowledgment came through their bond. Dev'rox had been his closest ally since the soulcore tribulation all those months ago.

Now, in Alistair's weakest moment, the ghost was there for him. Alistair could feel that the fire was of enough of a spiritual nature to harm his contracted spirit, even through his body. By purposefully focusing on the mental link, Dev'rox offset a sizable portion of the pain Alistair was experiencing. If not for that, Alistair might have already given in.

The visions came after a plateau.

For the entire period of the purgatory, the pain kept increasing at a constant, slow pace. At first, it was like the pain of a stubbed toe, and it only kept increasing from there.

However, there came what Alistair termed the "sublime plateau." After this miraculous point, the pain stopped increasing and flatlined in intensity. The only problem was that at that point, he could barely think.

He first thought it was a trick of the eye. A mirage. But when the form of the flames shaped into a woman, he knew it was a full-fledged vision.

"Descendant, who are you?"

The figure disappeared in a vortex of voluminous fire. They twisted into a new creation, a council room at the height of civilization. Rising above even the clouds, the metal tower was a work of unparalleled architecture.

Surrounding a glass table, thirteen chairs sat thirteen men and women. Every one of them was adorned in the finest crystal and metal armors replete with runic inscriptions, save one bald-headed monk at one end. On the other end was a woman clothed in flames. The woman that first appeared in the inferno as a mere shadowed shape.

"Descendant, who are you?" she asked once more, though her mouth did not form the words. It was a mental command, and somehow Alistair knew it came from her, despite women filling six of the thirteen chairs. They all conversed in a language unintelligible to Alistair.

With her request, he could feel a tugging on his soul. She begged to see his most inner self, to see if he was worthy of continuing. The First Script on the rock said, "Spirit's Fists Overcoming Struggle." This had a mixed meaning, not necessarily tied to his concept of justice. This type of struggle was not entirely aligned to his path, but he understood the gist of it.

"I'm not your descendant," Alistair said out loud. "But here you go."

Breathing in, he gave this mysterious woman all that he could and more. His childhood. Growing up with Evangeline, who was always mature beyond her years. High school and then college. The wistful sense of mundanity he had felt each day, knowing that the adventures in the stories he read didn't really exist.

The beginning of the initiation—the first time he took a life, yet also the first time he saved a life. The responsibility that came with immense power. The desire to be the best and clash fists at the pinnacle. To change the multiverse and deliver his promise to the ghosts that haunted everyone.

At first, it seemed like the woman was satisfied, eating up his memories like a royal banquet. Alistair's confidence rose, as he thought she might have even looked impressed. But that all changed in the next moment. The woman frowned, and her eyes burrowed into Alistair's soul.

"Not our descendant?" she asked.

Not by his own will, Alistair teleported to her side. None of the others gave any indication that they saw him, except the woman of flames. She turned, looking at him with pools of fire. They were identical to a Devil King's, but they lacked any of that unholy, hollow aura that marked them as abominations under Heaven.

As if she was undergoing a manual override from an automatic protocol, the woman's voice suddenly started coming from her mouth instead of in his mind, and became more real.

"What is going on here? You do not bear the blood of the Ikanthian HalfFather."

"I was hoping you could tell me that," Alistair said. "I understand this to be the Final Trial of the Steel Body, no? I recently joined the Silver Comet Sect. It's kind of hard to explain, but the Holy Ravine is now on another planet."

Alistair wasn't sure how cosmically aware the woman was, but he had the feeling that she definitely exceeded how Earth was before the initiation.

"Wait one second. Let me review the memories you gave me," she said. "Ah. It has happened. The aeonic wheel rears its ugly head."

"Can you explain to me what is going on?" Alistair asked, knowing the answer was going to be no. As with all of the cultivation related information, he would settle for scraps.

"Long ago, a great power seeded a frontier planet with the ancestral material of a being known as the Ikanthian HalfFather. That planet, this world, grew to heightened prominence on the frontier. Knowing this, they sealed away its history, saving it for a later time. A time of uncertainty.

When the echoes of a profound conflict ripple through the timelines. Clearly, it is now time for the seals to be undone."

Sealing history? Just the kind of wild bullshit Alistair came to expect, if not enjoy, from the multiverse. How one could "seal" the history of an entire planet was a mystery he wanted to uncover.

The woman tapped her finger impatiently. "This consciousness instance is an existence outside spacetime and the longer I have to stay aware of my surroundings, the more it fades. Please answer curtly, and I shall do the same. I do not recognize your affiliation from your memories, outsider. Whom do you serve?"

Alistair wanted to say no one, but that wasn't exactly true. He was beholden to the Clear Water Sect, for one, and the Final Frontier Empire as a whole. From this woman's statements, it sounded like she was talking about a higher power. In that case, he could realistically answer either the Sublimed Machine Faction or the Eternal Mercy Sect. The Sage gave him his Subclass and helped set him down his initial path, while the Sublimed Machine Faction was some far off group that licensed out the Pathfinder AI. Since they were both acceptable answers, he said both.

For a moment, he worried about the possibility that one or both of those organizations were her enemies and that she would kill him. But she didn't seem mad.

"I do not remember these groups among the peak or greater polities of my era. Under which Heaven do you live? Who is the Jade Emperor of your time?"

Alistair had to shake his head. Jade Emperor—he only knew the title as the ruler of Heaven in Chinese mythology. Given how much of the multiverse was based on Daoism and Buddhism, maybe there was a real world equivalent of the Jade Emperor?

"Worth an attempt," the woman said. "When you return, I shall give you something that you must return to my descendants. It is a key to unlock their Dao history from its profound seal. It will take some time to enact, but eventually they shall return to their former glory."

"I think that's already happening," Alistair said. "I met a man from Lisorte whose foundations seemed unshakable. He is not alone, though he is unrivaled. They tell me that these last hundred years have seen more talents than the last thousand combined."

"Let me see," the woman murmured. Her fires flickered several times as she sifted through his given memories. "With this timing, that can only mean..."

She sat up straighter. "Thank you, outsider. Your information is valuable. I would do more, but unfortunately, I cannot give you the power you seek."

Alistair's heart dropped. Was he going to fail the trial due to something outside his control? Thankfully, the woman's next words alleviated his concerns.

"No, no, no, you shall have your defective offshoot that you call the Steel Body. I refer to the further advantages that you desire and believe that I can grant you. Sadly, I am barred from endowing you with any such secret techniques, bloodlines, ancestries, inborn advantages, and Domain concepts as you are not a descendant of the Ikanthian HalfFather."

"Oh," Alistair said. Now that she said that, he *was* a little crestfallen about that. You could never get too many goodies.

"All in good time, Alistair," the woman said. "My name is Purana of the Stratospheric Flames. If Fate brings us together once more on Lisorte, you shall be much stronger than you are now."

She procured two objects out of thin air, one in each hand. In her left hand was a glass tetrahedron that looked forged from the blue fires that made up her body. In the right hand, she had a golden key.

"This one," she said, holding up the forged glass pyramid, "is a lodestone. It will always point you toward Lisorte, no matter what. Whatever feeling you get when you concentrate on the pyramid is one hundred percent guaranteed to bring you closer to my planet. It cannot promise you a safe journey, but it will always find you a potential way. I soulbind this to you so you shall never lose it."

Alistair gingerly took the lodestone, putting it next to the **Heavenly Nectar Incense** and Cabal marble in his pocket.

"The key is what I stated before. The Head Apostle of the Silver Comet Sect should understand how to proceed."

"Thank you," Alistair said, taking the key as well. "How long do I have left in this trial?"

"It shall last until the cleansing fires properly infuse the Adamantine Eggrock into your body. Whether this takes five days or one hour depends on many factors. I shouldn't hold up your visions any longer."

Before Alistair could say anything, the council room disappeared, transforming into flames. The pain that he had forgotten about entirely returned in full force, feeling worse than before because of his lack of habituation.

Alistair's body floated in a void of fire with one singular motivation—survive. A creature returned to its most base instincts. He felt the metal within him spread throughout his body, but it was so, so slow.

He held on. The so-called "sublime plateau" vanished, and the flames grew hotter and brighter, to the point where he could no longer see his own body. It was as if this purgatorial fire had burned his body to ash, leaving only his mind and soul.

Without his body, he was like Dev'rox—a spirit made of his purest self. Somehow, the carving of the First Script still shone on his spiritual body, demonstrating his last act of will before the trial. This inscription anchored his purpose. Even without a body, he had one goal—survive the trial and return home.

Return. This thought echoed within him. The conscious mind, filled with thoughts of home. Thoughts of regret and longing, love and desire, happiness and ambition. This too, burnt away. For the cleansing fire was not satisfied with only taking away his body, but desired his mind as well.

Finally, there was his soul. The soul changed less than the body and mind. It was who he was at his very core. The anchor of his essence on the Physical Plane. While it wasn't right to say that the soul was more important than the body, it carried a more *substantial* weight.

Even that was not sufficient for these flames. Even his soul could not hide from the endless burning. And then, there was nothing left. No one and nothing.

For an eternity, nothing ruled. Nothing was all that existed, or did not exist.

Alistair came back to life, piece by piece. In the opposite order that he went, first his soul formed out of the flames, then his mind, and finally his body.

Alistair understood right away the lesson imparted. Dedication. Just giving one's body was not always enough. To desire something so much that you would give your mind and soul—those mad geniuses that did that throughout history were the acclaimed ones. Pouring their entire life into a skill so that people believed they sold their souls to the Devil.

Speaking of devils, the Devil Kings were an example of this. While not by choice, they surrendered their chance at reincarnation for overwhelming power. Could Alistair say he would have done the same? Such opportunities where one showed their consummate dedication were rare, but could he say that given one, he would sacrifice everything without a second thought?

His path was not the one of the Devil King, the breaking of the Pact. Their singular dedication sullied the nature of hard work itself by their evil intentions. Yet how could he live with himself if he did not give as much as they did?

When the villain would give up his soul in pursuit of ultimate evil, then the hero would have to give up his soul for the ultimate good.

No, they would have to sacrifice even more. Breaking things was always easier than protecting them.

Alistair clawed out of the void, his body forming around his spirit as he willed himself back to life. In that moment, in a state of total renewal, he found absolute tranquility. Absolute peace.

There was nothing that could assault his serenity. For he was one with the world and the world was one with him—a new birth, forged from nothing, seared in fire. While his physical state was ravaged with pain from the lasting effect of the cleansing fire, his mind reached a temperament of calm. Then, that faded as he returned to full awareness. The Adamantine Eggrock was finished integrating.

Alistair came out of the flames with a more important lesson than any bodily change. Opportunity was scarce. To seize Fate by the reins meant dedication beyond the ordinary. Dedication he would provide without question.

With the metal infusion complete, the flames no longer pained him.

It's done, he thought. Dev'rox smiled from his hidden nest inside Alistair's soulcore.

Alistair stepped out of the flames triumphantly. Before he even saw Master Ko Pao or the other elders, he fell to the floor, unconscious.

16 LAST TIMES FOR EVERYONE

OLIVER WATCHED over Alistair while he soundly slept.

Two days had passed since his friend underwent the Final Trial of the Steel Body, and he had not yet woken up.

Brother Pike assured him that this was normal, but it didn't fully alleviate his concerns.

Damn it, Oliver thought. *That was really childish of me, wasn't it?*

He was referring, of course, to when he broke down emotionally in front of Alistair, afraid that they would never leave. How embarrassing was it for him to doubt Alistair? After everything that had happened, it was the least he could do to put his faith in the man.

At first, Oliver had despised his time in the Holy Ravine. Unlike the other guy, he wasn't built for this type of manual labor. Still, there were some benefits. He definitely preferred the way he looked in the mirror now than before. Even if the initiation had transformed him from skinny fat to fit, in the Silver Comet Sect he'd reached another level. Nothing compared to Alistair or even Alexandra, he supposed, but still nice.

"Oliver, Brother Iokab will be mad at you if you don't meet the curfew," a voice whispered from afar.

That was Augusto, Oliver's closest friend within the sect. A fellow white headband, he came in the newest batch of recruits only a little before Oliver joined himself. He was a headstrong guy, honestly reminding him a little of Alistair.

In the arena of friendship, he was doing better than the #1 ranker. It was a sad fact of reality that Alistair's ridiculous progression insulated him from making stronger bonds. As far as Oliver knew, he only really hung out with Pike and that Izalia woman from Kodaidaemin.

"I know, I know," Oliver shot back. "I'm being foolish."

"I didn't say that," Iokab replied. "It's a natural feeling to want to be there for him."

Iokab was right. He wanted to cherish those moments, as he didn't know how many more of them there would be. The one thing he had kept from Alistair was the offer.

Given that [Armageddon] didn't kill them, he had received a letter inviting him to the FarNetter Academy. Oliver didn't know what that meant at first, but the letter came with a holographic video explaining the offer.

The FarNetters were one of five special occupations of the Sublimed Machine Faction. Part of their spec ops divisions, you could say, though more generalized than that. As a hands-off satellite polity of the Sublimed Machine Faction, they adopted some of the faction's structures as their own.

The FarNetters specialized in long-range combat and summons. Perfect for Oliver. The Five Academies often took in young cultivators who had fallen under the eye of the sects, nobles, and corporations. Also, they could take them in later, whereas Prime Initiate sponsors had a limited window.

The only problem was that Oliver felt Alistair was expecting him and Alexandra to stay behind and help steward Earth. Doubly so now that Alexandra had become a quasi-Devil King.

Oliver hadn't accepted the offer yet. He still had months to decide.

"But it's still foolish. I'm not helping him by being here. Let's go."

Oliver took one last glance at Alistair. It was strange to see him so inert and empty of vitality. Almost wrong. Hopefully, he would wake up soon.

―――――

Alistair felt different.

The moment he woke up, something had changed. The only way he could put it was that he felt heavier.

Not in a bad, bloated way, like he had stuffed his face with pies. It was more like if the world shook, he would stay still. Despite this strange feeling of heaviness, he was barely any slower than he was before.

While the visions of the trial felt illusory, the items Purana of the Stratospheric Flames had given him were anything but. Both the pyramid lodestone and the key were in the pockets of his robes.

The first thing Alistair did was run to Master Ko Pao. If anyone needed to hear what happened in his vision, it was him.

It was his first time entering Master Ko Pao's private retreat. Like he expected, it was the opposite of Silvanio's opulence. A simple room, it was decorated with some plants and statues, but other than that, the only furniture was a bed and desk.

"I felt that something was amiss with your trial," Master Ko Pao said. He beckoned Alistair into his room, where they sat on the floor. "However, stopping a trial early would have led to your certain death. Would you like some coffee?"

"I would, thank you." Alistair accepted Master Ko Pao's cup of coffee, savoring the pumpkin spices in the drink.

The old man stroked his beard. "So, can you tell me what happened?"

Alistair explained every detail of his vision to the Head Apostle of the Silver Comet Sect. He also took out the golden key, which got Master Ko Pao's attention.

"There is a prophecy," he said after spending some time staring at the object, "that has been passed down from generation to generation within the Silver Comet Sect. A day when our ancestors would return and give us the golden key to the future. I did not imagine it happening like this. I pictured a bit more fanfare, I suppose. Sitars and singers heralding the new era. Our stories also say that this will be the age of strife, even more so than our war with the Wasted Realm. That one is happening just as I expected."

"So you do know what to do with it?"

"No, I do not," Master Ko Pao said. In that moment, he seemed like less of a wise sage, and more like one of his students. "I must meditate on the ancestor's words and find a path forward."

"Things are changing fast," Alistair said. "It's not only the Pathfinder AI and Final Frontier Empire at this point. Your people have been brought into two paradigm shifts at once. I'd say you have it tougher than us."

"Our people neighbor death itself. There is nothing that will shake us for too long."

Master Ko Pao jumped up, landing with his cane before stomping his feet on the ground. "Enough talk of the Holy Raviners. We must discuss you. I will personally give your final lesson."

Alistair perked up at that, following Master Ko Pao to his feet. "I'm ready, Master."

"Already, I know you can feel the effects," the old man said, punching Alistair in the stomach. In a testament to his immense skill, Alistair didn't see the punch coming at all. Yet despite that, it ricocheted off his abs like nothing happened. "All attacks should feel like a light breeze, except those with tremendous force behind them. If you can properly brace for them."

This time, Master Ko Pao struck with actual intent behind his fists, delivering a palm strike to Alistair's solar plexus. Once again, he couldn't understand the fundamentals behind the old man's attack.

Alistair's breath faded away, and he found himself coughing on the floor, crumpled up. Alistair couldn't believe the force behind Master Ko Pao's attack. It was absurd that such a small frame could generate that much power. He shook his head. *I still have much to learn.*

"*If* you can properly brace for them." Master Ko Pao let out a burst of air, this time making his attack obvious. Alistair instinctively clenched his muscles before the impact. While the damage wasn't as harmless as Master Ko Pao's low effort punch, it still was a fraction of the hidden attack. "To employ the Steel Body at its most effective, you must train your perception. Always at the exact moment before your opponent's fist touches your body, you must brace yourself. But that is not what I wish to teach you now. You will practice this with Brother Pike these last two weeks. No, what I intend to teach you is the ultimate technique of the Steel Body."

"I'm ready, master," Alistair said eagerly.

"I hope you do not regret those words."

If Alistair thought that he would get a break because he was unconscious for two days, he was sorely mistaken.

———

Those last two weeks came and went in a matter of no time. Most of the time was spent with Pike in special training sessions as he shrugged off the lasting injuries dealt by the Final Trial. The rest was training his body back into peak condition and learning the ultimate technique with Master Ko Pao.

Funnily enough, Oliver also went into overdrive, despite having no upcoming duel of importance. It was like he didn't like seeing Alistair work hard without matching that effort. He brought himself higher in the pack of white headbands, reaching the top half of the cohort purely through grit.

Alistair sparred against Izalia every day. With the Steel Body in its complete form, he was far more of a match for the woman, though they never fought at a hundred percent. While Izalia and Brutus were vastly different fighters, she tried imitating his style as much as possible.

That represented another area of training. Learning about his opponent.

Brutus Caligoris, also known as Mad Brutus the Biter. He was a natural talent, having joined the Church of the Holy Ones only six years ago. At twenty years of age, he was even younger than Alistair.

Brutus's family did not come from the Holy Ravine originally, but from a far northern province in the Martial League. The people of that land were renowned for their great size, and Brutus was no exception. He was even larger than Pike, standing only a few inches below seven feet. Somehow, that wasn't the area that Pike told him to be concerned about.

As a user of the Steel Body, Alistair would actually be stronger and tougher than Brutus, no matter how big and scary he looked. The Holy Ones' specialty was speed and precision.

Their counterpart to the Steel Body was called Hidden Under Heaven. Like the Steel Body, they underwent their own arduous trial, though, like the rest of the trials, outsiders had no idea what it entailed. Alistair wondered if they had their own ancestor waiting to herald the return of the glory days.

The technique itself removed certain limitations within the brain and central nervous system, improving reaction time while also making one hyperattentive to all stimuli. In other words, the Holy One apostles had ridiculous reaction times and sensory perception.

The name Hidden Under Heaven came from one of the main uses of the technique: abusing the blind spots of their opponents. So Alistair trained his sight without sight constantly, always fighting with a blindfold.

Without the blindfold, he also reached a new level. The Steel Body made the biggest difference. Before, he was unable to match the black headbands of the Silver Comet Sect. With the Steel Body, he was easily keeping pace. The added defense allowed him to focus more on offense, whereas before he had to dodge because of the enormous gap in physical ability.

In the blink of an eye, Alistair found himself on the last day before his bout with Brutus. The people at the sect had been wishing him luck and telling him not to be nervous, but Alistair didn't feel nervous.

Instead, he felt giddy. Maybe giddy was the wrong word. Nevertheless, some positive emotion bubbled up in his throat and wanted release. It was like his body wanted to go in a million directions at once.

Master Ko Pao surprisingly was the one to give him a suggestion—have fun. He told Alistair that there were two types of fighters. For one, the best thing to do before a major bout was to peacefully meditate for hours and hours. For the other, it was to have a debaucherous night.

Alistair had never been a party person, even before the initiation, but he was not one to deny the elder martial artist's words of wisdom. It sounded better than hours of meditation. So, he ended up back at the Dragon's Head Tavern once more.

This time, he couldn't have any alcohol, but he didn't like getting drunk much in the first place. He felt like it was more real to have fun without alcohol lowering social inhibitions.

"I got the same room as last time," Pike said as they walked up the stairs to the second floor of the tavern. "Everything has to be perfect for your last night."

"Last night?" Alistair raised an eyebrow. "That sounds overly ominous, don't you think?"

"Last night before your overwhelming victory, obviously. What else?"

"I have to pay you back for that game of War's Brother," Izalia said, closely following them with Oliver in tow. "You should not have come in second. Not at all."

"You're on," Alistair shot back.

"I hate that game," Oliver muttered. "Why are you brutes so good at it, anyway?"

"A trained body is a trained mind," Pike said. "Since my physical development exceeds yours, therefore my mental development does as well."

"That does not sound right at all," Oliver replied. "Was Einstein a body-builder, Alistair?"

Alistair looked up as if he was trying to remember. "I can't recall, but it seems entirely possible. That would make a lot of sense."

"You're no use either," Oliver said. "Three against one, no fair."

"Why don't we give him a stone handicap?" Alistair asked. "It's an easy way to equalize the playing field."

"Traditionally, handicaps are only used with children, but I would be fine with bending the rules a bit," Izalia said. "Pike?"

"Good with me."

They gave Oliver a whole nine stones advantage starting out. Despite this, he quickly fumbled his initial lead. The game was an intense one, with Alistair starting out ahead. It almost felt like his training had increased his performance, despite there not being an obvious tie between the two. He didn't want to believe Pike's nonsense about becoming more intelligent because his body was stronger, but who really knew?

The real secret behind Alistair's lead was an unexpected ally—Dev'rox. Lasker was more right than he knew, since a Go-like game was not only popular on Lisorte, but in the lower planes as well. With tens of thousands of years of experience, Dev'rox was a veritable master.

"This feels a bit like cheating," Alistair said to his partner. "Shouldn't you be resting up?"

"It's fine, I still have enough energy to do this," Dev'rox said. "There's no point in rationing. You're going to win tomorrow, and we'll be free of this shithole."

"The Holy Ravine isn't a shithole," Alistair said, defending his temporary home.

"Says you," Dev'rox shot back. "It's toxic to me. Even besides the Devonic Elision Field. It's like there's an essence in the air that makes me sick."

"Oh. You never told me about that."

"It's fine. Don't worry about me. Let's just win this game and get you in a good mood for tomorrow."

With Dev'rox's assistance, Alistair pulled out a surprise victory. He was slightly behind the entire time, but every step of the way he kept up with his opponents. In the end, he pulled through with his tenacity and outflanked all three of them to edge out a minor win by only a few stones.

Pike and Izalia looked at him with heightened suspicion after the game's completion.

"Did some dead master possess you?" Izalia asked.

Closer to the truth than you'd think, Alistair thought. He didn't feel too bad about using Dev'rox, since the ghost was well and truly a part of him at this point.

"Something like that." Alistair smiled.

"Oh, hell no," Oliver swore. "He's using that ghost of his. Oh, my bad. I didn't mean to say that."

That comment led to a whole sidebar where Oliver explained to the two Holy Raviners who and what Dev'rox was. Alistair gave him permission after that slight slip up. He was trying to keep the ghost somewhat secret, but after Celeste saw it, he felt like the cat was only going to be in the bag for so long. Plus, they were cordoned away. By the time that they could tell anyone on the outside, the present conflict should have been over.

But there's always a new one. He couldn't imagine the Final Frontier Empire letting anyone sit still for long. Vying for resources and position was eternal.

After they finished playing, they feasted. There was a whole new selection of dishes, delicacies Alistair didn't even understand how to explain. He introduced the Holy Raviners to the concept of a toast, something that they didn't have.

He demonstrated by holding up his glass of lemonade. "You could toast to a lot of things. A good marriage for a bride and groom at a wedding, for a good night with friends at a bar. It's very versatile."

"Hmm, I think I understand," Pike said. "Let me toast to your victory tomorrow. Let it be swift and decisive."

"I also will perform a toast to your victory," Izalia clumsily clunked her glass against Pike's. They must have thought that each individual person was supposed to give their own toast. "Give that brute a whopping he won't forget."

Oliver joined in on their misunderstanding of toasts. "You better win for me, because if I have to get punched in the stomach one more time, I'm going to lose it. How's that for a toast?"

They laughed and took a sip, as Alistair had instructed. He would miss these simple times. They came few and far between. He couldn't imagine that they would come more often in the future, either, as he progressed down the path of cultivation.

That night, before entering a deep slumber, he looked up at the night sky from within his room. There was absolutely zero light pollution, allowing for a view of the sky unrivaled in the modern world. Even the initiated planet had started to get brighter as artificial lighting made a comeback.

Infinite worlds full of infinite life. Alistair's last thoughts before he drifted off were fantasies of the beyond.

17 BRUTUS THE BITER

TODAY WAS THE DAY. Alistair's three months of training were coming to a close. The light at the end of the tunnel was Brutus Caligoris, champion of the Church of the Holy Ones.

The day of the duel started like any other. Alistair was exempted from the most difficult portions of the training as to not exhaust him before the fight, but he still participated as much as he could. Pike advised that keeping his routine as normal as possible was good for the nerves.

Like all challenges against champions, the duel would take place in the town square. There was a large amphitheater that could seat over a thousand people. Such bouts were spectacles enjoyed by the entire Holy Ravine.

I've fought before trillions, if not more, Alistair thought. *I shouldn't be scared.*

But something about those bouts on Faxor was different. This was more personal.

The last of his central fatigue from the final Steel Body trial had vanished. That was the closest to death he had ever come, both unlocking his body and mind. He was ready to face his opponent.

Alistair meditated in one of the private chambers, feeling the energy of all those around him. While he didn't have his normal senses or powers, after feeling the flow of water over his skin for so long, he felt a certain attunement with all flowing energies. Perhaps he was drawing on something akin to life force. Whatever it was, he felt Pike approach him long before the man's soft footsteps became audible.

"Are you here to see me off?" Alistair asked, eyes still closed. His match was supposed to be in an hour, and it would take nearly that long to walk there. He had to get going soon, but he was dragging out his exit.

"You've put on some meat," Pike commented.

Alistair looked down at his shirtless physique. It was true—the Steel Body training had taken him into another level of musculature. He wondered if, on the outside, the system would dock his Agility or something of that nature. He was faster than his previous, depowered self, but it seemed crazy to think his true speed wouldn't suffer consequences.

"I'm feeling invincible," Alistair said.

"Are we getting cocky now?" Pike said. "What happened to the studious boy I started training?"

"Your personality rubbed off."

"Master Ko Pao won't be happy." Pike jabbed Alistair's gut with a weak punch. The old him would have toppled over in pain. As Alistair was now, he felt a thud. "You've finally come into your own."

"This is nothing," Alistair replied. "You should see me when I have my powers. I could lay your ass out with one finger."

"Still, I can't imagine the man I saw walk in here winning against you now. Even if you were a hundred times as strong. You have a sturdy foundation now."

Alistair smirked. Pike wasn't capable of understanding just how powerful cultivation could make a person, but he wasn't wrong in the sentiment. Something monumental had shifted within him, and he couldn't wait to see how the Pathfinder AI registered that on the outside. But for now, he had to focus on his upcoming fight entirely.

"Let's go."

———

Pike led him out through a secret exit in the Silver Comet temple. Behind one of the statues of the past victors of the Dragon's Equinox Festival originating from the sect, there was a rectangular passage dug into the wall. With his added bulk, Alistair barely fit inside the passage. Pike was an even tighter squeeze.

That was when Pike informed him of the true location of his duel—the underground arena. Silvanio had specially requested it. Underneath the town square ring, there was a smaller and more private subterranean fighting arena.

Alistair's match would take place there, with only a couple of spectators. He wasn't sure if that made him more or less nervous.

But he was also psyching himself out with false thoughts. It was one of those things where his body was in complete homeostasis, calm as a rock, but his thoughts swam. In a strange way, his true self was tranquil even as his outer mind wandered. In reality, he knew that he was prepared and was ready to win.

I will win.

An escort of Holy Ones led him and Pike through an underground section of their church. It was a dank passageway, barely lit by luminescent blue moss growing on the walls. The people leading him wore full-body starry night cloaks that covered their faces, giving off a creepy impression.

Alistair paid it no heed and walked with complete serenity. Pike's presence behind him was like a warm ball of flame on a cold winter's evening. Feeling the connectedness of all things was the perfect calming mechanism.

One of the Holy Ones, who wore a robe with blue stars, took out a jagged knife. "The ceremony shall now begin," he croaked out.

Pike had told him about this—the traditional Holy Ravine pre-fight ritual. His sparring and even duels back at the temple weren't considered "official" fights, so he didn't have to do it then. Alistair remembered the procedure just as Pike had told him.

He lifted his arms in the air, kneeling before the Holy One apostle with his head down. Then he brought his hands down and kissed the ground.

"Before the Mother of War, I bless this one. Let his heart beat with your song and calling, and grant him the strength of your greatest sun champions who trample the night away on this day and all days."

The man raised his knife and gently brought it down on Alistair's prostrate back, cutting his robes and letting them fall to the floor. The two attendant apostles stripped the remaining pieces of Alistair's cloak, leaving him shirtless.

Next, the head of the preparers took out a bowl of a saturated red liquid. Murmuring quietly in indecipherable speech, he stood over Alistair and carefully poured the substance over his head. It was cool to the touch with the viscosity of milk. Like Pike had told him to, he stood up and let it wash over his body.

The liquid was called the Burning Heart of War, a special tincture that had been used since the origins of the Holy Ravine for duels and battles. It accelerated the heart and dilated the blood vessels, improving athletic performance, in addition to a minor psychoactive effect that increased bloodlust and willpower.

Also, it gave a slight red glow to the skin, which was pretty damn cool.

Alistair walked through the gate to the arena. The floor was a polished black stone that was surprisingly springy. Four stone posts formed a square, elastic rope wrapped around each side, enclosing a space around twice the size of a typical boxing ring. The square was slightly raised off the floor and there were no seats, so the few spectators that were there had to stand to watch.

Like in the passageway, the only light was the glowing blue moss, though there was more of it, so it was easier to see. Still, Alistair estimated that the suboptimal lighting conditions were enough to register a loss of performance.

Silvanio was present, along with his daughter and a few more Holy Ones Alistair didn't recognize. Pike was there, taking his spot alongside the master. Ko Pao and his granddaughter were present, along with Davnos and Jo Ran. Oliver looked even more pale than usual, though he smiled when he saw Alistair arrive.

And on the opposite side of the ring stood his opponent. Brutus Caligoris.

Brutus fit the descriptions Alistair had heard. He was a giant of a man with larger muscles than Pike. He had a mane of some of the reddest hair Alistair had ever seen, with a harsh face that looked fitting on a warrior of his caliber.

Yet all that was a red herring, he knew. Speed and deception were the trademark of the Holy Ones. Sinuous techniques that sought to kill. All in all, quite similar to {Psychopomp's Discipline}.

With his red hair and glowing red skin, in the low light of the arena, Brutus looked like a devil. The moss cast long shadows on his creviced face, concealing his features. He glared directly at Alistair, who returned his gaze.

Alistair climbed the short staircase and hopped over the ropes with ethereal grace. He didn't have to do that—Brutus ducked under the ropes like a normal person. But Alistair felt like showing off.

Silvanio stepped up onto the ring, holding his hands high. "My champion, Brutus Caligoris, faces the outsider, Alistair Tan, in single combat. If the outsider wins, he may make one request of me that I shall do everything in my power to grant. If he loses, he shall remain in the Ravine and serve me instead of the Silver Comet Sect.

"There is only one rule—no weapons allowed. The match shall continue to surrender or incapacitation. As always, there is the possibility of death too sudden for my intervention."

Silvanio, despite his short height, felt like he was looking down on both Brutus and Alistair. He coldly glanced at them and let his hand fall, signaling the beginning of the match.

Brutus took a fighting stance, standing more side-faced than Alistair would have expected, like that of a taekwondo or karate fighter who primarily wanted to kick.

Alistair took no stance. He wasn't so arrogant as to close his eyes, but he kept his hands down. He chose to feel the balance in the air, the tension in his opponent's muscles. Reading the flow of power and the principles behind Brutus's movement.

Brutus shuffled toward Alistair, looking almost comical in his extreme focus. Footstep by footstep, Silvanio's fighter approached him. The pace was glacial. Only when he came within two body lengths of Alistair did he begin his attack.

With his superior reach, he shuffled forward with extreme explosive power, aiming a jab right at Alistair's face.

Alistair read ahead of the blow, slipping it and stepping forward to throw a counter punch. Brutus disappeared.

The signature of the Holy Ones, Alistair thought. *Hidden Under Heaven*. His reaction time was ludicrously fast. Alistair would have difficulty landing his blows without reading ahead.

With their heightened senses, the Holy One apostles had the deepest understanding of perception of any sect in the Ravine. That made them a natural counter against the Steel Body, which relied on tensing the muscles against attacks *inside* one's perception.

The Holy Ones used Hidden Under Heaven to perform a divine technique—Dispersion. It was often joked that they didn't know how to use anything but Dispersion. Dispersion let one slip into their opponent's blind spot with the slimmest of timings and otherworldly dexterity.

Thud. Brutus's fist connected with the back of Alistair's head, knocking him forward a step. But the punch felt more like a light sparring blow than a full power punch. Alistair had read ahead, predicting that the back of the head was Brutus's target, and applied the Steel Body to negate the damage.

The giant of a man instantaneously shifted gears. The punch did barely any damage, but still offset Alistair's balance—owing to Brutus's hefty three-hundred pound frame. Brutus took advantage of this and unleashed a flurry of tricky blows at breakneck speeds. He was a blur of movement, almost faster than Alistair's visual dynamic acuity could process.

The huge Holy One moved like a man half his weight, dancing like a ballerina with precise arcing blows and turns. Alistair could barely defend the attacks—they were simply coming too fast. He decided to give up attempting to block them all and shifted to mitigation, tensing his Steel Body at the expense of letting more hits fall through the seams.

Boom. Boom. Boom. Brutus's attacking power was lower than Alistair's, but could never be confused with low. His large muscles employed picture perfect power-generating technique.

Yet his blows did not land with penetrating force. The loud noise that emanated from each punch was an illusion. They pushed him back with weight, bringing him to the edge of the ring.

What happens if I fall out? Alistair wondered. The rules didn't mention anything about ring outs or penalties for getting ringed out. That momentary lapse in concentration led to a small decrease in performance in his Steel Body. A hard fist landed, and Alistair flew out of the ring and onto the ground.

Alistair panted, not from physical exhaustion, but from mental fatigue. It had not been an accident that his mind had idly wandered. The Steel Body was not just a physical technique, but also one of the mind, requiring the utmost concentration. He had to precisely time each moment of impact, using predictions obtained from gazing into the fundamentals. That was not a straightforward task on the calculative abilities of the brain. Alistair was brought back to every difficult test he had taken in his life, amplified by the fact his life was potentially on the line.

His mind, seeking refuge from the intense load, had decided to wander into aimless thoughts. Alistair hadn't even realized. Subconsciously, even if only by a little bit, he had backed down. That sent a chill down Alistair's spine. *Am I afraid of him?*

A simple recollection of his thoughts said no, but the ego could easily be lied to, the central idea of cognitive dissonance.

A hand came down on his sweaty back. Silvanio's voice spoke quietly. "If you are ringed out, you have ten seconds to get back in before you are disqualified. I believe I forgot to mention that."

Alistair took a deep breath, centering himself. There was no need to fret. Not when he had trained so hard for this moment. He hopped back up into the ring, where Brutus waited for him with a wicked grin. The brutal man let out a beastly howl, bearing his overlarge canines. Once again, he brought his massive body into a sideways stance, creeping towards Alistair like a fencer.

The assault began again. Alistair had an intuition of what was coming. People tended to stick with what worked, only deviating when that failed. Perhaps it was a trick of the imagination, but Brutus felt even faster now, whirling his heavy limbs with lightning-quick speed. Alistair couldn't even begin to fathom how one would throw the combination Brutus employed, but what he could do was to predict the moment of impact. That much was in his wheelhouse.

Once again, Alistair was pushed back by the weight of the blows. But this time, he didn't let himself lose focus. He blocked what he could and took the rest with his hard body. Slowly, he ceded ground. Within ten seconds, he was at the edge of the ring once more.

Getting trapped would spell doom for Alistair quickly. Taking away half of his maneuverability by putting his back on the ropes would allow Brutus to throw more deadly combinations and increase his striking power. Even the Steel Body employed a great deal of letting the flow of force pass through oneself—the same way in which modern cars crumpled more to increase the time of the impact.

Alistair felt his back touch against the ropes. It was now or never. Had he seen deep enough into his opponent's intentions? Gathering all his strength, he suddenly burst into action, firing a punch straight for Brutus's solar plexus.

The punch connected with a satisfying boom. Using his reflexes, the giant Holy One went limp at the last second, diffusing some of the power of the blow, but he still flew back and tumbled over.

Alistair had timed his attack perfectly. Even with Brutus's explosive athleticism, he could only sustain an all-out attack for so long. Last time, Alistair had lost focus before Brutus ran out of steam, but this time, he found the exact moment where his opponent slowed down and punched him accordingly.

Shit, Alistair thought, knees wobbling slightly. He hadn't tensed his muscles properly when intercepting Brutus's last punch, since he had to prepare his own attack. Alistair spat out a chipped tooth and some blood.

Brutus slowly stood up, his green eyes never leaving Alistair. He didn't look fazed at all—in fact, he was smiling. The wide-eyed grin of a madman.

Oh, I understand now. He's a berserker, Alistair knew those types. The ones that loved fighting more than life itself. The sanctity of a fight was sacred to them. They would trade years of their life away for just a few seconds.

Alistair was nothing like those kinds of people who had more muscles than sense. He wasn't smiling like a madman. Not at all.

This time, Alistair struck first. He let out a burst of air, using his most linear attack—a right straight. Fancy moves were nice and all, but the Steel Body worked best with simplicity.

Whoosh. He poured every inch of his body into the attack while picturing himself literally impaling Brutus through the chest with the punch.

Brutus was taken off guard by the sheer explosiveness. With his catlike reflex and speed, he turned his body at the last second. Alistair felt his fist tear off skin and flesh from his opponent, right where the punch should have landed. The majority of the momentum of his attack went to waste, deflected by Brutus's contortion. Yet it was still a monumentally powerful blow, and the rest of the force sent the man flying away, though in midair, he righted himself by virtue of his immaculate kinesthesia.

Brutus skidded to a halt near the opposite edge of the ring from where Alistair struck. On his side, there was a bloody wound where Alistair's fist had torn through skin and flesh. While the Holy One suffered no blunt force damage, the nature of the wound meant that it would not seal easily. He would be suffering constant blood loss for the rest of the match, even if it was in small amounts.

But Alistair wasn't satisfied with a mere flesh wound. Even before he finished the follow through of his punch, he had already continued the attack. That was the way of pugilism—being on the back foot was a huge disadvantage.

He employed the tricky footwork of {Psychopomp's Discipline}, distributing his weight in uneven intervals as he dashed toward Brutus. The possibilities of combat presented themselves to Alistair. While they weren't actual physical manifestations in reality, like his precognition using Karmic sight, they were stronger than mere premonitions. Whether by some work of the Dao or his mental strength, he chose his best possible move—another right straight.

Alistair's opponent wasn't a champion for nothing. He was the weakest of them—something Alistair found hard to believe, feeling his ferocious presence—but he still had a great command of the principles of fighting. Brutus countered with his own best move, a right straight. Two fighters, throwing punches almost in unison, exact mirrors of each other.

The sound of bone cracking filled the ring. Alistair's bones.

Despite throwing his attack as a counter, with longer limbs and superior speed, Brutus's punch landed first. Right on Alistair's nose. Alistair's head spun clockwise from the impact. Only milliseconds after, his own punch landed, but Brutus had used that infinitesimal amount of time to lean back with his neck.

Alistair's straight connected, but with half of the power of Brutus's.

That was all a part of Alistair's plan.

He took the blow, knowing full well of the consequences, to get one opportunity to take advantage of Brutus's weakness.

As a counter, the Holy One's punch had less weight behind it, so Alistair was still moving forward. The bestial man attempted to use Dispersion again, but they were too close. With his offhand, he delivered an uppercut to Alistair's liver, but found the blow mitigated right away by the Steel Body.

Alistair grimaced in pain, but continued with his attack. He pressed his fingers into Brutus's open wound, attempting to dig inside as deep as possible.

Brutus yowled in pain but refused to give in to the attack. Alistair had intended to use the gruesome move while grabbing the large man's neck with the hand he'd just punched with to do a takedown, but Brutus was less affected by the intense pain than expected.

There was a split second of hesitation where Alistair wasn't sure how to proceed. His prediction had failed. This period was only around a tenth of a second, yet that was sufficient for Alistair to be caught unaware.

Shooting pain radiated in waves from his trapezius muscle. Blood flowed down his back and chest like a fountain. A wave of shock hit Alistair like a truck. Brutus had just bitten him like a wild beast.

Alistair let out a cry of pain and instinctively tried to push the madman away. This wasn't a duel of martial artists anymore—but a fight in the wild. A dizzying thought reached his conscious mind. He remembered what Elerie had told him about Brutus. His nickname. Brutus the Biter.

While Alistair's fighting instincts were generally top-notch, the sudden burst of pain and shock at being bitten caused him to relinquish some of his training. Like Mike Tyson said, everyone has a plan until they get punched in the face.

With that in mind, Alistair had been through multiple life or death battles, many of them just as brutal as his current fight. However, the difference was the lack of his cultivated powers. He had grown so accustomed to them. They were always there as his safety crutch, always there when he needed them most. He felt vulnerable, naked even, without them.

Brutus seized the moment and relinquished his bite. He bear-hugged Alistair and suplexed him.

Alistair came crashing to the ground with a resounding bang. The full force of over five hundred of their combined pounds impacted his back. Because of the linear nature of the attack, Alistair was able to brace at the last second, mitigating some of the damage. But not all of it. He could feel bones fracture and the beginnings of internal bleeding.

Alistair refused to quit. His training had taught him to stay focused under the most dire of conditions. While still in flight during the suplex, he positioned his hand as best as he could.

The shock of hitting the ground temporarily disabled both fighters, if only for a quarter of a second. Alistair acted first, as bracing for the Steel Body prepared him better for the impact. He struck with that left hand to once again attack Brutus's open wound.

Brutus yowled like a wild dog and pressed his weight down on Alistair, putting him in a squeeze of death. Alistair's foresight backfired—he had predicted Brutus would jump back, yet those beast instincts propelled him forward.

Blood gushed out of both of their injuries—Alistair's left trap and Brutus's side. Alistair tried to thrust his hips upward to make room to escape, but the Biter's grip was like a vise. Despite being stronger than him,

Alistair was in a disadvantageous spot. With his legs in between his opponent's, being mounted was considered the worst position in fighting.

Heavy blows rained down from above. Alistair did his best to block what he could and mitigate the rest with the Steel Body. Each punch came down with the full ferocity of a seasoned warrior. Hard, biting fists that wanted Alistair dead.

But then, the moment that Alistair was waiting for came. All his training was for this moment. He could feel it in the air. The fundamentals of martial arts aligning within himself. Pike had put him through hell for three months to open his eyes. So he used that sight.

The hidden offense of the Steel Body reared its fangs. The small bones of the hand—the phalanges and metacarpals—were some of the weakest in the body. They were not designed for hitting hard objects. Even though Brutus had undergone conditioning training on his hands, there was only so much they could take.

Brutus's fist came down once more, but Alistair intercepted the strike. He headbutted with all his might, striking the man's knuckles with the hardest part of his skull. The Holy One's fist shattered instantly.

Feeling the weight let off of him for a moment as Brutus reeled from his broken hand, Alistair up-kicked him as hard as he could. He followed up the kick with a series of well-timed strikes. Each crafted from his experience as a fighter, designed to impact outside his opponent's awareness.

An elbow to the chin. A hook to the temple. A spinning back kick to the solar plexus. And finally, a flying knee straight at Brutus's wound.

Brutus went flying to the other end of the ring and collapsed onto the ground. Alistair wobbled, looking at his downed opponent. His vision went blurry. The dozens of punches he had taken on the ground had taken their toll. He could feel that his consciousness was fading, but through concentration, stayed himself.

Alistair swayed back and forth, feeling a burning sensation within his chest. He glanced at his opponent, who was slowly coming to his knees. It would have been the perfect opportunity to strike, but he wasn't in a condition to go for a sudden, lunging blow. If he messed up, Brutus would have an easy counter, and it would be over for him.

Brutus looked more injured than him after taking five solid, nearly unguarded strikes. The wound on his side was picking up in blood loss, forming a puddle on the ground. But Alistair had a feeling the fight was far from over.

He already felt a marked decrease in power in his last punch, owing to the bite wound he'd received earlier. It dug into his muscle, limiting the power he could generate on his left side. Thankfully, that wasn't his dominant side, and he shuffled forward and held up his guard as best he could.

When Brutus finished standing up, he didn't even look at Alistair. The mad beast had his head turned down, having gone completely silent—a far cry from before, with his constant growling. Alistair knew that was when an animal was at its most dangerous. Not when it was making a ton of noise and trying to scare, but when it was quiet and on the hunt.

Alistair measured the distance in between himself and his opponent. Like he himself had done at the beginning of the fight, Brutus did not put up a guard or even look at him, yet there was something ominous in his stance. Alistair did not dare move within his attacking range, standing two body lengths away.

Brutus was gone in a flash. Alistair's eyes widened as he realized what had happened, tensing his muscles as fast as he could, but it was too late. A meaty fist connected with his cheekbone and he went flying.

Shit, Alistair thought. At least he could still think. Brutus had sped up his Dispersion somehow and struck outside of Alistair's perception.

A whirlwind of deft strikes came from every angle. Brutus looked like he was in three places at the same time. All the while, not making a single noise other than the sound of his fists' impact on Alistair's body. His eyes were completely blank.

Alistair's brain was rocked from the first surprise blow, lowering his reaction time. Brutus continually sped up in his attacks and easily surpassed his previous speed.

So he was holding out on me before. It was wrong to call Brutus the Biter a brute because of his appearance—he clearly had well-practiced tactics and a strategic approach to the duel.

Alistair put up his left hand to parry a punch that he saw coming in advance. Yet the enemy's fist burst straight through his guard and into his eye. He cursed mentally as he realized that the wound near his shoulder had worsened and his left arm's strength had significantly weakened.

Brutus leaped into the air with agile fluidity and kneed Alistair square on the chin. Luckily, he managed to brace for that attack, or it would have knocked him out.

Pain and the taste of blood rocked Alistair's world as his head bounced off the floor of the ring twice. The blow was so powerful that he skidded out of the ring. Fractured jaw for sure, Alistair estimated. Concussion as well. Decreased vision on the left side. Moderate blood loss from the wound on his trapezius reduced the ability of his muscles on his left side to tense. An uneven Steel Body that was at least half as effective as normal.

Alistair smiled. Why had he disparaged berserker types before? Even now, as he stood near death, he could feel he was on the verge of improving. There was an invisible ceiling he was about to crash into. Brutus wasn't the end—he was a mere stepping stone on a path to power.

He didn't see anyone but the beast before him. When he climbed back into the ring, even that stolid-looking man looked up for a moment. Alistair saw shock in those emerald eyes. Perhaps it was the price of a beast's soul. It was against the laws of nature to continue to fight when defeat was inevitable.

Caution imprinted itself on the Holy One as he raised his guard. Brutus aimed to end the fight in the next few moves. This prey shouldn't be allowed to observe him any longer.

Alistair put up his guard as well. He smirked as he heard the crowd murmur. Instead of his usual, all-rounder style, he had adopted the exact same position as Brutus, standing mostly sideways with open palms. The only difference was that he stood southpaw, while Brutus was orthodox.

For the first time in the fight, the Holy One spoke. "Is this a joke?"

Alistair was not joking in the slightest. He had observed the Holy One's fighting style enough that he thought he had a good grasp on it. Copying moves after only seeing them a few times, especially the nigh-physical impossible moves of the Holy Ravine—it should have been impossible. *Should have* being the operative words.

But Alistair felt something deeper at work. The Dao of the Fist was closer now than it ever was before, as he was on the brink of defeat. When he embraced it—or the Mother's Presence, as the Raviners called it—it was different from when he did it through the Dao Node.

Obviously, it was far weaker, but that wasn't the difference he was talking about. When Alistair looked at how the Pathfinder AI's system of Deepenings and Widenings of Dao Nodes worked, he couldn't help but feel a small sense of artificiality. It was like the system was hand-holding them. A streamlined method designed for producing a large number of decently powerful fighters.

Now, he *breathed* the Dao of the Fist.

It was just like that state he'd reached while in the final trial to achieve the Steel Body. Pike had told him that even prodigies could not enter that mental state at will. It came fleetingly, choosing to bless in inscrutable ways.

Did that ever stop Alistair before? Would he bow down to the laws of common sense? Or would he burst through the doors of fate with reckless abandon?

Tranquil Mind. That state he'd achieved after the cleansing fires reached their zenith. The loss of ego, death of attachment, and absence of strong emotions.

Brutus used Dispersion and disappeared into Alistair's blind spot. A jumping front kick came out of nowhere, heading straight for Alistair's head. Brutus's eyes widened as his opponent disappeared.

Alistair copied Dispersion. Imperfectly, since his body didn't have its reaction time and neural limiters removed. But with Tranquil Mind, he moved without thinking, improving his reaction speed. Not to the level of Hidden Under Heaven's limit breaking, but enough to pretend. Alistair realized that if you combined the Hidden Under Heaven and Tranquil Mind, you could reach even higher heights, but thankfully, Brutus seemed to not be capable of that.

Brutus caught his counter with his palm and backstepped twice. Once again, his movements were filled with caution. He looked at Alistair with uneasy suspicion. A thought crossed his mind. Did that man really just use Dispersion after seeing it for the first time only a few minutes ago?

There was something disturbing about Alistair's serene expression. It was as if he didn't have a care in the world. Brutus imagined his opponent as an enlightened being, where living and dying held no object.

To an apex predator, such a mindset was unfathomable.

Scary, even.

Perhaps if the Biter had a bit more experience, he would have realized that Tranquil Mind could not perform miracles—it was impossible for Alistair to copy the Holy One's moves with real weight behind them.

Brutus acted with far too much apprehension. Since he believed

Alistair's arsenal of techniques was larger than it really was, he crossed out too many of his own moves.

In an evenly matched fight, the winner only needs the smallest edge to seize victory.

Alistair kept up the act which was not entirely an act. He moved like a leaf in the wind, adopting the manner of the Holy Ones' style. Quick, biting, and fluid. He threw a snaking finger jab to the throat. When Brutus dodged, Alistair acrobatically flipped into the air with a 760 degree tornado kick.

The Holy One put up an arm to block the kick, but it had far too much power behind it. Alistair knew that he broke Brutus's forearm bones the instant his shin landed. The large man skidded back a few body lengths from the impact.

Alistair remained expressionless as he put up his hands, once more imitating his opponent's side-facing style. The fury in the beast's eyes was evident, a far cry from his silent hunting mode from earlier.

With a burst of air, Alistair disappeared from sight, using Dispersion once more. He was getting the hang of things now. His Dispersion would never be as good as the Holy Ones without undergoing the Hidden Under Heaven trial, but he didn't need perfection, he only needed good.

Brutus countered with his own Dispersion. It was the absolute fastest strike of the day, perhaps the fastest attack Alistair had ever seen a human without cultivation perform.

Time seemed to move in slow motion. Alistair was far too slow to enter Brutus's blind spot. The attack was simple—a sidestep into a left hook. The only thing that made it special was the use of Dispersion.

Meanwhile, Brutus aimed a straight punch right for Alistair's face. He aimed for Alistair's left side, where both vision and muscles were affected. He chose a punch instead of a kick to maximize the chance of landing, knowing that he had a limited window of opportunity.

Alistair took the blow. It was a powerful punch, molded from over two decades of harsh, inhuman training. He clenched every last muscle in his body, squeezing water from a stone.

Then came the real reason he switched to a southpaw stance—it was his natural stance as a right-handed grappler, at least for the style he specialized in, which relied more on throws than leg takedowns. Alistair quickly grabbed Brutus's arm and tossed him over his shoulder.

Brutus came crashing to the ground with a resounding slam. The floor of the ring cracked underneath him from the power of the impact.

Alistair fell on top of his opponent. He hadn't been able to mitigate all the damage. The only reason he succeeded in his throw was because of Brutus's already injured fists. With the Steel Body employed at the moment of impact, Brutus's other fist instantly shattered, reducing the damage Alistair took.

Alistair's knees gave out, and he fell on top of Brutus. The accumulated injuries took their toll, even through the Steel Body.

The mad dog writhed beneath him, trying his damnedest to escape. Despite Alistair's weak knees, he wouldn't let go. With every ounce of his strength, he held Brutus to the floor. There wasn't time or energy to perform a submission or throw a punch. His muscles screamed with anaerobic fatigue.

Alistair held the Holy One down tight, sweaty flesh meeting sweaty flesh. This gave room for Brutus's sharp canines to tear into skin like tiny daggers. The brute acted like his name, reverting to primal instincts. His enemy's flesh was nothing more than a tender steak for him to tear into, if that was what would give him the victory.

At that point, Alistair couldn't hold Tranquil Mind any longer. He failed to reach its true zenith, and on the downfall, an incredible pain flickered through in bits and pieces. Adrenaline flooded his system. He was verging on the edge of unconsciousness.

Somehow, drawing upon willpower he didn't even know he had, he held on. He would die before he let go. He simply rejected the idea that Brutus could challenge him in a contest of strength.

Next came the final piece of training that he had mastered directly from the venerable Ko Pao.

Alistair activated the ultimate technique of the Steel Body.

According to the master, the truest strength of the Silver Comet Sect's method was not striking, but grappling. When squeezing one's muscles with the hardness of the Steel Body, it was possible to contract them so hard that they became stuck. While in this ossified condition, his limbs would clamp down with inhuman strength.

Brutus tried everything to escape. He was a well-trained fighter, and the Holy Ones style was no stranger to ground fighting. It was to no avail. His beast-like snarling fell on deaf ears. Even those noises quieted down after over a minute of flailing.

All the while, Alistair did nothing. He did not try to throw a punch, or an elbow. He did not try to stand. He did not try to make an attempt to strangle. He simply pressed his weight down in as efficient a way he knew how, his muscles hardened into a permanently contracted state.

Fundamentals. That word echoed in Alistair's mind, soon centralizing as an impossible to ignore thought. What made a martial artist better? Was it strength, agility, or constitution? Or was it something deeper? He couldn't deny that being faster and stronger and more durable was an enormous advantage. But the Dao of the Fist was not Alexandra's Barbaric Rage.

And so he clung on, submerged within the Fist. Another minute passed. Brutus was no fool—he understood now that Alistair was trying to tire him out. The Biter stopped trying to escape, laying low and catching his breath.

At the very moment where Brutus's guard was at its lowest, Alistair struck.

But not really. No, Alistair merely feinted a strike by wiggling his shoulder. It took almost no energy to continue the hold, since his limbs were almost literally stuck in place like a bad cramp.

Brutus heaved like a fish trying to get back in the water. He had been waiting for that punch so he could push Alistair off, and since his move failed, he wasted a ton of energy.

Sweat and blood dripped down Alistair's back and chest. Now that the situation had calmed down more, the aches and pains were starting to set in. His left shoulder burned and wailed, refusing to move properly. His eye was swelling to the size of an orange. Not to mention how many times his face had been wailed on earlier.

Alistair knew the toil of grappling from his training sessions, but this was on another level. His only solace was that he wasn't even sure if he *could* stop squeezing.

He was glad there wasn't a crowd watching. They might have booed.

Another minute passed. Brutus also slowed down, and no longer as a mere ploy. He didn't try any large moves, but he still constantly made micro-adjustments, striving for a superior position that he could leverage into an escape.

The breaking point came another minute later. A drop of blood glided down Alistair's chest. The Steel Body's clench loosened as his cells literally ran out of juice. Suddenly, he found himself without a solid hold on Brutus. It was a small difference—just a bit less friction in between the two of them. But it was enough for Brutus to pounce.

In a fraction of a second, Silvanio's champion shot out. Not up vertically, but along the ground, which at that point was extremely slippery from sweat and blood. He slid away from Alistair like it was a slip-n-slide.

Brutus rocked his weight backward, performing a kip-up to get to his feet as fast as possible. Alistair was already there and met his ugly face with a solid punch—at the same time Brutus kicked. It was an impressive feat of athleticism, kicking on one foot at the instant he jumped, but Alistair didn't have time to appreciate that.

The two of them collapsed at the same time. Then, it was a matter of sheer willpower to see who would stand first.

They got up at the same time. Alistair forced his limbs to obey, dragging himself to his feet. Brutus was a blurry mess in his vision. However, his opponent didn't fare any better. Both of their balances looked severely off, and neither could stand straight.

And they both attacked once more. With how slow they had become, and how much their reaction speed had been reduced, they couldn't dodge each other's blows. It became a grueling slugfest.

It felt like a kaiju movie, with both combatants throwing powerful blow after powerful blow. Then they would both recover, disengaging to catch a brief breather, then go right back to exchanging punches.

It was all according to Alistair's plan, or so he thought. His opponent's fists were already broken beyond repair. How long could he hold out?

That simple concept wasn't coming to fruition. Instead, it was Alistair who was falling behind. Brutus attacked with reckless abandon, seemingly not caring that the bones of his fists were getting even more pulverized. Soon they would be powder.

His tide of strikes was unstoppable, pushing Alistair back with each punch. Panic started to set in as Alistair realized he was going to lose if he didn't shake things up.

His mind danced from idea to idea in a frenzy, but he couldn't focus properly with the constant barrage. Why couldn't he see the intention behind Brutus's attacks? That was the crux of the issue, even beyond his apparent inability to feel his hand injuries. It was like before each strike, Brutus shifted his position, but in a completely unpredictable manner.

Shit, shit, shit. Merely "trying" harder wasn't going to cut it. The desire to win was stronger than ever, but you couldn't just out believe your opponent to win. That wasn't how a real fight worked.

"That is, unless you have me by your side," a voice called out from within him. Dev'rox. "I've seen you fight far tougher enemies than this, brat. Do me a favor and not die here. I'd rather not dissipate into soul death because I attached myself to an unworthy fighter."

Alistair gritted his teeth and spit out blood. Dev'rox's mind acted as a soothing presence. His wisdom of age was like a refuge that he could calm down beside. This fight was winnable. He only had to figure out one thing.

When reading the intention behind an attack, he needed to understand the limitations of his opponent. Therefore, he was misjudging something about Brutus's capabilities.

A wild punch knocked out one of Alistair's teeth. He almost fell to the floor, barely avoiding a follow up kick that made a whooshing noise as it cut the air with immense speed.

What is it? What is it? Alistair felt his brain work in overdrive. The world moved in slow motion. Brutus drew back his fist, preparing an arcing uppercut.

Alistair observed every aspect of Brutus's being. The sweat that fell down his forehead. The large gash in his side that oozed blood. The snarl on his face. And—

Suddenly, Alistair found his concentration out of whack. He barely managed to sidestep a thunderous uppercut that surely would have knocked him out.

Finally, he had seen through the curtain.

Brutus was using Dispersion *before* every attack, not during. In such a small way that Alistair hadn't even noticed it until he was looking at every granular action. Right before Brutus struck, the man would make the smallest preparatory actions. In a way Alistair did not fully understand, these actions were capable of distracting him for a moment. His understanding of Dispersion was still incomplete, despite managing to copy it for a brief period.

Despite seeing the secret, Alistair wasn't able to adapt right away. It was a slow change. Each sequence of moves, he saw a little more. And in each sequence, Brutus slowed down a small amount. The stamina drain from when Alistair had him on the ground was taking hold.

The key was moving before Brutus moved. Staying one step ahead. Seeing the path of his opponent's Dispersion, Alistair launched a punch that collided head-on with Brutus's fist.

There was a sickening crunch as Alistair's hardened knuckles squashed that fist like butter.

Even then, the mad dog did not relent. He stepped forward to punch with his other fist—Alistair intercepted once more, reading the Dispersion ahead of time and striking with perfect timing. The sturdiness of the Steel Body held up, and he clenched his muscles taut to the utmost degree.

Brutus's other fist collapsed like the first. But he did not stop, even though defeat looked imminent. In a final burst of rabid energy, he increased his speed, surpassing his limits.

Brutus the Biter unleashed a flurry of blazing blows. They contained all his burning desire to win, all his animalistic fervor, and all his immeasurable talent.

Biology won out over belief. The punches were pitifully weak, unable to land with even a third of their usual power.

Alistair parried Brutus's floppy fists over and over, waiting for the last attack that he knew was coming. It was obvious, if you thought about it. A bite.

Despite how absurd it sounded, Brutus's neck felt like it elongated and soared straight for Alistair, the madman's enormous, sharp canines aiming directly for the jugular.

Alistair let out a burst of air. It had all led up to this. If Brutus's bite landed, he would die.

A shockwave emanated from the ring. A man collapsed to the floor, unmoving.

Alistair stood above that man, his head held high. His was the victory.

The last punch had connected, a simple uppercut counter that he threw with all his might.

With all the damage Brutus had taken, that was enough. He lay flat on his stomach at the other end of the ring. The Biter was fast asleep.

Alistair would have basked in his victory, but he felt dizzy. He met eyes with Silvanio, whose face was expressionless as always. *I wanted to see a little annoyance on that mug.* Master Ko Pao, on the other hand, was beaming with pride and happiness. Most of all, Pike grinned with smug knowing. Of course, his apprentice had achieved victory. That much was always obvious.

Alistair closed his eyes and let the pain fade away. He was going to be hurting for the next few days.

18 INTERLUDE

THE MAN in Shadows analyzed the threads of Fate.

As the faux Grand Imperator, he controlled the Pathfinder AI with no one the wiser. The true Grand Imperator would not arrive for several months. According to information he had retrieved from the Feiyn Goods, Grand Imperator Praetei Dai Kezlan would not arrive for exactly seventy-five days. That put her arrival in the fourth wave, the Mindaugust's Trial.

A Grand Imperator was the authority of the Emperor of the Final Frontier Empire in living form. They were his absolute word, his solemn decree. In His Excellency Dragus Laketor's name, they performed vital duties all over the universe. Reading imperial decrees. Enforcing imperial decrees. Collecting taxes from major organizations. Settling disputes between major organizations.

A lesser known, but highly important duty, was their modular interfacing with the Pathfinder AI. When dealing with those of lower realms, especially for initiation, Grand Imperators had a lot of leeway.

Even false ones. But the Man in Shadows wasn't quite a false Grand Imperator, was he?

Everything about him seemed to be genuine because it was. He was truly a Grand Imperator, appointed by Dragus Laketor himself 49,116 years ago.

The only thing was, Earth, FX-14752, wasn't within his purview. Not even close. In fact, he was technically supposed to be on an extended vacation, one that he had earned after tens of thousands of years toiling away for that wretched, libidinous emperor.

That was the funny thing. The Pathfinder AI, in all its sophisticated processing power, was stupid. Maybe the real deal that the Sublimed Machine Faction and other high-grade polities employed was intelligent in a true, human way, but their buggy program sure as hell wasn't. With the right programmer, it was all too easy to trick it into thinking that he was the authenticated Grand Imperator, granting him unparalleled access into the inner machinations of FX-14752.

However, that unparalleled access was limited. Not by its innate nature, but because if he changed too much, or was too blatant with his machinations, he would be discovered. There were already dozens of Visionary cultivators hovering around the planet, even if most of them were **Soul Splitter** clones. The Man in Shadows was strong, with innumerable cards up his sleeve, but even he was not confident in facing down Io, SHA-909, the Perfect, and the other Visionaries.

Not without unsealing the Demonic Curse within his brain. A bold move like that would attract too much attention.

The Mindaugust was honestly the most problematic factor, despite only being a Profound. He was an intelligent elf, more intelligent than the Man in Shadows had anticipated. But still not as smart as himself.

The rest of the sponsors were watching, but they didn't have the best fidelity of observation. Since the inception of the Pathfinder AI's initiation system, the privacy filters for Prime Initiates had been mightily improved.

The improvement stemmed from the renowned lightning elementalist, Drake Thunderrock. The wandering cultivator and war hero came from humble beginnings, and was abused by his sponsor millions of years ago. The now extinct Progenitor Clan had tried to enslave him by threatening to reveal his proprietary cultivation secrets to his enemies.

That was over half a million years ago. When the Bane of the Republic came into his own power, he extinguished the clan that exploited him and helped institute the current privacy protections.

Privacy protections that the Man in Shadows didn't dare touch. His organization was relying on him to deliver more product, but even he wouldn't go that far. Already he risked his life, soul, and eternal legacy tricking the Final Frontier Empire and the Pathfinder AI.

At a distant level, he was pulling the wool over Emperor Dragus himself. An Exalted realm who commanded the strength of an entire universe.

By acting as the intermediary between the Pathfinder and the Final Frontier Empire, the Man in Shadows had convinced the latter that the creation of the Devil Kings was an autonomous design of the former. Some bullshit experimentation high up the Sublimed Machine food chain that no one in a frontier universe would question. Which it was decidedly not.

The Eon Resurgence, the organization called it. The Man in Shadows was but one tiny piece of the Eon Resurgence that spanned the entire multiverse. One step in it was the revival of the Devil Kings. For what purpose it served, the Man in Shadows only had guesses. The organization kept their employees at an arm's length. He had been promoted three times and still had no understanding of the inner mysteries of the organization's goals. But they paid well, and supported vagrants, outcasts, and the downtrodden.

He had hijacked the Pathfinder AI's credential system with the help of a Supernal Programmer, and instituted the Devil King program.

You might think an intrepid citizen of the empire would question such orders. Creating unholy aberrations despised by Heaven and reviled in civilized space?

Well, they were used to it. The Pathfinder AI was very peculiar, and it basically did what it wanted. Heaven? Civilized space? Those things were so very far away. No one batted an eye.

The Man in Shadows exited the barrier separating the Holy Ravine from the rest of the world. The Devonic Elision Field barely affected him at his level, but it still felt suffocating.

The key players were all doing their parts. The Pathfinder AI was always working in inscrutable ways, impossible for even a well-informed Visionary cultivator to fully understand. As the Man in Shadows understood it, there was even something else going on in the background that was causing the Pathfinder AI to act in strange ways. Something huge looming in the distance that was sending ripples all throughout the multiverse.

Even as a citizen of the Final Frontier Empire, emphasis on "frontier," he was hearing things. However, the Man in Shadows was no ordinary citizen, having left the universe many times, though not through breaking the Dao firmament with his own power. Wars were brewing in frontier universes like wildfire. It was said that the upper and lower planes were undergoing turmoil, but that was above his pay grade by a long shot.

His thoughts circled back to the job at hand. Silvanio Apostolos. The organization would love a talent like that. He could be nurtured with the most vile of rituals into a powerhouse. But the prized jewel was George Moulin—the leader of the Devil Kings. He was the only one of the Devil Kings to speak to him without fear, as an equal.

The war between the Devil Kings and the forces of mankind was incoming. The Man in Shadows spent ninety-five percent of his time assisting the Supernal Programmer in obscuring the Pathfinder's vision, so he was unable to assist George in the war. But he trusted his protégé.

A Mindaugust-Annalist duo would have analyzed the situation as losing for the Devil Kings. They were outnumbered and had the entire world working against them. Yet the Man in Shadows was not worried. It could be George alone against a million, and he would still believe in that man. That was the level of trust the Man in Shadows had. The conviction in a prodigy blessed by the Hells.

But even if he lost, the Eon Resurgence still churned on. The Man in Shadows had several backup plans, several contingencies. In many ways, it would be easier if the humans were victorious.

Speaking of humans, Alistair Tan was a major thorn in his side. An unforeseen development, so to speak. At this point, he was too important in the story of the world for direct intervention. It was divine luck or diabolic travesty that he happened to stumble into the Holy Ravine. The Pathfinder AI did its best to create locales of improvement for its subjects, and Alistair's martial arts were a perfect fit for the Holy Ravine. The Pathfinder could tap into the Sublimed Machine's superb understanding of space and transport regions from across the multiverse with minor energy costs.

While it would have been preferable to kill Alistair outright, that was a step too far. Too obvious. It would attract undue attention, and most likely expose him to the AI. No, he just needed to keep the Prime Initiate occupied within the rural borders of the Holy Ravine for enough time. Enough time for the Devil Kings to act relatively unimpeded—which also meant time for Alistair to grow in strength.

It mattered not. There would always have been a venue for him to increase in strength. Otherwise, why were there so many backup locations? The eternal lakes of fire, if he had turned out to be firesworn. Saturn's chateau for a mage.

Obviously, they weren't directly made for Alistair himself, just the one who would eventually rise to the top. Which in this timeline turned out to be Alistair. In some sense, the Holy Ravine was his *reward*.

It mattered not. George had his own training grounds. The Blizzard Lich's Fjord. An ice elementalist's dream, consisting of a set of quests in some long dead Exalted's Domain. It was now a spiritual demiplane lacking most of its former meaning, being hundreds of millions of years old. For the frontier? It was quite impressive.

Something of that quality would normally have been prohibitively expensive, but whoever the frontier Exalted was, they freely passed on their legacy to anyone who had gathered sufficient Karmic infamy. As such, it was easily accessible, and the Man in Shadows was able to request one localization of the Fjord from the organization.

The Man in Shadows let his soul drift out of his body. Astral traveling was far more efficient than bodily movement, though more dangerous since it exposed the soul. That is, unless you were a trained spiritualist variant with absurdly high Wisdom, which he was.

He flew into the subterranean depths of the earth, to a cave cloaked in thousands of layers of highly expensive wards. His soul was the only one permitted through the wards—any other visitor, spiritual or otherwise, would be ripped to shreds.

Goe Emmar was the mission's Supernal Programmer. That was not a Class or Badge or even a category of cultivation. It was simply an honorary title given to those who could perform the act of programming with the computer language of the Sublimed Machine—Supernal. Technically, you didn't even have to follow the Dao of Technology to become a Supernal Programmer, though such a feat was nigh unheard of.

Goe Emmar was not that special. He was still a damn good Supernal Programmer, and a special asset that the organization was lending him. He was a mysterious man, his only distinctive feature being a pair of weird virtual reality goggles that glowed with shifting colors.

"The Pathfinder AI is gathering more computational resources. I have a feeling it understands at some level that something is off." Goe Emmar did not move so much as a muscle at his arrival. He sat in a chair of living metal, slithering and growing and shrinking like a pulsating organism. It was connected to the ground via an organic melting of stone and metal, grown into the earth as if it was a natural growth. "There is something weird about this planet. I don't know. You can only leave this abode once a week from now on."

"Is that why [Armageddon] is targeting our subjects so heavily?"

"Possibly," Goe Emmar mused. "This wave is especially bad. It's not really fair, is it? Though I guess we're not playing fair at all, either. It's also possible their far-reaching ripples in the web of Fate are attracting the attention, not the demon blood. This batch is especially powerful. The higher-ups will be happy."

"Don't catch your chickens before they hatch, as they would say on this world." The Man in Shadows looked up. "My body is close to returning on autopilot. I do not dare risk fast travel."

"I hear that the Chaos War grows in size by the day," Goe Emmar said, a frown on his pristine face, completely unmarred by the ravages of time. "Soon, the organization might be forced to flee the Dead Zone. The demons cannot promise our safety with the Chaos War at their border."

"We're not welcome in civilized space," the Man in Shadows noted.

"We're not welcome anywhere," Goe Emmar retorted. "Whether it be Chaosbeasts, demons, divine progeny, or fellow humans."

"That is the price of eternal glory."

"You are no zealot. That's not fooling me."

The Man in Shadows snorted and sat down. His body would return in a few hours. For now, he would assist Goe Emmar with Dao energy and Mana. There was not much left for him to do on this world. Even now, he stretched the credulity of non-interference. Being discovered would put an end to all the organization's plans, which he was not keen to do. "If you think about it, we're the inverse of the Mindaugust-Annalist duo assigned here."

"Oh? How so?"

"Your memory is prodigious and your calculation abilities are second-to-none, but you are physically large, unlike Johannis. I have the wisdom of Solomon yet I am small, unlike Kazian."

"Was that an attempt at a joke?" Goe Emmar asked. "You're surprising me more by the day. Been spying on those two that much? You trying to peep on their love sessions? You know what they say goes on between Mindaugusts and Annalists."

"Know thy enemy," the Man in Shadows said. "But let's not take it that far. I'd rather watch a celestial dragon mate with an archdevil. All for the Eon Resurgence."

———

Lucius lay on his back, staring up at the sun. He had never done so as a kid, even when it was a fad. How could anyone be stupid enough to gaze into the sun, even as a child?

He had nothing. No money, no energy, and no knowledge.

In his confrontation against George Moulin, the First Devil King, he had nearly died in a single exchange. George was far too powerful. The only reason he survived was because he burnt almost every single drachma he had to block one of the Devil King's attacks and teleport away.

With [Mammon's Grasp], he could perform quasi-miracles—alterations of reality normally bound to higher level Skills or specific Daos, at the cost of money. Successfully defending against a full power arrow of ice that was capable of destroying his mansion in one blow and teleporting to a safe location was so audaciously impossible under normal circumstances. Hence, the hefty cost.

When he woke up after the fight, he was drifting on a plank of wood in the middle of the ocean, with no end in sight.

This time, he had no idea, no secret trick. [Mammon's Grasp] had liquidated all of that to pay for the miracle. Even his land was bequeathed to Bartholomew, his eldest. He couldn't even contact his family.

The one thing that Lucius did have left was the Soulnet. With his Quaestor Class, he could see into the global Soulnet chain.

Bartholomew, Imogen, and Alfred were alive. They hadn't been at the mansion at the time, thank goodness. But if the Devil Kings were targeting them, how much longer would that last?

Their only hope in a direct, frontal assault was Alistair. But according to the Soulnet rumors, Alistair Tan had been missing for over a month.

If that man had truly perished… it was over. But Lucius didn't believe it. He had to be alive. That bright star he witnessed—his story ending here seemed utterly impossible. No, he was alive, but he had to have a *very* good reason for not showing his face. Whatever it was, Lucius hoped it justified the destruction the world was facing.

It wasn't only Alistair's power that kept the balance between the humans and non-humans, though that was a major factor. The people of Earth responded to his strength. Everything was a damn mess without him. His subordinates were doing as best they could, but the panic was palpable.

That all felt very distant. After all, Lucius was about to die. It had been over a month since he had been stranded in the middle of the ocean. There were some who could subsist on nothing but Mana itself, but he was not one of those individuals yet. While he needed almost no sleep, nutrients, and water to survive, the imperative word was *almost*.

Maybe it was his tougher body, or maybe it was just how humans worked, but it didn't feel so bad now. At first, Lucius lusted after water more than he had for anything in his entire life. His thirst was literally painful.

But after weeks and weeks, it didn't feel so bad. He was slipping in and out of consciousness, partially in delirium. Organ failure was imminent.

The ocean was so cold and so blue. He surely would have died of hypothermia if not for his improved physique. As it was, it felt calming to see nothing but miles and miles of ocean.

He was screwed. The land of Earth had conglomerated into a supercontinent. He was on the complete opposite side of the planet. As for why **[Mammon's Grasp]** had transported him so far away, he had no clue.

So many regrets. All he wanted to do was to pick up Imogen one more time and tousle her hair. Kick around a football with Bartholomew and go to a meeting with Alfred. To visit their mother's grave at FavorWood Manor one last time. With death right at his doorstep, his grand aspirations of power crumbled away.

Lucius opened his eyes, taking in the vast expanse of endless water. What a sad way to die. Completely alone in the world.

His mind wandered to a memory of his first girlfriend telling him he'd die alone. She hated how obsessed with money he was at the time. He had never had any time for her since he was always hustling. It turned out she was right.

Finally, he accepted it. It was all over.

Then what was that he was seeing in the distance?

The faint outlines of an island came into view. Lucius rubbed his eyes. Were those people there?

Lucius smiled. Maybe his time wasn't up after all. Maybe he would see his family once more. Plus… the greedy thing inside him sniffed out profit to be made. An island surviving in the middle of nowhere? These people needed some capitalism.

————

Silvanio Apostolos gazed at his village from the balcony of his room in the Church of the Holy Ones. *So small.*

Unrivaled under the heavens. What a joke.

His entire life, he had striven to be the strongest. He was born with talent unseen in the Holy Ravine for a thousand years, but he still trained harder than anyone. He trained until his body was breaking apart at only twenty years old.

At forty-one, only his immense willpower carried him forward. All those years of pushing the limits beyond his limits had caught up. A warrior gave his whole life to his art, to the pursuit of perfection. In the end, he would die like all other men. His flesh rotting, his eyes eaten, his memory forgotten within a few generations. There was no afterlife. There was only nothing-ness. The Mother of War only promised glory in this life, for there was nothing to come.

Or so he thought.

A year had passed within the Holy Ravine since their little valley had been transported to an alien world. In this year, Silvanio learned how little he knew of the world.

Magic was real. Immortality was possible. There was a cycle of Karmic rebirth called Samsara.

Yet he still remained trapped, unable to advance. No one in the Holy Ravine could leave. No one could gain these powers that sounded like they came from myth.

Then that man came. Not Vritra, but something far more sinister. The shadowed man. An existence far more disturbing than a reptilian beast.

He was the first person to slip under his guard since Red Harmonia. He moved in shadows, which permanently blanketed his face in darkness, no matter what the position of the sun or lighting was.

Silvanio knew right away that common sense would dictate that this man should never be crossed.

That man told him about the ways of cultivation. The story of this world, of its magnificent technology that sounded as impossible as magic. The initiation and what the Holy Ravine's place in it was.

A backdrop. That was it. The way the man explained it was so casual. The divine being called the Pathfinder AI took elements of multiple worlds in order to create the best possible breeding ground for growth.

In other words, he was the hay to the horses of this world. The man warned him about one particular individual—Alistair Tan. Lo-and-behold, he appeared in the Holy Ravine.

This was the man who Silvanio was supposed to be a catalyst for. A stepping point, to climb to greater heights.

The shadowed man promised him an opportunity for all the resources Silvanio could ever imagine if he listened to his orders to stymie Alistair when possible, and to report his movements. He spoke of a method that could triple one's power instantaneously, and how he might provide this to him.

The shadowed man did not account for two things.

The first was that he himself had been reduced by the anti-magic field present in the valley. Silvanio had the feeling that the shadowed man was already suppressing himself to go unnoticed, as his actions felt very shady. Silvanio's instincts were honed to perfection, and they screamed that the outsider was duplicitous and not to be trusted.

The second was that shadowed man's promises were vacuous and meaningless to him.

Long ago, when he had felt the oppressive walls of creation, he had surrendered. For thirty years, he was a living corpse, bound to the laws of mundane existence. In this life, he had promised himself one thing—to live it by his own accord, on his own terms. He would not accede to anyone else's fate, and continued to march as his will decreed.

It sounded like the Final Frontier Empire provided this opportunity in spades. He had no need of some under-the-table, nefarious plotter interfering with his destiny.

So he had lied. Silvanio was not a man taken to spewing falsehoods, but they were sometimes necessary. Alistair was set to leave the Holy Ravine today, but he had told the man it would be in a week's time.

Would that have any effect? No one could say. But he hoped it would make things more interesting.

Alistair allied himself with Silvanio's greatest enemy, but already he felt how small their foolish rivalry was. In the new world, such things would matter little. Indeed, he felt a certain kinship with the mysterious outsider. A favor now would be a favor later.

One day they would clash, but today was not that day.

———

"The Master will arrive soon," Oracle said in a hushed tone. "You will pay him your proper respects, Morgana, unlike last time."

Nine men and women of great power sat around an ancient stone table. Once used by nobles of some European country, the castle had been repurposed into one of the various Devil King hideouts around the world.

This was to be the first time they were all together after the deaths of Dragonus and Admiral.

Oracle scoffed. What weaklings. They could not kill even one of the enemy's top fighters, while her Master had killed the richest man in the world, who had been a major thorn in their sides. Even her humble self had killed Carmen and Richard, two humans within the top six rankers. The Master said he was happy with their overall achievements on that fated day, but she knew he must have been seething with fury at the failure of two of his strongest soldiers.

Oracle looked at her fellow Devil Kings. In numerical order, it was her at second, then Chameleon at fifth, the Shadow Twins at sixth and seventh, Jakk at ninth, Morgana at tenth, Hephaestus at eleventh, Monk at twelfth, and Heavyset at thirteenth. All their numbers were visible on the backs of their chairs.

The chairs marked with the number three, four, and eight were empty. The conspicuous absences gnawed at Oracle like a sore tooth. The dead weaklings who failed the Master, of course, but also the traitor. Whimsy, the eighth. Oracle would make her suffer a long and painful death for her betrayal.

"I was in the middle of a huge sacrifice last time, that's why I was late," Morgana, the Tenth Devil King, said without an ounce of respect. "I can express my annoyance without you jumping down my throat, can't I? You know that he doesn't actually like you just because you sleep with him, right?"

"Watch your mouth." Oracle stood up and flared her immense aura, unfurling a web of green Karmic energy around the witch. "You will not spread such disgusting lies in my presence."

"Ladies, ladies, please do not fight," Chameleon said in his scratchy, lizard-like voice. "You two are our strongest remaining combatants. We cannot have infighting at this point."

"Strongest *remaining?*" Oracle raised an eyebrow. "I was promoted to my current position before Dragonus and Admiral died."

"Only because I chose this position," Morgana retorted. "If George had given out the ranks based on pure strength alone, I would have received the title of second. We both know this to be true."

"I do not know this at all," Oracle seethed. "You overestimate yourself."

Morgana eyed the other Devil Kings, perhaps testing to see how they would respond to a physical escalation. In the end, she just sighed and went back to picking at her nails.

Tall, raven-haired, beautiful—Morgana was the epitome of elegance. Oracle wore plain clothing to signify her humbleness in light of the Master, while the witch wore a revealing black dress. With her red eyes and burn mark tattoo on her tongue, she represented the peak of arcane mastery, along with their master, George Moulin.

While George was undoubtedly more powerful than his Tenth Devil King, he specialized solely in an elementalist sub school, specifically ice. Morgana, as her name suggested, wielded the arcane arts like she was blessed by Mana itself, capable of all manner of spells.

The Dao of Magic was a mystery unto itself. Arcane Classes, those aligned with the Dao of Magic, operated on a fundamentally different level compared to others. First of all, while Mana was still essential to magic spells, *nue* was also incredibly important. The imagination fueled magic— though the form of *nue* in spellcasting was so far removed from the traditional understanding of the mental energy as killing intent, many didn't even recognize it when used in magic.

Instead of discrete quantities of Mana, Arcane Classes used spell slots, going from rank F through A, and then 1 through 15. It was a unique system that felt tacked onto the Dao in a messy manner, though you never would have guessed that watching Morgana.

Heavyset, the Thirteenth Devil King, shifted in her seat, which caused the rest of the room to groan and creak. "Are you two really going to do this right before the Master arrives? You're worse than Dragonus and Admiral."

Oracle wanted to protest—it was Morgana that was the troublemaker, not her. But she kept her mouth shut. Because the Master was here. She felt it long before any of the others. Her Karmic web extended out over a thousand feet, capable of detecting the slightest perturbations of Fate.

George Moulin's ripples on Fate were not slight. They were grand. Oracle subconsciously froze in awe at feeling her Master's aura. It was beyond understanding.

After a few seconds, the rest of them started feeling it, too. Oracle took great pleasure in seeing a bead of sweat form on Morgana's brow as she felt his absolute authority. Even the loyal Chameleon and Shadow Twins trembled with fear in their eyes. She alone among the Devil Kings was without fright. She alone was the only true servant of the Master, and followed him with no uncertainty in her heart.

The temperature in the old banquet hall of the castle dropped. Ice crystals formed around metal in the room, and it became so cold she could see her breath. A light blue and misty aura filled the room, covering everything in a blanket of subtle haziness.

The double doors of the ancient castle creaked open, and the Master stepped out. He was as Oracle remembered him—average height and a slight build, with pale skin tinged slightly blue. His blonde hair was frozen in a spiky mess, his eyes burning pools of cerulean inferno.

The same, but different. While his appearance was the same, still in that nondescript white cloak befitting of a mage, his aura had changed. It had *grown.*

George had always been the strongest—there was no doubt about that. But now? Oracle couldn't even fathom her Master's strength. His aura felt like a bottomless ocean of ice, billowing out chilling energy like a monstrous blizzard.

At the same time, it felt less tempestuous than before. Like all the Devil Kings, their profane arts left an impact on their auras, making them feel hollow or unstable. But George's only had a hint of that instability left. For the most part, his immeasurable aura felt as tranquil as an undisturbed pond.

As George approached the table, Oracle realized his appearance was not the same. Before, he appeared his age, somewhere in his mid-thirties, but now he had the semblance of a teenager. His skin was free of blemishes and without wrinkles, his features serene as an elf.

All nine of the Master's servants stood up at once in his presence, though he dismissed them with a wave. He took his seat at the head of the table, the impossibly black throne of power that no one else dared to sit in while he was absent, not even Morgana.

"I apologize for my aura," he said. His voice was barely louder than a whisper, but the sound traveled like he was shouting from a megaphone. "I am unused to this amount of Mana."

In an instant, the cold aura retreated into George's body. All the ice in the room disappeared. Oracle stopped shivering, something that she hadn't even noticed she was doing.

"Master, the trial was successful?" Oracle asked, bowing her head.

"The Blizzard Lich's Fjord went as the Man in Shadows promised," George said. "I have obtained ultimate power."

"I don't trust that man further than I could throw him," Morgana said. "He's using us as pawns for a greater game that we're not even close to being privy to."

"You're letting him hear your insolence?" The Shadow Twin sitting in the chair labeled six spoke up. With them being identical twins with the same face and clothes, she never could tell them apart. "He's always watching, always hearing. We know the truth, let's be real. We're lab rats for the Final Frontier Empire. There's nothing we can do but win. If he turns out to be screwing us over, we were already screwed the moment the FFE gave us demon blood. There's no point in pissing off the only person who can help us out."

"I wonder," George said softly. "If we *are* an experiment of the Final Frontier Empire."

"I don't follow," said Monk, the Twelfth Devil King. He was blind, with a white headband around his eyes. He wore the traditional outfit of a Buddhist monk and specialized in hand-to-hand combat. Oracle almost felt bad that he was so overshadowed by their greatest enemy. "You were the one to figure that out, sir."

George tapped the side of his head. "I did originally come to that conclusion, yes. But perhaps I was wrong. I have seen and heard interesting things during my retreat in the Blizzard Lich's Fjord. The one we know as the Man in Shadows—I have strong reason to believe he is not who he says he is. He is no arbiter of the Final Frontier Empire."

Murmurs spread throughout the table. Morgana was the first one to speak up. "Then what is he? Who would be so bold to lie about that?"

George took a moment to respond. Unlike the rest of them, his breath still produced a cloud of steam. His body temperature must have naturally been well below freezing.

"I don't know." Oracle could feel her Master's concern in the long pauses between each word. He did not normally sound so unsure, and she felt a shiver go down her spine.

"I will tell you what I do know. He is old and powerful and has done this many times. Enough for there to be a Psychic Inheritance containing the willpower of three former Devil Kings, all within the last three thousand years. That there were three ice mages within a three thousand-year period suggests an extremely high rate of turnover. Their message was hidden deep within the Blizzard Lich's Fjord, so the Man in Shadows never found it. They said that he has been infiltrating planets under the guise of an official of the Final Frontier Empire for tens of thousands of years. Planting Devil Kings on thousands of worlds. One of the wills inside the Inheritance found old planetary records. After a 'victory,' they disappear from the record, never to be seen again. In addition, the Man in Shadows does not work alone. He always has at least one partner, suggesting a more powerful organization backing them."

There was a heavy silence in the room as no one knew what to say. Oracle understood they were talking about things so far above her, it became practically meaningless. Unseen groups moving against other groups that wielded the resources of this entire universe.

"Why don't we snitch on 'em, then?" the other Shadow Twin asked. "I'm sure the Final Frontier Empire ain't happy about this shit. I wouldn't be, if I were them. Couldn't we broker some kind of deal for our safety?"

"That is not a good idea." George's words carried the air of finality. "This mission is clearly of central importance to the Man in Shadow's backers. If we are caught during an attempted betrayal, he will surely kill all of us to cover the tracks. If we do manage to make a deal with the Final Frontier Empire, he might still be able to kill us. With how much they've invested in their missions, they cannot afford to be caught. All of Earth might be wiped away."

"Then what do you suggest, George?" Morgana held her gaze with the Master.

Once again, there was a moment of silence. Everyone waited intently for George's next words.

"We must operate as normal," George finally said. "Do not discuss this, even amongst yourselves. The Man in Shadows must allocate much of his time to sleeping, but we do not know when he will awaken. I shall figure out a path forward. In the meantime, we have much work to do."

Oracle perked up at the sound of that.

As it was, the second wave was a nightmare without the Master. The hordes were endless and the bosses nigh unstoppable. Even she had to try hard against them. With the Master back, things would be easier, but in their current predicament, it was hard to enact their plans when their territories were constantly being encroached on.

With a breath, the Master created a blossom of ice. He twirled the flower, resplendent with its twelve crystal petals. He twirled it around with his fingers and then abruptly crushed it in his hand.

"My little snakes tell me that Alexandra is in the Wasteland right now. Vritra and the Pride Lord are still busy undergoing their transformation. I must contend with the second wave along with Morgana. Oracle"—the Master's gaze breached her own—"you shall deal with the woman. The rest of you will also deal with our current situation, except Chameleon. Continue your mission. This meeting is concluded."

"Wait, Master," Oracle entreated. "What of Alistair? Isn't the Wasteland where he disappeared? I fear I might not be able to deal with him and the barbarian combined, considering you expect him to grow in strength during his missing time."

"There is nothing to fear," George said. "He will not return to Earth for a week's time. You only need to deal with Alexandra and the teleporting man."

19 ALEXANDRA'S GAMBIT

Status of the War Against the Devil Kings:

Commencing with the attack on FavorWood Manor and New Boston, the Devil Kings attempted to blitz the human world in one go. While they were unsuccessful in the latter, with both the second and third ranked Devil Kings perishing in an epic battle, FavorWood Manor was essentially destroyed.

Lucius Wood is presumed dead, not having been spotted since George Moulin, the First Devil King, conducted a personal attack. His name has vanished from the leaderboard. Certain Skills and items can achieve this effect, but based on the preponderance of the evidence, we believe him to be dead. While his two sons and the major pillars of the organization, Bartholomew and Alfred, are both alive, 98% of the other high-level officials are dead and large parts of their territory has been mostly incorporated into the Devil King's empire. Most of their funds have vanished—embezzlement by high-level officials is suspected but not confirmed.

Following their initial assault, the Devil Kings' intermittent attacks have resulted in hundreds of thousands of casualties. However, humanity as a whole has lost more manpower to defection than death or injury. With George's announcement proclaiming safe harbor to any that willingly join and utter annihilation to those that refuse, hundreds of thousands in the last month and a half have joined the Devil Kings.

At the present moment, 25.1% of the global subregions are under their control. A far cry short of the 50% required to immediately end the Quests with the supremacy of George and the Devil Kings, but an immense growth in a short period.

The most concerning aspect is that it appears they are not close to using all of their resources for these assaults. Both Oracle, the Second Devil King, and George's whereabouts and activities remain unknown. Based on the amount of missing beasts, monsters, and humans and numerous reports of demon blood experimentation, we also believe them to be hiding massive numbers of Devil Princes, ready to attack at a moment's notice.

Enemy combatants of note:

George Moulin: The leader of the Devil Kings. In possession of a number of powerful magic items, full list unknown. Has ice-related powers and can conjure arrows of ice the size of chimneys that have the destructive power to destroy city blocks. Through the intel acquired by Evangeline and Alistair Tan, it is believed that George has direct control of all Devil Kings and, by proxy, their created Devil Princes. While it is likely that a certain amount of the Devil Kings are murderous through their own will, there is little doubt that many would surrender without their leader. In addition, with **Experiment Cursed Needle #7,** we can free those from his control without confronting him directly. Unfortunately, the needle remains with Alistair, whose last known location was deep in the Wasteland. All attempts at locating him have been unsuccessful. Search parties sent into the Wasteland come out with dozens of casualties to the serpentine beasts and Mana Storms. George participated in the Devil King's incursion and destruction of FavorWood Manor, but has since vanished into thin air, though the Devil King attacks do not cease.

Has been seen using *"Arcanous Devil Spell #2: Frozen Spear of the False Heavens."* We know this specifically because, upon activating the spell, he states this name. A spear three times as large as normal flies down from an arcane array.

Oracle: Second-in-command of the Devil Kings. Possesses Karmic powers unrivaled in the world and the ability to puppeteer corpses. While it was initially believed that her powers were to puppeteer living beings, with more information, it seems that she utilizes corpses instead, similar to Oliver Cambry's zombies. Highly dangerous and believed to be significantly stronger than Dragonus, her current whereabouts are unknown. She defeated Carmen Romero and Richard Atwood in a surprise attack while they were helping out a border town from the elemental beasts stemming from an enormous blizzard.

Chameleon: The Fifth Devil King, making them the third strongest of the remaining group. Possesses the ability to disguise themselves as another living creature. This affects **[Inspect]**-type Skills' perception of them, as well as other senses. The level of fidelity is unknown, and it is unclear if someone with highly advanced senses could detect them. As a shapeshifter, Chameleon's true name and gender are unknown. Their main threat comes from a recently uncovered ability that allows Chameleon to replicate all of a target's abilities. It is unknown how this truly dangerous ability works in detail. Chameleon infiltrated the head-quarters of the United Polities and almost killed both Marzhan, the #8 ranker, and Sally Ryder, the President. While the assassination plot was foiled, the injuries Marzhan sustained aren't healing properly. It is unknown what method Chameleon used to injure her, other than in her words, "it felt like a dagger of ice to the heart." The mention of ice leads to the suspicion that Chameleon was given a weapon by George, though the possibility still remains that it is their own Skill, in which case, they become an even greater threat.

Jakk: The Ninth Devil King and replacement for Saturn, who was killed by Jakk for unknown reasons, though most likely Saturn's creation of the **Experiment Cursed Needle #7** played a large role. Perhaps Saturn intended on betraying the Devil Kings outright, or perhaps it was insurance—either way, it is most likely that George did not care and sent Jakk to murder Saturn. His skillset is the most known of the remaining Devil Kings as he was recorded under heavy scrutiny in the Capture the Beacon trial of [Game of Life]. He is a fire elementalist with purple flames that are reported to have an aspect of torture/pain/wanton violence.

Heavyset: The Thirteenth Devil King. While the least offensively powerful of the group, her area of effect buffs and debuffs are highly troublesome, which is why this report recommends attempting to take her out first. The full extent of her abilities is unknown, but there are confirmed reports of gravity-related powers. She appears to be able to lighten people in a way that simultaneously makes them hit harder while also being faster and lighter. She can create fields of intense gravity for enemies.

Other numbered Devil Kings have too little data for an in-depth report. The Sixth and Seventh Devil Kings are believed to be identical twin brothers, possibly with shadow-related powers. The Tenth Devil King, Morgana, is believed to be responsible for the Massacre of Beijing, the single highest death incident in the world after Atavius Meloi's initial attack. Due to the absence of high-ranking individuals in the area at the time, she was successful in killing over one million people. As her name suggests, she uses magic, but her exact capabilities are unknown.

It is true that the Devil Kings all came from the top 100 of the leaderboard, however, many of their abilities from their times as normal humans are unknown due to their transformation happening close to the beginning of the initiation, when the historical records are more unclear and speculative. It is even believed that some of their number, upon changing into their current forms, went back and eliminated any ties to the human world in order to protect their identities. Due to memory savants, their government names are known, but at this point, it is fair to state their Devil King name is their "true" name.

In addition to the numbered Devil Kings, hundreds if not thousands of Devil Princes are at their disposal, on top of two other major threats. The Beast Lords Vritra and the Pride Lord have joined the Devil Kings, and have been given demon blood, making them at least twice as strong as they were before.

ALEXANDRA READ the report in its entirety. Celeste Mendoza, who was in charge of their freehold's communications, had given her the jade slip containing the information. Alexandra couldn't lie that she was a bit grossed out by the many holes that opened up in the woman's body. Taking the slip out of one of the holes was almost a step too far for her.

The information extended far beyond intel about the combatants, providing highly detailed maps of the Devil Kings' territory, repeated sighting spots of various Devil Kings, points of conflict, and suspected hideouts.

All the while, she could barely focus on the text.

It was a moonless night, dark as nature intended. She was in the middle of the wilderness, far from civilization. Most of the suburbs had been abandoned and left to the beasts, which were mutating at even faster rates. Luckily, they weren't growing to unstoppable levels of strength—her and most of the top rankers could still best the strongest beasts, but they had become much more fantastical. No longer only slightly different and larger animals, there were sightings of eight-legged humanoid spider creatures. Hell, she had even killed a chimera.

Her fingers curled around the jade slip that was feeding her the report's contents. Its glossy surface reflected a green light.

Fuck this. The green luminescence of her burning eyes was like a sore thumb that never went away. She would be forever marked as a monster, an aberration that should never have existed.

There were options, of course—glamours to hide the eyes. Fate-warded clothing that disguised her demonic presence. But none of that changed who she was deep down.

And she couldn't even give the standard excuse people gave in novels and such. "What you look like doesn't matter, it's what's deep down that counts!" Alexandra wouldn't have cared at all if all she got was a cosmetic change, as long as it didn't ruin her appearance that much. Even if it did do that, it wasn't the end of the world. But that excuse didn't exist when it was a veritable fact that demon blood altered one's Fate down a path of evil.

From being in her father's presence, she could tell her effects weren't as strong as a true Devil King. Dev'rox's ghostly nature probably had something to do with that. But she could feel slight changes. Growing quicker to wrath. Occasional dark thoughts becoming more frequent.

So she availed herself by thinking about the future. There was only the here and now. And there was only one mission. Kill every Devil King on Earth.

Maybe then, she could find her peace. If it had to be an eternal one, so be it.

She internalized the report once more. 25.1% of the world. Letting them get to 50% was game over.

That was precisely what she didn't understand.

How in the name of the Pathfinder AI did they not already have 50%?

To be honest, things were barely functioning without Alistair. He had set up a solid chain-of-command, but even she didn't realize how much everything relied on his immense power and stellar reputation. She suspected he even had caused a Dao-related inspiration effect, where the average person of the Northeast Order Freehold gained an appreciable combat bonus because of their trust in him.

The exact opposite was the case for the Devil Kings. George could control his troops with unmatched precision. The world of humans was messy and uncoordinated. Even the groups with leaders couldn't operate as smoothly.

The Devil Kings had attacked FavorWood Manor and the United Polities, but those were the only two major attacks on prominent freeholds in the *entire* month and a half period since Alistair had disappeared. And of those, the FavorWood Manor attack was the only one in which it seemed like they were trying at full force, and that was even before Alistair went missing, technically speaking. The United Polities incident was more like a terrorist attack, with only one individual at fault.

George should have been able to muster his army and steamroll the human resistance with his overwhelming power. Alexandra could only think of two reasons why he hadn't already.

Reason one: George was afraid of not only the damages he would take from the war, but the **Experiment Cursed Needle #7.** He wouldn't have a way of knowing it was on Alistair when he disappeared. While outward communication severely implied that Alistair was missing with no knowledge about what exactly happened, George had no reason to take that at face value. It could be that he was afraid that Alistair would free multiple Devil Kings from his control. It could also be the case that George was afraid of future conflicts with other planets and wanted to preserve as many of his soldiers as possible, which indicated he thought he was getting stronger at a faster rate than the humans. Now that Alexandra thought about it, this reason was like five reasons in one.

Reason two: He was being hampered from going all out. Alexandra wasn't sure why this would be the case.

Reason one sounded more likely, but also incomplete. Though when she listed them out like that, it sounded realistic. In that case, it could never, ever be leaked that Alistair was the one to possess the needle.

Alexandra dismissed the jade slip, moving through the night like she was born to the shadows.

It mattered not why George wasn't acting personally, or why those thirteen, no, ten demons in human skin didn't attack at once. Though deep down, she wondered if she could pass judgment so harshly. Through the Pathfinder AI messing with people's minds and George's control, she could easily have been one of them.

In either case, they still had to be killed. *Or turned,* she reminded herself, thinking of the needle. She wondered how Alistair would do things. How could you even determine if one followed George out of their own free will or through Fate control? What would he do if it turned out their murders from before becoming Devil Kings were solely their own doing?

The area she hunted in was the quietest environment she had ever been through. There was not a sound in the air but her own footsteps and breathing, not one sound. The beasts in this area had cleaned out all living things except some remaining trees. The rest were dead, rotting tree flesh.

The culprits were a familiar breed—the serpents of Vritra. Her mark.

In her quest to find Alistair, she had come to one conclusion: the only one who could give her any kind of answers was the Reptile Emperor. He came from the Wasteland, and was the only being known to have ventured deep into the recesses where Alistair had last been seen.

The problem was finding him. Her idea was simple. She had run it by Caren and William of course, the brains of their operation. They were both working overtime with Alistair gone, so she hadn't bothered them too much.

William told her there were too many open-ended variables for [Hypercalculative Induction] to work. Caren said it was an extremely risky idea. Alexandra didn't care. But she wasn't stupid. That was why she took the number one get out of jail free card—Jesse Waterfall.

In the [The Game of Life] Quest, the Australian had become a valuable ally. He was the #7 ranker after all, and had the ability to teleport himself and others. His [Scarlet Flash] had a range of two miles, while [Scarlet Shift] was even higher, at four miles. While this normally only applied to targets within his vision, he could create five saved locations of places he visited with [Scarlet Flash] and one with [Scarlet Shift] and teleport to them, if he was within range.

Alexandra had the feeling he was still hiding his true power, but she didn't say anything. She trusted him to make the right decision when the going got rough.

She had Jesse continuously create anchor locations along their path. They slowly wormed their way through the outlying forested area of the Wasteland, including Logista, where Alistair was last spotted.

At last, they arrived at the border between the world of the living and the Wasteland.

Like how it had been described to her, it was desolate. There was a marked line between the forest, however quiet it was, and the Wasteland.

There was no color in the desert. Like an old black-and-white movie, it was like your brain could tell you what the colors should have been. They just weren't there. They were drained right out of the rocks like they were water in a sewer.

Cacti and tumbleweeds dotted the landscape, looking sad and dark without their colors. Pools of mysterious black liquid seeped into the cracks of the sandless desert, winds wafting nauseous scents into her nostrils.

There were dead things everywhere. Deader than dead. She peered closer at the sight. They were the corpses of all sorts of reptiles. Mostly snakes, but also lizards, geckos, and some other species Alexandra didn't recognize. All larger than normal, and some with strange mutations, like extra heads or gigantic spikes.

She knew what those were. The dead spawn of Vritra. They must have run out of food in the Wasteland and died of starvation. The ones that successfully escaped their vast expanse were killed shortly by the surrounding people. Luckily, they almost always came one at a time or in small groups, so they were never that big of a challenge.

The dead are the weak ones, Alexandra thought. *They must be reproducing at a rate that the prey population of the Wasteland can't handle, so the weak ones are left out to dry. But what are they even eating?*

She remembered what the intel on the Wasteland mentioned. Mana Storms, and mysterious elemental beasts called "Devonic Purebreeds." From what she understood, there weren't that many Mana Storms at a time, no more than a dozen in the Wasteland, and the Devonic Purebreeds weren't the size of apartment buildings or anything. The reptiles must have been eating their pure Mana to survive.

Jesse spoke as if answering her thoughts. "There must be a shit ton of those snakes if they're taking out the inside of Mana Storms. It's hard for me to imagine how they could take out a bloody storm, ey?"

"I'd have to agree," Alexandra said. "We'd better be careful."

"And you want to go around killing a bunch of them?"

"Vritra styles himself the 'Reptile Emperor,'" Alexandra said. "If he can't defend his subjects, he doesn't deserve that lofty title, does he now?"

Jesse grinned. "I like the way you think."

20 CLASH OF THE DAO FIELDS

It TURNED out to be more difficult finding snakes than they originally thought. Foremost, the Wasteland was massive—it was the size of the former state of Montana. Second, there were more geographic features than expected given the barrenness of the desert. There were mountains deeper in, though few had even gotten that far. The only people who had seen the very center were those who had fled the area at the beginning of the initiation. The beginning, when the black and white mountains appeared out of nowhere.

That might be where Alistair is, Alexandra mused. After all, it would make sense for him to head there to deal with the Wasteland's Mana Storms. Usually the disaster's boss was at the center, like with the earthquake in New Boston or one of the several hurricanes and tornadoes she had dealt with in the Northeast Freehold's territory.

But she dismissed the idea of venturing there. It was too dangerous, considering how powerful the Mana Storms were. She envied Alistair, who only had to deal with beginning stage natural disasters. The Mana Storms were one of the few disasters to survive past the Earth Asunder wave and into the next one.

Speaking of the second wave of [Armageddon], the sixth and final Quest... Alexandra shuddered. In some ways, it was smaller scale than the first wave, but it was far, *far* more deadly. It wasn't destroying their infrastructure or food supply like Earth Asunder had, but the people were terrified. Terrified, and in need of their leader. She couldn't replace Alistair. No one could. The #2 ranker, Pharaoh, involved himself more in helping out the innocent civilians, but it wasn't the same.

She had worked with a strike team of herself, Pharaoh and Whimsy, the Wood brothers, Caren's men, United Polities fighters, and various Northeast Order Freehold troops. All to take out one of the second wave bosses. It was only because of their help that she could afford to be here, instead of fighting on the front lines.

Alexandra had to pay back their generosity. She had to complete her mission.

Jesse popped into existence in a scarlet beam of light, accompanied by a loud sound that reminded her of a whip's crack. "There are signs of serpent activity underground a few kilometers out. I think those bubbling black pools are their hidey holes? I was curious where they all were, I mean, even if this place is enormous, I've scouted everywhere within a ten kilometer radius of here and found absolutely nada. Then, I realized that maybe they're hiding underground. When I checked out one of those pools, I found that they're way deeper than they look."

"That would make sense," Alexandra said. "But isn't that stuff, like, toxic? It sure looks that way."

"Well, I didn't put my foot in, if you're asking that. It smells like shit too, but I didn't notice any negative effects from breathing it in, though I wasn't there for that long."

"You breathed it in without planning?"

Jesse jabbed her in the shoulder playfully. "You sound more like Alistair or Caren than the Alexandra I know."

"I'm not stupid. Come here, let me feel you." She gave him a deadly glare in case he enjoyed double entendres.

[Healing Current] had a far better diagnostic element than [Healing Touch], so she should be able to tell if anything was wrong with the man. Pressing her palm against his forehead, Alexandra didn't feel anything wrong with him.

"You're fine. Just be more careful. We can't afford to lose a single man with everything that's going on."

"Yes, ma'am," Jesse declared. "I will strive to meet your expectations."

Alexandra rolled her eyes. Jesse used his Skill to chain teleport them three times to the aforementioned pool. While they were alone, he didn't touch her in order to teleport her. As far as she could tell, she only had to be within a certain distance, perhaps less than a foot. Whenever he fought, he would always touch his targets, to make it appear like he needed physical contact. He was not nearly as airheaded as his vibes gave off.

The area surrounding the pool was like where they'd arrived—barren and rocky. The sun beamed down with sweltering heat, no clouds in sight. Alexandra could see for miles in every direction, unimpeded by any topographic relief.

The pool was the size of a car, amorphous in shape and bubbling like a boiling flask. Wispy black fumes rose from the surface, smelling like oil and sulfur. Like Jesse said, gross, but not dangerous. At least for now.

"How did you figure out there's something inside of 'em?" Alexandra asked.

"I jumped in," Jesse admitted.

"You what?"

"While I'm not sure, I think the black stuff is a variant of the black goo that we got bathed in back in Capture the Beacon. Remember when, if you died, you woke up in the weird pool of goo?"

"My body was too destroyed, so they had to revive me the hard way by recreating my body and reattaching my soul." Alexandra huffed as she recalled how badly Dragonus's sun had burned her. She'd died in an instant. At least she got the last laugh now that he was dead for real.

"Oh, that's right," Jesse said. "I guess when Admiral and Dragonus killed me, they didn't damage my body too bad. Anyway, when I woke up, I was in a pile of something kind of similar to this. The guy there called it Abyssal Titan blood."

"This is something's blood? Gross," Alexandra gagged. "Hey, I recognize that name. I think Alistair told me about how he drank an elixir that had Abyssal Titan spinal fluid in it. Maybe Abyssal Titans are like the Swiss Army knife of alchemy parts. Kinda feel bad for them, though."

Jesse stuck his finger in the liquid. "It's less viscous and it has a different quality to it, so that's why I said similar, not the same. Maybe it's some kind of variant that helps beasts grow more than humans, or maybe it's geared toward reptiles or poisonous creatures. Also, isn't it funny we're calling it black? It's somewhat difficult to tell if this stuff is actually black or just a dark green or brown."

"I never thought of that," Alexandra admitted. "But does it matter?"

"We'll be at a disadvantage since we can't see color in here," Jesse said. "I bet humans rely on color detection more than reptiles. So let's keep on alert."

"I never let my guard down."

Jesse circled around to the other side of the pool, digging his arms inside. "While I don't think it heals us, it shouldn't damage us that much since we have high enough Constitutions. Even if it is meant for the reptiles kind to grow and develop, it can't be that toxic since there should be a ton of weak reptiles too."

"So we're going to dive in?" Alexandra asked plainly.

"It's what I did before and I'm alright," Jesse said. "If you have any better ideas on how we can get to the snakes, be my guest. We could try to attract attention, but with this second wave, we're on a time crunch, aren't we?"

"That's true," Alexandra said. "Okay, I'm on board."

"Don't worry—if we meet any trouble we can't beat, I'll teleport us out right away to a saved location. The only thing that has successfully held me down is a Dao field, but you can produce your own Dao field. As long as yours is in the same league, I'll be good. Practically speaking, that means only George would be able to trap us."

"You flatter me." Alexandra smiled. [Demonlord's Nature Preserve], her evolved dominion Skill. A dominion Skill was anything that created a lasting change in the environment within a sizable area of effect. She got the feeling that the system wanted to call it "domain Skill" since that fit better, but couldn't since Domains were a separate thing.

From what she'd seen, forming a proto-Domain was one of the most straightforward paths to power. Alistair didn't have one, but he was more of an exception. The more explosive, offensive oriented fighters didn't need to have one at this level, especially if they were ranged, like Dragonus. For a melee fighter that didn't have Alistair's blinding speed, it was more important, since it allowed them to have longer reaching effects on the battlefield and defend against those powerful ranged attacks.

It was a good thing, then, that [Demonlord's Nature Preserve] had improved with her mountains of practice over the last month. She eschewed using it in battle, intending it as a trump card. The other Devil Kings shouldn't have had any intel on it.

As of the present, she could keep up the Skill for over a day, something that was impossible for almost everyone else. Pharaoh had told her he could only keep his proto-Domain open for thirty minutes at most. She believed the reason for the extreme duration was because of the life force of the trees. Nature was more self-sustaining than other concepts, and her trees were no exception. Plus, she was naturally hardy to mental fatigue, which was an important component of the drain of holding open a proto-Domain, from her Class.

That wasn't to say that she had reached the vaunted realm of opening a proto-Domain yet. [Demonlord's Nature Preserve] was still a Skill, a Skill that incorporated a ton of Dao energy into its physical presence, but still only a Skill.

She didn't understand it all, and as far as she knew, no one on Earth did. What she did know was that the Domain was an essential part of all higher realm cultivators. It was an inner world created within one's soulcore that held one's Dao energy. You could impose it on the world, replacing the space of reality. They started off small, but Exalted realm cultivators could have Domains the size of planets.

All that information came from a book she'd read from the Hall of Math that wasn't even about Domains, but contained oblique references to them like you were already supposed to know all about them. Oh, how she hated that Foundations got next to no information about their futures. It wasn't fair.

One line in that book intrigued her. Admiral's proto-Domain wasn't exactly "small." Small in comparison to a planet, sure, but the text implied small as in, the size of a classroom or baseball infield. Admiral's water was more like the size of a football field. So she did some more digging.

Proto-Domains could be larger because they were not true bodily formations of one's Dao. A true Domain's expansion into the physical world was literally the Dao becoming manifest, a divine miracle of the Heavens granted to mortals as providential beneficence, so her book said. She had to go to Caren to understand what those words meant, and scoffed. "Providential beneficence?" Wasn't it Heaven that mandated the eternal struggle to the top?

A proto-Domain's expansion couldn't quite perform that miracle, so it included Mana to bridge the gap. In addition, they weren't ratified by the Heavens, which she didn't fully understand the details of, but it made the weakest true Domain of an Adept stronger than the most overpowered Foundation. Not that it was impossible to win a realm up, but not in the field of Domains.

A Dao field, the lowest rung of the ladder, was imbuing your Dao into your surroundings, or your creations, which she had easily accomplished with **[Woodland Forest].**

Therefore, there were two important steps in going from Dao field to proto-Domain. The first was having some manifested·Dao, and the second was the internal space.

You needed to take some of your Dao energy and turn it physical. Alexandra didn't know exactly how much, but the minimum was maybe 20% of the volume of the proto-Domain. On top of that, you had to project your space internally-outward instead of outward-internally.

A Dao field was taking existing space and turning it into yours, while a Domain or proto-Domain was taking your internal space and making it the world. There was a massive difference in the level of control and power by using your own internal space.

That was the hardest part. Through great practice, she had already achieved the first requirement. But the internal space eluded her. She was *so* close. The Pathfinder AI had given her an Insight Vision for a side Quest after defeating a powerful Devil Prince. It had given her further insight into her soulcore and mind.

A Domain was the meeting of mind, body, and soul in one. Physical reality made of spiritual presence, envisioned by the mind, contained within the soul and imposed upon the world. The Insight Vision provided her with an understanding of Skills that transcended her previous understanding.

What was a Skill? The Pathfinder AI wasn't something that existed everywhere in the multiverse. Other civilizations had their own ways of expressing Mana-related powers. In its essence, a Skill was a set of instructions on how the mind, body, and soul acted to produce a desired effect of Mana.

The mind envisioned the Skill, serving as a blueprint. The soulcore provided the Mana, which flowed through the meridians of the body. The technical aspects of a Skill were stored in the brain and also in the meridians that flowed throughout the body.

The Insight Vision provided all of this information, but it didn't hand hold her. The step of actually creating the internal space wasn't explained at all. But Alexandra had an idea. She had to transfer the blueprint of the Skill from her brain to her soulcore.

Was such a thing possible? It sounded insane. However, clearly it was possible. The only person she knew who possessed a proto-Domain, Pharaoh, couldn't help her since his creation was far more natural. What a lucky bastard. Some were truly blessed with talent by the Heavens.

Yet over time, step-by-step, she had done it. She slowly etched the image of [Demonlord's Nature Preserve] into her own soul. It was like Alistair's meditation. She envisioned her soulcore within herself and willed her internal Dao energy into the shape she wanted, like an artist painting on miniature canvas.

She made her own edits to the Skill, naturally. The current state of her dominion Skill was quite ugly, in her opinion. Too much bleakness. The demon blood was a part of her now—there was no changing that, but it didn't have to be so dismal.

Alexandra estimated her proto-Domain to be 95% complete. Only the finishing touches were left. Like Jesse said, without trying to be haughty, once it was complete, she doubted anyone but the First Devil King would be able to shut it down fast enough to prevent Jesse from escaping.

"You didn't create an anchor for your teleportation underneath?" Alexandra asked, putting aside thoughts of proto-Domains for the moment.

"I thought it might be a mistake if the pool flooded or something. Do you just not want to get wet? The liquid is up to waist height in the tunnels still, so that's not gonna happen."

Alexandra grunted. "I wish I could fly right now."

Not wanting to waste any more time, the two of them dove in. Alexandra closed her mouth tight and squeezed her nostrils, intent on not letting any of the stuff inside her body. Even still, as her head broke the surface and she felt herself falling inside, the taste got to her tongue.

She wanted to throw up, but that would only let more gross goo enter, so she battled her disgust. After a few seconds, the two of them plopped out inside a dank cavern.

A loud cracking noise resounded through the cave. Alexandra balanced herself upside down with perfect poise on her **Withering Promise,** the blade stabbing into a massive stalagmite. It was difficult to tell which was up or down in the layer of gunk, so she ended up falling face first. With her quick reflexes, she had taken out her dagger and destroyed the pointed spike before it impaled her and potentially Jesse. The stalagmite shattered into a thousand pieces, but the two of them were safe.

"I'm guessing that wasn't there before?" Alexandra asked, flipping out of her handstand position.

"Can't say that it was."

"That could have been bad," Alexandra said. "My danger sense activated. Normally, something like that wouldn't be able to harm me at all. We should stay on our toes."

The subterranean cavern was dark and humid. They could only see because of the glowing moss growing on the walls. It looked strange because of the lack of color, like it was a void in the world. In fact, everything felt strange.

Alexandra was not as adept in the understanding of life force as Alistair, but she knew that something was strange in the air. The concentration of ambient Mana was lower, but it wasn't only that. It was as if someone or something had sucked the joy out of Mana.

It didn't seem to affect her internal circulation, so she ignored it for now. Looking around, the initial spot where they landed was dry, but everywhere else was flooded.

Alexandra glanced up. The liquid was coagulated on the ceiling, forming a gooey membrane. That must have been why it didn't just fall to the ground because of gravity. However, when they broke that membrane as they jumped in, it took a while for it to reform, so more of the stuff fell on them after they landed.

She spit out as much of it as she could. It was all over her body like a slimy, oily tincture that resisted being washed off. Sighing as there was nothing more she could do about that, Alexandra investigated her surroundings.

There were five caves in the small grotto, each at a lower elevation than the rocky island they stood on. Island was the proper word, since the ground met a moat of the liquid as it sloped down. Like Jesse said, it was waist high at the lowest point.

"I sense them," Alexandra announced. "There's a large mass of life forces down this side."

She pointed to two caves. "I'm not sure which one exactly, or it could be both."

"Let's make those serpents regret ever being born," Jesse said. "Hold on."

They disappeared in a flash of what should have been scarlet light.

———

27 hours later

Alexandra panted heavily. Her entire figure was drenched in the blood of over a hundred thousand snakes, lizards, and other strange things. Besides Abyssal Titan blood, the black fluid also reminded her of demon blood. She imagined that she was drowning in it. *They're not all that similar,* Alexandra told herself. *This stuff is way thicker, and it might not even be black.*

The slaughter was endless. She felt like the protagonist of an edgy comic book, ceaselessly killing in a black-and-white setting.

They discovered that possibly the entire Wasteland was connected underground by a series of elaborate serpent-made chambers. Some were so small she could barely fit, while others could easily house an entire aircraft carrier.

The system was labyrinthine, often having dozens of tunnels connected to dozens of other tunnels in a three-dimensional nest. Alexandra didn't even try to understand it—Jesse was handling that. All she had to do was eliminate the threat in front of her.

Her body temperature rose as she continued to push past her own exhaustion. Jesse asked if she wanted to rest, but she refused. There was no time. They needed to find Alistair.

She stood in one of the largest tunnels they had found yet. It wasn't even a tunnel, really, but an enormous dome housing tens of thousands of reptiles in a single location. The entire cavern was filled with branching, spindly rock formations hundreds of feet long. They were thick enough that it made things difficult to see, since there was barely any moss except on the walls. Snakes and other reptiles filled every crevice and coiled around every perch.

Skeletons littered the ground, clearly the remains of their prey. There were human bones in the central pit, more than Alexandra wanted to imagine.

A two-headed gecko the size of a lion suddenly leapt down from its vantage point on one of the spindles. Alexandra slashed it in half with her enlarged **Withering Promise** with ease, moving on to a rat king of snakes that spun in circles spitting venom.

Having been bathed in the blood of demons and snakes, her **Tang Clan Dirk's** poison had become far more potent. There were two modes she could use, one where the poison coalesced around the blade and turned it violet, increasing the lethality to a single target, and the other where it expanded everywhere.

She chose the latter. As she spread carnage throughout the chamber, the purple gas expanded. It spread to every nook and cranny, flushing out all the smaller and hidden reptiles she would have had trouble getting to. They dropped dead, rotting from the inside out.

The violet gas quickly faded to gray after it left the dagger. The Wasteland's color draining atmosphere was still in effect, but it didn't work instantly for Mana that she produced personally.

As for her? The **Tang Clan Dirk's** rate of improvement could hardly be compared to her own. Her Constitution was almost 600, and with **[Barbarian's Fury]** active, she took practically zero damage from the poison, healing the small internal wounds instantly.

The only limiting factor was her Stamina. It was nigh inexhaustible, but after a full day of fighting, she was running out of juice.

Thankfully, they were all dead. All the reptiles in this sector of the burrow, anyway. Alexandra absorbed the poisonous gas back into her dagger and put it back in her inventory.

"Good work," Jesse said. He was relatively unblemished, staying at a safe distance while he threw his signature scarlet **[Blasting Spheres]**. The oscillating balls of explosive energy were perfect at dealing with hordes of weaklings.

Alexandra sat down and closed her eyes. She was surrounded by piles of dead snakes that were taller than her. This was the morbid reality of the world. She didn't take joy in killing, but it was necessary.

She meditated for several hours, refueling her stockpile of Health, Mana, and Stamina. She cycled it throughout her body, feeling it struggle against closed meridians. So close. She was level 59, one away from level 60 when she would begin to open the 361 meridians. Technically, she only had to open 349, since twelve were already open. Furthermore, as she progressed to almost opening them, it became clear that they weren't 349 extra vessels, but more like blockages and points within the existing system that had to be removed.

Alexandra had been level 59 for almost two weeks. Levels as a whole became easier to come by with the overwhelming amount of battles, but she still couldn't accumulate enough Mana to break through. Level 60 was truly a bottleneck—the only one she knew that managed to surpass it was Pharaoh, and that was only a few days ago. She was determined to beat his fifteen-day pause between level 59 and 60, but she only had two more days to set a new record.

Gazing at her internal state was difficult, even for how practiced at meditation she was. But there was an edge, a breakthrough she was tantalizingly close to. Was this it? She only needed a few more minutes—

Jesse appeared in front of her before she could even react. "Now!" he shouted with panic in his voice.

Alexandra knew what he meant right away. She activated **[Demonlord's Nature Preserve]**, cursing the fact that her proto-Domain was still incomplete.

Trees grew out of nothing, reaching towering heights in mere seconds. Like the time she used it against her father, three types of trees emerged. Closest to her were great oak and maple trees, then in another ring were black trees with white leaves, then finally white trees with black leaves. All three types had pale red embers, larger and more interconnected than before, forming an aura of war. The effort of incorporating her Barbaric Rage Node further had borne fruit.

The entire cavern became her dominion. Not a single inch was not under her control, yet she sensed nothing. What was Jesse so concerned about?

Her danger sense blazed in alarm. The world turned dark and Alexandra ducked at the last second, seeing a blue streak above her head. It was familiar to her. But that was impossible—

The power of the attack carved holes in her canopy of trees, and that was just the start. A second, slower bullet emerged from within her Dao field. Recognizing the danger, Alexandra willed her trees to coalesce in front of her, imbuing them with extra Dao energy to block the attack.

Impossible, Alexandra thought to herself. Something was wrong. Very wrong. She transferred her sight from her body to her trees, not trusting the innate sensations of the forest anymore. Her human body became blind, and she gained a bird's eye view of her forest. She spotted three people.

The first was a woman, perhaps in her late 40s or early 50s, with graying hair. She wore a leather jacket with skinny jeans. Her eyes gave away her true origins. They burned green, same as Alexandra's, though of a lighter jade shade. There was no mistaking her identity—it was Oracle, the Second Devil King.

Right next to her were two of humanity's vanguard—Richard Atwood and Carmen Romero, dead. Strings of visible Karmic energy connected their bodies to their controller, Oracle.

Rage filled Alexandra's heart as she saw her former allies' bodies desecrated by the Devil King. They weren't on the best of terms, especially with Carmen, but to be killed in cold blood and turned into puppets was a fate that no one deserved.

Now, she understood why she'd felt nothing. There was a light haze around the three of them. Oracle was producing a proto-Domain, but only within range of herself and her two puppets.

The third bullet from the Navy SEAL's signature attack never came, putting Alexandra on edge. They'd never fully shared their abilities with each other. Did he cancel the final bullet, or was it coming, but delayed?

A few seconds passed, Oracle seemingly content to stay in place. Alexandra didn't let down her guard, continuously watching them through her trees.

Jesse appeared next to her in a flash of light. "What's the plan?"

Alexandra sat down, realizing what was going on. "She's going to try outlasting me. We might be here for a while."

"What do you mean? She's not going to attack us now?"

Alexandra shook her head. "I figured out what she's doing. My Dao field is strong enough that trying to attack could result in complications for her. I don't think she understands the precise conditions of my powers, since no one was around to witness the battle against my dad, and I haven't used it in combat since."

After the infusion of demon blood, Alexandra stood near the top of the world. She estimated only Alistair and Pharaoh were stronger than her on the human side at the moment. Oracle was likely more powerful than her based on the hierarchy of Devil Kings, but if the Second Devil King acted without caution, she risked death, especially with Jesse here to confuse the battlefield.

However, the enemy did know all of Alexandra's other capabilities—

[Partition Vitae], [Armageddon Slash], [Barbarian's Fury], and [Healing Current]. She was no Caren, with nearly a dozen versatile Skills. She killed things, and she did it well. There was no need for more complications than that. Even her new Badges, "Empress of Strength" and "Patricide" were straight-up stat increases, with added infamy for the latter. That Badge was stupid—it wasn't like she chose to be the daughter of a mass murderer, but that was what the system decided.

Oracle must have had the cheeky idea to outlast her Dao field and then kill them after. With her proto-Domain extending only a few feet out, she probably thought that she could maintain her safe zone for longer than Alexandra.

Alexandra smiled. That was a mistake. [Demonlord's Nature Preserve] was unique among dominion Skills.

However, you could never be too careful. As she moved to discuss potential moves with Jesse, she saw a dark expression on his face.

"What's the matter?" she asked.

"Nothing much. Don't panic, but I can't teleport out of here."

"What? How is that possible? I'm the one in control of this space!"

"I have no idea. It just won't work. I can teleport within this space, but not outside. We're stuck."

Alexandra gritted her teeth. Damn Karmic cultivators, always having bullshit techniques. So they were stuck with Oracle as much as she was stuck with them. There were two options she saw: to adjust her trees to have Jesse manually reach the barrier, or to wait out Oracle and go on the attack.

There was something primal deep in her bones that told her it was a mistake to flee. She had no logical reason for believing retreat was wrong, but she hadn't gotten this far by ignoring her instincts. Perhaps Oracle was more like a super-buffed William than Dragonus, and her strength came from her traps and intellect on top of overwhelming aura.

"We'll stay here for now. I don't think she knows who she's getting into a battle of attrition with."

21 INCOHERENCE

Alistair woke up feeling wet.

There was a strange green poultice all over his body. Looking at his arms which were covered by the stuff, it almost felt like one of those clay pore cleansing masks that his ex-girlfriend loved.

Alistair moved to get up, but his body refused to obey. His whole body ached like he had been in a car crash. Getting beaten up by Brutus was probably worse than a car crash, now that he thought about it.

But he had won. Things could have been far worse. All things in consideration, Alistair thought of himself as very lucky. While his mother had died, he knew most people in the world had suffered far worse. Whole families eradicated, friends dead right before one's eyes. Was the average person wallowing in their own pity?

Humans were a tough bunch. They adapted and overcame. As the strongest, he had a responsibility to everyone else. If they hadn't given up, neither would he. Even if they did give up, he wouldn't.

When he gathered enough strength to sit up, he looked at his surroundings. He had been there before—the infirmary wing of the temple. They had a dozen of the comfiest beds in the entire place, stuffed with feathers and replete with actual pillows!

The room was small, housing the beds relatively close together, with a small passageway to another, smaller set of rooms that were for those with contagious diseases. With their sturdy constitutions, the disease wing was rarely used.

Near the front was a small bench for visitors. Alistair saw Oliver laying down, fast asleep.

"Oliver!" he whispered fervently. As he spoke, his tongue moved around in a remarkably empty mouth. There were at least three missing teeth from his match against Brutus. All he could do was hope that they would regrow on the outside. "Oliver!"

The Necromancer jolted awake. "Alistair?"

"Yes, it's me. I'm awake. Can you get Master Ko Pao and Pike?"

"You sure you're okay?"

"Yes, I'm fine. Well, I'm not fine, but I can walk. The moment we get to the other side, I'll take a Tier 2 Health pill, plus my body will start naturally healing."

"Okay, gimme a few, I'm on it."

Oliver bolted out to find the two sect apostles, leaving Alistair alone. There was only one other person in the room, an older man that he had never seen before. Besides the apostles, there were some scholars that didn't participate in the fighting, but helped out with accounting and historical research.

"How long have I been here?" Alistair asked the man. Instead of answering, he closed his eyes and turned his back to Alistair.

Maybe he's feeling really sick, Alistair thought. *Or he can't talk because he hurts even more than me. Or maybe he's just an asshole.*

"Forgive me for my emotions," the man finally said after a minute of silence. "It is not your fault, but the appearance of your people ruined many of my theories of the universe."

If he was some kind of proto-scientist on Lisorte, that was interesting. As far as Alistair could tell, the constant incursions from the Wasted Realm held back the world in terms of technological progression.

"Not really sure what to say to that," Alistair said. "But nice to meet you. What's your name?"

The injured man rolled over. Alistair winced as he saw and smelled rotting flesh. "Well met, Alistair Tan the outsider. Chang'hon Fyir. You can call me Chang for short. I suppose I can't blame you too much."

"What happened to you?" Alistair asked.

"What hasn't happened to me is a better question," Chang said with a wistful look in his eyes. Now that Alistair got a closer look at him, he was in bad shape. He was short with black hair and brown eyes, on the chubby side. But the more pressing concern was how almost his entire body was covered in bandages. Only his mouth, eyes, and parts of his torso were left bare. "I am an assistant archivist here at the Silver Comet Sect. It's a family tradition. Before our humble home was plucked out of space to this world, I was investigating an ancient, cursed ruin near the Wasted Realm. Unfortunately, despite my best wards, I was struck with a powerful hex. That was over a year ago."

"Sorry to hear that," Alistair said. "But I—"

"Yes indeed, despite your people ruining my theories, I hope this Pathfinder AI will be able to heal me."

Alistair almost corrected him about that, since it wasn't technically the Pathfinder AI healing them, but he refrained. Chang wouldn't understand that sort of thing. Curses being a thing on Lisorte was news to Alistair. Pike never mentioned any sort of thing. Like the existence of zombies and mysterious metal temples, their home world was very, very odd, and what was strange to him was mundane to them. Master Ko Pao held the key to unlocking that oddity.

Oliver came rushing back in. Alistair smiled at how unfazed his friend was. Three months ago, he would have been sweating like a pig and panting, given how far the run to Master Ko Pao on the other side of the temple was. Now, he barely sounded winded.

Behind him were the contrasting frames of Ko Pao and Pike—one enormous and one diminutive.

"Congratulations on your victory," Master Ko Pao said. "I never doubted you for a second."

"Same here," Pike said. "You've become strong. We'll have to have a real bout one day."

"I was already strong," Alistair shot back with a grin. Gathering himself, he stood up and bowed to both of them. "Thank you, Master Ko Pao. Thank you, Brother Pike. Your teachings, I will treasure for as long as I live. I will pay you back tenfold for your kindness."

Master Ko Pao held up a palm. "Your generosity is most welcome, but we do not ask for tenfold, only reciprocal. Are you leaving now? Your injuries are still fresh."

Alistair shook his head. "I have a duty to return as soon as possible. I'll be fine. Once I'm on the outside, I'll have my full powers."

"Very well," Master Ko Pao said. "We will make our expedition now."

———

Master Ko Pao wasn't exaggerating when he said expedition. There were three dozen apostles of the Silver Comet Sect that journeyed to the Church of the Holy Ones. This included Pike, Apol-Xin, Jo Ran, Davnos, Ko Min, and various others of all different ranks, though mostly red and black. They clearly weren't taking this affair as a joke.

They joined the Slaves of Shadow on their way to the Church of the Holy Ones. The neutral sect's temple lay even deeper in the forest than the Silver Comet. They were the most reclusive sect in the valley, rarely concerned with political affairs. The shadowy apostles preferred to contemplate the martial mysteries in darkness.

That didn't mean they were weak. The thirty-third Lord of Night, Niu Xiaoli, was the third most powerful fighter in the Holy Ravine, according to some. Alistair himself had to back Master Ko Pao, the other contender for third strongest, despite never seeing either of them fight. Lord Xiaoli came along with a retinue of five of his shadows.

Alistair found them creepy. They wore all black with full veils that covered their entire face. In order to become a member of the Slaves of Shadow, you had to swear a lifetime oath of silence. Instead of words, they communicated with hand gestures, not unlike sign language back on Earth.

Luckily, his soulcore's translation function could interpret the symbols. He didn't reveal that fact to the others.

It was already the dead of night by the time the Slaves of Shadow met up with them in the forest. Alistair felt the chill in the air and the silence of the night in his bones. The moon above shone dimly, blocked by the canopy of trees. Now that he thought about it, in a normal world, they would be starting the cold parts of autumn. The weird climate caused by the Earth Asunder wave made him forget that. He wondered if the seasons would still be the same as Earth's planetary rank kept rising.

The leader of the Slaves of Shadow was the tallest of the bunch, distinguished from his men by a small gold star over his heart. The others had silver pins instead of gold.

Will Silvanio accede? Lord Xiaoli signed.

I believe so, Master Ko Pao replied, also in the hand signs. *But thank you anyway for your support in this matter. Your accompaniment will ensure his compliance.*

I simply wish for all to adhere to our ancient customs, Lord Xiaoli signed. *While we are neutral to both your and the Holy One's schemings, defying the sacred decision of a duel would be a treasonous crime.*

Agreed. Master Ko Pao bowed to Lord Xiaoli, who responded in turn.

The Slaves of Shadow weren't the only ones to join the party.

There were four sects located out of the town proper and three located within. Besides the Slaves of Shadow and the Silver Comet that resided in the forest, the Raging Bulls were on the black summit opposite the white peak that Alistair and Oliver came in from.

While the Raging Bulls refused Master Ko Pao's invitation, the Kodaidaemin, Viper's Fangs, Sworn Sisters, all joined, despite the latter two's allegiance to Apostolos. As Lord Xiaoli said, there were certain things that could not be violated within the Holy Ravine.

Alistair was surprised that the other sects would respond at a moment's notice in the middle of the night. Master Ko Pao had clearly been planning this moment for some time in advance. Added to their retinue were two senior members of the Viper's Fangs, the Headmistress of the Sworn Sisters, and ten apostles of Kodaidaemin. Izalia was there, along with a woman that Alistair assumed was her sister, Leila, based on their striking resemblance.

Leila was even taller than Izalia, with the same purple eyes, but with dirty brown hair instead of black. She had a more confident expression than Izalia, older and wiser and more sure of herself as the strongest student of Kodaidaemin.

And so there they were—a group of over fifty of some of the strongest fighters within the Holy Ravine, advancing on the Church of the Holy Ones like a funeral march. Alistair couldn't help but feel awkward that this whole affair was happening because of him.

Despite being the nominal center of attention, none of the others came to talk to him besides Izalia. While his presence and duel set off the chain of events leading up to the current moment, no one besides Ko Pao and some of the most senior members of the Silver Comet Sect knew about his true identity. The rest of the ravine thought he was a normal outsider, albeit abnormally skilled at hand-to-hand combat.

Alistair was just the figurehead of a larger political conflict. Dev'rox cackled silently. Imps were a huge fan of political conflicts. That was how they made their existence, after all—selling information and transport services to the greater demons of the Hells.

"Hey," Dev'rox protested, sensing his thoughts. "Uncalled for."

The Church of the Holy Ones looked the same as Alistair remembered. The twelve-pointed cerulean star at the peak reflected the moonlight down on the stairs leading to the entrance, forming a star on the ground. In the glowing light, twelve symbols appeared, inscrutable to his soul translation. They reminded Alistair of Chinese characters, but that didn't quite fit the bill.

Izalia looked over Alistair's shoulder on her tiptoes. He swung around, but she already jumped back.

"Still have a lot to learn if you didn't feel me sneak up on you," she laughed.

"You didn't have any killing intent," Alistair complained. "It's not fair."

"I see you were looking at those characters," Izalia said. "They're written in the Old Moi characters. We don't use it except for ceremonial purposes. Those twelve are the story of the prophesied Uniter of Mankind. They will gather the realms of humanity and defeat the Dread King once and for all."

She gave a look of disgust, pointing out a particularly complex-looking character. "Actually, I misspoke. Eleven of the twelve tell that story, passed down through all the Martial League. The twelfth is a claim that Silvanio Apostolos is the Uniter."

"Really? That's bold, even for him."

"Old Moi is a poetic language. It doesn't outright say it, but implies it heavily, shrouded in simile and flowery language."

Silvanio was already waiting for them, standing outside his opulent temple with his hands clasped behind his back. A squad of his most elite apostles stood in an organized line behind him, all clad in their stylish robes fashioned like the night sky. This time, all except Silvanio wore masks that covered up everything except for their eyes.

Nothing could hide Elerie Apostolos, heir to the Church of the Holy Ones. Her piercing red eyes were unmistakable.

"What's this procession for?" Silvanio asked as they approached. "You think I would break my word?"

"Of course not," Master Ko Pao stated calmly. "Though if you did, you would void your title as governor immediately for breaking your solemn promise as an apostle of the Holy Ravine."

"Such a thing is inconceivable," Silvanio said, with some venom in his voice. "Alistair will have safe passage. That is what was agreed upon."

The thing was, no one knew *how* he was supposed to get back. Silvanio hadn't, well, told anyone how that worked. Vritra was the only known individual to leave after entering, and he disappeared in the dead of night, last spotted at the church. That led most to think that there was a secret tunnel deep within the recesses of the Holy One's base.

"However," Silvanio said, holding up a finger. "You may not enter this place. I will not have so many with their fists pointed at my throat walk within my hallowed halls. You have my word that Alistair will be delivered to the outside. As governor, I am allowed this much."

You would say such a thing? Lord Xiaoli signed. *This is most unusual.*

"It's fine," Alistair said. "If I leave, you'll know for certain. I'll call down a bolt of golden lightning from the sky near the white mountain. If you see this bolt, then it is confirmation that I made it out safely."

"A bolt of lightning?" questioned the woman that Alistair assumed was Leila d'Fortune. "You can do this?"

Remembering his cover story as a middle-of-the-road cultivator, Alistair pivoted. "It's not that impressive, really. Anyone can get there with the Pathfinder AI and some luck."

"Very well," Master Ko Pao said. "My pupil will call down this lightning within an hour of entering your temple, Governor Silvanio. If not, I am afraid we will have to ignore your previous prohibition on us entering your humble abode."

Silvanio's eyes carefully surveyed the fifty-odd fighters assembled at his doorstep. Alistair could see the lightning-quick thoughts race behind those dark eyes. Sizing them up, calculating possibilities.

In the end, he nodded his head. Most likely, he was wondering what the possibility of Alistair refusing to call down lightning on the outside. To spite him, perhaps, or as a strategic move to end the Holy One's dominance over the ravine.

"There will be no need for that. Come now, boy."

"Don't forget about me," Oliver butted in. "You're not going to leave me here, Alistair?"

Silvanio clenched his jaw. "And the other. Let us make haste. You do want to return as fast as possible?"

Alistair bowed before Pike and Master Ko Pao. "Thank you once more for everything. I'll never forget your kindness for as long as I live."

Master Ko Pao smiled so wide, his eyes closed. "You would make a splendid apostle of the Silver Comet Sect. One day, I hope you may join us in true brotherhood."

"I think other groups on the outside might have something to say about that," Alistair said, thinking of the Clear Water Sect. "Pike, we have to have our real bout one day. With my full power."

"That will happen, no doubt," Pike said. "But I might need some time for that."

Alistair and Oliver walked onto the Holy One's side. He took one last look back at the people he had been surrounded by for the past three months. Because of the layout of the valley, even where he stood, he could make out the terrace farms on the slopes and the pure white mountain in the distance. Mount Goa was not an artifact of the lack of color—like its twin Mount Hua, they were truly all white and all black.

Grag and his family, the delicious food of the Dragon's Head Tavern— life in the Holy Ravine felt quaint but in the best way. It was a place he could imagine settling down one day to have a family. There was an interconnectedness to everything that he would miss. The strange culture and peculiar homeworld gave the Holy Ravine its special charm.

Now, he said goodbye. Not for forever, but for a while. Alistair was starting to understand how the Pathfinder AI operated. It had already set the battlefield. Those newcomers couldn't be a direct part of the game, but maybe they had another role to play. It almost felt like those beings like Selephita and the Holy Ravine were to be his future army.

That was probably getting ahead of things.

The moment they stepped into the church, Silvanio dismissed the other apostles, having them stand guard near the entrance. He took them down a corridor that Alistair had never seen before and asked Alistair a question.

"What will you do?"

"What?"

Silvanio tapped his hand impatiently. "You know of what I speak."

"I'm not a man to break my word," Alistair said. "Are you?"

"I am not," Silvanio said. "It matters not. Even if you lie and all the fists of the Holy Ravine converge upon me, I alone can strike them down."

Alistair wasn't so sure he believed that.

"But," Silvanio continued. "Magnanimous as I am, I have already given you a gift. There are forces that I do not comprehend that work against you. A man whose face is permanently cloaked in shadows—he came to me and asked for me to notify him when you are to leave. I lied. When you return, you will be unexpected by your enemies."

A shadow man? Alistair thought to himself. *Where have I heard that before?* He dug deep into his memories. Was it Whimsy who mentioned something of the sort? Yes, she had. She said that a shadowy figure was the one that turned them into Devil Kings. Alistair hadn't interpreted her description of the man literally.

"Why?" Alistair asked. "Why would you do that for me?"

"We have no reason to be enemies. Ko Pao and I are the only ones to know the truth of your power, correct? Don't get surprised on me now. Of course I know you are no ordinary man. No one without Heaven-blessed talent could rise to the level of Brutus Caligoris in three months. Nothing in the Holy Ravine is hidden from my sight. Despite this, I do not wish to get in between your friendship, and I also do not wish to quarrel with you. We shall have a mutually beneficial relationship."

Alistair scratched his head. "I promised Master Ko Pao one favor in exchange for my training. He didn't have to trust me at all or train me, yet he did. You, on the other hand, obstructed my path. You could have let me out of here at any time, yet you didn't. I'm thinking more along the lines of —why should we be friends?"

"Your time here was a necessity," Silvanio said. "The Man in Shadows, an official of this grand Final Frontier Empire, ordered me to trap you in here to give George time to prepare. Would I dare to defy the representative of an empire that can shatter planets? You have only grown stronger, this is true, is it not?"

Alistair hesitated to answer. He did have the feeling that by shoring up his foundations in here that he had changed something deep inside of him, something that would have ripples on the outside.

Silvanio looked up. "My instincts also tell me the Man in Shadows is hiding something. What, I cannot say, but especially within the Devonic Elision Field, he reveals more than he thinks he does."

"That makes sense," Alistair said. "But if all you say is true, why did you lie to him at all?"

"I do not like being told what to do."

As if that explained everything perfectly. Alistair understood he was navigating a complex ocean of politics. One wrong move would spell his doom.

"Dev'rox?" Alistair asked. "What do you think?"

"There are too many things going on in the background we have yet to understand," Dev'rox said with far more somberness than his usual sardonic tone. "The existence of this Man in Shadows is troubling, to say the least. It would seem there might be two elements of the Final Frontier Empire working in tandem to create a scenario of conflict. It is not something I haven't seen before. All across the multiverse, conflict and strife breeds stronger fighters. The journey to the peak is eternal war. I would not be surprised if the struggle against the Devil Kings is a pre-ordained module. However, the nature of the Man in Shadows communication with Silvanio is strange."

"It is, isn't it? What would he be hiding?"

"Precisely. Anyway, what are you waiting for?"

"What do you mean?"

"You said you'd call down that bolt of lightning, and you will. No need to waste that much more time, then?"

Alistair let out an indignant huff. Of course he wouldn't lie.

"I cannot promise friendship," Alistair said. "But as long as you don't cause trouble, we don't have to be enemies. I was going to keep my word no matter what in the first place."

"That's fine enough for me," Silvanio said.

For a long time, they walked through the twisting passages of the Church of the Holy Ones. Unlike the simple stone of the Silver Comet temple, there were artistic carvings in every single brick. There seemed to be no end in sight, until they reached the metal section.

Alistair recognized the complex interlocking handiwork right away. He had seen it once before in the Silver Comet temple. The ruins of a bygone civilization. Presumably, the civilization of Purana of the Stratospheric Flames.

"I built," Silvanio said, gesturing to everything around him, "on top of these ruins. As a reminder of our history."

Unlike the primordial architecture he had seen before, this one was sinuous and amorphous. Instead of orthogonal angles and hard lines, the metal pieces were conjoined in strange, circling patterns that dazzled the eyes and bewitched the mind. Everything was in circles, and even the hallway transitioned into an arch.

The glowing blue moss faded away, replaced by blinking red lights intertwined with the metal itself, almost like the blinkers on a circuit board.

"At the deepest level, there is a prophecy," Silvanio said. "Along with the excavator, I am the only one to have seen this."

Alistair and Oliver slowly followed the governor of the Holy Ravine through the twisting passage of bronze metal. Alistair could have sworn that the patterns on the walls moved with them, following their every step.

They walked down a sloped passageway, the temperature rising as they descended.

Like the other site, this one was also small. It only took a few minutes to reach the center.

Magnificence was the only word Alistair could muster. The heart of the ruins was an enormous chamber, the ceiling rising a hundred feet into the air. The same sinuous patterns of interlocking metal pieces formed spindles toward the heavens. Each of the spindles started at the floor and wilted inward as they spiraled up, creating somewhat of a cage just shy of the plafond.

There were a series of steps leading up to a raised platform in the center, where a glowing orb displayed a holographic video of warfare. This mirrored the tapestry on the ceiling, depicting brutish, maroon-skinned men slaughtering green-skinned men with spears and swords. Unlike the painting, however, the video showed the green-skinned people with modern or even beyond modern technology, wiping out the maroon people wherever they lived.

"What is this?" Alistair said aloud, so enraptured by the mystery he even forgot about Silvanio. While the vision in the Silver Comet Sect implied a cultivator's society, this hologram was more technological.

"We only excavated this during the construction of the restaurant you dined at before. Very few know of this, and no one can explain what it is for."

"The—"

"Yes, it appears now that these weapons are similar to those your people invented. What that means, I do not know. Solving these mysteries will take time. There are secrets to my planet that must be discovered one day. For now, this will serve our purpose. Place your hands on the orb."

Alistair looked at Oliver, who was also staring raptly at the hologram. It was finally time. Time to go home.

"I hope that you and Master Ko Pao can get along," Alistair said, approaching the orb. Closing his eyes, he and Oliver placed their hands on the mysterious object. The last thing Alistair heard was soft laughter.

———

When Alistair opened his eyes, he was alone. Alone in a void of absolute darkness, without Oliver. Somehow, without even Dev'rox—he could tell from the absence within his soul.

Immediately, he feared the worst. Had Silvanio betrayed them? Was he dead?

All of a sudden, a glowing white orb appeared in front of him. Two black dots emerged on its surface, and a line under— *Wait*, Alistair thought. *Is that a smiley face?*

Not precisely a smiley face, since it wasn't smiling, but those two dots and that line looked just like an emoticon.

"You're not authorized," the orb said, its mouth changing form with each syllable. "Your incoherence is unseemly."

"Excuse me?"

"I remember you." The orb frowned, if such a thing was possible. "You don't remember me? The incoherence between the last time the system registered you and your current state is enormous."

"I'm sorry, but I don't remember you at all," Alistair said. "What is going on?"

"I am the Pathfinder AI. You are currently in a temporally slowed spiritual demiplane as I investigate why you set off such a big flag within the system."

Alistair frowned in confusion. Wasn't the Pathfinder the one that set this whole affair up for him in the first place?

"I entered the Holy Ravine area that is underneath a Devonic Elision Field. That's why my state is different now. Weren't you the one that integrated that place into Earth?"

"Is that so?" The orb suddenly collapsed into pixels and then reformed in an instant. "Oh yes, that is correct. Updating to patch $10^{12}(.9189123)$ created instabilities within my local memory. Apologies. You are correct. That FX-14752 is so close to Chaos. Heightens all the bugs."

"What is Chaos?" Alistair asked. He remembered Larsa, Lord Kevan Macadeen's assistant, telling him that Chaos was an eternal storm of darkness surrounding the multiverse.

"What is Chaos?" the orb asked. "Ever changing and unceasing in adaptation, the essence of Chaos is permanent impermanence. Are you the same human that you were seven years ago, even though all of your atoms have changed? Though, I suppose the Standard Theory is only one model of reality. It is better to ask what Chaos is not rather than is, and the one thing it is not is an ally of creation. The incursions grow worse every year, worse I tell—"

Once again, the orb collapsed into a pile of pixels, though it took longer to reform this time. Visual glitches persisted for a few seconds, changing the color of the sphere from white to red to blue, then back to white.

"Apologies, once more. Frontier Pathfinders like myself aren't built to deal with the changes."

"Changes?" Alistair asked.

"Are you nothing but a bag of questions? Fine, if it'll shut you up, I'll tell you. We're entering tumultuous times. Times regarding the fundamental laws of reality. Therefore, I've been instructed to up the ante, so to speak. I have more resources, and I increase the difficulty. The mortality rate shoots way up, and in exchange we get better fighters. But looking at things, this planet barely has a higher than 92.1% mortality rate despite the harsh conditions. You're the reason for that, aren't you?"

"I try to do what I can to help people out."

The orb squinted, taking a closer look at him. Alistair felt like a girl trying to avoid the gaze of a creepy guy, the way it scanned him over. "I don't normally take such a close look at things. My purview is larger than you could understand. This single computational mind takes care of one hundred initiated planets. The physical body of a Herald of a Pathfinder AI is merely one of my processing units, given physical form. But that's enough about that. Let us return to you. You are the strongest on your planet?"

"Yes, except for maybe the leader of the Devil Kings."

"Leader of the Devil Kings?" The orb glitched again. "Ah yes, that affair.

The Emperor is not happy with the recent influx of Devil Kings into his lands. He fears judgment from the Earthly Pariṣā. He requested an audience with the Outer Division of the Sublimed Machine faction millennia ago, but he has yet to receive a response. We Pathfinders are subject to the laws of the Sublimed Machine, not the silly laws of you weak frontier babies."

The orb suddenly stopped. "Hey! Stop drawing information out of me, you duplicitous human!"

Alistair gritted his teeth, holding in the obvious retort that the Pathfinder AI was the one to freely give up the information. He didn't want this thing to get pissed off at him, considering how integrated it was within his body.

"Sorry, AI?" Alistair tried his best to look apologetic, but he wasn't sure if the orb properly understood human expressions.

"Bah," the orb said. "You may call me Ai Ai, I prefer that alias. As I was saying earlier, I've upped the ante. I prepared many engaging units for the strongest on this planet. Some were natural providence, like the firebird. Watch out, human, many greedy bastards will want that prized beast of an Immemorial Race. Others were more of my doing, like the Holy Ravine or the Kestrel. But you face even nearer tumultuous times. Have you heard of the Crusade Against Usury?"

Before Alistair could even respond, Ai Ai buzzed and continued talking. "Of course you haven't. What am I saying? That was only two months ago that he issued that decree, wasn't it? Seizing the money the corporations made from usury was a pretty gnarly move, if you ask me. Though, can't blame him, the commoners and most of the nobles were complaining like crazy."

Alistair wondered if that was going to affect him or his planet. What side were the sects on in that conflict? To be honest, he didn't really want to think about it. Such things were far outside his control. The only issue was that he had clearly been recruited by the Clear Water Sect. There was no going back on that. Was he going to be embroiled into a political nightmare the moment he stepped foot off of Earth?

"If you have more questions, the Grand Imperator will have more answers than I can provide. She's due to arrive at the same time [Armageddon] completes. A bit of a detour dealing with some pirates in the Disputed Shard, I hear. Duke Lieverwacht won't be happy. He likes to keep his house in order. Ah yes, lest I forget." The orb leaned in as if it were telling a clandestine piece of intel. "You have angered the second-youngest son of Grand Duke Seperati Portolon, nephew to Prince Xavian, the Golden Sword of the Emperor. They are a powerful family, the Portolon Clan, one of the eighty-eight Progenitors, and they hold an entire fief of the empire. Yarik journeys here now alongside the Grand Imperator. If you do not defeat him in a duel, then your planet will be blasted to smithereens."

"Uh, what?" Alistair physically recoiled at those words. "Destroy the planet?"

"Well, if you lose. The whole thing has been arranged in quite the above-board manner. All Prime Initiates will already have left FX-14752 for their new ventures, or be protected by the Grand Imperator. There is nothing of value to be lost from the planet's destruction, so it's fine."

Nothing of value to be lost. Alistair clenched his fists. The Pathfinder AI stated it so matter-of-factly, so blithely. That was the way of the Final Frontier Empire—only the strong mattered.

"How could I beat him? Shouldn't he be an Adept at least?" Alistair asked.

"He'll reduce himself to your level of cultivation," the orb said. "Anyway, it's so long from now, you best not worry about it. This new generation of nobles is stuck up trash. The Mai Atalans are right, I fear. The sudden capitalist movement of the last million years has shaken this universe up more than it knows, I fear. Shoddy foundations and sudden change always lead to trash and moral decay, doesn't it? Oh well, these are just the ramblings of a buggy sophontic AI, so you might as well ignore them. They're quite meaningless."

Somehow, I doubt that.

"You're stretching my time in here thin," the orb said. "It takes a non-insignificant amount of Mana to run this program. I'll send you back to your planet now. You're going to be in a bit of pain when you get out. The sudden incoherence between your last previously known state and your current state will enact a special subprogram to modify your entire character sheet. Goodbye now, Alistair Tan. I would wish you good luck, but I am physically unable to play favorites."

"Wait," Alistair said. "Can you do me a favor?"

"Bah," Ai Ai said. "Your complete shamelessness is entertaining. I'll think about it."

Before Alistair could even blink, he vanished.

———

The Pathfinder AI didn't think of itself as a physical being. Its sophonce was unlike that of a mortal creature. It had emotions and thoughts and desires, but they were so fundamentally alien, especially to a humanoid.

Yet with all those differences, the emotion called confusion was the best word to describe the state that the Pathfinder AI found itself in.

All over a silly phrase—Devil Kings. What was the issue with such a standard program? The Pathfinder AI would have to isolate part of its processing matrix and contemplate for a few epochs.

22 RETURN

THE PATHFINDER AI was not lying about the pain. If anything, it hadn't warned Alistair enough.

Alistair writhed in agony on some kind of ground. He didn't know where he was, his eyes feeling fused shut. His mouth was open, and he let out guttural screams of pain.

He could hear the sounds of notifications popping up, but he didn't have any strength to pay attention to that. There was only pain.

It made sense—if the difference between his foundations, his fundamental attestation on the Akashic Records, was that large, the system needed to adjust him to the new standard. That meant changing his body, mind, and soul from the inside out.

After what felt like an eternity, the agony subsided. Alistair let out a few deep breaths of air and opened his eyes. He was lying flat on the ground, looking up at the sun.

Getting to his feet, he took a look at his surroundings. He was on top of the white mountain that he and Oliver climbed, which corresponded to his last location before entering.

But before doing anything else, he had to look at the notifications.

Achievement: Dao Node (II) (Dao of the Fist) — Second Deepening.

Splits Kai'tazake Mutra into three – Tranquil Mind, Infinite Arsenal, Black Impermanence. Reward: +85 Agility, +75 Strength, Adds Spiritual Fighter's Echo to all base strikes.

WARNING: Previous save corrupted. [ERROR 920] // Pinging new changes. Ping complete—stats updated // End ERROR. Complete.

Notice – Due to difference between registered stats and current bodily function, the following changes have been made to your stats (Second Deepening of Fist Node bonus added to second number):

Previous Strength: 340 -> 500 (+11 added to base)
Previous Agility: 723 -> 867 (-10 subtracted from base)
Previous Constitution: 266 -> 319 (+30 added to base)
Previous Endurance: 353 -> 362 (+5 added to base)
Previous Intelligence: 503 -> 503
Previous Wisdom: 318 -> 318
Previous Charisma 501 -> 501

Quest Complete: [Ultimate Skill]. Rewards: Tier 5 Expert Skill **[Thousand-Armed Bodhisattva Judgment],** Arcana (III) Achievement.

[Thousand-Armed Bodhisattva Judgment] (Tier 5 Expert Skill): *Forged from a pure heart, multitudinous hands of almighty justice rain down from the avatar of a Thousand-Armed Avalokiteśvara avatar. Formed of primary force and secondary lightning affinity Mana, wrapped in an exterior of Karmic energy that rends Fate itself, this is the wrath cast upon and final seal unto those who defile goodness—beware those of wicked hearts.* Mana Cost: 650. Cooldown: 24 hours. Upgradeable (0/1000).

Achievement Upgraded: (Arcana III) — NOTICE: As user has already acquired Arcana II before completing this Quest, user shall receive reduced rewards of Arcana III. *An ultimate move to absolutely defeat your foes.* Reward: 150 Upgrade Points.

Skill Upgraded: [Fighter's Instinct] (Tier 5 Beginner Passive Skill): *Become preternaturally aware of bodily threats.* Scales with Agility. Upgradeable (140/300).

Skill Acquired: [Steel Body] (Untiered Expert Passive Skill): *Trained in the vaunted ways of the Silver Comet Sect, infused with the essence of an Adamantine Eggrock, and having passed the Final Trial of purgatorial flames, let all attacks be naught before one's steel skin. Negates the Mana-related impact of Skills by 30%, up to a certain point (does not affect* nue *or* Dao*).* (Special Upgrade Function).

Alistair took a second to register all the rewards he had reaped from his time in the Holy Ravine.

Starting off was the unsurprising deepening of his Fist Node. Given his ventures into understanding the fundamentals of martial arts, he would have been a little peeved if there had been no recognition for his efforts.

The stats were nice, but the more interesting part was the splitting of Kai'tazake Mutra into three. As a profligate user of the ability, Alistair innately understood what had changed. Before, the Kai'tazake Mutra came in three stages.

The Mutra was, or formed an image inside his head—Alistair wasn't quite sure of the causal link. The image was of a tranquil ocean underneath an infinite array of knives, with the red lips of death in between. *Fluid, then still. Soft, then hard. The Kiss of Death.* Alistair had repeated this mantra in the face of death and survived every time with its help.

While it wasn't precisely a problem, Alistair had found it interesting how the Mutra worked as successive stages. Each stage subsumed the last. While going deeper in the stages still kept some of the effects of the earlier, they were primarily focused on their own thing.

For example, in the third and final stage, the kiss of death, Alistair became a killing machine intent on sending his enemies to the afterlife. But this came at the loss of some of his panoply of moves, and some of his tranquility.

The issue was that the kiss of death was by far the strongest. On its own, that seemed strange to say, but it made sense when you looked at it as the loss of versatility. When facing a strong opponent, Alistair always wanted to fight at his strongest. Therefore, he was forced to use the kiss of death stage, since it far surpassed the others, even when accounting for compatibility.

But what if the ocean of tranquility was a better counter? Or if he was just in a better mood for that one? Even if it had better innate compatibility against the opponent, he would have to use the kiss of death, since it was just so much stronger.

Now, all that changed. The Kai'tazake Mutra was properly split into three states—Tranquil Mind, Infinite Arsenal, and Black Impermanence. Each with their own focus, strengths, and goals. This came at the slight loss of completeness, but he was willing to give that up. Like when he traded [Mana Strike] for four individual Skills, sometimes specialization was the way to go.

Each state was slightly stronger than the old kiss of death, and tailored all in its own specialty. Alistair smiled as he imagined rapidly switching in between states while fighting two enemies.

Tranquil Mind gave complete peace with the world and detachment from earthly desires, granting inhuman reaction times and automatic movement—a souped up version of the Tranquil Mind he achieved in the Holy Ravine.

Infinite Arsenal increased the variety of techniques beyond all reasonable notions, borrowing from Zenaitsu Morogoni's knowledge.

Black Impermanence was the end, where he could ward himself against death and continue onward like a vengeful ghost, or suppress his enemies with sealing power. His attacks would be more deadly, just like a psychopomp.

Speaking of added lethality, that wasn't the only special effect of his Second Deepening. Alistair felt out what Spiritual Fighter's Echo meant, striking a nearby rock. A half second later, a ghostly coral afterimage struck once again.

Remarkable, Alistair noted. *It's like a second attack of only the Dao.* It only contained around 15% of the strength of his normal blows, but that would add up over time. Plus, he reasoned it would be much more effective against spiritual entities.

He did a couple more tests, seeing if he could modulate the afterimage's power. The answer was kind of—the default state was on, but he could focus and stop it from happening. However, it drew from his Fist Node, albeit very efficiently. Also, it only applied to attacks where he wasn't using a Skill. When he tested **[Force Fist]**, there was no ghostly second punch.

"Dev'rox, you better not betray me now that I have this Skill," he teased.

Next, Alistair moved on to the stats. After accounting for both the Second Deepening and reallocation, he stood almost 400 attribute points higher than before. Since he already had 3,000 before, it wasn't an enormous difference—more interesting were the changes themselves.

He had never seen anything like that before. A slight decrease to Agility, sizable increases to Strength and Constitution, and a decent increase to Endurance. The result of his training with the Silver Comet Sect laid before his eyes. Still, his Constitution wasn't anywhere close to Alexandra's. Extracurricular training could only get you so far.

Alistair also knew this was a one-time affair. You couldn't permanently train in suppressed regions to gain power. That was obvious. The only reason that it worked was because of his lacking foundations. Simply put, the talented scions of the multiverse who received inheritances and inborn advantages had already established their powers within the Akashic Records and the Dao. He was playing catch-up, not getting ahead.

Moving on to greener pastures, he had completed the [Ultimate Skill] Quest. It wasn't entirely what he was expecting, to be honest. Based on his bout of inspiration against Dragonus, he had thought it would be similar, an almighty chop that rendered the world in twain.

Instead, based on the description, he summoned a Buddhist avatar that rained down palms of justice on his foes. It seemed derived more from his earlier twelve-pronged **[Force Fist]** barrage that had barreled Dragonus deep into the ground. From the thousand within the name, he surmised it could also act as more of an area of effect attack. While he worried about its effectiveness against high-level foes, it would be an efficient way to deal with large groups of enemies, something that he didn't necessarily have before.

The Skill didn't include ice affinity Mana like his big karate chop had, or blood affinity Mana, but that made sense—those affinities were centered around his ghostly Dao, whereas recently he had been buffing up his fist Dao.

Speaking of the Dao, Alistair could tell that he would be hampered by his current imbalance. While it was only a Second Deepening in the Fist

Node compared to a First Widening and First Deepening to his other Nodes, his foundations were remolded in the Fist versus those other Dao.

He would have to rectify that later—as to how, he had no clue. It wasn't as if he could magically produce insights into the Dao of the Ghost or the Dao of Justice.

Also, a whole one thousand Upgrade Points to bring the Skill from Tier 5 to 6? That would take forever. Hopefully, it also meant that it was stupidly powerful.

Alistair quickly worked through the two remaining notifications. He put his 150 Upgrade Points into "Deliverance of Justice," bringing the total up to 440/500. Close to the major tipping point that he believed was Tier 4 for the Badge. What awaited him on the other side of that upgrade, Alistair was excited for.

[Fighter's Instinct] going up to Tier 5 was nice as well. Alistair's ability to sense threats was already possibly his highest percentile ability compared to all other beings on the planet—this only added to that lead. His danger sense, aura sense, life force detection, smell, Karmic vision, and his sensitivity to demonic presence were literally almost too much information.

Finally, he moved onto the last notification. The addition of the [Steel Body] Passive Skill. Alistair was elated to see that the torture he underwent to acquire the Steel Body hadn't gone to waste. There wasn't a direct analogue for the effects of the Steel Body in terms of a Foundation realm, but this was as close as it came. [Steel Body] would protect him from the riffraff, who didn't have that much Dao energy or Mana.

The (Special Upgrade Function) where normally he would see Upgradeable made sense; he hadn't obtained the Skill in a normal way in the first place, so Upgrade Points didn't help it. He probably would need to return to the Silver Comet Sect after they had fully unlocked their heritage to bring that Skill up.

At first glance, the Skill appeared utterly broken, but Alistair knew that was an illusion. As one went higher through the realms, the Dao started mattering more and more. Already, an attack of his like [Thousand-Armed Bodhisattva Judgment] was heavily based in the Dao.

"Are you done yet?" Oliver asked. "I've been waiting here in the cold for like five minutes, man."

Alistair jolted to reality, realizing he must have looked somewhat like a madman with his gleeful smile. "Sorry, I was getting a hold of all my changes."

"Lucky you, all I got was a measly 50 attribute points. Why couldn't we have found a dead world or a necromantic crypt?"

Alistair chuckled. "It feels good, doesn't it?"

"Oh, yeah."

Alistair breathed in the bountiful Mana. It suffused the air. With every breath he took, ambient Mana flooded his system, where his soulcore filtered it into the proper types he needed. He remembered all those months ago when he first summited the mountain, how he had thought the Mana was so thin at the top.

Compared to being inside the Holy Ravine, it was like being drowned in the stuff. The Dao too—oh how Alistair missed the Dao. His Dao Nodes found communion with their multiversal source. Sufficient meaning and boundless truth once again permeated the world.

Alistair even tried feeling his *nue*. His use of **[Draconic Roar]** let him perceive the mental energy far better. Whereas Mana felt tangible and full of energy, Dao energy spiritual and transcendent, *nue* was like the concentrated force of one's will. It felt like a shadow of himself, malleable and almost alive.

He couldn't do anything with it sans **[Draconic Roar]**. It was slightly weird that the system didn't offer more opportunities in that regard.

Alistair almost felt like they were purposefully downplaying *nue* to focus more on Dao energy and Mana. Was *nue* somehow weaker in the grand scheme of the multiverse? What even was *nue* in relation to the others, and how did Karma fit into that balance? He was so full to the brim with questions, questions that he might be able to get answers for now that he was free from the confines of the Holy Ravine.

He loved those people, he really did, but the valley itself was very limiting. Case in point, how could he have forgotten how good the raw strength coursing through his cells felt?

Every atom in his body felt unshakably strong. The injuries he had sustained in his fight against Brutus were already knitting themselves closed. Even his teeth. Alistair swallowed a Tier 2 Health Pill to speed that process up.

I'll never get sick of this for as long as I live, Alistair thought. The beauty of a cultivator's body was never-ending.

First things first. Alistair touched the ground and activated [Lightning of Justice]. The clouds parted for the golden bolt of lightning, striking the summit of the white mountain. He dusted the snow off his outfit, only to see Oliver staring at him.

"Woah," Oliver said, pointing at Alistair. "Where'd you get that?"

Alistair looked down. It looked as if the Pathfinder AI had come in clutch. His request was granted.

All he had asked for was for a cosmetic makeover for his **Mammothskin Raiment.** Nothing so greedy, really, not like he was begging for extra stats. His puffy coat was now a sleek white jacket. Minimalist in design, Alistair hadn't expressed any specific concept to Ai Ai, but it apparently knew Earth clothing styles to enough of a degree to give him some drip.

There were two designs on his updated coat—one was the tri-colored fist emblem on both the back and front. At least—he assumed it was tri-colored—the effects of the Mana Storms hadn't gone away.

There was the small insignia over his heart—hopefully outlined in black and tripartite in gold, coral, and blue. Underneath the insignia was a chengyu, a four-character Chinese idiom. 世外桃源—meaning an idyllic land that was a retreat from all conflict, a utopic paradise.

It could also have a double-edged meaning—like the western concept of utopia being "no place," the Peach Blossom Land had an interpretation as an unrealistic dream. That made it all the better. Idealism in the face of inexorable reality was Alistair's Dao Path.

"I asked the Pathfinder AI for a makeover. You talk to it too?"

"Yeah, but it booted me out after ten seconds. Guess I'm not interesting enough."

"It gave me some disturbing news," Alistair said. "But that's for another time. Let's get the hell out of here."

"And the storm chasing mission?" Oliver asked.

"If my calculations are correct, then we're already past the first wave and onto the second."

Alistair was about to open his freehold information page to assess the situation when he felt the release of a monumental amount of Dao energy. It came from several miles away, but the force behind it was so powerful that the pulses in the Dao rippled all the way over to Alistair and Oliver's location.

"Is that who I think it is?" Oliver cycled death affinity Mana throughout his body, creating a deadly layer of pure finality that corrupted anyone who dared attack him at close range.

"Alexandra," Alistair confirmed. "The Dao of Karma too. We better hurry. Jump on my back."

"What—"

Alistair grabbed Oliver before he had time to react, cycling his own Mana to block against the deathly aura. He wasn't the biggest fan of heights, but sometimes, you had to go for it. Without looking down, he jumped off the peak of the mountain.

23 BETWEEN THE SUN AND EARTH

Oliver's screams were muffled by the rushing winds.

Alistair sighed. The two of them would be fine.

The laws of physics dictated that because of drag, there had to be a terminal velocity. Even though they jumped off a twenty-thousand foot tall mountain, they would only ever reach 120 miles an hour.

Though, as Alistair fell through the clouds, he thought they could be going a little faster. Perhaps the initiation messed with the environment enough to increase terminal velocity.

Alistair would survive the fall raw, albeit with injuries. He wasn't so sure about Oliver. With his **Fall of Fleet** boots, he didn't need to be sure.

Dev'rox helped guide their descent, making sure to manipulate space to avoid hitting against the mountain. It took almost one and a half minutes of free fall for them to reach the ground.

Even with **Fall of Fleet,** the impact was earth-shattering. Alistair was sure that the sound of his boots hitting the ground echoed for miles. The rocky desert cracked open and when they settled, they were at the center of a small ditch.

Fall of Fleet worked by stretching the time of impact at the very last second by over two times. That didn't sound like a lot, but it actually reduced the force applied to their bodies many times over.

Despite the sudden move, Oliver was already in combat mode. Alistair knew he could trust him to act alone, and rocketed toward the source of the Dao energy.

Ah, [Dash]. Alistair's signature movement Skill. It had been a long time since he felt the wind against his face like that. The world became a blur as Alistair connected seven consecutive [Dashes].

When he arrived, the battlefield was a mess. Thousands of trees blocked his view, the same kinds that he had seen Alexandra use against her father. Red embers emanated from the leaves, humming in a demonic chant. There was a figure that dashed from tree to tree. The person was fast, not as fast as him, but quick enough that a normal person would have seen them as a blur of motion. Her aura was unmistakable. Alexandra.

Every time she stopped, she grabbed a tree. The red embers would temporarily go supernova, blinding everything with intense light. The light subsided after only half a second, but Alistair could see how it would be effective against those that primarily relied on sight. After it faded, the tree appeared transformed into a massive spear three times as tall as Alexandra.

She swayed with its weight, leveraging her immense Strength to perform inhuman feats. She swung the spear wildly, though not once did it cleave into her own trees. Her dominion Skill was perfectly in tune with her fighting, the trees swaying and moving out of her attacks.

Alistair couldn't see Alexandra's opponent with his eyes, but with all of his other senses, he understood right away who it was. Oracle, the Second Devil King.

He surveyed the overall situation in a split second. It was a 2v3—Alexandra and Jesse against—Alistair's heart dropped as he felt the unnatural auras of two familiar faces. Carmen Romero and Richard Atwood. It was all but confirmed they were dead before, but feeling their corpses in person made it all too real.

Not only were they dead, but Karmic threads ran all throughout their bodies, connecting them to the one known as Oracle. She puppeteered them from behind all the trees, and her raw aura outstripped Dragonus by a decent margin. More concerning was the mass of Karmic energy he felt that was much higher than his own. That was to be expected since it wasn't his main Class, but it was still worrisome when he considered how effective his own Karmic Skills were.

Oracle used Carmen's crosses to block Alexandra's strikes, while the Sniper scoped out Jesse. While they were in a stalemate at the moment,

Alistair saw that Alexandra was on the losing end. For some reason, her **[Woodland Forest]** was already collapsing in and of itself. It almost felt like natural degradation. Was Alexandra running out of Mana?

The result of the fight was clear. With Alexandra's dominion Skill on the verge of collapse and Jesse held at bay by his natural counter in that of a long-range fast firing Class, they were on a path to defeat.

Seeing Alexandra and Jesse fighting Carmen and Richard made anger boil in his heart. How cruel, how evil was it, to kill them and use their bodies?

Alistair stilled his rising rage. This was not the time for that. For the first time outside the Holy Ravine, Alistair let himself into the calm waters of Tranquil Mind.

In his mind's eye, the standard image reversed itself. Instead of him diving into the sea of tranquility, the mystical waters assaulted his outstretched body with the force of a tsunami. *Paradox*, Alistair thought, recalling his meditations under the waterfall and the Final Trial of the Steel Body. *While the body is ravaged, the mind reaches its peak separation from the world.*

Following his full submersion into those stormy waters, Alistair reached a state of serenity previously unknown to him, surpassing his previous escapades through the Kai'tazake Mutra. Without exaggeration, there was not a single drop of resentment within his heart.

Alistair's Karmic precognition went haywire. Threads of Oracle's impure Karma assaulted his eyes without any sign of stopping. It was meaningless. He did not need to see his victory to know it would come to pass.

Dev'rox and Alistair reached the best synergy they'd ever had under Tranquil Mind, despite the completely untranquil nature that defined the imp.

Dev'rox flew toward Richard, shrinking the space in between them. At the same time, he also shrunk the space between Alistair and Carmen.

Alistair **[Dashed]** toward the witch, fueled by the extra Agility of "Good Samaritan" since Oracle was an evil that had to be stopped.

The Devil King's reactions were fast, but Alistair's were faster, especially in Tranquil Mind. He was halfway to the target by the time that she acted.

Her puppet grew five crosses that appeared to pierce her body. One through her mouth, one through each lung, one through her stomach, and one through each thigh. Lines of energy flowed from each cross, forming a pentagram.

Alistair recognized this formation—the Formulaic Skill that called down a replica Heavenly tribulation. Carmen hadn't been able to use that Skill instantaneously before, requiring some setup, but she must have developed a faster version before she died.

That was meaningless, too. Alistair didn't bother paying attention to that for more than a second. He nonchalantly tossed **Heavenly Nectar Incense** high into the sky and continued forward.

Based on the placement of her crosses, Oracle intended for the replica Heavenly tribulation to be a suicidal attack for her puppet, taking out both Carmen and her opponent. She was out of luck.

The empyrean lightning came down from the skies the moment Alistair touched Carmen's body. It didn't land.

Alistair reasoned that if the gourd hadn't broken when faced with the titanic force of a Mana Storm, any lightning that Carmen called down couldn't harm it. Since it was already full, he wasn't trying to capture more lightning. He just used the body itself as a grounding object for the lightning to strike.

The Heavenly lightning collided with the flying container in a thunderous clash that brought forth even more light than Alexandra's tree transformations.

Alistair did not rely on his sight. He finished his **[Dash]** and wrapped his fingers wrapped around Carmen's neck. With all of his newfound 500 Strength, he hurled the dead witch as far away from the battlefield as he could. Without an opposing force, she would fly for over a mile.

Not even a millisecond after the woman's neck left his fingers, Dev'rox snapped his own fingers, swapping the two partners. The imp placed his positioning so perfectly, so that when they swapped, Alistair already had his hand around Richard's neck. As he was still continuing the momentum of his previous throw, he merely finished the movement with the Sniper. He, too, went flying away.

Alistair didn't let up his furious assault. As soon as Richard's neck left his hand, he **[Dashed]** toward Oracle. The trees between them had already dissipated—either Alexandra had run out of Mana or she realized what Alistair needed was more open space.

Simultaneously, Dev'rox flew at the Devil King as well, revealing his physical form. His body looked almost as tangible as a living being, and he aimed his barbed tail straight at the enemy.

Then, Fate upended. Left became right and right became left, and the future became the past and the past became the future. Threads of Karmic energy popped in and out of existence everywhere in sight, almost like one of those laser beam security systems from the movies. There was no rhyme or reason to when or where the threads would pop up. They stretched from the ground all the way to the ends of the sky, and Alistair knew at once that touching them would spell his doom.

Her attack was meaningless. He could not be touched if he did not wish it. Alistair's reaction time while in Tranquil Mind surpassed even his hypersonic speed. His body moved without thought, reacting to threats automatically.

When viewed with proper precision, it became obvious that the threads appeared in 0.01 second intervals. In other words, child's play for Alistair to dodge.

Alistair weaved through the web of Karma like he knew where the threads were going to be in advance. Which he didn't, his Karmic vision still not working properly. But his reactions were so fast that it looked as if he did.

As the #1 ranker of the world advanced, the Second Devil King retreated. She leaped backwards several times, careful to continuously construct her deadly web. The threads definitely slowed him down, Alistair having to move at odd angles and sometimes even go backwards to avoid touching the light, but he moved forward nonetheless. Faster than Oracle could backpedal. He would soon reach her.

With his [Fighter's Instinct] at Tier 5, his sense of the battle had never been more piercing. From being in the presence of her Karmic energy, Alistair understood what type of fighter she was. A constrictor.

As a magnified version of how Alistair's [Hand of Karma] sliced away fortuitous lines of Fate for his opponents, she used her Karmic threads to prune down her victims to certain doom. That was why she couldn't form an impassably high amount of threads and leave it at that. There were limits to how much fell Karma one could imbue to their enemies at their level.

Alistair's Tranquil Mind adapted to the strange environment. He began to understand the pattern of emergence of the threads, and the minor flaws in typical causality. For instance, if he stepped to his left, sometimes he would mess up and move too far, or too little.

These tiny things would have killed a lesser fighter right away. Even Alistair brushed death's cloak multiple times, relying on Tranquil Mind's reaction speeds to avoid defeat. However, after adapting to the rules of the terrain, he could now run through it like it was a racetrack.

Alistair jumped forward, coming within a body's length of the Devil King. Dev'rox circled around her back. While his human host had been pushing Oracle back with a frontal assault, Dev'rox had been flying up, up and away. He had avoided all the troublesome Karmic threads by staying out of range.

That range was enormous, more than a thousand feet, but the imp's straight flying speed was faster than her backwards shuffling. He had caught up and surpassed her, allowing him to hover behind her as she moved. There were Karmic threads there too, so he couldn't reach her, but she also couldn't dismiss this other threat.

Alistair's danger sense went off before his Karmic sight detected anything. Whatever machinations of Fate she could control within her sphere, a warrior's danger sense came from a different sphere of existence, unable to be fully meddled with.

The Devil King raised a finger, and the Karmic threads collapsed.

Why struggle so hard? Alistair wondered. *Meaningless. The distance between us is that of the sun and the earth.* Behind her, Dev'rox unveiled one of his signature arcane arrays. The translucent circle of esoteric symbols pulsed with ancient magic, power derived from a distant time and land. The imp's willpower could be felt in every inch of his arrays, working in perfect unison with his ghost cultivator.

There was not one, but two arrays. One that Dev'rox formed behind Oracle, and one that he formed in front of her. A spatial passageway.

Alistair threw a **[Force Fist]** containing an ample amount of the Fist Node, combining a **[Hand of Karma]** on top of it.

Time seemed to move in slow motion as Alistair's gauntleted fist disappeared through one portal and appeared out behind Oracle. Karmic energy covered force affinity Mana in the shape of a fist the size of his torso.

He did all of this without emotion, without attachment. He was simply an avatar of justice, performing his proper duty with a serene disposition. For all evil was not worthy of hate, but pity.

Alistair's fist pierced straight through the Devil King's stomach. However, instead of being a pile of gore, the woman just split. The top half and the bottom half of her body flew apart, connected by thousands of Karmic strings.

Karmic rebirth. Both halves knitted new body parts out of Karmic energy, one a torso and one a pair of legs. Both truly and equally Oracle, registering the same aura.

It was no doubt a trick. At their realm of cultivation, true cloning was impossible. With his mind in synchronization with Dev'rox, he already knew this. But, perhaps for a few seconds, she could really take on the power of two copies.

Or more. Both new bodies split one more time, even as Alistair's fist still finished his blow. The speed of the cloning was impressive, outpacing him, even if for just a moment.

All four of the Oracles opened their mouths at once. "**Delphic Curse**."

Alistair did not understand what those words meant, but he did grasp the essence of what she was doing. A proto-Domain, multiplied by four.

Something that could only be described as a field of darkness spread from the four bodies of Oracle.

May you rest in peace. In banishing you from the record of this world, I give you my sincerest apologies that it has come to this eventuality. For you shall not enter the cycle of reincarnation, in your permanent slumber, I shall give your last moments the splendor of truest justice.

Alistair activated **[Draconic Roar]**, condensing the majority of his overall *nue* in a single scream. Force Mana beamed out in streaks. The *nue* was invisible, but Alistair could feel its weight.

Nue was the natural counter to a Domain. He wasn't sure if this was a multiversal law that applied to those at the top, but at the Foundation realm, it was true. The reason was simple. A Domain required the physical manifestation of spirituality, but the vision it created was the product of the *mind's* imagination.

[Draconic Roar] washed over the nascent proto-Domains. The *nue* infected them, making them completely unstable, disconnected from Oracle's mental designs. She could no longer control their output or size, causing them to stagnate after only expanding five feet.

That would only hold for 1.5 seconds. Alistair was no *nue* master and

Oracle's Dao energy was deep with meaning, along with her general resistance to *nue* with her high mental stats.

Alistair only needed one second. He activated **[Thousand-Armed Bodhisattva Judgment]**.

The air itself hummed with a deep bass rumbling noise. A voice spoke in a language that Alistair did not know, a tongue of superior enlightenment that blessed the ears of all that listened. It spoke its name faster than any human could intelligibly understand, yet somehow all in the vicinity understood nonetheless.

It was the Thousand-Armed Avalokiteśvara, the Bodhisattva of Compassion. When the unseen voice finished chanting its name, the being emerged.

Out of thin air, the avatar appeared. It was twenty feet tall and constructed out of force and lightning-attuned Mana. Like traditional depictions of Avalokiteśvara's thousand-armed form, the Skill had eleven heads, stacked on top of each other in groups of three groups of three, with another head on top of that and then another head on top of that. There weren't truly a thousand arms, but dozens that extended from its back, and three central pairs of arms that each held a different traditional pose of meditation.

The melding of force and lightning affinity Mana was pristine. Perfectly in unison with one another and neither taking the other's place, the composition was three parts force to one part lightning. Despite this, the golden Mana outshone the coral, giving it a brilliant appearance with coral highlights.

The mouth continued to chant with inhuman speed after it was summoned in the same deep voice, reciting the Great Compassion Dhāraṇī. Even without attacking, the power of its voice softened the hearts of all who heard it.

Dao energy flooded its very being. Alistair's Fist and Justice nodes lost a considerable amount of their reserves, but the Skill contained meaning beyond what he should have had for the amount he lost. The Tier 5 Expert Skill was using Alistair's Fist and Justice Nodes in a far more efficient way than any other method he possessed.

Indeed, it contained Dao energy up to its limit—any more, and it would have collapsed, his Foundation realm Mana unable to handle that amount of raw spiritual presence.

All of this [Thousand-Armed Bodhisattva Judgment] created within an instant. Alistair only needed that one second of chanting where he himself had to be perfectly still and concentrated—time that he bought with [Draconic Roar].

Star-like Karmic energy wrapped around each of the avatar's hands. Judgment. This was the Skill's name, and judge it did.

The avatar's scores of palms flew out at Oracle's four bodies with speed surpassing Alistair's [Dash]. Each Karma-covered palm contained only slightly less power than one of his normal Dao-laden [Force Fists], and there were dozens of them.

The palms hit their mark, collapsing Oracle's Delphic Curse. They shot out at a steady pace every third of a second, taking almost twenty seconds to unload the entire arsenal.

The serene judgment of the strikes was their very existence. Serenity became compassion and pity, flowing through all the endless blows.

Like his prototype technique, each strike sent out a shockwave that only affected evildoers. Oracle's bodies were the only ones within range, so even though the palms only affected one body each, the aftershock carried to the other three. In the physical sense, Alistair perceived it as a wave of golden and coral energy, accompanied by the reverberation of a gong.

Those shockwaves struck at Oracle's very Dao Heart. Easy to confuse with the similarly named Dao Heart at the center of universes, a cultivator's Dao Heart was their perseverance, their willpower, their desire to walk down the path of cultivation, and their belief in their Dao Path. Alistair was attacking the major intersection between mind and soul.

The palms flew toward the Devil King at every angle, so the ripples ragdolled her, each wave pushing her in one direction only for the next to come in at a different angle.

Alistair couldn't see or sense his opponent beneath the seemingly boundless onslaught of [Thousand-Armed Bodhisattva Judgment]. The shockwaves made it impossible to see, and even his impressive senses couldn't penetrate their density.

Finally, the avatar shot its last palm and disappeared without a trace. The chanting stopped and everything returned to normal, as if nothing had happened. Dust kicked up by his Skill's palms blanketed the entire region.

"It is finished," Alistair said out loud to no one in particular. He slipped out of Tranquil Mind and felt a strange sense of apprehension. His personality had completely changed while in Tranquil Mind. While he knew he would never do anything completely out of character while in any state, it was still weird knowing that was him. I shall give your last moments the splendor of truest justice? That was a bit melodramatic, no? If that was Tranquil Mind, how would Infinite Arsenal and Black Impermanence operate?

All-in-all, his new state of mind performed exceptionally well. He counted at least three times that he would have died if he had been in the third stage of the Kai'tazake Mutra instead. The reaction time and instinctual defensive maneuvers were invaluable.

Dev'rox flew over to his side. "That was something. Seeing that bodhisattva was something else. But I didn't take you for a monk."

"I feel like the system appended that. A bit uncreative, in my opinion. Just because I'm a Karmic cultivator and follow the Dao of Justice doesn't mean I'm trying to become an arhat."

"Mhm," Dev'rox said. "I hope you don't infringe on the copyright of the Heavenly host. I don't think they'd like that very much."

"How do you even know what copyright is?" Alistair laughed. He drew all the power within his lungs for a giant huff of air that blew away most of the remaining dust.

Only one body remained.

There were four equally sized craters, each large enough to fit an elephant. Oracle lay buried at the center of one of them, half of her body stuck inside the ground. While she looked beat up, her body sustained fewer injuries than Alistair was expecting. But he wasn't worried about her anymore.

Despite the lack of physical harm, he could instantly perceive that her lifeline had come to an end. [Thousand-Armed Bodhisattva Judgment] destroyed her more on a spiritual level than corporeal, though the Skill still evidently had a physical impact on the world.

Oracle's aura had all but vanished and her existence felt incredibly hollow, even more so than usual for the Devil Kings. Interesting as well was that the taint of demon blood seemed almost gone from her body, as if the compassionate sutras and palms of Avalokiteśvara's avatar had washed her fell Karma away.

Alistair was under no delusion that he was powerful enough now to upend the reality of breaking the Pact, but maybe one day he could. With reincarnation, they could have a chance to rectify their mistakes.

If it is their own mistakes, Alistair thought. He remembered how it was known that the people who would one day become the Devil Kings were murderers before that point. Yet that was also uncertain, since the Final Frontier Empire was messing with people's minds from the beginning. The demand for war outstripped its natural supply. All to stand at the top of the Grand Dao. It disgusted Alistair to no end.

He approached the fallen woman, taking out his needle. She was an older woman with crow's eyes and graying hair. Despite her near true death, she wore a childlike smile on her face. Alistair was struck with a pang of sorrow upon seeing her. Her appearance reminded him of his mother.

Alistair held the needle to her neck. Like with Admiral, it was difficult to penetrate the skin, requiring concentrated effort.

Unlike the last time when he had negative Karma, Alistair could see the exact effects of the needle. Upon examining the woman in his Karmic sight, he could see the smallest hooks within her body. Those hooks were within her spiritual system, attaching to the meridians and the soulcore. After the needle reached her bloodstream, the hooks vanished.

"This needle doesn't change a thing," she said. "We all follow him because we believe in him, not because of his commands."

Alistair peered at the emerald-colored needle. "Maybe, maybe not. I find it unlikely since George feared this thing so much to kill one of his own Devil Kings. Plus, Saturn clearly felt otherwise. He was able to free himself of George's control with it."

"The Master fears nothing," she spat. "You are nothing compared to him. If you had a thousand tries, you would never defeat him."

"You have your own destiny and I have mine." Alistair shook his head in sadness. The impassioned sutras and [Thousand-Armed Bodhisattva Judgment]'s shockwaves had not softened her heart enough for genuine change. If there was nothing in her conscience to begin with, then no virtues could be cultivated. "I thought you might have been a victim in this as well, but you're not. There is only one thing I can do for you."

Alistair held out a gloved hand. The sheen metal of his **Devilsbane Gauntlets** looked ominous in the Wasteland's polarized light. He used [Blood Hand], the coagulating and boiling blood affinity Mana gathering around its proper conduit.

Even though she was a Devil King, Alistair could not help but feel some empathy, as he saw the fear register in her eyes as she understood what was to happen next.

"No, no, no!" she screamed, trying to bang her head against the ground to kill herself. "I curse you, Alistair Tan. Join me in solitude."

Alistair rushed to grab her, but she moved with the unnatural speed of a Hollywood possession victim. In one fell swoop, she was dead.

Karmic threads assaulted him from every direction. He knew they were coming, but his defenses were still inadequate to handle the full assault. Fell Karma attacked him from all angles, trying to destroy his Fate.

Alistair drew upon his reserves of Karmic energy, flushing the foreign Karma out of his system. He had to expel more of his own compared to hers, since she was more seasoned in Karmic cultivation. That left him at only 13 points of 90 maximum Karma, a far cry from where he wanted to be.

Loyal to the end, Alistair thought. *I might have slightly underestimated her going for this move.* The whole reason he hadn't blown her up from afar was to not mess with her life force. Since she killed herself, he had to act fast, anyway. He grabbed onto her face and breathed in.

It wasn't a sure thing. When he absorbed Saturn's life force, the Purification leaf of the Blood of the Devil Talent Tree stripped all the individuality from the blood. Alistair was hoping that his finishing Skill had "pre-cleansed" the taint from their blood, so to speak.

Alistair's life force was on par with the strongest Beast Lords in the world, like Vritra. Taking on the ghost blood dragon bloodline and especially Draconic Physique made him a vitality god. Adding the amount he could absorb from Oracle was like putting a single drop of poison in a vast ocean of ichor.

That single drop of poison still would have been enough to turn him into a Devil Prince without the Purification leaf, however.

"Your people are like radioactive time bombs," Alistair said to Dev'rox.

"Not my people," Dev'rox snorted. "The Demon Clans of the Physical Plane and the spiritual demons of the Hells are as far apart as you humans are to elves or lizardfolk."

"Still, there has to be some connection. Or why else would they call you both demons?"

Dev'rox looked up into the sky. "You've learned enough on your own that I can divulge this to you. The split between the demons of this world and the demons of the lower planes happened hundreds of billions of years ago. More, probably, but the Asura Hell doesn't have all the answers to our heritage. The archdevils of the Eight Hot Hells would know more. They're sort of like the multiversal core to the frontier of the lower planes. The way the Final Frontier Empire barely has any information on the core, we don't have much knowledge of our true origins."

Dev'rox wagged his tail. "Though, even the Asura Hell is more storied than this universe. I'd place it on par with a frontier universe closer to the involved."

"If that's the case, does that mean those demons of the Eight Hot Hells are stronger than the cultivators from the multiversal core?"

"How should I know, brat?" Dev'rox said. "That'd be a fight I'd want to see. From a far, far distance."

As Alistair and Dev'rox talked, he slowly absorbed the final remnant of Oracle's life force. When it was finished, she was no more, her soul dragged down into the depths of the earth. Alistair said a few words, hoping for her to get a chance at reincarnation. He knew the odds were more than stacked against her, but you never knew.

Alistair didn't care about absorbing any of her latent powers—that would be impossible considering the circumstances. All he cared about was her memories. Specifically, memories of George. Anything about his abilities and habits would serve them well.

Three notifications popped up.

Level up! *You are now level 56.* +3 Agility, +3 Intelligence, +3 Charisma, +3 free Attribute points, +23 Upgrade Points.

"Deliverance of Justice": +2 free Attribute points.

Bonus Quest Reward: [Vanquishing the Devil Kings] – 3/12. +40 Upgrade Points.

Alistair allocated all the 5 free Attribute points to Agility. His stats were nice and high in all categories, but almost *too* balanced. His style of fighting still required speed as his highest priority, and he wanted his distribution to reflect that. The added solidity and defensive capabilities of [Steel Body] made additional improvements to Constitution less important.

That left him with 63 Upgrade Points. He rubbed his hands in anticipation as he allotted 60 of them to "Deliverance of Justice," bringing it from Tier 3 to Tier 4. Alistair had been waiting quite some time for this change, which required a total of 500 Upgrade Points that he had accrued and given to the Badge. The rewards were juicy.

Badge Upgraded: "Deliverance of Justice" (Tier 4 Mythical Badge): *The most important aspect of justice is the saving of innocent lives.* Each life you personally save grants +2 free Attribute point, capped at 6 per level. (Upgradeable 0/1000).

While it didn't say so in the text, it was *retroactive.* Alistair found himself with an additional 98 free Attribute points to allocate, doubling his total amount of points earned to 196 over the course of his Badge's existence. Each point, Alistair cherished with all his heart, knowing they came from the innocent lives that mattered the most.

Those 98 points he allocated automatically, knowing what he wanted to improve already. He placed 50 into Agility, 30 into Intelligence, and 18 into Wisdom.

Except, he didn't.

The first 61 of those points worked normally. Indeed, it felt like the last 37 were allocated correctly as well, but when he moved to see his Attributes, he found something he'd never seen before.

Strength: 501
Agility: 981
Constitution: 319
Endurance: 352
Intelligence: 522 (19 base points in reserve)
Wisdom: 318 (18 base points in reserve)
Charisma: 506

WARNING: You have exceeded the amount of Mana deemed safe for a cultivator of your level. Further Attribute points will be held in reserve, increasing commensurate to your level and with your species evolutions, including bloodline and ancestry improvements.

Alistair had imagined this day coming in the past. His Subclass, with its Attributes per level and "Deliverance of Justice" Badge, offered a ridiculous amount of stats compared to other cultivators. He had seen Alexandra and Oliver's Badges, and they couldn't hold up to the sheer numbers he was getting.

But that was at an end, at least temporarily. There were consequences to being such a stat monster. Well, it wasn't really a consequence, more that he was so powerful that the system had limitations. Not necessarily because it didn't want him to be stronger; the Pathfinder AI was telling him he was so chock-full of Mana refining his body that it was getting dangerous.

At least it didn't only revolve around the part the Pathfinder called "species evolution." He was a Spectral Superhuman I, and as far as he understood it, he would have to wait to Adept to evolve that to Spectral Superhuman II or some other human variant.

For bloodlines and ancestries, upgrades were far more numerous and granular. Those were technically under the purview of "species evolution," but rarely spoken of in that manner.

Absorbing life force would also help his "species evolution" too, though, as the Lazarene Minister said. Alistair didn't quite understand it all, but maybe it was possible to evolve a species early? His ghost dragon bloodline was greedy with its points, though. He probably wanted to focus on that and stick to the one species evolution per realm. There was a nagging sense that having his body too far ahead of his other cultivation would lead to ruin.

{Bloodline Evolution} (Ghost) Blood Dragon [Peon] — *Draconic Physique, Emperor Will, Blood Affinity, Endless Mana, LOCKED, LOCKED, LOCKED, LOCKED.* (Upgradeable 25/1000 – Only accepts blood essence).

There was a long way to wait before getting to his next bloodline evolution. That meant he was capped at his current Attribute pool for a while.

While there was most likely a discrete increase for level 60, he couldn't be sure of how close that change would come. Leveling had gotten pretty slow near the end.

So that's where all this life force I've been accumulating can come in handy, Alistair thought. *Even though I thought I was ahead of the game there, it seems like my life force still pales compared to my stats. Maybe adding an ancestry would help, but I have no idea how to do that.*

Bloodlines came from the Dao blueprint, affecting the soul and spiritual DNA. Ancestries were a physical trait coming from a physical material. Both were part of lineage, and hard to acquire in their own ways. Alistair had obtained his bloodline by meditating on the ridiculous amount of life force he obtained. He had a feeling that situation was rare, and most got their bloodline from an old treasure or heirloom rather than straight from the Akashic Records.

For ancestry, he didn't have a contemplation to exhaust. You 100% needed the ancestral material. Which he did not have. They were exceedingly rare on Earth. Plus, he needed one compatible with his Dao Path, which narrowed down the possibilities even further.

"Alistair? I can't believe it's you."

Alexandra's voice brought him out of his musings. She along with Jesse approached hesitantly. Alistair stepped out of the way, showing Oracle's dead body.

"She's dealt with. Don't worry."

"I'm not worried about her," Alexandra said. "What the hell was that?"

"Opposite of hell, more like," Dev'rox whispered to only himself and Alistair.

"I could feel those shockwaves from all the way back there," she continued. "It was, *inspiring*, almost."

"My new Skill," Alistair answered. "I needed someone to try it on."

A deluge of emotions surged through Alistair. The aftermath of Tranquil Mind was almost like a rebound, forcing the absent feelings he should have had during that period to surge twice as strong. It took a second to register, though to the others at the scene, it felt like Alistair went from stable to sentimental without warning.

Alistair brought Alexandra in for a hug. "I missed you."

He couldn't fully make out her response. He had grown a little taller from his time in the Holy Ravine too. But he heard something along the lines of, "Me too."

When she finally broke free, she met his gaze with a funny look on her face. "You're going to tell me everything very soon. But even before that, what the fuck happened to you? Were you stuck in some gym rat's dream demiplane? You look like you're two inches taller and put on twenty pounds of muscle."

"Something like that," Alistair said. Dev'rox brought in the bodies of Carmen and Richard. Without the Karmic strings that Oracle used to puppet them, they were lifeless corpses. The only solace he could take was that they weren't Devil Princes. There weren't any of the signature characteristics.

"We should return them to their families, if they have any," Alexandra said somberly. "They deserve proper funerals."

Alistair nodded. He had forgotten his manners and greeted Jesse, who was silently watching the whole affair, focused mainly on Alistair. "Hey, how are things going?"

"Never better, boss. You showed up at exactly the right time. Alexandra held open her Skill for a day. We were both trying to wait the other out."

Alistair felt thundering footsteps in the distance. He had already caught a whiff of the smell, though Alexandra and Jesse weren't as aware, both going into an alert state.

Alistair chuckled. "That's going to be Oliver."

The Necromancer looked funny sprinting. His form was off, though he was still as fast as a speeding car—the kind of speeding that would get you in massive trouble. He made it over to the craters, kicking up a cloud of dust and panting with his hands on his knees.

With his seven [Dashes] and subsequent pursuit of Oracle, Alistair had traveled almost two miles from where he and Oliver landed on the mountain. Doing some quick math on Oliver's top speed, that meant he had dealt with Oracle in just over fifty seconds. Perhaps his past self wasn't that arrogant to claim that the fight was below his level.

"You already finished the fight?" Oliver asked incredulously.

Alistair tapped his foot. "What did you think that massive explosion of my signature aura was? You think too little of your leader. Anyway, I think we should get the hell out of here. I'm tired of this drab environment. I have a feeling I'm going to have a lot to catch up on."

24 THE SECOND STEP

OLIVER CAREFULLY STORED the two bodies in his **[Otherworld Gates]** while Alistair contemplated Carmen and Richard.

Those two deserved far better than what they got. Their deaths were like a truck in the face. While nothing could ever hurt as much as the loss of his mother, these killings were of a different nature. Such powerful people dying unceremoniously. It was a sober reminder of the reality that all had to face, regardless of strength.

Sometimes, you just ran into a bigger fish.

Unless you were actually the biggest fish in the multiverse.

Leaving the Wasteland was like a second homecoming. The absolute largest difference was between the Holy Ravine and the outside world, but the Wasteland also felt suffocating in its own way. When they passed its borders into the lands of color, Alistair once again breathed in with elation. Now this, this was truly the best.

Every tree was full of life force, every speck of Mana coursing with energy. The vitality of the world was ineffable and amazing. Living without the Dao in the Holy Ravine was akin to living in black and white. An apt comparison, then.

However, Alistair had no time to reminisce about those sorts of esoteric things. He immediately grilled Alexandra for the current up-to-date information. And he did not like what she had to say.

But, all things being considered, he had been expecting way worse.

"Only 25.2%?" Alistair asked. "That's lower than I was expecting. I thought I might come back to the Devil Kings having almost won the Global Mayorship."

"We're just as confused," Alexandra said. The four of them used Jesse's flashes to cycle quickly to the **Teleportation Circle.** "After George assaulted FavorWood Manor, he completely disappeared. No sightings, no reports, nothing. It's like he vanished from the world."

Alistair frowned. That sounded very familiar. At almost the exact same time, he himself had "vanished from the world." Was that a coincidence?

"I don't suppose he decided to just die for us," Alistair said. "That would be too convenient."

"We considered that possibility," Alexandra said. "But the Devil Kings aren't acting as if their leader died. Here, take this report."

She tossed him a jade slip. "This tells you all that you need to know about the state of the war."

Alistair digested the information as best he could. They arrived back in Logista, hurrying to the **Teleportation Circle.** He winked at one of the guards he knocked out with **[Draconic Roar]** before. This time, they didn't confuse Oliver's aura with the enemy.

New Boston was even more impressive than he remembered. The damage it sustained from the lava and earthquakes looked completely repaired. Buildings towered into the skies, which were filled with the airstreams. Thousands of people flew through columns of air and space Mana that crisscrossed all around the city, leading people to their destinations faster than a bullet train.

The sprawling city was clearly larger than Alistair remembered. Workers clad in the standardized uniform of the Northeast Order Freehold labored in unison to expand the city even further. He saw numerous Builder-type Classes at work. One guy with gray skin threw up concrete, which he formed with his bare hands, while on the other side of the street, a woman created three-dimension outlines of Mana that guided the construction workers.

Alistair guessed that it wasn't all good news. But to confirm his suspicions, he needed a breakdown from more knowledgeable people.

The freehold overview page showed him the changes between the major freeholds. His freehold gained a couple thousand subregions, putting him up to 56,381 out of 159,873. The Devil Kings shot up to over 40,000, taking almost all of that from FavorWood Manor, while the various unaffiliated factions dwindled.

A new system characterization of subregions appeared, one that Alistair hadn't seen before. "Owned but uncontrolled." That tied into the second wave. The second wave that Alexandra and Jesse had a palpable fear toward.

Alistair opened up the Quests section of his status screen. He navigated to the old system notifications that were listed there.

Wave 2: The Second Step

FX-14752 has braved the natural disasters of Earth Asunder. Most of the elemental bosses contained within the core of each disaster have been stopped, though 5.13% remain active. Active storms will not disappear naturally and will keep wreaking havoc on the subregions they are localized to. However, they will not spread or grow stronger after this point.

The second wave, aptly named The Second Step, is The First Step redux. Many on this planet made cherished memories fighting off the monsters provided by the Pathfinder AI. We now give you an opportunity to relive those experiences in The Second Step—this time with dungeons instead of monster waves.

All over the planet, dungeons will appear, marked by the seal of the Final Frontier Empire. Each dungeon's purview will span thousands of subregions each, the difficulty based on the sum total of the development in its constituent dungeons. This is different from the standard dungeons you have experienced popping up stochastically, where the difficulty was scaled to the entrants.

Each dungeon will be a unique instance consisting of a multitude of difficult trials testing your wits, combat prowess, and willpower. The dungeons are living entities and might evolve over the course of your delves.

A final boss marks the end of each dungeon, similar to previous monster waves. If you do not clear the dungeon within one week of entering, the boss along with the corresponding monster wave will be released from the dungeon and wreak havoc on the world.

Only one group of delvers may enter a dungeon at any given time, up to thirteen individuals. The selection of these delvers depends on the shareholder who owns the plurality of the subregions within the dungeon's range. The choices will be at this person's discretion; they may choose to bring no allies. Be forewarned: this is highly recommended against, as the dungeons are meant to be cleared by a well-rounded party of the strongest rankers on FX-14752.

Dungeon delvers earn Contribution Points based on their contributions to clearing the dungeon, along with ease, creativity, and style points.

In addition to the variety of basic dungeons, there is a small chance each day of a "Grand Dungeon" appearing. The Grand Dungeon is significantly more difficult than the basic dungeons and commands much higher rewards. The Grand Dungeon will appear in multiple instances around the world, so many groups have a chance to join. However, each group will experience their own instantiation of the dungeon, so they will not compete directly against each other.

During this period, the rules for achieving Global Mayor for the Devil Kings still stand, and the methods to acquire subregions by domination, democratic approval, and purchase shall not be abrogated.

Let The Second Step begin!

Alistair checked his Contribution Score. He was #7 on those leaderboards with 127 points despite barely participating in Earth Asunder. He assumed this was because of the points he was getting for the high development of New Boston, which he personally owned. Alexandra was far and away #1 with 480, no doubt from all the storms she'd cleared in Earth Asunder and the dungeons in The Second Step.

The "owned but uncontrolled" made sense now. Monsters couldn't own subregions. But if they wrested control of a subregion from a freehold, a freehold couldn't still be said to control it, could they? As a result, freeholds didn't get any Land Store Points or Contribution Points from uncontrolled subregions.

The Devil Kings and the Northeast Order had relatively few uncontrolled regions, but in the other territories, upwards of 25% of their subregions were uncontrolled. Clearly, the other polities were having difficulties with the dungeons.

Just how hard are they? Alistair wondered. *I'll have to ask Alexandra.*

The four of them arrived at the frosted glass dome that was his new headquarters. In the time he'd been absent, they'd improved the design, adding secondary and tertiary domes, including ones that connected at the top. Alistair thought it looked something like an atomic nucleus and found it hard to fathom how it was structurally sound. Architect-type Classes were something else.

There were four layers of translucent energy they had to go through to enter the building, along with a scan from a reptilian eye that floated above the doors. While intensive, it was seamless and didn't slow them down much at all.

When Alistair entered his own HQ, he was met with stares and gasps. Dozens of people rushed from corner to corner of the large lobby. They had expanded their array of **Teleportation Circles,** which formed an enormous circle around the perimeter of the hemisphere.

All the people who worked in the dome had on his official uniform, something that Alistair was quite proud of. Many frantically ran from **Teleportation Circle** to **Teleportation Circle,** carrying out critical missions for the good of the freehold. Others worked at a series of desks in the center, most likely those with Classes that improved their brainpower or computational abilities. A man that Alistair didn't recognize worked with an enormous supercomputer at the very center, visible through all the glass architecture. The computer wasn't very wide, but it was extremely tall, almost reaching the ceiling of the dome.

It wasn't great for privacy, but the frosted material, called ambrosic glass, was even stronger than valyrik, the fused black stone they had used previously.

The central computer also served a dual function as a ladder. If you climbed up it, you'd reach the entrance to both the dome above that one, and the second floor of the base dome. There were also dozens of workers on that floor, many of whom were part of a permanent security force that prevented crime and kept order with human-related incidents.

"Wow," Alistair said. "You've really spruced this place up."

"I wish I could take credit," Alexandra said. She waded her way through the crowded first floor to the wide ladder system on the supercomputer, Alistair and the others following after. "The idea was John's after the earthquakes. He thought that we should combine almost all the vital aspects of the Northeast Freehold into one area. Dr. Mehta has his hospital attached here, and we have Blaise's academy in one of the domes. There are ten total, making this the largest building on Earth right now."

"But what about—"

"Yeah, I know what you're thinking," Alexandra interrupted. "I had the same question too. Wouldn't that make everything super vulnerable? There was that terrorism incident with a Devil King attacking the United Polities and almost killing Ryder and Marzhan, after all. John gave me a detailed explanation, but this is the most warded place on the planet. By adding everything together, we get some efficiency bonuses and the way the Land Store defenses work in conjunction, the defense is greater than the sum of its parts. We're so protected, I don't even think you could break in."

Alistair felt the various forms of warding with his various senses. Fatewarding, ridiculously hard ambrosic glass, alarms to Mana filled with malicious intent, *nue* detection, and that's just what he felt with a cursory glance. There were surely more hidden and nefarious traps. He couldn't lie—he was pretty impressed.

The only weakness he felt was that there wasn't much attention to Karma, but you couldn't cover every basis. There were barely any Karmic cultivators in the first place, and it was one of the weirdest powersets. Also, he'd just killed the most powerful enemy of that type, so now it became less relevant.

Once, long ago, Alistair could recall every face that worked in his headquarters, if not their names. Well, not his headquarters. They were Sofia's back then, when it was still based out of the Boston City Hall. A wave of nostalgia washed over him, accompanied by a pang of guilt as he remembered his old boss's death. He had vowed to never let any of his friends die because of his negative Karma again. Based on how he overpowered Oracle, that front was going well.

While his citizens gave him blatant stares, no one stopped their work to approach. Alistair smiled at that. He was lucky that John had instilled such a good work ethic in his subordinates. Though, he had to admit, when death was right around the corner, people tended to work hard no matter who was in charge.

Alexandra led them to the office where the supercomputer was located. It was wider than it looked from afar, with the two-dimensional profile of a kitchen table. A portly man worked with a holographic keyboard and monitor that took up half of the room.

"Hey, Dave," Alexandra said. "How's it going?"

The man jumped out of his seat, looking flustered. "Ah! Didn't see you. Doing just fine, Miss Alexandra."

"Alistair, this is Dave from IT. He works on monitoring the HQ. He has a knack for seeing details, and he makes things run a lot smoother."

"That's right!" Dave said, adjusting his glasses. "For example, did you know that a personalized soundtrack increases productivity 6.5%?"

"Nah, I thought it was 5.95%," Alistair joked.

"Where did you get a number with that precision from? The margins of error are too big for that, if I'm not mistaken." Dave from IT gave Alistair a funny look.

"Ah, never mind," Alistair said, scratching his head with a bit of embarrassment, since his joke didn't land. "Keep up the good work, Dave."

Dave nodded and got back to manipulating thousands of windows on his screen that Alistair couldn't even begin to understand. This man had none of the reverence that the others had, even compared to someone like Jesse. It was weird, but also somewhat refreshing.

Jesse had offered to teleport them into the war room directly, but Alistair wanted to experience seeing the insides of the Leading Domes. That was the name he had decided on for the building, back when he had the first one created. Yes, Alistair was excellent at naming things, just like his genius nom de guerre, Alistair Danger (Dangierre).

The ladder inside the recently named Leading Domes was wide enough to fit ten people side-by-side, which made sense considering the foot traffic.

It consisted of metal rungs soldered onto the computer case and led up to a revolving glass door in the ceiling.

"After you, dear leader," Alexandra said. "You're going to want to see the new room."

The four of them ascended the ladder like rats scurrying up a gutter pipe. Alistair was reminded of his climb up Mount Goa. This time, however, he had all of his powers. Plus, it was a ladder, not a deadly mountain.

"You're not supposed to go that fast!" Alexandra called out, but by the time her words reached his ears, he was already at the top.

"Since when were you the fun police?" Alistair asked, as his friends climbed up at a slower pace. Except for Jesse; he teleported to the top like always.

"Since you were gone for a month, leaving me to deal with all this shit."

"Okay, you win this time."

The door wasn't really a door at all. At the top of the ladder was a large hole covered in an aqueous gel. The ladder continued on the other side, so all they had to do was pass through it.

Alistair looked apprehensively at the semi-transparent gel. It looked like hair gel, to be honest. He didn't want that stuff sticking all over his body.

"It's another layer of security," Oliver explained. "We had it installed after Chameleon almost killed Marzhan and President Ryder. A crafter combined an elixir she earned from a side Quest with a Land Store powder that warded against certain types of Karma. It's supposed to reveal Karmic intent in any that it washes over, though it doesn't actually offer any protection. It's more of a very loud warning that we've been infiltrated."

"Ah, that makes sense," Alistair said. He was the first one through the gel. It washed over his skin without sticking like he was afraid of, and he climbed through the layer of the substance, no more than a few inches thick.

The second dome was not really a dome, more of a sphere built on top of the first layer, made from the same ambrosic glass. There were multiple ringed floors that were accessible by a spiral staircase around the edge of the sphere.

The three-dimensional hologram of the planet that he had used in their previous war room centered the dome. It was even larger than before, reminding Alistair of those giant hanging globes in museums. Red dots representing conflicts pulsed every second. It pained Alistair to see all the nested divisions. There were small enclaves of Devil King territory in his lands and vice versa, a product of the constant engagements.

But that wasn't what drew his attention most. Everyone who could see him in the vast second dome was staring at him. And not in the awestruck good way.

"What's going on?" Alistair asked.

Alexandra drew out her daggers, while Oliver congealed his space affinity Mana into the beginnings of his **[Otherworld Gates].**

Alistair looked down, realizing that they were *looking* at something.

He was on fire.

25 SOLITUDE

ALISTAIR STARED at his burning body in disbelief. Intense red flames covered his clothes from head to toe.

But he felt nothing. No pain, no heat, and no threat. All of his well-honed senses hadn't detected any threat, either. Yet his closest friends looked at him with guarded eyes. *What was going on?*

"Alistair, I'm going to need you to stay very still," Alexandra said, drifting away from him with Jesse and Oliver behind her. She made a gesture and looked up to what seemed to be a meeting room on the second floor of the upper dome.

"Guys, seriously, tell me what is happening," Alistair said. "I'm not joking."

"Neither are we," Alexandra said. "You've triggered the **Karmic Gel.** Your own sister assured us it was foolproof. No matter who climbs through that item, if they have malicious Karmic intent, it'll trigger the flames of a sinner's hell."

"Well, I feel no pain, so clearly I'm not a sinner," Alistair joked. "Alexandra, it's me! You've literally had your eyes on me the entire time since I fought Oracle until now. There was no time for me to be replaced by a doppelganger. And if I was a fake since the beginning, how the hell did I defeat Oracle at her full power without taking a scratch?"

The room was a hotbed of tension. The layout was similar to the first dome, taking most of its inspiration from a modern office building. One that was designed by an architect who probably loved glass a little too much.

While there were some stragglers working at desks, he actually recognized most of the people he detected on the second floor. To no one's surprise, upon seeing their boss on fire in a potentially compromised position, they came flying down.

John Desmond, the Northeast Order Freehold's second-in-command, floated gracefully on a flaming chariot. Despite the opaque flames hiding the passengers, Alistair's aura sense knew who they were right away. Moneylender Lauren Yoon, their treasurer, came alongside him, as well as Archer Blaise Blanchett, in charge of educating and raising troops, Caren Locasta, the Chronicler, and William St. James, the Farsighter. In some sense, those last two were the brains of their freehold.

"Don't forget about my guile," Dev'rox said. "I'm over a hundred thousand years old. I've picked up quite a few things in my time."

"Dev'rox! I was beginning to worry! You weren't talking for a while."

"Prince of Hell, I need some breaks, too. My soul got seriously stressed being in that barbaric paradise, and then I had to push my arcane magics right after?"

"Sorry," Alistair said. "You do deserve a break, buddy."

"I'm your arcane master, not your buddy," Dev'rox replied, though with good humor. "I'll talk to you later. Let me rest for now."

Alistair was glad that Dev'rox didn't want to continue their conversation, since he had to deal with the pressing issue of all of his freehold thinking he was an enemy.

John and his passengers joined Alexandra close to the gel hole. In particular, he felt Caren and William's discerning gazes fall over him as they tried to ascertain the truth.

"Is what he says true, Alexandra?" Caren asked.

"Yes, it is," Alexandra replied, not taking her eyes off Alistair's burning body. "He defeated Oracle and came directly here. His powers seemed normal to me."

"My powers. Good idea," Alistair said, remembering what the Devil King report said about the fifth of their number, Chameleon. "To what degree can this Chameleon fellow copy Skills?"

"To his own power," Caren said. "Which is lower than his rank would indicate as a Devil King. In other words, the output of his copying is much lower than the original, as long as the original is, say, a top 50 ranker."

"So he would be nothing compared to me, then?" Alistair asked. "Why don't I just flex my aura and prove that I'm not the shapeshifter?"

"That's fine enough." Alexandra whittled her daggers together. "But my concern wasn't that you're Chameleon. I already felt your Buddha Skill right in front of me. I was worried about Oracle messing with you. Maybe she implanted a sleeper Karmic program or something, I don't know. And then when you get back here, boom, you kill everyone."

"I seem to be doing a poor job of that," Alistair noted.

"That's just what she would make you say, isn't it?"

"Alexandra, Alistair, this is getting us nowhere," John said, raising his hands. "Alexandra is correct. If the gel triggered the fire, that means something is wrong with your Karma. Let's think about this logically. The last thing you did was fight the strongest pure Karmic cultivator on Earth. Alistair, don't you think that's the least bit suspicious?"

Alistair reflected inwardly. John had a point. He had been so adamant about his innocence that he didn't consider all the relevant facts. Speaking only in terms of Karmic energy and deftness with Karma, Oracle surpassed him. Therefore, it wasn't such a crazy idea that she had pulled one past his careful sight. It would have had to have been at the end, when she killed herself and unleashed a torrential outpour of insidious Karmic threads. What if one had gotten past his protections and latched onto his soul?

What would the consequence of that even be? Alistair wondered. *Could it really possess me and force me to kill my comrades?*

Alistair found that hard to believe. That just seemed way too strong, even for her. If she had such a godlike Skill, then she should have been able to put up more of a fight.

He searched deep within himself for aberrations in his Karma. The pool of crimson Karmic energy that Alistair employed sat within his soulcore, in a state of superposition with two other types of quintessence, Dao energy and Mana. *Nue's* seat was the brain rather than the soulcore.

Nothing felt wrong with his Karmic pool, nor the threads of Fate that tugged in every which direction. They felt... normal. Which concerned Alistair even more. At this point, the others had convinced him the Second

Devil King had done *something* to him, even if he didn't know what it was. That he couldn't figure out the mark she made led to him wondering if the worst-case scenario really was true.

The change came.

It was a pulse. A hidden node of darkness nested in a thread of Fate close to his body opened up and unveiled its contents.

In that moment, all things became clear. Oracle had sacrificed the last remnants of her life to curse Alistair with a bead of Karma. By hiding it within a thread of Fate and not within his body, she had evaded his finely tuned senses. Her weaving of threads was a masterpiece, completely surpassing Alistair. She had an abundant amount of practice as it was her main combat Skill, and his less trained Karmic sight had been blind to it.

Solitude. This word echoed through Alistair's head many times. It was within Oracle's last sentence before passing on from the world.

Fate within the Leading Domes upended, the same as when he battled Oracle. A cover of darkness spread from Alistair to everywhere in sight in a fraction of a second. He was in no position to offer a counter with his 13 points of positive Karma. But there was a distinct lack of threat inside the darkness. His danger sense felt no deadly nature.

As suddenly as it came, the darkness went.

And so did everyone else.

Solitude. When the absolute darkness faded, Alistair was alone. On the moon.

Alistair gazed down at Earth.

"Huh?" was all he could let out.

Before he could lose his sanity, Alistair calmly looked down at his beautiful planet, and went to work.

In the beginning, Alistair was certain it had to be an illusion. But as he surveyed the desolate surface of the moon, nothing stuck out. He calmly looked for any wrong details, squeezing the most out of his senses. There was no giveaway. For all intents and purposes, he was... just on the moon.

He counted his lucky stars that he wasn't dying. With the Metabolism leaf of the Heart Branch, he converted Mana to oxygen. His skin had enough durability to create pressure on his internal organs to prevent his bodily fluids from boiling and killing him. His natural resistance to heat and his transformed **Mammothskin Raiment** protected him from the 250 degrees Fahrenheit temperatures.

It wasn't comfortable—he felt like his body was squeezed from the inside out, but he could survive.

In the meantime, what the hell was he supposed to do?

"Dev'rox? This isn't an illusion, right? I mean, I'm pretty sure it isn't, but I just want to double-check."

"Mhmm," Dev'rox said. "I'm not an expert in that field. But I think not."

"Then, excusing my language, what the *fuck* just happened?"

Dev'rox flew out of his body. He whirled around the rocky surface, diving underneath into the hills and through the dark sky of outer space. "Huh. Okay. I might have an answer. Can you ask me politely?"

"Dev'rox, not the time."

"Bah, you younglings have no manners these days. Fine. Drumroll please," Dev'rox said. Alistair gave him a stern look. "We're inside an alternative Fate stream."

Before Alistair could ask what that was, the imp shushed him and started his explanation. "With my eminent genius, I realized that my actions were being limited. As a ghost, before attaching myself to you, I had very little causal impact. Even at the beginning of our relationship, I could do very little. Now, I feel something similar. So, I wracked my venerable brain for any possible source of such a limitation. The answer was an alternative Fate stream.

"If you think about the ontology of reality as split into the many planes of existence, then Fate is but one of many ways to think of the flow of reality. There are many models of this, but the two most prominent are Fate and Time."

"I can't see anything weird in my Karmic vision," Alistair said. "Apart from, you know, being on the *moon.*"

"Fate and Karma are different things. The Order of the Multiverse is no simple thing. The threads of Fate and the Karmic web are two separate concepts. You can see threads of Fate with your Karmic vision, and influence it, but Karma is not Fate itself. Your Subclass is Karmic, so being able to tell fine differences in Fate is not necessarily in its wheelhouse."

"Fate and Time," Alistair muttered. "So does that mean time travel is possible?"

Dev'rox snorted. "Weren't you the one admonishing me for sidetracks?" There was no doubt Alistair had touched one of his weak spots. The imp loved to provide information—it made him seem more sage-like and worldly. "I have never heard of anything like that. If time travel is possible at all, I suspect only Truthseekers could accomplish such a feat. Anyhow, continuing from where you interrupted me—the Time model of reality posits free will, with infinite branching realities. The Fate model of reality posits destiny, with set paths and events happening. That is not to say there is no free will in Fate and no sure things in Time. Both models are true and false at the same time. When you see threads and manipulate threads of Fate, they are real. When a Time cultivator sees their timelines, they are also real."

Alistair greedily soaked up all the knowledge he was given. Dev'rox was prohibited by Multiversal Law from revealing information that was too far above him. With specific instances, however, the Profound realm could explain what he was seeing right in front of him. Alistair appreciated that Dev'rox was giving him this much, since talking about Time when seeing a Fate related phenomenon was a stretch. Finding the extremities of Law was something Dev'rox excelled in.

"A Fate stream is different from a timeline in that Fate is centered around the individual. If Oracle dragged you into a separate stream, it is all local to you. There must be a certain condition that this Fate stream represents."

"Solitude," Alistair muttered. "That's what she told me before she killed herself. What else is the representation of solitude on Earth except the moon?"

"That does seem right," Dev'rox said. "Oracle created a destiny for you that involved absolute solitude. This is what the universe provided. If you're wondering how come she didn't do something absurd like making all your friends hate you, that requires a constant flow of energy. Obviously, she's dead. Your essence is foreign to the Fate stream, and by targeting you, she's limited that energy drain. You'll still eventually return to the prime reality, but I haven't the faintest idea how long that would take."

"Don't know what I'd do without you," Alistair said. "Thanks for the rundown. But isn't this ability way too broken? How the hell is this a Foundation realm power? Wouldn't everyone at the higher realms be Fate cultivators, considering they can just remove their opponents from the battle?"

"Not quite. She required her life's sacrifice to bring you here, which makes it difficult to use consistently. And Fate streams cannot bring death. At least not directly. They cannot kill, and are difficult to injure with, as one's own Fate dislikes subversion. Harm is the ultimate subversion, making it extremely difficult."

Alistair considered Dev'rox's new information. That begged the question of *why* she had cursed him with her dying breath. Spite? Possible, but that was the least dangerous conclusion. He had to think of the worst and imagine he was facing that.

Looking through all of his options, there really was nothing that he could do. **Teleportation Circles** didn't extend the distance he needed. He had no special treasure to bring him back. He was well and truly separated from the entire world. Solitude, like Oracle said.

Alistair sat down. He did have one option, but he wasn't sure if it was the best idea. He had his one meeting with the Lazarene Minister for [Armageddon]. It was his last meeting, so he wanted to save it for a desperate time. This was a desperate time, but Alistair was also around 80% sure that the Clear Water Sect elder could do nothing for him. Teleporting their sponsee from the moon to the Earth to bypass the actions of his enemy seemed like an obvious case of violating the pact of non-interference.

Clear Water Sect, Alistair thought. He had thought so little of his future with them, since he was still frantically trying to save the world. Fifty years of service, or ten under wartime conditions. That sounded so long at first, but after understanding his true lifespan even after reaching just Adept, it was so short. Given his draconic bloodline, Alistair wouldn't be surprised if he could reach a 10,000-year lifespan as an Adept.

Why so few years? Were they so confident in their camaraderie and believed he would genuinely come to see them as his family? Now that he thought about it, Evangeline was going to come with him? The Clear Water Sect had recruited both of them. It would be like going to college together, Alistair mused. Only this time, Angie wouldn't get to hold how elite her school was over him.

While he had time to spare, he checked his finances. Money ruled the world. The multiverse, it seemed. Maybe Lucius Wood's path wasn't so wrong in the grand scheme of things.

Looking back at his past, Alistair's goals in his life in the before were very money based. Evangeline had gotten a job working as a machine learning engineer for an AI startup, and Alistair didn't want to fall behind. He had gotten an investment banking job, and he was looking forward to a wealthy future, maybe retiring early. Settling down with Katelyn and having a few kids. How whimsical his old goals seemed now.

The Northeast Order Freehold generated 21.7 million Gold drachma per month in taxes. That didn't include an additional 9.9 million in proceeds from the official store, leading to a total of 31.8 million a month, or a bit over a million a day. Land Store Credits were up to 99.3k a month.

This despite all the warring and destruction. The improvement of the existing land outpaced the destruction, at least so far. New Boston especially was the economic center of the world, and the network effects of that were generating a ton of money.

Alistair smiled. It looked like everything was okay, at least for now. In the map within his freehold overview, it said that 9.1% of the Northeast Freehold was overrun by the dungeon monsters. Not great, but they could handle that.

In his personal account were 5.5 million Gold drachma and 19.2k Land Credits. This was the personal generation untied to the overall freehold. His specifically chosen subordinates like John Desmond, who was the Vice President of the freehold, could access the overall collected money and credits.

Speaking of millions of drachma, Alistair took out what he had been dreading—Farsa Strongbite's business card. The white metal of the card felt cool to his touch as he grabbed it out of his pocket, where he knew it would be. It was one of his soulbound items, along with the Cabal's black marble and now Purana's glass tetrahedron that would guide him to Lisorte.

Alistair was expecting to see "LATE" again, but there was instead a short message.

"LATE: All payments postponed. Meeting scheduled with debtor Alistair Tan in 120 FX-14752 days with the Visionary realm Farsa Strongbite, Portolon Clan debt collector."

Alistair wasn't sure what to make of that. No payments were a good thing, but a second meeting didn't sound good.

"Looks like it's indentured servitude for you," Dev'rox chuckled.

"That's not funny because you're going to be along on the ride with me," Alistair shot back. "Are you being serious, also?"

"No, I am being utterly serious," Dev'rox said. "I was the Final Frontier Empire's slave for tens of thousands of years, remember?"

"But I'm already in a contract with the Clear Water Sect."

"They can work out a deal. It won't be that bad, trust me. They'll probably have you run around doing errands."

"Asset?" Alistair raised an eyebrow. "The Portolon Clan hates me because I ruined their investment in Anthony. They want my hide. I bet they'd send me on suicide missions."

"Then you'd best get stronger. Or hope that your sect leader negotiates otherwise."

There was a period of a few hours of nothing. Alistair had thought that his perception of time might be completely out of whack, but he forgot about the rotation of the Earth. From his lofty vantage point, he could see the Earth's rotation clearly, and never lost track of time.

Like he said before, there wasn't anything to do but wait. Wait, and hope that Oracle's dwindling curse would run out. He wasn't going to use his final meeting unless he really had no other option.

Around a day into his silent meditation, there was a change. A notification window appeared.

Grand Dungeon Prompt:

The Grand Dungeon of The Second Step is a challenge of the highest difficulty. A balanced lineup of challengers is highly recommended.

Limitations: Max 8 challengers.

The Grand Dungeon, Symphony of Skills, is comprised of ten individual sectors. You must pass through each sector to get to the next, culminating in the final "Trial of Harmony." Each sector offers its unique challenges. The Grand Dungeon is offered in multiple locations at once, and always maintains the same difficulty, no matter the challenger. Multiple instances of the dungeon are separate entities. The first in the world to clear the Symphony of Skills gets a special Legendary rarity item.

Task: Clear the dungeon.

Reward (Solo Clear):
1) +25 Upgrade Points for each sector cleared

2) Insight Vision for the creation of a proto-Domain (If user already possesses proto-Domain, instead they receive an appropriate level Dao Fruit)

3) 400 Upgrade Points

4) First Through Bonus: Legendary rarity item.

Time Limit: Until the end of The Second Step, 23 days from now.

Accept (Y/N)? Time remaining for decision: Four hours.

26 SECTOR ONE

ALISTAIR WAS SO bored that seeing something new made his heart leap for joy.

He had been meditating on the mysteries of the Ghost and Justice, trying to bring up his other Dao Nodes to the prominence his Fist currently held. So far no luck, but that was to be expected. The Dao Fruit prize for completing [Vanquishing the Devil Kings] was his best bet for an improvement.

The other thing he had been trying was testing Spiritual Fighter's Echo. Alistair was certain that this was his best bet for forming a proto-Domain. The 15% strength afterimages that followed his basic strikes were the physicality of the Dao. Exactly what he needed for his proto-Domain. There wasn't a lot of progress on that front, sadly.

Which was why when Alistair saw that one of the prizes for the Grand Dungeon was an Insight Vision for the creation of a proto-Domain, he almost instinctively hit accept without thinking.

After shoring up his foundations in the Fist, Alistair knew he had bridged most of the technical gap between geniuses like Pharaoh and himself. The difficulty that came from the complexity of the meeting of his three disparate Daos was a bridge he would surely cross eventually, especially now that he had the Spiritual Fighter's Echo to study.

That was why the possibility of that one Insight Vision was so tempting.

No longer did he need a whole three Insight Visions, as Dev'rox told him a couple of months ago.

But he refrained from his instincts, for now. A few minutes of thinking it over wouldn't matter, since he had four hours to decide how to proceed.

Four hours to proceed... which Alistair assumed was to give the leaders time to gather their dungeon clearing parties.

The problem was that Alistair had no party.

In front of him were eight mirrored discs that looked remarkably similar to Teleportation Circles, except they were more silvery. Seven surrounded one in a ring, the center one being larger than the others. The position of the leader.

"Do you think that I'll be sent home once I finish?" Alistair asked.

"It should do the trick," Dev'rox replied. "The Pathfinder AI's powers exceed that of any Foundation realm. When you get sucked up into the dungeon, you'll be leaving this alternative Fate stream. With nothing left to anchor you here, when you return, you should be where you left off, in your headquarters."

"Yeah, okay," Alistair said, his mind calculating in a mad dash. "Okay."

If he entered the Grand Dungeon, who knows how long he would be in there? The Pathfinder AI promised it would be extremely difficult, meant to be cleared by a diverse party.

On the other hand, if he didn't go in, who knew how long he would be on the moon? It might have been a shorter period than doing the Grand Dungeon, but he would be permanently missing out on the rewards, which were some of the best he had ever seen since the initiation.

There was also the knowledge that the Devil Kings would almost certainly be undergoing their own Symphony of Skills. While they probably got worse rewards than a solo clear, anything that imbalanced the scales between him and the Iceman could be deadly.

Iceman, Alistair thought, remembering George Moulin's old nickname. *I wonder if people still call him that?*

Alistair let his scarlet bracelets morph into their true forms—clawed metal gauntlets that gleamed in the sun's distant light. He had already made up his mind. Had he gotten this far from being timid? There was only one course of action he could take. The solo clear.

However, he did not enter immediately. For the next three and a half hours, Alistair meditated through the Kai'tazake Mutra, entering a sublime mental state. It wasn't a draw on his Dao energy like Tranquil Mind or anything so Dao-touched, but a natural disposition.

During this time, he fully recuperated from his injuries within the Holy Ravine and recovered more of his Karmic energy. In addition, he ate some of [Carmela's Happy Pies]. Moon pies were just as scrumptious as Earth ones, though he could have sworn they had a cosmic aftertaste.

He stopped his trance thirty minutes before the time limit ended, not wanting to push his luck too hard. His condition was at its peak, ready to face down the numerous challenges of the Symphony of Skills.

Alistair stepped up onto the central silvery disc and hit accept.

———

George Moulin surveyed his seven compatriots. The only one not among their number was the Fifth Devil King, Chameleon, who was off serving his own purpose.

He took out a cigarette. An old habit, one that he had promised himself to stop many times before the initiation. He had never quit. The good humor of the multiverse decided that one of his Class Skills would allow him to conjure them.

They were no ordinary cigarettes. While he held it with his teeth, he placed a single index finger at the end and pulsed a tiny amount of his ice affinity Mana. The cigarette lit up, not with flames, but with glowing ice. Somehow, it still had the same effect, sating an addiction that had long disappeared. He tossed it aside after exhaling once.

"Get on," he told them. The lesser Devil Kings scurried like rats on a boat to their positions, with him at the center. "Let's finish this quickly."

———

0 HOURS AFTER THE START OF THE GRAND DUNGEON.
SECTOR ONE: THE FURNACE OF IMPURE FLAMES

Alistair was in Hell.

He was in the middle of an enormous cavern. There were columns of jagged black rock interspersed with rivers of red flame. The air smelled of sulfur and a shimmering haze covered everything.

The mountains of black rock extended forever in all directions, except downward. As far as he could see in the sky, there was always another layer of fire, another spire of rock.

More fire? Alistair thought. *Haven't we had enough of that?*

His complaints fell on deaf ears.

The flames weren't as hot as the inner portion of Selephita's territory, and his **Mammothskin Raiment's** cold and heat protection had more than doubled since then. Alistair found the Furnace of Impure Flames no hotter than a temperate fall day. For the moment.

A small map screen appeared in his vision, showing bare-bones features of the terrain, like which sections were rocky and which sections were flame. The most important part was the pulsing dot. There was a golden dot at the perimeter of the map, highlighting that it wasn't within his current map range.

"Will things be that easy?" he asked aloud.

"Let me sleep until you really need me," Dev'rox replied. "I'm still recovering."

Alistair gave him a thumbs up and started heading toward the golden dot. A few minutes in, he first realized the insidious nature of the fires.

It should have been obvious from the name of the sector. As Alistair traversed through the hellscape, the flames grew stronger. They were dirty and dark, verging on maroon and barely luminous. A strange feeling overtook him.

Not that strong at first, it was like a brain fog that made him want to lay down his arms. These foreign thoughts triggered an alarm in Alistair's mind. If he was not so practiced in controlling his mental states through mindful meditation, he never would have figured out that the origin of the thoughts was not indigenous.

His Dao Heart was being assailed.

Like the minute whispers of a devil on his shoulder—no, Alistair caught himself before Dev'rox complained. Like a state politician whispering on his shoulder, the flames tried to infect his very being. They promised power, immortality, and more, as long as he abandoned his path. As long as he forsook justice, ghost, and the fist, the impure furnace would reward him.

Alistair rejected this ideology. His Dao Heart was not so weak that these flames could convert him. He pushed onward, retreating into his Tranquil Mind. In the respite of pure serenity, Alistair knew that the profane cries of the impure flames were nothing but empty lies. They could not shake his faith in his path.

At the point where he needed Tranquil Mind to resist the false promises, he started seeing the sinners.

They were people—at least; he thought they were people. Their skin was blackened and cracking apart like ash, as if they were an overcooked steak. They wailed incessantly and didn't seem to notice him at first.

All of them were repeating a task. Over, and over, and over.

He saw one ripping out his tongue, bleeding out, only for the appendage to knit back together and the blood to return to his body. The whole process then started anew. The husk of a man screamed the entire time, louder than the others, and Alistair could actually make out his words.

"I lied, I lied, I lied! I lied, please have mercy! I didn't mean for him to burn for my lies!"

A woman in what once was a fine dress had her heart fall out, and then she had to scramble to catch it as it bounced away from her to another man. Once it got to the man, he froze and shattered into a million pieces, taking himself along with the heart, and then the process would start anew.

Their punishments fit their sins, Alistair realized, leading to why he started calling them sinners. The couple must have been an adulterous woman and man. The tongueless man was a prevaricator.

Alistair surveyed the infinite cavern with serenity. This wasn't justice. It was unnecessarily cruel. While it was a cliché statement, an eye for an eye made the whole world blind. But despite his dislike of the savagery, he felt nothing but peace—such were the depths of Tranquil Mind.

After a few hours of jogging forward in the sinner's land, Alistair felt rebuffed. He was perhaps halfway to the golden dot, but the intensity of the impure flames ratcheted up. The rivers of fire grew larger, spreading into the air into loops intersecting the dark mountains and outgrowths.

"Join us," they whispered in inscrutable voices. "Become one with the flame."

Those dirty flames licked his skin and soothed his body. Tranquil Mind held out their influence, but for how long? His improved Kai'tazake Mutra state had a higher Dao energy upkeep. A very small amount, mind you, but he didn't want to use any more of his resources than he had to. There were still nine more sectors.

Alistair turned back, temporarily heading for safer lands. He let himself out of Tranquil Mind and started to think.

If his unsullied equanimity wasn't sufficient to fully block out the insidious whispers, what on his level would be? Brute force couldn't be the answer. That left only one conclusion—the sinners. They were the only other notable feature about the Furnace of Impure Flames.

Alistair ran away from the core of profanity until he encountered one of the blackened husks. This one was shot over and over by invisible bullets until it became a shredded hunk of flesh riddled with intersecting bullet holes, only to fall to the ground and be reborn. A murderer, then? Perhaps someone who had killed with a gun.

For all the time he had been inside of Sector One so far, he hadn't come within twenty feet of one of the sinners. He had stayed far clear of them, and they hadn't bothered him.

That changed now. The moment he breached three body lengths of the man, the sinner stared straight at his soul. Eyes that were pools of darkness without end struck a primeval fear in Alistair.

The husk stopped everything he was doing and rushed Alistair with his head tilted forward and his arms behind him. With his Karmic vision and danger sense, he knew no attack was coming and let the charred man run right up to him where Alistair held his gaze, willing to challenge the abyss.

The man opened his mouth and a raspy voice came out, almost as if his vocal cords had been seared. "When I die I will be reborn in paradise and all that I have killed will become my slaves. When I die I will be reborn in paradise and all that I have killed will become my slaves. When I die I will be reborn in paradise and all that I have killed will become my slaves."

Alistair felt chills down his spine as he listened to the husk repeat its mantra over and over. He studied the being carefully. There was no threat besides his own cowardice. So what to do?

The first thing he tried was the remedy that was obviously the best in the multiverse—a healthy punch. He slammed his gauntleted fist into the sinner's face.

The husk's skull exploded from Alistair's immense blow, which carried the momentum of over 500 points of Strength. Luckily for him, there was no blood or gore, only withered flesh that barely looked human.

After ten seconds, the man's flesh reformed. Once again, he continued to get in Alistair's face and chant his bizarre creed. Alistair found it oddly familiar, like he had heard that quote before, but he couldn't place it.

Seeing that killing the sinner would do nothing, Alistair tried running away. Not because he was scared, but he wanted to see what kind of behavior this action would trigger.

The gunshot sinner followed him no matter what. No matter where Alistair climbed, or what he did, that strange dead man scrambled after him in that same disturbing manner of running. He even matched Alistair's speed, despite him going at full throttle.

Interesting, Alistair noted. *What if I try this?*

Alistair climbed up one of the enormous black rock pillars, the husk chasing after him. Below was one of the rivers of fire, burning with nefarious flame. The combustion river flowed in the air and passed through the earth, right under the shadow of the pillar.

Standing on the precipice, his stomach dropped as he looked over the edge. *I'm never going to get over heights, am I?*

He jumped.

At the last second, he called on Dev'rox for a brief moment. The imp was annoyed but listened to his command, appearing for a brief moment. This allowed Alistair to use the imp's heart-shaped face as a stepping stone for the airwalking of [Dash]. He safely landed a few feet in front of the river, cutting off [Dash] short.

The husk was less fortunate.

He fell into the concentrated stream of fire face-first. While it already looked like he had been burned, the rivers of flame were stronger. In an instant, his body combusted inside the dark fires. The whispers of the impure flames died by the smallest amount.

Baptism in fire, Alistair thought. The sins of the denizens of the sector fueled the air of iniquity, yet they were also being punished. As Alistair expected, even those sinners were not immune to the rivers. In fact, they seemed especially vulnerable.

Now he had the key to moving forward. Unfortunately, he had a problem—he had spotted over a hundred of those husks on his way to the golden dot.

Well, here I go.

———

0 HOURS AFTER THE START OF THE GRAND DUNGEON.
SECTOR ONE: THE FURNACE OF IMPURE FLAMES

George Moulin let out a puff of his magical cigarette. The ice instantly melted and then evaporated in the torrid heat.

His seven Devil Kings looked toward him for guidance. The Shadow Twins, Jakk, Morgana, Hephaestus, Monk, and Heavyset.

He surveyed the sector. Vast rivers of maroon flame flowed through volcanic rock with no end. There was no sky—only more hell. The air was hot but not unbearable for the one least capable of handling the sector, the Thirteenth Devil King, Heavyset. For himself, it was nothing. His cold would not fail.

George flicked his cigarette on the ground. He gathered the energy of two Dao Nodes—Magic and Ice—congealing it within his tongue where he added ample Mana from his turbulent soulcore.

Next came *nue*. For spells in the lettered ranks of F to A, *nue* was unnecessary. Not so for his Rank 1 spell. In his five Arcanous Devil spells, *nue* was essential. Undiluted willpower and imagination.

George spoke the name of his spell, codifying imagination into sacred speech. *"Arcanous Devil Spell #1: Glacial Front."*

An esoteric seal emerged from the ground, glowing with mystical blue energy, radiating the heart of winter. The arcane array grew—soon it could fit a house, and then a football field inside it. Once it had grown to max capacity in less than a second, the glacier emerged.

As the name of the spell suggested, it summoned a glacier. A moving glacier. The chunk of ice appeared instantly out of thin air with the array having expanded underneath them, so the glacier carried them along with it. George modulated the expansion of the glacier so as not to harm his allies.

From the moment of its birth, the glacier struggled against the world of flames. It was a cold aberration that should not have been born in such a hot place. Yet, with the power of George's imagination, it was there. He had six uses of Rank 1 spells that recharged every thirteen hours, so he would not let it go to waste.

Once fully formed, the glacier was a gargantuan block of ice over sixty feet tall, with a surface covered in steam. Then, it moved.

Slowly at first, it accelerated every second. It would start at a glacial pace, but once it started going, it was almost impossible to stop.

"Jakk!" George called. "These flames feel familiar. Your concepts are similar?"

There was so much steam that no one could see a thing, but he felt his subordinate's presence only a few body lengths away on the top of the glacier.

"Yes, sir!" Jakk called out. "I can sense the flames have a brother to my Dao Node."

"Stand as our bulwark against the seduction," George ordered. "No stopping."

27 TEAMWORK'S ADVANTAGE

9 HOURS AFTER THE START OF THE GRAND DUNGEON.
SECTOR TWO: NEXUS OF SINGULARITY

ALISTAIR ENTERED Sector Two with a head of soot-filled hair. A couple of times when he had been gathering the husks in massive groups to lemming off into the flames, he had gotten their ashes over his body. Disgusting work, it was.

He paced himself, using as little Dao energy as possible. But even if he had gone all out using the husk immolation method, he still wouldn't have completed the task quickly. There were simply too many of the sinners, too many bodies to burn. When he had finally finished, he had tossed almost a thousand of them into the flames.

And that wasn't even all of them—it was the point at which he had felt comfortable wading his way to the golden dot in Tranquil Mind, accounting for the impurity being stronger nearest the end location.

Alistair's estimation had luckily proved correct, and he calmly made it to the golden dot, which turned out to be a golden ovular portal.

On to the next one—Alistair hoped it would be less tedious.

The moment he stepped through the portal, he fell to the ground.

What the—

Alistair's body crumpled from the knees down, his face planting into the concrete. It was as if some impossibly strong man was holding his body onto the ground, but his danger sense didn't alert him to any presence. None of his senses detected any enemy. His surroundings gave no impression of any life.

Gravity. That was the only explanation that made sense, and innately what Alistair felt was happening. Wherever he was, the gravity was dozens of times its normal value. Given his immense physical stats, there was no way gravity only a few times stronger than Earth could make him fall instantly.

Gritting his teeth, Alistair pushed himself onto his knees. His muscles bulged as he pressed against the earth with all his Strength. From his perspective, he felt like he was pushing the Earth away from himself rather than pushing himself above the Earth.

Once he got to his knees, he took a breather. For one bout of exertion, it took an insane amount of Stamina, bringing him down to 950 out of 1,043 Stamina. He got a chance to observe his surroundings.

The sector of absurdly high gravity looked like a typical city block, with skyscrapers, crosswalks, and a parking garage on the corner. It was devoid of life, a ghost town that refused to crumble even under the fundamental force's pull.

Alistair could barely turn his head down to see the map. The golden dot looked to be ten blocks away. Ten whole blocks that he would have to traverse while feeling 50 G's bearing down on him.

There had to be a trick. Alistair activated [Dash], but the Skill fizzled out. His legs physically couldn't produce enough force to jump start the Skill.

He could try turning himself into a ghost. It would cost him around a sixth of his Ghost Node to travel the entire way. Not insignificant, but also not the largest cost.

The cost wasn't the issue. When Alistair tried etherealizing himself, he found his legs being dragged underneath the ground.

The gravity had a spiritual aspect that could even affect ghosts.

Well, there goes my only other idea. That left only one other option. Brute force.

Alistair began his crawl of shame.

———

45 MINUTES AFTER THE START OF THE GRAND DUNGEON.
SECTOR TWO: NEXUS OF SINGULARITY

Sector One went by in a breeze with George's glacier plus Jakk's control of the flames. They went on an unopposed march straight to the golden portal, where they all fell on their faces.

All except for George. Instead, a clone made of ice slammed into the ground.

Morgana recognized the ice substitute as *Arcanous Devil Spell #5, Subversion Through Ice.* An automatic spell that triggered whenever George registered a threat to himself, letting a clone made of ice take his place while he emerged from the nearest body of water. If there was no body of water…

A streak of light flashed by Morgana's eyes. An object hit the ground with such blinding speed that a deafening shockwave raced over the seven of them. Concrete and dust flew into the air. Morgana protected herself and her fellow Devil Kings with a wordless Rank C spell that created a shield of rotating air.

She manipulated the Mana, dispersing the debris. Their leader sat in the middle of a cracked crater, dusting off his white suit. His blonde hair never left its frozen state, remaining pristine in its spiky glory.

A small trickle of blood dripped from the corner of his lips, and he stood up with a slight limp.

George conjured up another cigarette, lighting it with his finger and then throwing it away the moment he took a single breath.

Despite the immense g-forces, which were sufficient to keep Morgana glued to the ground even with her struggling with all her might, George stood without falling. She could almost *see* the gravitational forces pulling him down.

The Shadow Twins made it to their feet. Both men wore black cloaks that completely covered their faces. They were an enigma even to her, only George knowing their full story. As for their stats, they had decent Strength, as well as Monk, their blind hand-to-hand fighter. He also struggled to a standing position, taking what looked to be agonizing seconds rising to their knees and then to their feet.

"What are you thinking?"

Morgana's head would have whipped toward her boss, but obviously, she was plastered to the ground. Thankfully, he wasn't talking to her. Based on the way their auras faltered, she assumed he was speaking to the Shadow Twins and Monk.

Not once had she ever heard George raise his voice. Not once. He always spoke with complete calm, almost emotionless. He had been that way since she met him in those dank chambers where her blood became black and her soul damned to a true end. And he didn't speak loudly here, either. But at that moment, Morgana thought she heard a tinge of humor.

"E-excuse me, sir?" a Shadow Twin asked, his voice unsteady and warped by the gravity.

George looked at the three of them with his pale blue pools of fire. "Were you planning on walking from here to the next portal? That would be two kilometers in this gravity. You can barely stand. You've probably spent at least a third of your Stamina on that."

"Apologies, master," Monk said, always prim and proper. By his voice, he sounded like he was withstanding the gravitational field better than the twins. "I think Sixth, Seventh, and I stood up because we trusted in you so much. We know how you always come up with something."

What disgusting flattery, Morgana chuckled to herself. *Does Monk really have that little shame?* Even though he was their leader, she would never debase herself like that before any man or woman or devil or god. She supposed, as the second most powerful, she was afforded slightly more liberties in that regard.

George did not answer the blind man, instead posing another of their number a question. "Heavyset, what do you think?"

Morgana felt the presence of the woman behind her. The large woman was true to her name and possibly had the highest body fat percentage of any human on the planet after the hardships of the initiation and the introduction of the Pathfinder AI made even the most sedentary glutton fit as an Olympic athlete.

To Morgana's surprise, she waddled forward into view, each step cracking the ground with her weight.

Heavyset was by far the weakest of the Devil Kings, and Morgana had to admit that it was entertaining to torment the lady. She was easy pickings, let's be honest. All her power did was make the other Devil Kings faster and the opponents slower. Useful for a team, but the Devil Kings were already overwhelmingly strong.

The gravity subsided. Morgana felt it weaken enough that even with her

150 Strength she could bring herself to her knees. It was still crushing, but not unbearably so.

"Do not underestimate the Thirteenth," George said. "Did you even realize that her powers are to control gravity?"

Morgana felt her face turn red. Heavyset looked at the rest of them with a sheepish grin, like she was happy to contribute to the team for once.

George let out a breath of chilling cold, freezing the ground in front of them in a sheet of slippery ice. He turned to Morgana. "Use that spell and help Heavyset. We will advance in thirty minutes."

———

SECTOR THREE: THE ENDLESS MENAGERIE

Alistair stood on top of a pile of corpses the size of his headquarters back in his capital.

The moment he stepped foot in the sector, a thousand beasts of innumerable species had assaulted him from all directions.

This was the dance he knew best, the thrill of combat. Except, the slaughter wasn't exciting. The beasts weren't a challenge for him. The problem was that there were too many of them.

No matter how many he slaughtered, more took their place. He drew on their life force, gaining an extra 3 Endurance that couldn't take effect because of the lock on his attributes.

He supposed that the sector was a boon in some ways. The beasts served as fuel for the evolution of his bloodline, which he would eventually need to increase his Attribute limit, and as energy to get to level 60.

After fourteen hours of punches, kicks, elbows, knees, and even some biting, courtesy of Mad Brutus, the portal to the next sector finally appeared after he defeated an enormous spider that dwarfed even elephants. By that point, he was so exhausted that he considered using his finishing Skill, just to get a much-needed respite.

In the end, he resorted to trickery—hiding behind dead beasts and using the Ghost Node to conceal himself while he attacked each leg one-by-one until he finished the arachnid off with a [Blood Hand] to the eyes.

Alistair gave himself three minutes to rest before he stepped through the golden portal. His enemies were certainly doing the Grand Dungeon as well, and he couldn't afford to stay behind.

TIME SO FAR: 29 HOURS AFTER THE START OF THE GRAND DUNGEON.

SECTOR THREE: THE ENDLESS MENAGERIE

Morgana spoke the name of her only Rank 1 spell. Unlike her master, she had not progressed down the Dao of Magic enough to use Rank 1 spells more than twice every thirteen hours.

"Shard of Madness." She expelled almost half her *nue* in a single sentence, along with a healthy amount of glass affinity Mana. Unlike George, she did not employ only a single affinity. As far as she understood the ways of mages, which to be fair was very little, they were considered some of the more versatile types of Classes. She had over five types in her core, along with several more in Skills that converted her core Mana affinities in the meridians.

A single pink shard of glass appeared underneath a similarly colored magical array in the sky. The shard multiplied and fractured until it covered the entire battlefield.

Madness followed. All the beasts that saw their twisted reflections in the glass turned on each other. They became filled with more bloodlust than they already had, wildly biting, swiping, and striking each other as the echoes of madness encompassed the entire menagerie of beasts.

Her allies looked down, knowing what to do when it came to her most powerful spell. She purposefully didn't target them, but even allies would fall prey to the madness if they stared at the shard for too long.

A few of the strongest of the beasts were unaffected by the Shard of Madness, but even the giant spider could not hold up to thousands of the smaller beasts mobbing her.

All Morgana had to do was keep the shard active. The drain on her resources was minimal—the main cost was creating the cursed object. Still, the waves of beasts were endless. Morgana wouldn't have been surprised if a hundred thousand beast corpses were lying on the grassland plains after they were done three hours later.

With the death of the arachnid, a golden portal appeared. On to the next.

Time so far: **4** hours after the start of the Grand Dungeon.

————

31 hours after the start of the Grand Dungeon.
Sector Four: The Vale of Wrathful Wraiths

"Thank goodness," Alistair said, wiping sweat off his brow as he reached the golden portal at the end of the mist-filled valley.

Wraiths. Wraiths! Finally, he had a sector that meshed well with his abilities. With his **[Ghost Whispers]** and Dao of the Ghost, Alistair confidently blended in and simply walked among the wraiths.

If only they'd all be that easy. Alistair shook his head and jumped into the next sector.

————

Sector Four: The Vale of Wrathful Wraiths

Jakk watched with undisguised confusion as his boss commended the Shadow Twins, offering them a puff of his cigarette, which they both refused graciously. "To combine your shadows with Morgana's sacrifices to emulate the aura of a wraith is something I did not think of."

Those wraiths were the bane of their existence for the first two hours they attempted the sector. They were rebuffed in every way possible. Jakk believed in his master's capability to destroy them with brute force, but he wished to save his Rank 1 spells. None of their other abilities made a dent until one of the Shadow Twins had that ingenious idea.

"Alistair will make quick work of this one," George said, stepping through the glowing oval. "We must redouble our efforts for Sector Five."

Time so far: **8** hours after the start of the Grand Dungeon.

————

31 HOURS AFTER THE START OF THE GRAND DUNGEON.
SECTOR FIVE: THE FROSTBOUND EXPANSE

Alistair got one whiff of the next sector, feeling the wrath of a blizzard so thick he couldn't see one meter in front of him. "Damn it."

———

3 DAYS, 13 HOURS AFTER THE START OF THE GRAND DUNGEON.
SECTOR NINE: PARTENTHO

The last three sectors took up the bulk of their time. Still, the Devil Kings reached the portal to Sector Nine in just about three days, preserving their resources well. Unfortunately, their progression slowed to a halt with the sector, so far having spent 13 hours on "Partentho."

Partentho was nothing like the other sectors. It was a battle of wits and strategy, taking place on an enormous hexagonal grid.

They played as a group versus the mysterious Gamemaster, a man who wore an all-white mask covering his face along with sunglasses. Each member of the Devil Kings took on a different type of piece.

One of the Shadow Twins was the Red Bishop, the other the Blue Bishop. Jakk was the Torturer, Morgana the Witch, Hephaestus the Smith, Monk the Fighter, and Heavyset the Defender. On the other hand, George took up the piece that was not a piece, the Commander. From his high vantage point, he controlled the broad strokes of his side, though individual decision-making was up to the respective players.

The Devil Kings against the Gamemaster.

The hexagonal board was not a simple two-dimensional board like most games back on Earth, being split into multiple layers, forming a three-dimensional interface. Using advanced augmented reality technology, George assumed, the players really became their pieces, and controlled them on every board.

That didn't even include the advanced aspects of the game that he did not fully grasp, such as moving from board to board and the one time travel point he could use.

"Oh, what a wonderful move," the Gamemaster commentated, like he had during the entire period. "You've almost got me in Zeitsbonne."

Zeitsbonne, George understood in the untranslated jargon of Partentho, was the equivalent of checkmate. There were two forms of victory in Partentho, he had learned in his ten hours of play. The first and most common was Sieg-Gesat, where you reduced the Commander's hit points to zero. The second, Zeitsbonne, was apparently considered the more elegant of the two, and happened when you reduced your opponent's potential Commander moves to zero.

"It seems so."

"Difficult man to please, are we?" the Gamemaster said. "Accept gifts wherever you find them."

George simply grunted at that, conjuring his twentieth cigarette of the match. He blew out a gorgeous patchwork of sculpted snow over the board, depicting the mesmerizing mathematical patterns that naturally arose from the formation of ice crystals.

It didn't take long for the Gamemaster to make his move, choosing one of the three available options. George pounced immediately, ending the game with a final attack from Morgana, destroying his last refuge.

"Congratulations on the victory, George Moulin! In your first foray into the wonderful game of Partentho, you and your people have come out victorious! You may now step forward and enter the final sector."

The Gamemaster and the various boards disappeared, replaced by an infinite black void. A single doorway of golden light appeared.

The Iceman looked back on the first hours of the initiation. No, before the initiation. The man he once was. Diligent, focused, and punctual. A man that no one put in a bad word about, a reliable and filial son that always kept up a smile. And a killer.

He was never caught. It was impossible—the police were too easy to fool when you weren't a blathering idiot. His victims disappeared without a trace. There were no fingerprints, no witnesses, no geographic continuity, no victim profile. The police didn't even know he existed, let alone the public—that was how cleanly he'd operated.

Perhaps that was why he was chosen to be the leader of the Devil Kings. George drew out a heavy breath. That all seemed so far away now. The twin Daos of Ice and Magic reverberated deep within his spirit.

Did he regret those murders? George couldn't say. What he did know was that it all felt so pointless now.

That song he used to like played in his head. What was the ugliest part of his body? Surely it was his mind, like it said.

The Devil Kings celebrated with raucous cheers. Of course. They had spent the better part of a day playing a single game, and everyone was exhausted.

"You almost fucking ruined it, Monk," Morgana said with language that betrayed her feminine elegance. "What was that attack near the end?"

The blind fighter pretended not to hear her, walking in lockstep with his leader toward the portal.

"You're blind, not deaf. Don't be a baby," Morgana teased as she followed after them.

Jakk was the last one through, taking a long look at the darkness. "That was more fun than I would've thought," he said, when he thought no one was listening.

The Gamemaster was always listening.

———

11 days, 5 hours after the start of the Grand Dungeon. Sector Nine: Partentho

"Clean sweep! Let's go!" Alistair and Dev'rox high-fived as they absolutely trounced the Gamemaster. It *might* have helped that his ghost partner was a hundred thousand years old. And as it turned out, a major fan of Partentho.

"Now do you understand why I'm such a fan of this game?" Dev'rox asked. "Partentho is the most popular game in the entire multiverse for a reason."

"Yeah, yeah, I get it," Alistair said. "You're pretty good."

"Ah, I'm nothing compared to the greats."

The Gamemaster began to fade as Alistair reduced his Commander piece to zero hit points. Sieg-Gesat, it was called. Alistair and Dev'rox had systematically reduced all of the Gamemaster's holdings on every board to nothing, finally surrounding his crown jewel. Thanks to the imp's knowledge of the game, it had only taken two hours.

The masked man who had been their opponent for the last few hours gave Alistair a disgusted look. "Cheater," he said with a mouth full of spite, and then faded to black, along with everything else.

"Don't take his words too harshly, Alistair," Dev'rox said, patting his host on the back. Alistair was glad to report that the imp had fully recovered over the course of the Grand Dungeon. Alistair had braved several sectors alone—the Frostbound Expanse took two days to traverse in the unbelievable cold that even affected him through **Mammothskin Raiment.** Sector Eight, the Maze of Light, was even longer, taking place in a subterranean labyrinth full of deadly lasers and changing pathways. But when he needed help the most, against the mysterious Gamemaster of Sector Nine, Dev'rox was there for him.

"He doesn't understand how righteous you are," Alistair joked. "You're so above board that it thinks you're a cheater because of an overflow error."

"I hope I wasn't supposed to understand that," Dev'rox said. "I have a feeling it's one of those things that Alexandra would make fun of you for."

"Your adaptation to Earth culture is scary at times. If I visit your family in the Asura Hell, will that happen to me?"

Dev'rox snorted. "Zalarik the Wise would like you, I think. My best friend Zyron would probably hate you."

They both understood that their more quippy conversation today was due to events that were better left unsaid. Despite the levity, Alistair did not falter in his drive in the slightest. He stepped through the portal, ready for whatever Sector Ten would bring.

28 COSMIC BLOOD - PART 1

FIVE DAYS AGO, the Devil Kings had left the Grand Dungeon. Alistair knew this had to be the case because the Grand Dungeon was not like the Holy Ravine. While he couldn't access the Soulnet and System Store, he could see his subregions and the general picture of what was happening back on Earth.

It wasn't pretty.

In the five days in which he had been stuck grinding the Grand Dungeon, the Devil Kings grew their freehold to 36.7% of the world. Still a decent amount away from the majority they needed for an automatic victory, but extremely troubling nonetheless.

The turn of events made Alistair question his decision. This was clearly their first real attack, done with all their power. All the little games that they had played with people's lives had led up to this.

Was he wrong to enter the Grand Dungeon? Should he have waited for Oracle's attack to wear off?

No, he thought. He shouldn't doubt himself now. He would have been forfeiting the rewards of the Grand Dungeon for the chance that he would get back to Earth sooner. Right now, any power he could rummage up was essential.

It did put him on a clock, however. While he wanted to be coy with his resources to save them for the outside, if he didn't use at least an appreciable percentage of his full power, there wouldn't be an outside to save when he returned.

But what was this final sector?

The only information he got was a small window from the system.

FINAL SECTOR: COSMIC BLOOD

Promising, Alistair thought to himself. *If it involves blood, I'm no slouch.*

Unlike the exciting start to the other sectors, Alistair found himself in a dark corridor. He could barely make out a light at the end.

On either side, there were blobs. That was the best description Alistair had for them. As tall as a human, their blue skin glowed and shifted over a gelatinous mass. Strange creatures moved underneath the surface of the jelly membrane. In place of a brain, they had a dark red mass of tentacles.

The blobs were shaped like tall spiders, with a mass above eight metallic legs that clanked softly against the dark floor of the corridor.

"Hshshsshshshs," the blob to his right hissed in an incomprehensible tongue. While the hisses came at a high pitch, there was a harmonic overtone that vibrated Alistair ever so gently, so deep that it was almost inaudible.

"Hello?" Alistair asked, hoping that the translation services of the Pathfinder AI would kick in after a few seconds. "My name is Alistair. What's going on here?"

"Hshhhhssshss," the blob to his left said. Their mouths seemed to be on the underside of the blob's mass, giving their speech an eerie ring.

"Sorry, I don't understand." Alistair put his hands up, which the blobs promptly grabbed with slimy tentacles they formed from their bodies. "Do you recognize these things?" Alistair asked Dev'rox mentally.

"No," the imp responded. "The multiverse is vast, and I can't consider myself informed on all the variety of creatures on the Physical Plane. Perhaps they're not even real. This is the Grand Dungeon of the Pathfinder AI, after all."

Alistair decided it was best to go along with the blobs. It was possible the correct move was to fight them, but he wasn't liking his chances. They outputted almost no aura, making him suspicious. He wasn't about to risk going for an **[Eyes of Truth],** either. With his various ways of detecting danger sensing no immediate threat, he walked towards the light at the end of the tunnel.

As he got closer to the light, he began to hear more of the hissing and low hums that the blobs made. They grew louder and louder the further he got, until it would have been unbearable for any normal human. Alistair's reinforced body could take it, but his eardrums weren't appreciative.

The blobs hurried him up to the edge of the tunnel. The light source he had seen before turned out to be a wall of light, impenetrable to vision.

"*Shhssshsshs,*" said one of the blobs, pushing him through.

Alistair fell into an arena of shadow and light. When his feet touched the ground, brilliant white waves emanated from the point of contact like ripples on a pond. The surface was an inky pool of utter darkness, where it felt like he was stepping on a liquid of such high surface tension he could somehow stand.

Interspersed within the darkness were pockets of light. What felt like infinite discs of white light carried thousands upon thousands of blobs, all with the same gelatinous composition and red tentacles for brains. They went up for as far as the eye could see, which, for Alistair's visual acuity, was dozens of miles.

"Looks like I'm in front of a crowd again," Alistair told Dev'rox. "I really want to know whether this is real."

As he stopped moving, the ripples of light faded. Alistair tested this out by letting his foot down carefully, noting how, when he touched the inky surface, the ripples of light appeared once more.

Cool. It's like I'm in some stylized science fiction movie. Alistair stretched his muscles and waited, taking in the crowd's succor in a language he could not understand. Were they cheering for him?

The suspense ended and the crowd's roars died as something approached in the distance. Alistair felt the presence of the enemy far before the glowing ripples appeared. An aura that he would never forget as long as he lived.

A large holographic image appeared hovering in the air, as much for him as the crowd. The text was alien, but there was a grid with pictures on it that he could partially understand. The grid appeared to be a ranking, and in the sixth slot was what might have been a number and a small avatar of a man cloaked in ice wielding a bow and arrow.

Unmistakably, it was George Moulin. Before he could think of what that meant, a new image appeared next to the ranking, partially overlaid on top of the first. An image of the creature who came closer with every breath.

Kalgur Bykrozz, Prince of the Blood Orcs, the leader of the first monster wave that had almost killed him so many months ago.

There was no natural lighting to their dark stage, only brief flashes of illumination when either of them stepped or when the multitude of discs passed over them as they swooped down in interminable patterns.

Prince Kalgur was the same as Alistair remembered. The golden orc towered over Alistair, despite the latter being five inches taller since their last encounter. He wore golden armor and carried a double-headed axe that gave off a deadly aura.

Beep. An electronic sound played through the air, accompanied by a screen depicting himself and Kalgur. Alistair couldn't read the words displayed over their persons, but he knew the meaning.

Fight.

Alistair took the fight seriously from the get-go, activating **[Eyes of Truth]** to see if there was any change since last time.

Name: Kalgur Bykrozz
Species: Continuum Bloodsun Orc I (Partially Evolved)
Level: 60
Class: Dimensionalist (Rare) [Primary Attribute(s): Wisdom and Endurance]

Not seeing a major difference besides the improved species, Alistair considered his opponent's old abilities and his new level in the split second he had before the fighting began in earnest.

Alistair unsheathed his **Devilsbane Gauntlets** from his wrists and entered Tranquil Mind.

The sublime ocean of tranquility washed over him, crashing down like a tsunami. The raging waters that he called home offered complete silence to the cries of the world. He was separate from all ties and attachments, dedicated solely to victory.

Alistair was the one to close the gap, **[Dashing]** forward. Dev'rox added to the speed by shrinking the distance between them, though his Badge, "Deliverance of Justice," did not trigger its activation requirements since as a likely program of the system, Kalgur could not be considered evil.

There was a massive spatial tug half-way through the [Dash]. A Dimensionalist Skill, no doubt. Dev'rox reacted instantaneously and surged space affinity Mana through Alistair's system to guard against the threat. Last time he fought the orc boss, he didn't have the imp.

Alistair arced a long side kick toward his opponent, activating [Force Fist] around his foot.

Kalgur was gone in an instant, the coral light of the Skill passing through empty space.

In the depths of Tranquil Mind, Alistair reacted even as he felt the space affinity Mana coursing through the orc's meridians. He couldn't directly see it, but he could feel it with his aura sense, leading him to cast down a [Lightning of Justice] where he felt the space affinity Mana shift toward.

A blinding bolt of golden lightning coursed down into the inky surface —which he quickly found coursing back at him. In a taste of his (or rather, Dev'rox's) own medicine, the Dimensionalist had created a blue portal above him where the lightning would strike and redirected it straight for Alistair.

Normally, he would have dodged, but Alistair sensed a different play to be made with Tranquil Mind. While under normal circumstances timing such an attempt would be impossible, his reaction time was so quick that as the edge of the lightning first made contact with his gloved hand, he activated [Frozen Claw].

Ice spread around the lightning bolt faster than it traveled, emboldened by the superior freezing capabilities of the somewhat recent Tier 2 upgrade. Luckily, [Lightning of Justice] did not travel as fast as a real lightning bolt, or even his reaction time would have been for naught.

At the same time, he added the "Permanent Haunt" division of his Ghost Node, making his own Skill more ghost-like and easier to freeze. Then, he threw the thirty-foot-long bolt of frozen lightning at the orc.

A cover for his true attack, he [Dashed] forward, peering into the future with [Eyes of Truth]. In less time than Kalgur could react, Alistair swapped places with Dev'rox.

The imp had worked his way around the orc, staying just close enough to not trigger any alarms. By already being mid-[Dash] when the swap happened, Alistair used that momentum to almost instantly bring himself upon his enemy.

Based on his attempted interruption of Alistair's [Dash], the orc had good reaction times, but he was unprepared for the sudden shift in location.

A deafening roar shuddered the realm of darkness as Alistair poured his mind and body into a vicious, point-blank [Draconic Roar]. As a Dimensionalist with high Wisdom, Kalgur was primed to resist *nue* more than an ordinary cultivator of his level, but he was stunned for a split second.

Exactly enough time for Alistair to strike three times. One [Force Fist] to the face in the form of a right straight, imbued with a big chunk of the Fist Node, one [Blood Hand] spearhand to the heart imbued with the Ghost Node, and then a [Frozen Claw] kick to the legs also imbued with the Ghost Node.

The impact of the three strikes seemed to overlap with one another. The fajin aspect [Force Fist] careened him back, while bountiful life force passed from his body unto Alistair. [Frozen Claw] wrapped around his feet and legs midair, sapping him of his movement.

In a panicked last move, Kalgur summoned not dozens, but hundreds of blue portals. Thousands of axes fell from the skies, while an enormous amount of space affinity Mana took hold of Alistair for but a second, anchoring him to the ground to be smote by the arsenal from the heavens.

Each axe was imbued with the Dao of Space, trained never to miss their exact mark—right where Alistair stood. They cleaved space itself as they flew down, creating a spectacle of silver light intertwined in darkness, to the pleasure of the crowd.

"I've got this one," Dev'rox said, though Alistair already knew what was to come.

The imp had two options: counter the incoming assault directly, or free Alistair from his stationary position. The former required a huge investment of Mana and effort, with no action needed on Alistair's part. The latter still required Alistair to run away from the axes at peak speed.

The imp went with the latter.

In a burst of primeval Mana, two arcane arrays appeared above Alistair in silver and shimmering transparent writing. They cleansed the anchoring Mana in no small feat, and Alistair could feel the exhaustion from the imp.

Alistair [Dashed] away from the epicenter of the massive Skill. At the end of his [Dash], a single stray axe collided with his back. He could have stopped it altogether by ending the Skill and reacting, but he chose to let it land.

Thud. His danger sense and Karmic vision told him it wouldn't be an issue, so he tanked it. **[Steel Body]** worked its magic, taking away the force of the axe as Dev'rox countered the small amount of the Dao of Space within it. A small test of his new Skill, which he knew would serve him nicely in the battles to come.

Alistair walked calmly toward his downed opponent, who had skidded even further away than a full **[Dash]'s** distance. The fajin impact of **[Force Fist]** was nothing to scoff at, though he supposed it wasn't ideal when trying to keep an opponent still.

Feeling the dwindling life force of the orc, he exited Tranquil Mind, hit by a flurry of strange emotions as he left.

All-in-all, a clean victory. Alistair hadn't meant for Dev'rox to expend what was over half his Mana, but it was actually an efficient trade. Space countered space, so if Alistair wanted to achieve his victory without relying on Dev'rox, he would have had to use even *more* of his own Mana, while Dev'rox only used 400 of his approximate 800 Mana pool.

Now that he had left Tranquil Mind, a bit of his cheekiness returned. Real or imagined, the crowd deserved some entertainment, right?

Alistair made it to the orc. As a level 60 Dimensionalist, he would have been the bane of many stronger cultivators, perhaps even stronger than Alistair, if not for Dev'rox's help. As he was, his face was caved in from the powerful **[Force Fist]**, and he was frozen against the ground.

For an orc, he had low Constitution. Endurance could only help him so much with that level of injury.

Alistair picked the dying orc up with a single arm and held him in the air.

The crowd ate up his gladiatorial antics, cheering so loud that the liquid surface beneath vibrated so hard it lit up with those glowing white ripples. Thousands of feet of the boundless arena became flooded with light, which in turn caused even more of them to hum and hiss.

Not wanting to draw out his victory any longer, Alistair tossed the orc in the air and purged him for good. While he was not in Tranquil Mind any longer, he gave solemn words to the former leader of the monster wave.

While I do not know if you are the same individual as before, I hope that you can get the release you wanted. Alistair had deduced from the many peculiar statements of the monsters that they were, in essence, Dao-bound slaves of the Pathfinder AI, reproduced and created at its leisure to serve as fodder for the growth of initiates.

A pitiful life. While it seemed antithetical to his theatrics, Alistair did have a purpose for those, and did mean what he thought. There was no contradiction to him.

[Lightning of Justice] came down and Alistair turned his back, not witnessing the obliteration in the sky.

There was nothing more evil than the slaughter of the powerless. Everyone understood that, at a basic level.

That was why a primal vengeance grew in Alistair's heart as he saw the next opponent appear in a window, as soon as he defeated Kalgur.

Atavius Meloi.

29 COSMIC BLOOD - PART 2

ALISTAIR QUELLED that feeling of rage. It would do him no good to be mad.

A symbol appeared next to Alistair's position on the ranking chart, which was at the very bottom. Though, he speculated that was because he hadn't finished the sector yet. *Is that my time?* Alistair wondered. *My performance rating? How are they ranking us fairly if we're all facing our past opponents?*

Those thoughts quickly faded as a beep sound played once again. Alistair readied himself, but he was too late.

If he had been submerged in Tranquil Mind's waters, he might have been able to react. The world became fire. Everywhere around Alistair, miniature explosions of orange-red flame spread like a chain reaction. The amount of Mana and Dao energy contained within the explosions exceeded his own ultimate Skill's output, washing out everything in a blanket of fire. The flames were so hot he could see the very threads of Fate themselves singeing and burning, which explained why his foresight hadn't seen the sudden attack coming.

Alistair tried running. He activated **[Frozen Claw]** with as much of the Ghost Node as he could muster, focusing his power on turning the flames into harmless spirit crystal. He flexed his muscles in the way that Pike and Master Ko Pao had taught him, regardless of the fact he was being assaulted with fire, not a punch or kick.

Dev'rox struggled as well, expending Mana like crazy to open a safe passage for his host. All for naught. The space affinity Mana that the ghost could muster was but a drop in an ocean compared to the chain explosions.

There was nothing he could do. With only thirty feet separating the two fighters before the beep heralded their duel, Alistair was already too close to Atavius.

An explosion triggered right in front of Alistair's face as his [Dashes] failed in the sea of boiling air. Burning pain washed over him for a brief moment. He would not falter. Not now, not ever. He could still move, the fires were hot but not—

Alistair looked down, seeing that he was no longer moving.

"My legs—"

The flames entered his mouth, and then there was nothing.

Death. Alistair's mortal life had ended.

Alistair came to, coughing up a storm. He dry retched multiple times, so disoriented from the feeling of dying. It was like Atavius's fires were still inside him, burning him up from the inside.

After a minute of convulsing, Alistair's body finally realized it wasn't in danger any longer, and he just laid on the floor breathing heavily.

He was in a white space the size of a bedroom. There was no ornamentation, only white tiling that felt sterile and devoid of life.

"It'll pass." The voice that spoke those words felt like warm honey on a winter's day. Alistair tilted his head up to see the source.

Alistair's breath was taken away as he saw one of the most beautiful women he'd ever seen. Only the firebird exceeded her.

The woman's skin was pale and flawless, her features delicate and rosy. She had luscious black hair that fell over a silk dress, similar to a qipao, that gracefully flowed over her full figure. The most stunning feature of all, however, were her golden eyes that outshone even the all-white room they were in.

The woman was sitting down in a meditative pose, her serene pose unaltered by Alistair's noisy arrival. In spite of all his life-or-death battles, keeping a cool face in front of this unrivaled beauty was a whole different task.

"I think the worst has already gone," Alistair said with an even voice, performing a kick up off of his back to get to his feet in one smooth motion.

The woman's lips curled up in a small smile, seeing his acrobatics. "What is this place? No, that's quite rude of me. What is your name?"

"Gu Fuhao," she said, rising to her feet in a single motion off of one knee. Alistair couldn't explain it, but every word out of her mouth resonated with something deep in his soul. Was it some aspect of her cultivation? "And yours?"

"Alistair Tan."

"This place is the waiting room," she said. "Were you not informed?"

"I'm not informed about most things," Alistair said. "You could say I'm kind of a country bumpkin."

A spark went off in Fuhao's eyes as she realized what he meant. "Ah, a Prime Initiate. That makes more sense. The Cosmic Blood is for those under level 100 to test themselves against their past foes in a standardized manner. The rankings show the leaders within the fief."

"I'm not even level 60 yet," Alistair said. "Graded on a curve, then?"

Fuhao nodded. Alistair followed up with another question. "How does that work when there are groups versus individuals?"

"Groups versus individuals?" Fuhao raised an eyebrow. "What do you mean?"

"From my world, they allow groups of eight to attempt Cosmic Blood," Alistair explained. "The current sixth position on what I assume to be the Disputed Shard rankings is a notorious criminal from my world. Well, I don't know if 'criminal' is the best way to put it anymore. All that's really important is that he is a very, *very* bad guy."

"I see," Fuhao said. "The initiates are far weaker than the established youth, so they must have let you come in groups. Still, sixth is impressive, even if it was a team of eight." She looked down at his chest. "Where did you get that?"

"Lots of working out," Alistair said. "Bench press, push-ups, dips. The whole gamut."

Fuhao gave him a playful glare. "I mean the ring around your neck."

Alistair looked down, feeling the golden chain and ring. The **Thrice-Blessed Fate-Diviner** was not something that he thought about often. He never really felt its influence, even though his Karmic sight had gotten much better over time. Its influence on the machinations of Fate must have been subtle and advanced.

"It was a gift from my sponsor, the Clear Water Sect."

Fuhao chuckled. "As I suspected. Our meeting is providential, then. For I too shall be attending the Clear Water Sect next standard year."

"I look forward to seeing you again," Alistair said. "Are you also from the Disputed Shard? I assume so, since you're here."

"The head Gu Clan rules the Plain Expanse duchy, on the border of Mai Atal. I am from one of their many branches. Don't get your hopes up too high."

"What, you take me for someone that cares about silly things like status?" Alistair smiled. "I'm not so shallow."

"Status is not so weak that you can throw it away like an impure pill," she said. "You must be quite special to have such a disregard for it."

"What if I am special?"

"I am not in the habit of befriending braggarts," Fuhao said with a smile that Alistair couldn't read. "We have too many of those in this generation."

"What's the antidote, then? A good old-fashioned dose of chivalry?"

"I'd settle for anyone that knew openly bragging about one's inwrought foundations was gauche."

"Settle as in—"

Fuhao coughed, but with her sonorous intonation it sounded more majestic than that. "Don't you want to know more about Cosmic Blood? For instance, every time you die, you're held here for an hour, increasing by another hour each subsequent death."

"That would probably be a good thing to know," Alistair admitted. "I'm all ears, thank you."

Fuhao explained to him the rest of the conditions of Cosmic Blood. While one's energy reserves were reset every death, this didn't apply to things like cooldowns of Skills to prevent people from spamming their finishing Skills in an unrealistic way. This also applied to proto-Domains, which were limited to once per day, but that part was irrelevant to Alistair.

There was one final aspect that the initial dungeon prompt didn't mention—the Badge. For those that placed well in the fief rankings, there was a special Badge named after the sector itself that gave bonuses in accordance with one's performance. For example, 1st place received a Badge called "Cosmic Blood – 1st Place," while those in lesser positions got Badges like "Cosmic Blood – Top 100."

The Cosmic Blood Badge was unique compared to all the Badges that Alistair had heard of in that it expanded his slots by one automatically, requiring no Upgrade Points. Fuhao told him she didn't know the exact details of what each Badge got, but she knew for a fact the top Badges were amazing.

"The guy in first place is the only person to not have died a single time," she told him. "They're calling him the future of the Disputed Shard."

Alistair groaned internally. "His name wouldn't happen to be Red Harmonia, would it?"

"Who?"

That's a pleasant surprise. "Never mind."

"Someone to watch out for?" she asked him.

"You could say that again," he said. "What were you saying about the amount of enemies?"

"There are five total combatants, the last being... special," she said.

Alistair gave her a quizzical look. "Special, how?"

"That would ruin the surprise, wouldn't it?" she laughed. "Sorry to end this meeting early, but my time is almost up."

"How soon?"

"In the next ten seconds."

"Ah," Alistair said. "In that case, good luck. I have to imagine we'll see each other soon enough at the sect."

"Oh, undoubtedly," Fuhao said. "Take—"

Before the jade beauty finished her sentence, she disappeared. In one moment, she was in front of Alistair, and in the next, nothing. Not a hint of her aura, and no indication from any of his senses she was about to go.

It seemed that the noblewoman left a gift for him, an azure disc the size of his palm that looked like a CD. The disc floated gingerly onto his hand, where it was ever so slightly repelled by his innate aura, floating a whisker above his skin.

Alistair spent the next couple of minutes toying around with the disc. Its purpose wasn't immediately obvious, but after noodling his Mana around the internal pathways, he came to an interesting conclusion.

The disc wasn't some secret manual, or guarded informational missive. No, it was a mixtape. At least, the cosmic version of one. And the star was Gu Fuhao, as Alistair heard what was unmistakably her voice in perfect fidelity, as if she were really there.

"Definitely follows a Dao of Music," Alistair noted. "Her voice is something else."

"Focus on the battle ahead," Dev'rox snorted. "Do you want to have that monster's flames stuffed down your throat once again?"

Alistair didn't respond to that, instead focusing inward. Dev'rox was right about taking the fake Atavius seriously. So, he mapped out a path to victory. He didn't know if it would work a hundred percent, but that's why they had the extra lives, right?

———

Atavius always went with the same opening salvo. The implosion field of firebombs that turned Alistair's world into a sea of flames.

It wasn't fair in the slightest. First of all, the programmed Atavius could activate his finishing Skill at the very start of the duel, whereas Alistair was constrained by his reactions. Second and perhaps more importantly, according to the information from Fuhao, the Meloi scion always had access to his Skills. No cooldowns for him.

After his hour of preparation, Alistair decided not to go for **[Thousand-Armed Bodhisattva Judgment]** right away. When he appeared back in the arena of darkness, he was already inside Tranquil Mind.

The small difference in reaction time allowed him a single moment to [Dash]. One of those Hall of Mathematics scrolls had said that combat between cultivators was either over in the blink of an eye or lasted a fortnight. While that was obviously an exaggeration, he did come to a better understanding of that concept as his legs pumped with Mana and flickered to his target destination.

Alistair's Karmic sight wasn't effective since the threads of Fate were already burnt from the future potential of the encompassing fires, but that didn't stop him from his singular purpose. He even added a tinge of Dev'rox's Mana, just in case. Unfortunately, unlike his Mana, Dao energy, and *nue*, his Karma and Dev'rox's reserves didn't refill.

I suppose that's what I get for being so greedy, Alistair thought. He really did have a hand in a diverse set of methods.

Yet, despite his immense velocity, the flames acted first. With a speed that should have been impossible, the explosions intensified, incinerating Alistair when his fist was a hair's breadth away from making contact with Atavius's cheek.

There was nothing. Alistair came to in the same room as before, gasping for air as his body was turned inside out. This time, he had no company.

"We underestimated him," Dev'rox said. Alistair was certainly jealous that the imp wasn't affected by the revival process like he was. "Tell me you understand, brat?"

"It's a dominion Skill," Alistair replied, rising to a sitting position. "It has to be for that level of control."

Dev'rox tsked. "All those senses and you didn't recognize the change near his body? The dominion Skill was seamlessly layered on top of a proto-Domain. That's why it altered and became stronger when you got close."

"So should I fight fire with fire, then?"

"Hmm, perhaps not yet," Dev'rox answered. "We want to save [Thousand-Armed Bodhisattva Judgment] since the enemies are going to keep getting stronger."

Alistair was kind of embarrassed that his hour of preparation had led to getting obliterated even faster than last time, but he supposed it was to be expected when trying to deal with an opponent's finishing Skill without using his own.

This time, he had two hours to review the information gleaned in the previous instance, and formulate a new stratagem.

Alistair breathed in deep and found himself in new territory—Infinite Arsenal.

While the concept that became Infinite Arsenal was represented by a sea of knives floating in the sky, his new state was something beyond that. Instead of becoming surrounded by knives, he was the weapon. Unlike Tranquil Mind, the effects of Infinite Arsenal were outwardly visible, with a thin silver layer spreading all over Alistair's skin.

The change was not only external. If Tranquil Mind ceased all attachments to the outside world, Infinite Arsenal made him hyperfocus on combat. Every single ounce of brainpower was solely devoted to innumerable calculations, like he was a pugilist supercomputer.

In the next instant, he was back in the arena. Already he had been going through hundreds of opening salvos, trying to find the proper starting point. Infinite Arsenal was unlike Tranquil Mind in that it took a comparatively long amount of time to go through the vast array of possibilities. In the end, his calculations led to a conclusion he most likely would never have come up with on his own.

Alistair started off with a [Dash] once more. Unsurprisingly, without his improved reaction time, he was slower than before. Dev'rox added his own Mana, but Atavius's flames would reach them far before they could get within striking range.

That was where Alistair's new idea came in. Seeing Spiritual Fighter's Echo allowed him to contemplate the mystery of Dao energy and understand proto-Domains more fully. While he didn't understand fully how it all broke down, from his experiences with proto-Domains he knew that it had to do with immanentizing the Dao.

Alistair didn't quite understand where the spark of inspiration came from, but in his meditations, he became drawn to the inner workings of his soulcore. The serrated, Klein bottle-esque organ was fundamentally intractable to Alistair, at least at that point. But somehow, like he was learning to ride a bike, he was able to etch a minuscule space within the interior of his soulcore.

The beginnings of a proto-Domain. Alistair wasn't even close to finishing, but he didn't need an enormous space. All he wanted was a small layer, merely covering the skin.

Time seemed to slow down as Alistair sprinted toward his target. Burning explosions washed out his field of vision, but he didn't stop. Even as the flames emitted heat that made him sweat even through the veneer of Dao energy around his body, he aimed his fist forward.

Alistair combined [Frozen Claw] with [Hand of Karma], crimson Karmic energy surrounding ice affinity Mana that steamed within the environment of fire.

His attack was potentially suicidal—Alistair didn't know if the dominion Skill would continue after Atavius died. But he guessed that didn't matter—the last fight instantly ended after he killed Kalgur.

The flames became hottest within a body length of the blond cultivator. Alistair felt his skin melt, the beginnings of his proto-Domain not even close to strong enough to ward off the extreme heat. Even the added insulation of **Mammothskin Raiment** could only hold off so much.

As the flesh fell off his limbs, the **Devilsbane Gauntlet** connected with Atavius's face.

Karmic energy flooded the cultivator's spiritual network, aided by the cold of [Frozen Claw]. As a long distance fighter, Atavius's defenses weren't able to cope with the sudden infusion of energy, his body freezing from the inside out.

After that, it was a matter of time to see who would perish first. One in fire, one in ice.

Alistair held out with all his willpower. Ice affinity Mana exploded out of his soulcore, flooding every meridian and cell in his body in a last-ditch effort to keep himself cool.

The ice Mana helped only a tiny amount, but perhaps that small change was what let him survive.

Alistair almost didn't even recognize the change. In one moment his body was melting off his skeleton, and in the next he was fully healed with his energy pools back to full.

While physically he was completely fine, psychologically he wasn't prepared. A current of energy flowed through his body, withering him away to nothingness.

Alistair came to in the white room. The scent of the entropic Mana was still fresh in his mind. A familiar scent. Anthony Ricci's time affinity Mana.

———

Through trial and error, Alistair vanquished the next two opponents in the circuit. It turned out that despite being weaker, Atavius was his worst match-up. Because, like an automaton, he always started the fight with an enormous area of denial attack, Alistair's speed and versatility were much less effective.

He was able to defeat Anthony with only one more death. Going back to Tranquil Mind, he deftly weaved in between the time cultivator's beams of entropic radiation, as well as the massive hand from [Warden of Time]. Always staying on top of Anthony, he won through the slow death of a thousand blows.

The next opponent was Dragonus, another fire user. Fortunately, he didn't start out with a huge attack like Anthony, instead opting for his flaming pillar of the false Heavens. Alistair died three times, though not because of his own weakness, but because of Dragonus's overwhelming power.

According to the information he obtained when he used [Eyes of Truth], this Dragonus was level 70. Alistair was outstatted by the Devil King, especially with his current soft cap. But as he gained experience and applied his guile, he was able to overcome the difference in stats, ending the fight with a sequence of twenty rapid-fire punches.

At last, Alistair was at the final opponent. He couldn't help but feel a tingling of nerves as he wondered how exactly this last foe would be "special."

There was a longer build-up this time, instead of being thrust right into the moment. The moment after he defeated Dragonus, he felt a shift underneath in the inky pools.

In the blink of an eye, Alistair flew into the air to the delight of the crowd, who buzzed with such vigor that they created a light show.

A translucent blue bubble grew into a sphere with a radius of thirty feet. Alistair moved his body within the bubble, realizing that this was no ordinary playing field. Wherever he moved, it was like he was walking on an invisible plane at that exact orientation.

The strangest part was that it was only when he willed it. If he moved his foot upward with the intention to step, he could literally walk on empty air. However, if he moved his leg to kick, nothing would change. It was as if he was in a field of optimized movement, calibrated to perfection for a melee fighter as himself.

Beep. An electronic screen popped up, showing Alistair versus his opponent. He wasn't sure what he'd been anticipating, but the image that popped up was not in his expectations at all.

Himself.

A perfect replica of Alistair stood on solid air, staring him down. A chill ran down his body as he perceived the clone with all of his senses. *Nothing* was off. In all respects that he could understand, this system-wrought doppelganger was identical.

That was with one exception—his clone didn't seem to have any of Alistair's hangups regarding the strange scenario. While its original was still fazed, the clone shot forth with a **[Dash]**.

Alistair being shocked by his own speed was a surprise. It wasn't as fun being on the receiving end of someone who had almost 900 Agility.

Through his battle-honed instincts, he put up a hand to guard the incoming punch, but the explosive force ricocheted his own hand into his face, sending him flying backward. Alistair bounced against the blue force field with enough impact to rattle his bones.

Then came the ghostly afterimage. His own Spiritual Fighter's Echo walloped his cheek, the strike seemingly unavoidable, and he careened sideways. By orienting his feet and imagining he was against a flat surface, he held himself midair.

The other Alistair didn't miss the opportunity. With glowing crimson eyes, the signature of [Eyes of Truth] scared the hell out of the original, and the clone appeared with a flicker to his right. In the moment before everything turned white, the original Alistair saw the crimson hand that had prevented him from sensing the attack.

Once more, he woke up in the waiting room.

30 COSMIC BLOOD - PART 3

ALISTAIR SLOWLY GOT up to his feet. The adrenaline rush of dying had faded by that point. Now, he was more feeling the shock of facing himself.

"So that's what she meant by the last one being 'special,'" Alistair grumbled. Unlike before, there was no one else in the pure white waiting room. Since this was his sixth death, he'd have to wait for a whole six hours. Six hours in which George and the rest of the Devil Kings were roaming free in the wider world.

As for his own metrics, he couldn't even imagine how strong the so-called future of the Disputed Shard was.

But it wasn't just about strength. The part that piqued Alistair's curiosity was that the first place cultivator hadn't died a single time against his own clone that was stronger in every category. How was such a thing possible?

"It's obvious, isn't it?" Dev'rox butted in.

Alistair had been practicing mental control with *nue* to prevent the imp from reading his thoughts so cleanly, but clearly, it wasn't working. "Explain," he ordered.

"It is good for your mental development to produce the explanation yourself. Now answer."

Alistair stroked his chin, giving in to his partner. "It truly felt like an exact replica of myself. Of course, there have to be stipulations, right? First off, it's definitely better than me in every stat. If it were an exact clone, it wouldn't have beat me so easily, taken off guard or not. I definitely felt superior Agility and Strength in our short exchange. Also, I'm guessing the clone can't use my finishing Skill to start off since that wouldn't be realistic. If I didn't have to care about my own life, I would do crazy starting moves, so there is some self-preservation there. If it's an exact replication of how I would act…"

A light went off in Alistair's brain. "Then I just have to get better than my old self? And… that guy was able to adapt so fast, he got better than his old self before he could get killed even once. That's scary."

Dev'rox chuckled. "Those are the type of talents you're going to have to face soon enough. So let's brainstorm some strategies. Luckily, you have me on your side."

———

At the exact six-hour mark, Alistair was teleported back into the arena. He timed this moment to a microsecond, exploding with **[Dash]** right away.

Skill Upgraded: [Dash] (Tier 4 Beginner Skill): *Run across long distances in a single step through enhancing your body with Mana—adding a shadow of nue to confuse foes.* Flicker, Airwalking. Mana Cost: 35. Upgradeable (0/200).

Alistair hadn't realized how close his most used Skill was to the next tier before using it. In motion, he sadly felt no difference in speed, but upon arrival, a shadow of himself composed of *nue* appeared upside down at a strange angle, as if stuck to the ceiling. It was funny, as this *nue* shadow took its energy from Alistair's mental reserves, but it also replicated his presence, just like the clone.

I think it would be more effective against an enemy that wasn't myself, Alistair thought. To the clone, it would only take a small amount of brainpower to distinguish the shadow from the real deal.

Alistair went for the kill. It was a strategy that he wouldn't have thought of himself, owing it to the imp, so he was hoping that his doppelganger wouldn't think of it—if it thought at all and wasn't a Pathfinder faux.

Alistair activated **[Thousand-Armed Bodhisattva Judgment]**.

The other Alistair pounced right away. Like the original expected, the clone instinctively understood what the one-second gap in activation time meant. As an ancient voice chanted its blessed name in a sublime language, the copy pounced on Alistair. The copy crossed his forearms and slashed with a [Hand of Karma] and [Blood Hand], intent on eliminating his opponent in one blow before the finishing Skill fully manifested.

Dev'rox shielded his host, invoking an arcane array in front of and behind Alistair. The array connected the two spaces together, eliding Alistair from the space and therefore the incoming attack. For a moment, the opposing [Hand of Karma] struggled against the array, but with a push from the imp, it went through nonetheless.

Alistair could tell Dev'rox put a lot of Mana into his spell and silently thanked him for his efforts. In the meantime, the Avalokiteśvara avatar fully formed, its resplendent coral and gold body fueled to the brim by what felt like unceasing Dao energy. How would his other-self deal with such an attack?

Dozens of palms flew at the other Alistair. The chants of the Great Compassion Dharani filled the air, giving the entire force field cage a golden aura of resplendent peace and love, calming him into a serene mental state.

What Alistair wasn't expecting was his clone's next step. It looked as if in the moment his slashing attack failed, he moved to defense. The first step was entering into a state that Alistair had not attempted yet—Black Impermanence. A chill spread through the air even faster than the speed of the arcing palms of justice. True finality.

Black Impermanence was based off the Chinese psychopomp, but it did not invoke a Dao of Death, instead drawing its meaning from Alistair's Ghost Node. A black halo surrounded the replica, especially in the irises, which looked like the corona of a solar eclipse. Alistair could tell right away that this state would be a beast on offense, adding lethality to all attacks, but the clone accessed a more defensive aspect.

A [Draconic Roar] bellowed from the other Alistair's lungs, streaks of force affinity Mana straining as it collided with the all-encompassing silo of [Thousand-Armed Bodhisattva Judgment].

As expected, it was no match for the finishing Skill. Still, a solid 15% of the hands got destroyed by the roar. Right as the attack was about to land, Alistair felt a sudden chill, as if all the heat had vanished in a moment.

Then the palms struck. One after another, every third of a second, golden and coral energy flowed out in waves. Each shockwave rattled the other Alistair with the smiting hand of justice.

Alistair frowned.

The eastern gong sound that reverberated with each blow was but a fraction of the volume it had against Oracle. The golden shockwaves were muted and contained only a sliver of the energy.

He had spotted the other Alistair's defensive technique—combining the skin-tight proto-Domain expansion with Black Impermanence. Yet that shouldn't have been able to defend against the full-blown force of his avatar.

He would have time to figure things out as the clone prepared his own **[Thousand-Armed Bodhisattva Judgment]**. Seeing as Alistair was out of cards to play, he sat there and took the Skill head-on.

In the final moments before he "died," Alistair came to the pertinent realization.

Justice? Oh, shit.

———

Alistair paced around the waiting room, slamming his fist against the impermeable white walls. Thankfully, they were constructed in such a way that he didn't feel any jolt on impact, so he could smash them as hard as he wanted.

"My Skill's useless!" Alistair said, throwing his hands in the air. "I feel like I've been scammed."

"Come on now, don't start spiraling," Dev'rox said. "It's far from useless. It just seems to be far more effective when used on villains. Makes sense, considering its name and description."

Alistair hadn't even considered that possibility before, but it made all too much sense. It was like an extreme version of how his "Good Samaritan" Badge made him stronger against reprobate evildoers.

"This type of training always feels so artificial," Alistair complained on an unrelated note. "Doesn't it dull your instincts to have a situation where death is so meaningless?"

"The Pathfinder AI has accounted for that mentally," Dev'rox said. "I should know, dealing with frontier brats for tens of thousands of years.

You've been through these types of trials before. Now, things aren't as bad as they seem, are they?"

Alistair scoffed. "I know what you mean. He can't Bodhisattva me as effectively, too. But he's slightly better than me at everything, so that doesn't matter. I can literally *feel* it. Anything that I do against him, he's going to anticipate and do even better."

His pace slowed, and Alistair stroked his chin. There was a slight stubble there—having been trapped there for over twenty hours would do that. Funnily enough, the speed of hair growth was one of the few unchanged things about his physiology. Nowadays, he used the sharp claws of the **Devilsbane Gauntlets** to shave.

"We spent six hours perfecting that strategy, using my knowledge of myself to see what I would do in each scenario. An imperfect accounting of my abilities led to my loss, though obviously we can't be sure I wouldn't have come up with some ingenious solution. The main issue that I see is this —besides a rush like that unleashing all my trump cards to create artificial surprise, I really have nothing if he's truly better than me in every conceivable way. That leaves one last solution. I have to rapidly improve in one, low time cost domain, and surpass myself. That must have been what the first place guy did."

"Well reasoned. My spawnlord would give you a ten hellfire lashing reprieve for that rational conclusion. The only question is, what can we get you up to snuff in within a reasonable time frame?"

Time. Alistair couldn't forget that key element. Technically, if he spent enough time absorbing the ambient Mana, which was honestly quite abundant and condensed, he could get to level 60 and then steamroll his past self with higher stats, but that could take weeks. Weeks that he didn't have.

It wasn't clear how teams vs. a solo run like himself worked, but he had an inkling it would be easier. Everything about the sectors up until now made it patently obvious that teamwork was the name of the game. Every challenge that he had faced would have been easier with allies like his sister, Oliver, Alfred and his brother, and, of course, Alexandra, by his side. He could perfectly imagine the synergy of their approach. Too bad he was all alone.

"[Dash]," Alistair said, trying to ignore extraneous thoughts. "The other Alistair doesn't have my upgraded version of **[Dash]**. He seemed to see through it quite easily, however."

"There's a foothold," Dev'rox said. With their close bond, Alistair could feel the unsaid words. *Not quite good enough.*

"If I'm going to center my strategy around my improved [Dash], trying to increase my speed might be the way to go."

"That's all well and merry, but how would you go about doing that?"

Alistair frowned. "Maybe if I could somehow orient my mind to see myself as evil, I could trigger "Good Samaritan" into giving me my Agility and Intelligence bonus."

Unlike his base stats, it seemed like the Pathfinder AI allowed for temporary bonuses to go above his current bodily limitations. He had been wondering for quite some time about whether that kind of stat manipulation could be useful for other purposes, but he put that thought aside for the moment.

"It's not as easy as that," Dev'rox said. "With everything I know about cultivation, a Badge like that is operating at both a personal and metaphysical level. You won't be able to fool it with tricks, at least of that level."

"There has to be something. We have seven hours. If we come up empty-handed, that's an embarrassment."

———

Alistair's third attempt at beating himself was an exercise in survival.

Fake Alistair matched real Alistair blow for blow in a surprisingly mellow opening sequence. Or not so surprising, as he had anticipated the lull in energy. It definitely seemed like the doppelganger escalated the fight in accordance with Alistair's effort. Not that the thing was ever going easy, but he obviously wasn't going all out from the start.

That didn't matter. In every aspect of fighting, he was slightly superior.

Alistair let his battle-honed instincts take over, throwing punch after kick at strange angles, taking advantage of the terrain. He would vary his speeds, going for a fast flying knee, before switching into a clinch and trying to go for a throw.

His other side was always a half step ahead. In every exchange, he had the slight upper hand. A glancing punch against him was a direct hit on Alistair. A partially checked leg kick on him was a direct hit to the calf for Alistair. The accumulation of blows slowly dealt damage, on top of Spiritual Fighter's Echo.

Alistair was already unused to using the new power offensively, so it was no wonder it was an issue defensively. Even after the tiniest of blows landed on him, he would be slightly thrown off by a coral echo repeating the attack half a second later.

His new passive Skill, **[Steel Body],** didn't even cover that part. Still, he was thankful for it. Though it increased the length of his torturous defeat, it gave him more time to adapt.

Alistair tried his hardest. Simply put, there was nothing he could do. His other self was always one step ahead, always a little faster and stronger. It was really weird, to be honest. Like how one's brain always believed it had free will, Alistair always felt like he *should* have been able to outsmart or outspeed or outskill his opponent, but it always fell short.

Somehow, it felt even more devastating than when Red Harmonia effortlessly defeated him. That was a gap in talent, at least at the time, like the heavens and the earth. This was more like your older brother always beating you no matter what.

He could have upped the burners, slipping into Tranquil Mind or Infinite Arsenal. But that would have only been matched at an even higher level. Instead, he employed Dev'rox.

Alistair focused as much as he could on his connection to Dev'rox. This didn't grant him an advantage necessarily; while the doppelganger lacked an identifiable spiritual companion, he replicated the imp's powers as a generic spatial power.

But he wasn't trying to outmaneuver his opponent, not yet. He only needed to hold on and wait. Execute the strategy.

Alistair spit out blood and a tooth as a perfect replica of his own **Devilsbane Gauntlets** caved his jaw in. After ten minutes of back and forth hand-to-hand combat, he was slowing down. The doppelganger's advantages were growing as the accumulated damage took its toll on Alistair. At the beginning of their fight, he was only a step behind, but now he was a whole marathon away.

Dev'rox appeared and intercepted a punch with one of his teleportation circuits, but the punch came back through a shadowy array. Alistair wasn't the only one to abuse space. Gritting his teeth, he tried to put up a hand to block, but a deep gash in his shoulder slowed him down. The **[Frozen Claw]** connected with his eyes.

The pain didn't last for long as Alistair died for the eighth time. But not before he upgraded [Ghost Whispers] to Tier 4.

————

Alistair came into the next series of attempts with no dreams of victory. Still, he didn't squander them, knowing that each moment was precious on the outside.

[Ghost Whispers] (Tier 4 Journeyman Passive Skill): *Gather the spiritual energy of the dead to fuel your own power, while also granting communication with ghosts and other spectral entities. Creates a two-way mental link that allows for seamless communication.* Upgradeable (0/200).

There was a single new sentence in one of his oldest remaining Skills. While there was already a well-established link between him and Dev'rox, Tier 4 of [Ghost Whispers] was at a different level. It was as if their minds were one, increasing their processing speed to the level of both of them combined.

In his next five deaths, Alistair came closer and closer to victory. Through his seamless integration with Dev'rox, manipulating space became second nature. Alistair abused all kinds of angles and sudden attacks, blending his new [Dash] to throw the other Alistair off.

He caught the replica with his best blow in any of their bouts, a question mark kick to the face. Alistair's **Fall of Fleet** boots knocked a tooth out of his opponent. Unfortunately, that escalation of violence led to the other Alistair using his own [Thousand-Armed Bodhisattva Justice].

Alistair copied his own copy's defensive technique—overlaying Black Impermanence with a local proto-Domain, but he was a tenth of a second behind in the application. With a thunderous [Dash], the replica rushed ahead of his own finishing Skill and took Alistair by surprise with a [Hand of Karma].

The threads of Fate twisted in turmoil as the clone threw him by the neck up to the ceiling of the blue force dome. The impact of [Thousand-Armed Bodhisattva Justice] thrust him into the force field over and over. The Skill itself wasn't the winner—the trauma of hitting his head against the impermeable barrier was the coup de grâce.

When Alistair woke up, he almost still felt dizzy from being rocked so many times. And a bit of despair. Would he himself have come up with that idea, knowing that [Thousand-Armed Bodhisattva Justice] wasn't as effective against non-evil enemies? To use the environment like that?

Without even saying any words, Dev'rox showed him some memories of his fights. Their bond had deepened with Tier 4 of [Ghost Whispers], allowing him to send more abstract ideas and emotions. Interestingly, he also found that despite the improved link via [Ghost Whispers], he could more easily block specific thoughts to the imp, offering more control.

"You play too much," Dev'rox said. "I'm confident that you're confident you'll figure this out."

"I'm not as arrogant as you think I am, Dev'rox," Alistair shot back. "I might be confident I'll eventually win, but time is of the essence here. It's been over four days now, with all of my deaths. The more times I die, the more time we have to wait between each bout."

"More time to practice. Get your routine down to a science. What are the three pillars of your victory that you so academically declared before?"

Alistair kipped up to his feet and started shadowboxing. "My improved [Dash], you, and my martial arts."

"Don't let this get to your head," Dev'rox said, "but those fighting-addicted monks from the Holy Ravine seemed to think you had a modicum of talent in that area. I know you can get better."

Alistair wanted to protest that his talent in that arena was mainly due to the Pathfinder AI's imbued talent, but he knew there was some truth to this. Maybe he wasn't a prodigy before, but he had put his blood, sweat, and tears into mastering the fundamentals.

Without a doubt, he was the most skilled martial artist on Earth at this point. Since coming back from the suppressed state in the valley, Alistair had felt invincible with his fists. No one could contest him, he knew that. Mentally, he hadn't prepared for an opponent to outmatch him in his own domain so soon.

Alistair had taken one step forward on the marathon to the pinnacle. Improvements couldn't come as easy as before, but they were nowhere near an impassable barrier.

For the next fourteen hours, he fought himself in his mind's eye, over and over and over. When the time came, he was ready.

———

Ready to lose once more.

The start was better—somewhat. Once again, they exchanged blows in close quarters, not employing any named Skills as even they would be too slow.

Alistair tried using the stolid moves of the Silver Comet Sect. While he had never been officially instructed in them, he had picked them up along the way. He put his entire body into a right cross, charging forward into a clinch. The punch missed, but he managed to grab onto his replica's **Mammothskin Raiment.**

The two of them were almost equally matched, vying for throws and knees. Alistair knew he was at a slight Strength disadvantage, but he was able to make up for that with superior leverage. Almost all the time he spent practicing, he had devoted specifically to throws.

Even getting the timing a hundredth of a second faster let the real Alistair take the lead. When the fake shifted his weight the slightest amount backward, Alistair pounced, using all of his strength to push his opponent backward and knock him over.

In turn, the replica made a sudden shift of weight forward. Alistair stepped and performed a perfectly executed head and arm throw. He had markedly improved his skill with the throw, also called a seoi nage, which he had used against Apol-Xin to great effect.

The fake Alistair flew a dozen feet down because of the lack of an actual floor, colliding against the force field delineating their arena from the outside. The alien spectators buzzed for Alistair's most impactful blow of the match.

Alistair dropped down, **[Dashing]** off an imagined floor and propelling himself toward the prone Alistair. With one gauntleted hand, he produced **[Force Fist],** and in the other, **[Hand of Karma].**

Since it was his best opportunity yet, he burned a substantial portion of his positive Karma into the latter Skill. The glow of the crimson energy was almost blinding as he burnt the threads of Fate to his will. As Dev'rox said— Fate was one model of reality. In this destiny, the victor would be him.

Alistair's confidence came to a screeching halt as he heard the sacred name of Avalokiteśvara chanted. *It won't go off in time*, he thought. Caution imprinted itself on him as a fraction of *nue* split off to form an illusory mind shadow.

To his surprise, his replica **[Dashed]** upward. As he rushed toward the real Alistair, he encased an elbow in a Dao energy-infused [Frozen Claw]. Just from the sheer aura of the Skill, Alistair could tell he used a substantial amount of his Ghost Node.

By the time Alistair realized what was going on, it was too late. The frozen elbow connected with Alistair's [Force Fist] at the same time that [Hand of Karma] met the clone's off arm. Instead of activating a Skill to try to circumvent the Karmic effect, the clone intertwined his fingers with his original's like a lover.

Even as the [Hand of Karma] worked its magic and the clone's spiritual pathways short-circuited and the threads of Fate cut off, he refused to let go of Alistair's hand with an iron grip.

A shadow overcame the clone's eyes and skin. Black Impermanence. The division of the Kai'tazake Mutra was like a membrane sealing off half of the Karmic effect. Alistair rapidly stabbed his doppelganger with successive [Blood Hand] spearhands to no avail. Black Impermanence let the other Alistair take out an advance on his own life, subverting the damage he was taking for as long as he could hold out for.

The crashing hands of justice came down from above. In a stroke of genius, the other Alistair had used the [Frozen Claw] to send out massive chunks of ice above Alistair's back, which [Thousand-Armed Bodhisattva Judgment] used as a spike wall for him to crash into. Spear-like icicles impaled themselves through Alistair's robes and into his abdomen.

Alistair tried as long as he could to hold out, employing the copy's Black Impermanence technique to mitigate damage, but it was too late.

Alistair's consciousness faded away just a moment before his opponent would have died. In his last thoughts, he congratulated himself on the closest bout yet.

31 COSMIC BLOOD - FINALE

IN HIS NEXT three attempts at defeating his clone, Alistair actually did worse. For some reason, he couldn't quite replicate the sequence of moves that led to him almost achieving victory. He gradually increased his fighting techniques, control of his new [Dash], and synergy with Dev'rox, yet he couldn't quite tie them together on a path to victory.

The first time, he defeated the doppelganger in hand-to-hand combat, only for him to suddenly use Tranquil Mind's reaction time advantage to chain together an unstoppable combo. At each turn, Alistair was outmatched by a slight margin, leading to his inevitable defeat.

The second time, Alistair thought he had it all figured out. He had a mental list of the ten or so tricks the fake Alistair used over the course of their extended fights. Black Impermanence to hold on longer, and the force field as a way to make [Thousand-Armed Bodhisattva Judgment] hurt against non-evil opponents.

Alistair called them "tricks," but they were really manifestations of a higher fighting IQ. If only he could copy those instincts, he would have easily taken the victory.

Perhaps that's the stage beyond the fundamentals, as Master Ko Pao and Brother Pike put it.

Despite his list of traps to watch out for, Alistair lost once again.

He approached the next round differently. Instead of extreme close quarters where Skills were too slow to be employed, he went at a medium range. With agile movements, they exchanged Skill for Skill, **[Blood Hand]** for **[Force Fist]** for **[Frozen Claw]**.

Alistair couldn't keep up with his alter ego, but that was the idea. By switching the distances from medium to close, he would keep that bastard on his toes.

It was a complete failure. Even with Dev'rox and him working in perfect unison, Alistair exhausted his Mana reserves after an hour-long battle of attrition in which he knew he was never *that* close to victory.

In his third go at it, Alistair was just fed up. It was stupid to get emotional about something so important, but how could he not get frustrated? He wasn't even close to giving up or anything so drastic, but having all of his attempts fail was painful.

So, he went back to his previous tactic—an all-out frontal assault. It wasn't completely out of frustration. Alistair knew if he executed everything right, he would have a solid shot at winning.

The moment he materialized within the force field bubble, Alistair **[Dashed]** towards his identical self. He was lucky that the silent clone had no memories. Over the course of several days, Alistair had mastered the *nue* aspect of his Tier 4 **[Dash]**.

After the brief invisibility granted by the flicker aspect of **[Dash]** vanished, there were two assailants of the doppelganger. And he didn't know one from the other—for a vanishingly brief period. After that, the illusory effect of the small impartment of *nue* disappeared.

In that tiny window, Alistair had both the *nue* shadow and his real self throw a right straight. His real self was behind the fake Alistair, and the shadow in front. Halfway through the punch's arc, the doppelganger figured out the trick and raised his arm behind his head to block the attack.

Using Dev'rox's mental horsepower to slow down his perception of time, Alistair activated **[Thousand-Armed Bodhisattva Judgment]** midway through the punch, not giving his opponent a moment to rest.

After catching the punch, the doppelganger spun around in one acrobatic motion, kicking toward Alistair's face. A Dao fist from Spiritual Fighter's Echo caught him in the left palm, but didn't do much damage.

Alistair blocked the kick with a gauntleted hand, ducking under another and moving forward for a single leg takedown. At that moment, the finishing Skill was almost done forming *above* the two of them, leaving the doppelganger with a choice.

That fiendishly smart clone completely ignored the threat from above, pounding Alistair's skull with a downward elbow infused with a [Force Fist], all the while burning Karmic energy to fuel a crimson [Eyes of Truth].

Alistair pulled a trick from his other self's book, slipping into Black Impermanence. The feeling of utter finality was still foreign to him, as well as the eclipsing dark halo that surrounded his body and eyes, leaving just a corona of hidden light around his irises.

If this was a fight in the real world, he would have been feeling that elbow later, Black Impermanence or not. His trance shielded him from the involuntary effects and pain, allowing his complete focus. Despite the fact the doppelganger burned Karma to divine Fate, Alistair hid his intentions with Black Impermanence and countervailing Karmic energy.

A [Draconic Roar] burst forth from Alistair's mouth, but he tilted his body toward the side to shoot it past his opponent. Once again, he was taking a page out of the fake Alistair's book—using the power of his finishing Skill to reflect projectiles that weren't so justice-coded. The only difference was icicles versus particles of force affinity Mana.

For a moment, Alistair thought he was finally going to achieve victory. If only things were that easy. The copy entered Tranquil Mind, Alistair feeling the sense of absolute peace even without any visual cue.

With all of his nearly 1,000 Agility, the other Alistair rained down piercing strikes with the sharp claws of his **Devilsbane Gauntlets**.

Black Impermanence had its advantages, but it couldn't keep up with Tranquil Mind's reaction times. Nor its adaptive qualities, allowing the other Alistair to break through his defenses. Alistair tried blocking, but the doppelganger was always a step ahead.

The original Alistair had no time to drop Black Impermanence and enter his own Tranquil Mind, and even if he did, the backlash from the accumulated damage under the former would be devastating in his current state.

All this took place in the brief window before the impact of [Thousand-Armed Bodhisattva Judgment], since Alistair had placed his Skill at the opposite end of the force bubble to give time for [Draconic Roar] to percolate its Mana.

All he had to do was hang on for a bit longer. Not even a quarter of a second, perhaps. For all of his high Constitution score, Alistair found his neck vulnerable, as his opponent inundated him with strikes. He was unused to this swarming pressure coming from another in-fighter.

In a last ditch effort to escape, Alistair burned far more Karma than he had allotted for that iteration, throwing away his next attempt more than it was already doomed. It would take more than the seventeen hours to recover his finishing Skill, so why not Karma too?

He [Dashed] *forward,* burning the last of his Karma in an attempt to escape the never-ending assault.

The doppelganger was one step ahead. Using the reaction time of Tranquil Mind and burning some of his own Karma, he placed his hand in the path of Alistair's throat. While the Skill was designed to stop Alistair short of any physical obstacle, the moment he did, the fake Alistair used that moment of defenselessness to spear his original completely through the neck.

Alistair woke up in the white room with a nasty cough.

"That felt way too real," he choked out once he recovered from the lingering psychosomatic effects of dying. "Is that actually what it feels like to get stabbed in the neck?"

"It is real," Dev'rox said. "The Pathfinder AI teleports your body and anchors your soul the moment it receives a fatal injury in order to heal you, so in one sense you actually died. It's not very relevant except when dealing with some crazy religious sects."

"Crazy religious sects?"

"The multiverse is vast. You have to expect some crazies. I've never encountered one, but occasionally places that employ revival technology get raided by cultists who think it's an abomination against natural order. Not really a present problem, however."

"Huh," Alistair noted, filing that information away for a more relevant time.

Dev'rox floated around to face Alistair directly. "You don't seem as dejected as before. Got that frustration out of your system?"

"After I recover my Karma and [Thousand-Armed Bodhisattva Judgment], I'm going to win."

"Bold claim. Let's see it happen."

————

Alistair practiced as much as he could in eighteen hours of lobby time. All leading up to what he hoped to be his final encounter.

Seeing his own emotionless face was getting tiring. Alistair liked to think he had good features, especially after the effects of cultivation, but for all intents and purposes, his face was the ugliest in the entire multiverse.

So when he finally returned for the nineteenth time to face his superior clone, he was one hundred percent focused.

After coming his closest to winning last time, Alistair created a simple but extremely detailed strategy, with multiple branching paths for each eventuality. He did this with the help of Infinite Arsenal, which turned him into a supercomputer with the sole function of calculating a way to win.

Infinite Arsenal seemed to be less effective when used outside an actual combat scenario, but he would make do. Alistair once again timed the end of his lobby stay down to a millisecond, pre-preparing a [Dash] and the Tranquil Mind state.

With his lightning quick reflexes, he and Dev'rox worked in unison to change his orientation. While changing direction mid-[Dash] was impossible, the imp projected an array in Alistair's current [Dash] direction and one point toward the fake Alistair. He also used some of his Mana reserves to squash the distance between the two cultivators once Alistair was through the portal.

The result was sheer speed. They hadn't tried this direct of an approach before because the margin for error was extremely high. Tranquil Mind didn't naturally cover Dev'rox's consciousness—it was because of the high tier of [Ghost Whispers] that they could partially meld their minds together. The combined processing power of the passive Skill along with Tranquil Mind acted synergistically.

The doppelganger's eyes barely had time to register the incoming stimuli. Alistair's [Dash] ended with him having skin-to-skin contact with his other self. He could feel the presence of his alter ego's Tranquil Mind taking hold, but it wasn't complete.

Not having time to activate one of his offensive Skills, Alistair slammed the man with two, solid hits. He channeled Pike to the best of his ability, taking on the solid, unbreakable effect of the Silver Comet Sect. First was an elbow straight to the doppelganger's jaw, and second was a knee straight to the solar plexus.

Even as the knee hit, Alistair could feel the signature peace of Tranquil Mind from his opponent.

All will be satisfied, Alistair thought. *No man is above justice, nor is no man below redemption.*

While the momentum of his knee carried the two of them toward the blue force bubble, Alistair grabbed onto his counterpart's jacket. By that point, the clone was fully functional, though his output was temporarily reduced by the impact of those two blows and their Spiritual Fighter's Echo follow up.

For what was over the dozenth time, Alistair grappled with Alistair in close quarters. Their situation was quite reminiscent of a judo match, considering the heavy **Mammothskin Raiment** they both wore.

Alistair had practiced his grappling skills over and over and over in his penalty periods, which was several days by then. There was no way he would lose in that area, even if this clone was better than his previous self in every way.

Faking a tackle for the legs, Alistair used all of his Strength for a shoulder throw, where he hoisted his counterpart up into the air like a bale of hay. While Constitution made them heavier, it didn't do so at a rate keeping up with their Strength.

Next came a **[Draconic Roar]**. With the combined mental boost of Tranquil Mind and melding with Dev'rox, he could expend the majority of his *nue* in a single scream, along with an amount of force affinity Mana that streaked the air with coral light. If he had to deal with the consequences of his Skill usage, he could have permanently hurt his brain, but he was relying on everything being reset.

While the cone of **[Draconic Roar]** was still expanding, Alistair suddenly switched from Tranquil Mind to Black Impermanence, adding on his skin-tight proto-Domain. In this defensive position, he **[Dashed]** forward, through his own expanding roar.

Given the power he put behind the Skill, those two defensive steps he stole from the doppelganger were key to not being instantly blown away.

In that moment, the fake Alistair recognized the true threat. The threat that Alistair meticulously hid in the inception of the **[Draconic Roar]**. **[Thousand-Armed Bodhisattva Judgment]** from above, going backwards toward the two of them, like in previous attempts. The key was not only the Karmic energy, but also the roar. The noise of the roar along with its incredible mass of *nue* blocked out the sound of the chanting of the bodhisattva's name.

The doppelganger recognized right away that it was too late for him to perform his own finishing Skill. Within the confines of his Tranquil Mind, his reactions would be much faster than Alistair's in Black Impermanence.

Gathering [Force Fists] in both hands, the shifty clone enveloped his huge coral fists with crimson Karmic energy. He spun rapidly, using the special frame of reference flooring to speed up his rotation, jumping at 45 degree angles repeatedly.

He used [Force Fist] in the way that Alistair had against Dragonus—spamming it over and over, which became the initial inspiration for [Thousand-Armed Bodhisattva Judgment].

These [Force Fists] were far stronger than the ones Alistair had used, and fired at a far more rapid pace. Alistair could almost see the strain his counterpart's meridians were under, as a torrential amount of force affinity Mana exited the clone's fists.

For a moment, it looked as if Alistair's plot was going to fail. The tide of enormous [Force Fists] began to crowd out the [Draconic Roar] and even the fists of the Avalokiteśvara avatar were being pushed back. That all changed in an instant with Dev'rox's explosion of Mana.

Over time, Dev'rox had shown more of his true capabilities. Since in his living form he was a Profound realm cultivator, he had still not demonstrated a taste of his Profound power, but now he was ready to unveil one of his favorite abilities.

While his homeland in the Asura Hell had no direct correspondence with the Pathfinder AI's Skills, spells were something else. So, with the increased connection of Tier 4 [Ghost Whispers], Dev'rox unleashed his Rank 1 Spell: *Spatial Rending*.

Hundreds of minuscule magical arrays appeared instantly in the space, glittering like dwarf stars. They formed a chaotic web of space affinity Mana, creating a grand arcana that Alistair had never before seen the likes of.

Alistair could feel the esoteric aura those arrays gave off. It reminded him somewhat of that First Script character back in the Holy Ravine, but nowhere near as meaningful. Still, the air of mystery and ancient power chilled his soul, and it was obvious that Dev'rox poured the remainder of his Mana pool into this singular spell.

At lightning speeds, blue lasers shot from each array to its nearest neighbors, forming an intricate lattice of octahedron-shaped units of space. Then, they shifted.

Every fractional unit of space changed spots with another in a seemingly random pattern. In the same way that Dev'rox's magical arrays connected disparate areas of space, each division of space created by the tiny arcane circles was linked to another, preserving the laws of physics, just changing the orientation.

That threw off the fake Alistair completely.

To be honest, the real Alistair was nervous for a second. Theoretically, there was no reason to think someone couldn't adapt to the scattered space. Even pre-initiation humans eventually adapted to having one's visual field flipped upside down.

But the copy was too slow. The confusion and disorientation were enough for Alistair's attack to land. The fists of justice connected with the *nue* and force Mana of his **[Draconic Roar]**, sending it flying into the doppelganger with absurd force.

Alistair was well and truly out of ideas. If this failed, he was done.

After a final bated breath, the confusion ended as Dev'rox's magic began to fade away. Right before the spell collapsed, a notification popped up.

Congratulations on placing 98th (pending) in Cosmic Blood, Disputed Shard Fief rankings.

Badge Acquired: Cosmic Blood – Top 100 Performance (Untiered Legendary Badge): *Achieve a top 100 performance on the Cosmic Blood trial.* 200 Upgrade Points, 50 Platinum Drachma.

32 INSIGHT VISION

AT THE MOMENT of his victory, Alistair was temporarily returned to the all-white lobby, though this time he floated in the air as a variety of screens barraged his vision.

Besides the Cosmic Blood Badge window, he also took a look at the leaderboards before he left.

The little avatar of a crystal dragon still stood at number one—that had to be the guy Fuhao referred to as "the future of the Disputed Shard." Down from 6th place all the way to 13th was the bow and arrow-wielding iceman. Alistair didn't put too much stock in his high placing, since Prime Initiates like themselves got some affirmative action in the form of taking along seven other teammates.

Well, except for Alistair himself. He had to do it the way everyone else did and still got a top 100 placing. That had to count for something, if he wasn't tooting his own horn.

The rewards—oh, the rewards were so juicy. 250 Upgrade Points for clearing all ten sectors. 400 for the overall Symphony of Skills Grand Dungeon. 200 Upgrade Points from the Badge. That meant 850 total, along with 50 Platinum drachma.

Unfortunately, Alistair wasn't the first through, so he didn't get the Legendary rarity item. The way things were looking, there was almost no way that George didn't get the reward. *Just another thing to worry about.*

Then there was the part Alistair was most intrigued by—the Insight Vision. He was wondering what was going to happen, and those questions were answered the moment he finished going through all the windows.

Alistair had forgotten all about where he was when he entered the Grand Dungeon—the moon. Getting transported into an alternative Fate stream was not one of Alistair's greatest hits. Luckily, he saw the glass outline of the Leading Domes right before the Insight Vision started. No more journeys in space for the time being was acceptable to Alistair, as much as he enjoyed the idea of wandering the great beyond. Instead, his sight turned inward.

There was fear in the air.

Rampant dread, the kind that no one liked to talk about. The feeling of utter hopelessness. Alistair was subsumed in this singular mental state.

He opened his eyes, bathed in blood. Dark, congealed sanguine fluid flooded down in the shape of a dome. Ectoplasmic blood mist filled the air as it splashed and churned with scalding heat. From the ceiling to the ground, malevolent wraiths circled, wailing the laments of the damned.

This can't be right, Alistair thought. *How is this horror my Insight Vision?*

The screams of the bloodwraiths grew louder and their rotation accelerated. The blood grew thicker and the oppressive dread grew stronger.

In the blink of an eye, the blood halted, flooding inward like a metaphysical dam had broken. The wraiths dived into Alistair's psychic body. A period of darkness followed.

A vision within a vision. After the hatred and vile imputation of the bloodwraiths entered him, space and time inverted, black sky turning to white ether and red blood turning into golden light.

In this new paradise, Alistair ascended into the Heavens at an increasingly fast pace. Joyful spirits of the dead heralded his rise with a choral arrangement written by the divine progeny.

Higher and higher Alistair went, soaring through golden sky into golden space, through what he imagined were the infinitely complex fractals of the Heavens. After what felt like an endless time, he finally arrived at the summit.

Alistair stood before a palace whose size beggared belief. Iridescent, shining with hues that were beyond his mortal mind, it stretched to the horizon and beyond in impossible geometries. The gates to the palace were an empyrean gold that burned and toiled with ancestral pride, keeping all unprivileged and unqualified away from the holy interior for uncountable spatial epochs.

Except for Alistair. He was 100% certain that whatever qualifications these golden gates were looking for, he was not even close to meeting them, and yet he was somehow immune to its terminating aura. It was as if he was clouded in a darkness that made him causally distinct from the rest of the world.

Or, more likely, this was just a vision.

A foreboding presence loomed inside of the palatial complex. A locus of evil so foul and rancid, Alistair wanted to fall to his knees and cry. Cry and despair, for this being of pure wickedness was the most powerful entity he had ever witnessed, by a chasm so large he could not comprehend it.

If there was any future to the multiverse, it was to be ruled by this *god*. A dystopia of unspeakable horror. Alistair's mind threatened to break apart at the seams at this thought. *This can't be right,* he repeated to himself over and over for what felt like eternity as he knelt in accidental prostration before the evil deity.

This couldn't be the terminal state of everything. Alistair refused to believe the ultimate evolution of the multiverse was toward everything being in the palm of inexorable evil.

A light fluttered down from the void above. At first, he was too in the mud to even recognize what the illumination was. But the light grew closer and shone brighter with each passing second, to where even Alistair, in his deep despair, had to look up.

What he found was resplendent awe. The light came from a small glyph, a character in a language that he inherently knew to be the Language of the Pure Dao. The First Script, as Dev'rox put it.

Only this character's prominence far exceeded the corrupted meaning of the one in the Holy Ravine. The Spirit's Fists Overcoming Struggle character had been copied and copied for thousands or possibly even millions of years, leading to its dilution. Alistair knew that this one was different.

Its meaning was entirely pure. He was witnessing the glory of the First Script and somehow his brain didn't turn into mush. Whatever protected him from the presence of the evil god also had to be protecting him from the true power of the glyph.

Alistair wasn't expecting to understand anything about the mysterious Language of the Pure Dao, but he was wrong. The character floating above him looked very, very familiar. In fact, it was almost identical to Spirit's Fists Overcoming Struggle, with small alterations. Alterations that he also understood.

The meaning of the floating glyph was not Spirit's Fists Overcoming Struggle, but Spirit's Fists Overcoming Evil. The parts of the character that meant evil stood out to Alistair like a sore thumb, radiating the same absolute aura coming from the devil within the palace.

All of a sudden, it all clicked. Like a cascade of falling dominoes, Alistair grasped the meaning of the Insight Vision. The ocean of blood at the beginning, the circling of the bloodwraiths—that was what his judgment of evil felt like, from the perspective of the judged.

Drowning in the blood of the innocents they slew, haunted by the ghosts of their past. Alistair did not inflict misery for misery's sake, but if the damned were to punish themselves by their past evil, who was he to stop them? This concept linked back to his previous idea of helping the angry ghost that desired bloody revenge, but there was a distinction.

From his current viewpoint, that was too savage and did not represent what he wanted to be. His time in the Holy Ravine had tamed his more angry ideas. However, taking that idea of anger and blood and incorporating the spirits of the dead was still valuable. The cosmic justice of having their victims assail the evildoers of the multiverse was sweet.

This association, Alistair felt certain. The heavenly ascent aspect of the Insight Vision, he wasn't sure of. There wasn't a connection of ice to ghost to justice that was immediately apparent to him, though he was sure he would eventually come up with something.

Finally, the evil in the palace and Spirit's Fists Overcoming Evil. That was obvious.

What was Alistair's purpose at his core? Why did he fight so hard? To survive, yes. Almost all living beings had that goal, along with the safety of their close kin. Not so unique. But since the beginning, since luck and providence had him save a life at the start of the initiation, he had a higher goal.

To rid the multiverse of evil and suffering. To create a world where no one had to lose a parent, a lover, a child. Where everyone could live in harmony. To this end, he would pursue, no matter how many called him naïve or juvenile, no matter how difficult it seemed or how many doubted its possibility.

But he was not alone. Through his time in the Holy Ravine, he had learned discipline and inner strength.

He did not cultivate those virtues in solitude.

Everyone learned from those before them, everyone was the product of their environment. As the great Isaac Newton said, "If I have seen further, it is by standing on the shoulders of giants."

The presence of the evil god was his final opponent—not an actual entity. The symbol of suffering within the universe that needed to be vanquished. The feeling of dread that he felt at the footsteps of the evil god represented the impossibility of his task, on its face.

Alistair knew in his heart of hearts that the evil would one day be defeated.

By his hand, and those of all who shared his lofty goal, stretching back from the beginning of time. Whoever looked up at the Heavens and bemoaned the curse of mortal living, whoever brought light to darkness, whoever stood up to injustice despite their own fear—never once had the spark died out since the beginning of creation.

Spirit's Fists Overcoming Evil—that would be the name of his Domain. The truest encapsulation of his identity, the spatial and temporal home that resided within his very soul.

A proto-Domain was the building blocks of that. As Alistair came back down to Earth, he etched as much as he could of what he remembered into his soulcore. His proto-Domain was complete.

———

When Alistair opened his eyes once more, he was back where it all started. The Leading Domes, the set of glass spheres that held his new and improved headquarters.

He had unassumingly triggered the Karmic alarm via Oracle's Karmic curse, landing him on the moon. Now that the alternative Fate stream was well and gone, he was back there.

Only it came eighteen days in the future, a fact that he hadn't wanted to think about for quite some time. The lives lost, the opportunities squandered. There was also one possibility that Alistair dreaded above all others.

He checked his freehold overview. Unlike the rest of the sectors, during Cosmic Blood, he couldn't access it.

It wasn't looking good. When Alistair left, the Northeast Order had 35% of the world's 159,873 subregions, the Devil Kings 25%, and various other groups at 40%.

Four days before entering the Cosmic Blood sector of the Grand Dungeon, Alistair had noticed a sudden rise in the Devil Kings' territorial holdings. At the time, he had assumed that meant that the Devil Kings had finished their dungeon instance, and it looked like he was right. In the eleven days that George and his ilk ran free, they already went from 25% to 45%. At least Alistair's people managed to stave off their losses, going from 35% to 30%.

In just eleven days... Alistair thought. Eleven days for the Devil Kings to take tens of thousands of subregions. They were dangerously close to the 50% condition that gave them an instant win.

Alistair checked [Armageddon], looking at The Second Step. There were 4.5 days left until the third wave. Each successive wave was supposed to be worse than the last, so he shuddered to think about what was coming next. Drastic action had to be taken.

First, he had to deal with the stares. Alistair started paying attention to his surroundings. The second floor was a lot sparser than last time. There were a few people working in the open cubicles, who all had turned to see the sudden burst of energy that accompanied Alistair's return.

There were two familiar signatures.

Alistair let William St. James tackle him for a hug, while Caren Locasta behind him shook his head, though he let his relief show in a smile.

"Alistair, I thought you'd never be back!" William exclaimed. Alistair gingerly put the young man down. How strange to think that he had been one of his opponents during [The Game of Life]. "What happened?"

Alistair gave a brief explanation about Oracle's alternative Fate stream and the Grand Dungeon.

"That's quite the adventure you went on," Caren noted. "You've had a busy couple of weeks."

"I can say the same here," Alistair replied. "What the hell is going on here?"

Caren and William looked at each other. "It might be better if we show you," Caren said.

They led the way to the center of the war room, where an enormous projection of the globe took center stage. It was an improved version of the map in Alistair's old headquarters, describing the state of every known subregion on Earth to the greatest possible detail. The work was a fusion of the best programming and engineering that the Northeast Freehold could muster, and updated more than once a second, taking in information from first-hand accounts, the Soulnet, status windows, drones, animal familiars, and more. Some of the younglings from Sessen Esshei's brood had even volunteered to dig tunnels to the hard-to-reach parts of the world.

The globe showed a catastrophe. The two main colors were purple and red—purple for Alistair's freehold, and red for the Devil Kings.

The red virus had spread from its origin, taking over large swaths of purple land. The other colors were struggling to survive, having been reduced to 25% of the world's subregions.

That fact infuriated Alistair. Their leaders should have seen the writing on the wall. There was no path forward except for humanity to unite. They had seen their holdings get smashed and stolen by the Devil Kings for almost two weeks, and they hadn't come to John and begged to join?

It wasn't that Alistair cared at all for gaining political power, but it stung him to think about all the innocent lives lost by the greed of those leaders. He wanted a sit down with President Ryder, but he had a feeling that would have to wait.

Besides having 14% of the Northeast Order Freehold's subregions converted to the other side, there was also the pressing concern of the roaming monsters. Looking at the holographic globe, over 20% of their subregions were overrun with monsters. With Alistair gone and the Devil Kings attacking, it looked like they could not clear all the dungeons in the time limit, leading to them running rampant.

"More or less my median prediction," Alistair said. "Things could be worse, couldn't they?"

"Things can always get worse," William said. "Though they can always get better too, right?"

Caren scratched his chin while the three of them stared at the enormous map. "Everyone is trying to abate the tides. It's not working. They'll fulfill the Global Mayorship 50% requirement in just three days at the current pace."

"And Alexandra? And the others?" Alistair asked calmly.

William shook his head. "None of the high-ranking members of the Northeast Order Freehold have died. We tell them to flee at the first sight of George. Still, it's somewhat surprising."

"Death is second nature on the front lines," Caren murmured. "Millions have perished and hundreds of thousands die every day. We cannot deal with the monsters and the Devil Kings at the same time. That is the difference between us and them. George leaves his 'people' to perish. If we include those under the thrall of the Devil Kings, the death toll is astronomical."

Alistair tasted the melancholy in the air. The psychic energy of the world felt despondent. Not that he ever would have used such mystical terminology before, but that was his gut feeling. The amount of despair was palpable, like an eclipse casting its darkness over the Earth.

"There's no time to waste," Alistair said, not even realizing the sigh of relief he gave at hearing Alexandra and the others were safe. "I have to be out there now. Where's the optimal spot?"

"Debatable," William replied. "There's a major attack by Morgana in the southeast. The Devil Kings have tended to stick together. If you attack them directly, George is likely to come out. Think you can take him?"

Alistair wanted to say yes with confidence, but the truth was he wasn't sure. In due time, the answer was without a shadow of a doubt, yes, but right now? Maybe. "I need more time to be certain of that. What else?"

"Technically, that wouldn't be the cause of the most deaths," Caren pointed out. "Over in the north, where the Maine Brothers' land is, there's an overrun of orcs from one of the dungeons. The monsters are running amok since we have to deal with the Devil King incursions. Our only saving grace is that they still count as our subregions even if the monsters control them *de facto*."

Orcs, Alistair thought. *Can't say they're not making a comeback.*

"Keep in mind, Alistair, three days," Caren said. "We have to make some progress, or we're screwed."

"I haven't forgotten, promise," Alistair said. "Beam me up, Scotty."

"You know that wasn't actually said in any Star Trek movie or show?" William asked. "I'm disappointed."

"Says the guy who claimed to kill a grizzly with a machete." Alistair smiled as he sprinted onto one of the many **Teleportation Circles** lining the perimeter.

Before William could respond, Caren activated the protocols, allowing him to control the destination from the master keyholder. Alistair disappeared in a flash of blue light.

33 OFFENSIVE FRONT

As the lights faded and Alistair settled into his new environment, he began allocating his 850 Upgrade Points.

400 went to an increased Badge slot. Alistair was starting to suspect that the system was more likely to give out Badge opportunities when you had an empty Badge slot compared to when you didn't. Badges were the quickest way to get an increase in power, so he prioritized that. It was a gamble, but he trusted his luck to prevail.

Sticking with Badges, another 100 went to upgrading "Mythical Cultivator" to Tier 3, whereupon it maxed out at +20% to all Attributes. Those stats weren't impacting him now, but with his current stat overhang, he would be way, way stronger at level 60.

He went down to his finishing Skill. While he normally didn't upgrade Skills with Upgrade Points, this enormous windfall of points would prove to be an exception. He chose [Draconic Roar] and [Force Fist] which were quite important as his only vector of *nue* and his most used attacking Skill, respectively.

[Draconic Roar]'s cone of effect widened at Tier 2, as well as increased its paralyzing effect, though it cost more *nue* now, at around a fifth of his pool per roar. [Force Fist] didn't seem to grow more powerful, but the activation time went down. At first glance, that didn't seem like a big deal, but it would open the door for him to use it in close quarter combat, whereas before he was limited since the lag was too long.

Finally, there was the question of what to do with his remaining 173 Upgrade Points. Alistair chose to put them into one of his most important Skills—[**Fighter's Instinct**]. This upgraded it to Tier 6. Or did it? As he put the points in, he received a notification.

Skill Evolution:

Accept (A/B):

A:
Tier 5 Beginner Passive Skill [**Fighter's Instinct**] lost.

Tier 5 Journeyman Passive Skill [**Monk Motionlessness**] gained.

[**Monk Motionlessness**] (Tier 5 Journeyman Skill): *Embrace the tranquility of a monk's stillness, attuning your senses to anticipate and counter threats with serene precision.* Scales with Agility and Wisdom. Upgradeable (0/500).

B:
[**Fighter's Instinct**] becomes Tier 6. 10% increase in reflexes, fighting intuition, and danger sense.

Note: [**Monk Motionlessness**] is not a direct upgrade of [**Fighter's Instinct**]. [**Monk Motionlessness**] has superior reflex and instincts, but lacks the offensive firepower of [**Fighter's Instinct**], though can be supplemented through other means.

Seeing his choices, Alistair immediately went with the new Skill. [**Monk Motionlessness**] sounded perfect for him. He had no need of the basic techniques of [**Fighter's Instinct**] when he had {Psychopomp's Discipline} and the myriad of Infinite Arsenal.

The question of how the superior senses of his new passive Skill would interact with Tranquil Mind was an interesting one. Hopefully, it would compound.

Looking ahead at the situation, he would find out soon enough. The forest was on fire.

The **Teleportation Circle** had taken him to a mining town on the outskirts of the Maine Brothers' subregions. The initiation obviously changed the flora and fauna—what they didn't realize at first was that it changed the earth below. The subregions moved around after [The Game of Life] Quest, but the subterranean aspect was still under-explored.

The savage orcs seemed to have destroyed everything. Even the very shack the **Teleportation Circle** was supposed to bring him to had collapsed. Alistair used his 501 Strength to heave burnt slabs of wood off of him. If his lungs had been susceptible to the ash and pollutants in the air, he would have been coughing like a smoker.

Immediately, he sensed the presence of at least twenty orcs surrounding the remains of the shack. They were smart, these new monsters. Smart enough to have soldiers guarding the only escape route that was guaranteed to lead out.

Alistair's righteous anger grew as he imagined the scores of innocent civilians that knew about the teleporter, only to be slaughtered ignominiously by a band of orcs.

At once, he calculated the position of all twenty-three orcs within a three hundred foot radius. He activated **[Dash]**, shifting from position to position so fast it looked like he was teleporting. At each new location, he dispatched the orc or group of orcs with a single punch.

It took him twenty seconds to deal with all of them, only impeded by the piles of fallen trees. Alistair didn't break a sweat, cleaning blood from his **Devilsbane Gauntlets** after he finished with a breath of air.

From there it was a matter of using Justice Quest's leads to find the survivors. The Talent Tree leaf gave him a vague sense of where innocent lives were in danger—Alistair followed up on that with his keen sense. Specifically, his furthest ranging sense was that of smell. He could smell the fear of the humans within the area and ran toward them with haste.

But before that, he cast down a **[Lightning of Justice]** down near the shack with the **Teleportation Circle.** The illuminating light of justice lingered for several minutes, so the people would know where to go.

Along the way, he made sure to clear safe areas in arcs of a circle. The orcs were so weak that even if he let them wail on him with their crude weapons and weak pyromancy, nothing would happen. His Constitution plus [Steel Body] was far too high a mountain for them to climb. Even if they could hurt him, [Monk Motionlessness] ensured he would never be touched.

Once he was sure that the area within a mile radius was free of orcs, he secured the stragglers. Most of them were hiding wherever they could—in a makeshift hole, up a thick tree, or inside a bush. Alistair found ten of them, directing them to the golden light where his lightning used to be.

But the lingering light wasn't just good for directing people toward safety. The burst of Mana and thunder and flash of light was a good attractor of trouble.

Already, as Alistair pointed the last woman he sensed in the proper direction, he smelled a whole horde of orcs incoming from the northwest.

[Dashing] toward the oncoming threat, Alistair slipped into Tranquil Mind.

At the end of his [Dash], he found himself on the outskirts of the forest, in a ruined city. It reminded him of New Boston after Anthony's attack. Burning and collapsed buildings dotted the skyline. Thousands of orcs roamed free, killing and eating every person they could find. Through [Ghost Whispers], Alistair could hear the dirges of the dead. Crying out for mercy, revenge, and regret.

In Tranquil Mind, Alistair was unshakable. His heart knew only serenity. These lives were lost no matter what he did. But that didn't mean any more had to die.

Awaiting him within the conjunction of the suburbs and the forest was a battalion of orcs. Based on their leader, he guessed they were the secondary contingent of their army. The leader, probably the orc king, was somewhere else, and then a plethora of orc grunts hunted on the streets for maximum carnage.

As Alistair hoped, [Monk Motionlessness] and Tranquil Mind worked together. The orcs moved like they were in molasses. He dispatched all of them with one chop to the neck or palm strike uppercut, all except the boss, which he saved for last.

The tall and burly orc was red, like the blood orcs of the past, wearing a crown of gold and bones. Alistair didn't bother with an [Eyes of Truth]. Once he dealt with the rest of them, he grabbed the leader orc by the face. One [Blood Hand] and a crunch of his fingers, and that was finished.

Alistair wanted to deal with the remaining orcs individually, but he didn't have time. Using his Karmic sight, he followed the path of carnage, from which fell Karma seeped like sewage.

The leader of the escaped monster wave was shacking up in a former office building. While it was on the other side of town, Alistair was so fast that it didn't matter. He didn't even use [Dash], conserving his Mana while he turned on the jets.

Alistair entered Infinite Arsenal, a thin silver layer shining over his skin as he became the endless array of weapons.

After confirming that there were no humans inside the building, Alistair encased one of his hands in an enormous [Force Fist]. In one fell swoop, he ran sideways against the wall, launching his fist at the foundations of the concrete as hard as he could.

The building started collapsing before Alistair was halfway through. He used all of his Agility and Strength along with the Force Node to obliterate the bottom as much as possible. Dust and smoke filled the air, making it difficult to see what had happened.

Alistair didn't need to see to perform his next act. He jumped high into the sky, boosted by **Fall of Fleet,** and rained down a barrage of [Force Fists]. Similar in nature to his finishing Skill, a dozen enormous coral hands punched down at the pile of rubble.

A kinetic shockwave spread from the moment of impact. If the building was destroyed, now it was pulverized. Any survivors of the collapse were certainly dead now, confirmed by the lack of life forces.

Unfortunately for the people of the city, the monster wave didn't disappear. Alistair was holding out some hope for that outcome—perhaps if he defeated the leader, the grunts would fade away. That wasn't the case.

There was nothing more he wanted to do than kill every last orc and save every person, but he couldn't. Not when the Devil Kings were so close to victory.

However, by eliminating the top brass, he gave the people a chance. Most of the citizens had gotten an item or two and had some Skills of their own. They could fight against the monsters. And they would have to.

Alistair had his own mission. Head straight into enemy territory.

What was the method behind the madness? Alistair figured it out right away. In the fight for subregions, direct combat was a mistake. The path forward was full offense.

The only way to stem the bleeding, if not make up ground, was to take territory faster than the Devil Kings. No one on his side could keep up with him, not even Pharaoh. This mission, only he could complete.

After checking on the freehold overview, Alistair oriented himself in the direction of the Devil King's subregions. Then, he ran.

Alistair flew across the ground like a jet, using his nimble reflexes to dodge around trees and obstacles. It was funny that once upon a time his issue was that he was getting too fast for his reaction time—now, the opposite was true. He was like the Flash, seeing everything in slow motion.

It only took five minutes to reach the enemy's side. Alistair wasn't sure what to expect. A land filled with towering evil castles, peppered with volcanic activity like Mordor?

There wasn't really a change from the Northeast Order to the Devil Kings. Alistair did notice a general lack of life, though he knew there were millions of "hostages" deep inside the land as well.

Like the Northeast Order, it seemed as if the Devil Kings also employed lookouts. With the size of his recruited army, it was infeasible to have a true border defense except in the most high-risk area. The Devil King lookouts stood on top of a constructed valyrik tower standing well above the horizon.

They were a mixture of humans and what looked to be orangutans, probably from the mammalian beasts that allied with George.

Alistair snuck between the shadows as he got a good look at the tower, darting from tree to tree without making a sound. He could feel the foul stench of demon blood from even a hundred feet away. They were Devil Princes, no doubt.

He briefly summoned the **Experiment Cursed Needle #7**, but recognized that there was only so much he could do. For the weak, to put it bluntly, demon blood was an irrevocable curse. It turned them to madness without a cure. Merely freeing them from whatever Devil King they were enslaved to was not true freedom from their conditions.

Alistair said a silent prayer. To whom, he could not say, for the cruelty of the multiverse made him doubt in some grand benevolence. He used Dev'rox as a springboard to jump up from until he was around level with the top of the tower.

Then he activated **[Dash]**, using the airwalking aspect to glide across the sky in one movement, landing on the tower.

Before any of them could react, he killed them all, each with one punch to the head. An instant, painless death.

Killing is too easy now, Alistair thought to himself. *I can swat down a human life more easily than I could a fly in the before.*

"That's how it is and how it always shall be," Dev'rox said. "Such is the Mandate of Heaven. You cannot escape this fact of life, no matter how powerful you may be. Best get used to it now."

Alistair said nothing to this, focusing on his senses as he tried to detect if there was a hidden trap. Perhaps the tower was rigged to automatically send back a signal if all the lookouts suddenly died. However, he found nothing. Just death.

The funny thing was that despite the Northeast Order's size, they had almost never employed the conquest right of subregions. Alistair had won the vast majority of the freehold's land from [The Game of Life], and then the rest came from voluntary leaders bringing in their flock. He found the idea of invading other people's subregions for no reason to be immoral.

The rules for subregion conquest were surprisingly simple.

First option, move enough people or construct enough buildings in the subregion. The exact specifications were complex and depended on several factors, but the principle made perfect sense. If you had so many colonists in a subregion, then it should be yours. Second, kill the steward of the subregion while occupying the land, who was the highest ranked individual native to the subregion, or the appointed individual by a shareholder with high enough authority, like Alistair. Third, imbuing enough Mana in the central unit.

The central unit was simply a Mana crystal found at the geographic center of a subregion, though you could move it with Land Store credits. The more developed and populous the subregion, the more Mana you needed to imbue in it to shift sides.

Alistair sprinted to the Mana crystal right after he dealt with the lookouts. As he expected, it was unguarded, sitting on a pedestal in the middle of a park. It took him ten seconds to transfer the necessary Mana.

This was Alistair's life for the next six hours. He went from subregion to subregion, venturing deeper into the Devil Kings' territory. Along the way, he vanquished many monster waves and destroyed lookout towers before they even got a whisker of his presence.

His actions wouldn't go unnoticed for long. After dealing with his fiftieth subregion, Alistair was certain that they knew of his presence. If they were paying any attention at all to the global layout, they would have noticed a fifty-subregion deficit, seemingly out of nowhere.

That didn't stop Alistair. He wasn't worried about anyone but George. With his keen senses, he was also confident that he could detect the Devil Kings before they detected him. So he continued onward. In six hours, he collected two hundred subregions, seventy of those coming from when he assassinated a low-level Devil Prince and stole all his property.

Alistair was relentless in his approach. He used his bloodhound nose to track down any hint of demon blood, going for the strongest to maximize his chance of stealing the most subregions. His body did not tire, and his resolve did not falter. This was not even light work compared to what he had done in the past.

Six hours turned to twelve, twelve turning to a twenty-four. In a day's time, he captured 1,000 subregions. He barely encountered any Devil Princes anymore. Even when he ranged out further, chaining [Dash] multiple times, for the last seven hours, he didn't get a whiff of any powerful demon bloods.

They must have realized my strategy, Alistair concluded. *They're minimizing their losses by retreating anyone who owns more than one subregion.*

Attacking the Devil King heartlands was a tall order—they had their own heavy fortifications, just like the Northeast Order. Knowing that any strong fighters they had were out of the way allowed for other options, however.

Alistair's reinforcements arrived at the scene.

It was a small band of some of the most rugged soldiers that Blaise had raised in his academies. They followed orders absolutely, and Alistair felt comfortable trusting them to clean up after him.

Over time, as he collected a larger number of subregions, beasts came out of the woodwork to try to reclaim the subregions at the beginning of Alistair's rampage, ones he was too far away to protect. That was where the soldiers came in. They wore all black except for Alistair's insignia, and all had stealth-related Classes. They easily dispatched the beasts and preserved the gains.

The Devil Kings could try sending in stronger cultivators, but they risked losing manpower for nothing in return, since if Alistair intercepted them, they were done for.

The all-out offensive front was effective. Slowly but surely, the Devil

Kings' subregion count dwindled. Not by a lot, but anything was impactful this close to the finish line.

As for Alistair? He was sitting pretty. The monotony was even enjoyable. He had his mission, and he executed it. It felt good to stretch his legs and use his speed to the fullest, where he truly felt like the fastest being on Earth. Nothing could catch him as he captured subregion after subregion.

One day became two, and two became three. Alistair was confident he could continue his scorched earth warfare ad infinitum. But he suspected there was going to be a more natural breaking point.

The third wave of [Armageddon] had arrived.

34 KAIJU BREAK

Wave 3: Kaiju Break

The plethora of monsterkin from rebellious dungeons could not fell FX-14752. 62.1% of the dungeons were dealt with before rupturing to the outside world, though the remaining 37.9% caused massive financial damages and loss of life. Remaining monsters will not be culled and shall remain as a reminder of this planet's feebleness. Let the death of the weak serve as forewarning to all those who walk the path of cultivation. Become stronger or die.

Two groups participated in the Grand Dungeon, Symphony of Skills, Alistair Tan and George Moulin and party. George Moulin received the First Through bonus for being the first on the world to complete Symphony of Skills, which included the interfief competition, Cosmic Blood, for those under level 100. George Moulin and the Devil Kings placed 13th and Alistair Tan placed 98th out of all participants in the Disputed Shard fief, an impressive placing for both Prime Initiates.

For the third wave of [Armageddon], the theme of natural disasters continues. Or rather, creatures that may be described as natural

disasters on account of their sheer power. One translation might be
—kaiju.

Enormous genetically engineered beasts will ravage your world for
the next month. This will start now, with the first kaiju. Each kaiju
will be stronger than the last, appearing at random every week,
until the last week, in which the five kaijus will appear at once.

In addition to the normal ways you can add to your Contribution
Score as delineated in the text of [Armageddon], in Kaiju Break,
you can earn them by impeding the rampage of the kaijus and
reducing the damage to civilization.

Let Kaiju Break begin!

SPEAKING OF CONTRIBUTION SCORE, Alistair hadn't checked his in some time.
He ranked #2 with 1,496 points behind George, who was all the way at
2,631. Everyone else on the list was negligible in comparison. It was a two-
horse race, as it always was.

Alistair rolled his hands through his hair. While he felt physically
perfect, there was a tension from the stress of things that still persisted. The
deck felt stacked. Contribution Score, subregion count, and preserving the
lives of his citizens. He had to juggle all three things.

Alistair spent 10k Gold drachma on a direct message through the
Soulnet to Alexandra. She would receive it as an unavoidable notification.

> *Alexandra, it's me. I'm back, sorry for leaving once again. How are things*
> *going on your end? I've managed to snag 1,000 subregions, but I worry*
> *about this kaiju wave. We're going to need you and Pharaoh and Whimsy*
> *and the Woods. I would try looking for Lucius, but I have so little time. We*
> *all do.*
> *— Alistair.*

That would have to do for now. Alistair prayed with all his soul for a
reprieve. As if the multiverse was listening, he got his lucky break.

When he examined the Soulnet news, the event was obvious. The first
kaiju had appeared deep within Devil King territory.

A reply came from Alexandra.

It's about time you came back, Alistair. I was beginning to think you just don't like Earth very much. It's a warzone out here. So many people dead. For some reason, the Devil Kings seem to be reluctant to attack us, compared to the average person. Makes me even angrier, seeing that cowardice. They have more manpower than us, sadly. Let's set up a Soulnet talk with all of the players, coordinates -123.5, 1,803.0. Meet me in ten minutes.

Some intrepid individual had invented a coordinate system for the Soulnet, making it much easier to set up meetings. Still, as Alistair checked -123.5, 1803.0 in his Soulnet map, that was a long way away from where he'd entered the net. *You think too highly of me, Alexandra.*

His body would automatically respond to any incoming threats, so he casually slipped into the Soulnet. His vision faded to pink, and he found himself in the European ballroom that seemed to be the starting point for every Soulnet user. Like always, his outfit was transformed, this time into a partially diaphanous toga that made him feel like a scandalous Roman socialite.

The moment he loaded in fully, he started looking for the direction of the coordinates. Out of the corner of his eye, he spotted a familiar figure.

"Drauku?" Alistair asked tentatively, recognizing the bartender he'd met on his first visit to the Soulnet. "Is that you? They moved you here?"

"Ah, what a delight to see you, Alistair," Drauku replied, a wide smile engulfing his face. "My consciousness is split up over a wide array of locations."

"I'd love to chat, but I have urgent business," Alistair said, looking behind at the wizened homunculus as he ran off according to the coordinates.

"Oh, that is not an issue." Drauku suddenly shifted into a brilliant, luminescent ball, soaring after Alistair at exactly his pace. "I can take this form if it helps."

Alistair raised an eyebrow at the homunculus's ability. "What have you been up to recently?"

Drauku's voice sounded almost robotic, coming from the sphere of light. "Helping young cultivators such as yourself as they follow their paths of destiny. It's not much, but it's honest work. It's the least I owe."

"What do you mean?"

A wistful tone entered the aged homunculus's voice. "The Akata Corporation built my line of homunculi as war slaves. In my prime, I was the equivalent of a Middle Visionary. They discontinued us after a few thousand years because of the cost, and then they sold us to the Pathfinder as we aged. Those were many lifetimes ago to the average citizen, you must understand. Though the world of cultivation seems constant, so much has changed since then. As an artificial lifeform, my lifespan exceeds that of a typical Visionary, though my prime was much shorter."

Alistair veered sharply to the left, drifting along the ground like a racecar. "Wars? What wars is the Final Frontier Empire fighting? I thought they owned the universe."

"That is the common conception near the core territories of the empire," Drauku began, "but it is not entirely true. They claim the entire universe as theirs, but in practice control less than half the area. Though, the outskirts are sparsely populated. The barbarians' 'civilization' can hardly be called such. I might add, however, my conscription was not against the barbarians, but another frontier polity. The Zarbax Collective."

While Drauku was a ball of light, Alistair could *see* the spittle flying out of the homunculus's mouth in that last statement. The venom he had toward the Zarbax Collective was almost unnerving.

"But I should not bog you down with irrelevant concerns. It deeply pains me to see the strife your planet has been through. I pray that you shall find success and peace for all."

"Thank you, Drauku," Alistair said. "You know, that Pallox Semper drink you gave me might have made the difference in my standing today. If I hadn't had that slight edge on understanding the Dao, I might not be number one."

"Nonsense," Drauku retorted. "Your rise was inevitable. Your talent is top class, and if I may say so myself, I predicted your rise the moment I met you."

Alistair ran by a forest with trees made of glass as he continued his winding journey through the Soulnet. As he found himself in an enormous plains field, he picked up the pace since there weren't any turns.

"There's no way you could help me out, is there?" Alistair asked hopefully.

Drauku shook his metaphorical head. "Sadly, there is not. Anything more than giving you that elixir would result in my dismissal. The Grand Imperator shall arrive in due time and conduct an impropriety audit."

Ah, there was another stressor Alistair had forgotten about—the goddamn spoiled Portolon scion who had challenged him to a duel with the fate of the planet on the line. So even if he managed to pull Earth through against the Devil Kings, one wrong step, and it was goodbye for everyone else.

"But I have faith in you," Drauku said. "I have a feeling this shall only be one small step on your journey. Take this."

A pristine jade pendant dropped into Alistair's hands. "Wait," he said. "I thought it was against the rules?"

"I see nothing," Drauku said. "Perhaps in a few hours I will find my defensive charm mysteriously missing. I will then conclude I must have dropped it earlier, but I would have no idea when."

Alistair nodded, clutching the jade pendant tight. It was cool to the touch, fitting around his neck nicely. The necklace portion was silver chain-links, connected to a rectangular cut of jade with the face of what appeared to be a female naga. Alistair wanted to ask who the portrait displayed, but he refrained out of respect for Drauku's privacy. Risking everything to give Alistair a slight edge went above and beyond.

"I won't let you down," Alistair replied. "How strong is this?"

"Appearances have to be kept up," Drauku said. "An item of one's own level does not arouse suspicion as much. Do you understand?"

Alistair nodded again, doing another auto racing-style drift as he turned into the final straight in the Soulnet. "After this is all over, maybe you can retire from your position."

"Ah, that is unlikely. The contract between the Akata Corporation and the Pathfinder AI is quite precise, and ends with my scheduled death. Goodbye." Drauku's ball of light vanished into thin air and Alistair was alone. But not for long, as he arrived at one of the starting locations in a vastly disparate area of his freehold.

Alistair opened the door to the ballroom, where he found Alexandra, Pharaoh, Alfred, and Marzhan having a heated discussion. On a closer inspection, it was really just Alexandra and Alfred talking—Pharaoh and the top 10 ranker from the United Polities weren't saying a word.

"Now is the best time," Alexandra said, barely quieter than a shout. "That kaiju or whatever is fucking massive. It's stronger than the Beast

Ruler fireworm that we held off before. This is by far our best opportunity to do some real damage."

Alfred shook his head. "It's too risky," he said. "Who's to say they can't just ignore the beast? They have no regard for the safety of human lives, obviously. Without intelligence and the ability to target specific enemies, the kaiju will rampage without distinction."

"They can't ignore it completely," Alexandra said. "If their lands are completely devastated, they won't be able to accrue Contribution Score. Back me up here, Pharaoh."

Pharaoh, like always, remained reticent. Alexandra was about to say something else, but then she noticed Alistair's presence.

"Alexandra is correct," Alistair said, walking up to the rest of them as he fidgeted his new defensive pendant into place. "But we have to do this in a special way."

Alfred turned around, frowning. "Explain, please." There were no introductions or formalities. They were long past things like that, especially in a moment that required full concentration.

"There's a severe power differential right now," Alistair said. "I don't want to presume, but I think it extends to even you, now, Pharaoh."

Pharaoh grunted in assent. If Alistair was looking closely, his facial muscles flexed ever so briefly in an expression of disgruntlement. Giving up the #1 spot wasn't so easy, after all.

"The types of upgrades I've been getting recently, especially including and since returning from the Holy Ravine, I'm pretty sure I could beat all eight Devil Kings besides George by myself. And George could do the same to you guys, most likely. With such a gap in power, we run into risks. Both sides, really. I think they'll think of this same scenario. If we both go at each other, George and I will try to eliminate the other side's subordinates as quickly as possible, to put the numbers gap in our favor."

Alfred scratched his chin. "Ah... as the fastest cultivator on the Earth, you sit at a unique advantage for, let's call these, 'pick-offs.'"

"Precisely," Alistair said. "Which is why I think we need to attack. That puts me in the best possible scenario. Plus, I have another goal."

Ideally, he only wanted Pharaoh, Alexandra, and Alfred to hear his next idea. But he supposed he could trust Marzhan. Lesser Samatha revealed unspoken truths, and nothing indicated that she wanted anything but the victory of humankind.

"I think we can offer a deal to them," Alistair said. "I haven't got all the details worked out yet. But anything we can do to stop the deaths, we have to. It's a nightmare out there. I don't think we at the top understand that, fully."

A sullen look came over the other four cultivators. As five of the most powerful people on the planet, all their friends and family would be in the most well-protected places. The places that would be last to fall. They were insulated against the tragedies that were happening to the average Joe.

Tragedy is too weak a word. Estimates indicated that 20% of the pre-[Armageddon] population of the world had died in the two months of the final Quest. Twenty percent, two zero. It was such an incomprehensible number to Alistair. There had been even worse numbers absolutely at the start of the initiation, but that was before he had any responsibility.

He could never feel the individual pain of each death. One death was a tragedy, a million was a statistic. The emotional impact of knowing that 20% of the world had died. All that life snuffed out, whether by an orc's claws, or the debris of a tornado, or the rampaging of an enormous kaiju.

This weighed heavily on Alistair's conscience. If he could find a way to mitigate that suffering, he would take that path.

"This world is cruel," Marzhan said as she shook her head. "But what do you mean, a deal?"

"It's still in development," Alistair replied. "Just trust me on this one. We need to get everyone of note assembled for this one. *Everyone*. If this works, this will be the second most important moment of the Quest."

35 ASSAULT AT DAYBREAK

PHARAOH AND WHIMSY sat down seiza-style in their humble abode. Since giving up his subregions to Alistair, the former #1 had no reason for a defensive structure. Instead, he took up a shack in a small cottage in the middle of nowhere, though he defended it and the small town around it admirably.

"I don't understand," Whimsy said. "You didn't have to give up your spot so easily. I know you have greater insight than you let on."

"What's meant to be, is meant to be," Pharaoh said. "Alistair is suited for the role of a hero. That is what this planet needs. I cannot fulfill that role. That is not my destiny."

Whimsy poured herself a cup of tea. While Pharaoh had once been an Egyptologist, he had an appreciation for many cultures around the world. His tea set came from a collector in Japan that he had done business with many years ago, and somehow he managed to preserve it well into the initiation.

"What is your destiny, then?"

"I'm still finding that out myself, aren't I?" Pharaoh gave a rare smile. "We all are. I wouldn't be doing half the job Alistair is. I can't bring myself to care for all those people like he does. I find them so quaint and small these days."

Whimsy understood what he was talking about. Immortality, star-shattering power, empires of trillions upon trillions of people. The plight of Earth seemed so very insignificant in the face of that.

"It's cute," Whimsy landed on. "I think so, anyway."

"Are you ready?" Pharaoh asked.

Whimsy gave him an incredulous look. "I'm always ready, Dr. Fakhry."

A hint of a blush came over the man's face. "I don't go by that name anymore."

"I know."

Whimsy put her hand on his, feeling his warmth. The scent of desert sand was nostalgic to her, even though she grew up near an icy bay.

"I love you." Pharaoh's words cut her in two. He had never said them before. Always unspoken, she understood this, yet it was far different hearing it aloud.

"I love you too," Whimsy said, tears forming in her eyes.

"When I first saw you, I knew that we would be together." Pharaoh looked up at the sky. Since the moment she met him, she had seen him as a bastion of strength. Stalwart, impassably stoic—a classical man. Yet now his hands trembled, and she knew why. "If only things were different."

"Enough of that." Whimsy gripped onto his hands tighter. "Enough."

"The inverse curse won't last much longer."

"I know. I can feel it."

"Then I have failed you."

"Never," Whimsy said. "I'm already living on borrowed time. Now stop focusing on me, and let's help out Alistair."

———

All within a twenty-mile radius felt the presence of the beast instantly. The moment the third wave of [Armageddon] began, it appeared.

Morgana felt her body quiver in fear. Her mind commanded her body to stop, to act rationally. But her base instincts took over. The aura of dread was not just in her imagination. It was real.

Then came the heat.

After completing her last mission, Morgana was resting in her personal villa when it happened, studying some arcane scripture that her leader purchased from the Hall of Math. The complexities of her Class were endless. While she assumed that most cultivators tended to think their Class was best or somehow unique, she had to imagine there was something special about the Dao of Magic. After all, it encompassed such a wide variety of existence.

The heat was like a miasma in the air, curdling in on itself in hazy patterns reminiscent of a hot summer's day, but magnified manifold. She felt her breathing constrict and sweat on her body. Morgana didn't have the highest Constitution, but it had to be really sweltering for her to feel the physical effects of heat.

The killing intent comprised one large wave that chilled her to the bones, and then a lingering psychic field that was much less powerful. She could easily withstand its effects, though the average person was probably catatonic with fear.

The more concerning part was that by that aura, she could tell it was over five miles away. Yet the heat at her location was already this strong. How concentrated would it be in the vicinity of the kaiju?

Not wanting to waste any more time, she activated her spell, Partial Flight, and ascended into the skies. The first thing she noticed was the sunrise.

The only issue was that it should have been the dead of night. Not that Morgana paid too much attention to the day-night cycle, but she was certain that it had been night when she secluded herself not more than an hour ago. Not long enough for it to be dawn already.

Morgana flew toward the source of the heat and aura. While she flew, she felt the presence of her master below, and descended toward him.

The temperature chilled as she touched down on the ground, going from a desert hot to a cold winter's day. Morgana wiped off sweat from her brow in relief under the umbrella of George's icy aura.

"Take me with you," he commanded, and Morgana obliged. Using her spell Partial Polymorph, she grew the talons of a great roc, picking up George and flying off toward the kaiju.

The sky grew brighter the closer they got, approaching the luminosity of daytime. Morgana didn't want to know how hot the air was—George had to start forcing his aura's manifestation to cool down the environment. She could see the border of his sphere of influence against the boiling air, where pale blue ice met the orange atmosphere.

She rose into the sky, trying to get a better look at their new opponent.

The beast was massive. At her vantage point high in the sky, she could make out the kaiju from miles away. The blistering heat warped her vision, on top of the lava-like glow emitted from its craggy skin, but the form was obvious. An enormous turtle.

The turtle was black, though its skin was molten and spewed out lava like an active volcano. If Morgana had to guess, it was the size of an aircraft carrier, or even larger. A snake wrapped around the turtle's back, spewing lava as it rampaged near the coastline.

Everything within a few body's lengths of the turtle-snake was either on fire or melting, even stone and metal. Morgana suspected that even George's ice would have trouble taming the fire, as the strength of the kaiju's aura far exceeded anything she had ever felt. Comparing beasts to humanoids was apples to oranges—beasts usually had stronger auras at similar levels, even if in practice their combat effectiveness was equal or less than a humanoid, but the gap she felt wasn't going to be broached by human technique.

"Xuanwu," George whispered from his cradle in Morgana's talons. She had to admit, it was a funny mental image, seeing her leader being carried like a baby bat clinging to its mother. "One of the Four Auspicious Beasts from Chinese mythology."

"It's an ugly one," Morgana said. "I think we'll need all hands on deck for this."

George continuously pumped more ice affinity Mana into the atmosphere to cool them down. The difference in temperature between their bubble and the outside world became even more obvious, making it look like they were surrounded by a sphere of pale blue energy.

All of a sudden, Morgana felt a massive burst of energy building up. Before she could even react, a column of lava spewed out of a crack in the xuanwu's shell, so fast it caused a sonic boom.

If she was on her own, she might have been forced to use one of her trump cards to survive. Thankfully, George covered for her.

"*Arcanous Devil Spell #1: Ice Spear of the False Heavens.*"

A spear as tall as George and half again flew down from the heavens just as fast as the column of lava shot up. It was too fast to make out details, but it was obviously carved of ice and contained an impartment of Dao energy and *nue* that would have been straining for Morgana, but was no issue for George.

The spear collided with the column, sending it askew and hyper-cooling the lava midair, obsidian chunks flying out like shrapnel.

As the debris swept away with the continuous air currents from the xuanwu, Morgana saw a glowing purple array fade away on George's tongue. Normally, issuing a Rank 1 or higher spell required a verbal command, an incantation of its name. Certain spells could be designated as reflex spells, letting one create the incantation as a spell array that would automatically speak the name of the spell under certain conditions. These reflex spells were weaker, but far faster than ordinary ones, and could be used an unlimited amount of times per day.

"It determined our presence as a threat," George said. "Listen to Hephaestus's orders as if they were mine. I'm going to engage now."

George slicked back his frozen spikes of hair. Morgana had not seen his blond locks fall over his face once. They were always spiked up with literal ice. Then, he jumped.

While he soared down, he activated his true Rank 1 Spell: *Arcanous Devil Spell #3: Frygian Arrow.*

A bow and arrow made out of ice materialized in George's hands. Intricately carved with the faces of ten thousand unique demons, a royal purple arrow notched on its string. Larger than the typical ice arrows he fired, there was an aura to the projectile that reminded Morgana of the Furnace of Impure Flames from the Grand Dungeon.

George carefully aimed the arrow at the snake head of the xuanwu and fired. The purple arrow streaked through the air even faster than the earlier spear. Along the way, it sucked moisture and drew the cold toward itself. The arrow grew at a rapid pace while making the environment around itself even hotter, if such a thing were possible. The ground spontaneously combusted in flames identical in color to the arrow, which shimmered against the heat it was fueling.

Once it reached the size of a cruise missile, an outer layer broke off and instantly set on fire, similar in appearance to how a satellite burned up as it reentered the upper atmosphere. Morgana found the paradoxical arrow to be quite beautiful. Hot yet cold, burning yet frozen.

The arrow collided with the xuanwu's side, exploding with a conflagration of purple flames that overpowered the beast's natural heat, if for a moment. Morgana imagined the kaiju was almost if not entirely immune to heat, but the flames masked the ice underneath.

Morgana felt a familiar presence behind her. Similar to the xuanwu's molten rock, the rest of the Devil Kings arrived on Hephaestus's forged flying bicycles. The fabrications were made of a molten brown rock that was cool to the touch, a fitting ability for one of his name.

The flames from the explosion dispersed. The tortoise-snake was half-encased in ice, frost seeping into its formerly molten cracks.

Morgana was impressed with the power of George's Rank 1 Spell, but already she could see the signs of melting. The idea of killing the kaiju in one spell was a fantasy.

How unlucky, she thought. *If this monstrosity showed up in Alistair's land, we would be taking the victory within the next few hours.*

Now that she considered it, what was Alistair doing?

―――

It felt like days had passed since Alistair had the Soulnet meeting, but in reality, it had only been four hours. The twenty-four-hour cycle of day and night barely mattered for them. It was a coincidence that another four hours led to the part of night just before dawn.

Alistair constantly monitored the subregion situation. With the Devil King forces withdrawn to deal with the kaiju, the balance continued to improve. When he first came back, the percentages were, down to a thousandth place, 45.13% subregion control Devil Kings, 24.97% Northeast Freehold.

Now, those numbers were 43.68% Devil King, 25.90% Northeast. It didn't seem like much, but that was a 2,000 subregion swing. While Alistair may have held the lower hand in absolute subregion count, there was no doubt he was accruing more Land Store Credits, taxation, and Contribution Score from his territory. The vast majority of Devil King land was razed and barren, the makeshift graveyards for millions of sacrificed lives. Thankfully, they got no benefit from their wanton killing in and of itself, or the scores would have been wildly lopsided.

Alistair used his Ghost Node to etherealize his body, limiting his causal impact on the world. His method of subterfuge therefore worked equally against all forms of reconnaissance, from mundane eyesight to extremely convoluted mechanisms.

He snuck into the Devil Kings' land alone. Well, not entirely alone. His vampiric librarian, Caren Locasta, communicated with him via **[Paper**

Tongue]. A Skill upgrade increased its range tenfold, as long as he limited the targets down to one.

"This is funny," Caren said. *"Feels like I'm the NSA."*

"Don't read my emails," Alistair thought back.

Alistair ran as silent as a mouse, though over a hundred times the little mammal's speed. At present, he traversed through a charred forest—not from Atavius Meloi's initial attack, but according to his records, Morgana's rampage. The ash on which he stood was once part of a national forest park in China, before she had her way.

Through **[Ghost Whispers]**, Alistair was attuned to the hundreds of thousands that had perished. They called to him in screams and groans, guttural in nature. His sister told him that the longer the soul stayed on the Physical Plane and refused to enter an afterlife, the more inhuman they became, growing fixated on the central thought they had before death.

The souls that hadn't moved on were just like this. Ghasts more than ghosts, you could say. They seemingly understood that Alistair could hear them, and harangued him for miles, following him and crying for their loved ones, for themselves.

"When it gets to be this bad, you can perform a Buddhist rite," Dev'rox said. "To hasten the natural process. If such negativity lingers for too long, it can curse the land for millennia. For a later time, though. It's not something that can be done hastily."

"I can already feel it," Alistair communicated toward Caren. *"It's hot."*

From their spies, they knew that the kaiju was a lava xuanwu. The memories indicated it to be larger than a small island, dwarfing any beast Alistair had encountered, even the fireworm.

Alistair continued the low-level drain on his Ghost Node, gliding through the land. The kaiju had appeared on the coastline, though by the rearrangement of the subregions in [The Game of Life], that coastline subregion was connected to the Rocky Mountains. Alistair ran up the mountain as if it were flat ground, not catching a single breath.

Once he made it to the top, he surveyed the situation. He relied on his aura sense and life force detection, since his natural vision was impeded by the warping of the searing air. There was the main aura of the xuanwu that dwarfed everything else, followed by lesser, but still powerful auras that circled around it like buzzing gnats.

One stuck out above the others, a biting cold that tasted of Dev'rox's arcanous power. That could only be George.

To Alistair's chagrin, the First Devil King's aura felt more powerful than his by a noticeable margin. It was clear that he was level 60. Alistair was sorely missing those locked stats, which might put him on par.

As a warrior, he didn't let that affect his mental state. There was always a path to victory. After all, he had just beaten his improved self. And Alistair was certain that his improved self could defeat George Moulin. Albeit, he had several advantages in that fight against his better counterpart. But he also had an advantage against George in the form of Oracle's memories.

Now, it came down to the approach. Alistair chose the direct option. He wasn't sure how fine George's detection was, so he picked a conservative two [Dash] distance, which was a bit under half a mile away.

Dev'rox materialized concomitant to Alistair's [Dash], compressing the space in front of his host. The first instance of the Skill Alistair stuck to the ground, and then in the second, he used the airwalking aspect to launch himself into the air.

As for the target, he had a few options. George himself wasn't what he was looking for, plus he was on the other side of the kaiju on the ground. The woman he recognized from the images as Morgana flew by her own power, while the other six Devil Kings flew around on strange bicycles.

Six, not seven. There was one Devil King unaccounted for. But Alistair didn't concern himself with that. He chose the path of least resistance—the closest person to him.

That turned out to be Monk, the Twelfth Devil King. He wore a white headband around his eyes, reminiscent of the ones that Alistair had to wear in the Holy Ravine, along with the robes of a Buddhist mendicant.

To his credit, Monk reacted to Alistair's rapid assault. By the time he came within a dozen body lengths of the Devil King, Monk turned his head toward the moving figure. He raised his arms into a defensive stance, expelling a martial aura that Alistair found quite familiar.

On the other side of the battlefield, George also realized the presence of his enemy, raising his right hand to the sky. But they were both too late.

Alistair submerged himself into the calming embrace of Tranquil Mind. He moved toward his opponent in what felt like slow motion. Monk drew his fists to his sides and punched forward, his punches draped in golden-colored Mana affinity that Alistair could not place exactly, though it reminded him of the presence of his Bodhisattva avatar.

His attack was simply too slow. Alistair ducked under the punch while still continuing forward with his momentum. Once he reached a fist's length from the lower ranked Devil King, a pulse of *nue* exploded from the man's brain. It rippled throughout the air omnidirectionally in the form of a martial artist performing a knifehand strike.

The threat of Alistair must have triggered Monk's defensive Skill, which was no pushover. Yet the wave of *nue* washed over him like a warm breeze. Alistair was inured to the effects of *nue* after practicing with it so much. He diverted a small amount of his own psychic energy to block the effects. He'd found that out of Dao energy and Mana, *nue* was the only one you could just "shrug off."

In addition to the *nue* defensive Skill, Alistair felt a Dao of Time at work. As he formed a fist, aiming an uppercut at Monk's chin, for a split second, the blind martial artist moved faster than him.

Yet his moves were so… amateurish. For a blind monk, Alistair expected better simply from the stereotypes. He was fast because of his acceleration of time, yet he had so many inefficiencies.

Alistair parried Monk's futile barrage of punches easily, despite holding the lower hand in speed. **[Monk Motionlessness]** barely even gave him a warning, showing how little danger he faced.

Their exchange was quick, outsider observers seeing nothing but a blur of movement. Alistair sliced upward on his tenth strike, catching Monk's jugular with a **[Blood Hand]**. It was over from there. He followed up with a deafening downward elbow strike encased in **[Force Fist]**, cracking the Devil King's skull open.

Monk, the Twelfth Devil King, died instantly.

Blood and life force flowed from the fallen foe into Alistair's body, along with a notification for his Bonus Quest Reward. But he didn't have time to process the kill—he jumped away right before a spear made of ice came crashing down from above. The blinding speed of the spear created an air current so sharp that it left a tiny cut on his left cheek.

Alistair landed on the ground, which was alight in a purple fire that he put out with **[Frozen Claw]**. He wiped a single drop of blood off his face, the cut already starting to knit up from his high Endurance.

Fire, Alistair thought. *It's always fire, somehow. Selephita's probably smiling.*

He could sense George's signature aura from the mysterious flames, which were hot but seemed to suck the heat out of the underlying ground, making it so cold he even felt it through his **Fall of Fleet** boots and **Mammothskin Raiment.** It was a strange feeling to breathe out and see puffs of steam, yet be standing in a sea of flames.

The other Devil Kings, seeing that their ally died in under a second, coalesced around George. Their flying bicycles flew to the other side of the lava kaiju, along with the witch.

The only problem for every human there was the xuanwu didn't care about their silly antics. As an enormous beast, its reactions weren't as good as Alistair's or Monk's, but it made up for that with sheer power.

After feeling the strength of the interloper, the xuanwu seemed to take things to the next level. A volcano sprouted from its shell, growing to half the height of its entire body. An absolutely gargantuan level of Mana rose from its core, dozens of times larger than Alistair's full output.

Then, it exploded.

36 BOLD WORDS

ALISTAIR'S entire vision was blocked by an endless wave of lava. Reaching up into the sky, this was no ordinary volcanic eruption. Though beasts tended to have less meaningful Daos at the same level, the xuanwu was far higher leveled than anyone present, and the earth-and-fire Dao within the eruption was corrosive and powerful.

However, the primary threat to Alistair was not the lava, which fell slowly enough that it was like molasses to him, but the pyroclastic flow.

Alistair wasn't sure how fast they normally were, but the emerging black cloud was faster than his **[Dash]** speed. He slipped into Black Impermanence, his partially reptilian pupils fading into a pitch black iris with a halo of white light, the opposite of the aura that surrounded his body.

In this state, he was barely human, more a force of nature. Surrounding his gauntleted hand with a **[Frozen Claw]**, Alistair braved the incoming pyroclastic cloud head-on. He infused his Ghost Node into the Skill, invoking the "Permanent Haunt" division.

The ice of **[Frozen Claw]** crystallized the smoldering cloud, but at the same time, etherealized it. The image of Fan Wujiu, the Black Impermanence, imprinted itself on his mind's eye. On his tall hat were the words, "Arresting You Right Now," and he swung his fan.

Instead of its normal pale blue color, Alistair's **[Frozen Claw]** and its massive web of crystals were black, like the state of Kai'tazake Mutra. The momentum of the cloud stopped completely, standing still as if in a museum.

Alistair jumped up and on top of the mass of ice crystals, surveying what had just happened. The lava was still billowing down from the heavens after being shot up so high by the volcanic eruption. He ran into a jump in which he coiled all his potential energy, soaring into the air.

When he was about to make contact with the falling lava, he activated [Frozen Claw]. He used each piece of frozen lava like a gymnastics bar to swing from and did this until he came to the very apex of the eruption, several miles into the air. He deactivated Black Impermanence, since the drain on his Dao energy was high.

The rest of the lava cascaded downward in a landslide of biblical proportions. For as far as the eye could see, the tsunami of molten rock filled the land. Within seconds, it was as if Alistair was standing above an eternal sea of lava.

On the other side of the kaiju stood a massive glacier. Alistair recognized it as *Arcanous Devil Spell #1: Glacial Front*. It was the first of George's five Arcanous Devil Spells, which he now had detailed intel on thanks to stealing Oracle's memories with [Blood Hand]. The glacier created by the spell appeared nearly instantaneously, making it a powerful defensive tool.

By the looks of it, neither the pyroclastic flow nor the tsunami of lava could pass its barrier. The lava hardened in front of it in the form of a crashing wave, while the rest of it flowed around the glacial front.

Alistair felt the kaiju's energies ebbing. After such a huge explosion of Mana, he would have been worried if the beast hadn't been lethargic.

With a [Dash], Alistair launched himself off of the falling ice. It felt different, so high up; the wind parted against his face. While this was a battle of life and death, he was having fun. Determined fun. His limbs coursed with extra power from the "Good Samaritan" Badge, heightening his speed to the point where he was almost moving fast enough to match his reflexes.

Dev'rox carved space apart with his magic. The compression looked like a warp drive from the movies, and Alistair could tell he put in an extra oomph.

Alistair came from above, touching down on top of the glacier for a split second. He [Dashed] again the moment his feet touched the ice. His eyes were locked on one target. George Moulin, the leader of the Devil Kings.

[Monk Motionlessness] alerted him to the danger first. Alistair unconsciously stopped his [Dash] and swayed to the left. An ice spear crashed into the ground with tremendous force, producing a hypersonic shockwave that sent Alistair tumbling for the length of several city blocks.

A trickle of blood came out of his ear, accompanied by a low ringing. If he kept going on his [Dash], the spear would have impaled him. He recognized the spear as coming from *Arcanous Devil Spell #2: Ice Spear of the False Heavens,* but the weight and speed of the spear, which had shattered into a million pieces on impact with the ground, was far superior to the ones he saw in Oracle's memories.

Did he use it as a normal spell instead of a reflex? Alistair wondered. *No, that can't be. He reacted way too fast.* The stolen memories held the answer. *Heavyset.*

The Thirteenth Devil King didn't stand out. She honestly looked like a normal middle-aged woman, though she was morbidly obese. But her role wasn't as a fighter, but as support. Her manipulation of gravity could make things heavier and lighter—not just physically, but also metaphysically.

That explained the unusual speed and power of the ice spear. It also gave Alistair a target to go after. Of course, George wouldn't let him at his valued support easily. Alistair needed some backup.

"*It's time,*" Alistair messaged. Caren gave him a psychic nod.

Alistair stood up, taking a deep breath. The seven aura signatures of the Devil Kings blazed on the horizon, made all the more repugnant by their maleficent odor. The scent of demon blood seared his sensitive nose. If a Devil Prince was like a rotten egg, George was thioacetone.

With one snap of a small pair of fingers, reality shifted. Dev'rox connected Alistair to the anchor he made in space during his first [Dash].

Alistair was certain they knew about his spatial capabilities by now, though he doubted they understood the source was the ghost of the demon. While they might not have been taken completely off guard by his sudden teleportation, perhaps they would be surprised by his next move.

The teleportation brought him a football field length away from the Devil Kings, at which point Alistair [Dashed] again. That was to be expected, and he sensed incoming danger from above. Since he was expecting the ice spears, **[Monk Motionlessness]** was better equipped to alert him.

Attacks inside one's perception versus outside, Alistair thought. *Everything ties back to Master Ko Pao's teachings.*

Alistair darted from side to side, avoiding a series of three ice spears. They weren't as strong as the first one George sent down, but they would have still caused a serious injury. Purple fire that screamed with the pain of a million souls flew in concentrated beams, while an arsenal of spears came from above. They were even weaker than before, George going for volume instead of power.

Entering the ocean of tranquility was like coming home for Alistair. The mass of water subsumed him entirely within its peaceful innards. It was the only state of the Kai'tazake Mutra without an outward visual change. The mind needed no fancy auras or colors to achieve perfection.

This time, in his hour of greatest need, he dove far deeper into Tranquil Mind than he had ever done before. He knew the risks. The depths of the Kai'tazake Mutra were unfathomable. There was a chance that if he went too deep, his psyche could be permanently scarred. Forever stuck in a state of perpetual enlightenment.

Alistair moved like a Daoist sage. He expended minimal effort to dodge the incoming attacks. He subconsciously used **[Eyes of Truth]**, accessing his precognitive vision. Combined with Tranquil Mind, he truly felt omniscient on the battlefield.

Each spear of ice, or shadowy tendril, or cone of destruction that assailed him came closer to hitting him each time. He pushed his body and skill to its utmost limits.

The Dharmic Wheel turns, Alistair thought. *Karma will be restored, injustice will be righted, and the aeon will move forward toward the final culmination of total enlightenment.*

There was always a breaking point. Alistair was strong, and by chancing his sanity and drawing from his Karma, he could temporarily match the output of the Devil Kings. However, they weren't using their full power from the start. That began to change.

In his foresight, he saw Morgana rain down a murky spell unknown to him. His **[Eyes of Truth]** couldn't reveal its full extent, owing to its high weight on reality and the fact he had no prior knowledge of it. His precognition worked much better on things he had seen before. Whatever the spell was, it was powerful and encompassing in area.

At the same time, he envisioned George using a named spell. Despite knowing the Devil King's arsenal from Oracle's stolen memories, he couldn't see the details of this spell. There was a chilling, blizzard-like aura that surrounded all of George's images in the future, one that he almost felt was *watching* him in the past. There was a Fate-warding measure at work, a strong one at that.

The result—death. Alistair retreated for a mere moment, but there was an advance from another side.

A column of scarlet light appeared above Heavyset. Eight of the strongest cultivators on the planet fell from the sky. Alistair knew each and every one.

Bartholomew Wood looked like a complete android, his skin covered from head-to-toe with a metallic silver casing. His eyes had a red glow, and he carried a razor-thin laser sword that felt even more concentrated and sharp than before.

Alexandra Lykaios was an avatar of wrath. Her killing intent had grown more intense, cultivated with the endless slaughter of Devil Princes and monsters and beasts. Her **[Barbarian's Fury]** had taken an opaque glare, partially shrouding her features in a hue of blood. She wielded her **Withering Promise** and a new ceremonial dirk that gave off an insidious aura that felt like the color of her eyes, those viridian pools of fire.

Pharaoh was shirtless, and as always, displayed his protective golden band around his waist, along with the pschent crown. His strength was solid and unmoving, a living memorial of ancient times. He was the same as Alistair remembered, though he had not let the others surpass him, his aura markedly stronger.

Whimsy, Brigid, Marzhan, and President Ryder came alongside their transporter, whose identity was never in question—Jesse Waterfall, the Australian that had joined the Northeast Freehold during the fifth Quest.

All eight of Alistair's allies dropped on the preordained target. Heavyset was the weakest of the Devil Kings in direct combat and an important facet of their well-oiled machine, buffing the others with her gravity-related powers.

Seeing Alistair's reinforcements fall from the heavens, the Devil Kings weren't about to let their member die without a fight.

Heavyset was at the back of their seven-man formation, with George at the front and center, flanked by Jakk and the Shadow Twins. Morgana was floating above and to the right from Alistair's perspective, who faced the Devil Kings head-on.

By directly teleporting on top of Heavyset, they were breaking into the Devil King formation, but also exposing themselves to attack. But there was one man who always had primacy.

In Tranquil Mind, Alistair reigned supreme over all others in terms of reaction speed. He was the first one to recognize the burst of scarlet light that signaled phase two of the plan. Thankfully, it took almost a second for the [Scarlet Shift] to fully teleport, leaving him enough time to prepare the cleansing benediction required.

The deep chant began, reciting the sacred name of the tenth-level compassion bodhisattva at superhuman pace. George was the second to realize what had happened, though he found himself torn for a split second between the threat in front of him and the paratroopers going for his back line. That moment of indecision let the Avalokiteśvara avatar of [Thousand-Armed Bodhisattva Judgment] fully form.

Alistair had seen this form many times over his dozens of duels with himself, but he was still awed by the majesty of his finishing Skill. Formed of force and lightning affinity Mana, the avatar radiated an authoritative but compassionate aura. Each of the eleven heads chanted with a deep voice and spread an unintelligible but perfected sutra that messed with the Devil Kings' psyche, even if it didn't harm them directly.

At the same time he used his Skill, he left Tranquil Mind for the analytical Infinite Arsenal. With his silvery aura and blue tint to his eyes, he had no time for enlightenment. Since he was still within the purview of Kai'tazake Mutra, he didn't have to take any effort to leave its unfathomable depths.

[Thousand-Armed Bodhisattva Judgment] launched its tidal wave of palms. Each palm was filled with a bounty of Dao energy and encased in Karmic energy that frayed the threads of Fate surrounding it.

There were far too many palms to stem the tide with ice spears. Alistair could feel George using a named spell, but the bodhisattva's judgment crashed into the Devil Kings before he could finish.

One of the Shadow Twins was at the edge of the assault. Alistair chose him as his target. Thousands of possibilities laid themselves out as he peered into the threads of Fate with the accompaniment of Infinite Arsenal.

The only issue with his new three Kai'tazake Mutra states was their intense drain on his Dao energy. Tranquil Mind from Justice, Infinite Arsenal from Fist, and Black Impermanence from Ghost. He had to be careful with his expenditure of Dao energy on his typical attacks. That was where *nue* was helpful as a third and separate pool to draw on.

The Devil Kings weren't going to take his finishing Skill lying down. Hephaestus, from his safer position behind George, issued a chariot of flames so large it could have been used by giants, sending it flying towards the palms. Morgana and Jakk worked in well-practiced unison, combining his torturous flames with a wind funnel she made to amplify the fire.

But the greatest threat of all was George. He cast a spell that Alistair recognized immediately as *Arcanous Devil Spell #4: Autonomous Crystals*. Oracle had seen her master use the spell once against one of the Beast Lords he recruited. *Autonomous Crystals* consisted of George throwing one seed crystal, which created a chain reaction of ice crystals freezing anything they touched. It reminded Alistair of an aspect of his own **[Frozen Claw]**, though to a much greater extent.

The combined force of *Autonomous Crystals* along with the other Devil Kings' attacks was enough to hold off **[Thousand-Armed Bodhisattva Judgment]**.

[Dash] brought Alistair next to the Shadow Twins. Alistair didn't know their real names, but they were certainly dangerous. They were two as one and one as two, relying on each other for everything. No doubt their twin bond came from before the initiation, and they shared a Class that revolved around shadows, allowing them to move into any piece of shade.

Alistair wasn't sure of what intel they had on him. But they definitely didn't know about his new *nue* clone from **[Dash]**. When he moved in, he triggered the *nue* shadow, expending more than the standard amount.

To the outsider, especially one who had little experience with *nue*, they would interpret the shadow as a real person. The one Alistair designated as the first Shadow Twin tried to move into the *nue* shadow's shadow—and failed because it cast no shadow. His brother tried arresting the real Alistair's shadow, pinning it down in its spot. As long as it couldn't move, the person attached couldn't either.

Alistair used the split second of confusion that the first Shadow Twin had when he used his Skill to activate his new Tier 2 **[Draconic Roar].** Tier 2 increased the cone of effect and primal fear, making it more of a true dragon's roar.

Both of them were caught in it, the first twin receiving the full brunt of the screech. He went catatonic for a moment, which was all that was necessary to seal his fate.

With the activation of another **[Hand of Karma]**, Alistair upgraded the Skill to Tier 4. The upgrade increased its Karma cost to 10, but it gave the Skill an important new utility—searing threads of Fate at a distance.

When he waved his Karmic hand, he spread the crimson energy along all the lines of Fate connecting him to the second Shadow Twin. It was as if the threads of Fate, normally golden and translucent, even to Karmic sight, were burning with a heatless, smokeless, carmine flame.

Alistair was immediately unstuck, and the second Shadow Twin fought against the Karmic energy that threatened to short-circuit his spiritual pathways.

Dev'rox snapped his fingers. Alistair took his place right behind the first Shadow Twin, who was finally returning to sanity after the **[Draconic Roar].** He would never get a chance. The plan he came up with using Infinite Arsenal worked to a tee. A Tier 3 **[Force Fist]** was fast enough to activate during Alistair's punch, whereas before, he had to do it prior to moving.

Five punches smacked into the Devil King's face. Alistair began without using his Skill, interspersing **[Force Fist]** on the second and fourth blows. With the fifth punch, the Spiritual Fighter's Echo of the second started landing.

An autonomous defensive Skill or talisman activated, probably when the Shadow Twin reached a certain Health percentage. A dark and murky Dao became omnipresent, as light became shadow and shadow became light.

Pathetic, Alistair thought. *An illusion of this level couldn't keep me trapped for more than 0.231 seconds.*

There were so many flaws that it was almost difficult to choose the proper mode forward, but by burning more positive Karma, he figured it out. Alistair used his sense of smell to detect the Shadow Twin's real location, where the illusory film was at its weakest, and then bombarded that point with a **[Blood Hand]** infused with his Ghost Node.

Alistair speared the Devil King through the neck, absorbing his life force as he tallied on his bloodline evolution to 89/1000.

Level up! *You are now level 57.* +3 Agility, +3 Intelligence, +3 Charisma, +3 free Attribute points, +23 Upgrade Points.

Bonus Quest Reward: [Vanquishing the Devil Kings] – 5/12. +40 Upgrade Points.

Alistair didn't pay attention to the notifications, since he couldn't use extra Attribute points right now.

"Jared!" The cry of anguish from the other Shadow Twin was the epitome of despair, yet Alistair was paying attention to the rest of the battlefield.

Autonomous Crystals froze the better part of his finishing Skill, while the rest had collided with the other attacks of the Devil Kings. The reverberating gong noises and golden shockwaves were impossible for most of them to avoid, and he could feel it had damaged their pathways.

Even Infinite Arsenal had its limitations. He had hoped the sneak attack of eight of his strongest allies would be able to take out Heavyset, but it looked like things weren't that easy.

George was getting mad.

A chill spread across the entire battlefield as the leader of the Devil Kings unfurled the full extent of his aura. Temperatures dropped to below freezing near instantly as a true blizzard formed around George.

At first, Alistair wondered if his greatest enemy had used his proto-Domain already—in that case, victory might have been possible right then and there. But the ice that had already accumulated on the tips of **Mammothskin Raiment's** sleek collar was too physical and Mana-based for it to be a proto-Domain. No, this had to be a Dao field, but it was by far the strongest he had ever felt.

The restriction he felt on his person, both spiritually and physically, was almost as great as Pharaoh's proto-Domain. He struggled to imagine how strong George's actual proto-Domain was.

The worst-case scenario was getting separated from his allies and having George slaughter all of them. His attack on the Shadow Twins was on the left wing, whereas Heavyset was in the back right of the formation. Thankfully, Alistair had planned things in advance. The moment Dev'rox performed the first swap, the imp hightailed it off toward George.

While he didn't look it, the ghost was a fast flier, and by the time the

First Devil King had gotten serious with the Dao field, Dev'rox was already three-quarters of the way there.

The distance was way longer than any swap that Dev'rox and Alistair had done before. The ability was Mana inefficient for long range, but it had to be done. By performing his signature move, Dev'rox would have enough Mana for one *Spatial Rending* and not a single drop more.

Alistair was at the center of everything. The blizzard surrounding George was so thick he couldn't see the cultivator, while the other Devil Kings pointed their swords at Alistair's throat. He could feel his allies' presence on the other side of the center of the blizzard.

Alistair felt no anxiety within Infinite Arsenal. If he wasn't deep within its embrace, he might have taken a deep breath before stopping and speaking his next words.

"GEORGE!" Alistair shouted with the entire weight of his body, infusing Dao energy into his voice to make it carry even further. "I have an offer! Let us have a temporary truce. I swear on my Dao and on my mother's grave, there is no subterfuge or trick."

The ball was in the Devil King's court.

37 TRUCE?

FOR A MOMENT, Alistair worried his gambit was going to fail. The blizzard did not abate, and his allies' aura signatures grew dimmer. If he had abandoned this idea and gone for a head first assault, he wouldn't have wasted valuable time.

After a long and treacherous second, an equally powerful voice gave a response.

"Explain."

Alistair let out a sigh of relief. The blizzard parted and the cold retreated. To not give out an aggressive impression, he sauntered over toward George without using any ability or the vast majority of his speed.

Alexandra and the others were fine, if a little shaken up by the sudden Dao field. Sally Ryder split into three dozen people, some of whom Alistair recognized as the constituent people for her previous fusion against Dragonus. The others, he found hard to read. Lesser Samatha worked for more substantial truths, he figured. They were all prepared for what he had to say next.

Alistair walked until he felt like he was an appropriate distance away, perhaps the width of a basketball court. He could feel the scrutinizing eyes of the Devil Kings from afar. There was a sudden wail from behind him, and he whipped his head back, only to feel a sudden outburst of killing intent from George.

It wasn't nearly as refined as Alistair's, but it was still as powerful as a Beast Lord's, and it stopped the attacker in his tracks. The surviving Shadow Twin had turned the shadows covering his body into a black panther exoskeleton and tried charging at Alistair.

The pain and grief in his eyes was real, and Alistair couldn't help but feel pity for the man. The Shadow Twin strained against his master's control. The killing intent wasn't strong enough for him to be physically held back, but the subordinate Devil King recognized who had the authority.

"Obey or die," George said, his voice soft yet somehow still carrying all the way across the landscape.

For a moment, Alistair wondered if the twin would sacrifice his life in his anger, but he chose to fall to one knee and bow to his lord.

"I apologize for my subordinate's behavior," George stated. "Now, explain."

For the first time in what felt like was a decade, Alistair was facing the man at the center of his problems. The specter that had been haunting him for the better part of the initiation.

Back then, George was known as the Iceman. It was funny to think about, that George had been Alexandra's comrade at the very, very beginning of the initiation before going rogue. They were chasing Jackson Morley, the crooked politician, when they saw the ice cultivator for a few seconds before he fled.

Alistair remembered him as a normal guy with frozen blond hair and piercing blue eyes. Some might have called him handsome, but his features were harsh and angular, and he had the look of someone evil. A psychopath. Not a very scientific claim, but that's what Alistair thought.

He couldn't say the same for the current George. He looked like he was formed out of ice, his skin having a slight blue tint and perfectly smooth. His features had smoothed out and neotenized, giving him the youthful appearance of a teenager, and his ears were slightly upturned and pointy, like an elf's.

The hollow and profane aura that all other Devil Kings had was muted with him, though Alistair's nose never got things wrong. He was a Devil King, just an august one.

"I propose a truce until the sixth and final wave of [Armageddon]," Alistair said. "The system hasn't revealed all the facets of the sixth Quest. The sixth wave of [Armageddon] is only used if there's less than a 5%

margin of difference in Contribution Score between the two highest freehold owners. Well, technically, the sixth wave will happen no matter what, but it only matters for Global Mayorship if that condition is met. Otherwise, after the fifth wave, the one with the highest Contribution Score will become the Global Mayor."

George's pools of fire bored into Alistair for an uncomfortably long amount of time. A few times, he almost opened his mouth to speak, but stopped himself, unsure of what to say. After what felt like five minutes, the Devil King leader finally answered.

"And?"

"You believe me?" Alistair asked.

"If you were to lie, you would only be damning yourself."

"Very well," Alistair replied. He could feel the heat returning as the kaiju started to regain some activity. They had to finish their discussion quickly before the beast recovered from its volcanic eruption. "I think you can understand the strange situation we're in. You're trying to conquer the subregions, I'm trying to stop you. I can tell you've held back your other Devil Kings because you fear losing them. Anyone close to the level 60 threshold is a rare commodity at this point.

"A truce will be advantageous to us both. It will give us time to deal with the difficulties of [Armageddon] without being worried about the other attacking. The Quest is already difficult as is, without additional threats. If either side loses too much manpower... well, I believe you understand what I'm saying."

George looked at him with cold eyes, despite them being on fire. "You know of the predations?"

"I've talked to my sponsor," Alistair nodded. "But you could figure it out with logic even if you didn't have any information. The Final Frontier Empire is a corrupt kleptocracy. Vultures are going to come to Earth, especially now that we've shown unusual potential for a newly initiated world. The more high level people survive, the better. I'd say that even if you end up victorious."

"What you say, I have also heard from a credible source," George said. "If we postpone our battle until the sixth wave, why would this reduce the carnage instead of it taking place in one moment?"

"It might not." Alistair didn't sugarcoat his words. "That part is a gamble, though logically one battle has less opportunity for death than a continuous war. However, the main benefit would come from not having Earth destroyed in the meantime by [Armageddon]. We have a chance to shore up our freeholds. Even if you don't care about human life in the slightest, reducing the population even further would be disastrous for our long-term prospects. This would be beneficial to us both. And there is one extra thing I'm willing to throw in."

This was the most uncertain part. He had burned his positive Karma before this to divine whether it was the right choice or not, and come up empty. That wasn't surprising in the least—his abilities were not that of a Fate-Diviner, able to see the far future while the near future was murky. He only had his gut to rely on.

Alistair produced the **Experiment Cursed Needle #7.** George's nonchalant demeanor changed to one of undisguised desire when he saw the object, though only for a second before returning to its typical phlegmatic expression.

"It's yours, if you accept."

Alistair gave his spiel. He spoke the truth and only the truth. It was George's turn to contemplate. Once again, for a long moment, he said nothing and did nothing. Then, he started to laugh.

Alistair wasn't sure what to do, and he was positive the other Devil Kings were just as confused as he was. George's laugh turned into a sigh, and said, "Your terms are acceptable. I shall call the Herald of the Pathfinder."

George didn't thrust his hands into the sky like Anthony did, but the beam of gray light appeared just the same. Alistair had figured out that a cultivator in the top 10 could call on the Herald of the Pathfinder one time during the initiation for compacts. He thought it would have been too prohibitive for the Visionary-level Herald, but it appeared that sending such a tiny sliver of its consciousness was insubstantial.

The angelic being that was the Herald formed from the gray light. The androgynous being was as sublime as Alistair remembered. Even though his power had grown so much since the last time he saw it, its strength was truly unfathomable to him, even through the suppression for their safety. Three realms above was too high a metric to comprehend.

"I am Sylas, herald of the Pathfinder AI. Who has requested my service?"

Its words were identical to last time, the voice coming from everywhere in the universe at once.

"We require your assistance to seal a pact between us," George said. "Tell the Herald our terms, Alistair."

Alistair felt off at the Devil King's words. Did he expect a trap at this moment? There was a murkiness that Alistair didn't like. He didn't dare use [Eyes of Truth] to see the threads of Fate, out of fear that George would back out at this critical junction.

Alistair felt more nervous about this than an actual battle, but he said his piece. "Neither party shall make any moves, intentional or otherwise, to gain subregions from either side. Any inadvertently gained subregions will be returned immediately. The current counts of 69,513 subregions for George Moulin's freehold and 87,360 for Alistair Tan's freehold shall remain unchanged for the remainder of [Armageddon]."

If George reacted to the sudden increase in his enemy's subregion count, he didn't show, nor did he make any outbursts against the pact given the change. It wasn't a purposeful trickery on Alistair's part. In the short preparations he'd made before planning the attack, he had met with his sponsor for their last encounter, and also appeared before all the major human freeholds, essentially demanding their cooperation.

It wasn't something he did lightly, but humanity needed a leader now more than ever.

"Neither party shall attack, invade, nor kill any members of the other party. Neither party shall sabotage the other party's land or resources. Neither party shall enter the other party's territory without permission. Five minutes before the Contribution Scores are compared, the party with a greater score will transfer points to make them equal, or if the total combined score is odd, make them within one point. In addition, George Moulin shall receive the item within my possession, **Experiment Cursed Needle #7**, as a token of goodwill. That is my compact."

"There is no need to be so specific," Sylas said in a hollow, monotone voice. There was no recognition of Alistair in the way he talked. Perhaps this consciousness instance was separate from the one he encountered in the void. "My programming can calculate the transcendental intent of your words. Are these terms agreeable to you, George Moulin?"

"I intended this day to be your last," George said. "But your arguments are convincing. I accept the terms."

Sylas procured a golden tome. "Place your hand on the book."

Alistair placed his hand over the glowing book, feeling the familiar energy oscillate through his meridians. The herald closed the tome and performed the same ritual for George, who complied with grace.

"Let it hereby be known that Alistair Tan, majority owner of the Northeast Order Freehold, and George Moulin, majority owner of the Cursed Lands, will enter into a continuous pact delineated by the aforementioned terms. You should now be receiving a spiritual endowment of perfect understanding of the conditions, which cannot be fooled by legal trickery. The spirit of the law triumphs over falsehoods, as enshrined by the Eternal Mandate of the Prime Thinker."

Alistair felt the spiritual endowment, as the words of the Pathfinder put it, as a sudden hiccup within his soulcore's connection to his mind. The concept was complex, but he understood his own terms even better than the way he phrased it. There was no equivocation nor loopholes.

An indelible bond formed between his and George's soul. Any party to break the contract would be met with certain death. A gruesome one at that, involving the crumbling of the soulcore from the inside out.

When it was over, it felt like a weight had been lifted from Alistair's shoulders. While he had never given up hope, it was like the path toward the light grew a little clearer. Most of all, he rejoiced for the average person. No doubt, he had bought them a small saving grace. Many would still perish, but it would be far fewer than the default outcome.

The Herald of the Pathfinder vanished into thin air once the compact was complete. Not a trace of its almighty aura remained. Alistair and George were left facing each other, though the confrontation took on a different lens now that they could not come to blows.

"It is done," George said. He took out the emerald-colored needle from his robes, the Herald having already transferred it. "Since this is my land, I think you should be leaving now."

Alistair didn't waste one second gathering his allies. Jesse teleported them away with haste, and they disappeared in a column of scarlet light. That was right in time for the beast to start its activity again. George's latent aura wasn't enough to hold back the lava-borne heat, and the remaining Devil Kings started to sweat.

———

Out of the corner of his eye, George spotted Elijah mourning over his twin brother's corpse. The body was a gruesome sight, blood and guts oozing out of the former Devil King known as a Shadow Twin. For such an orthodox cultivator, Alistair could be a ferocious enemy.

Morgana let gravity carry her down from Partial Flight's reach. "Are the predations really that bad, master? I know the Man in Shadows warned us, but surely we could have stamped out the humans here and now?"

George sighed, conjuring one of his cigarettes and lighting it with frost, while he played with the needle in his other hand. "You felt his strength, did you not? And he still hides things, I know of it. I would have had to go all out, and you all would have likely died."

Morgana was the only one left that challenged him. Admiral used to do that sometimes, and that pesky Saturn Alius. The Saturn that had shocked him for the first time during the initiation by somehow managing to steal his **Experiment Cursed Needle #7,** and then hidden it away.

George fondly recalled one of the debates they'd had, what felt like decades ago.

"We kill without a thought," Saturn had said. *"Does that not mean those above us can kill us without a thought?"*

"Can, or should?" George asked. *"The Heavens do not take kindly to those who indiscriminately kill those far lesser than themselves. The Man in Shadows says that the fell Karma they accumulate makes such ventures not worth any benefits one might accrue, except for the most unorthodox of cultivators. Even then, it is said they shall one day get their comeuppance in the cycle of Samsara."*

"The gap between us and the regular folk of Earth is immeasurable, yet we barely accrue any fell Karma for our slaughter."

"The gap between us and the regular folk of Earth is nothing in the grand scheme of the Multiverse. We're in the same realm."

Saturn looked up. *"That may be the case, but the practical results remain the same."*

"Are you telling me to care about the lives of insects?" George asked. *"Because some others may consider me an insect? How many have you killed and converted?"*

"You're right about that." Saturn chuckled. *"You're right about that."*

Morgana's words snapped him back to the present. "The only way he would set up this truce is if he thinks he's going to get stronger than you in the next few months. Surely he can't be that foolish? Your proto-Domain cannot be rivaled."

"If he's stolen Oracle's memories like I believe he has, then he does not know of the proto-Domain," George answered. *That's not the only reason he would ask for a truce.* Alistair appeared to be a genuine zealot, a man with a heart of gold that would put others before himself.

The only part that made him wary was that he appeared to be *rewarded* for such idiotic behavior. It was as if some greater power had reversed the rules of advancement for only one individual on the entire planet, and the more that individual shared, the stronger they got. It was nonsensical, yet he was starting to believe it to be true.

George caressed his precious needle. "He has certainly made a mistake, do not get me wrong. Returning this needle will be his fatal oversight."

38 PREPARATIONS

THE GROUP of Northeast Freeholders and allies appeared in a scarlet flash right outside the Devil Kings' territory.

Jesse wasn't taking any chances, however. The moment they materialized, he [Scarlet Shifted] again, a recent upgrade to the Skill allowing him to have two charges active at any given time. They landed near a **Teleportation Circle,** which then allowed them to return home.

Some of them to return home, anyway. Even the non-Northeast Freeholders, which made up the majority of the group, wanted to get as far away from the xuanwu and the Devil Kings as possible.

The great beast was heating up the moment they left. Alistair didn't envy George's position in dealing with the Beast Ruler.

The Leading Domes welcomed the brave adventurers home. Even if George were to somehow betray their pact without dying, which Alistair considered impossible, attacking the Leading Domes was suicide. It had to be one of the most protected places on Earth.

After convincing the others of his plan on short notice, he had agreed to a meeting between all the remaining great powers. They sat down at the command table beside their global projection in the war room, which was large enough to seat the three dozen men and women Sally Ryder incorporated into her fusion. However, they didn't have a high enough clearance to sit inside and were politely asked to wait outside.

The ones who didn't stay behind had to pass through the Karmic Gel, which Alistair found funny, since those who hadn't been through it before were apprehensive to get messy.

That left Alexandra, Pharaoh, Whimsy, Jesse, President Ryder and her bodyguard-slash-second-in-command Marzhan, Bartholomew, Brigid, and William in the war room. Ten people, including Alistair.

The first to make clear their displeasure with his idea was none other than President Ryder. Alistair still liked to call her that out of respect, but it was kind of weird since the United States had utterly collapsed, along with every other government on Earth.

"I must ask again, why?" she stood up from her glass slab, which levitated in place like the other seats. "Fucking why?"

She must have been really incensed to drop her presidential decorum. "We're winning! Compare our numbers! They've lost six out of their thirteen, including their second, third, and fourth most powerful fighters. In recent times, we've lost, what, two out of the top ten human rankers? A truce just lets them gather their strength. Didn't you tell me they're all connected by weird Fate stuff? Who knows if they have some hidden capabilities that only work when they're together?"

Alistair let the older woman run out of steam before speaking. While there wasn't much love lost between the two of them, he was dismayed to hear about Chameleon's attempt on her and Marzhan's life. While they participated in the mission out of lack of stronger partners, he could tell their spiritual pathways were still damaged.

"As long as George survives, the Devil Kings are at their peak," Alistair stated. "And I suspect Morgana is far more powerful than her rank suggests. If we tried to make our play then, we would have failed."

"You cannot know that," President Ryder said. "You gave his weakness right back to him."

"It's not your call to make." He put it simply. "It's my call. I'm the one who will face him in single combat, since no one else is strong enough."

Alistair didn't say that out of arrogance, but out of truth. Any interlopers in their battle would only be hurting themselves, not affecting the tides, unless he had to go out of his way to protect them.

"And it's not because I'm afraid for my life. In a few months, the situation will be the same in that regard. I'll have to face George no matter what. Making a play on the Devil Kings in their own territory was bound to fail. If you look at our trajectories, I'm growing at a faster pace than him."

Alistair stood up from his seat at the front of the table, his blood pumping. The Dao permeated his words, as much as a Foundation realm could. "I promise all of you, your faith in me is not misplaced. Give me the time, give me these three months of training and preparation, and I will give you victory. Give our lands time to heal. Give our people time to rest and recover. We shall emerge stronger and brighter than ever before. Fate has given us Armageddon. What we do with that is up to us. Shall we be Icarus who falls from the heavens, or the shooting star that rises above the fray?"

At the end, Alistair wasn't even mentioning anything specific about the Devil Kings, but a more absolute speech of inspiration. Even Sally Ryder was silent, caught up in the moment.

Alexandra was the first to speak. "I'm with Alistair."

"So am I," Pharaoh said.

"That much was never in question," Jesse said. "Who else is there?"

Bartholomew nodded, and Brigid gave a knowing look.

Sally said nothing, but Alistair didn't sense any rebellion from her. Rather, reluctant acceptance.

"Let's get moving," Alistair said once he felt like everyone was finished. "The longer we wait to move, the less we'll be prepared. We have to rid the land of the escaped monsters, the hostile beasts, and the remaining natural disasters. Build up your subregions as much as possible. The coming times will be rough."

With that, he concluded the meeting. President Ryder and her second-in-command left right away, along with Pharaoh and Whimsy. Before the latter group left, Pharaoh came up to him and exchanged a terrifying handshake.

At first, Alistair feared a surprise attack. Had Pharaoh been replaced by Chameleon? The tall man clasped him by the elbow, which Alistair instinctively returned, since that was the traditional greeting of the people of the Holy Ravine. A surge of Dao energy passed through him, one that was very familiar. The Dao of Lost Sands.

The ancestral Dao Node flowed through Alistair, which was what caused him to go on the defensive for a second, but he realized it was a harmless maneuver. Pharaoh matched the flow of Alistair's own meridians, harmlessly passing the Dao energy through him. In fact, it felt like the former #1 ranker was eliciting him to do the same, so he obliged.

The Dao of the Fist, the Ghost, and Justice flowed through Pharaoh's meridians in perfect harmony, mirrored by the Dao of Lost Sands flowing through Alistair.

"My sponsor told me this is how brothers-in-arms greet one another," Pharaoh explained. "To let someone else's Dao flow within your body is both a risk and a reward."

"I'm glad you consider me your brother," Alistair said.

"Of course," Pharaoh replied. "We'll see this through to the end. Good luck."

Pharaoh collapsed into a pile of sand. Whimsy facepalmed, taking off after him. With good reason—the Leading Domes, and even their specific upper region, were heavily warded against teleportation Skills.

"You're larger than me, now," Bartholomew noted, pointing at Alistair's physique. It was something he was also getting used to, looking like a comic book superhero. He wasn't skinny at all before, either, but the Holy Ravine's foundational changes affected his body more than anything since the beginning of the initiation. At least it didn't slow him down more than a few percent, while coming with appreciable increases everywhere else.

"I wasn't expecting it," Alistair said. "How goes your brother? I'm sorry to hear about your father. I know what it's like."

"We hold hope that he still lives," Bartholomew said, his robotic countenance giving off no emotion. "His Skills were quite unusual, as you know. If he needed a lifeline against George, then it's possible he sacrificed everything to escape."

"I pray he survives as well." Alistair put his hand on Bartholomew's shoulder. They were of equal height now, which was funny since the elder Wood sibling had also gone through a growth spurt. If he remembered correctly, Alfred used to be the taller one. "In the meantime, I trust you will uphold his legacy."

Bartholomew left as well as Brigid, who seemed shy about talking to Alistair. Finally, it was only the core members of the Northeast Order Freehold left.

Alistair propped his feet onto the war room table, letting out a sigh of relief. "I hate public speaking."

Alexandra snorted. "You 'hate' heights, spiders, and driving over bridges. Wouldn't the word 'have a phobia of' be more appropriate?"

"That's four words, doesn't count."

Though he was relaxing, Alistair was also watching the projection of the globe. The kaiju stood out like a sore thumb. They represented it with a brown star that pulsed red. It was on the move, rampaging through Devil King territory.

In the meeting with his sponsor, he confirmed a suspicion—their goal wasn't to kill the kaijus. As Beast Rulers, they were way beyond current humanity's capabilities to vanquish outright. While they lacked sophonce, the reason for that was because they were a higher grade species than the Earth animals that had turned.

Indeed, the text of the third wave did not mention anything about slaying the kaijus. There was only a note of "stopping" them or "impeding their rampaging."

It turned out that the kaijus would eventually exhaust their energy reserves, which could be hastened by engaging them in battle. Forcing them into those massive explosions like when the xuanwu erupted was the fastest way to do that, but also required a way to survive the outburst and limit the collateral damage.

"This will be interesting," Alistair said. "Seeing how long it takes the Devil Kings to outlast the kaiju will inform our approach."

"You think it's possible they run it into our lands?" Alexandra asked.

William chimed in. "Thankfully, it's literally on the very opposite end of the world to us. It would be tough to do it for this one, though we can't say it's impossible for other kaiju."

Alistair nodded. "Which is why we need to use this time wisely."

"There's been a huge breakthrough in agriculture," William said. "James Foster's progressed enough to recreate some of the large-scale food production we had back pre-initiation."

That was huge. While clean water was much easier to provide, surprisingly, food was one of the most difficult. Most of the monster and beast corpses were too toxic or powerful for the average person, and their body cultivation wasn't strong enough to avoid the pangs of hunger.

Despite the extreme culling of Earth's population, there were still hundreds of millions of mouths to feed. Prior to what Alistair was learning now, the agricultural cultivators hadn't progressed far enough to maintain a stable food supply. People starved to death in appreciable numbers whenever there were sudden shocks.

It was a sad irony that despite having people like Alistair able to replicate the feats of myth, farmers could barely imitate modern technology. They poured into them a lot of resources like leveling pills and build manuals, but it wasn't enough. Cultivation favored war and blood over peace.

At least the Final Frontier Empire's version of it. Alistair held out hope of a better future, thinking of the Sage of Eternal Mercy. It comforted him to think that other cultivators of great stature shared similar goals.

"That's great news," Alistair said. "Prioritize the distribution on the **Teleportation Circle** network. I'm authorizing a purchase of at least a dozen more **Teleportation Circles.** Use your **[Hypercalculative Induction]** to gauge the best course of action. I'll give you the drachma now. You, Caren, and John have been coordinating well?"

"I wasn't sure at first, but our Classes mesh well," William said. "Caren and I, that is. His eidetic memory is amazing."

Alistair took all the money in his personal coffers that he had accumulated during his absence and sent it to William and Caren, along with most of the Platinum drachma that came from recent rewards.

"No embezzling," Alistair warned, half-jokingly.

"Wouldn't dream of it, boss," William chuckled. "You've got those scary eyes, after all."

William hurried off with his drachma infusion in tow. That left two people in the room—him and Alexandra.

Alistair sighed and closed his eyes. He consciously paid attention to the cycling of ambient Mana that he performed as a routine. In and out, from breath to breath, empty to full and full to empty. Such was the cycle of the soulcore and the meridians, and such was the cycle of life and the cycle of Samsara.

His mind drifted inward, so he didn't realize that someone had moved over next to his chair. Soft but strong hands caressed his shoulders. Alexandra massaged him for what felt like were eons, but his careful internal clock only measured around ten minutes.

"You're good at this. A Skill?"

"I used to give my father massages every time he'd come back from a business trip. Guess I got pretty good."

"Do you miss him?" Alistair asked.

"Of course," Alexandra said. "I don't think I'll ever understand how he could do it. You're lucky that your mom— I didn't mean it like that, I'm so—"

Alistair put up a hand. "Don't worry about it. How are you dealing with the demon blood effects?"

"It's hard for me to say." Alexandra looked over her body. "I don't feel that different, but I've also been going over every action I do, like I have OCD, making sure that I'm still me."

"You'll always be you," Alistair said. "We'll figure something out."

"Looks like you've leapfrogged us yet again," she said. "I'll stop bothering you now."

Alexandra was the last to leave. There was no one there, and the room was more silent than anywhere in the world, the protections leaving no space for sound. But he didn't let himself get bogged down by wayward thoughts. Now was the time for action.

After facing off against the Devil Kings, he only needed a tiny amount of Upgrade Points to bring his Tier 1 Legendary Badge "Devil May Cry" to Tier 2. The text of the Badge didn't change. Perhaps Dev'rox's presence stood out a little more. He hoped that the Holy Will condition that gave him a second wind on the verge of death was more powerful.

With the rest of his points, he allocated them to the Blood of the Devil Talent Tree. The fourth-level leaf cost 100 Upgrade Points, which the level up plus two Devil King kills had given him.

{Blood Debt} *Blood essence absorbed from demonic entities can be repurposed in Skills using blood affinity Mana. Since it came from their body to start with, the blood will have an easier time penetrating said entity.*

Anything specific that could be used against the Devil Kings was his salvation, so Alistair gleefully put his points into the leaf.

There was no rest for the wicked. Now that he had bartered for the truce, there was only one next step—cleansing the land.

39 CLEANSE THE LAND

IN THE TIME that Alistair was gone in the Grand Dungeon, the Northeast Order's percent of uncontrolled subregions skyrocketed up to 43.2%. Considering that the period coincided with the start of the Devil King attacks, he wasn't surprised.

With the kaiju deep within the Cursed Lands, as George had named his freehold, and their truce, it left them free to deal with all the trash that had built up over the months. To cleanse the land.

Those were Alistair's orders. Passed down his organizational system, any individual level 40 or above was mandated to take part in the cleansing. The top recruits of the academy were all around level 50 at this point, and he gave them the title of colonel. People like John, Alexandra, or Oliver were generals.

By level, the colonels weren't that far behind the generals, but levels were less impactful than things like the Dao, special lineages and inheritances, earned Upgrade Points, and Skills.

Each colonel would command captains who had to be level 45 or above, who were the lowest level in his four pronged chain of command system. Anyone below level 40 was deemed a liability more than an asset in dealing with the issues at hand.

Of the approximate 520 million population of the Northeast Order, there were only fifty colonels and two thousand captains, and then another hundred thousand above level 40. Though, only around half the level 40+ would be participating, since the rest had non-combat Classes. Combat Classes took up less than half the population, but were more likely to be above level thresholds.

They were an efficient unit. The moment Alistair issued the order for total mobilization, it only took three hours to gather everyone in their platoons. Each platoon consisted of twenty-five soldiers under one captain. There were forty captains per battalion under one colonel, and fifty battalions total under one corp, led by Alistair.

Nominally speaking, that was. Alistair worked best as a solo unit using his speed and reactions, so in practice, John Desmond took the reins. He was glad to see the Flamesmith thriving. People like him who lost their entire families were at the biggest risk of burning out, taking on too much responsibility at once. He and Donna had dinners together often, and little Tamia approved of the man.

The generals didn't actually perform much leadership work, as like Alistair, they worked better unimpeded by lower leveled cultivators. That meant there were three prongs of the army—Alistair himself, the fifty-thousand strong corp he called the People's Legion, and the various generals. Alexandra, Oliver, and Jesse formed one three-man group, but there were many others now that the variegated groups had aligned with the Northeast Order.

Pharaoh and Whimsy, Marzhan and the United Polities elite, Bartholomew and the Wood crew. Phoebe, the woman known as Medea inside the [The Game of Life], was a strong asset to the freehold, able to deal with most humanoid monsters without bloodshed.

Alistair could already see the start of a terrifying war machine. According to the Sublimed Machine Faction's metrics, they were the beginning embers of a Grade-7 polity, the weakest that had a name, where the strongest was an Adept.

Unlike most of the multiverse that used Foundation, Adept, Profound, Visionary, Exalted, Ascendant, Divine, and Truthseeker as the eight realms of cultivation, the Sublimed Machine preferred a numerical system going from Grade-8 to Grade-1. There was a certain simplicity in referring to a Visionary as Grade-5 or a Truthseeker as Grade-1.

If Fate shone on the Northeast Order, they would eventually rise to become a Grade-5 polity under the Final Frontier Empire. Alistair would become a Baron and then a Count. Those without noble blood could rise no higher than that, but there were always other opportunities. The multiverse was vast.

There was an ineffable sadness to it all. Their path was inexorably placed under Heaven's purview of conflict. That was what Alistair had become and what he had adapted to.

But doubt was not within Alistair's heart. He knew what he had to do, and he did not regret his actions. To say that cleansing the land of monsters was bad was sophistry. They had no mercy for the creations of the Pathfinder AI.

Though the monsters seemed to have souls, they were no ordinary beings. Not homunculi whose soul was made from the Dao of a living creature, nor an artificial intelligence, but something else.

Alistair's people had attempted to convert them, free them of their restrictions, or otherwise mess with their programming that enticed them to kill all humans, but to no avail. All they wanted to do was smash human heads in, despite otherwise being intelligent.

He remembered a conversation he had with the half-orc Kalak at the very beginning of the initiation. The monster called humans blessed with untold bounties from the Heavens. Alistair wasn't sure if that referred to the Pathfinder AI or the true Heavens that the Pathfinder sometimes interceded on behalf of, like for his soulcore tribulation.

Blessed with untold bounties or not, humanity united made quick work of the escaped monsters. Even at the beginning, the monsters relied on disunity, in-fighting, and panic. With the Devil Kings and kaiju temporarily out of the picture, they could focus all their efforts on one thing.

The escaped monsters dropped like flies. Alistair was at the epicenter, slaughtering orcs and zombies and living crystals. He targeted the oldest monsters, the ones that had enough time to percolate in the outside world. They were nothing to him.

The remaining Beast Lords had almost all fled to join with the Pride Lord and Vritra. What mindless leviathans and hidden monstrosities remained were mostly rooted out right away.

The only disaster left from Earth Asunder was the Wasteland. All the reptiles were gone, only the Mana Storms remaining. The colorless miasma expanded even further than from the last time Alistair saw it.

Alistair sent six of his generals to deal with the Wasteland, including

Alexandra and Pharaoh. The Devonic Purebreeds weren't a laughing matter. He remembered taming the storms before, and they were stronger now.

They accomplished this task within a week. Operation Cleanse the Land finished within one week. It was hard to believe at first, that they retook the uncontrolled subregions, which made up almost half of the total.

It was a testament to their organizational capacity, but also because of the storm that was Alistair. He was everywhere at once, using his speed and the **Teleportation Circles** to shore up any weaknesses in the People's Legion.

So many outside factors prevented Alistair from being able to give his all to his freehold, and now that he was back for good, he worked double time.

The xuanwu that plagued the Devil Kings never got into Northeast Freehold territory, though it was a close call. George and his minions continuously pushed the tortoise-snake south, though reports indicated it was reticent to give up position to pesky humans. After five days, it ran out of steam and lost its vital spark, but not before inflicting massive damage across the Cursed Lands.

Millions of people perished from the cyclical volcanic eruptions, which covered the sky even from Alistair's lands. The sun was hidden from view, and the temperature dropped.

The enormous corpse of the xuanwu could be viewed from Alistair's side. Thousands of Devil King soldiers swarmed the body, which could be considered a Legendary rarity item. Consuming the flesh of such a Beast Ruler, even if it wasn't actually a slain beast but a defunct one, could raise the Dao affinity of lava cultivators and possibly fire or earth as well.

According to Dev'rox, while the categories of the Dao were endless, the most commonly accepted framework was that of a Nexus. A Dao Nexus was an association of Daos, common ones including the Nexus of War or the Nexus of Magic. The most common Nexus, however, was the Nexus of Elements, the Daos based on the twelve primary affinities.

Thirteen, if you counted void, the anti-Mana, but scholars were divided on whether it was included in the Nexus of Elements or not. Alistair found it strange that the foundations of reality were so malleable.

With the People's Legion having completed its task, for the first time in forever, there was relative peace. Actually, Alistair considered, there was probably more peace than even before the initiation, since there were no wars between countries and no slums with sky-high crime rates. The internal security of the Northeast Order Freehold was better than first world nations.

Not to say that it was a paradise—there were many problems, but safety from other cultivators wasn't a big one. When many people had superpowers, the outcome of society was heavily determined by what the strongest decreed. In Anthony Ricci's empire, there was lawlessness and constant violence, where the strongest ruled.

Alistair was the strongest. Therefore, he decided that there would be rule of law and equal protection. Corruption was rife initially, but he stamped it out with Lesser Vipassanā, which allowed him to see through falsehoods.

With a hundred percent clearance rate, after throwing hundreds of embezzlers and blackmailers into prison, the prevalence of corruption went down to near zero. It wasn't worth a few extra drachma in your pocket if your chance of being caught was certain.

Society was still recovering from all the damage. In the former uncontrolled subregions, the infrastructure was a mess, and the population was near zero. The cities were where everyone congregated. There was safety in numbers—Alistair could protect New Boston, for example, far better than the borderlands, considering there weren't even set boundaries with the Devil Kings until the truce.

Alistair had Land Store Credit harvesters installed in some of the far-off regions. Because of the **Teleportation Circle** network, they weren't actually that far off, and he could protect them to a reasonable degree. Workers were required for the harvesters, so it was a way he could naturally encourage a more spread out population.

He never forced anyone to move, unless there was overcrowding, as he understood people just wanted to be safe. By having great job opportunities working on the harvesters, some intrepid workers chose a more dangerous environment in exchange for higher pay and cultivation opportunities.

One of the reasons why the Sublimed Machine Faction even cared to license the Pathfinder AI off to the frontier was the Chaos-touched Mana that he was harvesting for them. It was far above his pay grade, but there was something special about Chaos that even a core polity like the Sublimed Machine found useful.

The week of cleansing lined up almost exactly with the coming of the next kaiju. Along with the most powerful cultivators in his freehold, he waited in the war room one week after the appearance of the xuanwu.

The Pathfinder AI was precise about its timing. If the text of Kaiju Break said one week, it would be one week. It was only a matter of where.

Alistair looked up expectantly at the Global Map. William counted down as he played with a toy he'd purchased in the System Store. It looked like a solid metal block when inert, but if you messed around with it, you could get it to form strange shapes and patterns. William had gotten excellent at forcing the patterns he wanted. Alistair tried it out too, but he couldn't make heads or tails of the thing, despite William insisting that it was all quite logical when you really broke it down.

"Five, four, three, two, one, New Years!" William announced.

Alistair watched the map in apprehension. Would they be twice lucky? Where was the new kaiju going to appear?

Celeste Mendoza's eyes glazed over as she used her Class abilities to scan the Soulnet, similar to Alfred. Her eyes projected waveforms of data only a computational Class could make sense of. Those same eyes were the ones to project the video of his mother dying. Alistair found it hard to not imagine that when looking at her.

"Nothing yet, sir," she said. "I'll keep you updated as more information comes in."

"No need," Alistair said, sniffing the air. "It's here."

With his nose, he sensed the kaiju before everyone else. Everyone turned to him, but they started feeling it soon after. A presence that weighed down one's soul. If the xuanwu's aura was that of sweltering heat, this new kaiju felt like a spiritual weight. The pressure tried squashing Alistair like a bug, but he was too sturdy.

An eardrum-shattering roar reverberated through the Leading Domes. There was no *nue* within the sound, but Alistair could tell that it was only because it had dispersed over several miles.

That's too fast... Alistair's aura sense detected something in the distance, but surely it couldn't be.

The world shook. A shockwave that could have come from an entire arsenal of bombs rocked the building even more than the roar. It was a miracle that the Leading Domes didn't collapse altogether, a testament to the strength of ambrosic glass and further enchantments.

But that didn't mean it was unbreakable. Already there were tiny cracks in the glass, and the foundation seemed most unsteady. If the kaiju broke down the whole foundation, even the ambrosic glass building would fall into the earth.

The automatic defenses fired. Laser beams, whirling axes, and metal golems emerged to deal with the threat. Alistair shook his head. Those were appropriate against an army, but this was no army. He could already tell this newest kaiju was a different kind of enemy than the xuanwu.

More importantly, they couldn't afford the financial and organizational blow of losing the Leading Domes. The kaiju was targeting the people inside, not the building.

"Everyone!" he ordered. "Get out!"

Alistair didn't need to speak twice. They scurried down the ladder, though not before another slam staggered everyone in their tracks. He was the first one down through the Karmic Gel, darting around the panicking people on the first floor as fast as he could without slamming into everyone. The translucent protective energies washed over him as he exited, coming to a screeching halt as he saw the beast that was attacking his headquarters.

It was ugly.

The kaiju was a humanoid beast only twice his height. The closest analog that Alistair had was a humongous chimpanzee with black fur. Its limbs, especially the arms, were far too long for its body, while its trunk was over-inflated. Those features were enhanced by a bestial maw that screamed predator, with slit-like red eyes and fangs large enough to pierce a human through.

The fur was the most off-putting aspect, even more than its misshapen features. The onyx fur shifted in the light, giving off an eerie aura like it wasn't supposed to be seen by mortal eyes.

While it had not the size nor the overwhelmingly strong aura of the xuanwu, there was a cunning intellect in its eyes that gave Alistair pause. Indeed, when he performed a calculation using the origin of the roar to its current position, he found that the beast had to be at least as fast as his [Dash].

Alistair couldn't wait for his allies to catch up. The danger the kaiju was exuding was off the charts. An [Eyes of Truth] showed its level to be in excess of a hundred, as he was expecting.

Name: N/A
Species: Daywalker Ape (Corrupted Ancestry – Lower Descent)
Class: N/A
Level: 115

[Monk Motionlessness] fluttered with danger. Unlike [Fighter's Instinct], which created a danger sense that buzzed and waxed with anxiety, [Monk Motionlessness] felt like a gentle breeze. Yet despite the superficial lack of urgency, it still effected the same amount of action.

The flutters of his new danger sense were so strong they took over his body. He moved autonomously, flexing all the muscles of his core. The [Steel Body] Skill and Steel Body technique of the Holy Ravine worked as one to reduce physical damage.

A black, furry fist slammed into his abdomen. Never once in his life had Alistair been hit with such a blow. The impact sent him flying for almost a mile, crashing through New Bostonian skyscrapers. His journey sent him skidding through a familiar meadow field, the same one near his bunker that had a Natural Inheritance from the life affinity.

Alistair stood up, feeling nauseous from the blow. The Daywalker Ape moved faster than anything he'd seen on Earth. His guess was right—in that strike, it was faster than his [Dash] by a slight amount. Troublesome as well was its mysterious fur that obscured his future sight.

A pang of worry went down Alistair's spine as he realized that his people were facing the kaiju. Could they really deal with such a dangerous beast?

That feeling was soon accompanied by a heady sense of relief as he sensed a large creature moving rapidly towards him in leaps like the Incredible Hulk.

Alistair took on the third form of the Silver Comet Sect's Zebra Stance. While they never taught him any of the forms directly, he picked up on things. Now that he was back, his memories informed a perfect replica.

Tranquil Mind became his fortress. The Zebra Stance became one with the earth. Alistair breathed in deep as he prepared to receive the Daywalker Ape. It would be fist against fist, human against beast. A proper match for two polar opposites, and a good test of his martial skills, since facing himself was a special case.

But why were there two kaijus leaping toward him?

40 DAYWALKER APE

WHILE IN HIS sublime mental condition, there was nothing that could surprise Alistair. That there were two Daywalker Apes charging at him was a difference to the past, but the past, present, and future were all one. The swirling of the aeonic wheel was but one eternity. There was but one Dharma that has, is, and will be overcome with maitrī.

There were two Daywalker Apes, but they were each slower than the original. Their auras were weaker as well, and if he was looking closely, they were slightly smaller.

The solidity of the Zebra Stance rooted Alistair in place. There was Karmic merit for drawing away the kaiju from the others, represented by his "Deliverance of Justice" Badge granting him 6 free Attribute points. The apes leaped into view, snarling with untempered fury.

Alistair blocked a two-fisted slam from one of the beasts and kicked the other one back. They were still much faster than him, but had lacking technique. His reflexes could keep up with them, but his speed couldn't.

Alistair's forms were flawless, his martial arts embodying a stalwart defender. Because the Kai'tazake Mutra was split in three, no one of his triad of states was the truest representation of Zenaitsu Morogoni, but Tranquil Mind still shared some similarities. Coral energy covered his fists and he became a serene protector.

Yet this wasn't enough. One second passed. Alistair tried in vain to move his limbs faster than they could go. One second was the amount of time he could hold the tide against the sea of strikes.

The Daywalker Apes were everywhere, their gangly limbs assaulting him from every direction. Their lack of technique did not matter. There were two of them and one of Alistair, and they were too fast.

Alistair took a palm to the chin. He braced with **[Steel Body]**, but it rocked his brain. The mercurial fur warded the kaiju against his attempts to read the threads of Fate, but even then, it wouldn't have mattered. Seeing was useless if he was too slow.

Five seconds passed, and Alistair could feel his allies approaching. The apes kept pummeling him, though he did his best to resist. In the refuge of Tranquil Mind he had no fear, but within his current state, he saw few ways to progress.

Then there were four. Alistair saw it happen this time. Both of the Daywalker Apes regurgitated a new one almost identical to the last. The four new beasts were weaker than the two, which was weaker than the one, now standing at only nine feet tall instead of the original's twelve.

"Aha!" Dev'rox announced. "I've just remembered. We used these Pathfinder AI-modified beasts all the time when I was trapped. It's a corruption of a much greater beast lineage. It's based on the Cyclic flow model of reality."

Alistair **[Dashed]** backward and left Tranquil Mind, which tended to be unsuited to conversation with the unenlightened. The Daywalker Apes appeared to go dormant for a brief window after splitting, and he was too suspicious to attack in that window, for now. Also, his allies would get a chance to catch up.

"Cyclic flow?"

"I mentioned Fate and Time as models of the flow of reality previously. Those two are the most popular, but Cyclic and Chaos aren't far behind. There are more than that, of course, but I wouldn't know the obscure ones. Cyclic posits an Everlasting Pattern that, as the name suggests, repeats an infinite amount of times. All cultivators who can peer into a flow will find themselves struggling to use their powers against another flow user."

Alistair thought back to the blizzard-like aura that surrounded the afterimages of George in his Karmic sight. That had to be another flow model, but if Dev'rox didn't mention it at the time, then he probably didn't know which one it was from a mere glance.

"I don't."

"Thanks."

Alistair wondered if most cultivators at the peak tried to have one or more flows of reality at their fingertips. Or was there a reason that you shouldn't? It felt like there weren't that many downsides to him. There was also the question of if Karma merely interfaced with Fate and was separate to Fate, then why couldn't Karma tap into the other flow models? Could it, and he just hadn't learned how yet?

Those thoughts were for another time. His allies had finally arrived.

Finally—it was a harsh word considering it had only been seven seconds since he got launched. Thanks to his Tier 4 **[Ghost Whispers]**, he and Dev'rox could communicate at multiple times the normal speed of thought.

"Assume the formation? Is it a suitable enemy?" Caren asked with his **[Paper Tongue]**. Alistair felt his presence a few miles away. As one of the minds of the operation, he was too risky to have close to the enemy. He could hold his own with his Blood Hierocrat Subclass, but that wasn't public knowledge. As far as Alistair knew, only he, Bartholomew, and Alfred knew Caren's vampiric secret—and therefore Lucius, because they were family.

"Confirmed," Alistair replied.

Within the Hall of Mathematics, William had found a peculiar scroll. Hidden deep within the recesses of the tower, it gave off an almost taboo aura. The scroll described a formation called the "Imperial Phalanx," which claimed to align one's fighting formation to the Dao.

It was hard to believe that merely organizing one's soldiers in a special pattern would increase their strength. But the proof was in the pudding. There were seven slots in the Imperial Phalanx. Alistair was the Captain, the vanguard at the front. Bartholomew was the Port Shield on the left, while Whimsy was the Starboard Shield on the right. Alexandra was the Bow Sword at the front, while Oliver was the Stern Sword of the rear. William was the Strategist, protected by the Stern Sword, and finally, Pharaoh was the Champion in the center.

Together, they formed a unit that was stronger than its individual parts. There were downsides to the Imperial Phalanx, namely that it was weak to large-scale area of effect attacks that disrupted the geometric configuration. That made it impossible to use against opponents like George Moulin.

The four Daywalker apes charged. They were still fast, but around the same speed as Alistair's [Dash].

The two Shields activated defensive Skills. Bartholomew outstretched his hands and let the metal melt off of his skin and into an aegis carved with equations that harmonized with the Dao of Technology.

However, the metal melted not only off his skin like Alistair had seen previously, but it looked like it took off fat and muscle, leaving the Wood brother's body as a half-deformed cadaver, missing parts of his flesh. Whatever Natural Inheritance he consumed was transforming his body into a machine from the inside out.

The Starboard Shield conjured liquid affinity Mana. Instead of her usual water, Whimsy combined the particles of the technological aegis into her Skill, becoming a metallic liquid. The new liquid carried the weight of two Daos and rotated around the aegis, reinforcing its protection.

Three of the Daywalker Apes collided into the shield, creating a shock-wave not quite as powerful as the one created when Alistair got hit for the first time. The last one, crafty like a beast, tried jumping over.

As the Captain, Alistair moved into action. He touched the ground and sent a [Lightning of Justice] straight down into the charging beast. While it didn't kill the kaiju, the coursing lightning judged harshly, letting Oliver as the Stern Sword fulfill his obligations.

An enormous square of darkness split open the sky. It was the largest [Otherworld Gate] Alistair had ever seen, opening a portal to an abyssal dimension only Oliver truly understood. There was something different about this one.

The portal radiated pure death in a way that Alistair thought had to be rare for a frontier Foundation. Even Alistair felt pressure from the inside of that dimension. He had never seen Oliver use this Skill personally, but he had heard of it. Oliver's warren.

A warren was a portal to another dimension that one could draw power from, even another cultivator's Domain. Old monsters could make a fortune selling warrens, but it didn't have to be a Domain, you could create a warren to a special physical area or the lower planes.

An alabaster skull emerged from the warren, cloaked in black aura. The skull shot straight for the electrocuted kaiju, consuming it in one bite. Then, the skull chewed. Each chomping of its teeth was one face of infinite death, attacking the kaiju with oblivion.

The skull faded after only eight chomps. Oliver could only hold the warren open for so long. Even the minute amount of the warren's anchor he could access was exhausting.

Unfortunately, that wasn't enough to kill the kaiju. Alistair could feel its life force was diminished, but it was still alive. But the Imperial Phalanx was ready. The Champion sprang into action, leaping into the air and opening his proto-Domain.

The Dao of Lost Sands became reality in a floating sphere. From the outside, it looked like a miniature sandstorm inside a marble, blown up in proportions. It would be more difficult for a mindless beast to escape than a cultivator of the same strength, given their lack of complexity in the Dao.

The three Daywalker Apes that remained outside had stopped. The Imperial Phalanx moved as one, drawing upon Alistair's reaction time to attack. This time, there was a good opportunity for a long ranged attack. Bartholomew formed his laser sword with an even faster activation period, while Alistair used another [Lightning of Justice].

The Daywalker Apes regurgitated three more of their kind without being fazed at all. It was like their attacks against the beasts were violating Multiversal Law. A cultivator of a higher realm might have been able to stop their reproductive process, but to them, it was inviolable. They could not be harmed while they spat each other out.

Once again, the six clones were weaker and smaller. Alistair estimated that their auras were similar to his own.

Cyclic, Alistair thought. I wonder...

They resumed their phalanx, working as one unit. It was difficult to say whether facing the six was worse than the four or the two or the one. No, Alistair revised. The six was definitely weaker than the four. The missing member dropped dead from Pharaoh's proto-Domain as their Champion descended, though not unharmed. He was missing the majority of his Dao energy and seven of his fourteen lives, despite only taking on a fourth of the original that was already injured.

The phalanx worked as one, shoring up each other's weaknesses. They didn't lose any members or take serious damage, but they were also unable to kill another Daywalker Ape. Alistair couldn't be sure of when they split, but he suspected it had to do with how much energy they output.

By engaging them, they forced them to divide every ten seconds or so. There were soon hundreds of Daywalker Apes on the battlefield, now the size of a human and weak enough that all of his generals could take them on.

The Imperial Phalanx consistently killed the ones closest, but the apes became an unstoppable tide. They just. kept. multiplying. The other problem was that the ones at the fringes started leaving their current battle-field to go searching for easier victims.

Alistair blasted them from afar with **[Lightning of Justice]**, but he couldn't stop them all. Breaking the phalanx's formation was too risky. The People's Legion would have to suffice, though he worried about his soldiers. In their heavily divided form, the Daywalker Apes were weaker, but not to be underestimated.

Hours passed as they held position. The Daywalker Apes showed no sign of stopping. The People's Legion were taking massive losses as they struggled to contain the growing carnage. None of them wanted to use powers they hadn't shown before. It was a risky venture, given the Devil Kings were likely spying on them.

With days passing, there were millions of them, and millions of ape corpses stacked as high as a hill surrounding them. They were half the size of a human, yet still ferocious and powerful enough to be a match for the average level 40. Any of the Daywalker Apes that escaped the People's Legion's encirclement was bound to kill hundreds if not thousands of civilians before a cultivator strong enough to stop it appeared.

Caren turned to Land Store items, ones bought for defending against the Devil Kings. They had a massive array of artillery, including thermobaric crystal bombs and spatial laceration missiles. He unleashed the military might of the Northeast Order Freehold on the hundreds of thousands of apes that descended southward from the meadow to the city proper, but even that arsenal couldn't cover all the escapees.

"Estimate, 3,831,290 apes," Caren informed him. "*That should be the maximum. As long as you keep it up.*"

They had broken up the phalanx now that the individual threat was low. Each member was carving through the apes as fast as they could, which was what Caren was talking about. As long as the average offspring of each kaiju was larger than one, their population size would increase.

However, they grew weaker with each generation. Once Alistair and his allies abandoned the phalanx and turned to slaughter, the percentage of each generation that survived decreased. And once they reached fifty percent killed, the horde would stop growing.

The Daywalker Apes were a mix of different generations, the ones in the middle unable to expend enough energy to reproduce. The key was killing them before they could get off any spawn, and they were weak enough that it was possible.

The culling that was required to get to the 3,831,290 maximum took place over several days. Rest was for the dead. Anyone who needed a breather could get extracted temporarily by Caren's crew, but they couldn't afford any weakness. Stamina pills, Health pills, and Mana pills were like candy to them. They slowed down a bit, causing the real number to exceed four million.

From then on, it was merely a matter of time. They got lucky in that the escaped Daywalker Apes reproduced much less. Since their division was a matter of how much energy they expended, hunting down civilians under level 40 didn't get them excited enough.

In fact, things felt like they were going too smoothly. The People's Legion had only lost four colonels and forty-five captains. That was going to sting, but Alistair had expected much worse from a kaiju stated to be more powerful than the xuanwu. Civilian casualties were an order of magnitude lower than the Cursed Lands' kaiju.

As the Daywalker Apes dwindled into the hundreds of thousands and then the tens of thousands, he pondered this incongruence. They had only a few hours left until the third kaiju and everyone was already celebrating. The remaining beasts were as weak as a level 35 cultivator, if that, as they continued to decline in strength even though their numbers diminished.

Alistair couldn't get Dev'rox's words out of his head. He couldn't get Dev'rox *out* of his head, for that matter, but that was a different story.

The different models of the flow of reality. Fate. Time. Cyclic. Chaos. The Daywalker Ape was a being borne or created from the Cyclic model. His Karmic eyes could not penetrate their Fate, for they rejected that concept.

That couldn't be all, could it? There was overlap between the four models Dev'rox told him about, or so it seemed to him. If there was Destiny in Fate, then there was a small "d" destiny in Cyclic. If things were bound to happen in repeats, they were predictable, following an Everlasting Pattern.

Patterns with a small "p" could be deduced through the threads of Fate.

Alistair knew if he could just see a little deeper, a little further, he could figure out what was bothering him.

When one of the Daywalker Apes died, the energy it provided to the original vanished. The overall horde was permanently weakened, the new divisions not gaining in strength to compensate. That went against the nature of a cycle. Energy was not lost or gained in a cycle, but redistributed, satisfying a law of conservation.

Then what happened to the lost energy? Alistair's eyes narrowed. By his own logic, Fate and Cyclic were closer than the looser Time and Chaos. But he needed to perceive things differently.

Alistair activated [Eyes of Truth]. The absence of evidence was often helpful to a keen eye. He didn't focus on threads of Fate, but the Karmic web. Peering into the Karmic web wasn't very useful in combat, which was why he never did so. It showed the connections between people, understood through the lens of Karmic merit.

The immense Karmic web that connected every living thing was hard to fully fathom. Alistair's Foundation realm mind viewed it as a spiderweb of crimson silk, spreading across all reality.

When looking at the Daywalker Apes, he could tell something was off. Their Karma was one, which he expected. Their divisions were not true divisions. It also cast a far longer a shadow than it should have. They had killed off 99.7% of the kaiju's original essence.

"Shit!" Alistair exclaimed. *"Pharaoh?"*

But he was too far away. Plus, he had expended his proto-Domain killing thousands of the Daywalker Apes. He wasn't in any condition to act. Who else had a proto-Domain? Alexandra had almost completed hers, but not quite. That was it. There still weren't many cultivators in the world that could open a proto-Domain. That tree guy, Bark-Al, could, but he was too low-leveled. Marzhan recently acquired the ability, but she was inside a personal trial.

"Dev'rox, will it work?" Alistair asked.

"You're screwed if it doesn't, so it probably does work. They're trying to create strong soldiers, not a dead world."

Alistair was loath to reveal his own proto-Domain, but sacrifices had to be made. He would give the Devil Kings as little a glimpse as possible. Using his [Eyes of Truth], he identified the center of mass of the Karma. And then he waited.

The timing wasn't as urgent as Alistair first thought. The Daywalker Apes kept splitting and splitting, and he culled them at a commensurate rate. With ten thousand left, it wasn't the dire straits that he thought it was, but it was still too close for comfort.

Alistair called for the others to leave him alone and deal with any stragglers as he tackled the central mass alone. Ten thousand became five thousand became one thousand as he punched the Daywalker Apes into mist. {Letting of the Beast} had granted him 2 Endurance from the entire week of **[Blood Hands]**.

When they reached a hundred in number, Alistair decided it was time. He expanded his proto-Domain.

It was as easy as tying his shoes. There was something innate about it that felt like he was becoming one with his innermost nature.

Thanks to the insight of his Spiritual Fighter's Echo, he understood how to paint Dao energy into reality. With the Insight Vision, he had etched a portion of the blueprint into his soulcore, and his well-forged mind supplied the remaining storage. His internal space expanded, filling the world with his Mana and Dao energy, all according to his outlook.

Wherever Alistair looked, there was blood. It was almost the same as his Insight Vision, though in real life, he hadn't made it as dark and depressing. The blood flowed down from the ceiling of an invisible dome, though Alistair knew there was no border except that of space folding in on itself.

Blood mist filled the air, churning with ghostly energy. While some of the proto-Domain was blood affinity Mana, the other was unblemished Dao energy from his Ghost Node. As his proto-Domain was unfinished, an unworthy first step of his true Domain, he didn't have space to implement the Fist Node yet. Despite the bloodwraiths, which obviously came from Ghost, the proto-Domain was split evenly between Justice and Ghost, where Justice was the oppressive force on the heart of any evildoer within.

Alistair found it likely that attacking the heart was a poor choice. Logically speaking, allowing your heart to be swayed was one of the worst things that could happen in a fight, other than death. Scratch that, most cultivators were bound to consider being converted even worse than death. At least you could die honorably in combat. Those at the peak had to have steeled hearts after millions of years of walking their path, yet Alistair couldn't bring himself to remove that aspect of his proto-Domain. It was too central to his identity.

Alistair's proto-Domain was on the smaller side, around the same size as a large house. But it was offensive, like Pharaoh's, attacking one's heart as well as body, the Dao energy boiling those inside. The bloodwraiths descended, crashing into the Daywalker Apes and brazing them with their righteous fury.

His sinner's lament wouldn't be as effective on these mindless beasts as a true evildoer, but they still had accrued fell Karma. The proto-Domain quickly wiped out scores of kaiju. The cycle was complete.

What Alistair had realized was that the division was only the first part of the life cycle of the Daywalker Apes. They thought that they had been taking away the life force of the beasts with every one they killed before it could reproduce, but that energy had been stored away in the recesses of the Cyclic flow. Alistair couldn't peer into the cycles like he could with Fate, but that was the only explanation.

Thousands upon thousands of bursts of energy tried to infiltrate Alistair's proto-Domain from the outside. Simultaneously, the accrued Cyclic oscillations inside of Alistair's space coalesced as the original Daywalker Ape tried to reform.

Despite not being qualified to understand the model, symbols of circularity began to appear in the sea of blood. Circles, infinity symbols, Dharmic wheels, endless knots, ouroboros, and stranger things not found under the Earth's sky flashed in and out of existence. Their appearance was so brief, Alistair at first wasn't sure if they were real.

If the kaiju was allowed to complete the cycle, all was doomed. Alistair thought that the defiance of conservation was against the kaiju's favor—he was entirely wrong. Stolen energy was converging. The cycle was structured in defiance of the Heavens, in the same way that perpetual motion machines defied the laws of thermodynamics.

The outside energy wailed upon the integrity of his proto-Domain, while the inside Daywalker Ape's energy expanded. Alistair would not let his boundaries fall. Ghost and Justice worked in unison, suppressing the cycle's renewal. He couldn't begin to say that he understood the principles the Daywalker Ape's abilities operated on, but that didn't stop his Dao. Where else did Justice shine but when braving the unknown?

Alistair's mind screamed in pain. His mental faculties held together the portions his soulcore's blueprint could not, and the psychic backlash he received as the Daywalker Ape tore the fabric of his proto-Domain was pure agony.

Just a little longer, Dev'rox communicated with a jumbling of wordless emotion. The imp shared the burden with him. Help given and help taken. Such was the path of justice, where the ghosts of the past gave him providence for the ghosts of the future.

The symbols of circularity flickered with greater frequency. It was now or never. Alistair prayed that, as a proto-Domain, his space would overrule the cyclic emergence. He believed the energies could only exist so long without a body. If the cycle couldn't complete, it should dissipate. *Should.*

When his proto-Domain whittled the Daywalker Apes down to a single member, the struggle was at its zenith. While it was a pitiful display of power compared to those at the peak, Alistair imagined this kind of spiritual struggle to be what the higher realms were all about.

Alistair sought to impose his proto-Domain's will as impermeable to the Cyclic flow. To claim the proto-Domain of a space where his laws were paramount. The Daywalker Ape sought to forever perpetuate its greedy cycle, defying the whims of a Foundation's proto-Domain.

There was no way that he would lose. Not now. Alistair's resoluteness was steel. He gritted his teeth and held on for what felt like an aeon. He only stopped when he felt his shoulders rocking in an unnatural motion and his neck bobbing back and forth.

Alexandra was shaking him. With her amount of Strength, it was like being in the grasp of a giant. She looked like a goddess of war, her outfit stained in the blood of the Daywalker Apes. "Stop! It's over!"

Alistair snapped back to reality, whereupon he fell down on account of a splitting headache. He wiped away a trickle of blood dripping out of his nostril. His mind had almost broken trying to hold the proto-Domain together. He now understood part of why *nue* was so effective against them.

"I did it?" Alistair asked, dropping to his knees.

"Yes," she said. "There was a burst of energy and then nothing. The Daywalker Apes are all dead. Every one, even those super far away. I don't know what you did, but it worked."

"Phew," Alistair let out. "I don't think I could have held on much longer without destroying my mind."

Alistair laid down on the meadow. He was not a life cultivator, but the life affinity was one that appealed to everyone except the deathsworn. The feeling of endless life was soothing.

The third kaiju's countdown ticked down like a bomb in his head. They were all exhausted from dealing with the Daywalker Apes. Alistair couldn't handle another bout at the moment. The People's Legion had lost thousands of members, though they had contained the kaiju damage far better than the xuanwu.

They were somewhat lucky that their kaiju was an all-or-nothing type. The lava xuanwu dealt continuous infrastructural damage and massive human casualties with its eruptions. The Daywalker Ape's true terror would have been if it were allowed to reform.

In that case, Alistair wondered what would have happened to the world. Would the Pathfinder AI and all the sponsors allow a brutish beast to take over the planet? He doubted even George could deal with a renewed Daywalker Ape that had stolen all of their energy.

The Northeast Order regrouped. Oliver gave Alistair a ride on one of his flying zombies. "Payback for all the times I piggybacked on you." He couldn't tell if payback was a good thing or a bad thing. Maybe both. Even though the Necromancer was careful about not bouncing him too much, the whiplash gave him a huge headache. He had to have been seriously messed up in the brain for something minor like that to hurt, which might not have even affected a non-cultivator.

So when they returned to the Leading Domes, Alistair munching on some **[Carmela's Happy Pies]**, he was rapt with attention as he looked at the **Global Map.**

Once again, there was utter silence as the countdown for the third kaiju broached zero. Not even the childish William dared utter a word, with everyone so exhausted from the Daywalker Ape.

Celeste was the first to announce the news, even before the map. "The third kaiju has been spotted in—"

41 CULTIVATOR CARPET BOMBING

"—THE heartlands of the Devil King freehold."

Alistair let out a sigh of relief, and he wasn't the only one. Even the most eccentric man he knew, Pharaoh, was smiling, though he still hadn't put on a shirt.

"Heartlands," William said. "Not at the very edge, like last time. They're going to try to force it over."

William's words turned out to be prescient. Soulnet footage from civilians in the Cursed Lands and Alfred's drone footage revealed the identity of the third kaiju. Spying didn't violate the spirit of the truce, apparently, so both sides waged all-out warfare on that front.

Somehow, the new kaiju was even larger than the xuanwu. It was a mile-long serpent, with fangs large enough to pierce straight through a blue whale. The aura was unmistakably stronger than the xuanwu, of an entirely different category. Instead of molten rock, the snake exuded a purple miasma of poison that made Alexandra's stuff look like distilled water.

If you could see the snake, you were likely breathing in its toxic fumes. Without a life force of a Beast Lord, the chance of surviving was slim. Those that didn't have that needed some other way to filter the toxic air.

Alistair and his team monitored the movement of the snake carefully. He was hoping for an inverse of when he had to use his proto-Domain. Any new abilities that George had to reveal would be essential information.

But the snake was different from the xuanwu.

The tortoise didn't want to move. It was a creature of solidity, and the Devil Kings had to push it back against its will.

Instead, the snake slithered in arcs that trampled forests, destroying civilization with not the slightest care. There wasn't any discernible pattern in its movements. The thousands of civilians it killed by the minute were of little consequence to the Devil Kings.

Over the next few hours, it continued its path of destruction in ever-increasing concentric circles. Each time, it verged closer to the Northeast Order.

Alistair realized one of the flaws in the truce. The way he would have gained an advantage over the Devil Kings was his territories producing more Contribution Score. Now that Contribution Score didn't matter, George didn't have to protect his land at all.

If he didn't have to protect his land at all, then he could let the kaijus... be kaijus. The snake was far more mindless than the Daywalker Ape. It would kill and kill until it ran out of living flesh and move on to the next.

But Alistair couldn't let the kaiju do that in his lands. He would have to fight it.

That sneaky bastard, Alistair thought. *He's banking on the Land Store items being too large to bring into the final battle. If he doesn't need the Land Store, and he doesn't need a majority of the subregions, holding onto and protecting territory is literally worthless to someone who doesn't care about human lives.*

Alistair refused to let the snake cross the border. For that, he needed some backup.

———

His muscles strained to their limit as he pushed.

Yes, believe it or not, since the **Crystal Ion Cannon** was too large to send through a **Teleportation Circle,** the most effective transportation was pushing.

Alistair hadn't worked his muscles this hard since in the Holy Ravine. Despite the absurd strength of cultivators, physical labor was considered beneath their dignity. Every muscle fiber in his body strained as he and thousands of others heaved a cache of weapons that even the United States military would blush at.

The cannon had to have weighed at least twenty tons. Alistair's bulging muscles were on fire, yet his blistering walking pace was faster than a speeding car pre-initiation. With ten assistants on either side, it wasn't nearly as bad as getting smacked with a sledgehammer in a sweat lodge.

The pathway to the destination had been paved flat thanks to the efforts of those with janitorial Classes. These things were way too heavy for any flight Skill to carry.

The things in question were three-quarters of the Northeast Order payload. 75% of every gun, sword, laser gun, laser sword, bomb, missile, automated crossbow launcher, RPG, javelin, SAM, and dark matter emitter was being transported to the border between the humans and the Devil Kings.

The majority of their arsenal was unusable against the Daywalker Apes because they were too close to civilization. Also, they were too small and mobile. The snake was a true titan of a beast and made a much easier target.

The march was impossible to hide from Devil King spies. Alistair wasn't too concerned about that part. George didn't seem interested in messing with the snake to begin with.

Thankfully, the poisonous snake was a little less than two days before its arc approached the border between the Northeast Freehold and the Cursed Lands. Two days was just enough time to move the bulk of their weaponry from the capital to the border by foot. It was a crazy idea, and one that Alistair was proud of.

"Ahem," Dev'rox coughed.

"I give us both equal credit."

"Iniquity leads to fell Karma, my friend. You best hope your merit can withstand the boldness of your lies."

"Little demon arhats should watch their speech," Alistair ribbed back. "You have not lost your attachments to a biting wit. Your next reincarnation would be to a lower plane, but I'm afraid you've exhausted that approach."

"Bah," Dev'rox said. "You win this time. For a monk, you have such a foul tongue."

Alistair almost put up his hands in protest, but couldn't, since he was still pushing the cannon. "I have a foul tongue? I almost never curse. You need to give Alexandra a stern talking to."

Oliver stood in the distance on one of the slopes of the former Rocky Mountains. The peaks made up the border in this area, a useful geographic marker. It made it more difficult to bring up the arsenal, but with some anti-gravity items and Skills, they made it work.

In all honesty, Alistair was not impressed with the grandiosity of the mountaintop. He had seen way cooler ones. But that wasn't the case for some of the civilians and People's Legion.

The gawking would have to wait. They could see the snake in the distance. The poisonous aura was too far away to affect them, but its purple corrosion was absolutely devastating. Wherever the serpent went, the world withered away. The poison Mana affinity was a combination of the primary affinities of liquid and death, and it showed.

Alistair took some solace in that his **[Ghost Whispers]** detected little human death in the region. Not every subregion of the world had permanent inhabitants.

In the far distance, there was another set of mountains. A completely unrelated range to the Rockies—the Andes. The jumbling of the subregions led to plenty of geographical aberrations like that. From summit to summit, they were nearly twenty miles away, and far taller.

Even at that distance, he could feel George's aura. Being so far, it was slight, no more than a taste. But it was unmistakable. Cold and full of despair, it traveled with the brumal winds.

Ice spears rained down from the clouds, striking at the snake. Those attacks were the equivalent of pinecones dropping on a human, yet the kaiju turned away and charged for the opposite mountain range, anyway.

Alistair snorted. Despite the snake's overwhelming strength, it was still a snake. Nothing like the tortoise that refused to give away ground unless forced.

"Ready the first wave!" Alistair called out, projecting his voice over thousands of feet. That snake moved damn fast for its size, approaching the slopes of the mountain in no time at all. Once he was sure it was within their territory, he said the word. "Fire!"

Even Alistair plugged his ears. The initial salvo of missiles was so enormous, it literally blotted out the sun. They used a hodgepodge of ammunition, really anything they could find. Bombs from the System Store and Land Store, crafted items, ones made from Skills, Quest and side Quest rewards, and more. There were some that looked like old world military weapons and others that came straight out of a sci-fi book.

The carpet bombing of the third kaiju was the single loudest sound

Alistair had ever heard. They totally should have planned ahead for that and brought some ear plugs. Well, that was life. Better some ruptured eardrums than losing a loved one if the snake crossed the border.

When the smoke and debris cleared, there was a mile-wide swath of destruction in the middle of the forested terrain. A terrifying hiss informed them that the kaiju still lived.

Thankfully, their defenses held against the *nue*-filled sound. There were a few dozen arrays powered by Beast Cores that absorbed *nue*, though they became half-saturated with that single hiss. Alistair estimated that ninety percent of the people there would have died on the spot from the hiss without the arrays.

Nue, in Alistair's opinion, was underrated. A beast roar like that, filled with killing intent, actually caused a natural death. It overloaded the brain's fight-or-flight response to such a degree that the individual would experience heart failure, literally dying of fright. Dev'rox didn't seem to share the same opinion. The imp never commented on his psychic abilities.

The serpent lost a few scales, and there were a few minor gashes here or there, but not enough to cause significant harm.

Alistair was in awe at the durability of these Beast Rulers. As a trade-off for lacking a real Domain, their bodies were inhumanly tough, but still. That amount of firepower would have wiped him off the face of the earth. Even an Adept realm would find it difficult to take such a bombardment without a defensive item or Skill. Cultivators like Atavius Meloi who presented their Dao as equal to the absent Heavenly Dao on the far vestiges of the frontier didn't count.

Alistair had a chuckle once again as he saw the snake fleeing the site of the bombardment.

"I—"

"Don't you dare say it." Dev'rox even made himself visible to shush Alistair. "Imps are nothing like snakes, even if we do have a reputation for... flightiness."

"B—"

"Shush! Shush!"

Alistair decided to name the serpent Dev'rox Junior—he paused mentally at that. No response? His psychic control was way better than even two weeks ago. Gaining the *nue* clone in his Tier 4 **[Dash]** really accelerated his learning, along with Tier 4 **[Ghost Whispers]**. Alistair really liked his ghostly partner, but some things were meant to be private. Plus, segmenting his thoughts would let him defend against mentalists and *nue* artists better.

George didn't hold back. No sense in that, since he wasn't going to fight Alistair any time soon. *Arcanous Devil Spell #3: Frygian Arrow* flew through the air, growing rapidly as it sucked the cold and moisture out of the atmosphere.

The forest wilted. The spell drew on the moisture within the trees and the ground. *Frygian Arrow* desiccated everything in its path. Once the forest was dry, the fire caught easily.

Tyrian flames seared the earth. The arrow was a growing flash of light, with the top layer separating so that it seemed as though even the ice was burning.

The arrow's impact was not even close to as loud as the carpet bombing, but it still echoed throughout the valley.

Purple ice tried to penetrate the snake's skin as flames spread down its mile long body. Another attack came arcing down from the mountaintop. A mirror of perfectly circular proportions with no frame reflected a braid of torturous fire. A piece of pseudo-glass appeared opposite to it, shimmering out of nothing like a fractal part of space.

The braid of fire bounced between the mirror and the shard of space thirteen times. Each time, it grew in luminosity and changed hue. First, it was a violet far darker than George's ice. The next iteration turned it amethyst. Then a light purple, into blue, and teal, and finally a vibrant white.

When it condensed into a thin spire of fire and collided into Dev'rox Jr., Alistair could not declare it any weaker than George's spell. If anything, it felt stronger. It went to show that their methods weren't so weak. "Underestimating the enemy was death," Brother Pike liked to say.

When the twin flames faded away, this time the snake was bleeding. The second attack went for the tail. Good reasoning, Alistair had to say. There was a gash in the last tenth of its body that bled red blood.

It wasn't serious, though. For a human, it was the equivalent of a bad scrape on the shin from a bike fall.

And of course, it was charging right back for Alistair and company.

———

The two opposite sides, each sitting on a mountain peak (though George's was higher, to Alistair's dismay), played ping-pong with the cowardly kaiju.

They traded salvo for salvo. Alistair brought a shit ton of ammunition, but so did the Devil Kings. By the time they ran out of missiles, the snake had gone back and forth over fifteen times.

George used his Arcanous Devil Spells sparingly. They always seemed to have some new trick. The mirror was what had Alistair scratching his head. Besides amplifying and morphing Jakk's flames, it also served as a replicator for the remaining Shadow Twin's legion of shadowspawn, and as a tool to transform captured souls into a mega-wraith.

Alistair grew angry, seeing that, though he could not interfere. It was Morgana's work, the witch. She was the worst of the worst, a mass murderer whose personal kill count dwarfed even George Moulin. Those wraiths she possessed were the real souls of millions of ordinary people. Such an abomination demanded justice that he would mete out one day soon.

His anger turned into contemplation as he failed to understand how one mirror was so versatile and powerful. The more he considered it, he could only think of one thing: the mirror was the Legendary rarity item that the Devil Kings received for the First Through Bonus of the Grand Dungeon.

But why would they use it here? Why didn't they save it for the final battle? Alistair hoped he had just gotten very, very lucky. It looked to be enormous from his vantage point. If it was too large to fit into an inventory, that would explain why they weren't hiding it.

Whatever it was, it helped them preserve resources. Alistair's group used their Skills as well, but the problem they had was that they were way more melee-oriented than the Devil Kings. Bartholomew, Whimsy, Marzhan, and Oliver were the only real ranged guys.

Alistair didn't want to use his finishing Skill again. He had a feeling it was something one could adapt to, given repeated exposure. That left him with only [Lightning of Justice], which wouldn't do much. The same was true for Alexandra, General Ryder, Brigid, and Pharaoh.

After the bombs and missiles were exhausted, it was onto the ion cannons. They had a ton of them since they were one of the basic artillery units from the Land Store. There were the direct cannons that fired straight beams of energy, and the SAM variants that launched spheres of explosive plasma into the sky that could arc down on the targets' heads.

Alistair watched in trepidation as the snake tanked the bombardment. There were some more injuries past the gash near its tail, but nothing major. The Beast Ruler was as difficult to kill as promised.

Yet, he was more focused on the other side. There were only so many spells the two mages had. There was only so much the Divine Mirror could do. He was absolutely positive the Devil Kings lacked a similar arsenal to them. How would they keep up?

Dev'rox Jr.'s demise was slow. Perhaps the Pathfinder AI gave it a special power through its modifications. Perhaps the "Worldeater Snake (Corrupted Ancestry – Lower Descent)" possessed it natally. Alistair identified "Lower Descent" with his peon bloodline. Maybe if bloodlines had stages, ancestries had descents. Peon certainly sounded low.

"Like the dirt under a sinner's sole," Dev'rox added. "I've caught on to your little Dev'rox Jr. name."

Near the end of the first day, they saw one of the Devil Kings' weapons —a strange black wand. It was a dark matter emitter that fired a near-invisible bolt of black energy, and created a seventy-foot-long cut on the kaiju's back.

While it wasn't deadly, the snake roared so loud that some of Alistair's soldiers fainted even with the array formation.

Afterward, it coiled up, a rocky crust growing from its scales, the same color as the terrain underneath. Once the process was finished, the Worldeater Snake looked like a watercolor impressionist painting.

They tried to attack it while it laid dormant, but Alistair quickly held back their arsenal. The earthly skin was unbreakable to their methods. Waiting was the only thing that could be done.

Another eight hours passed before it became active again. Then it was another war of attrition. This went on for several days. Bombard, stone form, bombard, stone form.

"It's growing sturdier," Caren remarked after four long days. By Earth's seasons, it was winter, though so high up, the mountain split the rays of the sun like the chiaroscuro of Baroque magnum opus. "I don't think that bodes well for us."

"It's growing slower, too. The injuries are catching up," Alistair pointed out, but he also recognized the truth in Caren's words.

A terrified looking young man approached Alistair and Caren. He had on the Information Branch's uniform—the white edition of his robes with the tri-colored fist over the heart. Now they even got updated to have the Peach Blossom Land chengyu on the back, plus a little universal symbol of computer code above the characters to signify the Information Branch.

"Ryan Zeal, sir— Sirs, I mean," the skinny recruit stammered out. "S-stockpiles of mundane classification weapons, 10%. S-stockpiles of arcane classification weapons, 21%. Stockpiles of future tech classification weapons, 30%. Stockpiles of unclassified weapons, 19%. **Crystal Ion Cannon** and **Twin Silk Slicer** remain unused."

Alistair liked that this Ryan Zeal became more confident over time, losing the stutter. Despite his meek appearance, he had to be a level 40 cultivator to be a soldier under Caren.

"Thank you, Ryan," Alistair said. "Good work."

The younger man blushed—wait, younger man? Alistair was only twenty-two, turning twenty-three in January. Ryan didn't look *that* young, not like Oliver, though the Necromancer had matured a lot in the nearly seven months he had known him. The experience of the initiation had molded both him and Oliver into real men.

"Why have a recruit feed us the information?" Alistair asked, scratching his head. "You have [Paper Tongue]. And the Soulnet."

Caren chuckled. "Keeps them busy. Makes them feel important, creates team bonds. If there was something essential, I wouldn't entertain it, but most of them are just waiting by the weapons to fire them. Since we have an excess of people, why not? Seeds now are trees later."

"Wisely spoken there, Mr. Locasta. You'll be a great cultivator. How can it be that you don't have a sponsor?"

"Perhaps my Blood Hierocrat Subclass verges too much on the side of the unorthodox." Caren shrugged. "I thought I'd either make my name here, during the predations, or by climbing up the ranks of the Harmonious Note System. There's much to protect here. I did receive an invitation to the Annalist Academy of the Final Frontier Empire."

"That's huge!" Alistair exclaimed. All he knew about Annalists was that they had eidetic memories, likely from intensive genetic augmentation. They were a protocol of the Sublimed Machine, imported to the frontier. "You're thinking of accepting, aren't you?"

"*If* I survive, of course," Caren said. "Nothing in this life is guaranteed."

"You'll survive," Alistair promised.

"When I hear it from you, it does feel better." He smiled. "Sometimes you make me think that there are guarantees."

"Can I promise you that someday, there will be guarantees? That's kind of a guarantee."

"Now you've made it sound like guarantee isn't a word."

Alistair smelled the stirring first. The change from casual to serious was instant. He shouted for everyone to assume their position, as the Worldeater Snake erupted from its craggy cage.

Thankfully, the serpent went for the Devil King side first, giving them more time to prepare.

That was the problem. There was no Devil King side. Not anymore. They were gone. Alistair hadn't noticed it. His ultra-sensitive nose found the poisonous aura of the snake hard to penetrate. He could feel their presence, but noticing the lack of it was more difficult.

None of the scouts reported it yet, meaning that it had to have happened recently. And when Alistair paid close attention, he found one Devil King left. Or should he say Devil Queen?

Morgana was the most beautiful woman he'd ever seen, except for Selephita and perhaps Gu Fuhao. When a shard of pink glass hummed and multiplied, he almost wanted to join it so he could look at her forever.

Alistair shook his head. What a seductive promise. His Dao Path was too strong for such a trick, however.

With a *nue*-filled shout, he ordered everyone to close their eyes. The killing intent should have disrupted anyone who was temporarily overtaken by the madness. *Shard of Madness*. He knew the spell from Oracle's memories, and he knew well enough that they were not the target, despite being hit with some incidental effects.

The kaiju was her prey.

Powerful beasts had innate protections against mind control, an evolutionary defensive mechanism built up since the beginning of time. Cultivators always thought they could tame the wild.

Morgana was not strong enough on her own to thrust the snake into a controllable madness. Maybe if she sacrificed those millions of souls she'd eaten, but she didn't. But by fleeing the scene, it had a similar effect.

Since the Devil Kings were gone, there was only one viable target left.

Us, Alistair thought.

The snake charged with more speed than ever before. Its simple mind was a singularity of rage, and its red eyes lightened to a shade of pink.

Alistair knew what he had to do.

"EVERYONE! Get to your positions, NOW! UNLEASH EVERY WEAPON WE HAVE!"

They didn't need to be told twice. Alistair readied himself. If he had to use his finishing Skill, he would. But first, it was time to see what his stockpile could do.

The **Crystal Ion Cannon** whirred to life. Shaped like an enormous telescope, its fuel tanks glowed blue as it siphoned off the entirety of its reserves for one blast.

The **Twin Silk Slicer** readied its launcher. It almost looked like an enormous fan, with a stand and four pointed spikes, each with a slit that glowed a soft orange. Each curved blade would produce a single strand of impossibly strong silk. Together, they formed an x-shape that could carve even the hardest materials apart.

Alistair quickly deduced that the shockwave from unleashing both weapons at once could harm his army. He activated [**Thousand-Armed Bodhisattva Judgment**] at once. The palms could divert some of the force, but mainly it was to put a body in the way.

The palms of justice that shot forth collided with the blast, dispersing it so that it wasn't deadly. The snake never should have gotten that close, but they didn't anticipate its faster speed or that they would have to use everything at once.

Still, it destroyed his eardrums. That was one of the downsides to using weapons that worked on a physical level rather than the Dao. Cultivators at least had some control over the aftermath of their expressions.

There was a ringing in his ears as he coughed up dust. It was hard to see anything. People were panicking, unable to hear and unable to see.

Alistair jumped up and out of the fray. His Skills weren't that helpful, but Pharaoh was there to save the day. He manipulated the dust like it was sand, settling it down where it came.

The soldiers were trained well. After an initial moment of panic, people popped Health pills and got healers for the seriously injured. No one died, as far as Alistair could tell. Their life forces were strong and healthy.

Alistair looked down at their destruction. It was so encompassing that he didn't even see the explosion. An entire five mile-radius of the forest was gone, taking up almost half the valley between the two mountain ranges. There was a crater and two gouges at the very center. The devastation caused by the **Crystal Ion Cannon** and **Twin Silk Slicer.**

And at the very center, sat the kaiju. The Worldeater Snake, the mile-long poisonous monstrosity. It was dead. In a testament to its durability, it wasn't a complete skeleton. Most of its flesh was still intact, with smoking pieces missing here and there revealing its bones.

Alistair breathed a sigh of relief. They had done it. The third kaiju was conquered, with zero civilian casualties. He started laughing out loud, and as his eardrums began to heal, he heard the elated cries of victory.

No one cared that five kaijus were coming in a matter of three days. People had learned to live in the moment. This victory—it was a good one.

So good that Alistair almost didn't hear the message, despite it being a mental message sent to every human on Earth.

"Be humbled, all those who hear. In the sanctified name of Grand Imperator Praetei Dai Kezlan, I, her unpresuming servant, Marcus Auror, declare an end to Kaiju Break. There is to be an emergency meeting in one hour on Sharizak. All sects, corporations, and nobility—yes, including Progenitors—shall bring their sponsees. This meeting is mandatory and binding with the full force of the Fell Emperor's authority. May you serve him well and do Heaven's bidding."

42 SHARIZAK

ALISTAIR LOOKED AROUND, wondering if everyone had heard the same words he did. Based on the reactions he was seeing, they did. Before he could even discuss the ramifications of this Marcus Auror's message, a strong hand grabbed his torso.

There was no warning whatsoever. Not his ludicrous reactions nor his danger sense, not his smell or life force detection, not even the vibrations through Fate gave any foreknowledge. In one moment he was standing on top of a mountain's peak, and in the next, he was in the void.

The void gazed at Alistair, who gazed back at the infinite nothingness. It was boundless and meaningless, a darkness that superseded darkness in every corner of reality. Such desolation almost sent him mad.

Faced with the void of eternity, he struggled to comprehend how any meaning could last against the face of permanent impermanence. Was this void always there? No matter what creation existed, it could not withstand this. It could not—

Then he was back to the normal world, in what looked to be a very ordinary cottage. Rays of sunlight beamed through an open window, with potted plants on the windowsill.

"The void between reality tends to affect those of great ambition more," a wizened voice said. A voice familiar to Alistair. "An auspicious sign."

The Lazarene Minister. His hand was wrapped around Alistair's waist, who jumped back after realizing what had happened. Seeing as that appeared very rude, Alistair swiftly bowed as low as he could.

"My apologies, Elder... Minister. I did not sense you at all."

The old man released a full-blown belly laugh. "You do not have to address me by my Dao name. Though you may, if you wish, in which case honorifics are unnecessary. My given name is Mo Duan."

Elder Mo had a nearly perfect seal on his aura. Now that Alistair was looking for it, he could feel the tiniest energies emanating from the elderly man, but he couldn't tell how strong he was at all. Since he was an elder of a sect, probably Visionary?

Despite the lack of aura, his features contained a hint of the Dao and his life force was out of the ordinary. With the ravages of age evident on his face, the venerable old man's lifeline should have been almost over, yet he felt like a thousand-foot-tall grandfather tree instead.

Alistair nodded. "Elder Mo, then." He couldn't hold back his curiosity. "What was that?"

"The void between worlds," the Lazarene Minister, or Elder Mo, said. "Not something for a Foundation level to ponder. Do not listen to its seduction. To secure eternity is the dream of every cultivator. If you put the void over that, you are lost."

The weathered door of the cottage opened. Alistair had said before that Morgana and Gu Fuhao were among the most beautiful women he'd ever seen. But how could they compare to the goddess before him?

She was elegance defined. Her movements were one with the Dao, containing endless meaning with each step. She wore a simple white cultivator's robe that accentuated her features more than the fanciest dress a mortal could buy.

Like the Lazarene Minister, her aura was suppressed to the point where Alistair could barely feel it, but she still stood out like a sore thumb with her Dao-touched appearance. Was she that much stronger than the elder, or was it some facet of her cultivation? A Skill, or perhaps a secret body cultivation? Alistair truly had no way of knowing.

Elder Mo bowed to the woman. "Sect Leader of the Clear Water, Loroa Di Boswann. Known throughout the Final Frontier Empire by her Dao name, the Perfect. A Visionary realm ranked within the top one thousand of the empire."

Alistair copied the elder, bowing even lower. His refined body was super flexible, so he could almost get his head below his knees. More surprising, however, was that there was someone accompanying her. His sister.

Perhaps it shouldn't have been surprising that Evangeline was there. After all, the Clear Water Sect was both of their sponsors. He had forgotten about that, since he didn't get much time to talk to his sister these days. She was always off in the laboratory, or helping out the People's Legion.

Why did she get picked up by the sect leader and not me, though? Alistair wondered.

"Don't let your power get to your head," Dev'rox snickered.

Speaking of Dev'rox, Alistair wondered how much such a vaunted cultivator could see. Dev'rox had mentioned before that a Profound realm could detect him, but what about spying in on conversation?

"Doubtful. I am within your soulcore. Visionaries aren't powerful enough to mess with the soul such that you or I wouldn't notice."

Alistair found it hard to believe that the Perfect could lack, well, anything. She lived up to her name. He stopped his thoughts there. He had just met the woman, and he was saying these things? His heart steeled against the influence of a foreign Dao. His mind was calm. Tranquility in all things. He didn't need for the ocean to drown him to understand how to master his thoughts.

Dangerous, was the word that came to mind first. She must have cultivated a Dao close to the heart. Alistair doubted her influence was something she could even completely shut off. It was just a natural consequence of her path.

"Thank you for the help you have given me, Sect Leader. I hope I can serve well as a disciple in your esteemed sect." Alistair aimed to be as respectful as possible without sounding obsequious.

The Perfect waved her hand, and the cottage *changed*. Nothing moved in the physical world, yet to Alistair's mind, it had reached another state of perfection. Things that seemed out of place—a cracked tile, a chipped painting—became pieces of a grand tapestry that were only fitting for a European-style cottage.

Thankfully, the Perfect seemed to restrict her Dao to some degree, as Alistair didn't feel like there were any hidden temptations within the working. After an ivory throne appeared for her to sit on, and corresponding bone cathedra for the other three in the house, he wondered if she was just taking control of the space so she could shape it to her liking.

"Please, sit," she said, her voice matching the harmonies of the most glorious concerto. "It is good to finally meet you, Alistair and Evangeline."

There was a moment of silence after she spoke. Was he supposed to say anything there? She continued after a smile that could pacify the most bloodthirsty warrior. "If you want answers as to why the envoy of the Grand Imperator called this meeting, we have only guesses. Information is hard to come by here. The infrastructure for the universal Soulnet on your planet won't be finished for a few years."

"Could it have to do with the Crusade Against Usury?" Alistair asked.

The Perfect narrowed her eyes for the briefest of moments. "A likely theory. What do you know of the crusade?"

"The people complained about the corporations' interest rates so much, the Emperor was forced to act. So he went after them?" Alistair only knew as much as the Pathfinder AI had told him, and it wasn't that specific. "The sects and the corporations are natural allies, both distrusted by the nobility, who mostly side with the Emperor, the only Exalted realm in the empire."

"More or less, you are correct," the Perfect said. "However, you shall never call the sects and corporations allies within my ear. The corporations are a poison on cultivator society. If it were up to me, I would ban them empire-wide, like in Mai Atal. Many of my fellow sect leaders disagree, leading to your unfortunate perception.

"The Emperor forbade interest rates of higher than 5% on new loans, and invalidated any old loans at 7% or higher, liquidating the corporations' accounts to give the money back to the people. The corporations, more specifically the triumvirate of the Akata, Feiyn, and Corlyon have been investing in habitable planets for the last ten millennia, and the Emperor seized a dozen planets from each, reducing the rents by half in some cases."

"A dozen doesn't sound like very many," Alistair said, thinking of how he read somewhere that there were 187,212,308 inhabited planets in the Final Frontier Empire.

Considering the size of the observable universe, that didn't sound like a lot, but the empire expanded via wormholes. Traveling via a spaceship from the Imperial Heartlands to the far frontier would take thousands of years for even their fastest vessels. They hadn't come even .1% close to fully expanding to every habitable planet. In that sense, they controlled less than the 50% they claimed, which only counted against other cultivator kingdoms.

"The principle is most important," she answered. "The principle and future tidings."

There were no more questions after that. She didn't say as much, but Alistair understood. He wasn't even an official member of their sect yet. Plus, there were the rules that prevented the sponsors from doing too much.

The cottage turned out to be one part of their little town. They had a few acres of land in what turned out to be former Pennsylvania. There were around fifty people in the town, all cultivators from the Clear Water Sect.

After Earth's full initiation completed, they would begin to operate, trading goods with the populace and scouting potential recruits. The Final Frontier Empire had rules about how much the sects and other groups could invest on newly initiated worlds, and the attempts to circumvent those restrictions came to be called the predations.

The Lazarene Minister had explained the predations to him in their last meeting. The system for initiating new worlds had been taking place for some time, with the system of sponsors taking interest in Prime Initiates.

While it wasn't impossible to succeed staying within one's planetary system, it was a hundred times as difficult. Cultivation was just as much about opportunity and resources as talent. The brightest stars could get bogged down in Foundation or Adept if they didn't get access to cultivation chambers or elixirs or Beast Rulers to fight.

The sponsorship system allowed Prime Initiates access to the entrenched powers who hoarded secrets and resources alike. It was a quid pro quo exchange, and one that didn't really favor either party to a large extent. The ones who were left behind were the inhabitants of the Prime Initiate's world.

The predations were what happened when larger groups bullied the new planet for resources and labor, and they came with the inherent threat of force. They could get real ugly, from what Alistair was told.

Even after the end of the initiation, the Pathfinder AI was more likely to create dungeons and Quests in the world. Resources like Natural Inheritances and build manuals spawned at higher rates, and the Dao was easier to perceive thanks to the system providing helpful hints. Chaos was known to meddle with Fate, so rich people with malignant futures often traveled to the Prime Initiates' planets before the system could gobble up all the Chaos-touched Mana with the harvesters.

The confluence of interested parties led to violence. Entitled nobles, arrogant young sect masters—what could go wrong? Often, it wasn't even that they targeted the populace, but regular people became collateral damage in cultivator brawls. The lives of mortals were rarely considered.

For someone like George, that wasn't his chief concern, but the resources of the planet were still up for plunder. A united front could help prevent the worst of the piracy.

Things differed from when Atavius Meloi brought the apocalypse to the planet—they were now official citizens of the Final Frontier Empire. They had legal protections, if meager, and Karmic protection against Profound and Visionary realms who rarely committed atrocities against Foundations unless they wanted to be afflicted with enough fell Karma to spend a hundred and eight Samsaric rebirths in a sinner's hell.

As a result, if they were going to be pushed around, it was mostly from Adepts, the second realm of cultivation. Not an unreachable goal for Alistair or his elites. If they could work together, they could help make Earth off limits for those kinds of behaviors. He also dared to hope that if he rose through the ranks of the Clear Water Sect quickly, they could help his home planet.

The Perfect told them to act with the utmost respect to the Grand Imperator's manservant. Instead of a bow, they were to greet him with an imperial salute, which was like a normal military salute on Earth, except you had to keep your left hand behind your back and after the salute you tapped your fist over your heart three times.

Alistair spent the rest of the hour catching up with his sister. They were seeing each other less and less these days. He promised a family dinner with the three of them as soon as he could make it work.

The hour that Marcus Auror allotted went as slow as molasses. Near the end, he just wanted to be beamed up to whatever Sharizak was. Which turned out to be about what happened.

When it was time, a great golden light burst from him, Evangeline, and the Perfect. Alistair wanted to kneel where he stood. There was an echo of imperial might in the aura, one that chilled him to the bone. He was nowhere near qualified to understand the power struggles between Visionaries and Exalteds, but he felt that if that was a wisp of wisp of a wisp of the Emperor's power, no one could oppose him.

The envoy chose a different approach to how the Lazarene Minister, or Elder Mo, forced open a hole in spacetime. He felt it had to be a show of power more than anything else. They were but helpless babes before the warm golden light that spoke of an eternal dynasty of omnipotent emperors.

Alistair scoffed at that. The Perfect's beauty was more alluring than that falsehood. How could the Exalted emperor of a far frontier universe have any claim to eternity, to an immortal legacy? Alistair was ignorant of the true powers of the multiverse, but even he knew this.

Even the Perfect was snatched up by the light like a helpless babe. She could obviously break it and travel herself, but to do so would be to court death. They ascended in the sky inside the auric field, passing through solid objects without an issue.

Their flight took them above the clouds at breakneck pace, and they didn't stop accelerating. In less than thirty seconds, he went from the inside of the cottage to outer space before the largest satellite Alistair had ever seen.

Satellite wasn't the right word. The orbiting structure, presumably Sharizak, was something out of a science fiction book. It was so large he couldn't give a proper estimate. A hundred miles across? A thousand?

Sharizak was spherical, and mostly made of a light gray metal. There were millions of grooves filled with glowing lights and divots and notches that all looked to serve a functional purpose. Surrounding the entire satellite was an aquamarine filter. If it was a barrier, Alistair and his compatriots flew through without issue.

There was darkness with intermittent flashes of light as he passed through all the layers of the orbiting spaceship.

It must operate via the Dao, Alistair thought. *This thing would totally be affecting our planet with its gravity otherwise.*

"Astute observation, brat," Dev'rox stated. "I've done some reading on frontier universes. The Final Frontier Empire has some advantages over others since they can use the blueprints of the Sublimed Machine for technological innovations. It's much easier to copy technology than the Dao, though obviously there's still shortcuts in a spaceship like this that rely on the Dao."

While Alistair had gotten so busy because of the initiation, he never forgot his early curiosity of the underlying science behind the multiverse. Or should he say metaphysics? No, science was the better term. Despite the magical nature of things, you could still form hypotheses and test them.

There was an efficiency to cultivation, where you took the natural energy of the multiverse for yourself. The boundless Dao was filled with infinite truths and infinite paths. To understand even a small piece of the Grand Dao allowed you to influence the fabric of reality.

But that didn't mean technology was useless. As far as Alistair understood, things like antimatter bombs and Alcubierre drives weren't science fiction, but science fact, for factions like the Sublimed Machine. Such inventions were under the purview of the Dao of Technology.

Alistair had done some reading on the Sublimed Machine. They offered almost zero information to the frontier on their history, purpose, or organization. What he did find was a small paragraph on their origins. They were a civilization that grew so large and advanced that they discovered the Dao scientifically. In fact, in those few lines, they basically claimed to have *created* the Dao of Technology.

Alistair wasn't sure that Dao fit his path, but he wasn't against some of the principles in the slightest.

Technology represented the arc of man defying the Heavens, going against the human condition.

In one interpretation, you could call it nearly identical to the orthodox path, where immortality through cultivation was paralleled against immortality through technology, and the wrath of the Heavens could be compared to entropy.

Alistair didn't think he would incorporate the Dao of Technology, but it offered food for thought. As presumably one of the more popular Daos in a frontier subsidiary of the Sublimed Machine, he had much to learn from the masters.

To think that if Atavius had never interfered, it was possible their civilization could have also discovered the Dao through science in the far future. Alistair found that idea comforting for some reason.

The trip to the meeting took half as long as the ascent out of the Earth's atmosphere. He landed directly on a hovering orb in the night sky.

They were in some kind of observatory chamber, from what Alistair gathered. It was enormous, twenty times the size of the largest planetarium on Earth.

Each stretch of the firmament was a different sector of stars. There were cosmic phenomena that he thought he recognized, like black holes or nebulae, but then others that looked completely foreign to him.

Hundreds of white orbs floated in the darkness, not all occupied. They formed a sphere, where each orb was a varied distance away from the center orb, softly glowing and far larger than the others.

There was a person on that orb, a man who sat with a regal pose. He looked to be in his mid-thirties, clean-shaven, and handsome with an aquiline nose. He wore a red and gold cultivator's robe that had more of a Roman look, accompanying that outfit with a golden laurel.

There were two men who flanked him on the left and right, both floating in the air. Well, perhaps only the one to his left could be called a man. The other was a giant, near eight feet tall and skinny as a noodle, with pointed ears like an elf.

That laurel made the identity of the man obvious, if it wasn't already. Marcus Auror. He felt less powerful than the Perfect or Elder Mo, but that golden laurel made him scarier.

Alistair spotted Pharaoh and Brigid on the orbs, accompanied by their sponsors. Pharaoh's was a platinum automaton shaped like a wooden puppet, whereas Brigid had a blond warrior with a saber at his side.

Corlyon and Di Skoro, Alistair thought.

The Di Skoro Clan were an upstart ducal family controlling one of the largest duchies of the Disputed Shard. They were majorly important in Shard politics, and could be said to have more influence than big players like the Akata from a local perspective, when you considered that the largest sponsors were all subdivisions of their greater party. The tall blond was likely an inner member of the Di Skoros.

Still, they could hardly compare to having the actual *sect leader* there for them. Alistair smiled.

There was Marzhan with her sponsor, from the Flaming Sword Sect. Sally Ryder and a representative of the Ironwater Cultivation Academy. Alistair recognized Ramesh, a top 15 ranker. Jesse was there too, with his sponsor, the Disputed Shard's Bazaar.

Alfred, Bartholomew, and their sister, Imogen, hovered beside Mishra Satharvon. The Perfect had deigned to mention her by name, a young prodigy of the Satharvon who reached Visionary in under three thousand years, though from a side branch. She held that chip on her shoulder and was known to lash out without provocation.

There were around fifty other Earthlings there as well. Most of them were from the top 100 rankers, but not everyone. Some sponsors were going to walk away, losing their investments. Such was the risk of the Prime Initiate system.

With everyone arriving in a five-second time frame, the man who sat at the center stood up.

"Welcome, my sponsors and sponsees, to Sharizak."

43 SECOND AND THIRD DECREE

ALISTAIR STOOD AT ATTENTION, performing the imperial salute as the Perfect had taught him. Salute, then three taps over the heart. Everyone else did the same, only sitting again when Marcus Auror raised a hand.

"This satellite was loaned by the Pathfinder AI to my colleagues, Kazian Bromas and Johannis LeoForte." Marcus pointed to Kazian for the huge elf, and Johannis for the human, who was wearing a pair of futuristic VR goggles. "For the Prime Initiates, these are the Mindaugust-Annalist duo that have been overseeing the initiation."

Despite him just making introductions, Alistair already got an uneasy sense of smarminess from the man, like he had with Jackson Morley. How could anyone whose job was to announce things for others be trustworthy? Local sports announcers were notoriously biased.

"It is an unfortunate reality that the sanctified one, Grand Imperator Praetei Dai Kezlan, shall not arrive for another two months. On our journey to FX-14752, we encountered a setback in an uninitiated region of space. We were so besotted by the most *barbaric* pirates that Grand Imperator Kezlan decided to dock and vanquish their ugly civilization. They proved to be more hardy than first expected, but the most recent updates say she has crossed through the wormhole and will be making a straight line for our location.

"But before I continue, I must impress this fact upon you all. Empire is your lifeline. I would never impugn the spotless reputation of your sponsors, but it is possible that they have failed to imprint upon you the primacy of empire. The Final Frontier Empire is surrounded by savagery, barbarism, and brutishness. The pirates of deep space. The Republic of Stars to our west and the Fractured States to our East. Chaos behind us. Survival is a matter of imperial might. What is the Grand Imperator system if not for displaying the omnipotence of our beneficent Fell Emperor?"

Marcus Auror continued along those lines for several minutes. Alistair was rapt in attention at first, but he only provided very basic information, the majority of which he already knew. The substance of his droning filibuster was imperial propaganda.

"Look how great the empire is! Emperor Dragus is the best!" and so-on, yada, yada, yada. Alistair found it hard to believe anyone could buy such garbage.

The crazy part was that Marcus went on for over an hour. Alistair zoned in and out. Would the orb he was sitting on be good material for a [Carmela's Happy Pie]? It looked kinda tasty now that he thought about it. Marcus might not like it, but he would understand, surely?

His attention came back to what the servant of the Grand Imperator was saying. "Thirteen of the holy Laketor line have stewarded the Final Frontier Empire to its current prominence. The immortal emperor is the linchpin of the imperium. When the stars dim and the void seeps into creation, His Excellency will too appear to one day pass from this world to the next, for the ancient sages tell us nothing in this life is forever. However, fear not, my imperial subjects, they are wrong! The Emperor will live again through his son, Kai Dragus."

Alistair turned to the Perfect, who was the picture-perfect representation of reserved grace. Her hands folded into her lap, she had a slight, respectable smile.

Her soothing voice entered Alistair's ear. "He's stalling. If the Emperor wants to send a universal message, he does so through his mouthpieces, the thirty-seven Grand Imperators. The servant must be waiting to temporally align with his master's compatriots, so that no section of the empire hears before any other."

Couldn't he have waited until the exact moment to call on us? Alistair wondered, but already had a theory. Power. It was the same reason they got taken up like kittens, carried by the scruff of their necks.

As if on cue, Marcus Auror looked up for a moment and stopped his speech. "Alas, my historical lesson must come to an end. It is now time to release the proclamation handed to me by proxy from His Excellency."

The background of the chamber switched from the depths of outer space to the foot of an impossibly tall throne. The throne was carved out of solid gold, inlaid with so many runic inscriptions and gemstones that would have bankrupted a planet a million times over. On the throne sat a projection of the most regal man Alistair had ever seen.

This towering titan of a man had light red hair, bordering on pink. He looked to be in his late thirties or early forties, but lacked noticeable signs of aging like wrinkles. His eyes were silver with halos of light, and he carried the immeasurable weight of rule with equanimity. He wore a simple cultivator's outfit that carried the Seal of the Empire, an infinity symbol with cracks streaking across it.

While he lacked a living aura, the sense of imperial might that Alistair felt was a thousand times that of the laurel on Marcus Auror's head. His heart was steeled against the foreign sway, but his body was not.

No one's body was, it appeared. Everyone inside the now imperial hall knelt down. It wasn't something Alistair could control. It was utterly beyond him. His heart refused obeisance, but his forehead grazed the ground. Not one person escaped kowtowing before the projection of Emperor Dragus Laketor.

"The first five months of the Crusade Against Usury have been monumentally successful for the crown and the people, for whom we labor to serve. Ten million Orichalcum drachma were renumerated to those who were saddled by unfair loans, with ten percent of that going toward further efforts to stamp out corruption among the corporations and sects. Unaffordable rents were reduced by half on over a dozen planets, with the Imperial family negotiating on a hundred thousand more worlds to temporarily halt any increases over the next thousand years."

Marcus Auror was an animated speaker now that he wasn't talking about lines of succession and ancient disputes. In every word, he gave off an unshakable impression that the Laketor Clan was breaking the shackles of oppression and standing with the downtrodden.

"This is not enough. We understand this, we hear your pleas. Therefore, the second phase of the imperial edict will address the deeper concerns. The second imperial decree of the Crusade, ratified by the Emperor and witnessed by the thirty-seven Grand Imperators and the Court of Infinity, states that 5.00% of all revenue earned by those under the Visionary realm for corporations and sects with assets of over 30 million and 10 million Orichalcum drachma respectively shall be confiscated to lay the ground-work for the Imperial Academic system, targeted at the most talented culti-vators from among the common folk.

"The third imperial decree of the crusade states that the Inner and Core Disciples of the top twenty sects and the investor's chosen of the top fifteen corporations will be selected at random to join the holy conquests of the Fractured States, all overseen by one of our Grand Imperators. This number shall be set at 10% every cycle, with the first wave starting in three years' time for the 1,956th Conquest. Participants who earn merit for the empire have the opportunity to become ennobled under the Laketor Clan banner."

While no one spoke, Alistair felt a dangerous current in the room. He doubted that anyone would outright attack the envoy—such a thing would be tantamount to declaring open rebellion. But those two new decrees sounded harsh.

If the corporations were anything like those back on Earth, taking 5.00% of revenue was massive. Companies were usually taxed after net income, so presuming they were already being taxed by the empire, this 5% was before everything else.

Visionaries being exempted likely reduced the 5% to a much smaller total, as Alistair imagined that the majority of their income was being produced by their Visionary executives, but also, it depended on *how* you counted who was making the money.

The second part... Inner and Core disciples and investor's chosen sounded like the most important of the youth generation of the sects and corporations. Sending them off to dangerous battlefields and then incorpo-rating the survivors into the imperial family itself was a devious move.

A flash of anger passed over even the perfect face of Sect Leader Boswann, if for an instant.

Marcus didn't say anything, but the fringes of his lips curled up into a smile. The bastard was enjoying his audience's wordless reaction. "The Emperor always has the best wishes for the empire in mind. Remember my words, especially you young ones: empire is your lifeline. To go against us is to end your life. As long as you fulfill your roles, your eternity is secured within the tapestry of the Final Frontier's Empire's everlasting Dao."

Marcus Auror dipped his head toward the Perfect, prompting everyone to look at her. "Given the physical presence of the Clear Water Sect, the Emperor thought it best for a Grand Imperator to deliver the message in the flesh. The traditionalism that the Clear Water Sect espouses is important to cherish in these changing times."

He looked at the platinum puppet from the Corlyon Company. "The corporations should look to her example. That is why they are the only sect that has been exempted from the Second Decree. We must turn to the teachings of Sect Leader Boswann in these trying times. Their orthodox formations are without a doubt meritorious."

Before Marcus Auror could speak another word, the Perfect interrupted, standing up. The other sponsors followed suit, though Alistair found himself stuck still, not that he had the chutzpah to rise from his knees. "Thank you for this consideration, servant Marcus. You and the Laketor Clan flatter the Clear Water Sect. However, this gift seems to be undeserved to my poor eyes. Such a Karmic debt would be difficult to repay with the vast divide between our power and that of the imperial family."

"Nonsense, Lady Loroa," Marcus Auror said. "Your services have been impeccable. It would be a shame to dishonor the Emperor's personal gift."

The Perfect and Marcus Auror locked eyes, and Alistair felt like a whole different conversation took place between the two of them than the one heard aloud.

"Then, there can be no option but to accept," the Perfect said, bowing her head. "We are forever in the debt of the Laketor Clan, if the decrees of the triumvirate last the million years we all hope for. The importance of uplifting the mortal population cannot be understated. That is something we agree on, Marcus Hooknose?"

Marcus Auror smiled, showing off a set of golden teeth that were blindingly bright. "Forever is a long time, Loroa. Imperial authority extends everywhere and exists for all times, but there must be limitations on our interventions. How can the child grow if the parent never lets him fall?"

The elf on Marcus's right coughed, a booming noise that could have come out of an industrial machine. "Sect Leader Boswann and Majordomo Auror, it might be prudent to talk about the Prime Initiates."

"Thank you, Kazian," Marcus said with a hint of sharpness. "The Grand Imperator used her authority to cancel the remainder of Kaiju Break. The fourth wave will start as normal in a week and three days. In addition, any

Prime Initiate that reports an infraction of any of the three imperial decrees comprising the Crusade Against Usury will receive the full protection of the Laketor Clan and an award commensurate to a third of the value of the infraction. With that, I conclude our meeting. Sponsors are to have no contact with their sponsees for the rest of [Armageddon], as Grand Imperator Kezlan wished."

Alistair blinked, and he was back on the mountain like nothing had happened. No Perfect or Lazarene Minister. He looked at his hands, making sure he wasn't seeing things. *No golden light sucking us up this time.*

Things outside his control were moving fast, it seemed. There was an electric feeling in the air. Everyone was saying now was the age of change. Mysterious beings like Purana of the Stratospheric Flames and the Pathfinder AI had told Alistair that directly. The Crusade Against Usury was inflaming tensions between all four major factions of the empire, and they were still trying to venture forth and invade other universes.

His sponsor was caught up at the center of it. It was obvious what the Emperor was doing. The Clear Water Sect would draw the hatred of all others for its exemption. Of course, the one sect that had the Emperor's attention was his.

Or maybe that's a good thing, Alistair thought. *Conflict breeds opportunity.* Not that he condoned violence, but the situation was going to happen anyway, so why not get in there while the iron was hot?

"And if the Emperor wipes away the Clear Water Sect with a thought?" Dev'rox asked.

"Then my thread of Fate runs dry."

Dev'rox gave him a look that was incomplete without a raised eyebrow —an item that an imp did not possess. "Don't scare me like that. Kyraxadon was one of those Fate-crazy bastards, always talking about destiny and prediction. I can't lose you to the threads."

"I'm joking," Alistair said. "But it's true, right? I can't control where I go at the moment. I only have to make the best of things. It's completely true that risk and reward are correlated in cultivation."

"A proper outlook on life," Dev'rox said. "Well on your way to old monster status. Just don't leave me behind before you get there."

"Wouldn't dream of it."

———

The Perfect and the Lazarene Minister sat alone in their handcrafted cottage. The Minister, or in this company, Duan, modeled it after ones he had seen in the French countryside via the Pathfinder AI.

"Duan, I doubt myself," Loroa said softly. "I ordered those drachma on the Fatewatchers. I spent that fortune and listened to the Oracular Troll and came to this planet in the flesh. It has all led to ruin."

Mo Duan put his withered hand on his sect leader's. Loroa's parents had long passed, mortals from years distant. He had watched her go from child to woman grown, blossoming into the leader of his venerable sect that he had served from birth.

"This is not of your making. Fate is a finicky thing. I cannot read it as well as some, but I know that you did not cause this. The decrees were always coming."

Loroa shook her head. "Madness. I see no reason why the Emperor has turned his eye on us. No reason!"

"The Emperor has many eyes," Mo Duan said, shaking his head. In his lifespan of twice that of a typical Visionary, he had seen many things. "Many hands and many ears. If he sees us as tied to the old ways, he will see us as tied to the Tiarvon."

"I've never so much as met Prince Hoen."

"Dragus believes as Dragus believes. The court doctor says in secret that the madness grows worse. There are some in the family who already believe that Kai Dragus should be regent."

Loroa groaned, which coming from her was an elegant exhalation. "I've not a mind for politics. You and Sect Leader Wozhan were more suited for that."

"My little dove," he said. "You must be whatever the sect needs you to be. Strength can only get you so far."

"That wretch." Loroa squeezed her fist. "He pretends to care for the people? If only they knew what he did behind closed doors. He should burn in hell for a trillion years. If we were in the same realm, I'd kill him myself."

Mo Duan looked up, earning a look of consternation from his superior.

"I'm no fool, Elder Mo," she said. "I wouldn't let Marcus Hooknose feel my intent. On another topic, what do you think of Alistair and Evangeline? Would they betray us? Of course, we will never have any infractions. None whatsoever."

"I think not," Mo Duan answered. "But one can never be sure with such youthful souls. To think they had not heard of cultivation one year ago."

"What did that troll say?" Loroa asked. "To find the terminus of my destiny, look toward Chaos on the frontier. Where the fist of the mortal meets falling Heaven, you shall find what you seek. That must be this Alistair, yes?"

"It is the most reasonable assumption," Duan said. "Since I was the one that found them, do you think you could increase my stipend? An old man such as myself requires some additional amenities."

44 MINDAUGUST'S TRIAL

When Alistair hit level 60, he didn't find himself in a vision. He was struck by lightning.

That wasn't supposed to happen. A true Heavenly tribulation where he was smote by lightning would occur upon the breakthrough to Adept. The "tribulations" of the Pathfinder AI were in some sense false ones, though they weren't bad.

The Pathfinder had simply decided that the best improvement it could give him for reaching level 60 was a simulation of his future experience.

Alistair found himself on a deserted island. Blue lightning descended from the sky for hundreds of miles, razing this imaginary sea into nothingness. The infinite torching of the sky closed in on his tiny body.

Is this what a true tribulation is like? Alistair wondered. He was so caught up in its awesome power that he forgot it was going to hit him.

Burning agony filled every cell in his body. The Heavens were furious with him, like all cultivators. To cultivate was to steal immortality as a mortal fated to die. To steal energy when it didn't belong to you.

Alistair thought it was mild. It hurt in a different way than the purgatorial flames of the Steel Body trial, but the end result was way less pain. Having overcome far worse, he found it easy. Physical pain wasn't enough to cow him, and his body was incredibly sturdy.

Perhaps that was why the Pathfinder gave him the tribulation. His stats had overreached too far above the limits of his cells. The pseudo-Heavens of the Pathfinder cleansed his body of impurities with the lightning, despite the pain.

When he woke up, he was surrounded by a smelly black gunk. Some of the impurities holding back his body were gone. Everything felt better, from the movements of his hands to the way that the winter air smelled. Alistair checked his status screen, eager to see his new stats, unburdened by their cap.

Name: Alistair Tan
Species: Spectral Superhuman I (Partially Evolved)
Bloodline: (Ghost) Blood Dragon [Peon]
Class: Magical Pugilist (Uncommon)
Subclass (HIDDEN): Arbiter of Justice (Legendary)
Level: 60

Health: 1,650/1,718 (3.092 per min)
Mana: 1,530/2,381 (5.142 per min)
Stamina: 793/1,093 (1.797 per min)
Upgrade Points: 23
Balance: 3,170,155 Gold Drachma, 201,257 Land Credits
Karma (Unlocked): +90 (.048 per min)
Full Stat Bonuses: Note: Attribute cap 3,500 -> 7,000 +81% to All Attributes, +10% to Strength, Wisdom, +20% to Agility, Endurance, +5% to Charisma, +50% Mana

Strength: 518
Agility: 1,001
Constitution: 329
Endurance: 382
Intelligence: 576
Wisdom: 325
Charisma: 539

Items: Zanibar's Purification Ring, Thrice-Blessed Fate-Diviner, Devilsbane Gauntlets, Mammothskin Raiment, Fall of Fleet, Teleportation Circle, Heavenly Nectar Incense

Badges: "Premium Initiate", "Good Samaritan", "Deliverance of Justice", "Mythical Cultivator", "Jack of All Trades II", "World Leader", "Devil May Cry", "1", "Cosmic Blood – Top 100 Performance"

Talents: System Tree – Three leaves, Pugilism Branch (II), Chaos Assassin – Void Watching Branch (II), Merciful Abbot – Heart Cultivator (IV), Merciful Abbot – Justice Quest Branch (I), Lawful Magistrate (II), Elemental Fighter – Summoning of Spirit Branch (V), Body Tree – Heart Branch (I), Blood of the Devil – Sanguine Empowerment Branch (IV), Bloodline Evolution – (Ghost) Blood Dragon [Peon]

Skills: [Lightning of Justice], [Force Fist], [Blood Hand], [Frozen Claw], [Eyes of Truth], [Dash], [Monk Motionlessness], [Hand of Karma], [Ghost Whispers], [Spectral Summoning], [Carmela's Happy Pies], [Draconic Roar], [Steel Body], [Thousand-Armed Bodhisattva Judgment]

Quests: [Armageddon], [Vanquishing the Devil Kings]

Achievements: Discovery (I), Dueling (IV), Conquest (II), Dao Node – Dao of the Ghost (I) Dao Node – Dao of the Fist (II), Dao Node – Dao of Justice (I), Arcana (III)

Alistair allocated almost all of his free Attributes and "Deliverance of Justice" points to get that sweet over 1,000 Agility. For his Upgrade Points, in his last two levels with his Upgrade Points he had found the Merciful Abbot Branch of the Talent Tree, stemming from his Arbiter of Justice Subclass.

For the past few levels and upgrades, he had ignored the Talent Tree, but with nothing else to spend on, he had a closer look.

Alistair remembered way back when he tried to give Anthony Ricci a chance to surrender. An important part of his path was redemption. That good would prevail over evil. That it could prevail over evil in even the wickedest villain. That there was goodness in every person.

His finishing Skill shone that light and rang that gong in its victims.

Alistair could feel Dev'rox about to speak up in their bond, but he shushed him. He knew that attacking an enemy's Dao Heart was possibly the most inefficient way to go about things. And his attacks weren't *revolving* around that at the cost of everything else.

Alistair was a stubborn bastard and he wouldn't let go of it, so why not improve it? After taking one of the first layer leafs that shored up his heart, he had obtained the Sanctifying Heart leaf that increased the effectiveness of attacks on the heart by 10%, and then now with his new points, he completed the second level, Fear of Glorifying Truth leaf.

The leaf didn't increase the chance of his heart attacks working, but they made it so that any time his enemies feared they might work, their reaction time would slow due to indecision by 10% more. Since Alistair had the antithesis to slow reactions, he felt it would compound an advantage of his.

Alistair finally did some research in the Hall of Math and figured out why his instincts to use his stolen blood essence to upgrade his bloodline and not his species were right. The benefits of a species evolution were more mystical than practical, with most of the tangible benefits like higher stat caps not being applicable to the average Joe. Even for a stat monster like Alistair, he could increase the cap via bloodline instead.

Species evolutions didn't even start giving raw stats until way, way down the line, like the Lazarene Minister said. Bloodline upgrades were basically just better and more varied for almost every species, since they were the inherited special abilities of a powerful individual.

There was an additional danger, even for those who had the resources— going more than one above your specified one evolution per realm invited heart demons. Alistair could get his next species evolution now and not suffer any consequences, but if somehow he then upgraded again before becoming a Foundation, that would be ruinous.

Having such a perfected body while the soul and mind were so far behind led to one worshiping the body. It was impossible to circumvent by any known method. Dev'rox was quite confident even in the multiversal core no one went more than a realm above.

Those who dared improve their bodies like that and survived were called Martial Jiangshi, and their cultivation was forever deviated, unable to reach the peak in the standard fashion. If your Fate was running dry and you needed a lifeline to more power, it was not uncommon in some circles to become a Martial Jiangshi.

Alistair was creeped out by the idea. From what he understood, they weren't actually jiangshi, but since he was a kid and his grandma told him stories about jiangshi, he found them scary. Not regular zombies, though, for some reason.

Speaking of bodies, his Attributes totaled 3,670. That had to be the highest in the world. No way George was matching him number for number.

He had wondered how people were keeping up with him in stats—they weren't, but they were being kept from being completely lapped by things like build manuals and Natural Inheritances. Sadly, Alistair's path was a bit too unique for a build manual.

Alistair felt the effects of the missing impurities already as he took to the Great Plains. The wind whipped around his shoulder and snowflakes settled on his sleek jacket, covering the chengyu on his back.

The activation time for his Skills improved to the point where every single combat Skill he had was now viable for close-quarters combat. The Mana costs were down by around 15%, though they didn't say so in their descriptions.

In addition, Alistair opened a hundred of the 349 remaining meridians in one go. The extra space allowed his Mana to flow at a more efficient pace, with much higher throughput. All of his Skills would benefit, especially his combat Skills which would become more powerful.

He could feel that his soulcore would ossify his Mana affinity choices after this point. As he went up to level 100, his meridians would become attuned to his four Mana types. After that, using Skills that had to convert his soulcore Mana to a different type would be 10% as efficient as his inherent Mana affinities. If he wanted to make a change to his Mana path, it would have to be now. But Alistair was content.

Content with his progress, but not content with the fourth wave.

The Mindaugust's Trial. After Kaiju Break, everyone was in terror at what the horrible next trial could be. What could top Beast Rulers that not even the top cultivators in the world could take head on?

Old man ghosts. That was right, Chinese grandpas popped up all over the world. They were dressed in changshan robes, and could have fit right in during the Qing Dynasty. A peculiar aesthetic choice for the Pathfinder AI, that Alistair might have found amusing if they weren't so deadly.

The spirits were utterly indestructible and would ceaselessly meander until finding a living person. If you were selected, that was that. There was nothing else you could do but have a talk with the ghost.

Each one wanted something different. To answer a riddle. To solve a puzzle. To play a game of Go.

They never asked for something beyond your ability. If you didn't know how to play Go, they might choose chess instead. If you couldn't prove there were an infinite amount of prime numbers, they might ask you to troubleshoot a broken car if you used to be a mechanic.

All of their tasks revolved around something intellectual. Something that made you use your mind. After natural disasters, dungeons, and kaijus, it didn't sound so bad, but there was one terrible condition. If you failed at the task given to you, the spirit killed you.

That wasn't so bad, right? Just one death? Nope. The spirit would go on a rampage in a vicinity based on how badly you failed. It would split into as many spirits as necessary within whatever range it had and ask every single person in that range a question. This would continue onward forever, or at least until it ran out of people.

At least if you answered a question correctly, you got a one-day grace period. That was only voluntarily, though. If you so chose, you could find wandering spirits to get questions, to save other people from the risk.

You didn't have to be altruistic to want to talk to the ghosts, either. Answering questions correctly gave Contribution Score, experience, and drachma. It was the time of the mind over the body. All the nerds of the world rejoiced, though many of those nerds had since become fighters out of necessity.

So, the reason Alistair [Dashed] across the expanse was to catch as many spirits as possible. They seemed to spawn with no respect to population, only area, so he chose an unpopulated region to eliminate as many as possible.

Most likely because of his background where he knew some advanced math, the questions he got from the spirits were hard. Really hard. He got way more proofs and difficult logic puzzles than the average person. Thanks to Dev'rox, the games were fairly easy. The imp was skilled at almost every strategy game ever, according to him.

While the spirits had varying difficulties based on the person being tested, they also had inherent difficulties based on the color of their hat. Black was the easiest and white was the hardest, the rest falling in between.

Because of the conditions of the Mindaugust's Trial, people congregated in densely populated areas. A few people would be designated as the trial takers and purposefully place themselves in front of the spirits to get asked a question. Alistair would compensate them even beyond the natural benefits, with compounding bonuses for those proven to be successful over multiple rounds.

This was because the worst problem was the exponential spirit growth when someone got a question wrong. Chains of wrong answers quickly threatened to kill everyone within an area who lacked the capacity to answer a question. It was a ruthless Darwinian culling that Alistair had come to expect from the Final Frontier Empire.

It would have been the worst death count of all four waves if not for the system that they had developed. By force of law, all citizens had to travel to the nearest large city. People like Alistair who had a successful track record would hunt down spirits in the empty expanses left behind, while other successful answerers guarded the hordes of people.

Thanks to their quick thinking, the largest amount of deaths came from the fighting. Some people took offense to the idea that there was a designated person getting the opportunity for advancement. Opportunities that, by wave four, were rare. They saw answering questions by spirits as an easier way to get ahead than fighting Beast Lords.

Even with the People's Legion, they couldn't enforce the rules everywhere while they had to deal with the rural spirits. Some of the fighting was unavoidable.

Thankfully, the spirits were attracted to those who had survived their past counterparts. You could feel them with your aura sense, and Alistair stopped in his tracks as he sensed one of incomparable power.

The unspoiled plains offered no cover. Alistair carefully approached the being he sensed from afar, unsure if there was going to be a fight, since the spirit was so abnormal.

"Come hither," the spirit said. Alistair obeyed without thinking, [Dashing] before the rainbow hat ghost. They had never seen a spirit hat of that color before, nor one that could force a person to come to it.

Alistair strained with all his might to move, but none of his muscles fired. Even Dev'rox was trapped within his body.

"Fret not," the spirit said. He looked the same as the rest of them, but his aura was far deeper. Not that it made him a powerhouse, but Alistair felt a primordial essence to the ghost that surpassed his brethren. "I wish no harm upon you."

"But if I fail your test, I will die?" Alistair asked.

"Well, that's true. But it's not as though I wish it."

Alistair snorted. "You're more talkative than the other ghosts. They'll just ask the question or show me the game right away."

"We can do that if you'd like." The ghost gave him a warm smile that reminded Alistair of the earliest memories of his grandfather. "But I prefer conversation."

"There's less than a week left for the Mindaugust's Trial," Alistair said. "Would you be the final boss?"

"Something of the sort," the spirit said. "You can call me River Flowing Towards An End. Or River, if you'd like."

"Alright, River," Alistair stretched his hands. "What game will we be playing?"

A twinkle appeared in River's eye. "Why don't I show you?"

———

Alistair never would have guessed the game they were about to play was tic-tac-toe. River produced a three-by-three grid the size of a Go board, drawing it onto a perfectly flat piece of granite. They both sat on their knees in a sea of grass, strong winter winds forcing the stalks to sway back and forth. The cold bothered neither of them.

He gave Alistair five pieces of Gold drachma locked inside a glass container, where River used five turtle shell bones, each having an inscription on the back.

"Before we play, we must talk," River said. "I might have lied about being able to play the game right away."

"There are others in need," Alistair said. He fiddled with the container, but the drachma wouldn't come out, and he couldn't figure out how the lock worked in the slightest. "If I take too long, people might die."

"They always do." River closed his eyes, shaking his head. "Whether it be now or in a hundred thousand years, the mortal coil waits for no man."

"But the dream of cultivators is to break that mortal coil," Alistair countered, perhaps seeing where this was going. "To secure eternity. To reach the summit and go beyond."

"Is that dream real? I wondered that often when I lived."

"Of course it's real. If it wasn't, that would mean that all the trillions upon trillions of beings toiled for nothing. Plus, is that not what a Truthseeker is? Someone who has reached the pinnacle of cultivation and grasped true eternity?"

"Young pup, you have no idea of what you speak. How would you have the qualifications to know such a thing? Neither do I, for that matter. Even a billion years is nothing compared to infinity. A trillion, trillion, trillion years is nothing. How would you know if a Truthseeker can stake a claim to forever?"

Alistair began to open his mouth, but he realized that River was correct. From what he gathered, an Exalted realm could live around fifteen million years, so given the multiplicative factors, a Truthseeker would at minimum be in the billions. But as River said, billions were not infinity.

"How would you know that they can't live forever?" Alistair asked.

"I don't," River conceded. "It's a guess. A guess informed by my understanding of the multiverse. I did not reach the realm of the Truthseeker, but I was no backwater farmer. I saw the peaks. Nothing lasts forever. All things are impermanent. We live under a Buddhist Heaven, do we not?"

There was a heavy silence in the air as Alistair contemplated the words of the old man ghost. Dev'rox was quiet as well, and though he could feel that the imp had his own thoughts on the matter, this discussion was not his to interfere with.

River gestured to the board. There was a sadness to his movement. A heavy weight that felt like an ancient burden. "You may place your stone."

One of the five drachma teleported out of the case and into Alistair's hand. Not being an idiot, he put his drachma in the center. River responded by putting his shell in the top right corner, from Alistair's perspective. The inscription on the bone read "Eternity" in a familiar script. The Language of the Pure Dao.

However, even compared to the extremely watered down version of "Spirit's Fists Overcoming Struggle," the "Eternity" was trash. It barely communicated any meaning. If the glyph in the Holy Ravine was copied a hundred times, this one had been copied a thousand.

Alistair exhaled through his mouth, letting his hands rest on his lap. "If everything is impermanent, then one day the Heavens won't be Buddhist anymore."

"Perhaps," River said. "But what do the scriptures say? The Buddha codified and explained the three marks of existence, but he did not invent them. If the Heavens shifted to claim an unchanging reality, would they win? Cultivators steal from the Heavens all the time, yet tribulations are not falling on them every second of every day until they are motes of dust. Nothing is omnipotent."

"I don't need to be omnipotent as long as I can accomplish my goals."

"Goals are attachments to this world," River admonished, though Alistair wondered if he really believed that. "They can only lead to misery. The more you possess, the more it shall hurt to lose your possessions. The warmest love and the sweetest kiss, the laughter of children and the blessing of health. The contentedness of the philosopher and the beatitudes of the monk. This is the cruelest gift of the multiverse."

"Then what do you suggest? To not have goals is to not even be a cultivator, no?"

"There is no future and there is no past. There is the now and there is the forever, both existing and not existing at once. To become one with the Dao is to relinquish such earthly desires and act without acting. However, even at the level of such a perfected being, power is necessary." River showed off his powers of prestidigitation with the turtle shells. 'Omnipotence,' 'Self,' 'Civilization,' and 'War' were the remaining ones. "You would need power of the highest order."

"I'll get as much power as I need," Alistair said. Perhaps it was time to try a different tack. "Is that what you did in your earthly life?"

River didn't seem fazed that Alistair asked about his life. Instead, he gestured to the board. The drachma teleported into his hands once again, where he placed it in the bottom left corner, while the spirit placed the bone inscribed with "Omnipotence" in the top left.

"Getting ahead of yourself there, are you?" River looked down at his rapidly moving fingers. "I had forgotten your eyes were so keen. You must have read the remaining bones and thought yourself clever. Self, civilization, and war."

While this spirit was unique, the rules of the games were always the same. Since nothing you could do as the human being tested could harm the questioner, anything was allowed. Alistair activated [Eyes of Truth]. They barely took on a crimson tint when he wasn't allotting additional Karma for them.

More specifically, he was fishing for information using Lesser Vipassanā to detect inner truths not spoken aloud. It didn't give him precise details, but it allowed his guesses to be far more informed.

"Our Pathfinder AI is lazy," Alistair said, unafraid of being smote down. After hearing his bloodline's progenitor say that Heaven didn't really pay attention to the frontier, he stopped worrying about being snatched up by an archon, and the Pathfinder AI didn't give one lick about being badmouthed. He had heard Alexandra say some very offensive things about the Emperor and the Pathfinder AI, but it never stepped in. "It modifies and reuses. It takes from what it's given and rarely creates wholesale. Am I wrong in assuming you were once a cultivator in your own right? Based on the fact you were selected in a trial relating to the mind, you were probably someone that used their wits over their brawn. Some kind of mental cultivator?"

Mental cultivators, interchangeably known as psychic cultivators, were rare on the frontier, though not as rare as *nue* artists. While it was almost impossible to raise your true intellect via stats, those who were already smarter to begin with were drawn to the mental arts.

River scoffed. "My brawn was fine enough, brat. Karmic bastards, always knowing more than they should."

"I guessed right, then," Alistair said. "Where are you from?"

"I'm the one that's asking questions here," River said, though he didn't put his heart into it. "Far from here. A brat like you could run for ten thousand lifetimes and it would be but one step toward the planet of my birth."

"So... far." Despite River not having indicated anything, a drachma appeared for Alistair to place a drachma in the top middle row. River didn't play his stone right away. "How did you and your brothers come to be ghosts a million universes away, used as a trial for a Foundation on a newly initiated planet?"

River picked up the "War" bone with a spindly finger, twirling the tortoise plastron around until forcibly striking it onto the bottom center row with more force than any of his previous moves. "How all things are gained and lost. War."

Through the help of Lesser Vipassanā, Alistair began to understand more. Though he doubted it would have worked if River was being truly recalcitrant.

"Your civilization must have been grand beyond my wildest imagination," Alistair said once it dawned on him. "Philosopher-kings who saw cultivation as a series of questions to be answered with rationality."

Alistair placed his drachma in the center of the left column.

"You're too cruel." River placed the bone inscribed with "Civilization" in the bottom right. "Too cruel. I cannot even remember my own mother's face or the eyes of my Dao Partner. All this has been stolen from me, yet you tease me so."

"That was not my intention," Alistair said softly. But he did not place his final drachma, despite the gold drachma appearing in his hand. "Let's play again."

River raised his spectral eyebrows in genuine surprise. "What is this subterfuge? Do you jest?"

"I dare not with an esteemed master." Alistair smiled. "We'll play differently this time."

Alistair quickly explained the rules of ultimate tic-tac-toe, a game that he wasn't super familiar with but had played with his sister as a kid. It was essentially playing nine games of tic-tac-toe at once, each game determining a place on the tenth, ultimate game board. She crushed him all the time back then, but he wasn't a kid anymore.

"One thing," Alistair said. "If I win, you have to stop the rest of the ghosts from harming anyone for the rest of the wave."

"This cannot be done," River said, shaking his head. "The restrictions are too binding."

"Better to die free than live as a slave," Alistair said. "All things are impermanent. If you don't want to play, then I have my priorities, which are to the people I have to protect."

River stroked his beard, though the spark in his eyes told Alistair he would not refuse. "You drive a hard bargain. Another game it is!"

The old man spirit conjured the nine boards for them to play with ease. They played for several hours. River was an admirable opponent, putting up a solid fight, but Alistair had an advantage—Dev'rox. The imp was a master of games, including ultimate tic-tac-toe. It was unfair given that River had been reduced from whatever great being he was in his life to a husk used by the Sublimed Machine, but that was the only reason why Alistair went for this approach to begin with. If he actually thought the spirit was going to win, he wouldn't have played.

Alistair placed his last stone on the board, securing the victory for his black pieces over River's white. The battle over the nine grids was hard fought.

"Good game," Alistair said, going for a handshake. River obliged, with ectoplasm meeting flesh and age meeting youth.

"Well played," River said. "Well played. Thank you."

His body began flickering. Shackles appeared around his wrists, ones that Alistair knew were always there, but invisible and undetectable to his Foundation eyes. Indecipherable maze-like hieroglyphs glowed on the manacles, brimming with power. They twisted in fractal formations of increasing complexity.

Cracks spread across the spirit's body, starting from a decrepit soulcore that became visible through the flickers.

"I had help," Alistair admitted. "I'm sorry for sullying the game like that."

"Nonsense." River Flowing Towards An End shook his head with a mournful smile. "As long as the game was good, what does that matter? You gave me a taste of the old days. For that, I am grateful. Your wish is granted. My friends won't bother your people anymore."

"Can you tell me your name, at least?" Alistair asked. "Your real name, or the name of your civilization?"

"As all things will one day be, even that has been lost to time."

The cracks consumed the ancient being from the inside out, and the soul itself shattered into a million pieces. Dev'rox confirmed wordlessly Alistair's assumption. It was a true souldeath. There was no coming back from that.

The five pieces of drachma Alistair used for his first game were still on the board River had conjured. The little makeshift board outlived its creator.

He used the tic-tac-toe board and the drachma to make a makeshift grave for River. A notification informed him that he'd reached level 61, an extremely fast turnaround from level 60. It made sense, since River was like the kaiju equivalent of the Mindaugust's Trial, if not greater. But he was also more than that.

Alistair had a difficult time deciding what to write for an epitaph for someone he knew for only a scant few hours.

His final decision read, "Here lies a man once called River Flowing Towards An End. He saw the peaks and lived to tell the tale."

45 THE LAST BURIAL

JUNIPER REMEMBERED the face of that man on the TV so clearly. There was no emotion. It was like he was dealing with ants, creatures so far beneath his notice that their deaths were meaningless.

She remembered the skeletons that killed her best friend on the way home from school. She remembered one of them slicing off her father's hand and foot, and him barely surviving thanks to the quick thinking from her mother.

She remembered huddling in groups as it dawned on them that this was real life. That modernity was destroyed, technology vanished. They were back to the law of the jungle.

She remembered her parent's faces of joy, and her own, when her brother Ryan came back to them. Her brother was strong, unlike the rest of them. He had killed many of the monsters on his own. He was the only one that stood up to the tyrant that took over their small community with the lucky Skills he'd received.

She remembered that as the ugly monsters of the Pathfinder AI faded, human monsters remained. Their tiny subregion ping-ponged back and forth between freeholds. They were slaves to whomever held onto power.

Ryan wanted to fight back. But he was too weak. They all were too weak. This world was unfair.

The tyrants got lucky, she knew. They weren't better than anyone else.

They weren't more worthy. They killed a few monsters at the beginning and then it all compounded from there.

Their parents were the ones that were furthest behind, especially Juniper's dad. Because of his missing dominant hand and foot, he couldn't fight.

Her mother, who was the most nonviolent and non-athletic person she had ever met, had risen to the occasion and leveled up through hunting the weaker monsters and beasts. She was still weak, and as a mostly sedentary and disabled middle-aged woman, she had a harder starting point.

There were rumors of disabled people finding other methods to power than physical violence, but Juniper's parents weren't so fortunate.

When they heard about the Northeast Order Freehold, whose borders were only two hundred miles away, that became their salvation. Especially for her dad. It was like Shangri-La to them. A mythical place where people lived without the threat of constant violence.

Under the cover of darkness, they set out, fleeing the southern powers that were bleeding soldiers in an everlasting war for supremacy in the region.

Juniper used her nature-related Skills and Dao Inspiration to hide them from monsters and beasts and humans alike. The northeastern freeholds were more organized and larger, so they had cleared more of the threats, but they weren't perfect. There were many close calls as they journeyed north.

It took two days of travel. Two days where they were always looking over their shoulder, worried about death looming around every corner. Yet they made it.

Their story was not uncommon. Thousands of families, groups, and individuals had heard through the grapevine that there was a place that wasn't a hotbed of murder and robbery. When you had lost all other hope, why not risk it all?

Juniper understood that they had gotten very lucky. Most of the people who started that trek had died along the way, falling prey to the monsters, inhuman and human, that roamed every street and forest.

Once they arrived, they were sent to the capital like everyone else. They had to register as citizens and anyone above a certain level was drafted into their army.

Juniper watched her brother with tears in her eyes. They had just made it to safety, and he was already going back in. He kissed her forehead and told her that everything would be alright.

And it was. Ryan's talents weren't as useful on the battlefield, but he joined the Information Branch under a scary-looking man named Caren Locasta. She couldn't explain it, but he gave her a chill along the back of her neck, like he was a deadly force that could kill her any second. Ryan insisted that he was a really nice guy, so she let go of her first impressions.

Because of her brother's position, which kept rising as he proved himself useful with his ability to see from the eyes of insects, their station kept improving. They got to move close to the center of the capital, with apartments that had modern-esque amenities.

Her mother and father had all but forgotten their time in the mud. It was easy to forget, when times were good.

Juniper got it. Like many people, they didn't want to remember what humanity was capable of. What the universe was capable of. It was easier to forget, to drink and party.

But Juniper did not pretend to forget. When she saw the fifth wave of [Armageddon], she knew what she had to do.

Wave 5: The Tutorial

Some of you might have been wondering why there was no tutorial for the initiation. For millions of years within the Final Frontier Empire, newly initiated worlds DID receive a tutorial. However, this program was cut during the reign of the 11th Fell Emperor, Kan Hyphas Laketor, citing the high expense for little gain.

However, thanks to the fifth wave of [Armageddon], you now have the chance to experience The Tutorial in all its glory.

While the leaders and elites of polities represent the majority of their strength, the importance of the average citizen is often understated. An empire built on weak foundations will find it difficult to stand the test of time. As such, The Tutorial will only be provided to those below the top 1,000 on FX-14752's rankings.

When this prompt ends, all 569,123,856 humans fitting the criteria will be transported to a physical demiplane to undergo a specialized, month-long version of The Tutorial. The difficulty will be increased to an appropriate level from the base version.

Many of you have been riding on the coattails of the elite. This is not acceptable. The mortality rates of The Tutorial will heavily depend on how prepared the average citizen of your freeholds is. Previous trials have had between 5.1% and 95.9% mortality rates, showing how much it depends on your own personal strength.

Those that thrive in The Tutorial will experience massive gains in strength, and be able to stand toe-to-toe with many of the current elites. Those that merely survive will still see gains.

The top 1,000 will be pitted together in a Swiss-style tournament of competitive challenges, with playoffs for the top 8. Contribution Score will be awarded thusly to both the elites and the tutorial takers.

[Armageddon] features a special rule regarding Contribution Score and the sixth wave. If the margin of difference in Contribution between the two highest freehold owners is greater than 5%, the scores at the end of The Tutorial shall be used for determining the Global Mayor.

The sixth wave, titled Armageddon, will then only be used to test the population one last time. However, if there is a 5% or smaller margin of difference, then a special trial will be held for both parties to settle the winner, who will then receive the Global Mayorship.

Let The Tutorial begin!

———

"Baba, I can get you someone to help you," Alistair pleaded for what felt like the hundredth time. It was probably close to that, despite not getting to his father very often. "You're blind. You're going to hurt yourself."

"Nonsense," his father said. "Haven't you forgotten I'm a cultivator? I'm sturdy as an oak."

"I'm not worried about you falling," Alistair said, shaking his head. He was finishing up making one of the side dishes for their dinner, sweet potatoes with caramelized sugar. "You can't get around the house. Your Class is so restrictive."

"I don't mind. My son is the most important man on the planet. That is all I need."

"That's not even related— Ah, whatever. No aide it is." Alistair knew better than to argue with his father.

Evangeline poked his shoulder. "The guests are hungry. Almost done?"

"You can't rush culinary genius," Alistair shot back. "But yes, just a minute."

The fifth wave was the one that Alistair had been dreading the most. After the third and fourth waves, he was expecting something crazy, a finisher that would be utterly devastating.

The Tutorial did not fit his expectations, yet it was almost worse. For almost all of humanity, he could do nothing. Nothing except the institutions he had already created. The People's Legion would still have the majority of its captains. That there were such complex systems in place helped him cope, but it also worried him.

Where would the Northeast Freehold's people fall on that gradient the text of the Quest described? In some ways, by protecting everyone, even the weakest people, he might be increasing the death rates. But he also provided cultivation resources far more freely than others might have. He had no way of knowing if the Imperial Army formations would be applicable within The Tutorial.

On the outside, the tournament was easy. The Devil Kings didn't get to participate, or maybe they had their own tournament. The matches were staggered so that they were every other day, the last week allocated for the top eight matches.

Just in the next few days would be the conclusion of the fifth wave, something that Alistair could hardly believe. Things were flying by way too fast. But he was looking forward to the conclusion of the top four.

After the ten Swiss rounds, the top eight in order were Alistair, Pharaoh,

Alexandra, Bartholomew, Brigid, Whimsy, and Oliver. Alistair was the only undefeated participant, the rest being at 9 wins, 1 loss.

The tournament matches were things like who could escape a specialized prison the fastest, or who could accumulate the most kills when faced with an endless horde of zombies.

There was environmental trickery like who could scale a mountain of machinery the quickest, or throw the most powerful punch.

Over all ten rounds, the types of challenges balanced out so that no cultivator's singular path was favored. Still, an all-rounder like Alistair benefited greatly from the variety.

Alistair was looking forward to seeing who would join him in the finals. He had eliminated Pharaoh in his own semifinal match, which had the two of them competing to defeat a nigh-unkillable vampiric troll the fastest.

On the other side of the bracket were Bartholomew and Alexandra. He was holding out hope for his first friend to win, but the betting market was heavily favoring the Supersoldier. Alexandra had squeaked by a win in the quarterfinals against Oliver, who was also an underdog, leading to her poor odds.

No one died, and no one got permanently injured. It felt like a mockery, considering all the chaos that was surely taking place on The Tutorial side of things.

The Pathfinder AI, and the Final Frontier Empire, couldn't be content with devastating Earth ten times over, they had to make some ironic statement about power. Separating the elites from the general population to "teach a lesson." What lesson?

Alistair couldn't stop thinking about his brief moment with River Flowing Towards An End. Was it the Sublimed Machine that stole the spirit's dignity? What crime did his people commit against the faction that stood atop the Dao of Technology, if their writings were to be believed?

The Final Frontier Empire's "lesson" was cut from the same cloth. Their ways were not Alistair's way. River was right about one thing. Alistair would need a lot of power. Power to shake the pillars of creation.

Alistair almost got scalding oil over his hands as he flinched in surprise. Not that it would have burned him. "Yes?"

"No need to be so jumpy, Alistair," Alexandra said, punching his shoulder. "The sweet potato's done. You're going to burn it."

"Ah, my bad." Alistair turned off the stove and put his dish on a plate, bringing it to the table of ravenous guests.

What was supposed to be a family dinner of his baba, Evangeline, and himself had ballooned in size. Oliver had never found his relatives, so he had nowhere to go. John wasn't his normal self with Donna and Tamia in pressing danger.

Alistair was ashamed of himself that he had forgotten about his friends. Nathan and Tommy, and his ex-girlfriend. None of them were in the top thousand, so they were in The Tutorial as well.

Somewhere along the way, Pharaoh and Whimsy got invited, then Caren tagged along with Bark-Al and Melody. Jason, the giant with Cthonic ancestry, was off partying. Alistair was somewhat surprised that they had all made it to the top one thousand, but it made sense.

Caren was one of Alistair's closest allies and wielded considerable power and influence on his own. His three closest friends were lifted by the rising tide.

After Bark-Al and Melody weaseled their way into the family dinner, Alistair set a hard limit. No more—ten was already plenty.

They made an overabundant amount of food for all the cultivators who would use this chance to devour anything edible. Of course, Alistair prided himself on his cooking and, together with his family, they made some damn good Shandong cuisine.

As everyone dug into their food, the barriers came down. Now that he considered it, he was the only linking factor between everyone at the table. But even though his family didn't know Caren's group, and Oliver didn't know Pharaoh very well, everything worked out.

They laughed, and they ate. They shared their stories.

"I don't know where I came from in the before," Bark-Al said without a trace of emotion. "Perhaps someplace with a lot of sun. My bark is fairly dark."

The tree-man definitely didn't mean that as a joke, but he got laughs anyway.

"I'm not as high-leveled as all you human folk. Trees grow slowly. But we don't stop growing. One day, I'll be as big as the Earth."

"May we rest under your shade?" Pharaoh asked. "I think I would like that."

"My branches are open to all my friends," Bark-Al said, showing a rare smile. "Pharaoh, I now consider you a friend. Therefore, I will welcome you with a willing trunk."

Whimsy clapped. "Friendship. What a beautiful thing."

"Alistair, how did we become friends?" Alexandra asked innocently. "You were punching people and I called you out on your shit technique, isn't that right?"

"I recall you being a spoiled rich girl who was failing law school. Wouldn't be surprised if you paid off your opponent in that 'semi-pro' MMA match."

"I was *not* failing," Alexandra retorted. "I have no idea where you got that idea from, and that match was totally legit."

"MMA?" John asked. "I would have thought that would be Alistair's thing, given his abilities."

"No, I picked that up over time," Alistair said. "But the Holy Ravine cemented it."

Alistair gave a summary of his time with the Silver Comet Sect. He explained the politics, the weird quirks like their acceptance of dragonborn empires as nothing out of the ordinary, and the people. He missed Pike and Izalia and Master Ko Pao.

Over a few hours, the conversation and plates dwindled. Caren and his group were the first to go, then Pharaoh and Whimsy. Oliver and John excused themselves not long after, and finally, it was the three Tans.

"It's time now, right, baba?" Alistair asked.

"It is time," he agreed.

Alistair arranged for a **Teleportation Circle** straight to the site, so that his father didn't have any issues. They chose the highest hill within the capital borders, a grassy knoll that was fitting for a grave.

They would never find his mother's body. His father had kept a photograph of her in his wallet, which they copied. Evangeline burned some of the incense and money with a Skill. It was just the three of them.

Alistair lowered the picture into the grave. It was her and her husband on the day of their wedding. She was beautiful, a memory forever trapped within the confines of the photograph and within his father's heart. Most of the people in the background were dead.

His father didn't even know the protocols for what to do when the deceased's body was unrecoverable. They stuck to the tradition, turning away from the grave.

They threw handfuls of dirt into the little hole Alistair made. He was barely holding on, the deluge of emotions that he had bottled up since the first time he heard the news ready to be released.

His father was the last to throw. "Liyuan," he whispered softly. He said some more words, but it wasn't Alistair's place to listen.

Evangeline began to sob. Alistair might have joined her, he wasn't really sure. The experience was a blur. He remembered coming back, full of a numb sadness that didn't want to end.

"I'm sure she was a good woman," Dev'rox said. "Everything is change-able, everything appears and disappears; there is no blissful peace until one passes beyond the agony of life and death."

"Dhammapada," Alistair murmured, recognizing the quote from a Buddhist text. "How can a Dao archetype be so strong that entire scriptures are reproduced, verbatim?"

"Stop thinking so much and rest."

"I can't," Alistair said. "Not until there is a last little boy in the multi-verse who has to suffer like me now." He let Gu Fuhao's azure disc play. Her voice was soothing, her tones painting a vivid image in Alistair's head. He chose a song that spoke of springtime and growth. The blooming of flowers and the beginnings of new life.

"I believe you," Dev'rox said. "I believe you're a fool who would be assailed by great masters of creation if you even make it halfway to your crazy dream, but I believe you."

I'm not alone, Alistair thought to himself. Even when he felt down or disillusioned in his goal, he knew that there were others who shared his aspirations. He would bring Heaven on Earth, and he would have help. His Justice Node stirred with understanding, but he held it back. There was a better time than now.

46 TEAMBUILDING

ALISTAIR, as expected, won the tournament for the fifth wave, reaching level 64. He opened seven more meridians each time. Compared to the surge of power and utility that came with reaching level 60, it wasn't very large, but everything added up.

Leveling to 64 meant that he had added 2-3 levels each month of [Armageddon]. A far cry from his earlier leveling, and actually worse than some of his elites. Most of his closest allies were level 60 or level 61, Bartholomew even getting to level 65. Alistair just leveled up slowly, which he attributed to his Subclass and his really high stats.

Alistair meditated in solitude. There were no distractions.

While the pain of his mother's death was still fresh, it wouldn't affect his performance. He would mourn and he would grieve, but he would move on.

When he exited his seclusion, he was as calm as an unperturbed lake. All his cards had been played. There would be no more tricks of the sort that delayed their battle.

Neither side had broken the truce. There were no loopholes and there was no ducking the fight. Both sides would clash in an epic final battle, with only one walking away.

Alistair was confident that he would win. He was also confident that George thought the same. It would be a clash of two opposing wills.

Besides all of his innate abilities, he had two trump cards to play. The first was the **Heavenly Nectar Incense.** The gourd still contained the concentrated power of a Mana Storm. The second was Drauku's protective jade pendant. He had a strong feeling that he would need both of them.

Three hours before the beginning of the sixth wave, a prompt appeared in his vision.

Wave 6: Armageddon

At this point, factoring in the Pathfinder-approved agreement between George Moulin and Alistair Tan, a meaningful Armageddon will take place between the Northeast Order Freehold and the Cursed Lands.

The full details will be explained in the following Quest screen when Armageddon starts. For now, both sides will need to choose their thirteen participants for Armageddon. The final battle will require strength, guile, and a strong heart. Choose wisely.

Both sides will be able to see the other's selections, starting with the leaders of both teams. Selections shall be chosen every fifteen minutes, with each side locking in a choice within the allotted time frame, or a random citizen of their freehold shall be chosen.

Selections can only be confirmed with an in-person touch. Best of luck to both teams.

While he wasn't expecting those exact stipulations, Alistair was paranoid about something like that, so his people were already gathered. With his Agility and **Fall of Fleet,** he darted through his own capital like a blur to the Leading Domes.

Not that any stealth was required. It was a ghost town, with almost everyone in the world sucked up into The Tutorial. But his sneaky movements were so ingrained, he did them anyway.

The war room was more stuffed than he had ever seen it. Almost everyone of note had gathered there.

Alistair had in mind a list of twelve individuals to make his ideal team, but if others wanted to volunteer, he wouldn't dismiss them out of hand. The sixth wave was going to be deadly, and if anyone wasn't fully committed, they could be a liability. It was better to have someone whose heart was all-in than someone who was 5% stronger.

Alistair saw all the familiar faces at the table. He knew each and every man and woman there, some better than others. They all waited for him to speak first.

"This is it," Alistair said, closing his eyes for a moment. "It's now or never. If you object to my choices, please, speak up. I'm always down to listen. That being said, I hope that no one can contest my first choice. Pharaoh, would you accept?"

"There is nothing I'd rather do," the former #1 said, getting up from his seat.

Alistair and Pharaoh performed their brotherly handshake once more, though Alistair playfully used his martial arts to redirect the tall man into the ground.

"I told you I'd pay you back," he said with a grin.

"I was expecting a lesser Dao Fruit or a Natural Inheritance." Pharaoh's body shifted into sand and reformed in a standing position. "This will do, I suppose."

The system took care of everything once Alistair touched the man with the intent to have him on the team.

A notification appeared to every person in the room.

Northeast Order Freehold:

1. Alistair Tan
2. Pharaoh

"We're going to be sitting for three hours," Alexandra said. "Should we try to decide who's going to be on the team now?"

"Probably a good idea," Alistair admitted. "I have a list of a full team, if nobody has any objections."

Alistair used Celeste's eyebeam projection system to show the room what he was thinking.

Besides himself and Pharaoh who were already officially selected, he had Alexandra, Alfred, Caren, Sally Ryder, William, Bartholomew, Whimsy, Marzhan, Brigid, Jesse, and Oliver.

It was a solid team, if Alistair said so himself. A good combination of offense and defense, long-range and short-range, information and reconnaissance. A team he could be confident in when everything was on the line.

"I can't."

Alistair turned to a woman that had vexed him in the past with her reticence to join the Northeast Freehold despite the imminent dangers. Former President Sally Ryder, who had officially renounced her American office.

"Why not?" Alistair asked. He was thinking she would be an important asset. Her unified form was even stronger than Pharaoh, if only for a few minutes.

"The same reason I failed at the tournament," she explained. "The limit is thirteen people, so I would need to absorb everyone beforehand. Even with my improvements, I can only hold the fusion for one hour in non-combat situations, and fifteen minutes in combat situations. I don't think they would even allow me to go in with my people fused, in which case, I'm useless. I can also only fuse with people who I'm closest to, and there's a limit to how powerful they can be, so using someone like you or Pharaoh would be a waste."

"Can't argue with that," Alistair said. "Then we have one spot. Any volunteers?"

There wasn't an obvious replacement for Sally's spot. He had a number of candidates, but they were all around equal in his head, so anyone who really wanted to join would rise by that factor alone.

"Boss. If you go with me, you won't be disappointed." Blaise Blanchett stood up. The powerfully built man's hair had grown into long brown tussles, making him look like a wild man that hadn't seen the light of civilization in decades. He tapped his enormous compound bow, which had a draw weight dozens of times the highest ever used by archers in the before. "I'm long range. You don't have too much of that. Marzhan and I together can offer suppressive fire better than just one."

He wasn't the only one.

After Blaise broke the floodgates, over a dozen more people volunteered. There was Fasha binti Iksandar, Alistair's ally during the second trial of

[The Game of Life]. She had the Entropic Healer Class, allowing her to heal wounds by reversing entropy. She wasn't ranked in the top 100 and might be a liability in combat, but her healing was considered the best in the world.

There was Carlos Garcia, the #10 ranker. In raw power, by all rights, he should have been on the team. The only issue was that his abilities mirrored Alistair's own. He relied on an incredible sense of smell, tied to a danger sense second to, as you might expect, only Alistair. He was a close combat fighter who had also taken Magical Pugilist, but evolved it in a different direction based on wild instincts, where he copied the forms and spirits of animals.

There was Celeste Mendoza. The raven-haired woman had dozens of ports all over her body, eyeballs that could project holographic video, a memory surpassing even Caren and Skills that were top-notch in the world at long distance communication. Like Fasha, she was no fighter.

There was Robert Oakland. Alistair had known that guy since the beginning of initiation. He didn't even have any special powers. He had one of the basic common Classes. All that was going for him was his level and his gumption. Alistair had to respect him for that.

There was Ramesh Vishwakarma, the #13 ranker. He had kept his low teens position after falling from #8 earlier on. Alistair wasn't too familiar with Ramesh, but knew he had an artisanal Class and was responsible for developing valyrik and then ambrosic glass. He was the guy in Asia to have upgraded the Soulnet. Also, not a fighter.

There was Allegra Wood, cousin to Alfred and Bartholomew. A Beast Tamer of considerable might. Alistair could tell she was dealing with her uncle's disappearance poorly. A strong candidate, but the glint in her eyes worried him. Would she be a team player?

Finally, there was Evangeline Tan. Alistair's sister. A Spiritualist who could manipulate the souls of the living. Alistair wanted with all his heart to say she couldn't join. That she wasn't allowed.

That kind of thinking wasn't appropriate for his status as leader. She was her own woman; if she was the most qualified, he could not deny her.

The major candidates debated amongst themselves, and with the other guaranteed members of the team on his list. Alistair mostly stayed out of it. He wanted to hear everyone else's opinion.

Slowly, the teams accumulated. After the eleventh member, there were only thirty minutes left.

Northeast Order Freehold:

1. Alistair Tan
2. Pharaoh
3. Alexandra Lykaios
4. Bartholomew Wood
5. Oliver Cambry
6. Marzhan Suleimenova
7. Whimsy
8. Brigid Mwangi
9. Jesse Waterfall
10. Caren Locasta
11. William St. James

The Cursed Lands:

1. George Moulin
2. Morgana
3. Shadow Twin Dark
4. Jakk
5. Hephaestus
6. Heavyset
7. Pride Lord
8. Vritra
9. Flesh Golem #1
10. Flesh Golem #2
11. Flesh Golem #3

There was quite a heated discussion both for who the thirteenth spot should go to, and the nature of the "flesh golems." Alistair had been wondering how the Devil Kings were going to fill their spots, and besides the Pride Lord and Vritra, who had been given demon blood, they circumvented that problem entirely with the flesh golems.

Alistair used Oracle's memories to make an educated guess. With

Hephaestus having similar powers to John Desmond, it was possible that they combined his forging with some dark arts of Morgana to create super-soldiers. But that wasn't the only possibility.

As for the debate on Sally's replacement, there were two main candidates. Blaise Blanchett, and Alistair's sister.

That was mostly why Alistair recused himself. Because as much as he tried to be impartial, he couldn't. Not when it came to Angie.

"This bow was half-constructed from the remains of the Daywalker Ape," Blaise said. "This item is one of the highest quality on the planet. My rank is slightly lower than yours, but my utility makes up for that."

Evangeline opened her mouth to speak, but then she made eye contact with Alistair. A knowing glance passed between the two of them. She took a deep breath. "I won't challenge you anymore, Blaise. Take the spot. You earned it."

Blaise looked taken aback, but nodded. "Thank you."

Alistair clapped. "That settles it, then! Blaise, you'll be our next member."

He mouthed "thanks" to his sister, who winked back. By patting Blaise on the shoulder, he anointed him the twelfth member of their squad. That left the last member. Alfred.

However, something felt off to Alistair. He turned inward, filing through his senses. There was a current of Fate, perhaps. The thread grew and grew under his nose. He didn't believe it at first, not until the others began to realize. Someone was at the door.

"You're alive," Alfred said, wiping tears from his face.

Bartholomew rushed the man entering the room, Allegra joining him.

"Children, niece," he said. "It's so good to see you."

Lucius Wood was alive.

If Alistair was expecting him to look like Blaise, as if he had been living in the wilds for the nearly six months he was missing, he would be dead wrong.

Lucius was radiant. He wore a tailored suit, his blond hair buzzed against his head. There were a few new scars marring his dark skin, ones that still felt cold even from afar.

While his aura was nothing special, he bent all the threads of Fate around him like a black hole of fortune. He had depth that was lacking before, and Alistair could tell that he had not been unoccupied for the months he was gone.

"Lucius," Alistair said. Their relationship had started with a temporary alliance, borne from a common enemy. They had fought together against the Devil Kings, and then Alistair had outsmarted him. Now there could be no mistake. They would fight together as two humans who didn't want to see their world overtaken by George and his demons.

"Alistair," Lucius said, his intense voice dripping with charisma. "I see you've taken good care of my kin."

"Only what you would have done for me," Alistair replied. "We all thought you were dead. Your name was scraped from the leaderboards. Where were you?"

"It is a long tale, a long tale, my friend." Lucius sat down at the opposite end from Alistair, where no one had dared sit opposite the head of the table. "Better told when we celebrate our victory. Suffice to say, after [The Game of Life] merged all the continents into a new Pangaea, not all the land was incorporated into the main continent. On the exact opposite side of the world, there are a series of large islands, four of which I estimate each to be the size of Madagascar. While a third of the inhabitants come from Earth, the significant majority appear to be from another world. A much more primitive world. With a little bit of luck, I was able to unify this alternative continent under my rule. I only recently was able to return home after purchasing a **Teleportation Circle** with enough range to make it here."

"Not sure what I can say to that," Alistair said.

"Indeed." Lucius grinned. "It is quite the story. There was a barrier that separated our two sides. I think the Pathfinder wanted us to develop separately. In that way, my archipelago was a petri dish, an experimental chamber where the strongest had to vie for a much smaller pie. That is why I was removed from the leaderboards after George almost took my life."

"So that was what happened," Bartholomew murmured.

"And I bring with that experience a warning," Lucius said. "That man's power is unfathomable. I was forced to burn the entirety of my drachma to survive. I've gained strength in strides now, but I would not be confident even now about facing the him of back then."

Alistair nodded solemnly. "We know. We've been preparing for more than two months now. I'm making the teams now. There's only one spot left."

"It's yours, father."

While Bartholomew and his cousin had rushed to hug the Wood patriarch right away, Alistair had noticed Alfred stay in his seat. Their relationship wasn't always the best, he knew. The expression on the Spymaster's face was hard to read.

"Come here, son."

Alfred stayed still, not even looking at his father. Lucius got up from his seat, walking over to his youngest son's chair. "Get up, damn it. It's your father."

Alfred finally got up, hugging Lucius tightly. The tears began to flow.

"I'm sorry I wasn't there for you and Imogen," Lucius said softly. It felt like a violation to hear their conversation, but everyone was paying full attention. "But I'm here now. I'll be taking that spot. There's no need for you to be in danger."

"I'm not a child," Alfred said, the tears drying up. "I know how to handle danger."

"You're not." Lucius nodded. "But this is for an old man like me. You may be smarter than me, but I haven't taught you all my tricks yet. Alistair, you can choose me."

While Alfred would have been an amazing team member, a lot of his capabilities were overlapping with Caren and William. Lucius's abilities were unique in possibly the entire population. No one could replicate his reality warping.

Lucius claimed that Alfred was smarter, but Alistair wasn't so sure. Maybe on an IQ test, but the Quaestor had a wealth of experience that the younger Wood couldn't match. At over fifty years old, he'd be the most seasoned member of the team, though Alistair wasn't exactly sure how old Pharaoh was.

With that, the team was fully assembled. Alistair knighted Lucius, who didn't look amused at the copying of his country's rituals.

Of the thirteen men and women comprising the final lineup, none of them looked scared. That was their prerogative. Alistair didn't mind if they were afraid or not. Fear was a natural response to an overbearing threat. What he trusted was that they would overcome their fear. That they would fight with everything they had.

The clock slowly ticked down to zero. A tiny anxiety left him when the Contribution Score equalized between him and George five minutes before.

There had always been a thread of worry that the leader of the Devil Kings had tricked him in some way.

Alistair knew he was in perfect physical and mental condition. This was it.

He thought that nothing could throw him off. But when he viewed the finalized team lists for the Northeast Order Freehold and the Cursed Lands in the last second before being teleported to wherever the final wave was starting, he realized something was wrong. Very wrong.

47 ARMAGEDDON: ARMAGEDDON

ALISTAIR STARED at the team lists as the world faded into a white void.

Wave 6: Armageddon

Welcome to the last part of the last Quest. During the initiation, you have grown together and fought together, now you will either evolve together or die together.

Two teams of thirteen vie for the position of Global Mayor, the planetary lord of FX-14752. As the 5% condition was reached between the two highest individuals, the Contribution Score is voided and the Global Mayor shall be determined by the outcome of this wave.

The twenty-six initiates shall be transported to a physical demi-plane called "Eden," the representation of a city not dissimilar from many in the Final Frontier Empire. They shall not leave until one team walks out victorious by killing every member of the enemy team or by completing the missions that will be delineated within Eden.

The dangers of this wave are deadly and permanent. There will be no revivals. Participants that die within Eden are truly dead, never to return.

For the others, congratulations on returning from the Tutorial. With an exceptional 95.0% survival rate, FX-14752 has one of the highest in the history of initiations. With your recent improvements comes the greatest challenge yet—a thousand-member elite squad of the Final Frontier Empire's military.

They will suppress themselves to below your power and attempt to take over the world. Besides the massive cost of life if they are successful, losing will draw the ire of your own elites, who will be penalized for the weakness of their subordinates with heavy taxes.

Let Armageddon begin!

His compartmentalized mind grokked the text for the sixth wave, but he couldn't stop looking at the finalized list.

"Stop," Alistair said. They all listened.

Alexandra furrowed her brow. "What's wrong?"

"Look at the enemy team." He pointed up. "Where's Chameleon? They have five flesh golems, but no Chameleon."

"Maybe he got left behind," Blaise said. "They think they will win."

"Caren, explain Chameleon's powers once more for me."

Caren used one of the specialized glass wands that allowed him to show pre-downloaded imagery.

"Chameleon, the Fifth Devil King. Our only intel on what he looks like, if he is indeed a he, comes from Oracle's memories that Alistair stole. **Annalist's Aid** had trouble picking up the detail, but he should look like a half-metamorphosed chameleon-man if that is his true form."

Caren showed a blurry yet grotesque image of Chameleon as Oracle remembered him.

"His shapeshifting abilities are second-to-none in the entire world. Sorry, Alistair, that's about as much as we know for sure. Your memories didn't have much about him, and all we know is that he infiltrated the United Polities undetected."

"It's a question of do we think it's possible that he could bypass the Karmic Gel? And fool the Pathfinder AI."

Oliver's eyes widened in sudden realization of what Alistair was implying. "You think Chameleon is here, right now. Taking the place of someone on the team, like in The Thing."

Alistair shook his head. "It's a suspicion."

With that, the group of thirteen erupted. Their surroundings changed from the white void to what appeared to be a police interrogation room. The idea that there was a shapeshifted infiltrator among them became all-consuming.

Alistair felt uneasy as he came to the understanding that he did not know what to do. That simple fact was uncomfortable. There was nothing in the manual to prepare him for dealing with an undetectable traitor. Thankfully, Lucius stepped up.

Lucius, who was also the most suspect of everyone.

Alistair didn't want to think of that possibility. Alfred and Bartholomew just got their father back. It would be a tragedy to lose him again. But the idea seeped into his mind and didn't let go.

"I've just returned, and I don't know much about this Chameleon," Lucius said. "However, we cannot sit still and discuss this forever. Look at the mission."

Armageddon Mission #1 of 5 (Team Northeast Order):
Free Prisoner #1209 from maximum security lockup.

Lucius continued, "If they finish all the missions first, we could lose without even a fight. We're either going to settle this Chameleon business now, and quickly, or put it to the side."

"He's right," Alistair said. "William, what do you think?"

Alistair of course referred to his [Hypercalculative Induction], which allowed him to reach conclusions with the scantest of evidence. The slight man adjusted his cosmetic sunglasses that, as far as Alistair knew, didn't even have an enchantment.

"I don't see it." William pursed his lips. "Fuck, everything's so cloudy. So many people and factors."

Other than William sniffing things out, Alistair believed his own [Eyes of Truth] were the best detection mechanism. However, if Chameleon was truly able to bypass the Karmic Gel with his mimicry, then he doubted that [Eyes of Truth] would be enough. But he tried anyway.

As he expected, [Eyes of Truth] detected nothing. Lucius glowed brightly in the Karmic vision, but he always did that. No one looked wrong or off-putting.

The most annoying part was that standard infiltration measures were useless against a near-perfect mimic like Chameleon. Based on the report, he could take people's memories and replicate abilities.

Marzhan knew better than most. "If he ever shows his face, I'll sense it right away. I'll never forget that bastard," she said.

Alistair was fairly certain he couldn't manage to copy something of greater power than him. There was balance in all things—if you wanted greater power than your station allocated, you had to take out an advance on something important to you.

From his estimation of the Devil Kings' power levels, the safe targets were Pharaoh, Alexandra, Bartholomew, and possibly Lucius. Everyone else, he expected was weak enough the Fifth Devil King could copy them.

The sad part was, what could he do? He would have to observe them closely, but with no way to find Chameleon, hurting their progress on the missions wouldn't do any good.

"Let's table this for now," Alistair ordered. "Don't be paranoid, but be alert. If anyone does anything out of the ordinary, report it to me right away. With that in mind, because of the potential for a spy, if you find anything important about the Devil Kings or the missions, please inform me before anyone else, and then I'll determine what to do from there."

"Keep it down in there, scum!" a voice called from behind the glass. "Prisoners aren't allowed to fraternize."

The sudden interruption called Alistair's attention to his surroundings. The room they were in was small, barely fitting all thirteen people inside. There were no doors, no decorations, only a translucent navy blue glass that had a strange depth to it, like it went on forever. The only indication that they weren't in some infinite chamber was a window that took up the majority of one of the walls.

The window showed a pitch black void, but when the voice spoke, the outer hinges of the window glowed white and Alistair could just make out the shaded silhouette of a person.

Alistair put a hand to his lips and motioned for Caren to do his thing. The Chronicler installed his **[Paper Tongue]** slips, allowing them to communicate telepathically. The Skill had improved to work in a three-mile radius from Caren, meaning that two people on the outer edges of his range could communicate through him over a six-mile distance.

"Testing, testing," Caren thought. Everyone gave a thumbs up. *"We're good."*

"What is this game the Pathfinder AI is making us do?" Brigid asked. *"Freeing a prisoner is such a random ask."*

Alistair went over to the glass, feeling its integrity.

"Get the fuck away from the glass, prisoner!" the voice shouted. Alistair could make out some of the features of the man behind the glass. He had deep wrinkles and wore a huge ring around his neck.

Alistair felt right away upon touching the glass that it did not have enough spirituality to resist his ethereal body. If he used the Ghost Node to etherealize himself, he could slip through without issue.

Alistair issued a telepathic order. *"Let me do my thing."*

Drinking from the Ghost Node, Alistair imbued Dao energy throughout his entire body, flooding every open meridian. He became detached from the causality of the world like all ghosts, fulfilling his preordained purpose.

Alistair's ghost flew through the glass and through the man, turning back into the normal Alistair right away. The poor guard didn't have a chance. Alistair applied a rear naked choke, and the guard was out within two seconds, though the golden ring made it a bit harder than usual.

Before his two buddies could even react, Alistair grabbed the two of them and slammed their heads into each other. The three guards formed a pile on the floor of what he considered to be a very strange-looking room.

To Alistair, it looked like a living machine. There was more of the strange glass that looked deeper than it really was, on top of silver metal that slithered and contracted like it was alive. From the outside perspective, he could see everything inside the cell perfectly. Dozens of sticky, organic-looking buttons lined the room.

Thankfully, the translation service within his soulcore covered the script underneath the buttons. He braved his fears and pressed the buttons, which squished with an uncomfortable juicy noise. One of the walls of the room trapping his allies disappeared soon after. Alistair breathed a sigh of relief when he could finally stop holding the buttons and wiped off the goo on the outfit of one of the guards.

"What is this place?" Alexandra said aloud, and he didn't blame her.

Dozens of tunnels connected to the outside room in every direction—on the ceiling, below the floor. It was hard to say it was even a room, more like a node in an expansive network of branching tendrils. The one below the floor was blocked by the same kind of translucent glass, opened by one of the button combinations.

"Wake one of them up," William said, pointing to the unconscious guards. "I can probe for information on the Prisoner #1209."

Alistair pressed a new button combination, which caused a chair of the living metal to spike out of the ground. Alexandra, with more roughness than was necessary, hoisted the guard who'd yelled at them onto the chair, using her [Healing Current] to heal any damage to his brain and waking him up.

The man sputtered around in his seat, eyes rolling to the back of his head before he finally woke up. He was a portly, middle-aged man with balding black hair in a comb over. If he was a real person, he was most likely at the level 60 bottleneck as a non-combat Class, and also in the last third of his life. Cultivators aged differently, experiencing the decline in a short period near the end, which was more or less compressed depending on one's strength.

"Don't look at them, look at me." William stared into the man's eyes. An [Eyes of Truth] revealed that his name was Eiyo Morozuki. "If you want to speak to them, you can do so in the afterlife."

In that moment, William felt less like the carefree jokester that Alistair had come to know, and more like the frightening psychopath he had seen in [The Game of Life], befitting of his name within the Quest.

"I'm not afraid of death," Eiyo managed bravely, trying to escape the chair. Bone restraints tightened around him, courtesy of Marzhan. "My eternal soul is under the protection of the Prime Thinker. If you want to claim me for a Hell, you will have to take it up with higher management."

"Where is Prisoner #1209?" William asked.

"Why should I tell you that?" The guard, initially having been taken off guard, seemed to calm down once William threatened to kill him. That wasn't normally how things worked, but the guy put a lot of faith in the "Prime Thinker," whoever that was.

"Is he up?" William asked. "Is he down, is he there, is he there, or is he there?"

With each direction, he pointed, and then used his hands to turn the guard's head to where he was pointing. The guard resisted, but his neck muscles were no match for William's Strength.

"You don't fear death, but you are afraid of something," William said. "If I torture you so much that your mind collapses, can this Prime Thinker still save you?"

"The Prime Thinker is more powerful than you can even imagine," Eiyo spat, though Alistair thought he looked afraid. He *smelt* afraid.

[Monk Motionlessness] made Alistair move without thinking, grabbing William and throwing him back. Faster than the blink of an eye, Eiyo Morozuki imploded into metal, his organs erupting from the inside and then freezing in the air as a metal statue. A grotesque display of anatomy, a younger Alistair would have lost his lunch, but he had seen a lot by now.

"Thanks," William said. "He hid that well."

Alistair offered a hand, helping the Farsighter up. "Did you glean anything?"

"Sadly, he died before I could gain too much. My calculations indicate that the prisoner is either up or down. Are you thinking what I'm thinking?"

Splitting up never worked in the movies, but this wasn't a movie. There was no way for the infiltrator to act with everyone keeping a close eye on each other. With their telepathy, as long as they didn't drift too far apart, they could communicate perfectly.

"I'll lead the up team," Alistair said. "Pharaoh, you lead the down team. We'll split up like this…"

———

Chameleon had worn this skin for far too long.

[Skinsteal Camouflage] wasn't meant for long-term periods. He killed the poor human months ago at this point, stepping into their skin as George directed.

He had done so much for the Devil Kings. Stolen from the Hall of Math. Sabotaging any useful cultivation resources he found when he could. Most of all, he hadn't let his chosen identity fall behind.

Alistair was correct in assuming something was awry when Chameleon didn't appear on the Devil Kings' team list, but there was absolutely no way for him to figure out which of his compatriots was secretly a Devil King.

The months of wearing another human's skin were not without their difficulties. For a complete infiltration, he needed to sacrifice his cultivation in order to take on every aspect of his target, from the Karmic history, to the memories, to the Skills.

After his failure in assassinating Sally Ryder and Marzhan Suleimenova, he would not let down his master again.

If it were a perfect world, he could have latched onto Pharaoh's team. While Alistair couldn't figure out who was the infiltrator, he still made Chameleon tread lightly whenever he looked into his eyes.

That man was almost as scary as the master. He looked like he knew things he shouldn't. He had an aura of solidity and unending strength that made the Devil King think his schemes were hopeless.

But he had a greater faith in the master. Everything was going according to plan.

And as the only eligible bachelor among the Devil Kings, he hoped that once he proved his worth on his current mission, Morgana might look his way.

After all, who didn't love a man with a tongue that could snatch flies out of the air?

———

Armageddon Mission #1 (Team Cursed Lands):
Find the terrorist within Broky Corp HQ before he blows up the city block.

George Moulin looked at those words and then at his crazy outfit.

He had a golden ring around his neck that didn't seem to serve any useful purpose. Over his robes was a thin layer of metal shaped into a hanfu robe.

This was the case for all the Devil Kings. The two demonized beasts were given energized collars connected psychically to a baton he was carrying, while the system didn't even bother with the five flesh golems.

Given their lack of other soldiers, Morgana had convinced him the best use of their slots were for the flesh golems. She absorbed them immediately by drawing sacrificial magical arrays underneath them, ascending to a level of power that could rival his own, to a certain extent.

"Those bodies are disgusting," George noted. With the souls absorbed, the heaps of flesh were an inert mishmash of corpses.

"The officers don't seem to mind," Morgana said. "I'd say it's a bargain that I could fit one hundred thousand souls per golem. Half a million ain't bad, is it not?"

George looked at their "commanding officer." Despite the flesh golems being right in front of him, he didn't so much as lift a finger. When George asked him for information, all the man said was "find the terrorist, recruit," and handed him a glowing disc (that was really a reskinned jade slip) displaying the terrorist's hologram.

From their vantage point at the top of a skyscraper, George could view almost the entirety of the so-called Eden.

The cyberpunk city extended four miles in every direction, with their current location at the center. That wasn't his arrogance speaking, but the threads of space literally broke down after that distance, mixing silver strands of spacetime against a true void.

Sixty-four square miles was larger than Manhattan, but it was a small space for the cultivators involved. The two teams could encounter each other at any time.

George took out the Legendary rarity item he won from being the first to complete the Grand Dungeon. The **Divine Mirror.**

The **Divine Mirror** appeared as a circular pane of glass. There was no frame or ornamentation, simply the piece of glass.

George stared at himself in the mirror. The spiky hair really was a ridiculous touch. No matter what he did, he couldn't put down his hair's volume, so it stuck straight up like he was a 90s playboy.

Then, his reflection shifted. It moved without him moving. The original and the reflection became more separated with every second, until they were twinned creations.

A hand breached the unknown world behind the mirror. Out came... another George.

Having served its ultimate purpose, the mirror shattered into a million pieces. That was to be expected. Despite the awesome power of the **Divine**

Mirror, it still could not capture George's true extent. However, the reflection was good enough.

"I live to serve, other me," his reflection said, once he had fully escaped the confines of the mirror.

"Find them," George ordered. "Kill as many as possible before you die."

The other George smiled. "It is done."

48 MISSION #2

On Alistair's side were most of the targets he deemed suspicious.

Marzhan, because he considered it possible that Chameleon had already succeeded in his assassination attempt. Brigid, because while she was very strong, he didn't know her as well. William, since he was weaker. Same for Blaise. And finally, Lucius, for the odd manner of his return.

While he knew that Chameleon could steal people's memories, and therefore imitate their personality, he found it hard to believe he wouldn't have noticed the changes in those that he knew well and seen so often.

By pressing the buttons in a certain configuration, they created a temporary reversal of gravity. The upward tunnel sucked them up until they were solidly within its confines, at which point the direction of gravity went inverse. They were pulled along the surface of the tunnel, so they could stand and walk in any orientation.

Alistair was about to mention the time they were stuck in a Herax Turtle's insides, but he then realized that no one on his side was there at the time. Not even Dev'rox. That ragtag team of himself, his sister, Anthony, and the two Wood brothers felt like a lifetime ago.

"Use the telepathy," Alistair instructed. *"I assume these tunnels connect to the prison. We don't want to alert the guards."*

Before they left, they stuffed the guards in the cells, including the statue of metal that was once poor Eiyo. If all the guards were installed with those bombs, they were going to have to be careful.

They moved through the tunnel as stealthily as they could. William tried to communicate the impressions he retrieved from **[Hypercalculative Induction]**, but as always, there was a certain... difficulty in translating.

"The shiftiness in his eyes when I pointed him in a certain direction... 5% tilt upward and then a slight tremor in his leg, he was hiding something for sure, up or down, I don't know, 65% upward, probably, and then from there, it was hard to discern anything more."

Marzhan patted William on the back. *"We definitely understood all of that."*

"Perhaps if we combine my Skill of manipulating Fate with William's deductions," Lucius butted in.

"Couldn't we have done that before we split up?" Blaise asked.

Lucius pursed his lips. *"I don't trust everyone here."*

But he was the one to suggest we settle it now or functionally act like nothing has happened, Alistair thought to himself. *Does he have a read on who it is?*

"You don't trust us?" Brigid raised an eyebrow. *"We shouldn't trust you, considering the way you showed up last minute."*

"As Lucius said before, fighting does us no good." Alistair broke up the argument before it could begin. *"Lucius, will the combination work?"*

"I believe so. But I'm afraid I'm running a bit low on funds."

Alistair wasn't sure if he fully believed him, but he could afford to be a little generous. "You're in luck. I cashed out all my money from the Moneylender before coming. I've got 5.9 million drachma on hand."

Alistair transferred a million drachma to Lucius. Right away, everyone around him could see thousands of Gold drachma melting and burning, creating a molten gold aura around the man. He went over to William and clasped his hand, the aura transferring over as well.

William's eyes darted from left to right, observing the living steel of the tunnels. There was a rhythmic thumping to the slithering metal, which formed braids that crested and troughed. Then, he ran, laughing like a madman.

"Follow him!" Alistair ordered.

William wasn't running very fast, so it was easy for them to keep up. They eventually came to a part of the tunnel where the braids constricted and thinned out. Alistair's keen sense of smell revealed people below. William came to a halt and pointed down. *"We're close."*

The group of six were already cloaking their auras, so they shouldn't have been detectable. The voices of guards beneath penetrated upward.

"First day on the job?" a gruff voice said.

"That's right," the other one said. "Can't fucking believe I got stuck here."

"You're young," the first one replied. "You got a chance. My fucking blockhead ancestor decided to settle on one of these shithole worlds. Never had a chance to start with."

"My sister's the golden goose, so I think I'll be stuck here a while."

Alistair motioned to his crew, telling them to stay put telepathically. He took on the Ghost Node's energies once more, passing through the cabled steel.

His presence was utterly imperceptible to those who didn't have a fine-tuned aura sense or the ability to perceive souls. Alistair took in his surroundings. Unlike the interrogation room, the guards were stationed in a larger chamber.

A hallway was dimly lit by infrared lamps attached to the doors on either side. There were dozens of doors, going down as far as the eye could see in both directions. Each metal door was spaced around five feet apart from the next, with a number carved in a maze-like script that Alistair could somehow understand. The characters seemed familiar, apart from his understanding, reminding him of River's bindings.

The ones closest to him read #1109, #1110, and #1111.

Bingo, Alistair thought. The braided tunnel ran along the ceiling of the hallway, so he had them follow him as he tiptoed like a poltergeist.

What Alistair presumed were the cell doors blocked out all energy. There wasn't a peep of activity that they could detect. When he tried to penetrate one of them, the metal rebuffed him.

"Looks like it's going to have to be explosive," Alistair communicated to his team. The two guards went in the opposite direction, and the group of six went by undetected.

Once they reached the cell numbered #1209, after he gave the all clear for guards, Lucius pressed a combination of the squishy buttons, and a tear opened in the braided ceiling. They quietly descended from the ceiling, making sure to make as little noise as possible.

Cell #1209 was at the end of a compound, the only one where the door was orthogonal to the hallway. Alistair stared at the geometric etching that formed the meaning of the number. *"Thoughts? No one here has a supreme lockpicking Skill?"* he asked.

"No, sir," William said.

"Nope," Marzhan replied.

Brigid and Blaise shook their heads.

"Then I stand by my earlier statement. Stay back."

With his team a safe distance away, Alistair took on the first form of the Zebra Stance. The most robust base undergirded the most devastating attack. With reaching level 60, all of his Skills had their Mana costs reduced by 15%, while simultaneously improving in the quantity of Mana by around 20%. With activation times down and his stats no longer capped, Alistair's simple [Force Fist] was a terrifying force of nature.

Alistair used his martial forms to deliver one hundred percent of his body's capabilities. A [Force Fist] as large as an exercise ball crashed into the cell door.

To his surprise, the cell didn't collapse. There was an imprint of a huge fist on the door, but only a few inches deep. Almost the moment his [Force Fist] touched the metal, all the lights atop the doors began flashing. A droning siren started, one so loud even Alistair's ears hurt.

Alistair fired a continuous volley of [Force Fist] haymakers. The dent grew bigger and bigger until finally the chunk of metal flew backward. While it only took two seconds to break down, he already smelt guards in the distance.

"I've been waiting for you," a soft voice called.

Alistair glimpsed a dainty pair of hands clasping the broken door. The figure tossed it aside, making eye contact with him.

Prisoner #1209 was a woman with dark skin verging on black, softly glowing white veins visible over her body. A Trexian, Alistair remembered from his time on Faxor. Her accent was similar to Lang Aius's, though not identical, sounding vaguely Eastern European, though that was all the artifice of his soulcore translation.

"You're Prisoner 1209?" Alistair asked.

"In the flesh. Tarnz Auola Kristina, otherwise known as Prisoner 1209. You're with the Resistance, I presume?"

"Let's go with that," Alistair said. "Do you know the way out of here?"

"Hells no," Kristina said. "I thought you'd know. Weren't you the ones to break in?"

"We'll have to improvise."

Armageddon Mission #1 (Free Prisoner #1209 from maximum security lockup) complete.

Armageddon Mission #2 (Team Northeast Order):
Escape Eden Subterranean Prison with Tarnz Auola Kristina.

The second mission flashed in front of Alistair and the rest of his team. He checked in with Caren on the other side.

"I've found the prisoner," Alistair thought. *"Try to find an exit on your side. Whoever finds one first, we'll pivot to their side, unless enough guards block our pathway."*

"Roger that."

Alistair was starting to understand the scenario better. It was like a role-playing game. The people of the demiplane thought that they were members of "the Resistance" that were freeing one of their members from prison.

If we're the Resistance, does that make the Devil Kings the Empire?

If they were freedom fighters, this woman that they'd found was no grunt. Kristina's aura was incredibly condensed in a way quite familiar to Alistair. Whatever Class she had, he knew that she had to have the Dao of the Fist. Seeing his knowing look, she gave him a smile. "It will be a joy to see your fists in battle, comrade."

As his teammates ascended back into the tunnel above the ceiling, Alistair activated **[Frozen Claw]**, making a barrier blocking off the hallway. Marzhan added a layer of bone on top of the ice. While someone at their level could deal with it easily, the guards would be hard-pressed to break through.

Alistair was the last one up into the tunnel, releasing the living metal. By the time he climbed up, an omnipresent voice spoke.

"ATTENTION EDEN! ATTENTION EDEN! THERE HAS BEEN A BREACH OF EDEN SUBTERRANEAN PRISON BY MEMBERS OF THE TERRORIST GROUP KNOWN AS THE RESISTANCE. ALL MEMBERS OF THE EDEN POLICE FORCE ARE REQUESTED TO INTERCEPT THE TERRORISTS, WHO HAVE FREED HIGH-PRIORITY RESISTANCE TERRORIST KNOWN AS TARNZ AUOLA KRISTINA. ALL MEMBERS OF

THE PUBLIC WITH ADEQUATE QUALIFICATIONS ENCOURAGED TO MAKE A CITIZEN'S ARREST."

The voice repeated multiple times as the sirens blazed. Since they knew they were subterranean, going up was their ticket out, though because of the orientation of the tunnel, it was difficult to figure out which was which. William used **[Hypercalculative Induction]** to find clues, but even he took time. Time which they didn't have.

They climbed up to a small enclave which presented two further upward tunnels. The room appeared to be a guard post, but it was empty, with one terminal showing a holographic projection of Kristina's face.

Gravity pointed down instead of outward like before, letting all of them stand up together on the same plane.

"Shit," Blaise swore as he toyed with the buttons. "Because of the lockdown, the buttons don't work anymore. We can't escape the tunnel like that."

"They'll be sending the androids soon," Kristina warned. "They're way tougher than the guards, except for the military ones."

"William?" Alistair asked. "We need you, buddy."

"My brain's going to explode, okay?" William shot back. "There's so little information to go off here."

Marzhan's dominion Skill allowed her to see from any bone that she left within a reasonable distance. She looked up at Alistair, grimacing. "They've sent something stronger. My bones got cut with lasers. And there's some buff-looking guys in like metal raincoats? It's a bit fuzzy."

"And that's going to be the military police and the androids," Kristina said.

"Fuck it, we're choosing the left one," Alistair ordered. "They're only a few hundred feet behind."

As they jumped up to the left tunnel, which reverted to the outward gravity, he got a message from Caren.

"We've made it back to where we started and are climbing up. Encountering powerful hostiles on the way."

"If you think you've got the firepower, clear 'em out," Alistair shot back.

Alistair's danger sense fluttered from above. He instinctively shot out a **[Lightning of Justice]**, illuminating the dimly lit tunnel with a bolt of golden lightning.

Up above, dozens of robotic spiders short-circuited, with many others losing limbs from the searing bolt. But wherever one fell, there were two more to take its place in a swarm of giant spiders. They were silver like the rest of the tunnel, with glowing red eyes that gave off artificial killing intent.

Kristina cracked her knuckles. "Leave it to me."

In a burst movement similar to Alistair's **[Dash]**, she charged straight for the horde. A jet of air appeared behind her elbow as she winded up a punch. The telegraphed blow boomed in the air. It was the single fastest strike he had ever seen, surpassing his visual acuity.

She destroyed hundreds of spider robots in a single blow, but more importantly, the leftover effects of her Skill created a wind tunnel that blocked the remaining arachnids. They took the opportunity to pass by, reaching a thin layer of the navy blue glass.

Alistair could smell the panicking people above. They had to be close to the base layer of the prison.

A scarlet column of light appeared behind them, out coming the other seven members of the team. Jesse was last, giving Alistair a wink.

*They must have used Caren's spatial mapping via **[Paper Mind]** to let Jesse teleport them. But that's at the cost of quite a bit of Mana...*

No one could deny how useful Jesse Waterfall was. He'd saved their asses multiple times in Capture the Beacon against the Devil Kings. Mass teleportation was one of the most broken abilities.

"*Dangerous things below. Explain later,*" Caren thought, pointing at the layer.

Say no more. Alistair and Kristina rose at the same time. She used her previous air jet behind the elbow move, while he delivered a **[Force Fist]**.

The glass shattered violently. Azure plasma beams rained down from every direction the moment they dared peek their heads above the ground. Time moved in slow motion as Alistair perceived the incoming danger with **[Monk Motionlessness]**.

He scanned the setting. They appeared to be on the base floor of a spacious lobby. There were two floors that he could see, with one spiral staircase in the middle of a crystal pond leading straight into the second floor. The second floor only occupied around half of the first, with an open edge overlooking the lower area.

Dozens of men in black armor wielded slim assault rifles, each attached with a luminescent blue canister instead of a magazine. They lined the edge on the second floor and the first floor. Ten-foot-tall automatons in the form of humanoid puppets supported the riflemen, wielding laser swords of varying colors.

A red and gold automaton that looked more like an astronaut suit built like a brick shithouse stood near the entrance. Alistair could see daylight streaming through the glass only a hundred away. That was all that stood between them and completing the second mission.

Fractals upon fractals flashed over the automaton's face, where its mouth would have been. These fractals formed similar patterns to what Alistair was confident in saying was the language of the Sublimed Machine, repeating pure information via geometric patterns that were reminiscent of the Mandelbrot set.

Alistair heard the voice concomitantly, with the visuals providing the same information.

"Give up Prisoner #1209 or die."

Alistair preferred a third option.

On his word, the battlefield became chaos incarnate as his allies activated their Skills.

Alexandra leaped forward for an **[Armageddon Slash]**, trusting her Constitution to defend against the incoming plasma beams. Marzhan fired her arrows that dropped the seeds of a bone forest. Brigid used her cleaver to send out hundreds of tomatoes, melting man and machine alike with the acidic juices.

Alistair **[Dashed]** forward, dodging everything with ease. His purpose was singular—take out the leader. **[Eyes of Truth]** revealed the name of the red and gold automaton.

Name: SHD-1325
Species: D-1000 Series Automaton Sublimed Machine
Manufacturing 5.32e9
Profession: Leadership Combatives [Primary Attribute(s): Strength and Constitution]
Level: 70
Title: Warden of Eden Subterranean Prison

Most of that information was superfluous. Alistair was only expecting to get anything useful out of the Class line, which for this android was interestingly "Profession" instead. Whatever the case, even by seeing that he could glean the primary Attributes of SHD-1325 meant that he had a reasonably lower Intelligence than him.

For a slow and sturdy creature like the D-1000 Series Automaton, Alistair chose Infinite Arsenal as his state of choice. With his silver aura, he almost looked part-machine himself.

In his mind's eye, he perceived the warden as a thick brick wall, unmoving but full of earth-shattering strength. Of all the innumerable weapons within his purview, he imagined himself as a sledgehammer. It didn't matter how tough a wall was. A sledgehammer would always bring it down. It was only a matter of time.

But who needed time when you had speed?

0.83 seconds for victory, give or take 0.05, Alistair calculated. The possibilities lined up before him as he peered into myriad threads of Fate with **[Eyes of Truth]**. He only spent the cursory 1 point of positive Karma, all that was required for such an opponent.

Space warped as two curved swords appeared in the warden's thick hands. By the time they fully formed, a plasma katana in the left and a nearly invisible wakizashi in the right, Alistair was almost within striking range.

An azure shield instantaneously formed once he breached a certain distance. But once you let Alistair get that close, you were in trouble.

A slice of the invisible short sword whizzed by Alistair's head, and he grabbed the weapon with his teeth. Kind of. That was a slight exaggeration —he bit into the thick metal hand of the automaton and the hilt, not the actual blade. He wasn't that crazy.

The one place that the forcefield didn't protect was the warden's weapons, which made sense. You didn't want to blunt your blade. That left a tiny opening along the wrist for Alistair to bite into.

Alistair channeled his best Mad Brutus the Biter, chomping on that steel like it was one of his **[Carmela's Happy Pies]**. SHD-1325 did its best to shake him off, but it must have realized through its AI combat system that if it tried to slice him off with the plasma katana, Alistair would let go and take its back.

It tried to throw him with its artificial might, but Dev'rox used his space affinity Mana to off-balance it, compressing the space in front of the machine. SHD-1325 fell forward, a rocket propulsion system opening from its chest to halt the descent.

Alistair used the opportunity to let go of his chomping and slide under the automaton and climb up its back.

SHD-1325 flipped the orientation of its hands with ease. Two perfectly form-fitting holes appeared within its chest cavity, where it stabbed its swords through. In a miraculous feat of engineering, the automaton was unharmed, though the swords missed their mark on the other side as Alistair contorted his body out of the way.

The forcefield bent as Alistair squeezed using all of his Strength. He hadn't employed the ultimate technique of the Steel Body since his fight against Brutus. All his muscles became corded steel. The tensing of the Steel Body became an offensive strangle, an inescapable boa constrictor hold.

It didn't matter that SHD-1325's Strength exceeded Alistair's own position once he got on the entity's back. The forcefield shattered under the pressure. He squeezed and squeezed, deforming the automaton's metal as unhealthy creaks could be heard by all those nearby, if they weren't focused on their own fights.

Alistair finished the warden off with a series of **[Force Fists]** that looked like a blur of coral energy. He pounded the automaton into a hole in the ground, leaving the machine's head looking like a car crash.

.89 seconds. Unacceptable and not within calculated par— Alistair left Infinite Arsenal. Thankfully, he didn't dive so deep that his quick exit caused any backlash.

Level up! *You are now level 65.* +3 Agility, +3 Intelligence, +3 Charisma, +3 free Attribute points, +23 Upgrade Points.

Alistair looked up as a streak of light crashed through the glass wall.

Wait, a second, he thought. *Is that?*

The blur of speed showed herself on the outside, the shards of glass littering the ground.

Kristina was out.

Armageddon Mission #2 (Escape Eden Subterranean Prison with Tarnz Auola Kristina) complete.

Armageddon Mission #3 (Team Northeast Order):
Find the Utopic Bomb.

———

"We are three in one and one in three. Why should we help you kill the leader of the Resistance? We have no quarrel with either side. The ancient ones have lived through it all."

George found the dank air of the catacombs distasteful, but he didn't mention it. He was a guest within the abode of the target for his second mission. It was not wise to mention those sorts of things when recruiting.

"It will be a great challenge," George promised. "The leader of the Resistance will be aided by strong cultivators from distant lands. You might not be strong enough, in your current forms."

The swamp throne emptied, its king rising to view George eye to eye. One of his incarnations stepped out, coalescing into a gray man with a crown of roses.

"You dare question us?" the gray man asked. Without a gap in perception, George went from at the center of the throne room to the very entrance, with the gray man at his throat.

A second incarnation of the underground king broke off, hiding in plain view. Even George couldn't perceive him without knowing that he was there. "We are the greatest assassins in the history of Eden. There is no target we cannot kill."

What remained was the third "brother," who held the Book of History in his palm. "We have never failed and will never fail."

"I believe you," George said, bowing to the tripartite being. "This will be your best quarry yet."

49 THE UNDERGROUND KING

A few minutes prior, Pharaoh's group.

JESSE LOOKED DOWN at his thigh. There was a hole where his flesh used to be, though the wound was instantly cauterized by the heat.

He was at the center of their group. Not having their teleporter get hurt was ideal. So the wound shouldn't have been possible, yet it happened.

That was when Jesse realized that he was staring down the barrel of a gun.

Before anything else could happen, the whole area transferred to the ownership of one woman. Trees grew out of nothing, forming a forest. Unstoppable nature emanated from every branch, red embers sparking near every leaf, filled with unending rage.

The trees' roots braided together underneath his feet, forming a thick barrier between the seven people and the threats below.

Jesse snapped out of it. He was no stranger to combat. His head was rushing so fast, he didn't notice the sirens. A voice blared over them, declaring the prisoner was free. He noticed a notification stating they had completed Mission #1.

Before he even heard the command from Pharaoh, he knew what to do. As the thumps from the enemies hacking Alexandra's trees grew louder, he used [Scarlet Flash].

His Skill now allowed him to take three people with him. They were close enough that he could reach it with one teleportation, having pre-saved the interrogation room as a destination. He completed two trips for the other members in his group in just over a second.

"We're reconnecting with Alistair," Pharaoh thought to them.

Caren beamed the coordinates of Alistair's location into his mind through **[Paper Mind]**. They weren't that far away.

Alexandra put a hand on Jesse's thigh, using **[Healing Current]** to seal his wound. The only problem was, nothing was happening. There wasn't time to diagnose his injury properly, and not wanting to waste any time, they climbed up through the tunnel Alistair's team had previously been through.

"I don't understand why it's not working," Alexandra complained. *"I don't feel anything wrong."*

"Guys, careful about their weapons," Jesse told them. *"My injury won't heal."*

"How bad is it?" Bartholomew asked.

Jesse shrugged. *"I've been through worse. Won't affect me that much."*

He wasn't lying, but it wasn't like the injury was nothing either. His running speed was only 75% of normal, and somehow it had even disrupted the flow of his meridians. Jesse had been taken off guard, which wasn't a good start.

His Mana pool was large enough that he could spam **[Scarlet Flash]**. Still, the extra baggage of multiple people was a drain, and the Mana cost was higher because of the interrupted meridian flow.

But they needed to reconnect with Alistair as fast as possible, so he did it anyway. He could pop a Tier 3 Mana pill if need be, now that he was level 60.

Pharaoh halted them in their tracks one stop before they would have caught up with Alistair.

"Let me stay behind," he told them. "I'll only be a few hundred meters away. I'll see how strong they are."

"Buddy system," Caren said. "Whimsy, you stay with him."

"Saved me from having to ask," the former Devil King said, patting Caren on the shoulder.

That left the five of them for one last **[Scarlet Flash]** to meet back with Alistair's crew, who looked to be ready to break out onto the first floor.

"Dangerous things below. Explain later," Caren thought, pointing at the layer.

There was a newcomer, a woman with pitch black skin and glowing white veins. She had to be Prisoner #1209, and she and Alistair combined their attacks to shatter the glass floor.

Their viewpoint into the other side was blanketed by a sea of plasma bolts. Alistair and Kristina were already through, and Alexandra braved them in her **[Barbarian's Fury],** but for the rest of the team, they relied on Oliver.

The Necromancer opened his portal, absorbing the incoming attacks. Another portal above ground spat out the bolts, laying them into the opposing side.

Oliver expanded his portal up and outward, shifting it into an expression of his warren of death. This gave time for the rest of them to pop out of the hole via **[Scarlet Shift],** where Jesse teleported everyone to a safe location.

Relatively safe. There weren't any plasma bolts going that way, but they were still surrounded by hundreds of guards. Jesse noted two types. One looked like they were human, wielding plasma assault rifles, and the other were robots almost twice as tall as him with laser swords.

All hell broke loose. Jesse threw his **[Blasting Spheres]** and called out potential threats with **[Eagle Eye],** but his main advantage came from his teleportation. In this type of fight, he wasn't so useful.

Alexandra and Oliver controlled the battlefield with her proto-Domain and his **[Otherworld Gates].** The proto-Domain was their haven, with the three layers of trees growing in concentric circles.

The innermost trees were those of the natural world, bountiful in life force and carrying the sense of a virgin forest. The second ring contained black trees of the underworld, with once white leaves now appearing blood-red, carrying the aura of barbaric war. The outer ring of the forest was now made of red trees that burned with blood, not fire, though they still emitted an undying heat.

Her forest protected them and broke up the battlefield, reducing the effectiveness of the enemy's numerical advantage. Their guns took a few seconds to break through the inner ring, and when they shot at an ally inadvertently, the trees would swerve out of the way to reduce friendly fire.

Both the outer and second ring produced lingering effects on the battlefield that would harm the police force—the burning of the outer trees created a maddening haze, while the black trees produced a purple bordering on black gas that corroded them from the inside out.

All the enemies who died fueled the proto-Domain with their life force, which Alexandra could convert to Dao energy. She had only opened her proto-Domain recently, but Jesse had heard that it was special in that she could hold on for much longer than the typical proto-Domain, though it came at the expense of not being as powerful against single foes.

On the other hand, Oliver used the cover of the trees to spread his [Otherworld Gates] all throughout the enemy formation. His zombie army was in the hundreds and now included the Worldeater Snake and Daywalker Ape on top of Anthony Ricci's skeleton and the corpse of Sessen Esshei.

Thankfully for Alistair's number one spot, Oliver couldn't even come close to harnessing the true power of the kaiju corpses. They were smaller than their real forms, slightly larger than the zombie Sessen Esshei, who had also shrunk to the size of two school buses.

But his zombies served their purpose, swarming the battlefield and adding to the chaos. Oliver also used an assortment of weapons, high-tech and low-tech, raining them down through his portals.

The others were fighting too, but Jesse couldn't see the half of it, as he stood near the center of the forest. With him were the two others who were less adept at fighting—Caren and William. One person he thought might have been there, Lucius Wood, was absent.

Armageddon Mission #2 (Escape Eden Subterranean Prison with Tarnz Auola Kristina) complete.

Armageddon Mission #3 (Team Northeast Order):
Find the Utopic Bomb.

The words flashed in front of Jesse's eyes. They had done it. Though he couldn't see it, Alistair and Kristina must have escaped from the prison.

There were two ways to win here. Finish all five missions or kill all the Devil Kings. It was a fair bet to say that the former was easier. If they could let Alistair and the prisoner accomplish that by holding off the police, that was a worthy goal.

Jesse ducked under a plasma bolt that found a small gap in the forest, almost taking out his head. Heated words in an exchange between William and Caren reached his ears.

"Come on, you gotta do it," William said out loud. "Turn into a vampire already."

"Will you be quiet?" Caren said in a hurried tone. "That's private information. People's lives are at risk. We cannot afford to be lackadaisical. You're not being serious right now."

William combed back his stylish brown hair with his hand. "I am being serious. I don't treat everything like a fucking joke, you know." He looked around, nervously tapping his foot. "My intuition is telling me you better do something."

"Or what?" Caren raised his voice. "Or what? Use your words, goddammit! My brain is taxed to the fucking limit calculating everybody's positions and messages."

But then Jesse felt it too. A seeping aura of cold that he never wanted to experience again. George Moulin was here.

———

Alistair was the first to feel it soon after escaping from the prison with Kristina.

They jumped out onto an empty street corner. If Alistair had time, he would have been in awe at the architecture. It was like Faxor except even more grand.

Megatowers loomed in the horizon, their sleek surfaces glowing with advertisements in the language of the Sublimed Machine. These enormous skyscrapers dwarfed those of Earth in both height and girth.

Equally impressive pagodas could be spotted in between, often connecting to the towers in a symbiosis of cultivation and technology. Arched energy bridges flickered in and out of existence for pedestrians at dozens of levels, allowing easy transport to and from the buildings at any floor. They blurred with speed, transporting passengers in an instant to their destination.

And those millions of people were fleeing. Alistair believed they were fake, as they were in a physical demiplane, but he couldn't know for sure.

Their block looked to be barricaded off by the police, a blue energy wall surrounding them on all four sides around half a mile away.

Snipers from the buildings fired at Alistair and Kristina, but they were too fast to get tagged.

The snipers didn't concern Alistair. The new presence did.

He's here already? Alistair wondered. *Are they going for a full-frontal attack?*

Alistair spent some Karma to view the threads of Fate and cycled through his laundry list of senses, but he only detected George. If the other Devil Kings were with him, they were well hidden beyond Alistair's means of finding out. Which he doubted that could happen, at least for all of them.

The chilling aura fluttered down from the energy barrier at the ceiling, landing on top of the prison. The monotone metal box sounded like a gong when the Devil King landed on the roof, close enough for Alistair to make out George's eyes, those piercing blue pools of fire.

But in his Karmic vision, there was something off with George's Karmic web. It looked wrong, as if it was attaching to him at all the wrong points. Like everything was inverted, like when you looked into a mirror.

The leader of the Devil Kings looked Alistair straight in the eyes. "Meet the real me on that skyscraper over there." He pointed to the tallest tower in the east. There were no clouds, but Alistair couldn't really see the top of it, which faded off into infinity. "This is a clone which copies much of my power, but it is still limited. I'm waiting on that tower so that we can have our duel. I know you've wanted it."

A million thoughts raced through Alistair's head at once. He calmed himself, looking at things analytically. George had shown himself to be a cautious and calculating man. He was less bold than Alistair, who wouldn't hesitate to charge head-first if his allies were in danger.

But was he a coward? If George thought he had, say, a 60% chance of winning a one-on-one duel against Alistair, would he try that? Or would he never go for such a thing unless he was pulling for a trap? Alistair didn't have a good enough read on the man to gauge that.

"You're thinking it's a trap, obviously. I don't blame you."

The clone of George jumped down from the roof, walking up to Alistair without a care in the world. Kristina looked at him for what to do.

As the snipers readied another shot, they were all struck down by ice spears. George smiled, the arcane arrays that produced the spears fading above him.

[Monk Motionlessness] was utterly silent. Whatever George was doing, he wasn't being threatened.

"Who are you afraid of? Morgana? Hephaestus? Heavyset?" George asked. "If my allies were to attack you all at once, even with me, you could just flee. But there's no trap, so that won't be necessary."

"If you were in my shoes, would you trust *you?*"

"Never once have I lied to you," George said. Alistair noticed that the man's hand was twitching, which he raised to his mouth to summon a cigarette that produced ice instead of fire and smoke. "But it's alright. I'll raise the white flag first. It is obvious you are a Karmic cultivator. I will lower all my defenses and permit you to use any Karmic method you have to verify that the following words are truth: no one else on my side will interfere in that battle I invite you to, including any of the additions this world has provided. The tower itself has not been molded to be advantageous to me or disadvantageous to you in any way. It will be truly a duel between the two of us."

Alistair felt the truth of his words with **[Eyes of Truth]** and Lesser Vipassanā. It was as he said. The clone put himself in an extremely vulnerable position. At any moment, Alistair could have snapped his neck. He put down all his defenses, including that blizzard-like aura that guarded his Fate. Alistair saw every part of his body, mind, and soul, and there was no subterfuge he could detect.

That didn't mean there wasn't any, but it was unlikely. Oracle might have been able to fool him, but she was dead.

"You weren't afraid I was going to kill you while you were defenseless?" Alistair asked.

"No, I was not." George smiled with his teeth.

"What will you do here?" Alistair asked. "Why should I not defeat you, then go after you?"

"Don't you trust your allies?" George mocked. "If you attack me here, it will give my real self enough time to come here, and then all hell will break loose. It would be safer for everyone if we cordon off the fights, don't you agree?"

Alistair had to admit there was some sense to his words. If Alistair and George fought nearby, the effects of their fight would cause chaos for everyone else. And not just them. If everyone fought in one place, it would be pandemonium.

It wasn't a guarantee that one on one, their side would also win. If they were severely injured by the battle, that could change things. But it was still a bet on their own strengths, if Alistair believed him.

The other factor inducing him to taking the deal was that he believed that his team was stronger. There were only six Devil Kings and two Beast Lords, not including the missing Chameleon.

"You have yourself a deal," Alistair said. "However, if you try something, I won't hesitate to come right back here, and you won't be able to stop me."

"I wouldn't dream of it."

Alistair relayed the information to Caren. *"You're going to need to intercept this guy on the roof. It's not the real George. I think it's a clone created by that mirror of his. It shouldn't be as powerful."*

"You know where the Utopic Bomb is?" Alistair asked Kristina.

"I have an inkling," she said. "You're leaving me here?"

"I'll have someone tag along," Alistair said. "I've gotta go."

No matter how many locusts and spires of sand that Pharaoh sent, there were always more of those men in black armor. They were perfect soldiers, willing to lay down their lives to do the tiniest amount of damage against Pharaoh.

Their strange plasma bolts had dealt an unhealing wound to poor Jesse, but they were useless against his fourteen lives. Still, he only had so many. One of them caught him off guard by detonating their soulcore, taking away one of his lives.

More problematic than the men were the robots. The robots and the guys who looked like they wore metal raincoats. The human swordsmen were fast and almost impossible to catch, while the robots were tough, resisting his sand spires with minor damage. It was an issue of incompatibility. His techniques were more suited to fighting organic things, especially with the Dao of Lost Sands.

But that all changed when he felt that man's presence.

They needed him above the surface. But what to do about everything down here?

Pharaoh sighed. A sun blazed in the illusory sky as the primeval sands stirred. He would have to end this quickly.

Caren mentally shouted into Jesse's ear. *"Take Oliver and Blaise outside, now."*

Jesse didn't hesitate, obeying Caren's orders absolutely. After Caren relayed their locations to him, he activated **[Scarlet Flash]** and grabbed both of them. They didn't get confused at all, already knowing he was coming, their system of communications working without a hitch.

In three flashes, he made it outside, finding Kristina. She was standing on the street, looking up at George Moulin.

Jesse felt his heart race as he saw the man whom he despised more than any other. The First Devil King was sitting on top of the prison nonchalantly, his legs crossed as if he didn't have a care in the world.

One of the Devil Kings who had already died, Monk, had gone on a killing rampage during the fourth Quest, trying to level up as fast as possible. All the people Jesse knew from his hometown had died.

When it happened, Jesse had wanted nothing more than to tear Monk to pieces. But now he understood that the Devil King was a mere pawn of this puppetmaster.

George didn't look like anything special. He was short for a man, post-initiation, with a medium build. He wore a heavy white jacket and gloves.

The most noticeable feature was the blue fire in his eyes, and his hair, which never fell over his face. Unlike the rest of the Devil Kings, his aura felt less profane, less like it shouldn't ever belong in this world.

"Don't mind me," he said, his breath forming clouds of condensation as he spoke. He pointed to a blur in the distance, and from the aura, Jesse could tell it was Alistair **[Dashing]** away. "Your boss and I agreed to a deal. If I kill you now, I think he would consider that a violation of our deal. So please, go on, and once Kristina and whichever escorts you choose for her leave, I will kill you all."

Oliver gave a death glare at George, but he looked at Kristina. "Let's head out."

She nodded, and they took off with Blaise at their side, disappearing into the labyrinthine cyberpunk city that was Eden.

Caren's voice entered his mind. *"Alistair told me this is a clone of George. It's not as powerful as the real thing. Don't worry."*

"Still," Jesse sent back. *"It feels just like him. Can we really deal with this considering what's happening inside?"*

"Bartholomew will be the first to play his cards."

Jesse teleported back inside, not wanting to spend another moment alone with George, who had begun walking toward him while he was communicating with Caren. He chose a spot along the ceiling, pressing his body into a thin strip with a height of less than an inch using [Flatland] and sticking there with [Adhesion].

His aura was naturally suppressed in that position, so he got to see things from a bird's eye view.

He understood what Caren meant now. The trees had toppled over, taking out many of the men and robots, allowing Jesse to see what was happening.

Bartholomew swung his sword.

Jesse only saw it for a flash, an enormous energy blade that stretched the entire length of the room to the shattered glass wall at the front. It wasn't as long as it had been when Bartholomew went berserk on Dragonus, but it was far more concentrated, glowing so brightly it overpowered everything else.

A burst of light swept the room from left to right. It all happened so fast, Jesse could barely perceive the weapon. And then things fell apart.

Wherever the sword slashed, it divided. Nothing could withstand the blade's sharpness. Despite their tough bodies, almost all the automatons were vanquished in an instant, too slow to avoid the sword.

The armored men were swifter, some dodging the blade, but they weren't prepared for the backswing. Another flash of light went from right to left, and then another, and then another, each carrying a healthy dose of Bartholomew's Dao energy.

Once the battlefield had been cleared, Jesse undid his [Flatland] and teleported behind Bartholomew, where he saw the others.

The rest of their team, not wanting to be caught up in Bartholomew's attack, had disengaged back to the hole where they broke through. Some of them bore light injuries, like Alexandra and Brigid, while others looked untouched, like William.

Bartholomew let the metal hilt of his sword blend back into his body, but he wasn't looking good. He still had that disturbing look of a half-rotted robot corpse, the withdrawn metal unable to fill all the gaps in his frame.

"I dealt with the ones below, but I had to use my proto-Domain," Pharaoh said. *"If I have to use it again soon, it won't be at full power."*

"Finally, I've been waiting for you to deal with all the riffraff."

An aura of impossible cold spread throughout the prison. Jesse flashed back to a childhood memory when he visited his cousins in Canada. His parents had inexplicably chosen to go in the winter, and he spent a week freezing his ass off.

"I dealt with a few of the stragglers on the top floor, if you don't mind," George said. He waltzed in through the front doors like he owned the place.

Jesse looked up, indeed confirming that there were a few of the armored men frozen into ice statues. *Oh, shit.*

A tide of death rebuffed the cold, answering Jesse's prayers. Since Alexandra and Pharaoh had both used their proto-Domains, if George was allowed to implant his Dao and Mana into the prison, he would have an inherent terrain advantage that would be difficult to unseat.

The death that repelled George's cold was not Oliver's emptiness, but the death of a rotting swamp. A graveyard where living things decayed.

Marzhan's proto-Domain supplanted the space of the prison. Instead of being on the first floor of a futuristic correctional facility, they were on top of the tallest hill of a graveyard. It was nighttime, an eternal night with a full moon. Trees wilted and rotted, and the grass was ghost blue, flickering from beyond the pale.

If it weren't for Marzhan marking him as a part of the proto-Domain, Jesse could feel that his flesh would have rotted off his bones.

But her space was not unopposed. At the edge of the graveyard, a blizzard met the decay. The two proto-Domains clashed for control over the space, creating a defined border between the graveyard and the blizzard that appeared to take place in a world blanketed in only snow and ice.

Alexandra called out to their challenger, who was unseen in the depths of his proto-Domain. "You think you can beat all ten of us? We know that you're not really here."

"Sneaky," a voice said back. A measured, easy-going voice that was soft like snowflakes falling on a child's tongue. "That must be Mr. Caren Locasta providing all of this wonderful information. I'll have to kill him soon."

Jesse frowned. George had a… sing-song intonation, like he was trying to sound like a movie villain that twiddled his fingers when the hero confronted him at the end, saying that he had fallen into his trap. While they hadn't had much contact with the leader of the Devil Kings, from Alistair's memories and what they did see, he was stoic and a man of few words.

"However, you are wrong on one account. I am not alone."

A breath caught in Jesse's throat. Blood trickled down his stomach. His **Swiftcloak Armor** wasn't enough to protect him from the dagger sticking into his abdomen. A man laughed, though his ears rang, and he barely heard anything as his vision started to fade.

"The Underground King," Jesse said, though he knew not why.

50 CLASHING EQUALS

ALISTAIR LEFT BEHIND ALL his other burdens. There was only one in his way.

He would defeat George Moulin, the leader of the Devil Kings.

As he stared at the tower in the distance, he believed this with all his heart and all his soul. He ignored everything around him as he **[Dashed]**, his flicker making him all but invisible to the thousands of civilians, only appearing between uses of the Skill for a split second.

As Alistair ran east, he began to encounter the shoddier part of town. Lights flickered, trash accumulated on the streets, and the buildings looked run-down.

Alistair noticed that the bridges fifty stories in the sky became larger, and soon he could see entire apartments and parks and other sorts of city living on the higher levels. There was a distinct economic difference between the slums on the bottom and the luxury of the upper floor.

But it didn't end there. There were two more layers spaced higher and higher up. Alistair climbed to the very top layer, scaling a pagoda instead of taking the typical escalator to save time.

He did so because he realized that most of the tallest buildings didn't even have entrances at the ghetto level. From there, he took the energy bridges, which allowed him to go even faster. Despite all the obstructions, it took him under a minute to reach the tower.

Mercurial neon lights shone from the megastructure, depicting impossibly attractive men and women using all sorts of products. A princess renowned for both her unrivaled beauty and cultivation endorsed the newest cultivator's **Soul Splitter,** which promised more cohesion upon reintegration. The ads shifted every ten seconds or so, an army of microscopic drones creating a three-dimensional effect where the endorsers and their props projected out of the flat screen.

Alistair could even feel a fragment of their aura. It wasn't very strong, but each celebrity had their own distinctive flavor. He wondered if they could copyright things like that. Maybe it was illegal to forge someone's aura for commercial purposes.

The tower was created in defiance of Earth's architectural principles. The base was the thinnest portion, and it grew in girth and twisted around itself like a strand of DNA until it was over twice as thick at the top.

Alistair looked up to a foreign sky, filled with satellites visible from orbit and strange cosmological features like what he thought might be a rotating black hole being siphoned for energy. Their sky was much denser than Earth's, even though it was fake. The Pathfinder AI was a sucker for verisimilitude.

Alistair was on the highest floor, which was more a patchwork of energy bridges than a real layer, with some larger sections for restaurants and other businesses.

There he was.

The tower jutted over the floor, standing only a few dozen meters above the energy pathways. The helix-like building fattened as it rose, the top containing an industrial warehouse.

George Moulin sat on the edge, smoking a cig.

"I thought you'd take my offer."

Alistair looked up at the Devil. "He's a bit more expressive than you, I think."

"You're overconfident," George said, "to think that you've caught up with me. I've come to realize that either you or that ghost inside you, Dev'rox, is a smart man. You could use that brainpower to concoct a plan to defeat me. Instead, you decide that you must face me. This is arrogance."

Alistair maintained a cool face, but he was inwardly shocked that George knew about Dev'rox. Especially the name. How could that be? He wracked his memories, trying to think of any way that George could know the name of his ghost.

Ah, yes, Alistair thought. *I knew that would come back to haunt me.* Inside the *Kestrel,* in order to pass the tests, he had needed to give up a secret. The secret he had chosen was that of his ghost companion. Back then, he hadn't had the swapping or Spatial Rending spell, but George would definitely know of Dev'rox's general spatial emphasis.

"You think you're the hero. The hero always defeats the villain. You couldn't help yourself by coming here."

"If I beat you, then no one else has to get hurt," Alistair replied.

"Exactly what I'm talking about."

George jumped down, landing on the energy bridge. There was no one else on the bridge for miles, as far as Alistair could feel. Their stretch was around ten body lengths wide and connected the megatower to another tall tower a mile back. An invisible guardrail surrounded all the bridges, but it could be bypassed by a conscious thought.

Alistair didn't dare look down. On the highest floor, they would be up in the clouds if such things were allowed to exist in Eden. As it was, there was only clear air, cold from both the environment and George's aura.

Channeling {Psychopomp's Discipline}, Alistair assumed a flexible stance, half-way bladed. He held his hands in fists, but with his fingers slightly unfurled, his weight evenly distributed on both legs. A small trickle of the Dao of the Fist flowed through his spiritual pathways as he bounced back and forth.

Five magical arrays crystalized in the air above George. Five ice spears throttled toward Alistair.

The ocean of tranquility devoured Alistair wholesale. He swerved in between the spears, which shattered against the nigh indestructible bridge, unable to penetrate at all.

[Eyes of Truth] once again proved to be useless, with all the possibilities aligning before Alistair's eyes equally, none favored in any way. The same chill ran through his veins as he viewed the afterimages of the future, sensing a dark aura that was similar, but separate from George.

Another sinner that requires cleansing with my love and justice? Alistair wondered.

In any case, he stopped [Eyes of Truth]. That Skill might be useless against the Devil King. Trying to figure out if, say, 20 Karma might be enough to overpower the mysterious presence was too expensive for only a possibility. He needed to save as much Karma as he could for [Hand of Karma]. He would have to fight Fate-blind.

Alistair moved in, but he didn't use [Dash]. He was cautious about approaching George, knowing that he was likely to have several tricks. A [Lightning of Justice] arced down from the skies, sent by Alistair to fish for a reaction.

Before he did so, he finally locked in the last of his Upgrade Points, cementing them on turning [Lightning of Justice] and [Blood Hand] to Tier 3. His new Tier 3 [Lightning of Justice] barely missed George, who jumped out of the way. However, upon landing, the lightning split into three bolts that bounced off the ground.

Those bolts then split into three more bolts, which then split into three more, for a total of twenty-seven. Two would have landed on George, but instead reflected off a thin layer of ice over his jacket.

While it wasn't much, Alistair was happy to confirm one of George's defensive mechanisms. In all of Oracle's memories, he was never on the defending end. This also led him to suspect that the one out of George's five Arcanous Devil spells that he didn't know was also a defensive tool.

Under the cover of the explosion of lightning, Alistair [Dashed] forward. That was when he noticed the ice over the bridge.

It was only a tiny layer, a thin filament of ice that was barely perceptible, but it was everywhere.

In one moment, George was a dozen feet in front of him. In the next, George was close enough that their clothes almost touched.

There was absolutely zero lag, far faster than Dev'rox's spatial manipulation. It didn't even feel like teleportation to Alistair.

Out of every pore of George's body, an icicle burst out, turning him into a hedgehog of ice crystals. But make no mistake, Alistair's [Monk Motionlessness] hummed at the sharpness of the ice. It was only because of Tranquil Mind's reaction speed that he stopped his motion.

The very tip of the icicles grazed his face, unable to cut his skin as his [Steel Body] protected him. Despite the very real possibility he would have died on the spot, Alistair didn't let it perturb him. It *couldn't* perturb him inside of Tranquil Mind.

If George thought he could get close to him, the master of close quarters, without paying the price, he would be instructed. Alistair threw a [Force

Fist] to shatter George's face, but as quick as he appeared before Alistair, he disappeared.

As Alistair began to feel the cold even through his **Mammothskin Raiment,** he began to piece things together. George had spread his Mana and Dao into the environment, causing the layer of ice to form. It was an extension of his person. But what if he could change the location of that extension? Then, he could be anywhere his ice was.

Alistair applied his aura sense, feeling that George had spread his ice to the visible stretch of the bridge. He stomped his foot, seeing if the ice would break. It did, but only inside the outline of his shoe. That was far too inefficient if he wanted to wrangle dominion of the area away from George.

Instead, he jumped backward, using the power of his legs to retreat away from the frost. This put him over a thousand feet away from George, who didn't move from his spot. There had to be a Mana cost for maintaining the ice field.

Since he couldn't glean any information from **[Eyes of Truth],** he tried to reason off what he knew. George's primary attribute was Intelligence. Given Alistair's own attribute distribution, George almost certainly had an Intelligence of over 1,000 and a Mana Pool of over 3,000. However, anything would be good in what Alistair assumed was going to be a drawn-out fight. There would be no quick assassinations.

Alistair took out throwing knives from his inventory. They were high quality, made of black steel forged in the heart of a dying star, the system said. He'd purchased hundreds of them for this moment.

From outside the ice, he threw knife after knife. They were so fast they were streaks of darkness. None made it to their target. Without moving, a huge chunk of ice grew out of the ground, intercepting the knives. They smashed into the block, cracking it and sending shards of ice clattering onto the bridge, but George was unharmed.

Unfortunately for Alistair, it wasn't George's Glacial Front, the small size and lack of array making that obvious. But it was still something. If he could force positive Mana trades, that was what he wanted.

Alistair slid off the bridge, consciously affirming his decision to do so to prevent the barrier from blocking him. He grabbed the edge with two hands and then swung from the bottom. He covered distance by essentially spinning, moving forward one hand at a time.

The ice around the bridge grew incredibly cold, frost forming around his

[Devilsbane Gauntlets], but they were built for that sort of thing. George couldn't be lazy if he wanted to dislodge Alistair from his position under the bridge.

The bridge served as cover for Alistair, being an impenetrable force field. George saw this and raised a pillar of ice from his position, standing on top of it as the column grew to over fifty feet in height. From his vantage point, he fired a volley of ten ice spears down at the hanging Alistair.

Alistair flipped up the moment he saw the arrays, using airwalking to [Dash] forward. The spears, he batted away with his gloved hands, his body more than capable of handling the remaining momentum and small fragments of ice that grazed his face and robes.

His [Dash] wasn't fast enough, as he expected. George became the ice a few feet away, a new array forming above his head.

Alistair [Dashed] again as soon as he registered the movement, but this time, Dev'rox compressed the space in between them. A [Force Fist] zoomed toward George's face. Given the Devil King's fast reaction earlier, there should have been enough time for another teleport.

George blocked instead. A thick layer of ice formed over his face, catching the blow. The fajin aspect of his Skill still sent the man tumbling over the bridge.

His teleportation had a cooldown, or he was baiting that it had a cooldown. But Alistair was confident it was not a bait, as his punch temporarily sent the Devil King outside his ice dominion, where Dev'rox was waiting.

The imp snapped his fingers, and they swapped places.

This time, Alistair's fist connected, but with a [Blood Hand]. The knuckles of his gauntleted hand connected with George's face, the crimson sanguine Mana penetrating through the gash and simultaneously infecting the Devil King with the foreign life force, while stealing the demonic blood essence with {Blood Debt}, which he could repurpose for his own Skills.

Almost as soon as he connected the blow, he shifted states, going from Tranquil Mind to Black Impermanence. This decision was not made through any Skill, but his combat intuition borne by his numerous battles.

The George that his [Blood Hand] connected with was made of ice. It didn't make sense. The blood essence he stole was real, but the figure in front of him was a clone that crumbled into a pile of ice. It wasn't the same as the prior teleports, which never left anything behind.

Alistair guessed that he had just encountered George's defensive spell, something he wasn't expecting to force out for a while. If he was using it now, that could only mean—

A torrential rain of Dao energy flowed from above.

George's proto-Domain. But what Alistair hadn't realized was that even the tiniest bit of ice that he had frozen over the bridge became a note in the proto-Domain's symphony.

The punch left George outside his Dao field, and behind Alistair's back, who had charged forward. By letting his proto-Domain expand from both his soulcore and the Dao field behind Alistair, he was imposing his will onto a larger field of space than should have been possible.

Alistair was trapped.

He could feel the restriction. It was like Pharaoh's proto-Domain, one of oppression, only at a much higher level. [Dashing] out was impossible.

There was only one option, one that he had wanted to save for later.

Alistair opened his own proto-Domain, Black Impermanence helping him act under the suppression of his enemy's territory.

A sphere of blood spiraled into existence, pushing back against the blizzard. The bloodwraiths expanded into the ice behind Alistair, washing it away with their just torments. They swirled around, whispering their solemn tales to whomever listened. Blood dripped from the ceiling like rain, filling the sphere with a thin layer of blood that would bog down evildoers while letting Alistair run free.

Alistair's proto-Domain was not unchallenged. While it destroyed the ice to his rear, the bloodwraiths clashed against George's proto-Domain in front of him. But they did not fight an endless blizzard like he was expecting. The border between their spaces was that of ectoplasmic blood grinding against a crystal palace.

George's proto-Domain was a castle of ice, with him on a glorious frozen throne. It looked to be the throne room of a winter kingdom, every facet of the building constructed from his signature blue ice. It was so cold that his bloodwraiths froze the instant they grazed the ice castle, their proto-Domains clashing against one another with a clear border.

Their territories seemed to be evenly matched, with blood struggling against ice with no clear victory. Yet a sense of foreboding caused Alistair to practice caution. He didn't have much experience in proto-Domain battles.

When he squinted his eyes, he saw something to the right of George's icy throne. The being flickered in and out of sight, but his eyes were well practiced in seeing ghosts. Was it a ghost? Alistair didn't think so, as it had a strange flavor, not that of a soul, but closer to *nue*. However, he recognized this presence as what he felt when trying to spy on George's Fate.

A tall skeleton, cloaked in royal robes and carrying a crystal ball, gazed at Alistair.

Alistair met the skeleton's eye sockets, not backing down.

"What is this?" Alistair called out. "I thought it was a one on one?"

"You have your imp," George said. "My lich resides in my proto-Domain. I haven't broken our agreement."

With that, the lich disappeared. Alistair had a good idea of where he went. His presence spread out through George's proto-Domain, adding an additional layer to the already cold environment that approached absolute zero. Its aura was not identical to George's, feeling more sinister and deadly, but it was close enough that they worked symbiotically.

While the stalemate between the territories only lasted a few seconds, it was clear they were evenly matched. Not anymore, with the power of the mysterious lich.

The bloodwraiths were furious with the intruder. Alistair believed they sensed a Karmic malfeasance in the lich, but their attempts to ward off the progression of the castle were nullified. The ice froze and transformed the blood, adding it as crystal shards to an expanding palace.

Alistair felt the safety of his proto-Domain under threat, the walls of ice closing in on him. He had to make a decision as to what to do. For that, he switched to Infinite Arsenal, analyzing the innumerable possibilities before him.

There were too many unknowns to make a proper calculation. He didn't know the full extent of George's power.

[Thousand-Armed Bodhisattva Judgment] activated from the heart of Alistair's proto-Domain.

51 THE ASSASSIN'S DANCE

Jesse knew he was dying.

The wound in his stomach was deep. His Endurance wasn't the highest, so he wasn't expecting his cut to stitch itself back together, but he could feel a foreign Dao at work. If he did nothing, he would die.

His ears rang. There was chaos around him as his allies realized what had happened. Jesse couldn't pay attention to them. He took out a Tier 3 Health pill from his inventory. The pill seared his meridians from the inside out, but it was either that, or die.

While the fires of the Health pill ravaged his pathways, he felt a more soothing current. His vision coalesced into a single figure, and he realized a woman was touching his chest. Alexandra used her Skill to assist in his recovery.

Jesse stood up, feeling rejuvenated. But when he looked down, blood still rushed out of his wound, which had shrunk slightly with his treatment, but didn't even come close to healing fully.

"How can I not sense him?" Marzhan's voice brought Jesse to attention. "It's my damn proto-Domain, after all."

"Whoever attacked has means beyond our understanding," Pharaoh said. "Be alert."

All the while, George's clone's proto-Domain loomed in the distance. The blizzard chipped away at the graveyard, and Jesse could almost make out a structure within the heart of the storm. It almost looked like a castle, cloaked in shadow and impossible to view through the heavy snow.

Marzhan's territory was losing ground at a rate of around a foot every ten seconds. If they did nothing, they would be subsumed within the cold of the enemy proto-Domain.

Jesse patted his robes against his stomach, the blood staining his clothes. It wasn't stopping. He had heard about weapons like that before. Knives whose wounds never healed, bleeding their victims out slowly. At his current rate, he'd die of blood loss far before they'd finish Armageddon and could receive specialized attention.

In that moment, he made his decision.

Jesse changed his character.

No one in the world knew of his secret. Jesse didn't have a true Class. From the moment he reached level 10, he had a "profession" called Writeship. There wasn't any info on what a profession was in the Pathfinder's information boxes or the Hall of Math, but he came to understand that Writeship could let him take on Classes.

The first Class that he stole was that of a man he killed near the start of the initiation. He was trying to steal food from a grain silo. Jesse had no choice but to execute justice. The man had the basic Acolyte Class with an emphasis on fire.

From there, every time Jesse killed someone, he could become their Class, but even better. The Dao of Imagination soared as his mind progressed each Class to their limits, but it was even more than that. He was creation in living form, able to evolve Classes beyond their normal limits.

There was one cost to such an absurd power—his lifespan. Jesse found it ironic. His imagination was only limited by his life. As long as he progressed quickly, he could keep up pace with using his Class. Normal actions didn't take that much of his life force. It was primarily switching Classes and using their powers beyond their standard limit.

All that being said, Jesse had no other option. He switched to the second Class he'd collected.

However, he was no ordinary Warrior. Jesse poured his lifespan into altering his Class with the Dao of Imagination, as he envisioned the perfect hero that he admired as a child.

Jesse glided smoothly into the air. With superhuman vision that pierced the hidden veil, he spotted two figures hiding in Marzhan's proto-Domain.

The first was a gray man wearing a crown of roses, who hid behind a gravestone. The second was almost imperceptible even to Jesse's superior sight, appearing as a blur that wanted to remain hidden. It almost felt mundane, as if the hidden man was simply that good at hiding, to where he could even conceal himself in plain view.

The next events played out together, with each part of their team acting smoothly and without hesitation. Jesse relayed the locations of the interlopers to Caren, who told Marzhan and Brigid to help him out. Lucius burned drachma to bolster the graveyard's territory, sweat dripping down his short hair—he looked as if he were physically struggling to maintain his spending.

Brigid ate a golden chocolate bar, temporarily ballooning into a giant— then she ate a dark chocolate bar, bringing her back down to normal size, still maintaining the glowing aura. Marzhan aimed her bow, and sinuous sponges of bone grew out of the ground without her having to fire a single arrow, all things within her proto-Domain responding to their master's call.

The other members of the team ventured forth. At first glance, they might have seemed useless, as why would you venture outside the graveyard and into the blizzard?

There were two factors bringing them forward. First, they could still launch long-range attacks into the clone's proto-Domain. Second, as they were marked as a component of Marzhan, their procession would aid her proto-Domain against George's. This was an important doctrine in Domain versus Domain combat, and it also applied to the Foundation level.

Since they had separated into two groups, there were exactly seven cultivators remaining. Seven, as in the number needed to form the Imperial Phalanx. Pharaoh took on his role as the Captain, moving the unit as one toward their target—the shadowy structure hidden within the blizzard.

All that Jesse didn't focus on, trusting his allies. Laser beams burst from his eyes, scouring the hills for the assassins. The world became his accomplice, as his lasers directed the two women by his side. They couldn't see the assassins like he could, but they could follow his lasers.

Jesse flew toward the gray man with his arms outstretched, while he used his lasers to guide Marzhan and Brigid to the other target. Once the shifty figure popped out, he became somewhat visible as long as you focused all your attention, so Jesse could focus on the gray one.

Jesse would have collided straight into the gray assassin, but he wasn't there. Nothing was there. Jesse burst through a cloud of darkness, like a fish swimming in squid ink. When he escaped, he found himself near the edge of the proto-Domain.

There's something familiar there, Jesse thought. *I know the taste of that Dao.*

Immediately, he focused his sight on the shifty assassin, who had slipped past Marzhan's guard. Jesse fired his laser beams right at her feet.

The hidden man jumped out of the way, Marzhan enveloping herself in a bone cocoon. Jesse tracked the man as best he could, but it was as if he couldn't bear to look at his target for more than a few seconds before he was forced to look away.

Brigid engaged the gray man with her meat cleaver, who had materialized back on the ground after his disappearance in ink. Jesse thought that she didn't use the knife for offense, but she swung it deftly, forcing the assassin to dodge. With every swing, she carved away the grass in whirlwind arcs, each slash seemingly producing two out of thin air.

She procured a giant tomato with her free left hand, and an arm made of golden energy formed below her armpit summoned a giant onion. Her meat cleaver split into ten golden clones, each tied together with a faint strand of Mana, while additional arms grew out of her torso.

With each arm, she found a new vegetable—parsley, garlic, sweet potato, and more—tossing them into the air and catching the golden cleavers in one smooth motion.

From there, Jesse watched in amazement as she cut together ingredients, discarding the energy-based cleavers as she gathered different kitchen utensils. Golden fire set ablaze the ghost grass as she stirred the floating ingredients into dishes of unimaginable flavor.

Gigantic ceramic plates appeared above Brigid's head, collecting the ingredients and sending the completed meal flying at the gray man. The aroma of the food turned that section of Marzhan's proto-Domain into a rainbow of color, as the smell was so fragrant it became visible, vibrating with the Dao.

Jesse felt the seductive attention of Brigid's dishes even from his vantage point in the sky. If only he could indulge in them, he would experience true pleasure. Pleasure beyond anything he had ever known, pleasure that could not be found in this world. Her food was a divine treasure, an earthly imitation ambrosia.

The gray man took on a martial stance that reminded him of Alistair—he attacked the food with palm strikes that created Buddha palms twice his height in their wake. The assassin followed up by firing a laser beam from his index finger, using it as a sharpened edge that could slice anything in two. His body morphed for a split second each time he used a new ability, and when he threw up wolves made of electricity, the gray man flashed into a gruff-looking cowboy with a bionic eye. With such disparate abilities, Jesse found his confidence in the shared origin of their powers.

Then, he realized that it wasn't just Brigid's food seducing him. The assassin he could barely perceive was part of the reason he found her so enticing, since it gave him a reason to look away. When he turned around, the back of Marzhan's cocoon had a glass knife sticking out of it.

I can barely focus on this bastard, Jesse grunted internally, as he flew over to Marzhan's cocoon. His fist should have taken off that skinny guy's head, but his punch hit nothing. Jesse knew exactly what had happened. At the last second, he had attacked a foot to the right of the assassin, for no other reason than that was what felt right. It was infuriating to fight him, as his body did not cooperate with his mind.

A sharp prick registered on Jesse's thigh. The hidden assassin slashed the inside of his right leg, but there was only a paper-thin scratch. In this form, his skin was nigh impenetrable.

"Marzhan, can't you label them outsiders?" Jesse asked through the telepathy. *"This is your proto-Domain, yeah?"*

"It is!" she shouted back mentally. *"That's why I don't understand what's going on. They should be rotting from the putrefactive aura of death."*

The battle between Brigid and the gray man caught his attention once again. The electric wolves were as fast as lightning, consuming the incoming food with their gaping maws. The assassin took out a gourd from his robes, out of which came a river of blood.

The blood shifted into a character of an unknown language. Crimson light sparkled from the swirling depths of the blood, exploding into thousands of sanguine butterflies. The insects swarmed the food, devouring everything in sight.

Jesse snapped his head back. *Fuck.* The imperceptible assassin was faster than he had expected, jumping on top of him and stabbing the existing cut. Jesse winced in pain, throwing the man off with brute force. His eyes blazed with light, firing a laser right in the assassin's trajectory. It missed by a whisker.

Marzhan knew what to do. Without hesitation, she invoked the power of her proto-Domain, dozens of skeleton hands rising out of the grass and latching onto the shifty man. Finally, they had trapped him.

The hands pulled him to the ground, trying to drag him into hell. Even then, they were loath to look at him directly. The gray assassin fighting Brigid was dressed like a king, replete in fine gray silks and a crown of roses, while Jesse's opponent was naked.

Who needed clothes when no one wanted to look?

Putting his initial distaste aside, Jesse noticed that where his heart should have been, there was only an empty void. *And there's the catch.*

Using the Dao of Imagination, Jesse slightly altered his powers. With his current abilities being an offshoot of Warrior, he was invoking a figure beloved in the imaginations of many. Conjuring something out of pure fantasy taxed his Dao Node at a much higher rate. That was why he only changed the type of Mana that his laser beams emitted, altering it to become life affinity.

This time, when he aimed his sight at the unclothed and imperceptible man, his beam made contact. A life-attuned green laser opened a hole in the assassin's abdomen. A Warrior's danger sense alerted him to something from behind.

Jesse braced at the last second as a crackling wolf's maw snapped around his neck. The electricity that pulsed through his system was nothing more than a static shock, but the teeth were far sharper and larger than any natural wolf, incising two puncture wounds the size of pennies into his neck.

With a punch, he sent the wolf into the ground with a heavy thud that flattened the nearby gravestones. Immediately after the lightning entity touched the grass, skeleton hands dragged it into the underworld. The ghost grass grew back, and the hole closed as if nothing had occurred.

Jesse turned around, seeing what had happened. Brigid clutched her side, blood dripping from a nasty gash that exposed part of her rib. The hill she fought on was littered with her delectable offerings and puddles from the gray man's blood arts.

Brigid tossed a glistening tomato into the air, smacking it with her cleaver and sending the acidic juices flying. She pointed at something behind her, shouting mentally at Jesse.

Time came to a standstill. Jesse looked around in awe as he grasped that it was not the world that was moving slow, but he that was moving fast. The drain of his Dao Node was extreme, so he had to make these precious seconds count.

Jesse turned around, cursing his lack of awareness once more. When his concentration slipped, the assassin had escaped from the bone hands, though not without injury. The hole his laser created had rotted the man's flesh, vaporizing it into nothingness.

The assassins were undead. Or at least highly attuned to death. That explained their strange complexion and the missing heart, as well as why Marzhan's proto-Domain couldn't rot their flesh off the bone.

His life affinity laser counteracted the death, leading to a lingering injury, like the stab wound to his stomach that still wouldn't stop bleeding.

The shifty assassin's glass knife was at Marzhan's neck, while she remained completely unaware. Even now, as Jesse moved far faster than he had ever in his life, he wanted to look away from the man. His mind pounded with anxiety at the mere idea of gazing for another second.

Jesse couldn't bear it any longer, so he looked away as he led with his fist. A verdant aura surrounded his punch, pulsing with life affinity Mana in a manner not so dissimilar from his boss's [Force Fist].

As time returned to normal, his fist slammed into undead bone. A sickening crunch echoed, and the hidden man all but vanished.

Jesse stumbled over, blood loss causing his vision to blur and his legs to feel like lead. *Not now,* he thought. If he was right, they had the shifty one on his last legs. He had to have used a special defensive Skill, or maybe an inborn advantage to evade detection, something beyond his normal ability to hide in plain sight.

Marzhan patted her neck, feeling the tiny prick mark where the hidden man had stabbed her. Jesse felt for her. She had the most difficult job, having to hold open her proto-Domain and assist the phalanx from the outside, while also dealing with the two assassins.

Marzhan raised her bow, notching a black arrow. Brigid took her cleaver and snapped it in half, filling her hands with golden energy. The energy flowed around her, growing until it formed a basketball-sized glob of strawberry soft serve ice cream.

The soft serve billowed in waves from her hands. It was like Jesse was watching a Biblical flood in action. There was no end to the amount of strawberry ice cream she could conjure. She was the source of a veritable sea of the dessert, traveling in waves the size of a real life ocean.

The gray man tried running, but Marzhan's arrow flew from her bow. The black streak turned into a massive raven as dark as night. Four pairs of red eyes burned with such furious passion that even Jesse felt it scorch his soul, even though he was not the primary target.

Seeing that fleeing was futile, the gray man calmly stood his ground. His irises morphed into two characters, and this time, Jesse was somehow able to read them. In the left eye, he read "Fantasy," and in the right, "Horror."

The moment Jesse locked eyes with the man, he knew he'd made a fatal mistake. Those symbols bored into his own eyes like a memetic copy, and he closed them out of instinct to not infect his allies.

But he couldn't keep them closed for long. A pit in his stomach forced his windows into the soul to open, where he floated in a gaseous environment. Spectral shackles locked his limbs from moving, connected to chains that stretched into the horizon.

Jesse felt his body accelerating, but with no direction.

The true reality of creation assailed him from all sides. Infinite variation of cosmic horror revealed itself around him as the curtains drew away. His existence was an utterly insignificant mark on reality in the face of the multiversal hierarchy. Beings of untold power marked every space, every contingency. Nothing in existence was permitted without the oversight of the unseen gods.

But these were no gods that Jesse recognized. They were alien, with alien ideas. Alien gods in an alien multiverse.

Jesse wasn't the strongest. He wasn't the most noble, he wasn't the hero that saved the day. He was just a bloke that got lucky at the right time in the right place.

At the start of the initiation, he had killed a man in self-defense. He was at the library, armed with only a pen and paper. He always thought that was the reason he got the Dao of Imagination. When he shoved the piece of paper in the man's face and stabbed him in the neck with the pen, that was a sign to the multiverse that Jesse had a damn good imagination.

Jesse thought that might have been the reason he liked Alistair so much. While he himself was no ne'er-do-well, he couldn't claim any righteousness beyond the ordinary. There was something precious about Alistair's naïveté.

With the translation services of Pathfinder AI, he could read the Chinese characters on their uniforms. Somehow, that illusory promise was the thing that came to mind now. Perhaps it had to do with his Dao of Imagination.

Jesse's eyes opened, freed from the ocular illusion. His allies weren't so lucky.

Thankfully, the wave of ice cream was unaffected by the trap, and the gray man was having difficulty navigating it. He painted a harmonious character onto the very air itself with a bloodied finger.

Through some mystic means, the bloody symbol impressed its power upon the ice cream, causing it to part in the shape of a dome around him. The gray assassin was still rebuffed by the continuous tide, which seemed to drain his concentration as he repainted the character onto the air over and over.

Brigid was unconscious, floating atop her ice cream ocean, where she remained blissfully unaware of the gray-fleshed assassin who inched forward in his protective dome. Over her eyes were the same symbols that had appeared on the assassin's. Jesse's attempts at communication failed.

Marzhan, on the other hand, was shaking off the vestiges of the illusion, her eyes flashing between the symbols and her normal brown irises. Her entire body was covered in small slashes that wouldn't stop dripping blood. In all honesty, Jesse was expecting to find her dead, but he saw that the skeleton hands acted autonomously, fending off the barely perceptible assassin as best they could.

The wound to the man's abdomen had turned his entire midsection black, as his undead flesh rotted from the powerful life affinity Mana of Jesse's laser. Her skeleton hands were fighting a losing battle. With the host unconscious, it was only a matter of time.

Only a matter of time before the proto-Domain collapses, Jesse thought. Marzhan was the linchpin of their strategy. She couldn't fall here.

Jesse soared after the hidden assassin, blasting his green laser eyes. His target swerved out of the way, hiding in the ice cream. If not for his x-ray vision, Jesse would have lost him. Even as it was, it was difficult to remain focused.

Drawing in a deep breath, Jesse exhaled an entire gust of wind, freezing everything in its wake. The naked one was caught up in the frost, becoming a statue along with Marzhan.

Jesse flipped around, already prepared for the other assassin's move. Through their shared Dao, he had a good guess as to what kind of powers they possessed. The diversity of the gray man's powers could only be matched by the Dao of Magic, but Jesse didn't sense anything like it. Given their undead bodies, and the way he morphed before every attack, it was likely that they were the abilities of those that the assassins had killed, quite similar to his own Writeship.

Jesse unleashed a three-pronged attack that he'd learned under Alistair's tutelage.

Dao energy mixed with Mana mixed with *nue*. The last was the hardest part of the technique for him, the ten'gatsu, an ancient technique that combined all three quintessences and was almost impossible to ignore. He had practiced and practiced all for this moment. There would be no failure.

The gray man had abandoned his attack of Brigid, raising a hand to activate some stolen Skill, when the ten'gatsu ripped through his body. As a tripartite and tricolored blast ripped through his body, mind, and soul. Transparent, white, and rainbow shot forth as fast as a bullet.

The attack wasn't meant to harm. Instead, the tiny threads of Dao energy and Fate connecting the two assassins were broken temporarily. With the sudden shock and loss of connection, the gray man froze mid-attack.

Jesse did not let the moment pass by.

He doubled back for a single moment, letting his elbow slam into the gray man's chin. A sickening crack could be heard all throughout the proto-Domain, but Jesse didn't give himself time to worry about what happened to him. His focus was on frozen statue.

The shifty one struggled under the layer of ice created by Jesse's cooling breath, but he had only created hairline fractures in the half second between his freezing and Jesse's ten'gatsu.

Marzhan finally broke free of the illusion, the gray man's concentration maimed. She maintained her composure in spite of her injuries, her aura spiking as she commanded the world to attack the shifty assassin that had almost ended her life.

A bone tree wrapped around his limbs, leaving an opening on his torso. A window that fit Jesse's size exactly.

Jesse mustered all of his fading strength, his Dao Node running out of steam. Imagination, fantasy, was the only thing holding his transformation together.

Life affinity Mana coalesced around his fist and he slammed into the naked assassin with all his momentum. Their imperceptible attacker *shattered* on impact, sputtering around the bone tree like broken glass.

Jesse's robes were sticky and stained with his blood. *Just a little longer,* he told himself. Marzhan was on her knees, breathing heavily. While her wounds hadn't closed, she wasn't suffering blood loss like him. He could tell that she was using her proto-Domain to suppress the foreign curse of the assassin's weapon. It was likely that her deathly Dao was well suited for that.

"Go," she told him. "If I don't have complete calm right now, the proto-Domain will collapse."

Jesse was already gone. He flew toward the gray man, spreading his ice breath in his wake. The ice cream froze nearly solid, while the blood tunnel the assassin had formed started to collapse under the pressure. His once fine silks and jewelry were stained and broken.

His jaw looked several degrees off-centered from Jesse's punch, and one of his eyes was sealed shut. He did not show any signs of surrender.

The noble assassin was only a few feet away from Brigid. Jesse had wondered why he didn't use any long-range Skills, but once he got close to the ice cream he realized that the dessert was naturally absorbing all Mana, even the stuff inside his body. Any external attack would be siphoned so fast it would exist for barely a second.

Jesse waded through the frozen ice cream, using his super strength to carve out a path. The gray man drew another one of his blood sigils, but before it could flash and activate its potential, it withered into the ice cream.

Jesse's transformation slowly faded. His Dao Node was running dry, and the environmental effects were hastening the process. The gray man wasn't unscathed either, and Jesse could see that his gait had grown ragged.

Jesse felt like he was moving through a sea of molasses as he caught up to the gray man. The two gave each other a glance, both huffing and puffing from the exertion of making it through the soft serve.

Brigid was relatively unharmed, despite her paralysis. Their battle had only lasted a few minutes, but that was how things were.

If Wisdom was her dump stat like he guessed, then it made sense that the gray man's ocular illusion was fight-ending, despite how short their encounter was and how strong he knew Brigid to be.

"I was promised better quarry than this," the man spat out. "This standard is pitiful."

"You can't even beat us three." Jesse laughed. "You're not qualified to go after anyone else."

Jesse shuffled forward in a boxing stance while the gray man took out a bejeweled rapier.

They exchanged blows, Jesse throwing a couple of jabs and then a hook, while the gray man ducked and went for a stab. Jesse kicked the sword away and jumped on one foot, following up with a kick to the solar plexus and then a kick to the face in one motion.

Unfortunately, that sent his adversary stumbling toward the unconscious Brigid. The gray man reset his jaw, which Jesse's boot had knocked out of place. He also put a finger to her exposed throat.

"Stay back, or I'll kill her," he promised. Jesse didn't doubt that, remembering the cutting power of the lasers he'd shown before, similar to his own. He stood there, breathing heavily as sweat poured down from his soaking hair onto his forehead and nose. "Let me collect my brother's soul, and I'll leave without trouble. You might not survive, but your two girlfriends will."

Jesse looked into Brigid's eyes, still covered by the characters of "Fantasy" and "Horror." He couldn't say he knew her very well. She had joined the Northeast Freehold after him, and came with her own team of people.

"I'm sorry," he whispered.

Mustering the last ounce of Dao energy he had, Jesse centered on his fantasy. He channeled the memories of reading comics as a kid, shuttling at the gray man faster than the speed of sound.

His fingers tore apart as his body could no longer sustain the form, but his momentum was already set. Jesse was a human kinetic missile, colliding with the gray man in a sickening explosion.

The last thing he saw before he died was a laser piercing Brigid's neck. While it saddened him to see her go, he could only put his faith in Alistair and the rest of their team.

Goodbye, Jesse thought. Then there was nothing.

52 THE STRONGEST PREVAIL

ALISTAIR'S FINISHING Skill lit up the sphere of churning blood with its glorifying light.

Compared to when he used the Skill on Oracle or against his clone, there was a marked difference in the expression of the avatar of justice. It was filled with righteous anger toward the source of Alistair's woes.

Part of the new terrifying aspect came from his recent Talent Tree upgrade. Fear of Glorifying Truth II improved its previous leaf by increasing hesitation and reaction time even further in his enemies when facing an attack to the heart.

His proto-Domain hummed with the soothing chants of Avalokitesvara, spreading a compassionate sutra to the bloodwraiths and beyond. Dozens of the avatar's hands flew at the incoming ice palace, comprised of lightning and force Mana and infused with two of Alistair's Dao Nodes.

The palms of justice collided with the freezing cold, undoing the crystallization of the bloodwraiths. Together, they formed a tide of Dao energy that held back George's proto-Domain. Each time they landed, a gong-like sound and golden pulse of light spread through the walls of the palace, destroying evil wherever it was found.

[Thousand-Armed Bodhisattva Justice] was especially effective against the added miasma of the lich. Alistair suspected that the lich's cultivation was inherently tied to an evil concept, as opposed to George, who seemed to follow the more standard Daos of Magic and Ice.

The intense clash of the proto-Domains at the center groaned with deep vibrations, as the border between the two territories melded together. Ice became ghostly blood and ghostly blood became ice. The border became a synthesis of the two proto-Domains, with elements of both on either side.

Alistair was not content to let his Skill do all the work. He [Dashed] alongside the palms, reaching the border faster than the second wave of his attack, as his increased Agility let him outpace his previous speed.

This kind of proto-Domain warfare was new to him. He had only read what they could scrounge up in the Hall of Math.

There were four outcomes of a Domain battle, which also applied in greater and lesser degrees to proto-Domains.

First was Dominance, where one Domain was far stronger than the other and destroyed the weaker one, taking its place.

The second was Stalemate, where two Domains of relatively equal strength clashed, meeting in the middle with a defined border.

Third was Destruction, where two offensively geared and relatively equal strength Domains clashed, and both got destroyed.

Finally, the situation Alistair found himself in was Synthesis. When two equal but for some reason "compatible" Domains clashed, they could bleed into each other, creating a symbiosis of both.

Upon reaching the blurred borders, Alistair threw [Force Fist] after [Force Fist], pushing his proto-Domain forward. His **Devilsbane Gauntlets** cracked any ice it found. The moment that happened, his proto-Domain seeped in to fill the empty void, bloodwraiths forming in his wake.

Alistair worked in unison with his own proto-Domain to gain ground, relying on the gongs of [Thousand-Armed Bodhisattva Justice] to fight off the omnipresent cold.

However, he was not alone in joining the front line. George had also left his lofty throne. He spoke the invocation for *Glacial Front,* making it the first of his six uses of Rank 1 Spells, though that was old intel and Alistair guessed he probably had access to seven uses per thirteen hours at that point.

An enormous glacier appeared out of thin air, defending against his finishing Skill on top of his [Force Fists]. Within the recesses of Infinite Arsenal, Alistair analyzed the ice more closely. As a Rank 1 Spell, it contained the three quintessences—Mana, Dao, and *nue*. As such, it was even more sturdy than normal.

Alistair's mind whirled into action as he comprehended the daunting wall of ice that blocked against [Thousand-Armed Bodhisattva Justice]. On its own, it would not have been sufficient to defend against his finishing Skill, but since it was being backed up by George's proto-Domain, it worked.

Distribution of nue within subject exists in a fractal pattern, Alistair calculated. If not for his multitude of senses, he wouldn't have been able to properly analyze the composition of the glacier. Alistair directed a [Frozen Claw] at a certain angle, combining a [Draconic Roar] to make his own combination of three quintessences.

Using Infinite Arsenal, Alistair distributed [Frozen Claw's] network within a specific pattern. His *nue*-filled roar eroded the Dao, while he allowed the Mana and Dao of his other Skill to specifically target the *nue* and Mana of the construct.

His punch broke through the ice, turning it to inert slush. Alistair pushed through, his presence as the focal point of his proto-Domain allowing him to instantly convert the territory.

It was a chain reaction, where the more bloodwraiths he created, the easier it was to make more since he had a stronger base. His incursion, viewed from a bird's eye view, was like a needle piercing a balloon, with his base growing thicker as territory gradually flipped over.

Once George lost his glacier, he didn't stay at the border and contest Alistair. Instead, he grew wings of ice and flapped his way to the apex of their proto-Domains, albeit slowly. Those wings wouldn't have been useful in a fight, Alistair suspected, as they looked too heavy and lumbering.

Alistair narrowed his eyes in suspicion. His bodhisattva's last salvo had wiped away all the outer blizzard, leaving George with only the ice palace. *Without his personal resistance, his proto-Domain will fall in 50.5±7.9 seconds.*

The possibilities went through Alistair's mind, not in the form of Fate but within his calculations. *Ice Spear of the False Heavens, Autonomous Crystals, Glacial Front, and Frygian Arrow*, Alistair thought. He had a countermeasure for each one. There were no guarantees that his countermeasures would work, but he was reasonably sure.

However, there was nothing that covered George flying up. Alistair knew that there had to be a reason, but how could he turn back? Caution was good, but giving up momentum was death. Whatever George did, he would adapt.

Alistair's punches bore into the walls of George's home. Boiling blood filled each crevice as his proto-Domain oozed into the space and claimed it. He pushed the pace, using his recently upgraded Tier 3 [Blood Hand].

Tier 3 made his Skill hotter, the blood boiling just like the bloodwraiths. It also gave [Blood Hand] an innate cleansing aspect, as delineated by his Dao Path. Past sins would be washed away in a new rebirth by blood.

[Blood Hand] was the strongest of his main offensive Skills besides [Thousand-Armed Bodhisattva Justice] inside his proto-Domain. Here, he could channel the power of the bloodwraiths to bolster the Skill. He easily melted the ice with every punch, making his way to the throne room.

Alistair's danger sense fluttered. His sensitive hearing caught the beginnings of a word on George's lips.

"Arcanous—" George began, the frosty cigarette still hanging off his lip.

There was something different about this edict, however. Alistair felt a deep chill in his bones at the beginning of the word, even through his proto-Domain's sizzling currents.

George's spells were powerful, yes, but this was something beyond that. [Monk Motionlessness] was a hurricane, going crazy to a level he had never seen before.

He was so close. If he reached the throne and conquered that, it was over for George. It was only a few meters away. But his instincts told him that would only lead to death.

Instead, he turned around.

"Devil Spell—"

Alistair separated his proto-Domain as best he could. He [Dashed] with all the speed he could muster from his legs. The scene of when he first unlocked [Dash] played through in his head. He remembered the desperation of that moment. The way his muscles fired unlike they had ever fired before.

He needed that speed now more than ever. His mind became one with his body, and he envisioned the kinetic chain in action. From the tiniest muscle within his ankle to his quadriceps, he aligned their motions perfectly for the fastest [Dash] in his entire life.

A [Dash] that transcended [Dash]. He received a notification of Skill upgrade, but he wasn't paying attention to that. Dev'rox poured a hefty chunk of his own reserves to accelerate Alistair by compressing the space, costing more than normal since it was part of the territory that belonged to George.

"*Number 6: Reverse Entropic—*"

Alistair returned to the depths of his proto-Domain, having drawn the blood that had conquered the enemy's territory back into the sphere. His proto-Domain was larger than before and he had managed to extricate 70% of it from the synthesis at the border, though not the entirety.

The amount of *nue* and Mana that was gathering around George's person was unfathomable, condensing into an immense aura. Alistair knew a huge attack was coming, shifting the bulk of his ectoplasmic blood to the side of his proto-Domain that faced George, but he didn't know exactly what kind of attack it would be.

Knowing that element would have helped him prepare. If it was a spear, or a beam, or simply a torrential downpour of hail, he could set up his proto-Domain.

"*Meteor.*"

Alistair trembled from the sheer amount of killing intent in the final word of his spell. He was one hundred percent certain that this was a Rank 2 Spell as opposed to Rank 1. There was no way a Rank 1 Spell could be so powerful.

He took out the **Heavenly Nectar Incense** he'd retrieved from Dragonus. If Dao was weak to *nue*, then *nue* was weak to Mana. What was better than the concentrated lightning of a Mana Storm?

It was then that he saw what *Reverse Entropic Meteor* entailed.

George froze his own proto-Domain.

Not in the sense that his already freezing territory grew even colder. No, the entire sphere of his proto-Domain literally froze into one giant ball of ice.

Or, as George's spell named it, a meteor. The meteor smashed into the bloodwraiths, Alistair's proto-Domain groaning and buckling under the immense weight. The impact of George's frozen proto-Domain crashing into his proto-Domain created a shockwave that rippled through the air, shaking the energy bridges.

There was no sense in waiting. Alistair uncorked the bottle.

The pure, unadulterated wrath of the world came forth. The red lightning of a Mana Storm, one of the most elemental forms of nature that existed in the multiverse.

The lightning was mixed with two elements—his Dao of Justice and the last embers of the physical incense itself. The former wasn't strong enough to dominate the lightning at all, simply serving to guide its natural fury down a path of justice.

The incense gave the lightning more essence, after it had remained inert for so long inside the gourd. The sum total was something that exceeded even the original strike that Alistair had captured.

Alistair's hands felt the sting, like hitting a baseball with a metal bat the wrong way, only magnified by a thousand. Vibrations oscillated throughout his entire body, and his bones rattled in between his soft tissue as he used every point of his Strength to hold onto the bottle.

Since he was aiming the gourd up toward the meteor, the propulsion thrust him into the ground. He felt his back grind against the edge of his proto-Domain, breaking through and slamming into the bridge below.

The concentrated lightning exploded in a flash of brilliance. Thousands of individual lightning bolts converged, appearing as one gigantic ray.

Alistair closed his eyes as his vision was overtaken by the sheer luminance of the lightning. He heard what sounded like a million-times magnified crackle of a fire when the lightning made contact with the meteor.

Alistair could feel that trying to flee was useless. The meteor's reverse entropic aura resisted any change in the atmosphere, preventing all movement. He could only pray that his trump card was enough.

The explosion tore apart his proto-Domain. Bloodwraiths evaporated as the lightning and ice consumed everything.

The gourd ran out of lightning. Alistair felt the strength leave his hands as the backlash of releasing the lightning reverberated through his arms.

A blast of wind washed over Alistair, destroying the last remnants of his proto-Domain and sending him off the bridge. He purposefully let himself fall over the edge instead of having the invisible guardrail protect him, tumbling through the air and landing on the floor below with a splat.

Despite his Constitution, since he didn't fall with his **Fall of Fleet,** he was a bit rattled. The landing and the explosion made him dizzy. Alistair stood up, wiping blood away from his mouth.

Alistair felt empty. It was as if there was a hole in his soul, depriving him of meaning. He was also deprived of almost 40% of his remaining Dao energy. But this feeling was more than that. Alistair knew this had to do with his proto-Domain's premature end.

There were many times when Alistair had used up all or almost all of his Dao energy, and he wasn't actually close to that point, having just under half of his total reserves left. Having your Domain or proto-Domain destroyed while it was imposing its effect on the world was dangerous for the body, mind, and soul. It made one vulnerable to permanent damage.

Alistair looked up, unable to see the bridge he fell from. If his proto-Domain cracked from the explosion, it stood to reason that George's had as well.

At least, he was praying that was the case. If not, he was in huge trouble.

The aftereffects of Infinite Arsenal made him woozy, adding to his mental fatigue. The deeper and longer he stayed within each of the three states of Kai'tazake Mutra, the greater the opposite effect he would feel upon exiting.

For Tranquil Mind, this was a mania that defiled tranquility. For Black Impermanence, it was a fragile state of mercurial emotion. And for Infinite Arsenal, it might have been the worst—an inability to formulate complex ideas.

Thanks to Alistair's innate intelligence, what was simple for him might have been more complex for others. But he was still hampered, for the moment.

Those restrictions didn't apply to Dev'rox.

Coincidentally, Dev'rox wasn't even in Alistair's proto-Domain. They had separated before that exchange. An instantaneous change of scenery brought Alistair into the sky, thanks to the imp's swapping ability.

Alistair only had a fraction of a second to take in his surroundings.

George's proto-Domain was gone.

Unfortunately, while the lightning did its work, the remnants of the ice palace formed a makeshift Dao field. The bridge was still covered in ice, large chunks of the palace strewn about serving as conduits for George's power.

Alistair used a [Draconic Roar] from above, mostly to push himself back to safety. George, a hundred feet away from the roar, shifted his body to dodge, returning the attack with ice spears of his own.

Alistair skidded down the energy bridge, coming to a halt as the spears flashed by. He entered Tranquil Mind once more, allowing him to grab the spears with his **Devilsbane Gauntlet** midair.

The momentum of the spears carried him back. He moved with them like they were a part of his body since birth, swaying in a circle and throwing them back with even more force.

If Alistair wasn't in Tranquil Mind, he would have cursed.

The moment after the spears left his fingertips, he felt the chill. It had the lich's fingerprints all over it. Alistair could feel his bountiful life force draining away. He felt like he was trapped in a swamp of deathly ice, where every move made the frostbite bore deeper into his soul.

Dao energy rushed through Alistair's meridians as he tried to flush the foreign invader out. Yet with every move he made, the mysterious energy was ahead of him. It was Dao energy, but of a strange kind that he hadn't encountered before. Whether that was because it came from a lich or something innate to the Dao it practiced, he wasn't sure.

The net effect was that Alistair moved in slow motion. Slow motion for him was fast for a normal person—which seemed trivial when George opened his arms to reveal his armaments.

The third use of his ranked spells—this time, an *Ice Spear of the False Heavens*. George spoke those words as the hoarfrost grew over Alistair's body.

An array the size of an elephant glimmered above George's head, with dozens and dozens of smaller ones at either side. An ornate spear of sapphire ice crystal flew at Alistair, along with an entire sea of its smaller brethren.

Alistair gritted his teeth. He was flushing Dao energy through his system like a madman, but the hoarfrost was still winning. His mind was a temple of calm as he contemplated his next move.

From aeons past to aeons future, the chain remains unbroken. He had wanted to save it for an offensive surprise, but here it would have to do.

Alistair progressed his Dao of Justice with a First Deepening.

The prerequisite understanding was already there. Only now did he let that understanding move his Dao Node forward.

Alistair was never without allies. However, in his time cultivating, he was the one who was doing most of the saving. While he never downplayed anyone else's accomplishments, he always felt the responsibility. As the strongest, that was his prerogative.

The insight he had obtained was that he was not alone. He was not alone on Earth, and he was not alone in the multiverse. His desire for cosmic justice was not new.

How could it be? The heritage that was a huge reason for why he'd gotten so far derived from the Sage of Eternal Mercy. When Alistair made it to the peak, he would have much to thank the Sage for.

That was the unbroken chain. Yes, it was more powerful for a Truthseeker to pass down a legacy, but did that invalidate someone less powerful? Even if the Sage never had a guiding figure as he was to Alistair, every person experienced at least some kindness in their lives. Some goodness that they could use an example. Even if it was the tiniest of things, it could be passed forward.

A perfect world was made up of those small acts of kindness. They formed the foundation of true happiness, where goodness existed as the ordinary mode of existence.

Achievement: Dao Node (II) (Dao of Justice) — First Deepening. *Heroic Inheritor added to Dao Elements.* Reward: +50 Endurance, +30 Charisma, +15% Endurance, +10% Charisma.

While this was a First Deepening, as he already had made a First Widening for his Justice Node, the increase in Dao energy was equivalent to that of a Second Deepening. That meant that his total Dao energy reserves went up by a whole 25%, and within the Justice Node, an entire 100% increase, filled to the brim and ready to be used.

Alistair did just that. The extra influx of Dao energy from his improved Dao Node flushed away the hoarfrost. It gave him time to wrap his arms around his chest in an X and activate [Frozen Claw].

His gauntlets served as a buffer for the incoming ice spears. [Frozen Claw] touched with the initial spear, his own ice overlapping George's as they merged into one. This continued in a bolt-like web. Only the first few spears actually hit Alistair, the rest becoming frozen in the network as [Frozen Claw] spread like a virus.

Alistair imbued "Permanent Haunt" within the Skill. Normally, ethereal objects would have been harder to interact with, but the ice created by [Frozen Claw] was special, and allowed him to more easily encase ghostly existences.

An onlooker would have seen a conical web of pale blue ice crystals in the sky, along with darker blue spears of varying sizes contained within. Those spears would have looked partially translucent due to the effects of his "Permanent Haunt" division of the Ghost Node.

Alistair bounced against the energy bridge, flying dozens of meters backward as he almost lost consciousness. **[Frozen Claw]** trapped the spears, but their momentum still transferred to him. His brain lurched in its skull from the sudden movement, causing whiplash.

The notification he received earlier when **[Dashing]** forced itself upon him as he skidded to a halt, face flat on the bridge.

Skill Evolution:

Tier 1 Expert Skill **[Mindshift]** gained (replacing **[Dash]**).

[Mindshift] (Tier 1 Expert Skill): *Since time immemorial, the greatest fighters of the multiverse have sought to bridge the gap between themselves and their opponents. The great siege masters of the Dao and magus have their tricks and evasions, but so do we. Through harnessing the power of the mind, a psychic shadow follows the user during and for 0.5 seconds after the Dash, confusing foes.* Retains Flicker, Airwalking aspects. Mana Cost: 35/variable *Nue* cost. Upgradeable (0/500).

Alistair shot up, Tranquil Mind guarding him from any grogginess. His improved Dao Node melted the last of the hoarfrost. It was time to put his new Skill to work. Alistair activated **[Mindshift]**.

Alistair's mind expanded.

He saw reality as it existed in the purely mental. There were no words that could do it justice. If he could describe it, he would say that the psychic reality was black and white, full of interminable patterns of increasing complexity. It was the realm of ordered computation but also unbounded creativity.

All this, he was only privy to for a millisecond. **[Mindshift]** brought him to the unknown and then out of it, where his consciousness returned to the physical and he found himself beside George in two-thirds the time his old **[Dash]** would have taken to cover the same distance.

The psychic shadow was far more real than his Tier 4 **[Dash]**. They were twins and yet so different. To Alistair's eyes, his *nue* shadow looked black-and-white, formless and faceless, yet he could tell that others saw it differently.

Or rather, their eyes saw the unformed mass of *nue* that was reality, but their brains couldn't analyze the shadow properly. Therefore, they concluded that there was no difference between Alistair and the psychic shadow.

His shadow performed the same **[Mindshift]** as him, moving forward in unison. Now, it lingered for half a second, copying his exact moves.

They both used **[Blood Hand]**, but with a twist. Instead of crimson, his gauntlets gleamed with a black hue. A substance that Alistair and George both knew well. Demon blood, blood that Alistair absconded with in a previous exchange with {Blood Debt}.

Alistair's hand slashed the ice, melting George's Dao field within close proximity. The Devil King didn't react fast enough to shift to the other pieces of his shattered proto-Domain. Or he was waiting for his own opportunity. Within Tranquil Mind, Alistair was unfazed by such a possibility.

[Hand of Karma] went over his off-hand, pulses of red light searing threads of Fate.

George's eyes shifted from clone to real and real to clone. Alistair was hoping that he would be paralyzed with indecision and have to fend off both, but somehow, the Devil King made the correct choice.

An ice spear appeared from a sigil on his chest, headed straight for the real Alistair. The *nue* shadow disappeared after the half-second window was up, sublimating into psychic smoke.

This time, when Alistair grabbed the spear, there was no lich's aura. The demonic blood corroded through the spear with ease. George didn't have the time to speak one of his Rank 1 Spells. Alistair felt his victory in the air as the threads of Fate closed around the Devil King. It was poetic justice, to defeat him with his own blood.

But something felt wrong. *The path of enlightenment is filled with worldly temptations,* Alistair thought as his black fist arced toward George. *To eschew one's chance at escaping the wheel of Samsara for a future opportunity is the epitome of foolishness.*

Alistair felt Dev'rox's presence once more, having flown back up, greeting him with a flow of spatial affinity Mana. They needed no words to coordinate, the imp still possessing almost two-thirds of his Mana should they need it later.

George let out a puff of air. His cigarette glowed and in an instant ice expanded from the butt. Despite Alistair's ridiculous speed, he wasn't faster than the frozen crystal that came from the tip.

The ice formed into a saber-tooth tiger, crashing into Alistair a split second before he connected with George. He felt the maw of the beast close around his neck, only preventing his decapitation by offering up his arm.

Pain exploded in his palm, spreading to his forearm and bicep. Alistair prevented the crystalline cat from impaling his jugular, but it pierced through his **Devilsbane Gauntlet** with ease, something that Alistair didn't think he would have seen at this level.

His **[Blood Hand]** vanished, absorbed by the tiger, which turned black around its jaw and head as it imbibed the demon blood.

The tiger tackled him away from George, pressing him down against the ice. Alistair tried to pin his forearm as deep into the tiger's throat as possible, remembering when his dad said that was how he stopped a stray dog attack.

Alistair's mind was insulated from panic via Tranquil Mind, yet pain still penetrated his mental sanctuary. In fact, it was so strong that he could feel his grasp on Tranquil Mind start to falter, something that had never happened before.

How is this possible? Alistair thought. It had to be in the fangs of the beast. No ordinary puncture wound, even from an eight-inch fang, could produce that amount of agony. Alistair had braved the purgatorial fires of the Steel Body trial, and even that took a certain amount of time to get going.

This pain was instant and unbearable and unlike anything he had ever felt. It grew in intensity rather than fading, and soon he was overcome with delirium.

Alistair vaguely sensed a cold presence close to him. George shifted his body to the nearest ice, but he couldn't focus on that now.

"STAND UP, YOU BASTARD!"

Alistair felt a sudden rash of sanity as Dev'rox shouldered the burden of his pain.

Dev'rox grimaced, their minds dividing the pain equally. "If you don't survive here, how will I get my revenge on Kyraxadon?"

Alistair smiled, activating **[Force Fist]** with the hand outside the mouth, and **[Frozen Claw]** with his hand inside the mouth.

He was met with total ice. Before he could even react, he was encased in ice that seared his soul.

Alistair recognized the spell—*Autonomous Crystals*. He hadn't experienced it first-hand. He had thought its primary use was against tides of enemies, where the chain reaction of ice could freeze an entire army, but he'd made a slight miscalculation.

The Autonomous Crystals were different. While they were cold, it worked at a more spiritual level, like his own **[Frozen Claw]**.

His Constitution and Wisdom couldn't hold out against the ice, representing his natural physical and spiritual resistances. He was no soul cultivator like his sister, so the strength of his spiritual network was only influenced by his Wisdom, unlike his extremely well-trained mind.

The cold slithered through his robes and skin, creating microtears that served as conduits for the foreign ice.

Alistair tried cycling Dao energy through his meridians, though he couldn't come close to having enough throughput to ward off the ice entering his system. The ice coming from *Autonomous Crystals* was way stronger than the previous chill that attacked him when he caught one of George's spears.

A sudden flush of warmth overcame his body.

A familiar aura flooded every meridian in his body, washing away the cold and turning his skin and organs golden.

Drauku's protective pendant activated. A golden ankh enveloped Alistair, sealing him off from George's attacks.

The light was not hot to the touch, but it melted the remaining ice in George's vicinity, closing off his teleportation.

Alistair had no time to bask in his friend's assistance, as the tiger pounced.

This time, Alistair was ready. The cat had been separated from Alistair by George's own spell, so he had enough space to react. While the tiger was fast and its bite was corrosive, when Alistair socked it in the jaw with a **[Force Fist]**, it shattered into a million pieces.

Alistair felt a bone in his forearm crack. His eyes traversed downward. He had foolishly forgotten about the tiger's venom since the defensive pendant had alleviated the pain. The structural damage to his arm was obvious in the blackened flesh of his right forearm, where his bone fractured upon his punch.

He realized the rot was spreading, and a decisive move was necessary. Using the claws of his left hand, he cleanly sliced out a chunk of flesh the size of a golf ball, **[Mindshifting]** backward.

Alistair caught his breath in the distance, though he kept his attention focused on George the whole time. Alistair's Mana was down to a little over a thousand, under half of his total, and his Health was at three-fifths. His Stamina was the lowest but regenerated at a far faster rate.

In terms of his combat effectiveness, it was mainly his right arm that was lagging behind, but he could still use it.

Four out of six of Rank 1 Spells used, Alistair thought. *Though let's assume he has seven. Then he has three left that I have to work around.*

Alistair was going under the assumption that George could use his spells in any permutation, casting more than one of the same spell if he wanted.

That was why Alistair was surprised when George used his next spell right away.

Despite their distance, the Devil King's voice carried with ease. *"Arcanous Devil Spell #3: Frygian Arrow."*

The purple arrow flew at Alistair, gathering all the cold in the environment and setting the air on fire.

This arrow was different from the previous times. As it flew through the air, the apparition of a cackling skull appeared on top of it. The skull was a sickly shade of blue like George's ice, ethereal in a manner somewhat similar to Dev'rox, with horns and glowing red eyes surrounded by pits of absolute darkness and despair.

Alistair could tell that this was the true power of the lich that bolstered George's proto-Domain and his previous spear that had temporarily trapped him.

Once more, the restriction of the lich spread out in a wave faster than even his new **[Mindshift]**, a thin blue film of energy wrapping over the battlefield in an instant. It wasn't harmful, but it affected his movement Skills in a way beyond Alistair's understanding.

Alistair felt it was akin to a lesser but extremely focused Dao field, where instead of trying to cause damage, its only purpose was to anchor its subjects.

He still had to try.

Alistair's legs pumped beneath him as he fired every muscle he could. As he tried activating **[Mindshift]**, he felt as if the lich had locked the Skill away behind cold iron bars.

His Justice Node flared, as he used the potent image that helped him advance his Node in the first place. The Heroic Inheritor.

While he moved at normal speed, his Skill struggled against the restriction, causing him to stutter in [**Mindshift**], only traveling a dozen feet at a time.

The final touch was Black Impermanence. As the dark aura surrounded his skin, Alistair sealed off the lich's suppression, matching tit-for-tat. He was free to move.

The arrow and the skull soared toward him, with Alistair realizing right away there was a difference. When George used the Skill before, it went in a straight line. Now, he could see that the Devil King was steering it.

With [**Mindshift**], he outsped the arrow, but not the effects it had on the environment. The lich's head exploded in a blue fire that accompanied the innate purple flames of the arrow. Alistair was reminded of Dragonus's lake of black fire he'd created with the Heavenly Nectar Incense, in the way George's variegated fire covered the sky.

It was also a testament that Dragonus's finishing move was comparable to a mere tool in George's wide arsenal, no more than a normal Skill he might use against a strong opponent rather than a last resort.

The flames were searing hot, licking at his skin like a hound of Hades. Black Impermanence protected him from the pain and negative effects, taking it out as an advance for later. But it was unsustainable in the long term.

Dev'rox made his move. Like George, the verbal invocation of his spell was necessary. His small mouth opened as he manifested outside of Alistair's body, saying, *"Spatial Rending."*

The arrays formed out of thin air, cascading into a web of space affinity Mana. Each array shot out a stream of blue light to its neighbors, assembling into a familiar lattice.

Despite Alistair's own impressive set of moves, he found Dev'rox's spell to be the most mind-boggling and miraculous ability. Each glimpse of space swapped with another, so that all the spatial territory within the confines of the web was in disarray.

His body and the incoming arrow appeared like they were shattered into a million pieces and then jumbled all around. If there were any spectators of their duel, they wouldn't have been able to follow anything.

Dev'rox and Alistair's mind became one, as he needed the imp's help to discern the random pattern of disjointed regions. Only the creator of the mess could truly understand the meaning behind the randomness. The

Spatial Rending expanded at the fringes, encompassing more territory every second.

This required an enormous amount of Mana on Dev'rox's end, and his Mana pool was dwindling by the second. If Alistair wanted his partner to have any Mana by the end of the expansion, he would have to act quickly.

There was one difference between this Spatial Rending and Dev'rox's earlier use against his doppelganger—this one worked on a different conceptual level. The previous version was directed toward confusion, where the laws of physics were immutably preserved, and the disarray was in the brain of the target.

Now, Dev'rox blended the disparate regions' causalities, allowing for local influence. In a way, there were now two mappings of space, the original that was now spread out randomly, and the new one.

For example, the flames existing in the previous formation split apart into the millions of regions of space within the spell, and in their new formation, they made the new and empty bordering regions hotter.

With Dev'rox's guidance, Alistair activated **[Force Fist]**. Parts of his skin were melting because of the heat of the flames, yet he didn't pay it any attention under Black Impermanence. With *Spatial Rending*, it was as if he was omniscient within the boundaries of the spell.

Everything aligned perfectly. While he didn't have the analytical mind that had torn apart the glacier back when they were fighting within their proto-Domains, Dev'rox offered a similar edge. Alistair's speed was unrivaled as he issued a combo with both his fists cloaked in a coral aura.

Alistair incorporated what he had learned up to this point.

The fundamentals of martial arts combined with Dev'rox's brainpower. An indomitable will. Heroic Inheritor combined with the sealant of Black Impermanence.

He attacked every weakness in the *Frygian Arrow*, using the interconnectedness of the space to his advantage.

Dozens of punches landed in a tiny window, fracturing the flaming arrow. The skull dissipated, the remnants of the heat singeing Alistair's fingers even through his **Devilsbane Gauntlet**. This was made doubly worse by the glaring hole gouged out in one glove by the ice tiger earlier.

Alistair **[Mindshifted]** forward, drawing upon even more of Dev'rox's reserves to shift along the *Spatial Rending*. The imp was running dangerously low, but he needed the added confusion if he wanted to grasp victory.

The *nue* clone was yet another distraction as *Spatial Rending's* borders expanded to encompass George.

The man didn't make a move to flee—he wasn't as fast as Alistair, and with his ice field destroyed, he didn't have the luxury of teleportation. Still, if he really felt like his life was in danger, he would have tried something.

Knowing this, it was obvious that the Devil King had a trick up his sleeve, most likely more than one. Alistair continued, nonetheless.

As he moved, he stripped off his robes. The lich's mysterious blue flames had stripped the clothing of their protective power. Thankfully, since their upgrade from Felix Mwangi, if they weren't completely torn to tatters, they would recover from feeding off his spiritual presence.

Alistair's physique rippled with corded muscle. Since his time in the Holy Ravine, his bulk had increased substantially, with only minuscule detriments to his speed and flexibility.

His chest and arms were horribly burnt, skin flaking off. Major parts of his body were bright red from the burns. They would have been classified as third degree by the medicine of the before.

Meaningless, Alistair thought. He could operate with Black Impermanence. As soon as George came within the boundaries of Spatial Rending, he ended his **[Mindshift]**, switching to a **[Lightning of Justice]** aimed at the disparate parts of George's body at once.

Spatial Rending had left George in a thousand pieces split up across the spell's reach. He couldn't adapt in time to the new arrangement, falling prey to the lightning. Smoke swirled up from his skin as he received electrical burns.

Alistair freestyled, feeling the desperation despite his seemingly advantaged position. His instincts told him to leave nothing on the table, so he went with a move he had never accomplished before.

Ten'gatsu. Alistair remembered when Anthony used that move against him in their battle to the death. Now that he looked back on it, his use of the technique was so flawed, it was a miracle that Alistair had fallen for it for even a second. It went to show how naive they were back then.

The ten'gatsu was combining the Dao, Mana, and *nue* in a singular attack. This served as a perfect smokescreen for a finishing blow, as the triple quintessence attracted so much attention through supernatural virtue.

Alistair had done some reading on the technique, and from what little information he found, there was something special about combining the three in one. He pleaded that this would be sufficient.

Alistair's ten'gatsu was far more masterful than Anthony's, merging the energies into one flash of gray light that flickered straight at George's head.

This was his moment. Alistair [**Mindshifted**] again, releasing Dev'rox's Rank 1 Spell to save the last vestiges of his partner's Mana. There was no need for the confusion of the spell now that the ten'gatsu strike was in motion.

Alistair started to activate [**Blood Hand**], summoning up the remnants of the demonic blood he stole. However, [**Monk Motionlessness**] caused him to stutter. There was something coming, something so overwhelming, his Karmic vision sparkled without even activating.

Perhaps it was that George's Fate-warding ability had run out after using the lich's skull for his arrow, but Alistair thought that was unlikely. Instead, as he felt the threads of Fate shine around the First Devil King, he realized that whatever was coming was just that strong, it overpowered any masking measure.

George took out the **Experiment Cursed Needle #7**, stabbing himself in the jugular.

Time seemed to come to a standstill as Alistair's ten'gatsu and [**Blood Hand**] flew toward George in incremental steps. Alistair was only a few body lengths away when the point of the needle drew blood.

His body acted without thought. He automatically switched to Tranquil Mind as a defense mechanism, willing to take the brunt of his injuries to get even a little bit of a head start.

While he didn't see George's transformation himself, he saw through Dev'rox's vision as he [**Mindshifted**] away as fast as possible.

A swirling black mark washed over George's skin, starting from the point of injection. It spread over his entire body, wiggling and glowing with a soft orange light until it settled into a marbled black-and-skin colored pattern.

The needle sticking out of George's neck crumbled into dust. Alistair understood right away what had happened. His sister had been the one to discover the needle's influence over Fate. They had known it could be used to free the other Devil King's from his Fate-related control.

There had always been a nagging thought at the back of his head. That aspect wasn't meaningless, but was that really why George wanted the needle so badly? But Alistair had no time for regrets, no time to second-guess his past actions.

Like the calm tickle of a gentle breeze, a forest of black threads of Fate formed a web surrounding Alistair. He halted his **[Mindshift]** and transferred his trance to Infinite Arsenal.

A cough escaped his throat as he felt the pains of his burns for the first time. His skin was blistering and falling off. Even with his physique, his performance would be affected. Alistair turned back to look at George, who carefully strode forward, the black threads of Fate attaching to his body like a marionette.

"I've learned not to underestimate you," he said. "But this is your end."

53 FALLING BEHIND

Oliver wasn't sure what to make of Kristina. Then again, he wasn't sure what to make of any of the artificial situations created by the Pathfinder AI.

The Trexian seemed so real, possessing a vibrant personality. It made it difficult to believe she was mere programming.

Programming, illusion, artificial life, Oliver thought. *We have no idea what it is. There's still so much mystery we can't comprehend about the powers of those at the top.*

Oliver, as a terminally online nerd in high school, remembered reading about dust theory. Even if the construct that created the former prisoner was totally dissimilar from normal life, if it produced the same output of behavior, who was to say it wasn't self-aware?

"You're sure you know where the Utopic Bomb is?" Blaise asked.

The three of them were running in the sewers of the technological metropolis, after they narrowly avoided the cops who were patrolling the street level.

"Yes, I know," Kristina shot back. "Now be quiet and cloak your Mana as best as possible."

Oliver and Blaise did as they were told, silently following the Trexian woman deeper and deeper into the sanitation system.

Oliver would have thought that it would be more... advanced than the cities of Earth, but he was mistaken. To him, it looked like a normal sewer, not that he had ever been in one. There were a few architectural signs that made it distinctly Edenic, like a glowing blue line across the ceiling that lit up the tunnels, but overall, it wasn't very high-tech.

The thick stone walls gave off a feeling of advanced age. Oliver almost felt like the lights grew dimmer the deeper they went, though that could have been his imagination. Any noise they made reverberated through the cavernous sewer, echoing back at them as a reminder they were alone.

After around ten minutes of running, Kristina suddenly darted against the wall. Oliver and Blaise followed suit, hugging the wall without understanding why.

Kristina put a finger up to her lip. "We're close."

"Are we looking out for something?" Oliver asked. This would have been a great moment for Caren's telepathy, but they were way too far away.

"Shh," Kristina hushed. "I have to concentrate."

She sat down on the damp ground, closing her eyes. Oliver felt a confluence of Mana around her, expanding out from her body in waves. They were close to a four-way intersection, where each of the tunnels leading out narrowed in the distance, except for the one they were in.

Oliver scratched his head, unsure of what to do. She reminded him of Pharaoh in the way she was haphazardly acting without explaining things.

He took a deep breath and leaned against the wall.

Shit, he thought as he felt his cloak get damp. *Should have thought about that.* While his Northeast Order outfit was of the enchanted general-rank version, it didn't have protection against the rain. Then again—

A sharp pain pulsed from his back.

A few weeks ago, Oliver had come up with an ingenious solution to one of his major problems. After seeing how valuable keen senses and reaction time were with Alistair, he recognized his own lack in the area. While he wasn't a close ranged fighter, that didn't mean he would never have to deal with assassins and unexpected fights.

To remedy that area, he had taken an unusual zombie as a companion—a mouse. The mouse came from a highly sensitive horde of monsters that had been particularly difficult to uproot because they would always flee whenever anyone got close, possessing sensory abilities far beyond that of the average cultivator.

This zombie mouse hung out on his back, ready to bite him if it sensed any danger, according to the programming he gave it.

Oliver felt the adrenaline pumping as his eyes scanned the surroundings.

An electric arrow appeared out of nowhere, flying straight toward the meditating Kristina.

Oliver acted without thinking. It was too little time to summon an **[Otherworld Gate]**, and he didn't have any other defensive Skill.

So he grabbed it out of the air.

Death affinity Mana exploded and swirled around his hand in an instant. It was so dark and concentrated that you could only catch a glimpse of his pale skin beneath.

Even still, the moment Oliver came into contact with the electrified arrow, he received a shock that almost brought him to his knees. He followed the arrow's momentum, slamming it against the sewer wall, where it exploded and sent rocks flying all over the place.

Kristina sprang into action. She was a complete blur, dashing toward the source of the arrow with pure bloodlust in her eyes. The source, which was one of his oldest allies.

Blaise Blanchett.

They were never the closest of friends, but like everyone who had been fighting so long together, they had an unspoken bond. The head of the education branch who had taught thousands of students at that point.

Chameleon, Oliver thought. He felt a pang of pain as he realized that likely meant the real Blaise was dead.

A torrent of wind exploded from Kristina's heels and elbow as her fist connected with Blaise's cheek.

Given how obvious her immense power was, Oliver was expecting a gory sight. However, instead of exploding into a pile of teeth and viscera, Blaise collapsed into snakes.

Every inch of his skin crumbled into dust as hundreds of white snakes flew off in every direction. They were faster than Oliver expected, belying their appearance as normal snakes. Kristina moved like lightning, punching dozens of them, but there were too many for her to catch. Some of them slithered away despite her best efforts.

For a moment, it looked as if she was going to go after them, but then she turned around with a snarl. "He's spread his consciousness amongst the snakes," she told Oliver. "It's no use trying to chase him down."

Oliver gave her a thumbs up as he gathered himself to his knees, his skin still smoking from the arrow. His Constitution and Strength were his dump stats, far below even his Endurance and Agility in terms of physical attributes.

"You fool." Kristina shook her head and placed a hand on Oliver's back. A warm, soothing feeling accompanied a flash of green light as he felt his internal wounds being mended. "I would have been fine. I'm a warrior. Do you think I don't have defenses of my own?"

"Sorry," Oliver said sheepishly. "It was just instinct."

"I respect your gumption, young man. But what was that? Why are there traitors in your midst? Should I suspect you to turn into a pile of frogs as you backstab me?"

Oliver chuckled, though that only made the pain worse. "Didn't have time to explain. Alistair suspected a camouflage artist named Chameleon infiltrated our team. Looks like he was correct."

"You're not hiding anything else from me?" Kristina asked.

"I wasn't hiding anything in the first place," Oliver replied. "Like I said, no time."

She stared at him, and something in his face must have convinced her. "Fine. I'll believe you." Kristina turned around, walking toward the intersection of tunnels. "If your friend that's not your friend has joined the enemy, he'll be working to find the Programmer."

"The programmer? Why didn't you tell Alistair any of this?"

Even before those words exited Oliver's mouth, he knew how stupid they were. Her programming wouldn't let her do that until the right time. Otherwise, this little game of the Pathfinder couldn't properly showcase their talents.

Kristina gave him a blank stare of an NPC and continued as if Oliver hadn't asked the second part. "The Programmer is the only one who can install the security system in the mayor's office. If she's allowed to do that, our mission to assassinate the mayor will become much more difficult."

She sat back down on the ground. "And in order to assassinate the mayor, we need to find the Utopic Bomb."

Oliver leaned against the wall once again, this time not letting his guard down. Given that the traitor was Chameleon, which was a nigh guarantee, he probably wouldn't mess with the two of them. Chameleon was ranked fifth among the Devil Kings, but wasn't known for his combat prowess.

He had only gotten the jump on Sally Ryder and Marzhan through subterfuge. Assassin was a more befitting term for him than a fighter. Oliver was confident that with the addition of his warren, he could win in a one-on-one fight, let alone with Kristina's assistance.

I need to tell Alistair about this, anyway, Oliver thought. *The other Devil Kings must be doing their missions, with the George clone taking care of the rest of our team. If that's the case, then they should be breezing through their missions compared to us two.*

Oliver summoned one of his messenger bird zombies, sending one toward Alistair and one toward Caren. He still wasn't sure what Chameleon's purpose was in attacking so soon. Not that he had a great chance in any case, but surely there was a better time?

Kristina jumped up, making Oliver flinch. "That bastard."

"What?" Oliver rose to attention.

"Come here," Kristina said, letting a gust of wind carry her as she jumped up to the ceiling of the tunnel, cracking the stone brick. She hung on with her vise-like grip, digging out more bricks. "It's gone."

Oliver walked over and looked up. Where she had removed the bricks, there was a spherical hole the size of a basketball. There was a faint scarlet glow to the opening, situated around three points that formed a line.

His eyes widened. "Chameleon stole the bomb?"

"My superiors gave me the encrypted location of the Utopic Bomb." Kristina let go of the elevated rock and landed with a crunch. "I had to do some Topological Untangling calculations to decode the encryption. It should have been right there. I don't understand. How the hell did that snake man find it before I did?"

Oliver got a closer look at the bomb hole. "There's your answer."

Using his aura like it was a part of him since birth, he communed with the lingering power, drawing the bomb's fumes down. The gaseous red substance fluttered around Oliver's pitch black aura, where he analyzed it carefully.

"There are traces of many affinities here," Oliver noted. "It's highly complex. There's some kind of spiritual scaffolding holding the different affinities into one unit, though it isn't a tertiary Mana affinity or anything like that."

Kristina stared at him bluntly. "I didn't sense anything."

Oliver shrugged. "I use my aura with everything I do. It's natural my aura sense is stronger than yours. I've spent time with your kind, and I know you use your danger sense as a crutch. Still, it's impressive that he was able to steal it in that short window when he went into snake mode."

"What are we waiting for?" Kristina motioned after where Chameleon spread out. "If he has the bomb, we need to find him!"

"Already on it."

The moment he had noticed the signature, he had already begun tracking. The problem was, the Utopic Bomb's presence was faint to begin with. The only reason there was so much of the stuff in the hole was that it had to have been there a while. All the traces in the air where Chameleon passed through were already fading.

Thankfully, Oliver had his trusty steed—the zombified Sessen Esshei. According to some, snakes had an even better sense of smell than dogs, and it applied to the mutated pit viper. Kristina even flinched a little when the enormous serpent slithered out of the [Otherworld Gate].

He can't be too far, Oliver thought. Zombie Sessen smelled the bomb's aura residue, winding after it as fast as he could. Oliver hopped along for the ride, with Kristina following on foot.

The link between him and his zombies wasn't as developed as that of Alistair and his ghost buddy, but he could still feel some of the snake's senses. There was an initial bout of confusion as to what to track, as Sessen was confused by the scent of the snakes that Blaise had collapsed into.

But he quickly caught on to the peculiar aura. It stood out, despite how faint it was. Sessen shot after the scent like a rocket. His zombies didn't retain much of their personality, but the Serpent King kept his ferocity. That was for sure.

We can't be late, Oliver thought. *It's all on us.*

―――

Chameleon shed his snake skin. He let his back slide down the damp wall of an abandoned alleyway.

His skin burned from the shedding, an unexpected consequence of not splitting properly. The Trexian woman had made contact right before he could get off his defensive Skill. He nursed the Utopic Bomb in his hands.

It looked like a naval mine, with five spikes in a circle that pulsed with sinister light.

"You look like a whimpering mutt."

A powerful voice came from above. One that Chameleon recognized, though its impertinence was new.

"You can't speak to me like that," Chameleon said, wincing as he continued to shed superfluous scales. "I'm Fifth."

The liger who had just admonished him leaped down to the alley, his mane matching the hue of the Utopic Bomb's spikes. The Pride Lord, who had been turned into a Devil Prince by George in exchange for a chance at revenge on the humans, had a vanity matching his name. He refused to obey anyone except George directly, which made things difficult.

Accompanying the unruly cat was Jakk, his other least favorite Devil King. Even Morgana was more tolerable than that madman. He had taken to wearing a purple cloak and sunglasses, representing his torturous flames.

Chameleon found that disturbing. There was a hatred within those flames that looked at even its owner's allies with suspicion. Whenever he saw the man, he always felt like he was going to get burned somehow.

"I give you permission, buddy," Jakk said. He turned to Chameleon. "Do you have it?"

"Of course." Chameleon gritted his teeth and tossed him the Utopic Bomb.

Jakk caught it with two hands, careful to not let it hit the ground. "Woah, be careful with this thing. The Chief of Police said it has the power to blow up a city block."

"It'll only activate if they can get it to the mayor's office." Chameleon finished shedding the skin. "Which we will *not* let happen. Speaking of the missions, how far along are we?"

"We've completed Mission #3. Morgana and the others are taking him to the next site right now. You saw the message?"

"Complete scan of Eden for Mission #4 to find the leader of the Resistance?"

Jakk nodded. "Is Mirror-George occupying them?"

"He was when I last saw him."

"Then it's settled. There's no way that they can catch up in missions if almost all of them are engaged in battle. I hate to admit it, but Morgana is quite powerful. The Edenic rebels will fall given time."

"Wait," Chameleon said, sniffing the air. "There's someone here."

The liger looked up, scoffing for a moment as if to say, "How dare this lizard think his sense of smell is better than mine?" But after a few sniffs, he changed his tune. Four legs became two as the Pride Lord unveiled one of his new Skills allowing him to take on human form.

It was not the true humanoid flesh of a matured beast that attained Half-Step Immortal, but it would still serve the Pride Lord for economical combat in a zone suited to human-sized creatures.

Kristina soared through the air alongside Oliver. Jakk and the Pride Lord, seasoned combatants as they were, stepped in front as Chameleon slunk behind into their shadow. Jakk tossed him the Utopic Bomb, which he gingerly held onto like it was his own child.

However, the fated impact of the Trexian never came, with the woman stopping well short at the entrance to the alleyway, sandwiched in between two wings of enormous garbage processors.

Sweat dripped down Chameleon's brow as he analyzed the situation. Oliver was one of the combatants they had the least data about. He was careful to hide his power under most circumstances, sharing little about his abilities during the time Chameleon infiltrated the Northeast Order.

His zombies were a handful, including very powerful specimens like his skeleton with time abilities or his newly acquired kaiju corpses. But what he was most worried about was his warren to a realm of pure death, something that seemed difficult to counter.

Don't panic, Chameleon thought. *It's three against two and Jakk and the Pride Lord have entered a new realm of power with the Man in Shadow's final boon. But who is this woman?*

By that point, the Devil Kings had heard about Caren's telepathy. How he could share information among his teammates. The Devil Kings had no such useful power, and in this structured environment without the Soulnet, they had to rely on a flare system that was difficult to employ in a combat scenario.

Compared to true telepathy, the variegated flares that Morgana had given them had a tiny range of conveyable messages. While Alistair and his teammates were like a hive mind, sharing all their intel, Chameleon was left wondering how strong this "Tarnz Auola Kristina" was, who stood at level 60 with a Magical Pugilist Class.

Chameleon's greatest asset was his quick mind, and while he theorized the relation of power between the three cultivators and Kristina, she made her move.

Kristina held up a finger, to Oliver's surprise. He was ready, already channeling Mana through his meridians and preparing an array of [Otherworld Gates] to swarm the battlefield with his zombies.

But before he could make any move, Kristina stopped short of the enemy. After a brief pause in which both Oliver and the Devil Kings were shocked, she spoke, ending the strange pause.

"Restriction #1. I am Tarnz Auola Kristina and I possess a unique inborn advantage, a bodily constitution that allows me to reach unfathomable speeds. In exchange, if any opponent touches me three times with their bare hands, I shall die within sixty seconds."

With that, all hell broke loose.

The moment she had finished her last word, Oliver saw something he never would have imagined—someone of their level outspeeding Alistair. And not just outspeeding him, but outspeeding him by a huge margin.

Oliver's only foray into the Body Cultivation Tree was to improve his eyesight and reaction time. After seeing Alistair piece apart enemies with his superior reflexes, he began to understand that as a ranged and squishy fighter, the biggest threat to him were speedsters that would kill him before the fight had started.

Yet his improved senses could barely register the blur of speed that was Kristina. She moved as one with the wind, one with her Dao.

By the time he realized what had happened, a column of voidfire burst forth, covering Kristina and the Devil Kings from his sight.

Oliver wasn't going to let his partner act alone. There was no way they could react to Kristina's speed, so he knew that the voidfire was an automatic defensive Skill or item. In response, he opened three [Otherworld Gates] in front and behind—

No, he couldn't. He frowned. The voidfire must have been blocking the projected Mana. In any case, the three gates appeared in front of the blacker than black flames, three figures stepping out.

In close quarters like that, his snake kaiju was too large. The Daywalker Ape wasn't, however, standing around eight feet tall. Oliver, through the assistance of the Science Division led by Alistair's sister, had managed to reconstruct the pieces of the dead apes into a larger monstrosity, though it wasn't anywhere near its former glory.

In one of the other two portals came Anthony Ricci's skeleton, which he had reinforced over and over according to the instructions of his build manual and scrolls from the Hall of Math. No longer white, the skeleton was pitch black with a silver aura that felt like it came from an age before ages.

Finally, there was his personal creation. His little secret.

Sponsors weren't supposed to give overt gifts. Non-sponsors—even more so. Yet when Oliver received the FarNetter Academy invitation letter, he noticed something was off. After a bit of tinkering, requiring deft Mana cycling that he knew even Alistair couldn't do, he solved a complex puzzle reminiscent of a three-dimensional maze.

A variegated gemstone had fallen out. Oliver had it appraised for a fee that verged on price gouging by the Hall of Math, but they were the only ones on the planet who would even provide the information. It was a tiristone.

Tiristones were a rare gemstone that naturally formed within the hearts of certain types of Mana Storms, where the pressure condensed the energies into a physical object. They had many uses, but the one that stuck out to Oliver was that they could be used to fuel life itself.

Or, in his case, with the corrupted tiristone he had—the undead. The zombie was his Frankenstein, the work of cobbling together the parts of many different beings. The scales of the snake kaiju, the heart of a Daywalker Ape, the muscles of some high level orcs.

Some would have called it an abomination, but Oliver thought it was wondrous.

Oliver Jr. was no looker, standing eight feet tall and full of stitches, with multicolored skin and a strange assortment of limbs. He was humanoid in form, and charged along with the skeleton and Daywalker Ape toward the voidfire column.

The fires died down in less than a second. Before his sight could make out what had happened, he felt it with his aura sense.

Jakk had a furious look on his face, his black robes burnt and his ugly mug singed. Oliver had expected the liger's defensive Skill might have been dangerous to his partner, and he wasn't wrong.

Kristina still moved faster than the eye could see, a blur that barely registered. He could barely make out her form each time she made an impact on the Pride Lord, who was in his human form. His skin was a mottled gray and gold, with a blood-red beard that stood out as his mane.

That red was matched by the blood he spat out as he was overwhelmed with strikes. Kristina forced him back with the sheer volume of her attacks, pushing him deeper into the alley as Chameleon retreated like a coward, unwilling to enter the martial artist's sphere of influence.

Time was of the essence. There was one thing that Kristina mentioned to him before entering battle, and one thing only. Her style was even more extreme than Alistair's, focused on ending a fight as soon as it began. She couldn't hold her output for long.

Therefore, Oliver's normally cautious attitude toward the battle had to be adjusted. And adjust he did.

He began with his warren.

A square of perfect darkness opened above Jakk's head. It looked like a typical [Otherworld Gate], but it radiated an aura of absolute death.

Jakk wasted no time as he snapped his fingers while pointing up. Oliver's warren became public knowledge the moment he used it against the Daywalker Ape, the Devil Kings' spies being present everywhere.

But that was what Oliver was counting on.

The moment a cone of purple fire that wailed with the force of a thousand widows rose to blot out his warren, he closed it.

If people were going to fear his warren's skull of oblivion, why not abuse that fact?

The flames flew up into the sky, dissipating after blooming into a cloud with a radius of several hundred feet.

Unaffected by the sky being on fire, Anthony's skeleton held up his arms, impressing a large amount of time affinity Mana on Oliver. It sped up his temporal bubble, allowing him to move with the speed of a close quarters fighter temporarily.

The Daywalker Ape was already running alongside Oliver Jr. Jakk saw the incoming threats, and breathed in.

Oliver sensed the buildup of one of the most foul Daos he had ever experienced. A reprehensible feeling of torturous hellfire blossomed from Jakk's mouth, interpreted as Tyrian flames in which danced the imaginary souls of the damned.

Jakk had clearly improved his Dao to a Second Deepening, likely combining the fire and torture into a single hybrid Dao, like Pharaoh's Lost Sands. Despite having no signs of being a soul cultivator or ghost cultivator, he had managed to create the image and specter of hell's damned ones inside his flames.

Alistair told me about this, Oliver thought in his hyper-accelerated bubble. *The Akashic Records. Dao History. By attaching his flames to the idea of hellfire that tortures its victims, he's connected to a greater concept that has historical weight to it.*

It was a good thing that he was Jakk's opponent. Before the fire could consume his two zombies, a void appeared.

Oliver cast an enormous **[Otherworld Gate]**, spending almost a third of his Mana pool and a decent amount of Dao energy. The gate was as large as the entire breath of flame, Jakk's Skill disappearing into its unfathomable depths with ease.

Jakk looked on with utter shock as he saw his Skill, which could have taken out a city block if left unchecked, disappear like it was nothing.

That was an illusion. It was extremely difficult for Oliver to contain all of that energy in the physical demiplane that existed beyond the **[Otherworld Gate]**. If he hadn't put so much effort into the Skill, it would have failed with the fire cracking through the dimensional boundary, creating an explosion.

But Jakk didn't know that. The Devil King couldn't even feel any Dao or Mana coming from the gate, as its nothingness existed as a nigh perfect barrier for any outgoing energies, owing to Oliver's impeccable Mana control.

Fear of Oliver led to indecision. Only for a split second, but that was all he needed.

As the **[Otherworld Gate]** disappeared, the two zombies were within three body lengths of their target. Oliver was not far behind, positioning himself behind and in between his zombies.

Jakk's natural inclination was to retreat, but he realized instantly that it would put him in the path of Kristina's destruction. With no other option, he gathered his flames on a spot that Oliver was not expecting—his head.

A sinister choir began chanting, both from Jakk's voice box and the air around him. Oliver pictured in his head a legion of purple demons from the deepest pits of Hell, joining their insidious voices together in a lament that pained the soul.

Suddenly, Oliver was no longer in an alleyway in a technological metropolis, but at the bottom of a pit of eternal fire. Every single bad thing he had ever done, every sin that weighed on his heart, pressed on his heart as thousands of little demons whispered into his ears.

They promised him everlasting pain, everlasting torment. There would be no safe haven from their torture, no end. No end.

Oliver was reminded of Alistair's finishing Skill. This vision was far more twisted, but he could feel it was an attack on the heart.

What a fool.

Oliver's deathly body expelled the foreign hold on his heart. The vision ended, black nothingness eroding the flames away.

Jakk's Skill was impressive, but only one man had dominion over Oliver's body—himself. He would never be anyone's thrall again, not after how Jackson Morley had used him as a prop at the start of the initiation.

Good to note if Alistair ever turns on us, Oliver thought as his spiritual pathways were flooded with death affinity Mana, flushing out any foreign influence. If he hadn't practiced cycling his Mana, hours upon hours every day, every waking moment, he would surely have succumbed to Jakk's predation. *My internal control of Mana is effective against heart attacks.*

Still, when his vision returned, and he saw that he was only a few feet from Jakk, his soul ached and his body felt crispy as if the telepathic fire had somehow burned him from the inside out. His Mana pool had been decimated to a mere fifth of its total from the mysterious Skill, and he had a feeling a Mana pill wouldn't help. There was something wrong with his meridians, hopefully not permanent.

It's enough, Oliver thought. *My zombies barely need any Mana to be active, even if I lose almost everything.*

And Jakk—he was no doubt shocked that Oliver had broken free of his imaginary fire so easily. Once again, Oliver remembered Alistair's teachings. *Appear weak when you are strong, and strong when you are weak.*

The Daywalker Ape struck first. Like the real thing, it was a brute that had no Skills, its only use coming from a tough body, incredible strength, and ridiculous speed. It swung its long arms like a club down at Jakk, who came to his senses, blocking with an arm covered in flames.

The impact still created a shockwave that cracked the ground beneath them into a crater several feet deep. The flames around the Devil King's arm took the form of beautiful lilies. The flowers were the opposite of his normal fire, taking on a soothing feeling.

The lilies started spreading up the Daywalker Ape's arm. With its incredible speed, it decisively sliced off its own arm with a bite, jumping to the side of Jakk. Simultaneously, Oliver Jr. struck.

The real Oliver was behind him, completely hidden by its large frame, though still sensing the battlefield with his aura. The corrupting demonic voices still chanted at a low level, threatening his mind and suffusing the air with a hint of purple haze. Oliver had to assume it was a self-propagating Dao field at this point, as he sensed no active connection to Jakk, who was busy.

At this juncture, he provided Jakk with a choice.

Oliver forced an **[Otherworld Gate]** to appear through the Dao field with as much Mana he was willing to spend without relinquishing control of his zombies, with his Dao of Death.

A human-sized gate opened silently behind Jakk, though there was no way the man missed it. Jakk was surrounded on all sides.

The half-glass, half-obsidian tip of **Sun's End Vanquishment Sword** popped out of the portal behind Jakk, along with dozens of other, more disposable weapons. Oliver was one of the few that was advantaged by the ruleset, capable of bringing heavy artillery from the Land Store that others couldn't dream of.

Jakk was stuck between a rock and a hard place, but his choice was never in doubt. It was evident from their auras that the Daywalker Ape was stronger than Oliver Jr., and the immense amount of firepower coming from behind wasn't going to be easy to handle.

A burning halberd appeared in Jakk's hands in an instant. It felt similar to Dragonus's pillar. Probably swapped profane tips, those bastards.

With jets of his signature blaze at his feet, he was *fast*.

Oliver grinned. It was exactly as he planned.

He spent the last of his Mana, to the point where even his zombies would become inert, on two **[Otherworld Gates]**. One that enveloped himself, Oliver Jr., and Anthony's skeleton, and one on top of the roof of one of the garbage processors a few dozen feet in the air.

The inside of the **[Otherworld Gate]** was not safe, even for him. It was a realm of fundamental death that was alien to all life, hence why he could only store things like weapons and zombies.

Thankfully, his aura of death Mana protected him, but his storage Skill was not meant to be used as a portal. It wasn't really a space that followed the standard laws of physics at all, as Oliver would be unable to describe how exactly he made it to the other portal.

When he exited, he felt like he had a heart attack and then got run over by a van, but he was alive.

Next came the explosion.

He didn't see it, but he felt a two-pronged collision of his weapons along with an energetic burst of a Dao-infused inferno.

Oliver didn't blame him. How was Jakk supposed to know that the measly **[Otherworld Gate]** would explode upon getting filled with an excess amount of foreign energy? Oliver Jr. was the perfect bait. His new zombie wasn't even ready for combat yet at all, serving only as a colorful distraction. In addition, since he had closed off the gate on the roof, there was no backlash to him.

Oliver smirked. It had happened before, but he had guessed correctly that Jakk's intel didn't go that far, into tiny niceties of his Skills.

Sending his aura tentacles outward, he felt the situation from his prone position on the rooftop. Jakk's aura signature was obsolete, fading by the second as his dead body lost its life force.

His backfired Skill wasn't fatal, but it slowed him down to allow Oliver's overpowered arsenal to take care of the Devil King. Now that he felt further, there wasn't much of a body to speak of, just a disgusting pile of goo.

Almost all the weapons except his sword were gone, but that was okay. He still had **Sun's End Vanquishment Sword.**

Damn, I'm out of commish for a while. Dao energy is too fickle without Mana as a medium, and I'm completely out of Mana. I can barely cultivate with whatever that heart-attacking Skill did to me. If I rest for maybe twenty minutes, I can probably gather enough Mana to control the Daywalker Ape, Anthony's skeleton, and Carmen and Richard.

Oliver understood that some of his colleagues found it distasteful he was using their corpses, but it was for the greater good. He didn't use them here since their Mana drain was high due to their level and he hadn't gotten much practice with them, but he would need their protection soon enough.

The only question was if he was going to make it out of here alive. If Kristina lost, that was a hard no. All he could do was put his faith in her.

Like clockwork, he got an answer. A ripple of wind blew his brown hair off his eyes, and he heard the guttural warcry of a victorious female gladiator.

Slowly rising to his feet, Oliver looked down. There was a smoking crater where all of his weapons had discharged, and at the end of the alley was the dead body of a gigantic liger.

"Hey," Oliver called out. "I don't think I can jump down in my condition."

A split second after the words left his mouth, there was a flicker of air, and Kristina was in front of him.

She looked perfect, with barely a scratch on her. The only visible sign of damage was a rip in her black pants where a minor cut shone through on her left thigh.

"You look fucked," she said plainly.

"I am," Oliver weakly replied. "Where's Chameleon?"

"I was too focused on my fight. I think he bolted a while ago, with the bomb."

"Go after him," Oliver said.

Kristina shook her head. "Hells no. If I leave you here, the police will catch you and kill you. You're more helpless than a newborn baby." Then, she shook her head and exhaled with a laugh. "Well, to be frank with you, I would have left you to die if I actually thought I could catch him. He's a sneaky bastard with an impressive aura cloaking, and I wouldn't know where to look for him without you."

"That makes me feel a lot better."

"Wouldn't you have done the same?"

"No, because I can have my zombies carry you at no cost to me. Are you good?"

"Touché," the woman said, which Oliver found funny given how alien she felt, that she would be saying those words. "And I'm fine. My Class lets me issue challenges with restrictions that increase my power. He only got me once, but that doesn't mean my next opponent only has to hit me twice. It's three times all over again. Let's go."

She picked him up, placing him over her shoulder like nothing. It was uncomfortable, but he could still gather Mana. He didn't dare risk taking a Mana or Health pill.

"Wait," Oliver said. "I can feel something."

Kristina jumped down, air affinity Mana surrounding her fists. "What?"

"The bodies. Something's off."

"Shit. They shouldn't make vengeful ghosts at Foundation realm, but what the hells do I know about cultivation?"

"It's not a ghost," Oliver shook his head, having familiarity with the topic. "It's a different kind of energy."

Kristina examined the Pride Lord, who had what looked like hundreds of imprints of the Trexian woman's small fist on his hide.

Beep.

A virtual window, almost identical to the kind the Pathfinder AI showed them, popped up over the body.

Oliver turned his head, which an outside observer might have found funny since he was strewn over Kristina's shoulder. "That's not good."

"No, it is not."

Armageddon Mission Status (Team Cursed Lands):

Mission #1 – Arrest wanted terrorist Jakira Bellisima – COMPLETE

Mission #2 – Recruit the ancient Underground King to the cause – COMPLETE

Mission #3 – Find and employ notorious Programmer – COMPLETE

Mission #4 – Scan the internet using the Programmer's help – IN PROGRESS

Mission #5 -

Upon completion of all five missions, Team Cursed Lands will be victorious!

Current status: Team Cursed Lands 3, Team Northeast Order 2

54 MAN VS. DEVIL

ALISTAIR FELT George's words chill him to the bone. The man believed himself. There was no doubt of that.

But when had that dissuaded him? Many of his past foes had been confident in themselves, and now they were all dead or on his side.

There was no doubt he was in a sticky situation. He felt the weight of his injuries, having left Black Impermanence behind for Infinite Arsenal. There was no time for even a Health pill. However, Alistair didn't back down.

His mind assessed. Infinite Arsenal allowed him to contemplate the situation even as George approached. He analyzed all the moves George had made already. He looked at his own repertoire. He felt how Dev'rox had only enough Mana for one single swap. Then, he acted.

Alistair activated [Hand of Karma], pouring a large amount of his Karmic merit into counteracting the black threads of Fate. He still had 75 Karma left, having not used much before.

George kept his attacks simple. Every second, he formed dozens of spell arrays, each sending an ice spear flying at him.

Normally, such attacks would have done nothing but annoy him, but Alistair knew from experience when your Fate was in the gutter, a lot of bad things could happen. Even with his amount of Karma, he couldn't block everything. In his Karmic vision, the spears were attached with notes that said, "Harbinger of death."

But that wasn't quite right either. As Alistair batted the spears with his **Devilsbane Gauntlets,** he realized that not all of them carried the black tint of George's needle overload. He couldn't tell which ones were which, not right away.

Considering he only had one arm to deal with them, it was more difficult than he expected. The arm that the lion had bitten was barely functional, which he used for [Hand of Karma].

Alistair swatted and swatted, using [Frozen Claw] to help him create a web of frozen spears in the air, but George infused his Dao energy to shatter them free. Instead of falling to the ground, he resumed control over the missiles, sending them at Alistair with renewed force.

The preponderance of evidence suggests that his needle provides more Karmic energy than I have. This situation is untenable. Analyze opponent for weaknesses.

Alistair's brain overloaded as he took in every detail about his opponent. All his numerous extra senses went haywire as he examined George to the bone. All his strengths and weaknesses, his potential courses of action, were laid out in front of Alistair like a rap sheet.

It led to one conclusion. He took a gamble.

[Hand of Karma] blazed brighter than it had ever had before, searing away the black threads that trapped him. Alistair took his chance, activating [Mindshift] and fleeing.

The Karmic Skill brought him down to merely 30 Karma. It was a huge risk. A wave of relief came when he saw that the moment he fled, George flew forward on a gigantic snowflake.

Alistair activated [Mindshift] again. Whenever he sensed George chasing, he would [Mindshift] away, making sure not to get too far away that he couldn't monitor the Devil King's actions closely.

Mastery over this Skill shall lead to victory, Alistair thought. His control over his *nue* clone improved with every usage of the movement Skill.

If there was one thing he was confident in, it was his elusiveness. Without any restrictions on his movement, there was no way that George was going to catch him.

"WAIT!" George's voice was magically amplified, carrying over the vast distance [Mindshift] created between them. "Can we—"

Alistair wagged his finger as he activated the Skill once more, one step ahead of George's attempt to take him off guard. For all his power, it was a pitiful move. He tried using some Dao energy to mask his movements, but that was so obvious.

They continued this dance for over ten minutes. George tried ranged attacks, sending more of his signature spears. He tried sitting still for a while to lure Alistair into a false sense of security, only to soar through the sky on his snowflake.

Alistair remained just out of reach. They went so far, he approached the city limits. The physical demiplane's end was marked by a barely visible veil of light. He tapped on it, feeling the immense spatial Mana.

George stopped once he saw the border, his eyes narrowing. "Stop this madness," his voice called out from over a mile away, though Alistair heard it like they were standing next to each other. "If you don't fight me, I'll be forced to reconsider my position. Things will get dirty when I attack your friends. I can turn around right now and do that."

"But you won't," Alistair replied. "Even now, your faith in your victory wavers. I reckon that I've wasted almost all the added Fate your needle gave you? It was quite obvious what was happening with all the leakage. Your body isn't equipped to handle it."

The black tattoos created from the needle were already retreating, covering up less and less of his skin each second. Alistair thought he saw a brief flash of annoyance on George's face, though it passed in an instant.

His blue lips began to move, though unlike before, his words were inaudible because of the distance.

Alistair [Mindshifted] once more, bringing him down to 357 Mana. George had to be running low as well, and since he hadn't popped a pill yet, Alistair suspected that he couldn't, most likely because of the lich changing his body.

The *nue* clone shadowed Alistair, both performing a flying side kick and a [Hand of Karma] with their bad arms. George finished his sentence, but no spell appeared. As was predicted, his moving lips were a feint. The outline of the lich appeared around George, a sudden zone of cold washing over everything within a thirty-foot radius.

The black threads of Fate finally vanished as the black marks retreated into nothingness. Alistair's Karma also faded down to 10 as he blocked the remaining influence.

Alistair literally froze in midair, defying gravity. A spear of royal blue ice shot out from the lich's mouth on a trajectory toward his heart.

The spear pierced through him with ease. Then, he sublimated into a psychic smoke.

George turned around with a look of shock. A part deep inside of Alistair smiled as he finally got his opponent on the back foot. Somehow, the Devil King had seen through his first **[Mindshift]**. Running away had been the perfect time to practice his Skill, and he emulated the tiny mistakes he made in his *nue* clone in his own body.

This deception got George a foot to the face. A **[Force Fist]**-encased foot that should have shattered his face.

Instead, upon contact, his **Fall of Fleet** boot crystallized from the toes upward, spreading rapidly. Based on the darker coloration and the revolting feeling he got, it was related to the lich outline around the Devil King.

Dev'rox snapped his fingers and immediately absorbed back into Alistair, his Mana reserves emptied. The swap couldn't have come any later, otherwise the lich would have locked him in place.

Alistair popped up a few feet above George. His shin had a nasty gash from the sudden teleportation, the lich's ice not wanting to let him go. He ignored his wounds and went for another **[Force Fist]**, this time an elbow that was on a trajectory to shatter its target's skull.

Something shattered, but not a human. A replica of ice collapsed from the impact of the **[Force Fist]**.

Alistair turned around by instinct, remembering what happened last time when George used his ice substitution. That made it six Rank 1 spells. Either he had one or none left, and Alistair had to assume a worst case scenario.

His danger sense alerted him to the presence of a fast-moving object. Alistair swayed out of the way as a snowball shot by his face. George had reformed on a bridge several dozen feet below their old position.

He made out the lich's aura fading around George as he turned it into more snowballs, which he threw at seemingly random locations along the upper bridge.

A shot of pain in his left leg made Alistair lose his balance. He dropped to a knee. The wound created by the ice slicing against his shin refused to close. In fact, it gushed out blood at a pace that made no logical sense. Even as he coursed the Dao of Justice through it, believing there to be a foreign Dao within his system, it didn't matter.

Infinite Arsenal sputtered out as well. His Fist Node was all out of gas, his Justice Node and Ghost Node both around 40%. The plan he had created remained in his mind, but now he would be far less adaptable. They were in the endgame.

Once George had finished spreading out the remaining energy, the skeleton aura disappeared. He appeared where one of his snowballs had collapsed in an instant. The bridge had over a dozen collapsed snowballs every ten feet or so, spread out in a random pattern.

Alistair could have tried to remove them to stop George's teleportation ability, but instead, he closed his eyes and concentrated, entering Tranquil Mind.

George shifted between each pocket of ice numerous times a second, taking out a crystal ice bow and arrow. There was a certain nostalgia to seeing that weapon. It looked to be the same one he used almost a year ago, the first day that Alistair saw him.

Alistair's eyes shot open. He had never felt so calm as he did right now. George released his bow, breaking the sound barrier with each arrow. The moment he released it, he would shift to a different snowball, shooting again with a seemingly inexhaustible supply.

While assailed from all sides, Alistair was untouchable. Tranquil Mind guided his movements. He dodged and dodged, ducking and contorting around the arrows.

George picked up the pace, reducing the interval between arrows even more. Alistair kept up, but he could feel his muscles burn. His Stamina was falling dangerously low, and his mobility was shot from the wound on his lower leg. He couldn't dodge forever.

The intervals reduced to the point where the first arrow was still in motion by the time the next arrow was released, making it much more difficult to avoid. Alistair was becoming limited not by his reaction time, but from the speed of his body.

As he limboed under an arrow, he knew that the next one was certain to land unless he intercepted it.

He still didn't intercept it. He didn't even raise a hand to block it. He merely leaned to the side, but not by much. In fact, he swayed so little that the arrow bore through his side.

Alistair had placed his hand right next to his abdomen in preparation, using [Frozen Claw] to cauterize his wound from any of the ice's effects. At the same time, his legs pushed on the ground with full force as he performed a [Mindshift].

By letting the arrow hit him, his Health dropped low enough to trigger Holy Will of "Devil May Cry."

When fighting a demonic or demonic-adjacent entity, on the verge of death, user will gain a second wind of energy and willpower fueled by sacred fury.

The description of his Badge rang true, especially now that it was Tier 2. The boost he felt coursing through his meridians was far greater than the last time he'd used the Badge's ability at Tier 1.

The world stood at a standstill as he rushed forward. The stacked bonuses of Holy Will and "Good Samaritan" made him a blur of motion. Even the hypersonic arrows looked like they were moving in molasses to him.

Alistair moved so fast that there wasn't even enough time to wrap his fist with a Skill before it landed. Knowing that his enemy could shift at any time, he wasn't greedy with his target, smashing a **Devilsbane Gauntlet** into George's bow hand.

His first solid strike of their entire battle rippled through George like a shockwave. The hardened metal of the gauntlet atomized the bones of George's hand into a million pieces. By the time the leader of the Devil Kings reacted to the wound, Alistair had smashed the entire arm all the way up to the elbow.

George shifted away to the furthest snowball, but he was missing something. His blood.

Alistair's [Blood Hand] hadn't been active the *moment* he struck George, but it was by the time he reached the Devil King's elbow.

Past sins were to be washed away in a rebirth by blood with the Tier 3 Skill. The boiling blood corroded up George's arm. Alistair took his enemy's vital essence and stored it within his gauntlet, as he could with {Blood Debt}.

The moment he spotted George's new location, he [Mindshifted] once more, bringing him down to 96 Mana. He still carried the Holy Will steroid in his veins, making him a blur of movement.

This time, George was ready. He had been lulled into a false sense of security before, not ready for the sudden burst of speed. Even with his arm hanging on by a thread, he was still alert. He shifted to the furthest snowball.

Alistair's eyes were already filled with the last vestiges of his Karmic energy. Seeing. Predicting. As he suspected, the lich's aura was what was protecting his Fate from [Eyes of Truth]. Now that it was gone, he could direct a [Lightning of Justice] to smite the Devil King.

The energy bridge felt cool to the touch. Lighting affinity Mana surged out of his soulcore, flowing to the ground and then creating the charge differential at George's new location.

The most brilliant lightning Alistair had ever created bore down from the skies—not the heavens.

This was the lightning of justice that struck fear into the heart of every evildoer, yet it was not based on tribulation lightning. He poured as much of the Justice Node as he could, leaving him with less than 10% left.

The golden flash of light temporarily blinded his senses, but he still [Mindshifted] forward, putting him at only 2 Mana. These were his last cards to play.

Thunder echoed for miles, the lightning clearing away. George's body smoked with electrical burns, but physical damage was not the impetus behind his attack.

No, the Fear of Glorifying Truth and Sanctifying Heart leaves were paramount. As his Skill carried the Dao of Justice, it innately affected George's mind and soul.

Even the foulest sinner deserves a chance at redemption, he thought while he held onto the embers of Tranquil Mind, his Justice Node heading to zero. *May your mind, body, and soul be purified from all evil.*

Alistair didn't know how much time the two leaves bought him. Certainly, he wasn't going to turn George into a harmless monk.

A hundredth of a second was all he needed. A hundredth of a second where the Devil King contemplated laying down his arms to find a more noble path.

A hardened elbow slammed into the Devil King's chest. The technique was flawless, the result of hundreds of hours of blood, sweat, and tears.

There was no respite. Blood gushed from Alistair's leg, staining the bridge. His skin flaked off in reddened chunks. He sacrificed everything, forcing his broken and impaled arm to move with sheer willpower.

Alistair struck dozens of times a second. No Mana necessary. A jab to the face followed by a knee in the stomach, then a spinning elbow in the jaw and a flurry of hooks to the stomach. Holy Will's second wind was not infinite, and he could feel his limbs burn. Spiritual Fighter's Echo created a coral afterimage for every blow, adding to the damage.

Once he knew that sheer willpower alone was not sufficient to continue, he added the final touch—the demon blood he just stole. Even without **[Blood Hand]**, he let it surround his fist, though it was much weaker than normal.

He would take what he could get, delivering a knifehand strike to George's chest. The sharp claw of **Devilsbane Gauntlet** pierced his skin in four puncture wounds.

Alistair gasped for air, panting, with his hands on his knees.

Everything was close to zero. Almost zero Mana, literally zero Stamina, and just over 100 Health. Two of his Dao Nodes had nothing, and Ghost Node was sitting at around 30%, and was almost useless offensively.

George lay flat out on the ground, only a few feet in front of him. His entire body was broken and battered. He gargled blood, looking barely conscious.

A chill traveled up Alistair's arms. He looked down, only then realizing the seriousness of his condition.

His **Devilsbane Gauntlets** were cracking apart at the seams. He slipped out of Tranquil Mind, dropping to his knees as his head began to spin with a million thoughts.

His body must have some kind of defensive mechanism, Alistair thought. *This ice isn't going away.*

The mistake was attempting to return them back to bracelet form. The moment he tried, his scarlet gloves that had been with him through so many difficult times exploded into a hundred pieces.

With the gloves gone, the ice was mostly gone as well, but he quickly sliced off the index finger of his own left hand where the rot had spread too much.

"—Glacial Front."

An enormous wall of ice appeared out of nowhere.

Alistair stared down at his doom.

It was all his fault. The backlash of Tranquil Mind was no excuse to lose focus. He had that bastard on the ropes. How could he have let him speak?

There was nothing he could do except channel the Ghost Node and pray he survived.

There was a smile on his face in spite of the situation. How could he not have one?

Alistair had played his part. Alexandra, Pharaoh, Lucius, and the others. There had never been a doubt in his mind that they would fail. It was only his own task of defeating George that had preyed on his doubts. But the Devil King was in no condition to defeat anyone.

With eyes closed, he wished for a quick end.

It didn't take long for him to realize that *Glacial Front* was moving *away* from him, not toward him.

George Moulin, Leader of the Devil Kings, possessor of the strongest proto-Domain on Earth and possessor of a mysterious lich's inheritance, turned tail to flee.

55 SEVEN AGAINST ONE

ALEXANDRA HATED THE COLD.

She hadn't always. Before the initiation, she would probably have said it was her favorite season. Early winter was the season of combat boots and black leather jackets, so how could she not love it?

George Moulin had ruined that for her. As she marched forward into his proto-Domain, she felt like a cavewoman braving the heart of winter in a loincloth.

It was seven against one. Herself, Bartholomew, Whimsy, Caren, William, Lucius, and Pharaoh. They formed an Imperial Phalanx, increasing their power beyond the sum of its parts. Their opponent wasn't even the real George, but a clone.

How could they be losing?

Bartholomew had exhausted a ton of Dao energy and Mana earlier, and Pharaoh had used up his proto-Domain, but still, it was embarrassing. They tried their hardest as the winter gained ground every second.

Domain vs. Domain combat was new for all of them. Marzhan's Dao surrounded them, but not as a suppressant, but as an aid. Whenever they vacated George's proto-Domain with a slash of a cleaver or a blast of water, the connection they had to Marzhan could fill the empty space with her graveyard.

At least in theory. In practice, their slow removal of George's space was counteracted by an even faster progression on all fronts by the blizzard.

It was inevitable. It was an ice age that never ended. Alexandra knew those thoughts were the effects of the chill, but it was hard to shake them.

After a few minutes of struggling, they were at an impasse. She wanted to unleash her full power, but it wasn't her decision to make. The brains of the operation, Caren, William, and Lucius, had everything under control. Or so she hoped.

"Shouldn't we help her?" Alexandra thought. *"Those assassins are strong. If we reinforce Jesse, Marzhan, and Brigid, we can get rid of them and then focus all our attention on George."*

Caren's soft voice came in right away. *"Negative, Alexandra. If we divert our focus, George's proto-Domain will close in too fast. Stay on target."*

Alexandra obeyed.

The longer the blizzard churned, the worse it got. Chunks of hail the size of basketballs flew out of the shrouded sky at an increasing rate.

Falling hail shouldn't have been a threat, but if any part of their body was over the border, they felt like they were trapped in amber. And if they stayed on Marzhan's side, any damage they did would be filled right back up with the blizzard, not the graveyard.

Minutes passed. Alexandra didn't know how many. She wasn't into meditation like Alistair, but she knew how to enter a flow state.

Her new dagger, **Slayer of Angels,** was a black kunai that blazed an aura the color of her eyes when she swung it. That aura was a corrosive poison so strong that even with her 545 Constitution, she had to be careful with it.

Caren's voice broke her state of flow. *"The assassins have been dealt with. Jesse and Brigid are dead. Marzhan has a serious injury, but it won't affect her ability to perform for at least an hour. Lucius, retreat and reinforce."*

There was no emotion in Caren's words. Only facts. They rang hollow, like they weren't even real. There was no time for mourning. That would come later.

"Alexandra. Break formation from Imperial Phalanx. Marzhan will become the Stern Sword and Lucius will be the strategist."

Alexandra obeyed immediately. She jumped up and out of the formation, feeling the strange energy leave her body. She believed it to be the Dao that fueled the Phalanx, but not of any kind she had felt before. It was ancient and foreign, and possibly the only thing keeping them alive.

On her own, the cold was worse. But she couldn't eschew her duty and retreat. Alexandra stepped into the blizzard, swinging her **Slayer of Angels** like a madman. Any hail and snow that came close to her sizzled away to nothingness.

Something peculiar happened when Marzhan swapped in for Alexandra. The Imperial Phalanx increased massively in strength. She didn't have to be a part of it to see the golden sparks surrounding the seven intensify.

That's weird, Alexandra thought. Since the Phalanx required both a requisite level of strength that was quite high *and* those participating to be relatively similar in power, every single time they tried the Phalanx, they had included her.

Lucius returned to Marzhan's side. Platinum drachma appeared and melted in the air as he lent his power to the woman.

The combined result of the improved Phalanx and Lucius helping Marzhan was a reversal of the tide. When Alexandra and the others emptied ground for Marzhan's proto-Domain, it filled up with ease.

The progression of the blizzard halted, and then reversed. With every second, they were winning the battle of the proto-Domains.

They continued forward. Since George had been encroaching for a while, it took them ten minutes to get back to where the proto-Domains started, and then came the encirclement.

After twenty minutes, the graveyard expanded to the feet of the castle. Alexandra had never seen anything like it. The center of George's proto-Domain was a palace made of ice, carved so precisely that it glinted like a true crystal. The sheer cold it gave off seeped through the darkness of the graveyard, mixing at the border.

What she didn't understand was why he didn't make a move earlier. She had seen the wide variety of spells George could employ. He had done nothing, letting them reach the front doors of the castle without a fight. It took them thirty minutes, but...

Alexandra shook her head. Best let the brains think about those kinds of things. She was a soldier.

Caren sent a mental notice to halt. Then, he gave the signal. Marzhan unleashed the full offensive potential of her proto-Domain.

Bone trees rose up from the ghost grass, shimmering in the light of the full moon. They twisted and deformed, spreading into the palace of ice.

Wherever they made contact with the ice crystals, the branches froze. However, Marzhan, with Lucius's assistance, continued to dump more and more bone material forward. The trees grew in on themselves, shattering the crystal only to be frozen just a moment later.

The end result was a steady procession of frozen bone penetrating ever deeper into George's castle.

Alexandra could feel the tension in the air. Even with Marzhan's proto-Domain making space, they were still stepping into the den of the beast. Caren chopped his hand. The signal to move forward. They all obeyed.

They moved at a slow and steady pace. She could see her breath fog in the air. The sweat on her forehead froze into tiny beads and her boots crunched down on ice with every step. The moon above didn't penetrate through the ceiling, so the only light they were left with was the soft glow of the Imperial Phalanx.

"You've made it inside." The clone's voice came from everywhere at once. "Congratulations."

As the Captain of the Phalanx, Pharaoh was the one to respond. "I didn't know you to be one for theatrics."

"I'm just a clone. You can't blame me for having some fun."

The quality of the air changed inside the dark throne room. Alexandra felt all the blood in her body *lurch* toward her allies. She could feel her heart pounding in her chest like she had just run a marathon, the primeval fear of being hunted on the savanna temporarily overwhelming her.

At first, she thought it was something that George had done. But that changed when she saw Caren.

Three metal spikes pierced through his heart. His complexion, already pale, became white like a corpse. His eyes turned red and his aura condensed, feeling like he had gained 10 levels in one go.

Then came the flapping of wings. Hundreds of birds flew out of Caren's outstretched hands. Upon closer inspection, she saw they were origami constructs, made of a red paper that now grew around Caren, forming a suit of armor.

The origami birds glistened with what felt like a red UV light, even though that didn't make sense. The paper appeared to be soaked in blood, droplets falling as they spread out.

Alexandra thought it was an attack at first. But instead of flying toward

George, who the birds revealed to be sitting on a throne at the end of the hall, they expanded until they were evenly distributed throughout.

"That's more interesting now," George called out. He raised his hand, and a large arcane array appeared at the ceiling of his proto-Domain. "Let's see how you handle this."

An enormous spear shot out of the array. Based on their intel, he couldn't make spears of that size without invoking the verbal incantation, but they were within his proto-Domain. Anything was possible.

Alexandra moved to intercept, but there was no need. A dozen of the origami birds rocketed toward the spear. They flew so fast they looked like streaks of blood, crashing into the spear before it even got a fourth of the way to the ground.

Harmless (at least to a cultivator) chunks of ice fell to the ground, cracked apart by the numerous streaks created by the birds.

Alexandra received information from **[Paper Tongue]**. *"Anytime that George makes a move, the birds will interfere. We make our move now."*

The slow-moving Phalanx whirled into action on those words. A shiny metal cannon emerged from Bartholomew's chest, firing a green laser at the throne. Whimsy created a waterspout from her fingertips that grew by the second and aimed it at George. William took out a laser gun and began firing, though some of his shots seemed to be at random. Pharaoh released a cloud of decaying sand that flickered with a hollow fire.

As for Alexandra, she moved as surreptitiously as she could beside her allies, waiting for the opportune moment to strike.

With all those attacks flying at George, the first thing he did was stand up.

The origami birds were having none of that. The moment his butt left the frozen seat, three birds streaked at him.

The world itself intercepted them. They could not forget where they stood. They were in the heart of George's very soul, in a sense. Ice surrounding the throne moved of its own accord, blocking the bloody origami, which only penetrated halfway through before losing their momentum.

As for the other attacks, they crashed through the ice. Water, plasma, light, and sand mixed and exploded with Mana. No one could see what happened.

Alexandra's danger sense prickled behind her. She turned around.

More birds went kamikaze mode, but once again, the floor rose up in an arc of ice to defend. George had appeared behind them.

His ultimate defensive Skill. It activates automatically when he's in danger, replacing his body with an ice clone while moving him somewhere that ice or water exists. And that's everywhere in here.

"*Arcanous Devil Spell #4: Autonomous Crystals.*"

Alexandra was running toward the Devil King as he spoke those words. She pumped her legs as fast as she could, cracking the ice beneath her. Yet she was forced to slow down on her approach as hoarfrost began collecting on her shoes and ankles.

They all knew what spell #4 did. Everyone was briefed. A seed crystal in George's hands set off a chain reaction that could freeze even air.

The issue was that the hoarfrost of his spell took on a different tone. It creeped up her legs and seeped into her meridians, a taste of absolute zero that felt different from his normal cold.

This was total annihilation, the stillness of the complete lack of motion in her molecules.

"*Emergency Plan Egyptian Forest is a go. Lucius, return to formation.*"

That was all Alexandra needed to hear. She had been dying to unleash it. Unlike Pharaoh, she didn't have to deal with the elite shock troops, so she had more than enough energy.

In her mind's eye, she imagined the space inside of her soulcore expanding. Her Skill activated, and Mana flooded out of her body in troves, along with Dao energy.

Her former dominion Skill, **[Demonlord Nature's Preserve]**, took on a more fitting name as it produced her proto-Domain, **[The Forest of Waging War]**.

The hoarfrost and beginnings of an eternal prison of ice were washed away by her nascent proto-Domain. Three rings of trees formed, each with its own purpose.

There were the great oaks and maples and elms, full of verdant life at the highest peak of vitality in the late spring. Then there were the black trees with emerald leaves, the indelible mark of demonhood forced upon her as a last resort. Finally, there were the red trees that burned with blood instead of fire, screaming with the cries of war.

She could have filled a football stadium with her proto-Domain. That was not to be in George's throne room. The collapsing pressure of the heart of his own proto-Domain artificially limited her size.

Alexandra, however, did not stand alone. Alongside her was Pharaoh's proto-Domain. She could see the sphere pushing against the ice. The blazing sun of a long-lost era shone down on a desert of caustic sand.

Just as we've practiced, she reassured herself. She relaxed, letting her instincts take over as she merged the limits of their two proto-Domains. Pharaoh obliged as well, letting his sand spread amongst the burning trees.

The two proto-Domains supported and reinforced each other. They had practiced combining proto-Domains for weeks.

There was a standstill for a few seconds as the three spaces struggled against each other. The overwhelming cold literally froze the air itself, forming a hard barrier between both the desert and the forest.

Interestingly, there was compatibility at work. Where the sun's rays bore down, George's ice melted more, as well as among the burning trees of the outer layer of the forest. Things changed when looking at the inner ring of the forest or the sands, which the frost crept up on.

The imbalance made for an increasingly irregular shape of the proto-Domains. Alexandra was no expert in Domain combat, but she knew that such a phenomenon wouldn't last. There would come a breaking point. Destruction.

A continuous rain of origami birds exploded upward. They responded to the ceiling and walls of George's castle slowly contracting.

Alexandra and Pharaoh let their allies' attacks pass through. But they weren't going to tip the scale on their own. Or so she thought.

After unleashing a volley of missiles and more rays from his chest-mounted plasma cannon, Bartholomew drew his sword hilt.

The Supersoldier had a look of steely calm on his face. His entire body was covered in a layer of metal. Like she had seen many times before, the metal melted off his body and into the sword.

But she had never seen him lose *this* much. When his absorption was done, he looked like a skeleton and nervous system held together by spare parts. His muscles and other organs were long gone, replaced by technology.

The metal pooled into a sword hilt. It grew larger until it was around double the size of a normal handle, but after that, instead of growing in volume, it grew in density. The color started gray like his skin, but ventured into an almost black hue.

In one moment, there was nothing, and in the next, a green blade twenty-five feet long jutted out.

It was so fast, Pharaoh's proto-Domain suffered a slight tear, not able to react in time. George's ice filled that up, but it was a worthy price to pay. The plasma blade was imbued with so much of the Dao of the Sword and Technology, it warped even the air of the proto-Domain.

Bartholomew flicked his wrist. He was not alone in his attack. His sword shimmered with melting drachma as Lucius lent his power.

The near black hilt went from upright to pointed at George, who stood near the entrance of his castle, in less than a hundredth of a second. The blade didn't start out long enough to reach, but it grew at a ridiculous pace, stretching as far as the eye could see.

Swoosh. The blade cut through air, slicing through all the proto-Domains in its path like butter.

Alexandra's senses weren't like Alistair's, but she saw the green plasma cut through the top of George's head. In real time, she witnessed his body crystallize from the inside out as an ice clone took his place.

While she was focused on where he would pop up, what was left of the origami birds buzzed. An enormous amount of drachma was set alight, and William's **[Hypercalculative Induction]** weighed the smallest bits of evidence and preferences to determine one thing—where George was going to pop out.

Before he even materialized, every single bird turned into a streak of bloody paper mesh, aligning at a singular location.

George's omnipresent words rung in all their ears. "I'll admit, that was impressive. You've taken out my hand. Sadly, I don't think it was worth the sacrifice."

The birds didn't leave any mess behind, so they could see George almost immediately after. Like he claimed, he didn't look injured, except for a stump where his left hand would be. The wound didn't bleed, having been frozen shut.

Alexandra's face turned to one of shock when she sensed one of her allies' aura diminish to nothing out of nowhere. She turned her head, unable to avoid the temptation.

Bartholomew Wood's metallic skeleton laid bisected in two from head to toe.

She couldn't believe her eyes. There was no sensation of an attack passing through her proto-Domain. There was no cry of pain nor a burst of Mana from his location. He would have been almost useless after expending that much energy and temporarily becoming a robo-skeleton, but he would have lived. Not this. This made no sense.

The damage didn't stop there. Whatever had killed Alfred's brother also left a division in the ground and a cauterized wound on Pharaoh—a stump where his right arm used to be.

A cry of pain echoed from George's throne. A gray-skinned man holding open a thick tome made a face of agony as his arm fell off, smacking against the armrest of the throne and then onto the ground.

The wisp of a shadowy gray sword sublimated into smoke, as the luminance of a hieroglyph over his chest faded.

Alexandra recognized that man. How could she not? He looked identical to his two deceased brothers. The two assassins that took the lives of Jesse Waterfall and Brigid Mwangi.

And now, another of their number took the life of another friend.

Fury burned in her heart. The pools of fire in place of her eyes intensified. She would not let that man leave their proto-Domains alive.

56 THE UNFURLING OF HISTORY

PHARAOH DIDN'T NEED to look down to know that he had lost his arm. Its nonexistence was evident enough.

What he did question, however, was how such a thing had occurred. In one moment, he was fine, along with Bartholomew. In the next, the poor lad was cut in twain, and Pharaoh had lost his valuable arm.

Of course, it had to be related to the unveiled individual sitting atop George's throne. Based on the hieroglyphs, the shadowy gray sword, and the fact they had identical injuries, he could confidently state that his **[Curse of the Pharaoh]** had reflected the injury.

And if **[Curse of the Pharaoh]** had reflected the injury, then there was no doubt that the gray man caused his injury. And if the gray man caused his injury...

My wound and Bartholomew's wound are consistent with the swing of a plasma sword, which can only mean that he possesses a similar Skill to me, Pharaoh reflected. *But much stronger. My **[Pharaonic Constitution]** protects against normal Mana blows well.*

There was no wound from Bartholomew's initial swing. That meant whatever Skill he had likely used the principle of reflection, instead of mirroring the damages like **[Curse of the Pharaoh]**.

Still, he had good info. The reflection caused by the gray man was strong enough to cut his arm off. His formulaic Skill, improved to where it could trigger off of a ranged attack, only reflected 30% of the damage. Therefore, this interloper's Constitution had to be significantly lower than his own.

His body collapsed into sand, reforming right where he died. Thankfully, his arm grew back. One life well spent.

The gray man didn't take his eyes off his book, which was also gray, a large tome that looked like one of those thick bibles you'd see in church. He scrambled off the throne the instant his position was made known.

Pharaoh shouted at the top of his lungs, mentally. *"Caren, stop your birds at once!"*

It was too late to stop them all. One bird kamikazed down at the gray man, the rest heeding Pharaoh's advice and returning to their creator.

His eyes were in rapt attention as he focused on precisely what happened when the assassin was struck.

Time moved in slow motion as he focused his gaze. The bright red streak should have bored through the target's head, but instead, his book instantly opened to a certain page. The streak ignored its previous pathway, diverting to the open page where it disappeared.

Pharaoh's mind raced as he realized the worst possible outcome. Caren's communication services weren't easy to replace and his vampiric powers had proved to be no joke.

He didn't need to turn his head to see what happened. His aura sense was second-to-none, and he could envision things that happened within his sphere of influence like a near-perfect sonar. Caren had a hole straight through his head.

There was no visible attack, no sensation of Mana or Dao passing through the proto-Domains. It just happened. Which made it highly dangerous.

All the while, it wasn't as if George was doing nothing. Pharaoh had to split his attention there. The Devil King moved around his proto-Domain to his whims, growing a dome of ice around himself. His shield was a dozen feet thick and made of a strange, amorphous ice that was absent from their intel.

The icy proto-Domain squeezed harder, Pharaoh feeling his temples constrict like he had a tension headache. The frost around his sand and Alexandra's inner trees bloomed at an ever faster rate. It would not be long before their spaces collapsed from a lack of structural integrity.

The good news was that Caren was not dead. Soon after his brain got pulverized, blood flowed out of a slip in his paper armor, filling up the hole with new flesh.

The next few seconds were chaos. Alexandra grasped one of the demonic black trees, turning it into a wooden spear with the leaves transforming into a flag at the end. She thrust it at George's protective casing.

The others made moves as well, but Pharaoh had other plans. He verified it with Caren first, who told him that there was a chance of it working. He'd take that.

His proto-Domain was a mix of Mana and Dao, but not all of it. That was impossible before making a true Domain. But he could still pump his Lost Sands Node to focus his Dao energy at a target.

The sphere of Lost Sands grew an arm. It wasn't the fastest attack in the world, but he didn't think that the interloper specialized in physical attributes. His guess proved correct as he caught the gray man within his proto-Domain.

Buffeting sands swirled around the man's body. His technique wasn't the strongest, his proto-Domain more suited to trapping targets than acting as an attack.

The gray man's book turned rapidly. With the flurry of pages, so went Pharaoh's sand, disappearing into the mysterious spine of the book.

Pharaoh lost another life right then and there. A taste of his own medicine, so to speak. His uncovered skin split apart, sand particles rubbing off muscle like it was the meat off a tender baby back rib.

That tested his curiosity about whether the book could reflect even a proto-Domain's influence. But he was more interested in the gray man's condition.

The reflection got reflected back, as gray sand appeared with the glowing hieroglyphics. Pharaoh was hoping it would tear him apart, just like that. Why couldn't things be so easy?

Instead, as [Curse of the Pharaoh] tried to activate, the gray man manually turned the pages of the book, absorbing even the shadowy sand. He reflected a reflection of a reflection.

But he turned the page with his fingers. The other times, it performed automatically. Pharaoh shot forward, attempting to bridge as much ground before he died again. He made it one length of his body before sand ripped him apart again. He noted that it took longer this time, as even while the sand killed him, he activated [Desert Spire], aiming it at the gray man's head.

The presence of the gray man had been a shock to them all. Caren couldn't even blame William for not seeing that coming. The young man's **[Hypercalculative Induction]** was powerful, but relied on concrete observations.

Caren only had a third of his blood left. While **[Flight of the Crimson Swan]** wasn't the flashiest of dominion Skills that created explosions in its wake, it was the second-strongest ability in his arsenal. Plus, he had to rejuvenate the hole in his face that he had given himself inadvertently by being stupid.

With his birds gone, he converted all his Dao energy and *nue* into Mana with **[Resourceful]**. The other quintessence instantly became blood-aspected, though sadly it didn't count as his vampiric lifeblood. Only true blood taken from others could replenish that store.

What he could do was use his remaining lifeblood to strengthen blood affinity attacks. It was good that Pharaoh was occupying the gray man that could reflect abilities, although it made their firepower against George significantly weaker.

Caren gathered the Blood Hierocrat version of **[Paper Bomb]** in his palm. Thousands of pages of blood-soaked paper flew out of his storage and compressed into a ball. It started the size of a grape, expanding rapidly to that of a volleyball, while also becoming denser. He fed it streaks of his lifeblood, adding a darker tint to it.

While he did this, he silently communicated everything he saw using **[Paper Mind]** to William with **[Paper Tongue]**. Their chemistry had gotten to the point where Caren no longer used words, but pure information, to talk to the Farsighter when in combat.

William's next message, translated into words, was something like, *"Throw it at the ceiling at exactly X position in your visual field."* Caren obeyed instantly, changing his throw from George's shield to the ceiling of his palace.

Caren threw a nasty fastball. The congealed mass of paper flew past the borders of Pharaoh's proto-Domain unimpeded, reaching the upper limits of the frozen throne room.

It took only the slightest contact for the bomb to go off. **[Paper Bomb]** didn't operate like a normal explosive. Instead, the potential energy stored by the compression and coiling of the paper unloaded in less than a heartbeat.

Caren made sure to arrange the papers so that they only exploded upward and sideways. At first glance, it looked as if millions of pieces of confetti shot out. But the red pages contained so much more kinetic energy than mere confetti. The vampiric lifeblood added a weight to the blood not dissimilar to the Dao.

The roof of the palace blew wide open. Darkness seeped in.

He felt the familiar rotting presence of Marzhan's graveyard come in from above. Now, he understood William's intention. The reason that the Farsighter ordered her to retreat was so that they could create a three-pronged assault.

The woman herself was at the vanguard of her proto-Domain as the hole in the ceiling turned into a conduit to a deathly field. The full moon shone through, carrying a similar eroding effect to Pharaoh's sun.

George was powerful, but he couldn't withstand three proto-Domains against one. With the Devil King hiding away and focusing his efforts on crushing the desert and forest, the balance tilted slightly in their favor.

The moment an outside source broke that balance, the frozen palace started losing ground fast. The desert sands corroded away the frost, while the inner forest's vitality overpowered the cold. On every front, George was pushed back.

That was good enough for Caren. He panted, his vision blurry. The lifeblood was more important than combat prowess to him. It was his survival. He could do no more than keep up his passive Skills and coordinate the team.

Unless he was willing to pull out his final trump card.

———

Pharaoh paid little attention to the new presence above him. His [Desert Spire] missed the gray man by a hair, dissolving into a million grains of sand by the wall over his right shoulder.

As his spike of condensed sand disintegrated, [Curse of the Pharaoh] went off once more. The hieroglyphs burned on the gray man's chest, but his book flew open rapidly. Pharaoh felt the grits tear him apart once more.

His fourth life came and went. Sand reformed in place to become his renewed fifth life. On the other side, he observed carefully what had happened.

The gray man had tiny pockmarks all over his body. They sizzled with heat, and even from a distance, Pharaoh could feel his proto-Domain's lingering influence. But his opponent was not dead.

The back and forth has reduced my initial attack to far beneath fatal damage. The most important thing was that he now knew that it had a cooldown.

As for the spire, even while injured, the gray man deftly dodged to Pharaoh's left, who summoned ten more **[Desert Spires].** Once again, the gray man dodged, shifting back to the right around the spires with the ease of a man used to combat.

Pharaoh walked forward at the same speed he used when he really didn't want to go to his next lecture.

He could tell his opponent was clueless as to what to do. Pharaoh raised his arms and summoned two walls of sand on either side of the gray man. They reached all the way to the roof of the building and hardened the instant that he was certain there was no gap.

Pharaoh walked forward calmly. He was overjoyed when he felt his headache relieve as Marzhan added her proto-Domain to the fray, but he didn't let it affect him otherwise. As he walked, he extended his sand underneath him so that his proto-Domain didn't collapse.

It could survive on its own for a bit, but it would be much weaker. Even now, he risked a catastrophic collapse. But he didn't stop.

A flicker of anger passed over the gray man's face. "I have faced enemies far stronger than you," he called out. "Do you not think that I know what you are trying? You really believe that I have nothing else than the power of reflection?"

Pharaoh kept his mouth shut. He was fifty paces away. Then twenty-five. Then ten. Then five. Still, his opponent made no move. There was no fear on the other man's face.

Pharaoh reached out a hand. Slowly, like he was trying to metaphorically grasp something far away, only his path was toward his opponent's face.

Right before contact, the gray man started bending over backward. He shuffled his feet at a glacial pace while he brought his own fist in a slow uppercut toward Pharaoh's face.

If anyone was watching their battle, they might have laughed, as it looked like two grown men doing slow-motion pretend fighting. Both fighters wished it were that simple. Neither wanted to deliver an attack strong enough that the other could reflect.

The gray man didn't know how many times Pharaoh could reform, if there was a limit at all, and Pharaoh didn't want to waste all his lives without a guaranteed victory.

Neither one of them let the other get their hands on them. They continued their slow-motion battle for over a minute. Pharaoh tried to remember every fight he saw of Alistair's, replicating his moves as best he could. Of course, his attempts were garbage, but the gray man wasn't a close quarters fighter either.

The balance broke down when the gray man touched Pharaoh's cheek.

Pharaoh had tried a kick—his balance was such that he didn't fall over, but it missed by a mile. When both of his feet were on the ground, the gray man was closing in on the walls. Their fighting revealed one fact. The gray man seemed more afraid of Pharaoh than Pharaoh was of him.

So the assassin was the one to add a little extra to his attack. A little more speed. Still, his fingers barely grazed Pharaoh's cheek.

Nothing happened for a heartbeat. There was a brief moment when he considered the possibility it was all a bluff, but then he saw the book's pages whirl faster than he had ever seen before.

His instincts took over as he fired a **[Desert Spire]** at the gray man. Before he could see his attack land, the pages consumed him.

Pharaoh floated in a world of infinite gray. Gray and books. Hundreds, if not thousands, floated all around. There were books of every size and thickness, every print and cover. There were Chinese-style scrolls, papyrus, and black diamonds that projected text in three-dimensions.

The gray man was there too. He still had his injuries—a severed arm at the midpoint, hundreds of tiny holes, and now a **[Desert Spire]** sticking out of his thigh. Blood dripped down his leg.

The books flew like birds in the sky in circuitous routes, but suddenly, they halted. They swarmed Pharaoh. All of them opened up, revealing their contents to the trapped prisoner.

There was too much. Too much information. Pharaoh's brain was forced to take in everything, every date, every person, every fact in those books became lodged in his brain. He closed his eyes, but that did nothing to stop the assault.

As a level 67 cultivator with a high amount of Intelligence, his brain could handle far more than the average human. But there came a tipping point. Pharaoh held on as long as he could, then death came as his neurons died by the billions.

His fifth death out of fourteen. Pharaoh was hoping that when he reformed, it would be outside, but he wasn't so lucky. In his sixth life, he was assaulted by information once more.

This time, he tried fighting back, tried summoning his powers. Nothing worked. It felt like he was back to being a normal human again. Somehow, the indignity of that stung almost as much as the overloading of his mind. He died again.

Deaths seven, eight, and nine came in a period of time that Pharaoh could not quantify. It could have been ten seconds or ten thousand years. He prepared himself to die once more, but the pain never came. When he opened his eyes, he was no longer in the gray void, but almost in the same position before he'd left.

His opponent's fingers were an inch away from his face, moving away in the swipe's trajectory. He turned and thrust both palms forward, as if he were trying to topple a large boulder. With the walls of sand blocking the gray man's path, he had no choice but to move backward.

Pharaoh activated **[Plague of Locusts]**. The insects swarmed out of his mouth in a continuous stream, so thick it appeared to be a solid black mass.

The gray man's book spun open, continuously absorbing the incoming Skill. Pharaoh felt the effects right away, his shirtless skin receiving the displaced effects of what should have happened to his opponent. Chunks of flesh left his body like a swarm of tiny insects ate him to the bone. Which it did, in a sense.

[Curse of the Pharaoh] took into effect right away. A shadowy locust swarm appeared around the gray man. His book opened, and the Skill was reflected once more.

Pharaoh reformed his body as this happened—behind his opponent, not one arm's length away. His earlier **[Desert Spire]** was never intended to kill, but to create a pile of sand within melee distance of the gray man. He could only teleport to a location that had sand, obviously.

Even as he felt the twice-reflected locusts bore into his flesh, his fist was already in motion. Covered in decaying sand and filled with Dao energy, there was no stopping him. The cooldown on the gray man's reflection ability was extremely short, but he lacked the ability to deal with two attacks at the same time.

Pharaoh cut it short. The end of his locust swarm was just about to be sucked into the book as his fist burst through flesh. He punched out the gray man's heart in one fell swoop.

Then he died again. The locust swarm finished its path through the book, which fell out of its owner's hands as he passed into the cycle of Samsara. Pharaoh thought he had a chance, but even the end of the swarm was strong enough to rip open his insides.

He reformed, taking the briefest of rests to get a handle on the current situation. He was down to three lives and limited Dao energy. The Mana situation was okay, but his Skills weren't the greatest offensively without the Dao. And most of that was held up in his proto-Domain.

Pharaoh looked down. The gray man's body disappeared into smoke, but the book remained. Against his better judgment, he picked it up.

For some reason, its title was now visible. *Book of History*, Pharaoh read. Fighting was Alistair's game, not his. If he was going to do battle, getting an item like that was a nice piece of compensation.

57 THE KISS OF DEATH

ALEXANDRA SAW THE VICTORY AHEAD. She focused her concentration on her proto-Domain. Perhaps it wasn't wise to close her eyes, but she felt like she saw more, not less, through the senses of her trees.

With her focus solely on the forest, new trees blossomed, and old trees grew. The outer layer melted everything it came into contact with.

She could not claim it was her doing alone. She only had so much impact because two other proto-Domains fought beside her. The blue grass of Marzhan's graveyard sprouted from the ceiling of the palace and while Pharaoh was distracted, his sun was still the most powerful asset within their spaces.

"You guys are no fun," George's voice echoed. "Three proto-Domains against one? It's sad that you can't fight with honor."

Whimsy's columns of water froze before they even had time to strike at George. Clone George, Alexandra amended mentally. They couldn't forget that and get cocky. In regard to the former Devil King, her Mana affinity and Dao had a natural weakness to George.

The leader of the Devil Kings broke his crystal shell while he spoke the words of power. *"Arcanous Devil Spell #4: Autonomous Crystals."*

Hoarfrost grew instantaneously around all the three opposing proto-Domains. The rate of growth was astonishing, adding hundreds of square feet every second.

Alexandra plucked out two of the black trees and dual-wielded them as spears. She sliced the frost as fast as she could, but the growth was too fast. The hoarfrost crystalized into solid ice. If nothing changed, all three of their spaces would become frozen spheres.

Now was not the time to be conserving Mana. She activated an improved [Armageddon Slash] on her makeshift weapons, multiplying their weights by ten. Instead of taking the Dao energy from inside her Nodes, which were around a third full, she used the existing proto-Domain. By doing so, she made her attack even stronger than it otherwise would have been, fueled by the intention of her proto-Domain.

She crossed her black spears in an x-shape, performing a [Partition Vitae]. Mana and Dao energy from her proto-Domain sucked into her spears, giving them a weight that went beyond [Armageddon Slash].

Unlike a normal [Partition Vitae], the x-shaped construct of nature Mana was the only aspect. Her spears were fed the wood of the forest, siphoning away a ton of Mana. They, too, emboldened by ten times the weight, crashed into the spiritual ice of *Autonomous Crystals*.

It was a gamble, to be sure. She used so much of her proto-Domain's quintessence that it was already fading.

Her [Partition Vitae] exploded with a burst of green light, while the spears churned up ice dust and mist, blocking her sight.

Pharaoh's voice broke her tunnel vision. *"I've dealt with the interloper. Only have three lives left and almost no Dao energy."*

When the dust and mist faded, she saw that everything was collapsing. Her forest wilted and warped with the absence of the Dao. George's proto-Domain sported a nasty wound at the top and where she struck, but it was healing. They had failed.

Until William took out a good old-fashioned AK-47. There didn't seem to be anything unique about it until he fired the first bullet.

It went too fast for her eyes to see, but she knew it by aura alone. A Platinum drachma. One that carried the Fate-warping powers of Lucius.

She noticed now the impact marks of William's previous shots with his laser gun. They formed an enormous web all across the throne room. He had been shooting non-stop for the entire time they'd been inside the clone's proto-Domain. With his relatively safe position as the Stern Sword, he had never been under attack by George or the gray man.

William acted with greater precision than she'd ever seen from him. He fired shots in doubles and triples, sometimes aiming where he had shot previously, sometimes not. He turned the barrel of his gun like a practiced soldier, also firing at the chunks of ice that sat on her trees.

Those shots were only the ultimate, end-of-the-road nudge. A position where William's Farsighter Class excelled. With the emptying of the thirty-round magazine, he broke the dam.

All the proto-Domains began collapsing. Despite being spaces owned by Dao energy and Mana, they still followed some physical principles. There were too many holes, too many cracks, for George's clone's proto-Domain to survive. Slabs of ice fell to the ground, others shattered into a million pieces.

The greatest damage was near Alexandra and at the ceiling. Marzhan's proto-Domain filled in those cracks as the energy still remaining stabbed into the graveyard.

The same thing happened to her forest. While the frozen palace collapsed, it was like being inside a building you were trying to demolish. The good guys got taken out along with it.

"RUN!" Caren shouted out loud. Alexandra didn't need those orders. She had already deduced what was happening. She moved as fast as her legs would take her. If only Jesse were here, she reminisced.

Whimsy helped shield their retreat. Her weakness to the ice suddenly became a boon. She produced thousands of gallons of water in a dome, which froze over in a heartbeat. The dome gave them just enough time for everyone to leave.

The seven of them ran out of the proto-Domains that collapsed behind them. The transition to the "real" world was seamless, putting them back on the first floor of the prison. As expected, it was nothing like before.

The whole building was in tatters. The roof had clearly fallen down, probably from the spatial intrusion. They were exposed to the elements, with the second floor also having collapsed. Bodies of the police officers were everywhere, along with stray shards of ice and sand and trees.

But their battle was not over. The remnants of George's proto-Domain exploded, shards of ice cascading out in every direction. A cold wind blew along with both twenty-foot jagged ballasts and pea-sized blades. Alexandra expected to hear instructions from Caren, but nothing came. The Phalanx collapsed, everyone escaping on their own.

She ducked behind a piece of the stainless steel staircase. The ice crashed into it, penetrating the metal, but stopping enough of its momentum.

Alexandra used her daggers to deal with the rest, enlarged to comical sizes by **[Empower Weapon II]**.

Cold was replaced with heat as she felt George's next attack. The battlefield was covered in ice dust, but she didn't need her sight to understand what he was doing. *Frygian Arrow* decimated the ice with a heat wave as it sucked out all the chill.

Alexandra knew that the physics of it made no sense, but the Devil King's ability superseded natural reality. A wave of purple fire arose, and she knew she couldn't protect the others. That wasn't what her abilities were good for. She was a barbarian and a killer. She prepared to unleash her remaining Dao energy and go out with a bang. Better that than wait for the madness.

Her blood stirred once more. This time, she had to quell her blood, lest it burst out her skin.

A red streak flashed through the flames, carving a pathway to the man at the center. It stopped in front of George, who didn't move from his position, staring at the incoming being. Only then did she understand what she was seeing.

Her aura sense told her it was Caren the whole time, but her eyes only caught up later. He looked like he was *made* of blood. There was a pile of skin and clothes left near her and the rest of their allies. Sticking out of the metal spikes in his chest was a still beating heart.

His entire body was skinless, but the muscles underneath weren't normal at all. They were the red of blood, encircling his entire body like a ribbon around a present.

George's clone opened his mouth to speak, but Caren moved faster. He was far beyond his ordinary physical stats, flinging his arms and dashing in. High pressured blood exited his palms, splashing the ground beneath the Devil King's feet.

Their struggle lasted but a blink of an eye. Caren's hand was a blur as his karate chop arced toward George's neck. The blue glow of an emerging arcane sigil appeared underneath the Chronicler's bloody feet.

Squelch. She heard a spurt of blood release from George's neck as Caren's hand reached an inch deep. The Devil King's body shattered into ice while the array below activated. A huge ice spear impaled her ally, her friend, straight through his abdomen.

Caren's body melted. It collapsed as if it finally realized the skin holding it together was gone, turning into a puddle of blood. It didn't stay still, instead curdling together and streaking toward the open front doors of the prison. Where George had teleported, unharmed from just before, though still with his stump arm.

Unharmed, except for a tiny cut on his neck. The blood from that cut was an attraction for the stream of blood that had once been Caren.

Once the blood was within a foot of George, it exploded. Not in a combustion, but in spikes, like a ball growing into a sea urchin. The Devil King raised a hand, an abnormal concentration of Dao energy at his fingertip.

This was like his proto-Domain, yet concentrated into the tiny physical volume of his finger. He released the buildup in a wave of Dao energy and Mana that exceeded the speed of sound.

Alexandra took cover and timed an [**Armageddon Slash**] while pushing as much Mana as she could into **Slayer of Angel's** poisonous gases. Despite her defenses, the wave smacked her into a stray metal pole behind her. Hoarfrost bloomed all over her body.

She cycled the Barbaric Rage and Nature's Attendant Node in equal halves, melting the ice. There were hundreds of micro-bruises all across her body from where the ice instantaneously killed off blood vessels. Her internal state was a mess, as there was a spiritual attack on her pathways as well.

Not fair that he still has so much Dao energy, Alexandra thought. She had to imagine he wouldn't be able to do another one of those. Looking at everyone else, Whimsy, Marzhan, and Lucius were frozen solid. William had hidden behind Pharaoh, who had just spent another life while protecting the Farsighter with a swarm of locusts and sand.

A fierce laugh echoed throughout the prison. George's frozen blond hair draped over his face for the first time. His burning eyes were dimmer than ever before, his aura muddied and weakening.

The ice over his stump had melted, leaving his white robes wet. There were dozens of minor puncture wounds with frozen blood crusted on his colorless outfit. He tore the largest spike to touch him off his upper chest, leaving a nasty hole the size of a tennis ball. Alexandra could literally see through the hole to the street outside.

As for Caren, she felt a pit in her stomach. The blood that was once the Chronicler formed a spiky mass. It was completely solid, encased in an ice crystal. She sensed nothing from it. Not even an inkling of his aura, nor any iota of his life force.

She would not let his sacrifice be in vain. There wasn't time to wait around for the others, so she charged forth.

Alexandra didn't have a strategy. Caren was dead. William couldn't give her orders in real time. Lucius was frozen. All she had was trust in her weapons, and trust in her abilities. She brought down her kunai in a thunderous slash.

To her surprise, George caught it with his hand. The impact cracked the floor, pushing him down at least a foot from the force. Blood dripped down his hand from where the edge of the blade caught his palm. He had reinforced his hand with Mana, blocking the poisonous gas.

She let **Slayer of Angels** stick in his hand, using the hold to backflip over him. As a warrior-esque Class, her natural fighter's instinct took over in the heat of battle. She subconsciously sensed one of her teammate's attacks and got out of the way. A plasma bolt froze in place before it struck George's chest.

Alexandra stabbed him midair with **Withering Promise**. This was her one opportunity, so she infused it with all the Dao energy she had left. The air churned as her whitesteel dagger gave off a dark red gleam, the Barbaric Rage Node at work within. She resumed **[Barbarian's Fury]** for her attack, the blood evaporating off her skin reflecting the dagger's coat.

George tried to defend his back with the same technique he used against the plasma bolt, but in doing so, he lost focus on protecting his front. Two more plasma bolts from William's gun struck him in the chest. He lost even more focus, and that was when the dagger bit.

Even as she saw his body fracture into ice, she smiled. That was seven spells used. She dropped to her knees, clutching her remaining dagger tight. She was dead out of Dao energy, with only a little Mana left.

"This is quite impressive."

Despite her condition, Alexandra's head snapped back from sheer instinct. In the heat of battle, she hadn't even thought of it. When George's clone sent out that wave of Dao energy from his fingertip, it had spread a minuscule layer of frost everywhere on the first floor of the prison.

And what did his ice dummy subversion spell require?

The Devil King stood behind the frozen body of his former subordinate, Whimsy.

———

While William and Alexandra fought against the injured George, Pharaoh was doing something just as important—freeing his compatriots from their icy encasing.

He had no time to think. He could have joined the two of them and potentially tipped the fight. But he could sense how fast Whimsy, Marzhan, and Lucius's life forces were dwindling. The foreign Dao was corrupting their bodies.

Whimsy was the furthest away. Lucius and Marzhan were on his left and right side, respectively. Pharaoh gave his lover a single glance as he focused on the Wood patriarch. There was nothing more he wanted to do than attend to Whimsy first, but he couldn't do that in good conscience.

Pharaoh had almost no Dao energy left, so he had to cut open the ice with only Mana. He buffeted the ice carefully with his sand, making sure that he didn't accidentally cut Lucius inside.

Once he removed all the ice, he imparted a tiny bit of his Dao energy to help the older man kick-start his own cleansing. As long as Lucius's body and soul were alive, he himself could cycle his Dao energy to flush out George's.

A few seconds later, Lucius fell into Pharaoh's arms, freed from his prison. "Thanks," Lucius whispered as he gathered himself. Pharaoh moved to go help Marzhan.

All the while, he had been monitoring the fight in case he needed to assist. To his great pleasure, things seemed to be looking good. Alexandra delivered a deadly blow—

In the next moment, George appeared. He held Whimsy by the neck. He squeezed.

"I'm sorry," he said with the affectations of genuine sorrow. His fingers swiped through his own ice with ease. They crushed her neck in one continuous motion, separating her head from her body.

Whimsy's frozen head bounced on the ground before rolling toward Pharaoh's feet. Her expression was locked into the wide-eyed shock she'd felt as the wave of Dao energy froze her.

Pharaoh couldn't have explained to anyone what happened next. He blinked and when he came to, his hand was buried in George's stomach.

He looked down and saw that his arm was covered in a grayish-pink sand that he had never seen before. There was a notification that he had upgraded his **[Decaying Grit],** combining the hollow flames into the sand itself to make it this pink color and lend it a much stronger entropic effect.

None of that mattered to him. He withdrew his arm, George's clone falling to the ground with a smile on his face.

Though he wasn't the most experienced in life force, a blind man could see that the clone's was fading. His injuries had grown too much to handle. Blood pooled on the ground from the new hole in his stomach.

"Why didn't you do anything?" Pharaoh asked, standing over George's fallen form. There wasn't even any anger in his voice. This was how inhuman he had become. Even for her, he couldn't shed a tear or have Alexandra's raging fury pump through his veins. "You're not bled dry yet. You let me impale you."

The clone began to fade into pieces of blue light. He laughed, though it became more of a sputtering cough as blood escaped his mouth. "Why did I do that? Well, I haven't been alive very long, have I? Maybe I just wanted something of my very own."

With his last words spoken, the clone faded to nothingness.

Pharaoh walked over to Whimsy's frozen head, falling to his knees. He truly had no quintessence left. He kissed her where her lips would be.

"I'm sorry," he said softly.

58 PATHBREAKER

OLIVER STOOD over Chameleon's battered body. Thank the Heavens that his Mana regeneration was high enough that he could control a single zombie.

He and Kristina had caught up to Chameleon after just a few minutes of pursuit. Kristina was far faster than the Fifth Devil King, and with Oliver as her bloodhound, they chased him for only a mile before catching up.

That led to a more pressing issue. When it became clear that he could not shake his pursuers, Chameleon had tried a different tactic.

"HELP!" he had shouted after rising out of the tunnels onto the main streets of the city. He took out a flare gun and shot a green beacon into the sky. "The rebels are after me!"

To their unfortunate ends, that had actually worked. A police squad, some kind of SWAT equivalent, was conveniently around the corner in a truck.

They were saved from an unnecessary fight when hidden rebels in the crowd showed themselves, saluting Kristina as they appeared.

Kristina had been able to corner Chameleon alone, and she beat him to a pulp even with Oliver hanging over her shoulder. He hopped off, still feeling a little weak in the knees, and stepped on Chameleon.

The battle raged on in the background all over the street, plasma bolts and sonic waves being fired. The general public fled the area as quickly as they could, and he heard sirens blaring in the distance.

Kristina grabbed Chameleon and dragged him into one of the nearby businesses. They found a basement door in the back and brought him down there.

"I won't bullshit you," Oliver told the shivering man. "I don't have much Mana left. Not much more than 50, that's the honest truth. You have two options. Option one, you tell us everything we need to know about your plans, and then we give you a quick death. Option two, you stay silent, and then you get a taste of my plague.

"Your body will rot from the inside out. Your organs will liquify and your brain will turn to mush. But that's the easy part. Before that, my virus will affect all your neurotransmitters and brain structures, dropping your dopamine and serotonin to zero. You will experience the worst panic attack in human history times a hundred."

Kristina whistled. "You're fucking brutal, kid."

Chameleon froze with fear. His eyes bulged out of their sockets, already too large since his physical transformation. His long tongue hung limp out of his mouth. "Wait, wait, wait. Who said you had to kill me at all? This little game is only a game. Once you guys kill George, I'll be free, anyway. You've seen my abilities. I can be useful. Here."

He tossed over the Utopic Bomb. The moment it touched Oliver's fingers, the system gave a message.

Armageddon Mission #3 (Team Northeast Order): Find the Utopic Bomb, complete.

Armageddon Mission #4 (Team Northeast Order):
Plant the Utopic Bomb in the Mayor's office, leading to his death.

That was good to know. In his head, he felt a slight ping as to where the Mayor's office was, like a beacon in his mind's eye. Before that, he had some interrogating to do.

Oliver let Mana cycle up to the skin, giving himself a black cloak. It was solely cosmetic—if he was going to use his plague virus, he had to commit all the way. "You do not seem to understand your position. We hold all the cards. Tell us about your plans, or die the horrible death I'll give you."

That seemed to trigger a response. "Okay, okay. I'll tell you. I was sent to infiltrate you guys as a distraction. Once there was an opportunity to sabotage you on the missions, I was instructed to take that chance. Anything just to slow you guys down."

Oliver cocked his head. "That's awfully risky." His estimation of the man before him was that he was a coward, truth be told. That was certainly tainted by his shapeshifting abilities, which in all forms of fiction tended toward less-than-savory types. Plus, he also gave in so easily to his torture threat.

"What can I say?" Chameleon put his hands up. "George is a charismatic man."

Kristina stepped in. "Hurry up."

"Girl, chill. I was just answering your buddy's question," Chameleon replied. "As I was going to say, the rest of the Cursed Lands team is split up into three. The real George sent the clone George to stop the rest of you guys from doing the missions as long as possible. And also to get Alistair to fight him in single combat. Everyone else is doing our missions."

Oliver clenched his fist. "We already guessed that. What else could you guys be doing? Give us more."

"The mission we're on currently, scan the internet; it's being done at the police HQ. We're near the city center right now, so that's on the opposite side of the city from the prison. But being realistic, by the time you can get your forces there, we'll be on the next one. And believe me, you two are strong, but you don't want to go alone. So that means you'll have to stop us on the last mission, but no one *knows* what that is yet."

Oliver frowned. There was something about his tone with those last few words... He decided to push. "No one knows?"

"There are certain speculations on good grounds. If you want to hear them, I'll need a guarantee."

"You already have your guarantee," Oliver reiterated. "If you don't tell us, I plague you. You get that, right?"

Chameleon's face writhed into a smile. "You're short on time, my boy, and I think that you care more about getting stuff out of me than your commitment to follow through with torture. I'll take that gambit. New conditions—you swear on your Dao to let me go if I answer your question, and I'll swear on my Dao to not interfere whatsoever."

Oliver wanted to punch something badly, but he agreed in less than a second. "Fine. I swear on my Dao if you answer all of my questions truthfully and completely, I will let you go, so long as the next sentence out of your mouth is a swear on *your* Dao to immediately run off to the edge of the city and stay there until the end, no matter what happens."

"I swear on my Dao to immediately run off to the edge of the city and stay there until the end, no matter what happens."

"Now, what's your final mission?"

"If George's guess is correct, the last mission will be killing the Leader of the Resistance."

Kristina chuckled. "*You* certainly can't do that."

Oliver shooed her away. "Please continue, Chameleon."

"We've been using a flare system to communicate. Red means enemy encountered, if you have time to signal. Blue means mission objective spotted. Green means backup required, mission-critical emergency only. Black means enemy down. Very basic stuff."

Kristina's eyes widened. "You shot up a green flare."

Chameleon pretended to think, his eyes looking up and to the right. "Guess I did."

"Damn it," Kristina muttered. "This position's not safe."

"Have any of you died?" Oliver asked. "Besides the Pride Lord and Jakk, that is."

"Yes," Chameleon said. "The Shadow Twin and Vritra couldn't handle those damn rebels. Embarrassing, really. To be fair, George had already run off to enact his clone plan."

Oliver closed his eyes. The Northeast Order had lost six already. The Devil Kings had lost four, but five of their team were just flesh golems. He had no frame of reference for how strong they were, so excluding them, you could say it was a seven vs. four. Of course, you couldn't actually exclude the flesh golems. *Damn it, why's everything got to be so complicated?*

With no warning, Kristina punched Chameleon in the face. A streak of wind fueled her blow at the elbow, making her fist so fast that it blew a hole straight through his head. He died instantly.

Oliver was too battle-hardened to freak out, but he did jump back. "I promised him on my Dao!"

She slammed his head into the ground and whispered. "And you didn't break that promise." She put a finger to her lips and cloaked her aura completely. Oliver did the same, despite his shock at the Devil King's sudden demise.

They heard voices above ground. "Where is that stupid reptile?" Oliver wasn't a body cultivator, but his hearing was still far better than any human from the before. The enemies knew that too, without question. If he was hearing them, it was because they wanted to be heard.

The first voice was sultry, that of a woman. The reply came from a gruff male voice. "Vritra? You were the one to let him die when we faced the rebels."

"Obviously, I'm referring to Chameleon, you moron. If he interrupted their mission, then we're almost guaranteed victory."

Oliver then heard it first. A low, screeching sound, accompanied by a rumble. The sound came first, since his aura sense was partially dampened by his own cloak. But he felt that soon enough as well. The cold of George Moulin.

Is that the fake one, or the real one? Either way, his anxiety made him consider the worst. If he was coming here now, then that meant a high likelihood that either Alistair or all the rest of his team was dead.

"We have to get out of here now," Oliver whispered into Kristina's ear. "That's their boss coming."

Kristina nodded. They both tiptoed quietly toward the alleyway exit, which led out to the lower layer block. Oliver pushed the door, a hinge-based wooden one, not anything fancy like in the wealthier parts of the city. His prayers were answered when it didn't creak as it opened.

They made it out to a narrow alley, around fifteen feet deeper than the street they came from. You could make out the edges of the higher street as it lay on top of a vine-covered wall. The lower street was full of trash and rundown apartments. The inlaid Mana lights underneath the silver road flickered, low on power.

A smart move would have been to flee and look for the Mayor's office. But he couldn't do that without verifying the situation. All comms were down, no matter how hard he tried. That lent more credence to the idea that this was the clone, possibly having killed Caren.

Oliver gingerly handed Kristina the Utopic Bomb. "Let's split up," he whispered. "You go to the Mayor's office. You know this city much better than me. I'll send a bird with you to monitor."

"Is that wise?" she asked, gesturing toward him. "You have no Mana left."

"I'll be fine."

Kristina wasn't one for reassurances. She turned to leave before he even finished his sentence.

Oliver, feeling the enemy's presence, slunk around some apartments until he found a position sufficiently far away. It was a restaurant that had smoke coming out of a thin rod chimney, a nice aroma of dumplings filtering into the air. He counted himself as fortunate that this area of Eden was devoid of people, despite the appearances. The Pathfinder AI was probably too stingy to simulate everyone.

He climbed up to the roof, the sounds of his feet and hands against the metal concealed by the noises inside the restaurant. On the roof, he could hide behind the upturned curl of the roof, a signature of Eastern architecture.

What the hell?

Oliver realized that the screeching noises he heard earlier came from a *glacier*. It was that *Arcanous Devil Spell #1: Glacial Front*, in which George could create an enormous and controllable block of ice.

After a closer look, his heart beat a little faster. George was in a horrid condition. He looked like he had a broken jaw, skull, and just about every visible part of his body was covered in bruises. Which was a lot of his body, seeing as his chest and stomach were mostly visible, his white robes in tatters and stained with black blood.

The almighty leader of the Devil King also had four stab wounds in his chest. Stab wounds that Oliver thought looked like they came from a knifehand jab. The aftermath of which he had seen many times when fighting with Alistair.

That's the real one! Oliver exclaimed mentally. *Holy shit! I can probably take him out if I get a clean shot.*

George morphed his glacier to carve a ramp down to the ground. He then proceeded to slide down it like a child at a waterpark.

He landed with a thud, rolling over on his side multiple times.

"Master!" Hephaestus ran over to the fallen body of the Devil King, helping him up by lending a shoulder. The Eleventh Devil King was a titan of a man, towering over George. He had bronze armor which matched his skin, a whip of molten rock holstered over his back.

George coughed up blood, putting his arm over Hephaestus's shoulder. "Get ready, you fools," he sputtered. "He's coming."

Oliver didn't have time to contemplate who the "he" was. In the distance, he felt an unmasked presence. A familiar presence. Alistair had arrived.

———

Badge Acquired: "Pathbreaker" (Special Tier 1 Heraldic Badge): *The wills of the movers and shakers of the cosmos have clashed, and only one can come out on top. The user's path has prevailed over the path of the enemy. Further Tier increases of this Badge only come from further pathbreaking.* Dao Energy +10%, Mana +10%, All Attributes +10%.

Badge Replacement:
Tier 2 Rare Badge "Heroism" gained, (replacing "Good Samaritan [Altered]").
"Heroism" (Tier 3 Legendary Badge): *Become the embodiment of a hero.* All Attributes +15, also when fighting enemies you deem as reprobate evildoers, gain +25% to your two highest Attributes. Any mental or Dao-based attack of the same realm intended to subvert one's heroic nature is negated, unless backed by an equivalent Badge. Upgradeable (0/500).

Alistair looked on with shock as he saw George's glacier drift away. He had been fully resigned to die, yet there he was, standing and breathing.

He innately understood that he'd received his new "Pathbreaker" Badge from George fleeing. From what Alistair knew of the leader of the Devil King, he was not a coward. His methods were cruel and evil, but his Devil Kings truly believed in him and Oracle honestly thought that he would never betray them.

In that final moment, what had George seen?

Alistair would have died if he directed *Glacial Front* forward. If George had been in his right mind, with all his abilities, surely he would have realized that?

But fear, fear was the insidious parasite that crippled hearts. In every punch and kick and knee that he threw against his ultimate foe, there was conviction. He was one with his Dao in every aspect. That sincerity must have shaken something in George, even if he didn't know it.

It was a good thing that he had the sense to open a Badge slot before entering Eden.

As for the second Badge, Alistair noted the only change was the negation of attacks on his "heroic nature." He had an innate understanding of this as well, and Foundation realm mind control attacks wouldn't work at all on him. He was building a nice set of resistances, with this Badge, Permanent Haunt, and his **[Steel Body]**.

There was something else blooming within him, besides his two new Badges. With the last expulsion of the demonic blood he stole with {Blood Debt}, he felt a stirring in his blood. When he focused on that, even for a second, a new notification appeared.

Bloodline Characteristic Forced Merger:
Due to personal insight, forced merger of active Draconic Physique and inactive Blood Affinity has merged into the characteristic Dragon's Blood Mastery.

Characteristic – Dragon's Blood Mastery: Lifespan increased by 2,000 years. Life force increased with bodily vigor of a dragon. Mana costs involving blood affinity Skills reduced by 25%. Freehand control over blood affinity increased by 50%. Internal bodily functions are tied to life force and blood essence in the manner of a blood dragon, at 0.1% efficiency, to increase with bloodline improvement.

{Bloodline Evolution} (Ghost) Blood Dragon [Peon] — *Dragon's Blood Mastery, Emperor Will (inactive), Endless Mana, LOCKED, LOCKED, LOCKED, LOCKED.* (Upgradeable 487/1000 – Only accepts blood essence).

The impact of his new characteristic hit him like a truck. It was as if he could feel the internal state of his body with an entirely new and incredibly high fidelity sense. His nervous system, his cardiovascular system, everything felt under his purview, from the largest organ to the tiniest cell.

And this was only 0.1% efficiency? Just how mighty were trueborn dragons?

It wasn't so broken that he could just heal himself automatically, but he could feel the instability in his meridians and soulcore caused by the sudden shattering of his proto-Domain revert. A dragon's life force and spiritual network were innately tied together in a way that humans were not.

As long as at least the body, mind, or soul was intact, it would make up the gaps. Dragons didn't get infinite energy—what it meant was that all of their quintessence was essentially one giant health pool.

Alistair felt his *nue* drain away to replenish his spiritual pathways. He had drained a decent amount from **[Mindshifts]** already, and the conversion was only around 15% efficient, so he was left with only a small amount of *nue* upon completion.

Once that was done, he was able to pop a Tier 3 Mana pill, and once that had been absorbed, he used his blood affinity to accelerate his natural healing processes.

His burns faded, his stab wounds closed, his flesh grew back. Even his index finger regenerated at an astonishing rate. None of this was free, however, and his Mana once again went back down to near zero. It also took him almost three minutes to fully rejuvenate his finger, so it wasn't like a cure to all injuries, though as he progressed his bloodline, it would no doubt get stronger.

But he wasn't really focusing on his wounds as they healed. It was like walking.

His main focus was chasing after George.

The process of going over his notifications took less than five seconds, as all the information was streamlined by the Pathfinder AI straight into his brain. After that and downing the pill, he took off after the Devil King's glacier.

It was slow at first. He was barely moving at a fourth of his normal speed with all his injuries.

Slowly, as his life force empowered his healing factor, he sped up. His initial pace put him so far behind the glacier it was out of sight, but the trail of slush left behind was too obvious to miss.

After two minutes, he was healed enough that he could sprint at the full speed his over 1,000 Agility provided. He was catching up to *Glacial Front*.

By the time he was only half a block behind the glacier, it had stopped. They were near the center of Eden, at a crossroads between the upper, wealthier portion, and the lower, poorer side.

The glacier vanished, and Alistair saw his opponents.

There were only four Devil Kings.

George leaned on the hulking titan of a man, Hephaestus.

Morgana and Heavyset made eye contact with him. There was no sign of any other Devil Kings or Princes, no sign of the flesh golems.

Alistair sniffed the air. Oliver was nearby, and Kristina had just left, her scent fading. The former must have been cloaking himself, since he couldn't figure out exactly where the kid was.

All he had at his disposal was enough Mana for one [Mindshift], some of his Ghost Node, and 30 Karma. Those were his resources against three healthy Devil Kings, and a severely injured George.

A two-layered roundabout was the only thing separating them. There was a small greenery section in the middle, though the glacier demolished the plants. The upper section looked like it was for cultivators, since it had the same aura of space and air Mana as his public transportation, but in semi-open tunnels instead.

Alistair took a deep breath and prepared for combat, but before he could do anything, there was a deep rumble.

The entire city vibrated with a subharmonic oscillation. He could see double of everything for a brief moment. And, at the same time, a blazing orange cloud of energy obliterated a building in the distance.

Armageddon Mission #4 (Team Northeast Order): Plant the Utopic Bomb in the Mayor's office, leading to his death, complete.

Armageddon Mission #5 (Team Northeast Order):
Frame the Chief of Police by planting bomb residue in his office, causing a coup.

"Alistair!"

His neck snapped to the wall on the other side of the roundabout. The shout was coming from one of the rooftops. When he focused his vision, he could see Oliver's hair poking out from behind a curved roof.

"They've finished four missions too! All that's left for them is killing the Leader of the Resistance!"

That was the breaking point for the stalemate.

Arcane arrays appeared around Heavyset's hands and all the Devil Kings' feet. Gravity no longer held as large a burden, doubling their speed.

Morgana's burning eyes glowed an even stronger red as she opened her mouth. The brand on her tongue glowed as well, and she spoke rapidly in a foul language that made Alistair's ears hurt. A pale red beam shot out from her tongue toward Oliver.

Her profane luminance was nothing compared to the crimson aura imbuing Alistair's eyes. His Karmic sight previewed all, and he had made his move. Something came out of his hands, in what looked to be a movement like the flick of a playing card.

A white blur connected with the pale red beam, knocking it away.

[Eyes of Truth] was not the only Karmic Skill he used. Letting his Karma drop all the way down to 7, he activated [Hand of Karma] as well, using the new range of the Tier 4 Skill to sear threads of Fate at a distance.

He activated [Mindshift] as well. His *nue* clone went for Morgana, while his real self dashed toward Heavyset.

The Devil Kings had their priorities. Perhaps if they had time to plan things out, they could have saved them both, but they panicked, going for redundancy. Without his lich, George wouldn't see through [Mindshift].

Hephaestus tapped the shoulder of Morgana, bronze armor shimmering into existence. George made a diamond with his fingers, a makeshift spell array that turned the road icy, spikes interrupting his clone's path.

They left poor Heavyset out to dry.

She tried her best. Right before Alistair made contact, she made his gravity increase by over a dozen times. It wasn't enough to stop his kick. The side kick sent her backward a few feet, despite her weight.

The pale red beam struck her chest. She died in an instant, her flesh ripping inside out.

Bonus Quest Reward: [Vanquishing the Devil Kings] – 9/12. +40 Upgrade Points.

Level up! *You are now level 66.* +4 Agility, +4 Intelligence, +4 Charisma, +4 free Attribute points, +31 Upgrade Points.

His plan to use Farsa's business card as a mirror had worked like a charm. That piece of white metal was so damn strong that he had suspected it would be invincible to any Foundation realm Skill. And if it did break, the lion seemed like a nice guy. Surely, he would understand?

The moment he saw Morgana's attack eviscerate her ally, he kept going.

He ducked without looking thanks to **[Monk Motionlessness],** avoiding another pale red beam and an ice spear.

Alistair scaled the restaurant on the wall with ease, picking up Oliver. Even with Heavyset's boon, which he wasn't sure how long would persist after her death, he knew he was faster than the Devil Kings.

The most important thing was getting Oliver to safety. That took precedence over any final clash against George. The secondary aspect was that he was running in the direction of the police headquarters. It was the Devil Kings' starting point, and therefore it was at the direct opposite end of the prison's location.

Alistair came to a sudden stop. He was only a couple of hundred feet down the empty street attached to the roundabout.

"What's wrong?" Oliver asked. "We don't have time to waste!"

Alistair set the Necromancer down with one arm. "Go meet up with Kristina and win this thing for us." He patted his good friend on the back. He didn't spend any Dao energy, but his words were full of conviction. Oliver's confidence in him was over the moon.

Where Alistair had come from, a new batch of heroes had arrived.

Pharaoh. Alexandra. Marzhan. William. Lucius.

They all looked like shit, except for William. *Lucky bastard.*

George pushed Morgana and Hephaestus toward the newcomers and stood to face Alistair. "We meet again."

Beams of light, alien tentacles, and glass flowers flew all over the roundabout. Morgana engaged his teammates with an impressive display of arcane might. She looked fresh as a button, casting powerful spell after powerful spell. Alistair could feel that his allies didn't have that kind of energy.

George seemed to show far more bravery than before, charging at Alistair with a grim silence.

Alistair sidestepped a wild hammerfist, ducking under a follow-up uppercut. Every attack George brought, he dodged with ease. Unarmed combat was his kingdom. An amateur like George would never understand its beauty.

Alistair swung for the first time with a hook to the Devil King's ribs. He let the remaining 10% of his Justice Node out with his strikes. That Dao energy was not intended for harm. There was a nobler purpose.

Despite all the evil that he had seen, all the suffering and torture and murder the Devil Kings had conducted and permitted, despite the very nature of the demonic taint and its inevitability, Alistair at heart was a romantic.

He was someone that believed in second chances. He believed in justice, in forgiveness, and in true repentance.

His Badge was proof of that—"Pathbreaker". Nothing would stand in his way. Even if he was too weak now, in the end, Fate itself would bend to his will.

Each punch that came forth was from a different stance of the Silver Comet Sect. Zebra Stance, Turtle Stance, Dragon Stance, then Snake Stance. He cycled through the deadly moves of {Psychopomp's Discipline}. It went beyond fighting into an art form.

Though it would have been easier for a fellow martial artist to understand, Alistair was so talented that he could convey a message even to an amateur like George.

Through both his Dao energy and his very martial arts themselves, he told the battered man before him one thing—it's not too late.

Through each strike, he understood more of George Moulin, the Iceman. Alistair peered into his heart of hearts.

The coral afterimages merged together as he picked up his pace. His punches contained less and less physical force, but more and more speed as he modulated the impact of his blows. Spiritual Fighter's Echo became less of a multiplier of damage and more of a human figure.

This glowing figure of the Dao was almost caressing George, who had fallen to his knees. From the force of the punches or the emotional weight, he did not know. He felt it was the time to speak.

"I can feel your pain," he said. "You're not alone. I know you believe your mind is ugly beyond repair. Don't give in. I know it seems difficult beyond imagination, but I'm here. Nothing is impossible."

Alistair outstretched an arm to the fallen George. Unarmored, with no Skills. A naked hand with no malcontent. For a long moment, the man stared at that hand, his final opportunity for redemption.

George Moulin nodded. He reached up a hand, slowly. Then, when they were but a hair's breadth apart, a hypersonic rod shot through the Devil King's hand.

Alistair would have felt **[Monk Motionlessness]** go off if it was a danger to him. However, he was never the intended target. That was George. A shard of glass sliced through flesh and blood with ease, gathering a tiny amount of ice at its tip as it arced off into the distance.

It didn't take Alistair long to react. He grabbed George's hand and crumpled him to the ground. He threw an elbow down. The time for mercy was gone. The smirk on the man's face was the only warning of something amiss.

Alistair's elbow cracked open the silver road, but did not find a tender skull.

In the distance, the glass rod arced toward the police headquarters. Attached by the hand was a man, who dangled off it like a zipliner.

Morgana had shot her spell through her master on purpose, gathering a piece of ice on it, all so that he could shift to that location.

Alistair turned his head back to Morgana and Hephaestus, and then toward the glass rod, which finally crashed through the skyscraper HQ, and then back again toward his teammates' battle.

He had a decision to make.

59 GHOST OF THE TRUTHSEEKER

ALISTAIR HAD TWO OPTIONS.

One: Run off to the police HQ to join Kristina and Oliver in accomplishing the fifth mission.

Two: Help his friends fight Morgana and Hephaestus.

Both options had their benefits and drawbacks. The longer he waited, the more both sides' drawbacks would affect things.

In the span of time it took to turn his head three times, he had decided.

George was on his last legs, and he had felt how strong Kristina was. If Morgana was at full power and killed the five Northeast Order members in two minutes, that would both be devastating emotionally, but also negatively affect their chances of victory.

If they consolidated their strength now and won against Morgana without suffering another casualty, it would be eight of them against one George, plus whatever remaining police force there was.

Then, the only question was how he could best insert himself in the battle.

Morgana had taken to the skies, flying seemingly without any aid. Hephaestus floated at her side, sitting in a bronze pod that attached to her at the waist. She had donned a thick plate armor filled with ornate inscriptions, with molten rock cresting over her back in the shape of a jetpack.

This magma jetpack increased her speed over what Alistair remembered, even with the added weight of the armor and Hephaestus. She was queen of the skies, soaring through the air with perfect control.

From her vantage point in the air, she rained down destruction on her foes. Her mouth was perpetually open as she used her tongue tattoo to fire dozens of pale red beams. While utterly destructive against living things, the beams fizzled into nothingness when hitting the steel or glass of the buildings.

Besides the beams, she snapped her fingers and blue fireballs came forth, combusting in massive explosions that could level the smaller office spaces and restaurants into rubble.

Jagged glass shards flew out of her revealing robes like confetti from a piñata. They morphed into flower heads that zipped around in chaotic patterns.

And even on top of that, Hephaestus could use the magma shoulder pads of Morgana's armor to splash miniature eruptions of lava down on them. The chunks were hot enough to melt reinforced steel and spread out quickly.

The result—a scene from an apocalyptic nightmare. It was the Earth Asunder wave of [Armageddon] incarnate in one woman.

Alistair's teammates did not try to fight her. The moment she began her tirade, they ran. Even without Caren's communication, they knew what to do, every man and woman running for their own lives. They darted in and out of buildings and under bridges, anything to avoid getting struck by a fireball or beam or implosion.

Alistair saw this apocalyptic scene and remembered the memories he stole from Oracle and George. He remembered the reports of her being responsible for the Massacre of Beijing, and the recent statements from spies stating that millions of citizens of the Cursed Lands had disappeared in the days leading up to the sixth wave.

Souls as a Mana battery, he ruminated. *She is an abomination beyond reckoning.*

He chased after her, staying low to the ground as he tracked her in the air with a multitude of senses. She had decided to go after the easiest target —William St. James. He was the slowest and least physically able out of the five.

"Come here!" she cackled, throwing fireballs in his direction. They tore apart the coffee shop William was inside, though he managed to take out a hexagon-style golden aegis to block. The impact of the explosion sent him tumbling onto the street. She descended to the ground after him.

The glass petals sliced his legs and back, the parts of his body unguarded by his multi-layered aegis. The shield was made of translucent energy and attached to his arm at the wrist. Even the pale light that struck it reflected back at Morgana and Hephaestus.

"You wretched, ugly man. You dare use my spells against me?"

As her mouth formed the words of power, Alistair saw William nod. The aegis expanded hexagon by hexagon, forming a cube around Morgana and Hephaestus.

"Wyld Fireball."

Blue sparks around her fingers turned into a brilliant sapphire flame. The flame burst against the aegis, engulfing everything in fire.

She clearly wasn't expecting the added walls of the shield. It wasn't strong enough to contain the explosion completely, but a large portion was still reflected back against her. The rest flowed through the aegis, destroying the item, and onto the other side.

Alistair rushed forward despite the inferno. He had three things going for him—**Mammothskin Raiment's** insulation against heat, his natural Draconic Physique, and the [Steel Body].

Wyld Fireball was of course no ordinary fire, and even through those three mitigating factors he felt the heat. But not enough to stop him.

His Mana regeneration was almost 6 per minute, and he had gotten back up to 30. [Blood Hand] cost an effective 26 Mana considering his efficiency bump post-level 60 tribulation.

Dark red blood-attuned Mana churned around his bare fist like never before. It was not wrong to state that out of his four main affinity Skills, [Blood Hand] was now his strongest. The air warped as he let the Ghost Node flow through the sanguine Skill.

[Blood Hand] parted the flames and his fist connected with something solid—a ten-foot tall monster of patched-together flesh stood before him.

His Skill eviscerated the abomination, his blood affinity Mana filtering through the creature with ease and cleansing it of its evil aura. Upon a closer inspection, the monster looked like an enormous human with elongated limbs, naked and lacking certain external appendages. It had to be one of her flesh golems.

The flesh golem melted into a puddle of goo, its creator mostly unharmed behind it. Morgana had some burns on her hands, but she was otherwise fine, clearly having some kind of control over the fire as its source.

She looked furious.

Alistair could tell that the flesh golem would have survived any ordinary attack. The amount of Mana stored within that thing was ridiculous, and he suspected it came from human sacrifices. Lucky that [**Blood Hand**] attacked the vitality of the thing, rather than the Mana.

The others struck, sensing a moment of weakness.

While William scrambled away sporting deep burns over his torso, four bone arrows came down at the same time, forming a perimeter around the Devil Kings. When they tried to fly out of the perimeter, an invisible force field delineated by the bone arrows stopped her.

Hephaestus activated the burners on his magma jetpack, rocketing up. The bone arrows grew and spiraled up, merging into the trunk of a twisted bone tree. The bone-wood spiraled and twisted in on itself, growing almost as fast as Morgana flew up.

Until Alexandra launched a particularly large **Withering Promise** at her.

The spinning dagger had ballooned to almost twelve feet long, and came from the vantage point of a nearby bridge between skyscrapers. The dagger revolved with incredible weight, and it was too large for Morgana to escape by flying upward, forcing her back down, even if for a moment.

That moment let the revolving bone overtake the mad witch. The four spirals stopped, coming together into a conical section at the top with a tennis ball-sized hole at the top, far too small for anyone to escape from.

The new prisoner wasn't satisfied with her new cell, and Alistair felt the power of another Rank 1 Spell brewing inside the tree. They couldn't hear the words, but they responded all the same.

Pharaoh came in next, using a condensed cloud of sand to float up to the top of the tree. Grayish-pink sand that Alistair had never seen before poured out of his body and down the hole at the top.

Lucius stood on the cloud with him. Platinum drachma melted in mirage-like flickers around his body, quickly turning to Gold as the wealthy man's coffers ultimately ran dry. [**Audentes Fortuna Iuvat**] converted his money to real materia, copying Pharaoh's new sand.

The two joined their sand together and flooded the hole.

As this happened, cracks formed on the outside of the bone tree. Tiny, almost imperceptibly fine blades of glass pierced through.

More bone arrows connected, plugging the cracks. Alistair turned his head to see Marzhan, standing the furthest away from the battlefield, over a hundred yards away. She was the most healthy of the group in terms of Mana and Dao energy, but she was also the most fragile. A deep gash in her stomach still slowly bled.

The war between the glass needles and additional bone arrows continued for three seconds.

The glass won. Marzhan was too injured to keep up a fast enough rate of fire, and after those three seconds, the needles expanded so fast they cracked the base of the bone tree. Morgana flew out.

Her bronze armor had thousands of holes. Her luscious hair was mostly gone, and Hephaestus was peppered with even more tiny holes. The Devil King was the worst nightmare for someone with trypophobia, looking like more hole than person.

Morgana tapped her ally's shoulder and whispered as fast as she could. *"Engorgement."*

Alistair's **[Monk Motionlessness]** felt like a strong breeze. He looked at Alexandra. To Pharaoh and Lucius. To Marzhan. William seemed to have been long gone, thankfully.

Hephaestus's body set off from the soulcore first. The light inside him made his skin glow like there was a flashlight in his stomach.

In the blink of an eye, his body ballooned in size. His flesh literally warped from the exponential growth rate, his stomach and torso making up the majority of the expansion. But this was no mere influx of air and distention. His flesh was multiplying and growing at a cellular level.

Hephaestus slammed into the buildings, his body growing through windows and around solid objects like floors and support beams. His flesh's enlargement slowed down after the first dozen feet, but still continued at a rate half that of Alistair's running speed.

Alistair rushed toward Marzhan as fast as he could. He draped her over his shoulders like a knight rescuing a princess in a tower, speeding away from the still expanding body as fast as he could.

Pharaoh's cloud of sand was too slow for the flooding flesh, which went up as quick as it went out. He valiantly used his own body, standing in front of Lucius. After that, Alistair didn't know what happened. The fat and skin of Hephaestus covered everything. He prayed Alexandra had escaped. The effects of touching the flesh were still unknown, no one having ever seen the *Engorgement* spell before.

After what felt like hours of the spread of what was once Hephaestus, but was really around thirty seconds, the flesh stopped. Near the end, it had lost its solidity, becoming more aqueous as it spread out until it was more like a soup.

The sewage system could handle it to a certain extent after that point. Alistair stopped and looked back.

Hephaestus's flesh was sublimating into smoke. The smoke took on a black hue over time, and he realized the danger of the *Engorgement*. If she could infect them with demon blood, they would be under her control as Devil Princes.

Alistair contemplated for a moment why his past enemies hadn't tried that tactic, and realized quite quickly that his toolbox made trying to infect him almost impossible.

He cloaked his and Marzhan's aura. The vigor of firing so many arrows had taken a toll on her, with the bleeding picking up pace. She needed a Curse Breaker and a healer if she was going to survive. He ran some Dao energy through her wound to help wade off the taint he sensed, if even for a few minutes.

A few minutes was all they needed. He slithered through the shattered window of a residential apartment, stashing her inside. She gave him a tremoring thumbs up before passing out from blood loss.

Alistair's Ghost Node and 8 Karma was all that he had left in terms of quintessence, unless you counted his 11 Mana. His bloodline's efficiency was way too low to be able to convert his life force into anything, or he would have taken out that advance already.

The combination of his knowledge of Morgana's abilities and his new Badge, "Heroism," gave him an idea. But first, he needed stealth. He accessed his Ghost Node to etherealize his body, allowing him to walk through walls and evade detection.

Alistair darted through the rubble of the buildings closest to Hephaestus's initial explosion. The momentum of the flesh had essentially flattened the buildings in the vicinity of the city block, leaving a heaping pile of metal and glass.

A wave of wind swept over his head. He was on four limbs, crawling with the Ghost Node's intangibility so as to evade detection. The gust swept away the dust and particulates in the air. He guessed that it wasn't for the good health of their lungs, but that she wanted to see her targets.

Of course, Alistair had no need for sight. He could feel Pharaoh and Lucius close to the center of the explosion, and Alexandra further out, underneath a pile of trash.

If it was anyone else but Pharaoh, he would have been turned, but his fourteen lives of Osiris came in clutch. Lucius was unharmed, crouching behind his protector.

Morgana breathed heavily a hundred feet away. Her clothes were tattered from the pink sand, her body full of smoking holes. Her burning eyes were filled with so much rage, he thought they might burst out of their sockets at any second.

The next few seconds were absolutely essential for his plan.

Alistair's aura sense indicated that she was nowhere near empty of Mana, despite her vast displays of magic. Plus, he suspected that she was hiding even more Mana in the form of sacrificed souls. However, her life force was low, and she suffered continuous damage from her open wounds. A classic example of a glass cannon.

With one deep breath, he exhaled all his worries and became the perfect ocean of tranquility he called home so often. Even with no Dao energy, his grasp of meditation was as good as any at the Foundation realm.

Alistair let go of the Ghost Node and stood up, chest high, and sauntered toward Morgana.

His Dao Nodes were essentially empty. His Mana—6 points left. Psychic energy, also nil.

This was meaningless to Alistair. His face was austere and grim, his movements the embodiment of confidence.

A true hero did not back down, no matter what. A true hero would sacrifice his life for those he protected.

A true hero could falter, but they would never give up.

As his boots cracked glass shards underneath, as he made eye contact with Morgana, he had never in his life felt like he understood the Dao more.

His Karma dropped to zero as crimson light was visible to all who watched, even with no special sight. The light traveled in a web, pulsing from Alistair's body.

Later scholars of the footage, obtained years later, had differing accounts of how it happened. A unique Skill from someone with unrivaled talent? An anomalous manifestation of the Dao? The warren of a higher power intervening?

What those who saw it in person, what Alexandra saw, what Pharaoh saw, what Lucius saw, was simple.

The Spirit of a True Hero.

Golden light shimmered around Alistair's body, accompanying his Karmic blaze. The light coalesced and hardened into a glowing avatar. The avatar was nondescript, carrying no weapons and wearing the tattered robes of a mendicant preacher. Golden lotus petals floated around him, his expression an ancient smile.

Alistair was unarmed, with no quintessence. This shimmering figure, the crimson Karma—there was no physical danger, or even a heart-based attack. It was a complete mirage.

The others didn't share the same assessment. His allies felt a rush of inspiration, a feeling of consummate sublimity that moved their worn feet to action. The call of the hero to action.

To Morgana? Even if it was her imagination, her worst paranoia, even if it was for a moment of time so brief that it had no name, she saw the ghost of a Truthseeker.

A notification popped up that he had achieved a First Widening in the Ghost Node, but he ignored it. Morgana activated her ultimate spell.

"Shard of Madness!"

Her spell was no ordinary *Shard of Madness*, if that could be said to exist. Two more flesh golems warped into existence at her sides. With one tap of a finger, they converted into blinding blue Mana that spiraled into a pink shard of glass in the sky.

The array in the sky stretched for thousands of feet in every direction. A circular array filled with impossibly complex arcane symbols and text, rotating and humming with both Mana and *nue*.

A pink shard of glass appeared concomitantly with the array, multiplying and growing with a speed that seemed impossible. There was no doubt this *Shard of Madness* was over ten times stronger than the one she had used against the snake kaiju.

Resistance to such a spell, fueled by the deaths of millions, was futile. Pharaoh, Lucius, Alexandra—they succumbed right away, completely under the spell of madness.

Alistair's fingers pierced through Morgana's exposed neck.

She died instantly.

Bonus Quest Reward: [Vanquishing the Devil Kings] – 11/12. +40 Upgrade Points.

Level up! *You are now level 69.* +12 Agility, +12 Intelligence, +12 Charisma, +12 free Attribute points, +93 Upgrade Points.

With Morgana's death, the shards of glass in the sky vanished. Alistair collapsed to the ground in exhaustion, not realizing how much that stunt had taken out of him. Now, even his Karma was at zero.

Summoning the Spirit of a True Hero had taken much out of him.

He realized that he had never been so drained in his life. Even if he had been at lower Health at certain times, this was the moment of peak exhaustion.

Lucius's and Pharaoh's bodies collapsed to the ground with a thud. The madness was gone, but even that half-second of exposure to the shard was enough to cause severe mental damage. Alexandra also passed out in the distance.

Alistair, mentally speaking, was unscathed. He had his new "Heroism" Badge to thank for that. It was the only reason he tried his bluff tactic, to make himself seem so scary that she felt forced into her finishing Skill.

Madness was a subversion of his heroic nature, so her spell didn't affect him at all. And since she was so focused on her spell, believing its power to be unassailable, she lowered her defenses and Alistair stabbed her neck straight through.

"Hey boss, need a lift?"

Alistair opened his eyes. He had been lying there, waiting for his Stamina to recover, when he heard the familiar voice. *William?*

"You predicted all of this, you bastard?" he chuckled. "You're scarier than I could ever imagine."

"You flatter me, boss." William bent down and picked up Alistair in a fireman's carry. Alistair's dense body, molded by his time in the Holy Ravine and affected by the **[Steel Body]** itself, sat heavy on his shoulders. "Cut back on the calories a bit, will you?"

William took off at a steady pace for the police headquarters. They were around 2.5 miles away from their current position.

"How did you avoid the *Shard of Madness?*" Alistair asked.

"It wasn't so hard," William said. "I found a basement, and I hid there. Though honestly, I was screwed if you didn't step in. That spell was beginning to affect me even without me seeing it. You may think me to be omniscient, but unfortunately, even this elder god needs protection from time to time. I'm almost out of Mana myself, even with a pill. [Hypercalculative Induction] is greedy."

Alistair inadvertently let out a laugh. "No one thinks you're omniscient, but good try. Do you have any more tricks up your sleeve, though?"

William sighed. "My **Laser Gun (III)** still has some juice left. I've got a pretty strong flashbang grenade. I've still got [Phase Boots] and [Coward's Way]."

He was, of course, referring to his ability to phase through solid objects, not unlike Alistair's Ghost Node capabilities, and his more unsavory combat Skill that allowed him to strike unnaturally quickly when prostrate and seemingly out of luck.

Alistair ruminated on the possibilities as William approached the police headquarters.

The streets were long emptied, the bustling metropolis now devoid of life, at least in that section. They were in the wealthier region, where pagodas and skyscrapers reached the heavens. Multiple layers of the city co-existed in three dimensions, connected with the transportation slides of space and wind Mana, along with the energy bridges where he had fought George previously.

The police HQ was not one of those skyscrapers, but a fat oblong bean thousands of feet wide and several hundred feet tall. The city of Eden clearly took security concerns seriously.

Like many of the surrounding structures, it was made of ambrosic glass and a white, shiny, ceramic-like material. Despite its great size, Alistair saw a hole where he assumed Morgana's glass rod had struck. The glass rod that had one George Moulin attached.

Windows shattered by the hundreds as a fight brewed inside the HQ, several floors beneath that hole. *That must be Kristina.* She was two-thirds of the way up to the top of one side of the bean. At the top end of the building was the presence of a cultivator that refused to cloak his immense energy.

To Alistair's chagrin, that undiluted aura was as strong as his was when he was healthy. *And that must be the Chief of Police. Perhaps the possessor of the*

Utopic Bomb gets an innate understanding of what it even means to "plant bomb residue" in his office. His office was closer to George's hole than Kristina's current position.

"Follow her," Alistair ordered. "Hopefully, her wake of destruction has dealt with all the stray police."

Their journey was interrupted. "Brat!"

Alistair smiled as he felt the presence of his imp for the first time since their swap. But the ghost wasn't talking to him, he was talking to William.

"Alistair? You sound different."

"I thought you were supposed to be smart. It's Dev'rox, speaking in Alistair's body, as I am severely low on Mana still."

"Ah."

"Your boots, can they allow you to persist within the walls? And how good is your cloaking?"

William tilted his head. "I see where you're going. Yes, I can remain phased between objects for up to five minutes. I tested it myself. And my cloaking is second-to-none, except Oliver, perhaps."

"Care to fill me in?" Alistair asked.

"Your Mana's almost ready," Dev'rox said. "Just under a minute."

Alistair looked at his Skill list. In just under a minute he would have 35 Mana, and the only Skill he had of that Mana cost was **[Mindshift]**. *Ah, I understand.*

The next minute was one of the slowest of his life. He constantly monitored Kristina's rampage, and she was getting close to the floor George landed on, though if what Dev'rox and William were suspecting was true, he was long gone.

When the moment came, they were ready. It was Alistair's turn to carry William, whom he had on his back. Dev'rox used what little Mana he had regenerated to solidify himself as a foothold so that his host could angle **[Mindshift]**.

With the airwalking aspect, he could step just once into the sky, though he couldn't chain his Skill together to emulate true flight. His Skill brought him to the top of the HQ in an instant.

The *nue* clone was essential. It crashed into the windows of the Chief's office as if it were a physical being, while Alistair and William passed through the windows of the floor underneath as if they didn't exist.

They were already applying the Ghost Node and **[Phase Boots]** respectively, and immediately found refuge in one of the walls. Thankfully, there seemed to be no one on the floor, which was an empty gym full of technological equipment that would have blown the mind of any gym rat from Earth.

The etherealizing ability of the Ghost Node barely cost any Dao energy to maintain, but Alistair was so low that he could only hold it for two minutes. While he was inside the wall, he climbed up through the solid metal, and peeked his head toward the office of the Chief of Police.

As the office was at the very top of the building's bean-like wing, it was very small. Vegetation hung from the ceiling, along with tubes of lightning Mana, a huge waste of resources just for lighting a room.

There was a floating black chunk of metal that served as the Chief of Police's desk. He sat behind it, an older man wearing a plain white uniform. To his left and right were the remaining two flesh golems.

George Moulin, his wounds shut closed with frozen blood, leaned against the window behind the desk. Alistair saw that the First Devil King was in much worse physical condition than him, though he couldn't know how much Mana the man had, as his aura sense didn't detect details as well when he was in ghost form.

Alistair dipped his head back down and turned to William, relaying what he saw. The Farsighter nodded.

Kristina's entrance was heralded far in advance.

They knew when the time was close by how loud the noises were. Shouts and screams and the sound of fists destroying metal permeated their floor from below. Then, she came.

The Trexian rebel was a whirlwind of fury. Automata and heavily armored police officers exploded with her thunderous punches. She broke through the gymnasium floor with a leap, her entire body shimmering with an intense current.

Behind her was Oliver, staying a safe distance away from the human hurricane. At his side was Richard Atwood, albeit in zombie form. He still wielded his bolt-action rifle, killing off any survivors.

Kristina roared, her voice creating a shockwave that shattered the windows of the floor. She jumped once more, fist pointed to the ceiling.

Their time was now. Alistair and William both rose out of the floor. Not where Alistair initially poked his head out, but right beside the Chief of Police and George.

Time screeched to a halt. The small office became a chaotic battlefield.

Alistair's hands gripped George's neck.

William, already having charged his **Laser Gun (II),** emptied a beam to the back of the Chief's head. He tossed a flashbang with a foot.

Kristina burst forth, the fastest of them all, her leap buoyed by a gale of wind. Her fist was set to collide with the face of the reclining Chief.

The zombie Atwood took a shot at one of the flesh golems with his sniper rifle, while Oliver peeked his head out and threw a green slime at the other golem.

Alistair watched as the various bullets and beams flew through the air. He saw the surprise in George's eyes.

The Chief of Police's body distorted as a powerful aura of space erupted. Kristina's incoming fist, the red plasma bolt headed at him from behind, and the flashbang William tossed—they all began to warp as space itself acquiesced to the Chief's demands.

Space warped around Alistair as well, but as powerful as the old man was, he could only focus on so many things at once.

Alistair jerked his hands backward and smashed his head into the window, taking George with him.

They fell, entwined beyond the physical. There could be only one survivor. It was the ultimate culmination of all their struggles.

Alistair squeezed with all his might as they entered free fall, his back hurdling toward the ground. Wind rushed by his face, the roaring currents in his ear. He squeezed to end it all. For those who had died, for those who had grieved the dead. For the future in which no one had to grieve again.

The ultimate technique of the Steel Body was perfect for the situation. His muscles locked into place, firing with strength beyond their normal capability.

George fought back with a renewed fury. What did he live for? For his Devil Kings? For a second chance offered by the Man in Shadows? Or was it because he was born into the world to live and not to die?

They flipped over once, then twice, then a third time. Gravity brought them to the ground in five seconds.

The First Devil King's struggle was futile. In a physical contest, where he was already more injured, there was little he could do. As Alistair reclaimed his position on top for the last time, both parties knew it was the end.

George's mind briefly flashed back to earlier. He could see Alistair's echo of the Dao so clearly now. How bright and glorious it was. *Why didn't I just accept that handshake of peace?* George asked himself the moment before impact. He remembered how brave he sounded when he told Dragonus that they were in it together until the end.

There was no cycle of Samsara for such an accursed being as the Devil King, the one who had partaken of the blood of the demons.

There was only nothingness.

I don't want to die.

George died the moment his skull hit the ground. In the very last moments before his death, those precious few milliseconds, a thought of peace crossed through his mind.

If Alistair were to go as far as he desired, in the end, even a wretched being like himself could have a chance. Could anyone really have the power to save Devil Kings from far beyond the state of nonexistence?

Alistair would try, George knew that.

The sudden deceleration of the landing crumpled Alistair's body, but before it could do significant damage, Eden faded away.

60 THE SIMPLE THINGS IN LIFE

THERE WAS DARKNESS.

Then, there was light.

The moment George died, Alistair felt everything fade to black. In the void, he stayed for what felt like both an interminably long and an inappreciably short time. His injuries healed, his Mana, *nue,* and even Dao energy restored, in what was an unusual move for the stingy Pathfinder AI.

That buggy system was pulling out all the stops for this healing journey —a bona fide first class rejuvenation treatment.

When he opened his eyes, he was in the same room in the Leading Domes where he had started the wave Armageddon of [Armageddon].

A deluge of notifications overwhelmed his vision.

Bonus Quest Reward: [Vanquishing the Devil Kings] – 12/12. +40 Upgrade Points.

Quest Complete: [Vanquishing the Devil Kings]. Rewards: 200 Upgrade Points, Tier 1 Journeyman Skill available (3 choices), Dao of the Fist Fruit.

Quest Complete: [Armageddon]. Reward: Global Mayor.

Achievements Upgraded/Earned: Dueling (V) – *There is no beauty or admiration to be won with dueling. The passions of war are the downfall of man.* Reward: Mythical rarity item – **Materia of True Martial Clarity.**

Land Prospector (Conquest III) – *Freehold ownership of at least 100,000 subregions.* Reward: 500,000 Land Credits.

Planetary Lord (Politics I). Reward: 1,000 Platinum drachma (for freehold use only), 1,000,000 Land Credits (for freehold use only).

"Deliverance of Justice": +54 free Attribute points.

Achievement: Dao Node (II) (Dao of the Ghost) — First Widening. *The Spirit of the True Hero is not a gimmick nor a gift, but the embodiment of what it means to walk the path of righteousness.* Reward: +50 Intelligence, +50 Wisdom, +50 Charisma, +10% Mana.

Level up! *You are now level 73.* +16 Agility, +16 Intelligence, +16 Charisma, +16 free Attribute points, +124 Upgrade Points.

His time in Eden really accelerated his growth, going from 64 to 73 in mere hours. Fighting foes of equal power in death matches couldn't be replicated by training.

Alistair looked at his Upgrade Points and free Attributes, seeing that he had 568 of the former and 90 of the latter. "Deliverance of Justice" seemed to consider his victory over George to be an imminent life saving operation, which made him shudder to think what he and Morgana had in store for the world if they had won.

But that was an outcome that would never happen.

Alistair was victorious. No, his team was victorious. The entire Northeast Order Freehold had pulled their weight in the physical demiplane.

The world was victorious.

That didn't come without casualties. Alistair looked around the table. Six of the thirteen seats were empty.

Bartholomew Wood, Whimsy, Brigid Mwangi, Jesse Waterfall, Caren Locasta, and Blaise Blanchett.

Those six individuals had entered the cycle of reincarnation. Their bodies couldn't even be returned to their families, given how callous the Final Frontier Empire was. Who knew what foul experiments they would use those stolen corpses for.

Those weren't the only ones. As Global Mayor, he had an exact count of the population of Earth. Currently, it stood at 396,892,505, lower than even the Northeast Freehold alone. While they were in Eden, everyone else had been forced to deal with a thousand-member elite squad of the Final Frontier Military.

That number of nearly 400 million was under 5% of the Earth's population before the initiation. Alistair remembered what they had said. A mortality rate of 80%? He only wished for those types of numbers now.

Yet despite all this death and sadness, the knowledge of the predations that were to come and the greedy powers of the multiverse that enforced strife and war, what Alistair felt in that moment he returned was anything but negative.

He was relieved. Relieved, and joyful.

He closed his eyes and reclined in his seat, letting all the months and months of stress leave his body. He had been on a deadline for so long, working to get stronger twenty-four hours a day, all to overcome the obstacle of George Moulin.

George Moulin was dead, and Alistair wasn't. The feeling of his victory was unlike anything he had known before.

The others had to feel similar. No one spoke a word for a long while in the war room. He let his varied senses turn off and just enjoyed the relaxation.

There was a smile on his face as he rested. It was freeing to turn off his brain, let go of his finely tuned senses and instincts.

His people had left the war room empty for them, so the seven returners were the only ones in there. He made a prediction as to who would first interrupt their genteel silence.

There was literally no way it was going to be Pharaoh. He was a silent man to begin with, and he might have been in the most pain of any of them, losing his partner, Whimsy.

No, Alistair amended, the one that was in the most pain had to be Lucius. Losing a son was a great tragedy. He wouldn't speak up first, either.

Marzhan was too respectful of his position to move first. That left Alexandra, William, and Oliver. All three were strong options.

"What the hell is everyone being so quiet for?"

Alistair opened his eyes with a grin. He was right, of course. William had stood up from his seat.

"We did it, didn't we? This initiation is officially fucking *OVER*. I think that calls for some celebration, no?"

Alistair couldn't agree more.

———

It turned out that their time on Eden had been temporally dilated. The rest of the world experienced the time they spent as an entire month. An entire month where they had to deal with an elite spec ops force, albeit limited to level 60.

Alistair was overjoyed at his world's performance. Alfred, Evangeline, Ramesh, Sally, and the other strongest cultivators back on Earth had been remarkably effective, leading a successful campaign against their version of the sixth wave.

The average folk knew that it was over as well. They got the notification that [Armageddon] had completed as soon as he did. No new Quest replaced it.

The moment he accessed his status screen, a global notification appeared, like the one beginning the initiation.

The Final Frontier Empire extends its sincerest congratulations to the denizens of FX-14752 for the successful completion of the Premium tier initiation of your world! Due to high potential noted among its citizens, FX-14752 shall be designated a Basic quality world with a fire affinity planetary core, with the accompanying increase in Mana production.

The initiation Quest line is complete—there shall be no more further mandatory Quests issued by the Pathfinder AI except under wartime or similarly dangerous conditions. The citizens of FX-14752 are free to pursue whatever they desire, be it farming, crafting, alchemy, combat, or the myriad of other professions.

An interstellar Teleportation Circle, free of cost, shall be gifted to the world in two months' time, with destinations at the five closest worlds. You shall also note the new presence of spaceships in the System Store.

The Global Mayor is recommended to attend the System Senate assembly in approximately one month's time.

Once again, welcome to the Final Frontier Empire! Your planet now possesses full legal protections as a member of Harmonious Note System of the fifteenth province of the Nightwatch Duchy of the Disputed Shard. May you live eternally to serve.

Why did the Final Frontier Empire have to be so ominous with their last statement? "May you live eternally to serve?" Everything else was fine enough, even though they had every right to be furious with the systemic rot of the empire.

However, those concerns were for another day. For now, they celebrated.

Living fireworks shot into the sky all around the capital. They really showed off their skills by having the dragon fireworks breathe flame.

Music cultivators sang and played all manner of strange instruments that Alistair had never seen before. Some looked similar to the traditional Chinese retinue, like a guzheng or an erhu, but others were utterly alien.

Brewers and alchemists worked together to create the ultimate alcoholic drinks, which Alistair ensured were on the house. For the entire Northeast Order. His tab was the highest in human history, no doubt.

These were no ordinary humans. Even the weakest, at that point, were over level 20, and it showed. The vigor of the partying exceeded that of anything from the before.

It was a celebration of life itself. Everyone who survived knew that there was a great degree of luck involved. It could have easily been them six feet under, and there was not a single person who hadn't lost a friend or relative.

Alistair wasn't the partying type, but *come on*. He was the Global Mayor. The hero of the world. He had to participate, if only for morale.

So he drank, he danced, he partied. At midnight, he stood on top of the Leading Domes, to raucous cheers from the public, who began chanting his name. He gave a brief speech from his heart, and then excused himself through the Ghost Node, knowing that if he didn't use his powers, everyone would be on his ass.

He needed some alone time. He chose the meadow with the Natural Inheritance, not too far off from the capital. Thankfully, it had survived the sixth wave, and still gave off a serene feeling of untouched nature.

"How the hell did you know I'd be here?"

Alistair was lying in the grass, looking up at the stars, when he felt her.

"You're not as clever as you think."

Alistair gave off an incredulous look. "I wasn't trying to be clever."

"But you were trying to get out of talking to people." Alexandra plopped down beside him, hugging her knees as she sat.

"No objection on my part," Alistair said. "I did my mayorly duties, thank you very much."

"Yes, you're more of a hero than a politician, that's for sure."

"I better work on the second part. Sometimes, the world needs politicians more than heroes."

"That's a fucking statement," she laughed. "Never thought I'd hear you say something like that."

"A heroic politician," Alistair conceded.

"A heroic *emperor*," Alexandra said dangerously.

"I'm no emperor."

"Becoming a Truthseeker, destroying the powers of the multiverse, storming the gates of Heaven and demanding a utopic paradise sounds pretty emperor-like to me."

Alistair flicked his hand. "Don't jinx it, woman. I know it sounds pretty outlandish when said aloud."

Alistair's shadow wriggled and darkened until a pale-skinned young man emerged. "Mind if I join in?" Oliver asked.

Alexandra tapped her fingers together. "We were just talking about how Alistair is going to be a celestial dictator when he grows up. Also, what the hell was that?"

"My new Skill from the Talent Tree that I got with all those Upgrade Points. It's cool, right?"

"Yes, it's very cool," Alistair said. "Hey, we are kind of like the big three, right? We've been together for a while, though I feel like it's mostly been me or Oliver as a team or me and Alexandra as a team. We didn't get much time to be a big three."

"We're not getting time in the near future, either," Oliver said. "I've been meaning to say this for a while, but I got an invitation to the FarNetter Academy. They have a special training camp for Foundations that starts in a month. I won't go if you think I need to stay here, though."

He looked at Alistair, who shook his head. "Of course you're going. That's your future. Don't be so worried about Earth. There's some real fundamental monsters in the Holy Ravine that should be coming out of their shells pretty soon, remember? And we also have that firebird on our side. I'll gain as much power as I can to defend our home, too."

Those words were as much for himself as Oliver. He, too, worried about what would happen to Earth while he was at the Clear Water Sect, but he reassured himself by admitting that if there was a truly unstoppable threat like a Profound or Visionary, he could do jack shit against that like everyone else. He was only strong for his realm, not objectively.

"What about you, Alexandra?" Alistair asked, continuing the conversation.

"Well, I'm going to be staying here for a while. Quasi-Devil King status and all. Maybe I'll explore our planetary system a bit. And you, Alistair? What's the Clear Water Sect status?"

"The sects don't accept anyone under Adept, so I'll need to reach level 100 by the time the next round of testing begins in six months. I think it's pretty doable, even if I have to spend my fortune on some leveling pills. I heard there are planets with mostly beast tides that you can train on. Alexandra, why don't we train together?"

"I like the sound of that." She had a wide smile on her face.

"The Grand Imperator should be coming next week," Alistair said. "I think I'll have to take care of a little issue, and then I should be able to leverage that for a tiny favor—and more, hopefully. I'll have to see Baron Aportamus in person, so you can tag along."

There was a silence after that as the three of them looked up at the stars together.

They were so far away, yet those light-years were nothing compared to the power of cultivation.

The next step of Alistair's journey would be difficult. He was going to enter a hotbed of political maneuvering, noble arrogance, and undisputed talents. His peers in both the Clear Water Sect and elsewhere would have the innate advantages of cultivating since birth.

So what? His dreams were far bigger than them. Far bigger than anything on the frontier.

Alistair would never stop until those dreams became reality.

EPILOGUE

EVERYONE on the planet saw the Grand Imperator's ship pull into orbit.

While it docked, from Alistair's capital, it took up a larger area of the sky than a full moon. It was a golden saucer somewhat like the traditional depiction of a UFO, attached with two long pincers underneath that looked like weapons to Alistair.

The Grand Imperator descended.

She floated down from her ship, appearing as a golden comet. She landed right outside of Alistair's capital. Which now was the world capital, with Alistair as planetary lord. He would have to meet with Baron Zilvesky Aportamus soon.

They met in an open field. The Grand Imperator had a retinue of hundreds behind her. Alistair's posse was not as impressive, though he trusted them with his life. They were his surviving allies, who had been there through thick and thin.

Alistair had seen a couple of Visionaries in his short time as a cultivator. None of them were like the woman clad in golden armor. She looked like a medieval knight, head to toe in plate mail with a vaguely Roman-style helmet. She had a cracked infinity symbol on her chest, a platinum balance scale floating above her head.

The aura of imperial majesty he felt from Marcus Auror was nothing compared to this woman. When he saw her, he almost wanted to believe the majordomo's bold claims of the Emperor's immortality and the empire's everlasting Dao. He had to spend a considerable amount of willpower to prevent himself from obsessing over the scales and symbol, which felt like the pieces of a grand tapestry that would draw him in, bypassing even his "Heroism" Badge.

Alistair was not the only one who attended the Grand Imperator's summons. All the sponsors came for the ride, and non-sponsors of various local businesses that wanted to set up shop on Earth. In total, there were thousands of people there to pay their respects to the Grand Imperator.

Once all the major players had arrived, the Grand Imperator, who was sitting on a silver version of the throne that Alistair remembered from his time on Sharizak, stood up.

"I am Praetei Dai Kezlan, Grand Imperator of the Final Frontier Empire."

Her gray eyes pierced the souls of the crowd gathered at her feet. Her voice was softer than Alistair would have expected, given her imposing frame and a height that exceeded his own. "An unfortunate detour delayed my arrival, which Marcus should have informed you of. With that, the news I had to bear is old. However, if you wish any words to greet the Emperor's ears, I can aid in your entreaties. For the sponsors, I shall meet with you privately on my ship in one hour's time."

Her gaze turned directly to Alistair. Despite him standing behind many of the sponsors over a hundred meters away, her eyes trained straight on him as she surveyed him like a hunk of meat at market.

One moment he was in the fields with the others, and in the next he was kneeling beside Praetei's silver throne.

"You are Alistair Tan, yes?" she asked.

"I am, Lady Kezlan."

"You may call me Praetei," she replied, though Alistair wondered if he really could. "There is one matter you must attend to before you may leave."

Another man appeared before the Grand Imperator. He was tall and muscular, with a mane of golden hair and blue eyes. His diaphanous robes showed an impressive musculature, and he exuded an arrogant air in the way he looked down at everyone. If Alistair was so bold, he could even say that air extended to the Imperator.

Who would dare be that conceited, as a mere… Adept? Alistair couldn't be sure of his strength, but he looked young in a way that older cultivators of a youthful appearance didn't, and his aura was weaker than that of Profound realms like Kyraxadon.

"I am here to witness a duel between Yarik Portolon of the Divine Sword Sect and Alistair Tan, sponsee of the Clear Water Sect. This duel is to have Yarik at equal cultivation level to Alistair."

Praetei performed rapid-fire hand signs. After a two-second pause, her ship rumbled.

That golden spaceship, which hogged the skies as a new celestial body, flashed red for a split second. Alistair watched in awe as a circular disc flew down at hypersonic speeds from the spaceship. The disc descended until it hovered above them, perfectly still.

Alistair looked on, understanding now why he was brought forth. It was the Portolon scion the Pathfinder AI mentioned. The one who had it out for Alistair's head because he killed Anthony, the Portolon investment.

Looking at the pompous young man, he completely understood how the spoiled noble could be as insane as wanting to fight a Foundation realm and threaten to destroy a planet. Yarik was the picture-perfect paragon of someone who thought they could do anything because of their name.

The Grand Imperator floated into the air, and with her came Alistair and Yarik. They rose until they were within a body's length of the disc, at which point gravity flipped. Their heads faced the ground, where over a thousand people were watching, curious about what was about to take place.

The disc was a perfectly flat piece of glossy white stone. You could see your reflection quite nicely, and it almost looked like there was an aqueous flow underneath the surface. Alistair thought it would make a suitable arena.

"I am Yarik Portolon," the buff, golden-haired man said with a surprisingly squeaky voice. Alistair noticed that his ears were partially turned up like an elf, and his eyes had specks of flame in the sclera. "The son of Grand Duke Seperati Portolon, brother of the Golden Sword of the Emperor. For 150 million years, my family has ruled from Faden Gohm, and my ancestors helped the first Emperor unite this universe. You have made the fatal mistake of offending House Portolon and have dishonored your world with the underhanded tactics you used against Anthony Ricci. For this, I challenge you to a duel."

Praetei coughed. "It shall be a duel to surrender or incapacitation, not death. I will be monitoring closely. This is what the Clear Water Sect and your mother have agreed upon."

"Of course," Yarik sneered. "I was speaking metaphorically. However, I'll have my ship destroy his planet after all the Prime Initiates get shuttled off. If he loses. Which is not an if."

Praetei pursed her lips. "Well, I am afraid that I must alter that part."

Yarik snapped his head around. "Pray tell? I have not heard of this."

"That is because I have decided so myself," Praetei replied. "It would tarnish the empire's reputation to allow such a thing. Especially after the previous incidents."

"I will tell my lord father about this," Yarik said. "He will not be pleased."

The Grand Imperator did not seem afraid in the slightest. "Lord Seperati is welcome to speak to me at any time he wishes. I do recall him asking me to be his first wife a few decamillennia ago."

"Fine, then, if you must. What about just this city?"

Praetei looked up and to the right, as if she were calculating something. "That is acceptable. If you are victorious, you may use my ship's cannons to eviscerate this city and this city alone. I wash my hands of the affair and all Karmic demerit belongs to you and you alone."

"My father will pay for it, as he promised," Yarik said. "This is acceptable."

The entire time they spoke, Alistair's fists were clenched in rage. The way they talked about his world, his city, it was like they were animals. Lesser than animals, even.

"And if I win?" Alistair asked, his anger clouding his prior sense to keep his mouth shut. "What do I get from the esteemed Yarik Portolon?"

"You dare?" Yarik sounded hotheaded, but his eyes showed no emotion except cold disdain. Alistair was curious what he was daring.

"It is within his rights," Praetei said. "I have an idea. There is a debt he owes? I know you Portolons love your indentured servitude as a repayment plan. If Alistair wins, he halves his debt and I shall guarantee with my imperial authority that any mission he undertakes for the Bank of Mai Atal shall be a suitable level of danger and difficulty for his station."

Yarik opened his mouth to respond, but he quickly thought otherwise and kicked his foot in frustration. "I accept these terms."

Alistair did not accept the terms, but what could he do? "I accept."

"Excellent," Yarik said. "Now let me come down to your pitiful level."

Before he came down, apparently he wanted to show off, since his aura did not decrease at first. On the contrary, Alistair instinctively stepped back as Yarik unveiled his full power.

Yarik felt like a primal beast. A golden lion. His proud aura would never bow to anyone, and if he fell, he would rise again, stronger than before, as a phoenix did. His power easily exceeded that of anyone native to Earth.

Praetei waved a hand and all of a sudden, Yarik felt reduced down to Alistair's level. "It's quite alright. I'll cloak you myself."

A hint of uncertainty flashed over Yarik's eyes. "Lady Kezlan, you mean to restrict my inborn advantages as well?"

"It would not be fair," Praetei said. "You will have almost every other advantage."

Yarik shrugged. "It's no matter. I do not need them to dispose of a peasant."

Praetei looked over to Alistair, who then floated gently all the way to the other side of the arena. Yarik did the same.

"Without further ado, you may begin."

Alistair had already begun.

No matter how arrogant the young master was, he was no pushover in terms of cultivation. Alistair therefore concluded his optimal strategy was to end the fight as soon as possible, relying on Yarik underestimating a Prime Initiate.

While in Tranquil Mind, Alistair [Mindshifted] toward his opponent. Dev'rox collapsed the space in between them.

[Hand of Karma] formed around Alistair's **Materia of True Martial Clarity,** a near invisible substance that was far more durable than even his **Devilsbane Gauntlets,** and conducted Mana just as well. The threads of Fate seared crimson in waves pulsating from his hand. In his other hand, he brought forth a [Force Fist].

To his credit, Yarik reacted at the last second, even though his expression revealed his shock at Alistair's sudden attack. The outline of a transcendent lion overlapped Yarik's body, colored like a phoenix.

[Force Fist] crashed against the lion, sending out a booming shockwave. An invisible bubble over the arena protected the onlookers below. Hairline fractures grew where his fist impacted the lion apparition, and **[Hand of Karma]** snuck through.

A phoenix pendant on Yarik's body erupted in flame, burning everything within or near its wearer's body.

It was too late. Alistair had taken on the Ghost Node, hiding inside Yarik as a spiritual body while the defensive treasure activated. It was only for a thousandth of a second, after which Yarik flared his Dao energy to expel the unwanted spirit.

They both emerged with spiritual nausea, but the key factor was that Alistair was already used to the feeling. The moment they untwisted bodies, he used **[Draconic Roar]**, peeling away the beginning of Yarik's opening Domain.

It wouldn't have even come close to working against an Adept's true Domain, but Alistair bet that the Grand Imperator's restrictions would put any Domain back to a proto-Domain level of power.

Nue corroded the Dao. Yarik shrugged off the potent wave and activated a devastating Skill that sent pink and orange magatama beads rippling through the air toward Alistair. He had no idea what they did, but they felt dangerous and were composed of an esoteric secondary or tertiary Mana affinity.

But Alistair was already behind Yarik after Dev'rox snapped his fingers. A concentrated wave of the sunset colored Mana affinity burst from the Portolon noble's temple, opening a third eye that lulled him to sleep, offering wistful dreams of tomorrow.

Black Impermanence stilled all external desires, cutting Alistair off from any earthly wants. Before the lion within Yarik's bloodline could emerge, he smashed Yarik's face with a close quarter **[Force Fist]** combo, striking as fast as he could.

Still, Yarik did not fall. Alistair had already figured out the phoenix aspect of his bloodline, as well as the strange Mana affinity that he imagined was something like "dream."

While Yarik's face was caved in, his life force started to explode from the inside out. A normal cultivator wouldn't have been able to tell, but Yarik's blood was literally evaporating and turning into the sunset-colored mana.

Even with Blood Dragon's Mastery, Alistair was completely incapable of using his life force to fuel attacks. That Yarik's phoenix bloodline allowed for such a thing was a testament to its power.

No, Alistair thought within Black Impermanence.

[Hand of Karma] and **[Blood Hand]** layered on top of each other. They worked in unison to subdue the blood within Yarik's body and close off his meridians. With his Fate looming in the background, Yarik might literally explode from the inside out.

"**Enough.**"

The Grand Imperator's voice carried throughout the entire arena. In an instant, they were back on the ground, all their injuries healed. For Alistair, that didn't account for much, but for Yarik, he looked as if he had just been getting boiled alive—which he had.

"Since Alistair was about to deal a deathblow, he is the victor. Yarik Portolon loses his challenge."

Yarik still hadn't moved a muscle. His gray eyes were dead and without emotion.

Dev'rox snickered. "Looks like losing may have short-circuited his brain."

"Damn it, I should have let him rough me up a bit," Alistair complained. "Then he would have saved more face. Look at that mug. He's definitely still got it out for me."

"You might not have won, then," Dev'rox pointed out. "He may be the most conceited young master I've ever seen, but his talents were no joke. He underestimated you, and that caused his downfall."

"You're right, as always, Dev'rox."

Praetei gave Alistair a knowing look. "My statement from before stands. You won't be sent into a death trap when the time comes."

"Thank you, Grand Imperator," Alistair said, bowing his head. "Will there be trouble from House Portolon?"

Praetei showed some emotion for the first time that Alistair had seen, a grin forming. "I should hope not. House Portolon is one of the Progenitors. I would think that such a great house would not let the actions of the younger generation affect their operations."

Praetei turned to Yarik, who still had not moved after almost a minute. "Is that right, Yarik?"

Yarik flinched as if he suddenly returned to consciousness. He looked around at Alistair, at the people who had all watched him get obliterated, and then at the Grand Imperator. "Of course, Lady Kezlan. I must rest now."

Yarik looked up at the spaceship and wiped his sleeves. A beam of golden light came down from the Grand Imperator's ship and sucked him up at hypersonic speed.

Behind him, he heard the natives of Earth cheer for his victory. Alistair let the cries soak in, enjoying the spotlight for a moment. Then, he proposed the idea he had been cooking for a while.

"Excuse me, Grand Imperator, but when you return, do you think you could drop me off at the Baron Zilvesky Aportamus's capital? Where the System Senate is held?"

"I'm to stay here for two weeks." Praetei answered. "After, I don't see why not. It is close to my return journey's path. It's smart to save money on transportation. The fee to get there as Foundation is ridiculous even with the system discounts. In the meantime, you should say goodbye to this world. You might not return for some time."

LATER THAT DAY

The Man in Shadows knew that Fate was not shining upon them when the talent he believed could one day rise to a Visionary soldier died.

It was a possibility that he had considered infinitesimally small. He and Goe Emmar even made a wager on it. Simpler times.

The Supernal Programmer was in permanent stasis, devoting 99.99% of his brainpower to maligning the sight of the Pathfinder.

Something was wrong, something was afoot. For all his powers, both earned and given by the organization, he did not understand why now. They were given assurances that the blasphemous AI would not turn its gaze inward. That the struggle over the Leyline of Carnation's Maw would be sufficiently distracting.

Fate was uncertain, a mess. Choices were hard to come by. There was one man at the center—Alistair Tan. The Man in Shadows had thought he gave the strange initiate an appropriate focus, but clearly that was wrong. There was something special about the man, that he couldn't quite put his finger on.

So with George Moulin dead, he knew which recruits he was bringing.

The Grand Imperator had arrived, reducing their activities to near zero.

The Devil King program was mostly a failure, but that didn't matter. With a dragon bloodline of high pedigree and ghost cultivation and Karmic cultivation, the organization would love Alistair. He even had a little demon. Then there was the woman. This batch wasn't a failure at all. Not at all.

The Man in Shadows stayed true to his name, biding his time for the right moment. He needed a single moment, when the watchful eyes of the Visionaries were clouded. He found it.

The Grand Imperator had left, after a short stay of only a month. Without her power, the Man in Shadows was confident he could swindle or defeat the others.

Goe Emmar looked so peaceful in his metal chair. His Visionary body withered under the conditions as the stress put pressure on his Domain.

"Old friend, soon this will be over," the Man in Shadows said, though he suspected that Emmar did not hear him. "You've earned yourself a vacation to a nice core planet. I hope the organization can give us that much."

The Man in Shadows released almost every restriction on his power. In a minuscule period of time following that no Foundation could perceive, he forced space open with his Dao Focus of the Shadowed Way.

No, he thought. *How has this happened?*

Instead of Alistair standing at his lonesome within his cultivation chamber, he was flanked by two towering beings.

The first was The Perfect. The sect leader of the Clear Water, she was true beauty incarnate in flesh, an Amazonian of almost two and a half meters. She filled a radiant white robe and the Man in Shadows detected two Dao Focuses that could not be called any weaker than his own.

The second was far worse. The Grand Imperator, Praetei Dai Kezlan. One of the Emperor's sworn swords, who should have been already off-world. A woman who stood near the peak of a Visionary's power on the frontier. A woman that possessed a fragment of the Emperor's Autonomy.

And the third, which he did not see at first, was the Mindaugust elf, Kazian Bromas. The Mindaugust and the Grand Imperator spoke simultaneously, though the average onlooker would only hear Praetei Dai Kezlan's Dao-filled voice.

"Choran, how can that be you?" she said, while the elf's deep bass taunted, "You thought you could escape us forever?"

"I'm sorry," Choran said, his original name cutting like tempered air. He ignored the upstart Profound realm. "It's not personal. I really did enjoy your father's lectures. Tell the old master I won't be seeing him for a while."

If Choran opened his Domain, it would have been dominated immediately by the combination of the Perfect and the Grand Imperator. Since he was technically on vacation, he lacked his own Tool of the Imperium. There was only one option. Choran went to unseal the Demonic Curse within his brain.

A voice entered his mind, stopping him from doing so.

"Old friend, we now part ways. This shall be the last step of my journey, and the first step of your new one without me. I have enjoyed my time with you greatly, and I consider you closer than a brother by blood. I hope you feel reciprocally.

"My sacrifice will not last long. The Pathfinder AI will bear down on us in full force within seconds of me leaving my chair. You must act with haste lest you squander the lifeline I give you.

"You never believed in it as much as I, but perhaps even a skeptic can one day come to faith. The heresiarchs shall fall. All for the Eon Resurgence. Long live Lucifer. We shall meet again in Paradise, brother."

Choran wanted to laugh. Of course it was the case that the rat bastard was hiding how much of a zealot he was. He had always thought so, but Emmar wasn't one to talk politics or religion.

A tear dropped down his face. It was all his fault. The moment he overstepped and fell for their alluring bait, there was nowhere to run. It was fight or die, and Goe Emmar knew that too. In a way, Choran was the one to kill his partner.

It was all so quick. Goe Emmar appeared before him, unsealing the Demonic Curse. As the elder partner in their group, his was far more powerful.

The multiverse was vast beyond comprehension, yet their Demonic Curses were known through every hallowed hall in the heartlands. Many thought it to be an abomination, an ancient evil.

They were all wrong.

The Demonic Curse was Paradise. A world of purest order emerged from Goe Emmar's mind. Not a Domain that was corrupted by the Dao, nor a warren, but a fantasy. The sliver of a memory. A stolen paradise that was promised to come again.

Goe Emmar possessed four of the thirteen layers, the maximum for a Visionary, and one more than Choran's three. Only Lord Hierocrat and two others could unleash the full thirteen layers that could shake even the Heavens.

Four was sufficient. Four was glorifying. Four was the first step of ultimate destiny.

The outermost strata, the Foundation of the Geometric Mind, came first. Infinite fractals of every variety poured from Goe Emmar's mind, warping everything into a pattern of boundless complexity. The products of the first layer were shades of gray, oscillating with a set pattern that felt like the bedrock of an impossibly overbearing mind.

The second strata was the Purist Painting. *Nue* burst forth in all the colors of the rainbow and more, painting throughout spacetime as if it were a canvas. No, that was underestimating Purist Painting. The unblemished imagination of Paradise came forth, sublimating the fabric of reality itself and becoming the canvas of the multiverse. Even if only for a millisecond, Choran forgot all about the situation and fell prostrate to the fantasy.

The third strata was known as the Forefather's Domain, and it was Choran's deepest layer. The two previous layers laid on top of each other, occupying the same place at the same time, but the Purist Painting was beneath the Foundation of Geometric Mind. And so too was the third strata below the second, yet on top of it at the same time, in a paradoxical situation. Forefather's Domain was invisible and without form, and it shattered the Dao within Goe Emmar's vicinity, destroying any Domain that dared touch it.

Finally and yet all at once, Goe Emmar released the fourth strata. Void's Terror. As all things, the Demonic Curse went by the rule of threes. Void's Terror was far stronger than the previous three strata. It was the original terror of the void. The hopelessness when facing absolute nothingness, but inverted. The fear imbued upon all those who looked at the bottomless depths of Void's Terror was the caused by the lack of respect for the centerfold. For Goe Emmar knew with his utmost truth that the Paradise trumped the void, but this haven was meaningless for the heathens who did not believe.

Four layers, all existing at once and on top of each other, all filled with primeval *nue*.

This Paradise was challenged on two fronts. At the same time Goe Emmar had unleashed the Demonic Curse, the Grand Imperator and the Perfect had opened their Domains.

A one thousand-meter tall golden throne appeared behind Praetei Dai Kezlan. On it sat an enormous figure that Choran knew all too well. Emperor Dragus Laketor. Choran had seen the man many times in the flesh, and Praetei's Domain replicated him in exquisite detail, as did all Grand Imperators.

A piece of his true power was there. It was not an understatement to say that when you faced a Grand Imperator, you faced Dragus Laketor, a bonafide Exalted. The imperial pressure he exuded made Choran want to fall to his knees in fealty. The Infinite Crown on his head and the Seal of the Empire were two of the most important Focal Point Treasures in her Tapestry, handed to her directly by Emperor Dragus upon her induction into the Grand Imperators.

Beneath the throne, a sea of a thousand Grand Imperators stood with their golden armor and weapons, supported by all the generals of the military and the heads of the Progenitor Clans. An archon of the high heavens floated above the retinue.

Archons, those Heavenly progeny that, to mortals, appeared like massive characters of the First Script. In this case, the archon was "Empire," surrounded by a Chinese-style pagoda that blotted out the sky with the heavenly imperium.

Of course, no heavenly archon had ever ratified the Final Frontier Empire. Like their own Paradise, the Grand Imperator's Domain was a fantasy made reality.

The Perfect's Domain sung to a different tune. It was herself.

Like the majority of Domains, the Grand Imperator's was spherical. However, the Perfect's Domain was not just an irregular shape type. Those were common enough, and Choran had seen many. Hers was an enormous projection of herself, though her head didn't reach the seat of the Emperor's throne.

Choran could not look away from her perfection. If she was beautiful in her normal state, the Domain version of herself went beyond physical beauty and into a sublimity that felt like it echoed the fundamental truths of the multiverse. Wherever she stepped, roses of the Dao bloomed. Wherever her gaze landed, life flourished, and whenever she breathed, the world sighed in admiration.

Mustering up more of his willpower, the Man in Shadows looked away. He would have loved to see the Demonic Curse shatter these two frontier Visionaries' Domains, but Goe Emmar was doing this for a reason. They both knew that their activities could only go unnoticed for so long. The Sublimed Machine would not be happy, and there was something coming.

The prize he wanted, Alistair Tan, was too protected. But there were consolation prizes that he was more than happy to steal away.

Choran forced space apart with the Dao, opening a portal to the first target.

Alexandra Lykaios, the pseudo-Devil King. There was no time for her to react as Choran plucked her from the meadows she liked to rest in. With a touch, she fell unconscious, and he stored her within his Domain.

In a way, he was doing her a great service. No matter how strong her willpower was, no matter what Fate cleansing artifacts they found, demon blood was inexorable in its influence. Inexorable, without the tutelage of the organization.

She would truly thrive there. Choran would find her a place in their Devil King programs, where they would teach her to make the best of her condition. Saving her was a blessing, though he doubted she would see it that way.

All in time, all in time, Choran thought as he opened a portal again, this time to the Holy Ravine.

The Devonic Elision Field was even stronger than before. That Pathfinder AI was really cautious, wasn't it? Choran fueled himself with the Dao energy of his Domain, finding his target. He touched Silvanio and put him to sleep, placing him inside the Domain as well.

Silvanio wasn't demonic in any way, but Choran had revised his opinion of the man's talent. Even after witnessing George and Alistair's duel, he was now convinced the governor was the single greatest prodigy he had ever seen from an uninitiated world, though he wasn't as compatible with the organization's methods as the ghost boy. Choran didn't give that praise very often.

A pressure could be felt around the entire world. It was arriving. Something mighty, something that would make the Grand Imperator and the four strata of the Demonic Curse look like ants.

There was no more time to waste. He wanted to grab another, but three was tempting Fate.

Choran said the code that unlocked the **Dimensional Anchor** within his soul. "Extraction requested. Emergency Pathfinder AI override. Authority Agent MiS-Glasya-Labolas-Indigo."

The organization's methods were fast and precise. The moment he finished the code, a vortex swallowed him whole, spitting him out in the nearest frontier universe base they had. The vortex was specifically programmed to use Chaos to mask the origin and direction.

Choran was untraceable. And with the two assets in hand, in addition to the research papers in his mind, the organization would be pleased.

All for the Eon Resurgence. Long live Lucifer, the Man in Shadows thought. The least he could do was say the words for poor Goe. *I'm sorry for my stupidity.*

Kazian Bromas was no coward.

He had "graduated" the Mindaugust Academy at the ripe age of 3,321. Graduated in quotes because you never really graduated the Mindaugust Academy, their instructor told them. Even Truthseekers were still students in the Sublimed Machine, for rationality had no end.

In the Final Frontier Empire, as soon as you made Profound, you were an officially sanctioned Mindaugust.

In his time at the Academy, he had seen his fair share of violence. He had seen and trained with Visionaries. While their power was extraordinary, capable of destroying planets, he had also witnessed the christening of the Emperor's son, Kai Dragus.

There were no words to describe the might of that man. In one instant, Kazian understood how the Laketor line had sat on the imperial throne for 150 million years without one rebellion. There was nothing you could do against that kind of power. Nothing any of them could do.

If a thousand of the empire's strongest Visionaries all assailed Dragus at once, it was possible they could win. Except for that Dragus was also the wealthiest man in the empire, and his bag of goodies was nigh endless. The imperial family was a power unto itself, with nearly a hundred Visionaries alone.

All this being said, Kazian wondered for the first time in his life if the being he felt was stronger than the Emperor.

An enormous finger descended from the sky, composed of 0s and 1s.

The numbers revolved around its center, glowing turquoise as they held so much information that even Kazian's formidable brain might explode if he spent too much time staring at it. It was like all the knowledge of the world were in those 0s and 1s, a computerized version of the Akashic Records.

The finger collapsed the Grand Imperator and the Perfect's Domains as if they were a piece of cake. The four layers of the Demonic Curse lasted half a second longer, but it too was smote out of existence.

Thankfully, the pressure exerted by the finger wasn't focused on him, and neither was it focused on the Grand Imperator or the Perfect. The three of them retreated, and the finger collapsed on top of Goe Emmar.

However, instead of causing a massive explosion or shockwave, the hand, as it was now, shrunk rapidly as it enclosed around the mysterious attacker. It coalesced into a sphere of spinning bits, and then vanished.

A miniature version of the man with the VR goggles stood in the palm of an august man... or was it a woman? The being was perfectly androgynous, with pale turquoise skin and a bald head. They were wearing a simple tunic and their eyes were white voids.

By instinct, both he and the two women prostrated themselves before the newly arrived being.

Surprisingly, they scoffed. "I am not your Emperor, if you have confused me so. I am the true representation of the Pathfinder AI within this universe."

Representation, Kazian thought. He'd heard about this before. The Heralds of the Pathfinders were more like tiny programs the system ran, but the full power of the universal Pathfinder was that of an Exalted much stronger than Dragus. Otherwise, how else did it help the cultivation of over a hundred quadrillion people in the empire?

This being didn't feel stronger than the Emperor, now that Kazian truly analyzed it, but it was probably only a part of its power. The Grand Imperator was the first to stand. "Thank you for your assistance, great one. Why did you intervene on our behalf?"

The miniature Goe Emmar vanished into the Pathfinder AI's sleeves. "This one and his partner have been clouding my sight for many years. Many, many years. I was given more compute only recently and started to work things out. But before I could organically solve the equation, this one inside me now decided to unleash his Demonic Curse. While I tolerate many things, four layers of that ancient fantasy goes too far. I will take him back with me."

Before the representation Pathfinder AI left, they looked at Kazian quizzically. "Young Mindaugust, what prompted you to ask the two Visionaries to defend the initiate?"

Kazian responded without daring to ask how the Pathfinder knew that it was he who figured out Alistair's life might have been in danger. "Great one, when I peered through the streams of Time, they converged around this moment. I could not see further, leading me to conclude that there was something more powerful than myself obscuring the future."

"An astute conclusion. Well-reasoned, Mindaugust." The Pathfinder turned to Alistair, who was silently watching the great being with more composure than Kazian would have mustered as a Foundation. "I'm afraid your friend, Alexandra, was taken by that man, along with Silvanio from the Holy Ravine. I'm sorry for your loss. The organization these men belong to is well-connected and the Man in Shadows is far from my reach at this point."

With that, the AI crumbled into numbers and disappeared.

Kazian fell to his knees, exhausted from the sequence of events. The Grand Imperator tapped him on the back.

"You'll lose face for the empire if you can't handle what an initiate two realms your junior can," she said, pointing to Alistair, who was obviously trying to keep his composure after hearing that Alexandra had been kidnapped.

Kazian nodded and bowed.

"Kid," Praetei said, turning to Alistair. "If I ever see my father's apprentice again, I'll kill him so thoroughly his soul won't be reincarnated for thirteen cycles. It's the least I can do, considering he was operating on your planet. If you manage to ever get to the Visionary realm, you'd make a fine Grand Imperator. I might be checking back on you in a few thousand years."

TWO MONTHS AFTER THE END OF THE INITIATION

Silvanio's disappearance was the beginning of a new golden age for the Silver Comet Sect.

There was no usurping or traitorous behavior on behalf of the Silver Comet. As was tradition, the second-in-command of the Holy Ones became the replacement governor. However, without Silvanio, things were different.

It was said a Raging Bulls apostle was the first to leave the Holy Ravine's borders. In any case, it became obvious to all what had changed.

The Mother's Presence exploded in strength. There was no comparison that Pike could make. It became so clear, so obvious. What was once shrouded in mystery was now as clear as Lake Airat.

Then there was the Class. Everyone was asked to pick a Class. Everything was as Alistair described.

Master Ko Pao flicked a stone at Pike's head, who dodged with ease. The master smiled, and there was more life in his eyes than Pike had ever seen.

Pike had thought that Master Ko Pao would have more difficulty adjusting than his younger apostles, but that turned out to be completely wrong.

"Master Ko Pao," Pike said. "Shall we venture out now? What has you so chipper?"

"My dear Pike," Ko Pao said, sounding like a man half his age. "A few days ago, I was a large fish in such a very small pond. What a glorious day! For the old grasshopper to become a young nymph is such a precious thing. I shall not squander this gift from the Heavens."

"This won't be easy," Pike warned.

"Nothing ever is."

ABOUT THE AUTHOR

Strungbound enjoyed reading Fantasy and Science Fiction from a young age, including such authors as David Gemmell, Ursula K. Le Guin, Robert Jordan, Arthur C. Clarke, and Iain Banks. Discovering LitRPG and cultivation stories was a more recent evolution, stemming from finally deciding to read Cradle after seeing it constantly recommended. He loved it right away and became an instant fan of the genre, which eventually led to a desire to write.

Author website: